‖ A Historical Saga ‖

DEEP TRIVEDI

Author of Bestsellers 'I am The Mind' & 'I am Gita'

I am Krishna

Researched from Scriptures

COMPLETE PSYCHOLOGICAL BIOGRAPHY OF KRISHNA

Trials & Triumphs in Mathura

A captivating story that will take
you on a breathtaking journey

Available in English, Hindi & Gujarati

Second Edition: 2025

Printed in India

Concept, Illustration and Design:

www.aatmaninnovations.com

Publisher: Aatman Innovations Pvt. Ltd.
Place of Publication: Mumbai

ISBN 978-93-84850-38-8

DEEP TRIVEDI

Deep Trivedi is a renowned author, speaker and master of psychology. He writes and conducts workshops with an all-pervasive perspective, guiding individuals towards the achievement of their full potential. To date, he has led millions of people onto the path of success and happiness through his works.

In his voluminous works, Deep Trivedi has extensively explained Nature, its laws, its behaviour, its psychology and the effect it has on human life. No aspect of life and human psychology has been left untouched by him. He states that lack of psychological knowledge and understanding is the sole reason for all the sorrows and failures that pervade human life.

He has authored the bestsellers 'I am The Mind', 'I am Krishna', 'Everything is Psychology', 'I am Gita', '101 All Time Great Stories', 'The Black Book of Soul', '3 Easy Steps To Win At Life', '200+ Shocking Truths About Krishna' and many more. His bestseller 'I am The Mind' has been published in several national and international languages. He has been awarded the Times Power Men Award 2018 for his immense contribution to society.

His command over the biggest psychologies of life can be gauged by the fact that he holds the record for 'Maximum Workshops on Human Life', 'Maximum Workshops on Psychological Aspects of Tao Te Ching', 'Maximum Workshops on Ashtavakra Gita' and 'Maximum Workshops on Bhagavad Gita', spanning 168 hours, 28 minutes, 50 seconds in 58 days in different National and International record books. He also holds the record for 'Maximum Number of Quotations on Human Life' (about 12038) on subjects such as Soul, Human Life, Psychology, Laws of Nature, Destiny and many more. He has also been awarded an Honorary Doctorate for his works on the psychology of Bhagavad Gita. His interactive workshops have brought about a revolutionary transformation in people's lives by addressing their day-to-day concerns. These workshops have been conducted in front of live audiences across India.

He is known for his special ability to touch upon the deepest aspects of life and explain them in a lucid language, leaving no scope for ambiguity. The distinct psychological-spiritual language and expression in his writings and workshops begin to have an instant effect on the mind of the reader or listener, which makes Deep Trivedi a pioneer in this field.

To know more about Deep Trivedi, visit **www.deeptrivedi.com**

DEEP TRIVEDI The Speaker

Deep Trivedi uses a unique combination of psycho-spiritual content, voice, language and expression, which effectuates an instantaneous transformation in his viewers and listeners. Innumerable lives have been transformed just by listening to him. This is the reason why he is known as the master of psychology.

Deep Trivedi sheds light on every subject related to life. His interactive workshops have brought about a revolutionary transformation in people's lives by addressing their day-to-day concerns. There is no aspect of human life that has been left untouched by him. He has spoken on Bhagavad Gita, Tao Te Ching, Ashtavakra Gita, Secrets of Nature, Mind, Soul, Time, Destiny and numerous topics such as:

- **Laws of Nature**
- **Time and Space**
- **Religion**
- **DNA-Genes**
- **Path of Life**
- **Day-Sleep**
- **Mind and Brain**
- **Personality**
- **Complex**
- **Phobias**
- **Guilt**
- **Involvement**
- **Expectation**
- **Partiality**
- **Acceptance**
- **Natural Intelligence**
- **Power of Transformation**
- **Marriage**
- **Freedom**
- **Future**
- **Hypocrisy**
- **Creativity**
- **Concentration**
- **Joy and Happiness**
- **Wealth**
- **Good-Bad**
- **God**
- **Ego**
- **Anger**
- **Self-Confidence**
- **Love**
- **Confusion**

Discussions and talks on the above topics and many more are available on **Deep Trivedi YouTube channel** and **Deep Trivedi App**

Contents

The Saga Behind the Research on Krishna

As the annals of history have innumerable references to Krishna's iconic personality, there can be no two opinions about the fact that he was a real and historical personality. I am making this statement specifically with reference to the trend among scholars to casually dismiss the life and personality of such legendary personages as being nothing more than a riveting story. This may indeed hold true in case of several other personalities, but Krishna is certainly not one amóng them. From a psychodynamic perspective, when the various threads of a story perfectly match the graph of an individual's personality, then such a person or his life cannot be considered to be a mere myth.

There are three factors which unambiguously prove the truth of Krishna's existence. Firstly, a fictional account has only one author. In other words, if a character is fictional, the entire life of the character is summed up in that one story narrated by the author. However, there is no single book or scripture which details the entire life of Krishna. The most discussed, popular and the oldest literary work that offers glimpses of Krishna's life is the great epic, the Mahabharata. However, this epic focuses mainly on Hastinapur, and thus, the narrative revolves around the Pandava brothers and their cousins, the Kauravas. The Mahabharata mentions Krishna only when he comes in contact with the Pandavas and Kauravas or Hastinapur. In the entire scripture, there is no reference to his birth or childhood nor is there any allusion to the last 36 years of his life. But one must admit that the Mahabharata is the only tome which brings to light all the psychological aspects of Krishna's intriguing personality. I am saying this because the awe-inspiring Bhagavad Gita is an integral part of the Mahabharata, which is included as a dialogue between Krishna and Arjuna. And the truths that Krishna reveals to Arjuna in this discourse not only stem from his experiences in life but are also an intrinsic part of his personality.

Other than the Mahabharata, fragments of Krishna's life are available in many other historical texts, and if arranged chronologically, we can piece together his entire life history. At this juncture, it is imperative to understand that out of the 100,000 *shlokas* (cantos) of the Mahabharata, only 8,800 were composed earlier than 3000 BC. The rest, that is to say, almost 90 percent of the *shlokas* have been added to the Mahabharata between 4th and 2nd BCE by different authors.

Fifteen major works, written over a 1000-year period after the Mahabharata war, have references to Krishna's life. The chief among these are the Harivamsa Purana and the Vishnu Purana, both of which have detailed descriptions of Krishna's life. And these are the only two books which can be considered the most important and reliable resources for those who choose to write or speak about Krishna's life. Nevertheless, I am presenting to you a brief description of the 15 texts—including the Mahabharata—which have been used to piece together the life history of Krishna.

Name of the Text	Accepted Date of Composition
1. Mahabharata	Out of the total 100,000 verses, the main 8,800 *shlokas*, also referred to as Jai Khand, have been composed around 3000 BC. The rest were added approximately between 400 and 200 BC.
2. Shatapatha Brahmana	Composed around 900 BC, this Brahman text, which is a section of the Yajur Veda, describes Krishna as a valiant warrior of the Vrishnivanshis (descendants of Vrishni).
3. Aitareya Aaranyak	Composed around 900 BC, this text is a part of the Rig Veda. This work also describes Krishna as a heroic warrior of the clan of the Vrishnis.
4. Nirukta	Composed by Maharishi Yasyaka around 600 BC, this text describes the Syamantaka gem, which plays an important role in Krishna's life.
5. Ashtadhyayi	A grammar treatise by Panini, this text was written in 600 BC and it contains meanings of terms used to describe Krishna and his life.
6. Garga Samhita	Composed in 400 BC, this text describes the birth and childhood of Krishna. However, in the 15th century, matter related to Brahmanism, *avatars,* rituals and worship was inserted into the book, corrupting its essence. Therefore, one needs to exercise caution while studying it.
7. Markandeya Purana	This text, written between 400-200 BC, also has many contextual references to Krishna.
8. Jataka Katha	Composed around 400 BC, this Buddhist text mentions Krishna in the Jataka Tale titled Ghat Pandit.
9. Arthashastra	This renowned political treatise, written by Kautilya in 400 BC, refers to Krishna as Vaasudeva, the son of Vasudeva.

10. Indika	The Greek scholar Megasthenes wrote this text between 400 and 300 BC, in which he describes a warrior, Heracles, of the Shurasena clan. It is actually a description of Krishna.
11. Harivamsa Purana	Composed in 200 BC by Ugrashrava, this text contains the description of almost all the heroic deeds of Krishna right from his birth.
12. Vishnu Purana	Composed by an unknown author in 200 BC, this is the oldest and the first text which describes Krishna's life right from his birth to his death.
13. Mahabhashya	Composed in 200 BC by Patanjali, this text sings praises of Krishna.
14. Padma Purana	In the Patal Khand (section) of this book, written in 200 BC, Krishna's birth and his childhood antics have been described contextually, along with those of Rama.
15. Kurma Purana	This text written in 400-200 BC carries a description of Krishna and Balarama, as well as the Yadu dynasty.

Please note that in these books too, there are several contradictions in the facts related to Krishna's life. Thus, while profiling Krishna's life, I have included only those events and descriptions that are in agreement with Krishna's character and personality. Let me make it clear that I am a psychologist, author and speaker, well-versed in spiritual psychology. And the meaning of spiritual psychology is that there are no secrets in the world, that is, there is nothing which cannot be known or revealed.

Indeed, reading the Bhagavad Gita from this unique perspective, one can readily understand that these words must have been spoken by a person who is firmly rooted in the highest levels of consciousness. Any person, well-versed with spiritual psychology, will vouch for this. And when the person who delivers the Bhagavad Gita is so wise, his experiences are bound to be powerful too, because psychologically speaking, anything that one states inevitably comes from his own experience, and needless to say, he has gained this experience from his life. Hence, any statement of a person is essentially a reflection of his life, and his personality, around which his entire life has revolved.

So, I would like to mention here that while writing this story, based on extensive research on Krishna's life, I have given greater importance to his nature as described by him in the Bhagavad Gita. It is a person's own psychology which is of paramount importance in his life, and it is his individual psychology that determines what he would do in a particular situation, or what he must have done. Therefore, what holds immense significance in Krishna's life is his thought process before taking a certain action or decision, and the reasons behind it. Honestly speaking, for a wise master of spiritual psychology, Krishna's entire life is clearly described in the Bhagavad Gita; all one has to do is match the threads of his life. And this is precisely the reason why, throughout this book, I have linked all the experiences and incidents of Krishna's life to his *shlokas* in the Bhagavad Gita; it is through these *shlokas* that he expounds upon his experiences to inspire Arjuna.

It has taken me five years to research and write this book and during this period, I have done nothing but live and breathe Krishna. Frankly speaking, during these five years, my consciousness was entirely immersed in Krishna and his Bhagavad Gita.

If I divide the descriptions of Krishna available in the various historical texts into two parts, the first part contains texts that were written during the BC era, in which Krishna has been described as a skilled warrior and a supreme human being. The second part comprises texts written in the post-BC era, which include works such as Sur Sagar by the poet Surdas and the renowned Bhagavat Purana. And it is only in these relatively new works that Krishna's life is depicted as being replete with miracles and the *Shringara Rasa*, or the flavour of romance.

However, I have always perceived Krishna as an immensely gifted, supreme human being. So, while researching my book, I have only referred to the ancient and more authoritative books. Of course, wherever I found a link missing, I have tried to bridge the gap by using psychodynamic extrapolations that I feel are congruent with Krishna's personality and story. Below is a list of the books from the post-BC era along with their descriptions:

Name of the Text	Accepted Date of Composition
1. Bhagavat Purana	Composed between 5-10 Century AD, the entire 10th volume and the beginning of the 11th volume contain descriptions about Krishna's life.
2. Harivamsa Purana of the Jains	This work was composed in the 7-8 AD by the Jain saint Acharya Jinsen and it carries a description of Krishna's life.

3. Geet Govinda	Composed in the 13th century by the famous poet Jaydeva, this poetic work speaks of the transcendental love between Radha and Krishna and glorifies their activities.
4. Padavali	Based on the Bhagavat Purana and Jaydeva's Geet Govinda, Vidyapati from Bihar has described Radha and Krishna's acts of love in this book, written in the 13th and 14th century.
5. Sur Sagar	Surdas, a poet-saint who was the follower of the Pustimarg sect, composed this work in the 15th century which mainly focuses on the childhood activities of Krishna.
6. Guru Granth Sahib	Out of the many couplets compiled in this book by various Sikh Gurus between 1469 to 1708 AD, 2492 are about Krishna's various acts.
7. Prem Sagar	Lallu Lal composed this work in 1810 AD, based on the Bhagavat Purana and the Vishnu Purana. It has hyperbolic descriptions of the acts of Krishna.
8. Shree Prem Sudha Sagar	This is a Hindi translation of the 10th canto of the Bhagavat Purana published by Gita Press.
9. Sukh Sagar	In this work, Makhanlal Khatri has translated the stories of the Bhagavat Purana in simple Hindi language.

Apart from these, this book also includes some incidents from a story on Krishna, titled *Meri Aatmakatha* (My Autobiography).

NOTE: For the convenience of readers, on every page that describes an incident in Krishna's life, I have also included a footnote which lists the books that it has been drawn from. It is hoped that this endeavour and captivating story will appeal to you and also inspire you. Most importantly, I hope that Krishna's elevated level of consciousness and his art of living prove to be instrumental in helping all of us take our life to greater heights. With this fervent desire, I offer this book to you.

DEEP TRIVEDI

Preface

'Krishna' is a name synonymous with victory and flamboyance, yet he has always been an enigma. The diverse facets of his personality make it difficult, or rather impossible, for anyone to grasp his personality in its entirety. Yet, the love showered on Krishna and the manner in which he is revered is nothing short of phenomenal.

Such is the uniqueness of his personality that for some, he is a lover, while for others he is a savant; some believe him to be an ascetic while others perceive him as a *Karmaveer* or a man of heroic deeds. Interestingly, whichever aspect of his personality one chooses to recognise or believe in, one cannot help but be smitten by it; although it is not that everyone is equally enchanted by him, after all, he also had - and still has - his share of detractors. His personality has such a paradoxical effect on people that on one hand, some learned followers of the Hindu religion have hailed him as the only 'complete-*avatar*', and on the other, the authors of Jain scriptures, as per their own understanding, reasons and perceptions, have relegated him to hell! But Krishna's personality is not contingent on any of these views. Who thinks what does not matter in the least to Krishna or his personality.

Although Krishna's personality does not depend on others' perceptions about him, in light of these contradictions, it is imperative to understand what exactly his personality was. It is also essential to know how he rose to become the King of Dwarka despite being born in a dungeon and having grown up in the shadow of death. Besides, there are several other questions that invariably pique one's curiosity about Krishna. It would also be interesting to know what kind of love he and Radha shared. Why did he leave Radha? Why did she roam the streets of Brij for the rest of her life like a woman madly consumed by her love for Krishna, who never returned? At the same time, it is important to decipher the mystery of this awe-inspiring personality, who, on one hand, has been accused of triggering an epic war like the Mahabharata, and on the other, has earned the distinction of being the supremely wise one who imparted words of supreme wisdom, which we know as the Bhagavad Gita. Krishna is such a multi-dimensional personality that there has never been a dearth of names he has been addressed with such as thief, manipulator, liar and trickster, and at the same time, a colossal number of people view him as Vasudeva, Madhusudan, Kanha, a supreme being and a supremely wise man! The numerous other questions which invariably make people curious about Krishna are: How many times did he marry? How many children did he have? What exactly is Yadavasthali?

This book contains the answers to all these questions. I have penned this work only after a long and thorough study of all the available scriptures related to Krishna such as Harivamsa Purana, Vishnu Purana, Shiva Purana, Shrimadbhagvat Purana, Markandey Purana, Kurma Purana, Bhavishya Purana and Mahabharata, among other historical texts, and after grasping the practical and psychological aspects of all the dialogues and incidents mentioned therein. I have condensed the 108 years of Krishna's life and all its significant events into this book, endeavouring to keep this account close to the true psychology of Krishna, and needless to say, I have given it the form of a story to make it an interesting read. I have tried to make the events in Krishna's life come alive for the readers, by elaborating upon the incidents as much as possible, keeping in mind the requirements of modern literature.

I am a psychologist and a strong adherent of spiritual psychodynamics and if viewed from a psychological perspective, whether it is an individual or his life, or any kind of incident occurring in his life, eventually, everything is a part of a psychological sequence. And Krishna's personality, in spite of its great aspects and complexities, is no exception to this. Even though psychologically, he has reached the greatest of heights, his state of mind is certainly not beyond comprehension. And I believe that the causes behind the event are far more significant than the event itself. Rather than knowing what a person has done, it is more important to know the reasons why he has done it. Therefore, in this book, I have given equal importance to Krishna's life as well as his state of mind. I am sure, this book will not only shed light on Krishna's life, but will also acquaint you with Krishna's personality and his evolution.

As far as I am concerned, the Bhagavad Gita has transformed my life and taken it to new heights; in fact, Krishna and the Bhagavad Gita are firmly rooted in my heart in their true essence. But in a departure from common belief, I am of the firm opinion that hailing someone as God creates a distance between him and us. Pronouncing someone as God incarnate is a grave insult to the effort that he has put in to nurture and enhance his potential, his wisdom, his capabilities and his spirit of enquiry. Because the truth is, all those who have accomplished great feats in this world have done it on the strength of their intelligence, capabilities and sheer hard work. It is very convenient to state that Krishna became great because he was destined to. Possibly, it may give you an excuse to conceal your inability to attain greatness. But in truth, by linking the greatness of an individual to his destiny, we insult his skills and hard work. That is the reason, in this book, I have attempted to shed light and elaborate upon all the virtues of Krishna, beginning from his phenomenal grasping power. And it is only by grasping the true essence of his life that we can learn from him and imbibe his qualities. Krishna too learnt from every person and each incident that came into his life. He scaled the peaks of love, concentration, *karma* (action) and wisdom, solely on the strength of his spirit of enquiry and determination. And this verily is worth learning from his life. As a matter of fact, this book, comprising a detailed account of his long, eventful life, contains the entire journey of his transformation from a simple cowherd boy 'Krishna' to the supremely powerful 'Jai Shri Krishna'. I affirm with conviction that yes, Krishna is the only 'complete' personality in the history of mankind, but I assert even more firmly that he has reached this state solely due to his diligence and virtues. Therefore, I salute not only him, but also his diligence and intrinsic qualities.

And as for me, I am determined to imbibe his qualities and endeavour to bridge the gap between his psychology and mine, so that I too emerge victorious at every juncture of my life; so that I too can spend my life in joy and bliss, and so that, inspired by him, my life too can be effectively utilised to help humanity, just as his did.

Researching on and writing about Krishna has taken me on an incredibly rewarding journey of self-discovery and I hope with all my heart that this book helps you embark on an equally enriching voyage. With this ardent wish, I offer this humble labour of love to you.

DEEP TRIVEDI

The Story So Far...

Very few have been able to rejoice in both victory and defeat...
I was one among them...!

Born in a dungeon in Mathura, I escaped the jaws of death when I was whisked away by my father, Vasudeva on a dark stormy night and taken to Gokula, a settlement on the outskirts of Mathura. It was in this quaint, little village that I spent my childhood in the loving arms of my doting mother, Yashoda; and as the days passed by, I grew up to be the apple of everyone's eyes. Although my childhood was fraught with danger, with the ominous shadow of Uncle Kansa always looming large over me, I was Krishna—the *karmaveer* who never gave up and gained victory over every adversity that came my way. Surmounting all odds and emerging victorious soon became second nature to me. When I saw worn-out traditions such as the *Indrapuja* being practised at the expense of human life, I opposed it with all my might and put an end to it. When a pack of wolves attacked my beautiful village, Gokula, I decided to relocate with my beloved *Gokulwasis* and found a new abode in Vrindavan at the foothills of the Govardhana, on the banks of River Yamuna.

As I grew older, my charm increased manifold, attracting all the *gopis* of Vrindavan, whose hearts whispered with just one name—Kanha. The heartthrob that I was, all the *gopis* were bewitched by my flute-playing and my endearing smile. But I, despite ruling the hearts of everyone, was smitten by the spellbinding beauty of Radha, who became the epitome of love for me. With time, she became not just my friend but also the one I looked upon for inspiration and guidance. For me, life was a beautiful journey of ups and downs where sometimes I fought demons like Keshi and Putana, and at times, experienced the peak of bliss by indulging in *raasleelas* with the *gopis* and my beloved Radha. I mused, this was how the story of my life would pan out—a cowherd of Vrindavan revelling in *raasa* with the *gopis* and locking horns with demons. But unbeknownst to me, Nature had a different plan for me!

An interesting and unexpected chapter in my life unfolded when I was invited to Mathura by my uncle, Kansa. Though I always knew he had been baying for my blood, I wasn't aware that it would all happen so soon. It so happened that when I reached Mathura, he employed all his might and every possible evil machination to erase my existence from the face of this earth…but I escaped unscathed. However, when he gave orders to kill everyone including my father and the *gopas,* I had no choice but to slay him for the greater good. For, I always believed that when someone becomes a threat to humanity, he must be eliminated. Now, although I had committed this deed selflessly, I knew that I was putting my life at great risk. I could feel it in my bones that I was just a few inches away from death, for I, an ordinary cowherd, had slain the king of Mathura in front of his own subjects. Standing on the precipice of certain death, I wondered, what step would his soldiers take now? How will the inhabitants of Mathura react to my bold move of slaying their king? Will I have to face their fury and receive punishment in the form of death? Or will my life be spared...?

Chapter 1

Turning Down the Throne of Mathura

As I stood tall in the royal gallery, chest puffed, arms akimbo, with the mighty Kansa lying dead at my feet, I noticed a few panic-stricken people rushing towards their homes, fearing the wrath of the soldiers. Yet, many others remained rooted to their spot, curious to witness the course of events that would follow. As the crowds thinned and a semblance of order returned, I experienced a sense of relief and regained my composure. And needless to say, the moment I relaxed, my gaze audaciously locked with Rukmini's. After the dramatic turn of events, she too seemed to have calmed down, and let me tell you, Rukmini appeared even more ravishing in her serene composure. I couldn't take my eyes off her. I was so enamoured by her innocent face that before I could stop myself, my hand rose of its own volition in an enthusiastic wave. Incredibly, she too rose from her seat, flashed me a wide smile and waved back. Oh, what was this? Was she actually waving at me? Rubbing my eyes in wonder, I peered at her and yes, there she was...smiling and waving at me. I was euphoric, for, never in my wildest imagination did I expect a princess to respond so sweetly. Oh, I could feel my heart soar to the skies! Indeed, it felt as if I was walking on clouds. Unfortunately, my happiness was short-lived. For, her brother, Rukmi was watching this spectacle and I'm not sure why, but he did not react favourably to her greeting me in this manner. Grabbing her arm, he pulled her down to her seat. My heart sank on seeing this, for, I did not like Rukmi using force with Rukmini...my Rukmini. I let out a long sigh, sadness engulfing me. Truth be told, Rukmi's behaviour made me realise that Rukmini was not mine, at least not yet. However, before I could recover from this dismay, I was jolted by yet another development. All of a sudden, the commander of Kansa's army decided to escort the princes, princesses and other women back to the palace. Accompanied by heavily armed soldiers, they were all led back; and sadly, Rukmini had to leave with them too. In other words, the commander's action made the sadness I was feeling stronger. Standing in the packed royal gallery, I sighed as I watched the woman of my dreams walk out of the festival ground.

Nevertheless, as soon as Rukmini left, my entire focus shifted to the events unfolding in the festival ground. This too was a peculiar attribute of my mind which allowed me to shift focus from one activity to another in the blink of an eye. In any case, this attribute was very much the need of the hour, for, it would help me keep a close watch on the fast-changing circumstances and the rapidly occurring events. With Rukmini's departure, I returned to my senses and with that, I became fully alert too. For, I could not ignore the possibility that a great, reputed king like Kansa could have many well-wishers who may have loathed my killing him. What if they decided to attack me to avenge Kansa?! Meaning, whether I liked it or not, there existed

a strong possibility of yet another conflict. And under such circumstances, it was certainly not safe to remain standing in the royal gallery. Thinking thus, I made a hasty retreat with bhaiya and headed straight towards the public gallery. Funnily, I had sprinted so fast from the royal gallery as if death itself was chasing me, close at my heels. And verily, such an eventuality could not be ruled out, for, an unexpected attack could take place only in the royal gallery. Indeed, I was much safer among the commoners. But I knew that no matter where I stood, I was not completely safe. It was quite a spectacle; I stood amidst the common people in the public gallery, while hundreds of pairs of eyes looked at me in amazement. However, soon, the crowd started trickling from this gallery, and the ground which was packed to capacity now looked almost barren, so much so that one could enter and exit it easily. On the opposite side, the royal gallery was nearly deserted and Kansa's vacant throne was also clearly visible from where I stood. Nonetheless, there were still about twenty to thirty armed soldiers standing guard around his body. I was not too worried, for, as long as the soldiers didn't advance towards me, I was safe. But yes, my eyes were glued to the royal gallery, watching the smallest movements and developments that were taking place. It was then that the wives of Kansa—Asti and Praapti—who were also my maternal aunts, walked to where Kansa's body lay and began to wail, beating their chests and lamenting the loss of their husband. They were, of course, justified in mourning their beloved husband and I saw no threat in their display of emotions. However, it must be admitted that their pitiable cries and loud wails were quite dramatic. The first queen, sobbing uncontrollably, howled, "You were so powerful, strong and exceptional! How could you die like this? After taking such good care of us and bringing so much happiness to our lives, how could you leave us to fend for ourselves? How will we live without you as widows? Why oh why have you abandoned us, relegating us to a life of loneliness and misery!" Seeing the elder queen lament in this manner, the second queen could not contain herself and cried even louder, "Why was your love not eternal? Why did you not take us with you? How will we live without you? What meaning would our lives have now without you?"

Watching my aunts bawl in this manner, it was only now that the realisation dawned on me that the great King Kansa was actually slain at my hands! Indeed, the events had transpired so fast that until now, it had all seemed like a surreal dream to me. Certainly, the killing of a king by an eighteen-year-old lad was no ordinary occurrence. Even more shocking was the fact that the king was slain by a mere cowherd from Vrindavan, a village that was itself dependent on rearing cows belonging to the royal palace! Truly, the situation was startling from every angle. However, at present, it was the loud racking sobs of my aunts that had put me in shock. Their continuous wailing had, in fact, thrown me in a completely new quandary. My head began to reel as all of a sudden, the scene of Lohita's wife lamenting over his dead body flashed before my eyes. You too might recall how her wailing had provoked the crowd. I was also well aware that a crowd often falls prey to sympathy, and in such situations, without thinking, it usually rallies around and sympathises with the person who is affected. And in the present situation, my aunts were undoubtedly the aggrieved party. Moreover, to my misfortune, I too was standing in the same crowd that stood watching my aunts wail. My condition had become peculiar indeed. Although Kansa was long gone, my life was still in peril. I was not safe anywhere, neither in the royal gallery where I was present a while ago, nor in the public gallery where I stood at the moment. Argh! This is why it is said that you must think twice before stirring up a hornet's nest.

Nevertheless, with no safe place in sight, I signalled the cowherd boys to come over, as I reckoned, in this hour of crisis, four of us were surely better than two. As for bhaiya, he did not seem overly worried. Wherever I went, he just followed me like a shadow, protecting and standing guard over me. In any case, he always found it easier to flex his muscles than strain his brain. And, of course, considering the perilous situation we found ourselves in, the use of physical strength was equally crucial. In the current circumstances, the need for employing muscle power could arise at any moment, especially considering the fact that my aunts were still wailing in an undulating crescendo. Indeed, they looked highly distraught. Their grief was justifiable too, as they were Kansa's wives after all. But for me, their relentless venting was now becoming a cause for concern. In fact, my mind had become numb, as I couldn't figure out what to do next. The situation had become so dire that, over time, their cries only grew louder. Caught in these thoughts, suddenly, one of my aunts cried out, "You always slept on a soft bed. Are you not uncomfortable lying on this hard ground?" Uttering these words, she began to wail louder. Really, now, what difference would it make to a dead person whether he was lying on a plush bed or the bare ground? They were weeping unnecessarily, stirring the crowd's emotions. As these thoughts crossed my mind, I began to feel exasperated when Kansa's mother arrived on the scene, howling at the top of her lungs. Argh! There seemed to be no end to my problems. The way Kansa's mother expressed her grief was also quite unique. Each time she looked at her son's lifeless body, she would faint; and on regaining her senses, she would cry out louder, "Oh, my son! My precious son!" before collapsing again. What an incredible sequence of events! Instead of improving, the situation was becoming more and more complicated. Interestingly, the people who were causing these problems for me were all my relatives! After all, Kansa's mother was my grandmother, wasn't she? And Kansa's wives were my aunts, which means my life was put in peril by my own relatives. I was unsure of whether I should walk up to my grandmother and seek her blessings since I was meeting her for the first time…or express my anger at her raucous display of grief. I was equally clueless as to why she was lamenting so much for a wicked son like Kansa. 'Dear grandmother! Please stop. Do you not understand that your crying will put your grandson in great peril? Grandmother, just try to remember, this is the same man who had imprisoned your husband—my grandfather—for so many years. So, why are you lamenting so much for him?' Ah, but who would explain all this to her? After all, these were just thoughts buzzing around in my head. I certainly could not go anywhere near my grandmother, for, that would put my life in graver danger. Oh, how unfortunate I was! This was the first time I was seeing my grandmother, and under such strange circumstances. In fact, it was also the first time I had seen my aunts up close. The two were siblings, which was obvious not only from their appearance, but also from the way they were crying. Be that as it may, but most remarkably, this day marked my first and last meeting with Uncle Kansa! In other words, I was meeting my close relatives after eighteen years, and that too, in such an unusual situation. Oh, how incredible Nature was, and how incredible was its child, Krishna!

All said and done, the collective mourning of my grandmother and aunts was fast becoming a threat to my life. Indeed, their weeping could take an adverse turn at any moment and incite the inhabitants of Mathura against me. And as for crowds, their behaviour is anyway unpredictable; swayed by emotions, they often fail to discern right from wrong and go to any length. Besides, it is an established truth that riots and mayhem are caused only because of such sentimental fools reacting in the heat of the moment. An even greater truth is that in such situations, man either becomes a sentimental fool or resorts to cruelty. It is always one extreme or the other—he doesn't know how to find a middle ground. This is precisely what I had said to Arjuna in the Bhagavad Gita, "Those who are cruel and tyrannical are definitely sinners, and I certainly destroy such fiends. But bear in mind, Arjuna, those who are swayed by emotions are sinners too; the only difference is, they cause their own destruction."[1] You would remember, at that particular moment, Arjuna too was caught in a vortex of emotions and was all set to destroy himself. That was why I had said to him, "Let go of all desires and attachments. For, any attachment that precludes you from performing your *karma* is worthless."[2] Whatever I had enunciated in the Bhagavad Gita was drawn from my life's experiences, which is why I say that the Gita is nothing but the essence of

---

1. Shrimad Bhagavad Gita, Chapter – 16, Verse – 19-20.
2. Shrimad Bhagavad Gita, Chapter – 3, Verse – 19.

my life's experiences. As you are well aware, it was my nature to learn from every circumstance, every incident and every person, and deeply reflect upon those encounters and analyse them. Therefore, seen from this perspective, the Bhagavad Gita is nothing but the essence of all the lessons I had learnt throughout my life. Besides, I was such an avid learner that even now, I was imbibing valuable lessons from the mourning of my aunts. For one, I could clearly discern that no matter how cruel a person is, he invariably loves some people close to him, and naturally, he also behaves well with them. What I am saying is, even the most inhumane person has a tiny flame of humaneness glowing in his heart. Going by this reasoning, Kansa must have certainly behaved well with his wives, which was precisely why they were so grief-stricken at his death. This implied that even wicked individuals are adored and loved by some. This also means that the relationship which two people share depends on their behaviour with each other; it is not dependent on their deeds in life or the kind of person they are. But in my opinion, this is wrong. Ideally, the relationship an individual shares with another should be based on their true self. If Kansa is wicked, then he should be considered wicked by everyone. Then it does not matter if his behaviour with my aunts was good; they should have remained upset with him. As for me, my relationship with a person has never been dependent on his behaviour towards me. I always gave importance to his behaviour and conduct towards all of humanity, and this is precisely the way it should be.

Another aspect I had grasped from the present situation was that nobody dies alone. With an individual's death, his entire family, all his loved ones and the people dependent on him also die in part. And the moment this realisation swept over me, I decided that henceforth, killing any human being should always be considered the last resort. As long as there is another alternative available to solve the problem, no one should be killed unnecessarily. Even today, although I had killed Kansa, I had done it only because I was left with no choice. He had tried to kill me by pitting me against a mad elephant, but I was not offended. Next, he had cunningly planned to finish me off by arranging a duel between Chanoor and me, yet I did not take offence or feel animosity towards him; because until then, his enmity was directed only towards me. However, when the fire of his hatred spread over, threatening to engulf all the *gopas*, my father and several *Mathurawasis*, I had no option but to kill him. What I mean to say is, I never considered the person who was hostile only towards me or hated only me, as my enemy. But when a person spreads his venom to poison the whole of humanity, I consider him to be my enemy. In other words, I consider the person who makes life a living hell for others as my real enemy. That is why at the time of slaying Kansa, I didn't think of Mother Devaki's pain or grieve for my murdered brothers. Nor did I harbour resentment towards Kansa for all the attempts he had made to finish me off. All these events had occurred in the past, buried in the sands of time, and Kansa was merely an instrument for whatever had transpired in the past. It was not in my nature to be vengeful, and seen from this perspective, I too was just an instrument to prevent something terrible from taking place. Therefore, Kansa's death at my hands should also be viewed as the result of me being a 'medium' in his killing, not as an act of revenge, enmity or ire.

Well, now that I have spent enough time on my ruminations, let me return to the strange events unfolding before me. The cruel Kansa was dead, my grandmother lay unconscious once again, and my aunts, overcome with emotion, were still weeping. And I stood at a distance, watching this emotional drama play out. Uncertainty hung heavy in the air, and given the volatile situation, it was hard to predict the emotional turn these events might take. As for my mother and father, they found themselves in the most awkward situation. Mother appeared grief-stricken; after all, she too had lost her dear brother. At the same time, she was perhaps gripped with anxiety too, as it was her own beloved son who had slain her brother. In other words, she had already lost a brother…what if she now lost her darling son as well? Father, meanwhile, was still sitting on the edge of his seat, his brows furrowed in worry. Caught between the devil and the deep blue sea, the poor man was in no position to utter a word or even grieve. For, it was his own son who had killed the king! Truly, I had put my parents in a quandary not just at the time of my birth but today as well, after having slain Kansa. The plight of Nanda and the cowherd boys from Vrindavan was even worse, for, although they were not party to my act, Kansa's threat to them followed by my slaying him had linked them to this event. So, it was certain that they too would be caught in the storm that was likely to erupt and face the consequence of any retaliatory action taken against me.

These thoughts were still racing through my mind when suddenly, the commander returned, flanked by a posse of soldiers. Surprisingly, he was accompanied by King Ugrasena, my maternal grandfather. Although my present deliberations came to a halt on witnessing this scene, I immediately started wondering what other unexpected events were about to transpire now. In my head, I began to converse with myself, 'Respected Commander, had my aunts and grandmother created any less commotion that you have now brought this gentleman too, to add to it?' Well, his arrival was just the beginning. Little did I know that a string of surprises lay in store for me. For, following close on the heels of my grandfather—the old king—all the princes from other kingdoms had also walked in. This surprise did bring with it a measure of happiness as well, for, along with the princes, the love of my life, Rukmini had returned as well. However, at this moment, rather than get distracted by Rukmini, I thought it prudent to focus on the new developments that were unravelling at such a fast pace. Because to even focus on my lifeline 'Rukmini', it was imperative that I first focused on saving my own life! Even otherwise, given the rapid pace of events unfolding before me, I could not let my attention stray at this moment. Really, this poor cowherd was feeling like a rudderless boat that was set afloat in the stormy sea, unable to fathom the course of events taking place at such a frantic pace. As for my grandfather, on closer inspection, he appeared to be a very simple man. But having said that, he too looked deeply unhappy. After all, he had lost his son. For a while, he just sat next to Kansa's lifeless body, lost in grief. Then suddenly, stroking his son's head, he stood up. As soon as he rose, he consoled my distraught aunts and also asked after my unconscious grandmother. And immediately after, he sent the commander to fetch me. Remarkably, Grandfather Ugrasena had done all of this in just a few minutes.

I obviously became a little anxious on being summoned, for, I really could not understand his intention. My heart beat with trepidation as I was suddenly gripped with a sense of foreboding. But irrespective of whether I could fathom his intention or not, I had to comply. Had I displayed even an iota of unwillingness to go, I would have surely been arrested and hauled in his presence. Thinking thus, I quietly started walking, accompanying the soldiers. Bhaiya also began following me. Understandably so, for, how could he abandon me at such a crucial time? And talking about my state, a million thoughts were coursing through my mind, creating a cacophony. Of course, I was well prepared for any unexpected attack, but what if I was arrested for assassinating the king? If that were to happen, all my caution and heroism would vanish into thin air. I was already quaking within on seeing the battalion of soldiers that had stationed itself next to grandfather. On one hand, a storm of thoughts assailed my mind, and on the other, I continued to keep a close watch on every move of my grandfather, because everything now depended on what he was thinking. Meanwhile, the crowd had already dispersed from the ground, with no more than four to five hundred people left behind, including us. The royal gallery, however, was filled to capacity once again, with a noticeable increase in activity too. It was quite evident that the next move was clearly up to my grandfather. Having left the public gallery, bhaiya and I were crossing the open ground and slowly moving towards the royal gallery under the vigilance of the soldiers. But despite the danger looming over me, in some corner of my heart, I could not help but feel impressed by my grandfather. I was most impressed with the fact that although he had been languishing in prison for the past so many years and had just stepped out, he still held sway over everyone. He still conducted himself with dignity and was in firm command of the situation. I had visualised him to be a sick, tired and dejected man after having spent so many years in prison. But my presumption of him had been entirely wrong, and when someone proves my presumptions wrong, not only am I impressed, but my interest in them is kindled too. Indeed, if a person could be understood easily or his actions become predictable, then how can he be called a human being in the first place? His stature is then reduced to that of a mere object which can be manipulated and used easily by anyone. In this regard, I must say, grandfather was the second person after *Acharya* Shrutiketu, whose personality impressed me so much. Well, wasn't it enough to have the opportunity to meet such a great person in my final moments? Otherwise, you are aware that so far, I had used all human beings as if they were mere objects or toys in my hand. Whether it was mother's love or father's silence, whether it was Radha's obstinacy or my brother's ire, everything had ultimately proven advantageous to me. Conversely, no one had ever been able to use me, nor would anyone be able to, simply because I was neither obstinate nor fixed in my nature. So, bear in mind, if a person has a rigid, inflexible nature or is stubborn about something, he can easily be used like a toy by others.

Well, now that I have given you a glimpse into my nature, let me also tell you a little about my art of learning. For, who knows whether I would be accorded such an opportunity again! You already know that for me, life itself was like a school, and I went on to imbibe whatever I learnt in life to transform myself. Indeed, it is an established truth that no child is born learned; it is life that teaches him all that he needs to learn. Therefore, I believe that an individual's progress depends solely on how much he can learn from life and how fast he can learn. Consider my life as an example; I never missed an opportunity to learn. In fact, I seized every opportunity to imbibe the lessons life taught me, and remarkably, I never had to learn anything twice. It was this innate ability to grasp combined with my ability to mould myself accordingly that helped shape my present personality. It was because of my constant endeavour to know my own mind and that of others that today, my eyes, my intelligence, my speech and now, even my smile were serving as the most powerful weapons in my arsenal. For, a person who can fathom other people's minds is capable of transforming them as well. Similarly, if a person has complete control over his mind, he can very easily control the minds of others too. Thus, the one who is the master of his own mind and can control the minds of others is invincible; indeed, no power in this world can defeat him! In fact, there is no knowledge beyond this that is worth acquiring. Just think, what learning can be superior to the one that allows you to control others? At the same time, it presents another advantage: your own mind always remains under your control. And verily, what could be a greater achievement than you being the master of your mind? Consider me for instance. My mind had always been under my complete control. That was the reason why, even though I was hopelessly besotted with Rukmini, I did not allow her presence to divert my attention even for a moment. Life is all about the choices you make. At the moment, I could either choose to let my gaze wander over to Rukmini or keep a watchful eye on the commander's actions. The choice was between winning Rukmini's heart and reading grandfather's mind. If I chose not to pay attention to Rukmini, there would be no great loss, but if I let my attention waver from the commander's moves, my life could be in danger. On failing to gauge my grandfather's mind, I could face incarceration for the rest of my life. To sum it up, "As long as one is alive, anything is possible." And this phrase was applicable not just to the present situation but to every place and situation in life. Meaning, there are not just one or two but countless choices to be made in life. If you think about it, the slaying of Kansa was also a choice I had made. It was either the death of all the cowherd boys, my father and myself or just Kansa—and the choice I had made was to slay Kansa. Oh, isn't this incredible?! Death was staring me in the face and my mind was caught up in ruminations—not just ordinary ones, but profound contemplations! Perhaps, a confrontation with death awakens one's supreme consciousness. And with the awakening of supreme awareness, a miracle occurred—my self-confidence returned! With the return of my self-confidence, I walked slowly yet purposefully towards my grandfather, thinking only one thought, "Let's see what he has to say!"

Walking in this manner, I had reached quite close to the royal gallery, every step of mine making the cowherd boys even more anxious. And don't even ask about the state of my mother; she had plunged into an abyss of despair ever since I had slain Kansa! Father, fully aware of the political ramifications, seemed visibly anxious too. The *Mathurawasis* who had stayed behind also looked restless, clueless about what would happen next. The situation in the royal gallery was no different; every face appeared ill at ease, except for grandfather. Along with the commander, all the princes who had come from the other kingdoms were also restive; nobody knew what would happen next. For, presently, the reins were in the hands of grandfather, and gauging his calm and composed demeanour, it was not easy to discern the storm brewing within him. What I mean to say is, it was not just me but everyone else too who was caught in this state of suspense. Let alone us, even Rukmini appeared restless. The only person unaffected by this intense emotional turmoil was grandfather.

Now, whether his calm countenance signified something good or bad would only be revealed once I reached the spot where he stood. And that wasn't far either; within moments, I had reached close to him. Bridging the distance between us, I presented myself before grandfather and the commander. Naturally, I first touched grandfather's feet with love and respect, exuding immense self-confidence. In return, he too embraced me affectionately. And as soon as he did, I felt my life force return—the love and warmth of his hug made it amply clear that my life was no longer in danger from the royal palace. Watching this loving exchange between grandfather and grandson, all the subjects breathed a sigh of relief too. As for mother and father, tears welled up in their eyes the moment grandfather pulled me in an embrace. With hope surging in my heart, I mused, 'This family, which has been apart for various reasons, is reuniting today. So, surely, my aunts too must have had a change of heart. Perhaps, they too would feel love and affection for their nephew!' With this vain hope, I turned my gaze towards them. But alas, forget about affection—they completely disregarded me. In fact, they frowned at the cordial manner in which grandfather had greeted me.

Well, this too was a special quality I possessed: regardless of the situation I found myself in, I always tried to glean the minds of those around me, so that on detecting even the slightest trace of malice and deceit that could harm me or others, I could address it before it was too late. And in this scenario, it was clear that my aunts were still furious with me. Oh well! Let them be upset! This matter was not an immediate concern to me, as they had no say in the functioning of the royal palace. Presently, the only thing that mattered was grandfather's opinion, and he had already displayed a positive attitude towards me by embracing me. Although, let me tell you, his warm greeting had taken me by surprise. But wait, the surprises were not over yet! It is rightly said that one surprise leads to another, and one joy paves the way for the next, because soon after grandfather had surprised me with an embrace, he amazed me a second time with what he said next. Stroking my head lovingly, Grandfather Ugrasena made me sit next to him. Then, looking deep into my eyes, he said, "Kingdoms are meant to be ruled by the brave. And you have demonstrated your bravery—first by killing the mad elephant, Kuvalyapeed, then Chanoor, and finally Kansa. You love the people of Mathura dearly, which is evident in your demeanour. And the fact that the *Mathurawasis* have also begun to love you is apparent from the atmosphere in this arena."

Saying this, he cloaked himself in silence, but I was left dumbstruck. Although I was pleased to hear this unexpected praise, I could not fathom the import of his words or where this conversation was heading. But I was convinced of one thing—there was no imminent threat to my life. And naturally, under the present circumstances, this realisation was of far greater consequence than trying to understand anything else. Although confusion was etched on my visage as I was still trying to gauge the import of grandfather's words, I noticed that the princes around us were most unhappy on hearing grandfather praise me. This puzzled me, for, try as I might, I failed to comprehend what they stood to gain or lose by what grandfather had said to me. While my mind was abuzz with all these thoughts, grandfather noticed the confused expression on my face, hence to relieve me from my predicament, he continued, "With Kansa's death, Mathura has become bereft of a king, and no kingdom can function without a king…even for a single day. Now, as a rule, whoever kills the king is entitled to his throne. Besides, you are my grandson and your father is in close relation with the royal family, so considering your capability, on behalf of all the inhabitants of Mathura and the royal palace, I request you to take over the reins of Mathura. This request of mine should be treated as one made by the royal household. I, therefore, humbly request you to accept the crown of Mathura."

I could not believe my ears! The events had taken a completely different turn than what I had expected. Even as I heard every word spoken by grandfather, all I could do was stare at his face with a dazed expression. Indeed, how could the senses of this cowherd, who until moments ago was certain he would meet his end, function after being presented with the idea of becoming a king? I had not only lost my ability to think, but my senses of sight and sound had also temporarily deserted me. I had come fully prepared for my death, to be ground into the dust, but instead, grandfather had elevated me to the skies! I stood unmoving, as if carved out of stone. On the other hand, as soon as grandfather put forth the proposal, the crowd roared its support from all corners of the arena, which naturally brought me back to my senses. Well, I may have returned to my senses, but I still could not believe what was transpiring. I, a mere lad, would become king?! When I could not make sense of anything, I pinched myself hard just to make sure I was not dreaming. But no! I could clearly see Kansa lying dead before me, and hear the crowd voicing its support; all of this assured me that I was not dreaming. But if this was indeed the reality, then it was necessary to compose myself. At once, I focused all my concentration on increasing my presence of mind, for, the time had come for this young boy to mature. Indeed, one could deal with this situation only by thinking maturely. Well, this was all about me, but in stark contrast to my composed demeanour, bhaiya and the cowherd boys were delirious with joy. Father had recovered a little too, but mother seemed largely unaffected. Regardless of her condition though, her darling son was well and truly trapped! With remarkable ease, grandfather had proposed making this cowherd the king, but for the cowherd, let alone becoming a king, it was difficult to even comprehend the events unfolding. Until moments ago, the future that lay ahead of me seemed to be that of a cowherd living his life in Vrindavan—and even that had been uncertain, as it all depended on whether I could escape from here alive. And now, just see, I was being offered a throne! Perhaps, no other person must have ever received the opportunity to make such a massive leap in the fraction of a moment. Let alone becoming a king, this was the first time in my life that I had even set eyes on one! So how was I, a poor cowherd, to know that the one who kills a king is entitled to become one himself? Nevertheless, I had to assess the proposal put forth by grandfather. Not only was it essential to analyse the situation carefully, but it was also imperative to give an appropriate response to my grandfather. With the trust he had placed in me, I felt it was necessary to demonstrate at least some amount of maturity. In other words, if the proposal was for a position that was far beyond my present status, then it was also essential for me to rise above and think beyond myself. It was little wonder then that my mind was tossed in a whirlwind of thoughts, as I began to evaluate every aspect of the proposal down to its minutest detail.

Oblivious to my inner turmoil, bhaiya and the cowherd boys were still dancing with joy, while the rest of the people in the arena were starting to warm up to the proposal. For that matter, I too was elated, and the two main reasons for my euphoria were: firstly, my life had been spared, and secondly, in a fraction of a second, the tide had turned, raising my stature in society and making me eligible for winning Rukmini's hand in marriage. Obviously, as soon as I was reminded of Rukmini, my gaze hungrily sought her out in the royal gallery. And I was not disappointed, for, she too was watching me keenly, her eyes sparkling with amazement. And the moment our eyes met, she not only enthusiastically waved at me, but also urged me to accept the proposal. For a brief moment, this pleased me immensely, but then I mused…what did she have to lose by way of encouraging me? She would not be impacted in any way; it was I who would have to become king. And in my heart, the love I had for her had its own place, whereas the future of the inhabitants of Mathura had its own importance. All in all, it was a momentous decision and I did not want to make haste in either accepting or rejecting the proposal. Before giving my answer, I wanted to consider all aspects and analyse both options carefully. But an exhaustive analysis of this matter in such a short span of time was no child's play. Standing at a crossroads, my train of thought was heading in two different directions. On one hand, my mind was caught up in wanting to thrill Rukmini by accepting the proposal, and on the other, I was determined to take steps only in alignment with my capability. Caught between these two conflicting thoughts, I focused all my attention on understanding the rapidly unfolding events so that I could analyse the situation correctly and make an informed decision, either in the 'affirmative' or in the 'negative'. But as I mentioned, deliberating over this matter in such a short time was no easy feat. Firstly, within moments, grandfather had elevated my status from an ordinary cowherd to one poised to become king. Naturally, this cowherd, who had only walked on uneven, rocky paths until then, needed time to accept such a sudden change in position. Secondly, this was the first time in my life I was facing an avalanche of unforeseen events at such a fast pace. No sooner would I manage to deal with the first, a second one would emerge, followed immediately by a third. And interestingly, the root cause of all these unforeseen incidents was grandfather himself. Now, I could very well recover from everything that had happened so far and even arrive at a conclusion, but my problem was, I just could not shake off his influence on me even if I wanted to. He had arrived just a few minutes ago, but even in this short span of time, he had managed to accomplish so much.

First, he had brought all the visiting princes with him in the arena, which clearly meant that although the king had been slain, the situation in Mathura was now under control. And verily, it was crucial to convey this impression to the visiting princes to safeguard Mathura's political identity as a kingdom. By bringing the princes with him to the arena, grandfather had not only managed to salvage Mathura's pride and honour, but had also saved the kingdom from sliding into anarchy. Perhaps, grandfather wanted to send out a loud and clear message to these princes and even to the inhabitants of Mathura, that although Kansa was dead, Mathura was no longer rudderless with no one to helm it. Otherwise, some people, moved by the mourning of my aunts, might have started sympathising with them and stood up in support of Kansa. On the other hand, there was no dearth of Kansa's enemies in Mathura either. In such a scenario, Mathura would certainly have been divided into two distinct factions, paving the way for a civil war. Also, grandfather's equanimity must be praised, especially the way he had addressed everyone. It was truly remarkable, for, each word was chosen with great care and precision. Come to think of it, it was after languishing in captivity for so many years that grandfather had finally breathed the fresh air of freedom, and what was the first thing he saw when he arrived at the arena? His heroic son lying dead on the dais! But despite the horrific scene his aged eyes had witnessed, he had not lost his composure. Was this not worthy of praise? Indeed, I had gained a valuable life lesson from his ability to remain composed. I had learnt from grandfather how to keep calm and composed under all circumstances. In fact, this lesson of maintaining composure which I had learnt today went on to become one of the greatest lessons of my life, one that stood me in good stead even later. For, it is only when a person loses his mental equilibrium in adverse circumstances that he falls into the pits of doom, whereas maintaining one's mental equilibrium is even more crucial under such circumstances. Another remarkable aspect about grandfather was that he neither wept nor mourned on seeing his son lying dead; he showed no traces of anger either. He had spared only a moment to pay homage to his departed son, conducting himself in a manner as if nothing major had happened. It was this ability of his that had brought the entire situation under control in a fraction of a second. This is why I say: the world is like a vast university, and every incident, every individual, is a teacher. Today, I had learnt many things, not only from King Ugrasena but also from Kansa and my aunts. In other words, the truth that we have no friends or foes in this world was being proven true. Sometimes, we encounter people who come to us as teachers, and at other times, we cross paths with those who appear as students. In fact, if we observe our actions carefully, what do we really do? We either spend time learning something ourselves or create opportunities for others to learn.

Well, you must be thinking that Krishna is speaking about everything under the sun, but he is not talking about his grandfather's proposal to crown him king. So, let me tell you that I was still busy contemplating over it… but is it ever easy to arrive at such a crucial decision? Just look at the scene unravelling here: grandfather was standing right in front of me, trying to read my mind by observing my expressions. Before me lay the corpse of Kansa which was the very reason why the question of my becoming king had been raised. On my right stood Rukmini and my aunts, while the princes were on my left. Amidst the large crowd, I could also spot Uncle Akrura, standing in a corner next to my parents. A number of voices could also be heard from the distant public gallery. As my gaze fell upon the gallery, I could clearly see the happy faces of my cowherd friends. And right next to me was bhaiya! Well, with so much happening around me, how could this poor cowherd deliberate over this matter? However, this cowherd was cunning enough to not have displayed any emotions when King Ugrasena had spoken, and even now, he stood silent, depicting a calm and composed demeanour. In other words, even after receiving such an unexpected proposal, my face was devoid of emotion. This was certainly the wonderful outcome of having practised the art of maintaining one's composure, a lesson freshly learnt from King Ugrasena. Otherwise, our expressions and behaviour usually give away our thoughts, and naturally, this proves detrimental to us.

Now, let me tell you one more thing: while I had complete control over my expressions, my keen eyes were constantly probing, trying to read the expressions of others. What I observed was that most of the people in the arena were on the verge of breaking into a celebratory dance at the prospect of me being crowned the king of Mathura. The cowherd boys were equally thrilled at the thought of their friend assuming the throne. Rukmini too seemed no less delighted. And what do I say about bhaiya! He had already assumed the stance of the king's brother, standing with his chest puffed up with pride. As for my parents, despite all these positive developments, they were still struggling to regain their composure. Once or twice, grandfather had even gestured to me, asking about my decision, and I too had gestured to him that I was thinking about it. Let me also tell you, while the inhabitants of Mathura were rejoicing, there were a handful of people whose expressions clearly conveyed their displeasure. Among those were my aunts, who were visibly upset on hearing the proposal. Indeed, how could they stand the idea of their husband's murderer being crowned the king of Mathura? In addition to them, most of the princes were also not in favour of this proposal. Rukmi, in fact, had shot up from his seat and was openly expressing his objection. Actually, I could empathise with these princes, for, it was only because of their lineage that they had become princes. Perhaps, their apprehension stemmed from the fact that if the crown were to be handed over to an outsider—especially a cowherd—and if this were to become a norm, what would become of these poor fellows and their future? Wouldn't it put a question mark on the very right of these princes to become king? But grandfather had to be commended, for, he had cast aside all traditions and was courageous enough to hand over the throne to a cowherd. Of course, the fact that I was his grandson must have also played an important part in this brave decision he had taken. On deeper reflection, it was also clear that Rukmi had another reason to oppose this proposal. Yes, you guessed it right! When he and I had been embroiled in a brawl the last time, bhaiya and I had given him a sound thrashing. Moreover, the fact that Rukmini was evincing immense interest in me could have also been a major reason for his opposition. But then, these were not the only people who were disgruntled. There were many others too, for instance, the Yadava elite such as Satrajit, Kritavarma and Satyaki, who were the chief guests at this function. Essentially, all the visiting princes and the politically influential people of Mathura who were closely connected to the royal palace were not in favour of making me the king of Mathura. But opposed to this group, the majority of the subjects had unanimously expressed their support for my nomination.

As usual, a difficult choice stood before me on this day as well. It wasn't just about becoming a king or remaining an ordinary cowherd forever, but also about whether I wanted to spend my life as a king or an impoverished cowherd. For that matter, who wouldn't want to become a king? Besides, if I became king, my chances of winning Rukmini's hand in marriage would also improve significantly. Clearly, on attaining kingship, I would be catapulted to a position on par with her in every respect. On the other hand, you are also well aware of how impressed I had been with the style, pomp and grandeur of princes. Just imagine, what a lavish life I would live on becoming king! I would not have to lift a finger to get work done, for, there would be a retinue of servants to take care of every need and comfort. Moreover, my name would resonate across kingdoms and I will be treated with honour and respect. Pondering over all these aspects, I could clearly see the personal benefits I'd enjoy if I became king. Having said that, I also understood that receiving a sudden opportunity to become a king on account of certain circumstances was one thing, while being worthy of becoming a king and being able to rule a kingdom and serve its subjects was a different matter altogether. I thus decided to shift my focus from personal interests to capability, and began to search within me the abilities that made me suitable to be a king...and well, I didn't have to look far. Standing before me was King Ugrasena and seeing his impressive personality and equanimity, I could not help but think that presently, I did not possess the qualities required to be a king. A king has to face trials and tribulations on a daily basis, with fresh problems cropping up every so often. Indeed, when a person struggles to look after his own family, it's clear that managing an entire kingdom is no child's play! Let's consider today's events for instance. Had I been in King Ugrasena's place, I would've been at my wits' end, not knowing what action to take. Regardless of what I did, I certainly wouldn't have been able to do what he had accomplished so effortlessly. Indeed, it would have never occurred to me to bring the princes to the arena. The way he had read the situation and taken control of it in a matter of moments clearly showed that to become a king required a different kind of intelligence and experience. Taking all these aspects into consideration, I had fully understood the personal benefits of being a king and had also recognised my current ability—or lack of it—for this role. Of course, if viewed differently, how long would it take for an intelligent and brave person like me to imbibe the qualities of a good and able king? So, did it make sense to let go of this golden opportunity to become king just because I was not fully qualified for the position? At the same time, why should I forget that this was a matter that pertained to my heart as well? No sooner would I become king, the chances of fulfilling my dream of tying the knot with Rukmini would increase substantially.

Oh, but do not think for a moment that I was preparing myself to become king. For, this was just the tip of the iceberg. There were many twists and turns that lay ahead. Agreed, the inhabitants of Mathura had expressed their unequivocal support for me, but what about the princes who were persistently raising their voices in objection? Then again, since they were visiting princes, how long would their protest last? They would soon forget everything and leave for their own kingdoms. However, the main opposition was from the Yadava chiefs, whose stance had made it clear that they could not stand the sight of me. And without their support, it would be impossible for me to retain the throne of Mathura. For, all things considered, the inhabitants of Mathura were completely under their thumb. In the future, they could very well switch their loyalties on being instigated by the Yadava leaders. Meaning, it would be easy for me to become king right now, as grandfather had already proposed it. However, continuing to remain a king for an extended period of time seemed difficult. What if I were made king for a few days and then chased out of Mathura? If that happened, 'King Krishna' would once again be relegated to herding cows and buffaloes! Jokes aside, becoming king would mean entering into a conflict with these powerful Yadava leaders on a daily basis, ultimately leading to unrest and anarchy in Mathura. So, even if I were to accept kingship considering my short-term benefit, it would only spell doom and disaster for Mathura. And my nature would never allow me to hurl Mathura into the flames of anarchy for my selfish gain. Now, coming to Rukmini, she was my dream, and it was just as pleasurable to continue dreaming about her as it was to see that dream come true. What is a dream after all? It is nothing but an opportunity to put oneself on the path of progress. It is not always necessary for every dream to turn into reality; dreams are meant to be cherished and treasured. Of course, if time and circumstances are favourable, there is no harm in realising one's dreams. But in order to fulfil one's dreams, one cannot stoop low to the levels of inhumanity! It is not as if dreams have to be realised at all costs. Dreaming is an art that paves the way for you to develop your capabilities and expand your vision. And if dreams too were to be fulfilled at the cost of degrading oneself, then how different would dreams be from desires? While dreams elevate an individual to greater heights, desires spell his downfall. To cut a long story short, the crux of all these deliberations was that, even though becoming a king would benefit me personally, neither was I qualified to become one nor did the current circumstances in Mathura favour such a decision. All in all, I could not accept the proposal to become the king of Mathura. Though I had taken time to reach this decision, I was satisfied it was the right one. Seeing me lost in thought, this time, grandfather decided to address me directly saying, "I have a personal request to make. Take as much time as you need to deliberate on my proposal, but kindly grant me permission to perform the last rites of my son, Kansa, with full honours."

Hearing these words jolted me out of my contemplation. I was stunned! Why was he asking for my permission? I was not the king of Mathura. Did this mean that grandfather had construed my silence as my willingness to become the king of Mathura? 'Oh, Kanhaiya! Waste no time and clear up this misunderstanding right away. Express what is on your mind clearly and explicitly, else they may just place the crown on your head and you'd be left standing like a statue!' Thus, gathering my wits, I quickly replied to grandfather, "I have slayed my uncle neither to demonstrate my valour nor with the intention of becoming the next king. In my opinion, his death should be seen as an outcome of his tyrannical actions. And I should be regarded merely as an instrument that delivered the consequences of his terrible deeds. As for the question of my becoming the king, let me make it clear that, at present, I am neither old enough nor qualified for the role, for, I have been raised as a simple cowherd boy. In my opinion, you alone are worthy of being the king of Mathura. There was a time not too long ago when happiness and prosperity reigned in every nook and corner of Mathura under your wise rule. Therefore, I request you to once again be instrumental in bringing joy back to the kingdom of Mathura. As for my uncle's last rites, he was a king, and his funeral should be conducted according to the protocol reserved for royalty. In this regard, I believe the royal palace does not require any permission from me."[3]

Speaking thus, I fell silent and noticed that even grandfather hesitated to accept the proposal I had put forth. Meaning, the matter of who would become the next king of Mathura remained as complicated as ever. However, it was decided in the meantime that the last rites of King Kansa would be performed with full honours. On the other hand, even though grandfather had not accepted the proposal, I could intuitively feel that the desire to sit on the throne had been kindled in his heart. Meaning, his hesitation in accepting the throne did not carry enough conviction. And the shrewd person that I was, I had noticed this clearly. Actually, grandfather's desire to reclaim the throne of Mathura and helm its affairs was quite understandable. He had been a successful king who had unfortunately been thrown into the dungeons and made to languish for years together. Therefore, at this stage in his life, it was natural for him to wish to become the king once again in order to prove himself. Meanwhile, there was another development that had taken place quite naturally. My suggestion to make grandfather the king had triggered a ripple of happiness through the ranks of the Yadava leaders. Their elation was understandable, for, they clearly did not want to lose the opportunity to be rid of me. Interestingly, no sooner had I voiced my decision than they began shouting slogans in support of King Ugrasena. They even started urging him to accept the proposal. As for grandfather, his reluctance was half-hearted

3. Harivansh Puran, Vishnu Parva, Chapter – 32, Verse – 18-53; Bhagavat Puran, Part – 10, Chapter – 45, Verse – 12; Vishnu Puran, Part – 5, Chapter – 21, Verse – 9.

anyway, so he soon gave in to the pressure of the Yadava leaders. Acceding to their request, he agreed to take charge of the kingdom. As soon as he nodded his head in agreement, I began to encourage the crowd to hail him. Thus, once again, preparations had commenced to put the reins of the kingdom of Mathura in the able hands of 'King Ugrasena'.

Finally, to my greatest relief, the matter was resolved! But before accepting the proposal, grandfather had put down a strange condition which astounded everyone including me. He stated that he would accept the throne only if I agreed to stay on in Mathura and promised to help him manage the affairs of the kingdom. Now, of course, there was no possibility of the Yadava leaders agreeing to this condition. But unfortunately, they were in no position to oppose grandfather at present. As for me, why would I object to the condition he had put forth? I was anyway keen to learn about the administrative affairs of a kingdom; moreover, I was his grandson…if I did not support my grandfather in his old age, who would? Besides, I had taken a liking to this city too. Hence, all things considered, there was no aspect of the proposal that would make me turn it down. For one, it was my duty to accept grandfather's condition; secondly, the proposal was very much to my liking. I, in fact, saw this new development as an opportunity to become worthy of Rukmini.

With my consent, the matter was settled—it was decided that King Ugrasena would grace the royal throne once again. In a sense, today was a momentous day for both grandfather and grandson, offering a similar kind of opportunity to each of us. On one hand, I, a cowherd boy, had the chance to become a king in mere moments; and on the other, grandfather, who had resigned himself to spending his life in prison, was crowned king in a matter of moments. Ah, isn't it incredible how quickly time shifts! In the blink of an eye, fortunes are reversed, turning a king into a pauper and a pauper into a king. This is why it is said that in this world there is no power greater than time. Well, grandfather and I had made our respective decisions, but bhaiya and the cowherd boys had become disappointed with my decision of rejecting the proposal to become king. As for the inhabitants of Mathura, it did not seem that it had made much difference to them whether it was grandfather or I who became king. All they wanted was deliverance from Kansa's tyranny, which I had given them already. Besides, I was not so well known or influential in Mathura that the *Mathurawasis* would be disappointed with my decision to decline the throne. As for the visiting princes and the Yadava elite, they had breathed a sigh of relief on my declining the proposal to become king.

Now, let me look at this entire episode from a different angle and tell you about the role played by others. And in that context, I must especially mention the praiseworthy deeds of the commander of the army. It was Mathura's good fortune that Jarasandha had played no part in the appointment of the commander of the army, which was why the commander was fully devoted to the welfare of Mathura and its inhabitants. He had shown keen intelligence and presence of mind by promptly freeing King Ugrasena after Kansa's assassination and escorting him to the festival arena. Speaking of the atmosphere in the arena, the majority of people had already left for their homes, anticipating trouble at any time, while a handful of bravehearts and curious onlookers still lingered. Of course, now that all the issues had been resolved one after the other, the atmosphere was also becoming normal. Mathura had found its new king, thus eliminating the risk of instability within the kingdom. The only matter that remained was performing Kansa's last rites with full honours. King Ugrasena had entrusted this responsibility to the commander, who quickly made all the necessary preparations. Surprisingly, a large number of people, including the princes, were still present at the ground, adhering to royal protocol. As for me, I had taken my place right behind grandfather, with bhaiya standing next to me. As soon as the preparations were complete, Kansa's funeral procession commenced, leaving the festival ground with full royal honours. Meanwhile, the news spread like wildfire, and the whole of Mathura gathered for the final farewell, everyone appearing grief-stricken. I had heard the expression that "with the death of a person, all his sins are washed away," and today, I was witnessing it too. Along with grandfather and me, several princes and members of the Yadava elite were walking towards the royal cremation grounds, with a crowd of around two thousand people following behind. Needless to say, King Kansa had become more popular in death than when he was alive. Well, the last rites were over and we had all returned to the arena, but soon, we had to face another issue—my inconsolable aunts. Indeed, my aunts' anger towards me was still a major cause for concern. Every time we faced each other, they would glare at me with eyes spewing embers. From the murderous look in their eyes, it was clear that given the chance, they would devour me whole! In fact, this was yet another, though small, reason why I had refused to become the king of Mathura. Their furious demeanour made it obvious that they would have never let me sit on the throne of Mathura in peace. Also, to my misfortune, their father, Jarasandha was the bravest and mightiest king of his time. So, even if I had agreed to become the king of Mathura, it was certain that my aunts would have instigated their father against me, causing me a lifetime of trouble. Oh, forget it! I will speak of my aunts some other time, but right now, let me talk about Rukmini whom I had seen accompanying my aunts. Although our eyes had met a couple of times, I couldn't fathom the thoughts racing through her mind. For that matter, was I capable of understanding anything at all at this point in time?

It was nearly evening by the time all the proceedings were complete, and needless to say, after the eventful day we had lived through, all of us were exhausted, especially bhaiya and I, who were tired to the bone. We had, after all, fought three successive fierce battles since morning and not a single morsel of food had passed our lips. Our condition was so pathetic that we were not even in a position to return home on our feet. Dragging ourselves with difficulty, we somehow clambered onto Uncle Akrura's chariot and set off homewards. Once home, it was a herculean task to even remove the clothes off our bodies and soak our tired selves in a bath. But we had to muster every ounce of strength left in our bodies to step in for a bath, as we had battled all day long and were thus drenched in blood. Well, once we soaked ourselves in the cool water, we felt life return to our limbs. And the moment we felt refreshed, pangs of hunger began to gnaw at us, driving us insane. This was the first time in our lives that we had gone without a morsel of food for such an extended period. Needless to say, as soon as the food was served, bhaiya and I pounced on it like hungry lions. Well, for that matter, earlier today, we had also attacked Kansa and his demons like hungry lions. So, we were simply continuing the tradition. Interestingly, for reasons best known to Uncle Akrura, his hospitality had a special touch to it today, for, we were served *Chhappan Bhog*, a meal comprising fifty-six food items. Indubitably, the marked change in the hospitality accorded to us and the scrumptious meal served to us were the result of our increasing political influence in the corridors of power at the palace.

No sooner had I finished devouring the *Chhappan Bhog* than sleep began to invite me into its beguiling arms. Hence, taking leave of uncle, I headed straight to my chamber and lay down on the bed. But despite the fatigue, I could not fall asleep and ended up tossing and turning in bed. My mind was caught up in reflecting upon the entire sequence of events that had transpired on this day. Indeed, it had been an extremely long and eventful day. I had left home in the morning to participate in the wrestling competition, but ended up confronting a mad elephant. Thereafter, I wrestled with Chanoor, and eventually, killed Kansa due to circumstantial compulsions. And if the duels I had fought weren't dramatic enough, grandfather had struck me with a thunderbolt with his proposal to crown me the king of Mathura. Incredible, wasn't it? Speaking of the proposal, for a short while between grandfather's offer and my refusal, I had become the king! In other words, this cowherd had certainly enjoyed the status of a king, albeit for a few fleeting moments. If nothing else, I could confidently say that I was no longer just an ordinary cowherd from Vrindavan. I had worn the invisible crown of a king, even if only for a brief time. In conclusion, today had been a day of victory for me in all respects. I first tasted victory on killing the mad elephant, and immediately after, I fought an intense duel with Chanoor, the most powerful wrestler in Mathura. Thereafter, I had even outwitted Kansa. However, all these victories paled in comparison to the victory I had achieved by way of securing Rukmini's admiration. Her repeated encouragement, her happiness over my victory, and her congratulating me over and over again were truly the greatest victories of my life. Indeed, for this cowherd boy from Vrindavan, who was a connoisseur of beauty, no other conquest could have been greater than attracting the attention of a princess!

But the question is, how did I gain this stupendous victory so effortlessly? On deeper reflection, I realised that many people had contributed to it, by becoming a 'medium' and driving me closer to this victory. Consider Uncle Akrura for instance. Had he not alerted me about Kansa's evil designs on our way from Vrindavan to Mathura, I would have been killed by Kansa long before. Why just Uncle Akrura, how can I overlook the contribution of that old man who had made a brilliant yet caustic remark about Kansa while we were wandering in the marketplace? Do you remember what he had said, 'The uncle has invited his nephew to the festival, but just see, he did not even have the courtesy to send a chariot for him. The poor fellow is walking around the marketplace on foot!' I'm sure you will recollect how this single sarcastic comment by the old man had instantly turned me into an astute politician. Had I not learnt politics in time, Kansa would have perhaps succeeded in his nefarious plans much sooner. Indeed, the truth was as clear as daylight. Thus, close on the heels of this thought, I began contemplating once again. Sleep had eluded me anyway, so I reckoned, why not ruminate over the sequence of events once again in the hope of discerning the reasons behind them? A barrage of questions had already begun to race through my mind such as, 'Is there a power that governs our lives? Were Uncle Akrura and that old man sent by that power? If I had not sharpened my awareness or learnt political tactics at the right moment, would I have been eliminated? Was there a connection between the lessons I had learnt and the fact that I was still alive? If this was so, then it meant that it was this very cosmic power that was governing all our lives. This also meant that it is verily this power that turns individuals or incidents into a 'medium' and sends us indications, guiding us on what to do, when to act and where to go. And if this is indeed the case, then our sole duty is to decipher these messages and act according to them. Yes! This had to be the case. For, it was precisely by learning and fathoming these messages that a mere cowherd from Vrindavan had the opportunity to take a giant leap in life to almost becoming the king of Mathura. And if that is really the case, then what about all those who fail to decipher these messages? Well, they are perhaps destined to be born as cowherds…and die as cowherds!

Having said that, it was just as well that I was brave, strong and courageous, else the mad elephant and Chanoor would have made me bite the dust in no time. The voice from within spoke up, 'Well, you had to survive these attacks on your life; that is why you turned out to be brave and courageous.' But how did I become brave and courageous? Perhaps, it was my habit of constantly learning and my selflessness that had largely contributed to this. But then, there are many people who are selfless and learn habitually too, but not all of them turn out to be brave and courageous, do they? So, did that mean that Kaaliya, Keshi and the mad bull were merely 'mediums' sent to build my courage and strength? If that were so, then instead of being my enemies, they were actually my friends! Viewed from this perspective, no one can ever be considered an enemy. This implies that this grand game of life is being played out only between two parties—the individual himself and Nature which governs his life. All the other people and things that stream in and out of one's life are mere 'mediums'. And if this is true, then whatever is happening is good, whatever transpired in the past was also good, and whatever happens in the future will also be good. Did you see? Today, my contemplation was soaring to entirely new heights. This impudent little mind had dared to fathom the mysteries of Nature. Perhaps, this was the result of having become a king, albeit only briefly! Well, whatever the reason may be, I could not ignore the fact that my contemplation and intelligence were not evolved enough to fully comprehend or unravel the mysteries of Nature. But so what? Today, I had taken a deep dive into contemplation for the very first time, and with the dawn of a new day tomorrow, more opportunities to reach new milestones would come my way.

Feeling a sense of calm from all the contemplation I was engaged in, I was just about to fall asleep when another question crept into my mind, jolting me wide awake. However, I was not able to contemplate on it. In other words, I was neither able to sleep nor contemplate. But it was essential to do one or the other; I could not just lie there forcing myself to sleep. Caught in this vexed situation, I mused, why not play the flute? It would become easy to clear my mind by immersing myself in its soothing melody; besides, it would be entertaining as well. It was definitely a good idea, so without wasting time, I picked up my flute and walked towards the garden. After a leisurely stroll, I came upon a flower-laden tree, its sweet fragrance soothing my jangled nerves. Sitting under its canopy, I could see the moon winking at me from between the branches. Oh, what an ethereal sight it was, enough to induce a beautiful melody from my flute! I thus became engrossed in playing, so much so that I don't even remember when the night melted away and morning tiptoed in. Perhaps, my flute had also become impatient to celebrate my victory. Well, I had fulfilled its yearning too, but what next? What I mean is, yesterday's events had completely exhausted me, and yet, instead of surrendering to the peaceful arms of sleep, I had spent the entire night awake. What more could I do now? A walk would perhaps help. Yes, this seemed to be the best way to drive away the lethargy that had set in from not being able to sleep. So, I did that as well! After returning from my walk, I saw that bhaiya had already bathed and was waiting for me in the veranda. The moment I set eyes on him, I remembered that we had to meet grandfather early in the morning. So, I hurriedly got ready and set out for the royal palace. At that moment, I was in a peculiar state of mind. I had faced enemies like Chanoor and Kansa, but this great enemy called 'sleeplessness' seemed unconquerable. Not just that, I was unable to shake off this menace called 'exhaustion' too, which had caught me in its grip since yesterday.

This was the first day after Kansa's death, and also the first time that we were visiting the royal palace. I had long desired to see the palace for so long, but until now, I had kept myself away from it out of fear of my uncle. However, as we approached it now, I could not help but be struck by its beauty and magnificence. Oh, I had never imagined it to be so impressive! This cowherd, who until this moment was under the impression that he lived in the best and most stately house in Vrindavan, saw his belief shatter on seeing the grandeur of the royal palace. Indeed, I watched with amazement the imposing structure, which appeared like an impenetrable fortress from the outside. The interior of the palace was even more magnificent, and for a moment, I was lost in its countless colossal chambers, huge pillars and beautiful paintings that adorned the walls. Truly, I was dazzled by the palace's splendour. Honestly, for a cowherd who had lived all his life in a mud house in a small village, this grand palace seemed no less than a dream. Really, there can be no comparison between a village house and a palace in a city! A city is, after all, a city, much like wealth has its own appeal, a palace its own magnificence, and a king his own authority! Seeing the grandeur of the royal palace, I was suddenly struck with a humorous thought. In jest, I said to myself, "Oh, you fool! By declining the royal throne, you have washed your hands off such a magnificent palace." Indeed, had I known this earlier, I probably wouldn't have declined the throne. Of course, this raillery was merely an attempt to drive off my lethargy, so do not take my rambling thoughts seriously at all.

As expected, the royal palace was in deep mourning, and we were immediately taken to grandfather's chamber. As soon as he saw me, grandfather crossed the distance between us in a matter of seconds and enveloped me in a warm, loving embrace. I too was overjoyed to see him. It was just yesterday that I had met him for the first time, yet in such a short span of time, our bond had already grown strong. We had developed a good rapport, which helped us understand each other well. After all, the relationship between a grandfather and grandson is always unique and special. Well, after indulging in some polite conversation, grandfather took us directly to the main assembly hall, which was packed to capacity. Along with all the nobility of Mathura, my aunts were present as well, wearing a wearied look, their swollen eyes a clear indication that they had spent the entire night weeping. It was only natural, after all, who can sleep in peace after having lost their beloved husband? But surprisingly, in spite of their exhaustion and anguish, they had managed to muster enough strength to glower at me. Even now, their demeanour suggested that they were ready to pounce on me and swallow me whole! Really, their malevolence towards me had left me dumbfounded and I was amazed to see that their anger was only surging with time. This too was a unique experience, for until now, whenever I had seen anger, it was of the kind that dissipated with the passage of time. For example, I had faced bhaiya's anger, father's annoyance, mother's ire, and even Radha's rage many times. But I had seen their fury subside as time went by. This was my first experience wherein I saw that anger, instead of abating, was intensifying over time. Well, despite the fact that this was my first such experience, I realised that if their anger continued to increase at this rate, then sooner or later, these women would surely create a problem for me. Even the behaviour of the Yadava elite did not seem favourable towards me. They certainly could not tolerate my closeness with grandfather. In other words, 'King Krishna' had stayed back in Mathura, considering it his duty towards his grandfather and with the intention of scaling new heights of the mind, but it did not seem that things would become any easier in the days ahead. At present though, I was sitting right beside my shield, that is, my grandfather, while people were still streaming into the assembly hall. Though everyone wore a sorrowful expression, the mourning of my aunts had scaled an altogether new level. Sitting amidst a court filled to capacity, they continued to cry bitterly, their grief-stricken cries reverberating all around. Their lamentation had troubled me even yesterday when Kansa lay dead at my feet, and hearing them shriek in this manner was vexing me today as well.

Nevertheless, let me apprise you of the situation that had suddenly undergone a change at present. Sometime after our arrival, the visiting princes began to flock in. Seeing them, I immediately thought of Rukmini, my eyes darting towards the entrance of the assembly hall, as if they had a will of their own. I was so eager to see her that my eyes, even though tired, having not slept a wink last night, kept gazing at the entrance, expecting her to arrive at any moment.

Did you see how my mood had taken a turn for the better and brightened up instantly? Once Rukmini's thoughts invaded my mind, there was no question of my paying attention to the mourning of my aunts. And due to this change in my mood, the entire situation felt a little bit strange. At the moment, about three hundred people were present in this grand and majestic assembly hall. To the right sat all the men, while the left side was occupied by a group of women including my aunts. Naturally, this group also included Mother Devaki, while Father Vasudeva and Uncle Akrura sat with us. Everything was proceeding peacefully so far, but while everyone else was sad and solemn, I sat half-turned in my seat, craning my neck and continuously looking at the entrance from where I expected Rukmini to enter. Fortunately, I did not have to wait for long, otherwise anyone watching me in this position would have surmised that Krishna had indeed gone insane, concluding that it was just as well that he had not been crowned the king! Well, who cares? Lovers are anyway known to indulge in crazed behaviour. And, just see, my patience paid off wonderfully, for, as soon as Rukmini entered through the doorway, our eyes met, and the moment I locked my gaze with hers, miraculously, all my exhaustion drained out of my body. She quickly glided her way to where my aunts were seated and joined them, but the rogue that I was, I continued to glance at her surreptitiously from the corner of my eye. The only difference was, sitting straight in my chair now, I had a full view of the princess sitting in front of me. Thus, I no longer needed to crane my neck to catch a glimpse of her. Sometimes, I too caught her glancing in my direction which made my heart skip a beat. In fact, the manner in which she kept stealing glances at me made me go wild, and I feared that my heart, pounding wildly, would burst out of my chest any moment now. Had the circumstances been different, I might have lost all self-control by now. In fact, to a large extent, I had lost my self-control even now. Losing all sense of time and place, I felt as if I was suspended in this beautiful moment forever, with just me and her in it. All that I yearned to do was look at her bewitching face, those large expressive eyes, the upturned nose, the rosebud lips which wore a naughty smile, and the manner in which she held herself with poise and elegance! And well, there was nothing wrong in it anyway! Unfortunately, our playful exchange of glances could not continue for long. A short while later, Rukmini got up and proceeded towards the exit of the hall. Watching her leave the hall, I became despondent, my gaze following her departing figure. Oh, why did she have to leave, while I was still seated here! I felt my heart being wrenched out of my body and my very life departing with her. Considering this state of mine, it suddenly dawned on me that I was hopelessly attracted to her. Was it not amazing that despite having never spoken to each other or being formally introduced, my vivid imagination had conjured up this neat, little game based solely on the conversation our eyes held with each other. Interestingly, this transgression had been committed by the eyes, but it was the heart that was being punished for it. I was so taken in by her charm that her arrival would make my heart dance with joy and her exit would plunge it into gloom. One look from her would drive me insane and if she ignored me, I would feel myself slipping into an abyss of despair, as if my very life had been wrenched out of me. I was still lost in these thoughts, when suddenly, I felt as if Rukmini was signalling me to step outside. For a moment as I watched her, I was dumbfounded, too dazed to even react. No, no, how is this possible! 'You are surely daydreaming, Kanhaiya! Why would Rukmini call you over…and that too, in the royal palace, in everyone's presence? Impossible! Krishna, you have lost your mind! You are of no use anymore. Kanhaiya, you are living in a fool's paradise. You are seeing things that do not exist. You would do well to remember your standing; so just keep quiet and remain seated.' Hence, I just sat there in silence, averting my gaze from Rukmini.

But alas, this was a restriction forced upon me by reason; my heart obviously had plans of its own. Thus, paying heed to my heart, my insolent gaze once again turned towards Rukmini. Was that a slight frown I noticed on her face? It seemed as if she was annoyed that I did not get up to go to her, and at the same time, she was still gesturing to me to step outside. Well, there was nothing ambiguous about it anymore. The princess was, indeed, beckoning the cowherd. I went delirious with joy—the gloom I was engulfed in a moment ago was now replaced by sheer bliss, my heart urging me to do cartwheels. So, without wasting a moment, I shot up from my seat and began walking towards her. I did not even make an effort to comprehend what was happening…or why. In any case, this cowherd was not refined enough to read the mysterious signals or comprehend the charming ways of princesses. The princess had summoned him and it was not for him to question or analyse, but merely obey her command. With brisk steps, I quickly reached the spot where she was waiting for me. However, the moment I reached her, without a word, she turned her back to me and began walking again, while my feet followed her of their own accord. Then, all of a sudden, she stopped and so did I. The sudden halt shook me out of my daze, bringing me back to reality, and with that, my senses returned too. On becoming aware of my surroundings, I found myself standing in a secluded corner of one of the long-winding corridors of the palace, far away from the crowd. Aha! So, the princess had already found a secluded corner for this beautiful encounter. Before I could think more on this, recover from the sudden turn of events or even celebrate, I found Rukmini gazing at me with great admiration. Well, it was only yesterday that I had executed three slayings, each more significant than the other, but one killer gaze from Rukmini was enough to sear the heart of even a valorous fighter like me. Truly, she had a knack for leaving her admirer gasping for breath. Neither had she used arrows or swords, nor had she resorted to tricks or treachery, yet one glance from her was enough to slay this lover and make him go weak in the knees. And while I was trying my best to recover from the combined effect of all this, she posed a question to me that made me swoon. With full authority in her voice, she asked me, "Why did you not accept the crown of Mathura?"

For a moment, I looked at her dazed, for, I had never expected this soft, delicate beauty with the most bewitching eyes to pose such a direct question at me. Today, my sharp 'mental calculations' were failing me terribly. All my remarkable qualities that I would flaunt with such panache had all but disappeared into thin air. Already on the verge of losing consciousness upon hearing this startling query, I was rendered totally speechless. My senses refused to function. Rukmini's piercing gaze continued to bore into me, numbing whatever little remained of my consciousness. Ah! Tell me now, how could I possibly shield myself from this onslaught even if I tried? And what could I say to her in response? However, realising that it was now or never, I gathered my wits and awakened my self-confidence. In fact, I admonished myself saying, 'Krishna, if you remain tongue-tied in the first meeting itself, how will you ever make her yours for life?' Truly, Rukmini had captivated me wholly in the first meeting itself. Or should I say, it was I who had willingly surrendered myself to her beguiling charm? Whatever the case may have been, at present, the reputation of Kanha—the darling of the *gopis*—was at stake. I was just thinking this, when the inner voice quipped, 'O fool! Just yesterday, you had learnt from grandfather the art of maintaining composure, so why aren't you putting that valuable lesson to use? Oh, for heaven's sake, she is just a princess of this earth, not some fairy who has descended from heaven!' Thinking thus, I quickly willed myself to become more confident. Taking a deep breath, I composed myself and, boldly looking into her eyes, spoke with full confidence, "Because I do not find in me the qualities required to become a king."

Hearing this frank admission from me, it was Rukmini's turn to look flabbergasted. Nonetheless, taking a deep breath, she spoke emphatically, "Wrong! In my opinion, there are just three essential qualities needed to become a great king. First, he must be brave enough to protect his throne.

Second, he should have the support of the people. And third, he should be concerned about the welfare of the people. And I see all three qualities in you."

I'm sure you must have understood how difficult it must have been for this poor cowherd to maintain his composure before this imposing princess of Kundinpur. Speechless, I just stood before her wide-eyed, listening to what she was saying. Today, I could neither find the words to express my feelings, nor think of a suitable response. What could I say? I had never engaged in a conversation of this stature before. You are already aware that I had been deeply impressed by Rukmini's powerful personality at first sight itself, and later, it was her innocence that had enchanted me completely. Moreover, her beauty had captured my heart long ago. And today, her courage and wisdom were bent on making me her slave. In other words, Kanha was totally slayed by Rukmini's charm. And when Kanha himself had been slain, what could he possibly say? Well, Kanha had been vanquished, but his vanquisher was still standing before him. So, with no reply coming forth from me, Rukmini decided to keep the conversation going. And this time, she spoke with an astounding firmness in her voice. Looking directly into my eyes, she said, "Let me state my clear opinion that your refusal to accept the royal throne of Mathura was not a very wise decision. Perhaps, you don't fully understand that for an ordinary cowherd, the opportunity to become a king—despite not being the son of a king—is itself an unprecedented, historic event. Do you realise, you may never get such a chance to make history again? In fact, the agony of not being able to become a king despite being fully qualified for it could even trouble you for the rest of your life."

Well, before I could fully comprehend the import of her words or even be impressed by the manner in which she spoke, her brother, Rukmi appeared out of nowhere. He no doubt glared at me with the nastiest expression imaginable, but seething with rage, he even grabbed my dear Rukmini's hand, almost dragging her away with him. With Rukmi's sudden appearance, the bubble of happiness I had found myself in just by being in Rukmini's presence burst, thus abruptly ending our beautiful yet enlightening encounter. With this incident, Rukmi once again made it amply clear that no matter how much an ordinary cowherd's heart yearned for love, a princess was still way out of his reach! Truly, Rukmi's rude behaviour shook me to my core, but despite this, my eyes continued to follow the departing figure of Rukmini. As for the princess herself, she was incredible indeed! In spite of all that had transpired, she appeared unfazed. And oh, what a daredevil she was! Before disappearing out of sight, she turned, threw a bewitching smile at me and even waved goodbye. Perhaps, this was the key difference between an uneducated cowherd and a well-educated princess. Circumstances had no power to ruffle her feathers! Well, I was not one to be so easily perturbed by circumstances either. It was just that my heart had betrayed me, making me a little weak in the knees. Indeed, Rukmini had left long ago, but I still stood rooted to the spot like a fool. And if I may confess, today, Krishna had also departed with Rukmini; what stood here was merely an empty shell of his physical being, and all that remained in this physical being were thoughts of Rukmini. At present, all I could do was lean on a pillar for support and let out a deep sigh, immersed in thoughts of my bewitching princess. Truly, every aspect of Rukmini was unique. How brave and carefree she had seemed when she had signalled to me to follow her! And right from the beginning of the conversation, she had assumed full command and expressed full confidence in my capability, while I stood before her like a smitten lover. Most importantly, even though she was a princess, she had taken a keen interest in ensuring a bright future for this ordinary cowherd. What balanced thinking, what maturity she had displayed for a person so young! She was not flustered even when Rukmi showed up unexpectedly. Even as she was being pulled away by her irked brother, she had not forgotten to wave at me. Of course, there was no way to tell if she was only interested in my capabilities or whether she was interested in me as a person as well. However, the state of my heart was quite clear—it wanted her at any cost. And to fulfil this desire, I made two resolutions at that very moment. One, I had to win Rukmini , come what may; and two, I had to make myself worthy of her. In short, even though I had not become a king this time, for Rukmini's sake, I would have to become one in the future.

But would this be enough to win her hand in marriage? What if our love was made to bear the brunt of her brother's ire? This bothersome, future brother-in-law was already annoyed with me; and seeing his behaviour, it was quite clear that he would leave no stone unturned to stop me from becoming his brother-in-law. Oh, just look at the way my imagination had begun to run wild, as if I had already become a king...as if Rukmini had already indicated her interest in marrying me, thereby urging me to think of a way to deal with Rukmi! Such a fool I was! This was like going to the royal palace to haggle over the price of butter even before purchasing a cow! Did you see, even here, I had used an analogy that reflected my life as a cowherd! After all, I was one. 'Oh, dear Krishna! It's alright to use an analogy that a cowherd would, but at least refrain from behaving like a cowherd! Look at you...instead of being present in the assembly hall, you are standing here like an idiot. Show some maturity and go sit with the others!' So, off I went to the assembly hall...but my mind was still elsewhere. Only my body had made it there. Still lost in thoughts of Rukmini, all I could think about was the unshakeable faith she had shown in my abilities.

Amazing, was it not? Even my own parents who had raised me had not shown such incredible faith in me. For that matter, even bhaiya, in whose company I spent all day, did not have as much faith in me. Therefore, obviously, the faith that grandfather and Rukmini had shown in me after just a few interactions, had astounded me. And as far as I was concerned, I had full faith in my abilities right from childhood. For that matter, when had I ever considered myself ordinary? Surely, I had not locked horns with Kaaliya, the serpent and Keshi, the demon just on a whim! Without a doubt, I had always considered myself capable, and there was never any question about it. The question that begged an answer was, why did only these two people show faith in me and not the others? This meant that to recognise someone else's capability, one must first be capable themselves. Be that as it may, I was so engrossed in these musings that I barely realised it was almost afternoon and people had begun to leave. Before long, the assembly hall was deserted. And as soon as everyone left, grandfather took us to the dining hall. Ah! What a huge and grand dining hall it was! I was awestruck. For that matter, it was not just the dining hall, but everything around me that was steeped in opulence. And I was taking in all these details with a keen eye. Oh, have you forgotten? It had now become necessary for me to not only notice and appreciate such objects of opulence, but also to understand how they were made. Do you see what I am hinting at? If you wish to bring home an esteemed princess, you would have to think of all this too!

Of course, this would all happen in due course of time, but for the present, pushing these thoughts at the back of my mind, I turned my attention to the pangs of hunger gnawing at my insides. Although I did not have to bother much, as we had already entered the huge dining hall, taken our seats, and the servants were ready to serve us the meal. Naturally, in such an environment, the euphoria I had felt upon meeting Rukmini began to fade. While waiting for the meal, my eyes wandered around the dining chamber. It could seat about twenty people at once. Our seats were not only soft and comfortable, but there were plush cushions too to lean on. As if that weren't enough, the dining table in front of us was also made of silver, as were the dining plates. Beautiful paintings adorned the pristine white walls of the dining area. However, there were only five people in the chamber at the moment—myself, bhaiya, grandfather, the commander and the chief minister. I'm not sure about the others, but we cowherd boys were over the moon. But oh, what was this? We, who sat in anticipation of a *Chhappan Bhog*, were served a plain and ordinary meal. Bah! My craving for a scrumptious meal vanished entirely. Such a grand palace and so ordinary a meal! Perhaps, it was due to grandfather's old age or the fact that the palace was mourning Kansa's death, but whatever the reason may be, this cowherd's fervent desire to partake of a royal *Chhappan Bhog* remained unfulfilled. Well, we ate whatever was served to us. The treat had ended and so had the love and affection! Now, I did not feel like lingering around the palace anymore; besides, I could also feel lethargy creep in. Naturally, the momentous deeds of the previous day and my sleepless night had begun to take their toll, so I sought grandfather's permission to leave.

Of course, I had to work hard to gain his permission, as he wanted me to stay in the palace. I too wished to stay, but my sharp political instincts suggested otherwise. The Yadava elite, already uneasy about my closeness with grandfather, could cause unnecessary trouble for him if I stayed in the palace. To be honest, I was eager to stay in this grand palace. But I knew it was far easier to convince myself not to stay than to try and reason with the stubborn Yadava clan. In short, the choice was between my desire to stay and grandfather's peace of mind. And naturally, grandfather's peace of mind was far more important to me. Besides, he too did not insist much on my staying back. He was under the impression that my refusal was on account of my enraged aunts. Well, this issue was settled, but perhaps grandfather, just like Rukmini, had fallen into the habit of constantly springing a surprise on me. I say this because just before I bid grandfather farewell, he gifted me a magnificent chariot. The gesture was so unexpected that I could barely contain my joy. Indeed, this wonderful gift from my grandfather completely won my heart.

My spirit soared upon receiving the chariot as a gift, and I was overjoyed for two reasons: first, I was thrilled to receive the chariot, and second, I was happy to have effortlessly reached the first milestone in my attempt to become worthy of Rukmini. Really, the standard of living in Mathura was so different when compared to Vrindavan! In Vrindavan, when father occasionally bought us a new garment, we would become delirious with joy. You might remember, the day he gave me a brand-new flute, I felt like I was floating on cloud nine. But here in this splendid city of Mathura, a gift meant no less than a magnificent chariot, and that too, a grand and royal one. Perhaps, that is why it is said that in a big city, everything is larger than life. Oh, but what's this? I instantly showed my petty-mindedness. As soon as I saw the chariot, I began daydreaming about Rukmini, wondering if there would ever dawn a day when she would ride beside me in this chariot. I had just begun to weave these sweet dreams when the charioteer signalled to us to climb aboard. Well, this was a matter of prestige for us, so bhaiya and I promptly climbed in and sat in the back seat. Honestly, the manner in which I sat, akin to the many princes whom I had seen riding in splendour, was a little too imperious. As soon as we settled down, the charioteer got the chariot moving and took us straight to Uncle Akrura's house. Funnily, the moment the chariot gained momentum, thoughts of Rukmini vanished from my mind and I was fully captivated by the chariot and its magnificence. Did you see how fast events were unfolding since our arrival in Mathura? Perhaps, this was the norm in a big city, and needless to say, it suited me well. I certainly enjoyed this way of life. In fact, it felt as if I had experienced more ups and downs in my two months' stay in Mathura than I had in the eighteen years I had spent in Vrindavan. Besides, in Vrindavan, I could have never imagined scaling the peaks of progress that I had achieved soon after my arrival in Mathura.

Engrossed in these thoughts, I barely realised that we had reached Uncle Akrura's house. As I stepped down from the chariot, I could feel exhaustion take over, so I retired to bed at once. But honestly, the chariot standing outside was not allowing me to sleep. With a brand-new chariot standing outside the house, how could the restless, impish Kanhaiya fall asleep? So, the nap was pushed aside, and as soon as evening set in, we rode the chariot towards the marketplace. Oh, what a thrilling experience it was to sit like royalty in the magnificent chariot, and watch it make its way through the market lanes! I felt as if I was seeing the marketplace of Mathura for the very first time. And oh, on our way back, I had not forgotten to stop by at Malini's for a refreshing, cool drink. How regally I had descended from the chariot and embraced Malini, who in turn had reciprocated with the same energy and warmth. Indeed, she was elated by her lover's progress, and she had every right to feel so. You might recall that I had met Malini on the very first day I had arrived in Mathura. The contrast between the Krishna of that day and the Krishna of today was nothing short of phenomenal! A *Vrindavanwasi,* who until yesterday was just an ordinary cowherd, had today transformed into Mathura's brave and valorous hero. And I must say, the biggest contribution to this transformation was Malini's alone. And it was because of this very valour I had displayed that everyone in the market was showing me respect today. Well, after my brief meeting with Malini, I headed home with bhaiya.

Today's trip to the marketplace was truly memorable. Not only did we roam around in great style, but we also got a taste of the regal lifestyle of princes. In other words, this cowherd had taken a significant first step towards progress. Later in the evening, we were all seated in the veranda after dinner. Though my eyelids felt heavy with sleep, my mind lingered on my newly acquired chariot. Meanwhile, bhaiya had already retired to bed after making some light conversation. But the restless one that I was, how could I fall asleep? And the reason was obvious: the chariot stationed outside was beckoning me. Alas, I could not hold myself back any longer! Thus, I called the charioteer and set off for the banks of River Yamuna. You already know that River Yamuna was my weakness, but as it was far from the city, I had not been able to travel there as often as I would have liked since my arrival in Mathura. However, now that we owned a chariot, there was no problem. Truly, a deep sense of calm descended upon me as I sat by the riverbank, my legs dangling in the cool water, in the darkness of the night. In any case, after the tumultuous events of the past two days, my mind craved peace and rest. Interestingly, on the way back home, I even tried my hand at riding the chariot and enjoyed it thoroughly. After all, if I were to take Rukmini out for a ride, I certainly couldn't have a charioteer accompanying us! A person does need a little privacy when in the company of his beloved.

On reaching home, I headed straight towards the bed. But alas! I was already robbed of my sleep due to my infatuation with Rukmini, and now to aggravate my restlessness, there was the chariot. Really, they had both become enemies of my sleep! But today, I needed to sleep, come what may. After staying awake for the past two nights, I was completely exhausted. At present, the body was no longer capable of assisting the mind. The mind may wish to fly to a hundred places, but the body functions in its own unique ways. So, I somehow managed to fall asleep. The next day, as soon as I woke up refreshed after a sound sleep, my intellect took over. I wondered to myself, 'How long could we possibly stay at Uncle Akrura's place?' It made sense to stay on until the festival was over, but now, I was unsure of how long we might have to stay back in Mathura. The decision of when I would return to Vrindavan was in grandfather's hands. At the same time, staying in the royal palace seemed unwise as far as my own security and the peace of Mathura were concerned. This being the case, the only alternative was to take residence at father's house. Besides, the reason I had avoided staying with him so far was also eliminated—Kansa was already slain! Well, I had slain him myself! And now that the decision was made, there was no need for my friends, the cowherd boys, to stay back in Mathura either. So, when I met them in the afternoon, I instructed them to return to Vrindavan. However, my instruction opened a whole new can of worms, as they began insisting that both bhaiya and I should return with them. Bah! What sort of a request was this? At present, it was imperative for us to stay back in Mathura. Thus, with great patience, I tried to make them understand that the prevailing situation in Mathura did not allow us to accompany them, but at the same time, I also assured them that we would return at the earliest. Almost all the cowherd boys were convinced, but Uddhava and Shripaad turned a deaf ear to my pleas and refused to go without us. What a strange situation I found myself in! Standing just outside the royal guest house, I was convincing them, while several *Mathurawasis* who passed us by were astonished to see us engrossed in such an animated discussion; many of them even greeted me from afar. Whether I knew them or not, there was not a single person in Mathura who did not recognise the slayer of their king. Well, I had a difficult time convincing the cowherd boys, but finally, my efforts bore fruit and they agreed to go. However, the problem was still not resolved fully. Just as I heaved a sigh of relief, Uddhava fired a clever salvo at me. With the intention of poking fun at me, he asked, "Do you have any message for Radha?"

Argh! What could I possibly say in response? So, ignoring his question, I chose to remain silent. Why react and give them the chance to drag the issue out? Of course, I knew this wouldn't end here. Once these cowherd boys started needling me, they wouldn't stop until they'd put me in an embarrassing situation.

And that's exactly what happened! Enthused by Uddhava's question, Shripaad jumped in to tease me with his tongue-in-cheek remarks. Deliberately raising his voice, he asked, "When people ask about what happened here, what should we reveal?"

Irked by his ill-timed question, I blurted out, "Whatever has happened, and whatever is happening now. Go tell them everything!"

Perhaps, Uddhava was just waiting for such a response from me, hence he piped up, "So, can we tell everybody about your exploits with Kubja?"

I replied, "Yes."

"Oh, even to Radha?" Uddhava quipped.

Hearing him utter Radha's name, I was silenced at once. Indeed, I had no choice but to put down my weapons and grin in embarrassment. Truly, no other pleasure in life can bring the simple, pure happiness that comes from bantering with friends. My mind was not at all ready to part with such friends, but parting with them was the need of the hour, so we had to. In life, things do not always transpire the way we want them to; at times, one has to convince oneself to flow with the tide, so I had done just that. Well, after extracting a firm commitment from bhaiya and me that we too would return to Vrindavan soon, the cowherd boys departed in a cheerful state of mind. But what saddened me was that Mother Yashoda and Father Nanda had also left with them. Nevertheless, we were fortunate to have Father Vasudeva and Mother Devaki, who felt blessed to have us stay with them. Honestly, the joy on their faces greatly alleviated the sorrow I felt on parting with Nanda and Yashoda. As father's mansion was quite huge, bhaiya and I were allotted spacious chambers of our own. These chambers were so grand that they just could not be compared to the ones in Vrindavan. Interestingly, the moment

I entered my chamber, I felt as if it belonged to me. However, there was one thought that puzzled me. Despite the love and care that was being lavished upon us, somewhere deep down, I failed to fathom why I could not feel as much affection for Mother Devaki as I felt for Mother Yashoda. Perhaps, the immense love that Mother Yashoda had showered on me for eighteen years as I grew up outweighed the love of my biological mother.

Ah, but let me put aside these sentiments and speak about the present situation in Mathura. All the princes who had arrived for the festival had departed by now, and sadly, my dear Rukmini had also left with them. Naturally, I was saddened by her departure, but what made it all the more heart-wrenching was the fact that we had not been able to meet one last time before she left. Perhaps, Rukmi had taken her back to Kundinpur on the same day that he had dragged her away from me so that our 'budding affair' could be nipped in the bud. Argh! Was he so daft to not realise that he would soon become my brother-in-law? Indeed, this sort of impudent behaviour does not suit a brother-in-law at all! I must say, it was because of this very brother-in-law that my plight had become indescribable. Truly, Rukmini's departure had pushed me into an abyss of sorrow. Everything seemed bleak to me, as I moved around in this melancholic state. Even though Radha used to quarrel with me frequently, at least she was always nearby. But Rukmini had vanished from sight! I had sunk into such despair that not only could I no longer find joy in Mathura, but my mind had lost interest in the world itself. Struck by love, I roamed around for a day or two wearing a cloak of gloom, preferring the solitude of my thoughts. But how long could I continue to mope like this? I mused, 'If the person you are pining for does not care, then why should you lose your sleep over them?' In fact, this was yet another facet of my personality—I could not remain dejected for long. Fun and laughter were intrinsic to my nature, so how long could sadness persist? And the best way to overcome sadness is to shift the mind's focus onto something else. Unfortunately, there was nothing new happening in the city of Mathura that I could engage my mind in. But I did not let that stop me. I began focusing on my daily tasks, and with that, life quickly slipped into a routine. Every morning, I would go to the palace and later to the marketplace to meet Malini. In the evening, I would take lessons in chariot-riding and have dinner with my parents.

Diverting my mind from my sorrows yielded a pleasant result too. Due to the routine I had fallen into, I quickly learnt to ride the chariot. With chariot-riding, happiness bounced back into my life, and the chariot soon became the centre of my existence, pushing all thoughts of Rukmini to the back of my mind. And now that I had learnt to manoeuvre the chariot on my own, I reckoned, 'Why do I need a charioteer?' Hence, I sent him back to the palace. Riding the chariot on my own was a thrill in itself, and now, all day long, I could be seen riding through the streets and by-lanes of Mathura in great style. One night, on a sudden whim, I set off with bhaiya towards the banks of River Yamuna. On our return, I rode the chariot through the deserted streets of Mathura at such speed that it felt as if the chariot was flying, talking to the wind. Excitement coursed through my veins, and every pore of my being seemed rejuvenated as the cool night breeze whistled through my curls, sending them flying wildly across my face. In fact, now that I had learnt to ride the chariot, I had begun to enjoy my stay in Mathura. But the killjoy that bhaiya was, he had no interest in staying here, and for obvious reasons too. Neither did he have any interest in politics nor in riding around in a chariot; he did not have a friend like Malini either. Although he would not complain, his cheerless demeanour was making it evident. At times, when he felt utterly forlorn, he would pose questions like, "What do you reckon? When will we be able to return to Vrindavan?"

I could empathise with his pain of being away from Vrindavan. His only problem was, he did not feel at home in Mathura. But this could be alleviated if I found something that would interest him here. It was crucial for bhaiya to develop an interest in some activity; else he would either drag me back to Vrindavan or make my life miserable in Mathura. Well, very soon, I found a solution to this problem as well. We began attending a local wrestling club, and no sooner did we start doing this than bhaiya became so absorbed in the sport that he even resumed his practice with the mace. We had already killed Chanoor and Mushtik, the best wrestlers of Mathura, so who in their right minds would now challenge bhaiya in wrestling?! But even so, he found immense joy in trouncing the inexperienced wrestlers of Mathura. Another stroke of luck was, as soon as bhaiya began practising at the wrestling club, he gained widespread fame and recognition for his exceptional fighting skills throughout Mathura. Indeed, bhaiya had taken to the wrestling ring like a fish to water. Phew! I was finally free. I no longer had to worry about keeping bhaiya company every day. He would go to the wrestling ring on his own to showcase his strength. For that matter, I too would often head to the wrestling ring accompanied by Kubja to cheer him on. Sometimes, egged on by Kubja, I would even step into the ring for a couple of bouts with the wrestlers. As for bhaiya, he had become so adept at wrestling that he would take on no fewer than five wrestlers at once, and only then would he feel somewhat satisfied. Occasionally, on his insistence, I too would practise with the mace. Incidentally, due to his fondness for the wrestling ring, bhaiya had almost stopped accompanying me to the palace.

Well, the good news was, he had become friends with a couple of sweetshop owners who also frequented the wrestling ring. In short, bhaiya was enjoying himself thoroughly, satiating not just his love for wrestling but also feasting on mouth-watering delicacies, which his new friends would provide him for free. Furthermore, his reputation as a wrestler was scaling new peaks of fame and glory throughout Mathura.

Meanwhile, I continued to visit the palace every day without fail, regularly attending the discussions being held with the council of ministers. Grandfather too lost no opportunity to encourage me and spur my enthusiasm. His constant words of encouragement helped boost my self-confidence. Gradually, I reached a stage whereby if I understood the point under discussion, I would not hesitate to voice my opinion on it. And if I received praise for my intelligence, my chest would swell with pride and my spirits would soar. After all, how mature could I have been at eighteen years of age? Although, I am not sure if I was really speaking intelligently or if grandfather was praising me every now and then just to encourage me; but regardless of the reason behind his praise, my self-confidence continued to surge.

One day, during an assembly of the ministers, the commander alerted everyone's attention to a grave issue. I too began to listen attentively. At any rate, grandfather had made a permanent seat for me next to his throne to grant me importance, while the rest of the chamber had arrangements for seating the courtiers. Coming back to the commander, he informed us that during Kansa's rule, a unit of soldiers had been commandeered from the kingdom of Magadha, which Kansa had later inducted permanently into his army. But now, after Kansa's death, the commander was sceptical about the allegiance of those soldiers to Mathura. So, the question that came up for debate was whether they should be retained or dismissed. In grandfather's opinion, these soldiers of Magadha who had been completely loyal to Kansa may no longer prove to be as loyal to the royal palace as before. However, arriving at a decision was not as easy as it seemed. For, if we terminated the services of the Magadha unit, it would mean antagonising Jarasandha, the king of Magadha; and no one wanted to make Jarasandha their enemy, especially grandfather. Therefore, his nervousness regarding this matter was totally justified. It was, after all, Jarasandha's power that had not only dethroned him earlier, but had also forced him to languish in prison for the past several years. However, when the commander explained the entire matter, we learnt that his anxiety stemmed from a far graver situation than the mere loyalty of these soldiers; he feared that these soldiers of Magadha might rise up in mutiny upon receiving Jarasandha's orders. Even the Chief Minister was quick to concur with the commander on this issue, but he was thinking far ahead of the present problem. In addition to the question of loyalty, he was worried about the royal treasury too. During Kansa's reign, the treasury had almost run dry, mainly because Kansa had never paid much attention to it. The Chief Minister firmly opined that "Considering the alarming state of the royal treasury at present, it is no longer possible for Mathura to bear the burden of paying salaries to these additional soldiers from Magadha."

Since the matter was serious and had several implications, a long series of discussions and debates followed. Both the problem and the discussions had piqued my interest, so I started listening to every word spoken with rapt attention. In fact, I kept committing to memory all the opinions expressed for and against the issue. Simultaneously, I had also begun to process all the information in my mind to tackle this problem. This was the first time in my life that I was witnessing such an intelligent discussion, and admittedly, it felt quite strange at first, for, I found myself oscillating between two contradictory viewpoints. When someone presented a strong argument to state a certain point, I would find myself agreeing with them wholeheartedly. But when someone else presented an equally strong case against it, I would find myself nodding in agreement with that too. However, this dithering did not continue for long, and gradually, I began to catch the nuances of all the arguments. You may find it hard to believe, but in just a short while, after listening to all the viewpoints, I had even formed a firm opinion on the issue. But I hesitated to offer any suggestions, fearing I might look foolish.

Towards the end of the discussion though, an astonishing thing happened. After all the arguments for and against were tabled and discussed threadbare, just as grandfather was about to proclaim his decision, he paused and asked me if I had any opinion on the matter. A thousand thoughts coursed through my mind at lightning speed. One loud and persistent voice pleaded, 'Kanhaiya, for heaven's sake, do not open your big mouth; you will make an absolute fool of yourself!' Another voice emphatically advised, 'Don't be silly! Why let such a golden opportunity to demonstrate your wisdom slip by?' I found myself badly trapped between these two voices, sometimes paying heed to one, and at times, supporting the other. Earlier, it was the arguments and counter-arguments during the discussion that had made me oscillate between opinions, and now, my own mind was vacillating between two extremes. Seeing me caught in a dilemma, grandfather encouraged me and said, "State your opinion without fear, Kanhaiya. Not only I, but the entire court is eager to hear your thoughts on this matter."

Well, I had no dearth of enthusiasm and self-confidence, and with grandfather's encouragement, I got all the push I needed. So, I stood up at once and began to express my views with full confidence. I said, "In my opinion, the depleted state of Mathura's royal treasury and the question mark over the loyalty of the Magadha unit is cause enough to dismiss these soldiers. And as far as Jarasandha is concerned, he has never been a well-wisher of our king. Mathura can perhaps deal with Jarasandha alone, but if the Magadha unit revolts, we will end up paying a high price for it. History bears testimony to the fact that it is always difficult to deal with traitors hiding within one's own ranks. Even a powerful king like Ravana was defeated primarily because his own brother, Vibhishana had betrayed him. Another fact worth considering is that Kansa, during his rule, had given too much importance and preferential treatment to the Magadha unit. The local Mathura divisions must have surely resented this, but they must have felt compelled to keep their resentment in check during Kansa's reign. But now that Kansa is no more, we may witness not just an outpouring of this resentment but also a resurgence of their hopes. And if that happens, the army would unnecessarily be split into two factions. And surely, a divided army is like having no army at all. Thus, in my firm opinion, all the reasons point to only one solution: dismissing the Magadha unit." After voicing my opinion in an unambiguous manner, I took my seat, but you will not believe this, my opinion drew a favourable reaction from everyone present in the assembly. To my surprise, not only did everyone praise me, but the Magadha unit was also dismissed with immediate effect. With this significant input, I not only became grandfather's favourite but also gained respect in the eyes of the council of ministers, who now viewed me as a wise and sensible person.

Just as I had hoped, the termination of the Magadha unit led to a positive impact on Mathura's soldiers as well, who celebrated the decision with great fanfare. With the dismissal of the Magadha unit, the people of Mathura also began to trust the royal palace. After many years, hope rekindled in the hearts of the *Mathurawasis* that the royal palace truly had their best interests at heart. And the reason for them thinking in this manner was absolutely clear. During Kansa's rule, all the atrocities on the inhabitants of Mathura were committed by these very soldiers of Magadha, so when they were dismissed, naturally, the *Mathurawasis* began to regard the royal palace as their well-wisher. Praise for King Ugrasena began resounding from all corners, and even I, his grandson, received his fair share of praise for putting forth the proposal. On one hand, I was gaining fame in Mathura, and on the other, tales of my heroic deeds were spreading far and wide, across the length and breadth of Aryavarta. As you are aware, I had already gained some recognition in Aryavarta when I had put a stop to the practice of *Indrapuja*, and now the slaying of Kansa had elevated my fame and recognition to a whole new level. The fact that a mere 18-year-old had killed Kansa was big news in itself. It is also worth noting that only a few great kings or distinguished *Acharyas* were widely known and respected across Aryavarta. From this perspective, I was the sole exception among the region's most famous and illustrious personalities. For, neither was I a king nor a prince, neither a minister nor a commander in an army, neither an *Acharya* nor a great artist. And yet, today, I was no less famous than any of these eminent personalities. This is the very reason why I emphatically state that it does not matter where a person is born or under what circumstances he is raised. What holds importance is how much he learns from his circumstances.

Well, things continued this way and I carried on with my usual routine. There was nothing else to do except going to the court on a daily basis, having meals with my parents, meeting Malini and riding my chariot. And now that I have mentioned the chariot, my newest passion, let me tell you about a positive change that had occurred in me—with my daily practice of riding the chariot, I had turned into an expert charioteer. Oh, what a splendid chariot it was! Pulled by two strong, white horses, it was completely under my control. Manoeuvres such as bringing the racing chariot to a sudden halt or swerving it at a high speed in a matter of moments had now become child's play for me.

Speaking of recent changes, a great opportunity for change soon came knocking at my door. And surprisingly, it was bhaiya who became a medium in bringing this opportunity to me. It so happened that one night, I had stepped out with him for a ride around Mathura, when on a sudden whim, he said, "Kanhaiya! This sweetmeat business looks quite profitable. Why don't we give it a try?" I liked the idea as soon as I heard it. In any case, I wanted to forge ahead in life, and you already know that the reason behind it was Rukmini alone. So, as soon as bhaiya put forth the idea, I drifted off into a reverie—Kanhaiya, a wealthy shopkeeper, sitting at his shop selling sweets! But dreams, after all, are only dreams. Confronted with the harsh reality of life, they quietly fade into oblivion. And this is what happened in our case too, for, after a preliminary discussion, I realised that we did not have enough money to set up a shop. All things considered, even though the idea seemed promising, we lacked the means to turn it into reality. With this, I also realised that it is not easy for penniless cowherds to progress in life. Although this did not affect me much, it saddened bhaiya a great deal. And you are well aware that I could face any difficulty or hardship, but I could not bear to see bhaiya unhappy. As a result, his gloominess pushed me too into an abyss of despair. At this point, however, time took a turn and proved that the winds of change were indeed blowing strong all around us. Grandfather was quick to sense my sadness, and no sooner did he enquire about the reason behind it, I revealed the entire matter to him without hesitation. Listening to my explanation, he first laughed out loud, then, running his hand tenderly over my head, said, "Is that all? Is that why you're so upset?!"

Before I could wrap my head around what he meant, he immediately gave orders for a hundred cows to be allotted to us from the cowshed of the royal palace in exchange for a nominal annual tax. And just like that, we were back in business! When I shared this news with bhaiya, he jumped for joy. Oh, he was unstoppable now! He sat down to prepare a list of all the delicacies he would sell at the shop. In fact, he was so excited that he couldn't think of anything else. Bhaiya usually had a calm temperament and it was not in his nature to be overly excited; but today, his enthusiasm had surpassed even my own. The blueprint of the business was prepared overnight, and the very next day, we first recruited a bunch of cowherd boys, who were tasked with the responsibility of taking the cows for grazing. Of course, now that we had turned into businessmen, we could not take the cows for grazing ourselves, could we? When father was apprised of our plans, he too shelled out some money from his savings to encourage us. With this monetary assistance, we soon set up a cowshed. Since we were cowherds by nature, there was no question of us shirking hard work. Brimming with enthusiasm, bhaiya and I toiled day and night. You won't believe it, but in just two months, we not only purchased a shop in the marketplace, but also stocked it with wares and kick-started our business. All kinds of delicious sweets made from milk, curd, butter and sugar-candy were available at our shop. With the passage of time, the business continued to thrive, and with that, our efforts and dedication towards it increased too. Within a short span of time, we had shops operational in all three main marketplaces of Mathura, with bhaiya at the helm of managing all three shops. And oh, what a sight he made! He would sit so pompously in the shop as if he was the most eminent businessman in all of Mathura. Meanwhile, our burgeoning business began to fuel the resentment of the Yadava elite, who already despised us for no apparent reason. Their attitude towards us made it evident that they considered us competitors who were eating into their business. Well, this may have been true, for, our new shops had more customers thronging to them compared to their long-standing, renowned ones. Now, whether it was due to the way bhaiya and I interacted with our customers, the quality of our offerings, or the stamp of royalty attached to our shop, the fact was, our enterprise was flourishing rapidly. We were no longer poor cowherds struggling to survive. With the success of our venture, a fresh chapter unfolded in our lives in Mathura, one that promised not just prosperity, but a future filled with hope and endless possibilities.

Chapter 2

Face-off with Jarasandha

Our days in Mathura were passing peacefully, and verily, what more could we ask for?! A comfortable house, delicious food, fine clothes, and above all, a splendid chariot in which I rode majestically around the city. Really, I could not tell if Mathura was gradually growing on us, or we were embracing it in earnest! Either way, the result was clear: we had become true *Mathurawasis*—just like the other inhabitants of Mathura. While we were relishing every moment of our stay in this city, we were suddenly greeted with more joy that came cascading into our lives. As was my daily routine, that day too, I was sitting in our shop in the main marketplace, when father's aide came in search of me—and you won't believe the news he brought! Mother Yashoda and Father Nanda had arrived in Mathura! My joy knew no bounds on hearing this news. Actually, Nanda was wont to visit Mathura every year to pay Vrindavan's annual taxes, but this year, he had brought Mother Yashoda along as well. Perhaps, the fact that mother was missing her darling son in Vrindavan must have compelled Nanda to bring her along and spring this pleasant surprise upon us. As soon as I heard the news, I jumped down from the shop's veranda and raced towards our house, my heart beating wild with excitement. A flurry of thoughts flooded my mind, the foremost being, 'how had my poor mother spent her days without her darling son?' And look at me, how callous I had been in not even bothering to enquire about her well-being! But what could I do? I was so engrossed in my activities in Mathura that I hardly had any time to think about anything else. But now, everything else paled into insignificance. The moment I received the news of mother's visit, I was lost in thoughts of her. In fact, I had even begun to converse with her in my head. What can I say, my bond with Mother Yashoda was such that her arrival was bound to send me soaring to the skies. Honestly, I hadn't felt this happy since my arrival in Mathura. There was no greater joy for me than knowing that, in just a few minutes, I would be standing before my beloved mother, in her very presence! Naturally, Nanda and Yashoda were staying with Vasudeva, as they had no other relatives in Mathura. And, of course, they would stay wherever Krishna, their beloved son, was.

When I entered the gate, I saw Mother Yashoda seated on the swing, her eyes riveted on the entrance, awaiting my arrival. Nanda was seated beside her, while Devaki and Vasudeva were seated close by. As soon as I entered the house, I touched my parents' feet in reverence, but mother instantly pulled me up—her brave son—and wrapped her arms around me in a tight embrace. And before we realised it, we were both swept away in a tide of emotions. With sundown, bhaiya returned as well, and the conversation thereafter continued till the wee hours. Oh, what joy it was to sit in the garden, with me comfortably settled at mother's feet, her fingers tenderly running through my curls, while the soft glow of the torches cast a radiance around us. In fact, this had become our daily routine. It seemed that Mother Yashoda had brought my entire childhood along with her. Every evening, we would all sit in the garden, while she would open a trunk full of memories of Vrindavan and I would hopelessly get lost in them—Vrindavan's soft, earthen by-lanes, the sparkling waters of River Yamuna, the beautiful lakes nestled amidst tall fruit-laden trees, the mighty Govardhana Mountain, the *gopis* and...Radha! Oh, life was magical then! Everything a person needed to lead a serene, blissful life was available right there. If I were to compare Vrindavan with Mathura, then Mathura was no doubt a bigger city. It offered us exciting business opportunities, a far more spacious house, a certain degree of eminence in the royal palace, and now, we had our own transportation too. At the same time, if seen from a socio-economic perspective, the city was full of possibilities for its inhabitants to carve a bright future for themselves. But if I were to stop comparing and talk about my preference, then I must say, Kanha liked both these places, as each was unique in its own way. The offerings of one place could not be found in the other. Indeed, the city and the village represented two radically diverse ways of life. Lost in these thoughts, I suddenly found my contemplation swerving in a new direction. I began to think, although I was born in Mathura, it was not really my decision to go to Gokula; the circumstances at that time had played a major role in this. Similarly, coming to Mathura from Vrindavan was not my decision either. It was my uncle's sudden outpouring of 'affection' towards me that had brought me here. Even now, it was not my decision to stay back in Mathura. It was grandfather's wish and Mathura's welfare that had held me back in Mathura. And when it was always circumstances that had decided where I would stay, why was I engaged in this futile exercise of comparing Mathura and Vrindavan, especially when I liked both places equally? But then, it was not I who had started thinking on these lines; it was Mother Yashoda who made me do it. From the day she had arrived in Mathura, she had been glorifying Vrindavan and poor me had begun reminiscing about the bygone days. But honestly speaking, life in Vrindavan was so peaceful, pleasurable and full of love, whereas life in Mathura was tough, insipid, friendless and fraught with struggles. Vrindavan was inhabited by simple and affectionate people, whereas the streets of Mathura were teeming with egoistic, selfish and manipulative individuals. Just see how quickly mother's arrival in Mathura had changed my perspective! The scales had now tipped in favour of Vrindavan. No, no, that is not true at all! It is just that I had allowed myself to be swayed by emotions. Otherwise, why would I care? For, as stated earlier, the choice wasn't mine. Both Vrindavan and Mathura were significant in their own way; I had compared the two just for the sake of it. This was all fine, but what was I supposed to do about this contemplation of mine which would just not stop? If I diverted my mind from one thought, it would promptly latch on to another. And ever since mother's arrival, this had turned into a nightly ritual. I would retire to bed only after hearing stories of Vrindavan from her, and then I would find it difficult to fall asleep, reminiscing about Vrindavan all night long. Although, one day, I was taken by surprise. Lost in deep thought, I was contemplating over Vrindavan and Mathura, when a question cropped up in my mind, 'Is it not possible for love and progress to co-exist?' Of course, it is possible. I will prove it through my life that it is indeed possible for love and progress to co-exist. For, I myself cannot live without either of these. I enjoyed Vrindavan's love-filled, peaceful way of life as well as Mathura's progressive, fast-paced life. And obviously, since I liked both, I wanted both. Why should I unnecessarily subject myself to the pain of not having one of these in my life? Now, although this was a pipe dream, it was definitely a positive one. And the pleasant outcome of this positive thinking was, on this night, I was able to surrender myself to the restful arms of sleep.

Since Mother Yashoda's arrival in Mathura, I had started having all my meals at Vasudeva's house, which also gave me the perfect excuse to savour every story that mother dug out from her treasure trove of memories. It also gave me the opportunity to sit in the garden and chat with her for hours every night. Mother Yashoda's narration would bring to life the golden memories of Vrindavan, and listening to her, I would find myself travelling back in time to experience the feelings each memory evoked in me. Ever since mother had arrived, this had become our daily routine. It could be said that in a way, mother's memories would spirit me away to Vrindavan. Every day, our gatherings would make for a picturesque scene, with Mother Devaki and Mother Yashoda sitting on the swing, Nanda and Vasudeva sitting close by absorbed in their own conversation, and bhaiya and I sitting on the floor in front of the swing, lost in Mother Yashoda's stories for hours together. Indeed, only a person who has indulged in the innocent joys of childhood can turn into a promising youth later in life. A youth aspires to progress in life, whereas a child merely wants to play. Hence, only someone who has revelled in the joys of childhood to his heart's content can walk the path of progress in his youth. Perhaps, this was the secret behind my rapid success after coming to Mathura. I can state with conviction that any child who has spent his childhood in a serious environment can never turn out to be a promising youth. And needless to say, if one fails to become a good youth, how can he be a good person in his old age?

Well, Mother Yashoda stayed with me in Mathura for just seven days. Amazingly, while she spent these seven days in Mathura, I spent this same period in Vrindavan...which was alright, but this made life in Mathura seem dull and lifeless. Indeed, there were no festivals or celebrations in Mathura. All it had was the humdrum routine, with each day melting into the next without any significant change. But thanks to mother, before leaving Mathura, she had at least etched the golden memories of Vrindavan in my mind, and in such vivid detail that those memories stayed with me for the rest of my life. Indeed, I have no words to describe Mother Yashoda's love! I was eternally grateful to her. In all these days, the angel that she was, she had not asked even once, "Son, when are you returning to Vrindavan?" As always, the happiness of her son was of prime importance to her, overriding everything else. It did not matter to her whether I stayed in Vrindavan or Mathura, whether I stayed with her or far away…she had ensconced me in her heart in such a manner that I could never be far from her even for a moment. Wasn't Mother Yashoda wonderful? In fact, I was the fortunate one, raised for eighteen years by someone who was the very personification of unconditional love. To see me smile, she had accepted with grace the sacrifice of her only daughter; where on earth would you find such a loving mother? Honestly, throughout the entire time that mother stayed with me in Mathura, I was tempted every single day to accompany her back to Vrindavan. But that was not possible as I had my new business to take care of. Besides, grandfather would not allow me to leave either. But then I reckoned, Vrindavan was just a day's journey from Mathura, so I could visit whenever I wanted. And now that I had a chariot of my own, it would take me just half a day to reach Vrindavan if I raced at full speed.

These fleeting thoughts had entered my mind only because I was feeling sad and homesick since mother's departure—nothing seemed to hold my interest anymore. Although I had bid mother farewell with a smile on my face, hiding the tears that threatened to spill, later in the day, I plonked myself on the banks of River Yamuna and spent hours listlessly throwing pebbles into the river. It was evening now, yet I couldn't find solace. This was still alright, but the actual problem began only now. Although I had managed to get through the day somehow, as night descended, I found myself unable to fill the void left by my mother. Over the past seven days, I had become habituated to sitting with Mother Yashoda, listening to her countless stories of Vrindavan, but now that she had left Mathura, this was just not possible. This thought was enough to make me angry and restless, and in this irked mood, I hurled one last stone into the water. But none of these antics were going to bring my mother back. So, with a heavy heart, I trudged back home. However, my condition worsened once I reached home, for, I had lost my appetite completely. Momentarily frustrated, I muttered to myself that it would have been far better had I left with mother for Vrindavan.

I found myself caught in a strange situation. Try as I might, I could not fall asleep; instead, I kept recalling Mother Yashoda's tales. Every time I closed my eyes, hoping for rest, images of a vibrant Vrindavan danced before me. Well, there would always be time to rest, I reasoned, so why not heed the wishes of my heart? Mother was not here with me, but at least I had fond memories of her in my heart. Oh, how happy both my mothers had been when I had taken them on a sightseeing tour of Mathura in my chariot! How could I ever forget the pride and joy Mother Yashoda felt when she saw my sweet shops? How could I forget the look of contentment on her face and the happiness that glowed from her countenance when I'd fed her delicacies with my own hands, from my own shop! After all, I too used to experience bliss and contentment when mother would lovingly feed me with her own hands! I silently asked her in my mind, 'O dear mother, why did you leave?' Another voice in my mind shot back, 'Well, if you miss your mother so much, why did you not go with her?' The question was valid, for, mother had at least come to see me because she missed me. But I had done nothing of the sort; in fact, I had not even thought of Vrindavan until now. Oh, how can I express the state I was in once mother had left, for, she had left behind a trail of memories of Vrindavan! Despite my best efforts, I could not break free from their lure. For that matter, I had found myself absorbed in thoughts of Radha too on several occasions in the past; these days, my mind was obsessing over Rukmini as well, but being enchanted by Vrindavan was an altogether different experience. This was because Vrindavan encompassed everything. Perhaps, that was the reason why I had not felt as much pain when I had parted from Radha or Rukmini, as I was now feeling on being miles away from my precious Vrindavan. Naturally, how could I not feel restless thinking about it? How could I forget roaming and playing on the banks of River Yamuna and around the Govardhana Mountain? How could I not remember my friends, the *gopas* and *gopis*? How could I stay without the love of my dear parents? And how could I live without my sweet Radha?

Ah! The moment her name popped up in my mind, I became engrossed in thinking about her. I'm sure whenever I visit Vrindavan, Radha will not even speak to me for the first few days, her anger getting the better of her. But how long would this last? As soon as I make her sit in my chariot and take her to Govardhana, or to the banks of River Yamuna, her anger would surely wash away in its cool waters. And the *gopis*! I'm sure they will start fighting among themselves to be the first to sit in the chariot; indeed, they might even come to blows over it! Ah, what fun it would be to watch Radha's sweet anger, the *gopis* quarrelling...! Do you see how, even without going to Vrindavan, I was deriving joy just from thinking about it? Just as I was experiencing the joy of living with Rukmini, even when she was not present with me. This was truly the secret behind my everlasting happiness. I had never given importance to meeting or separation on a physical level. In fact, I never believed in meeting or parting. For me, remembering someone or thinking about that person was just as satisfying as physically being with them. For, I firmly believed that if true love dwells in the heart, it is enough. Besides, meeting and parting depend on the other person's will and countless circumstances and reasons on their part, apart from one's own. But to weave dreams, one's own desire is enough. Similarly, to nestle true love for someone, it is enough to have just a pure heart. And let me tell you another specialty of dreaming: if your desire is strong and your love is pure, you can instantly start living the dream, the way I was doing currently. My heart was in Vrindavan, my mind was with Rukmini, but I was still here...in Mathura! However, this did not mean that I was unhappy here. No! Mathura had its own engagements, its own life and its own pleasures. So, let me make it clear that while executing my tasks here in Mathura, I would invariably become one with Mathura. And as for my memories and dreams of what I yearned for, I already had my flute with me as a cure. Radha's love had woven such magic into its notes that, on the wings of those melodies, I could soar and reach wherever and whenever I pleased. Whenever I missed Vrindavan or Radha, I would play the flute and the magic of the melody would instantly transport me there. Similarly, whenever thoughts of Rukmini made me restless, I would take flight on the winged melodies of the flute and soar into the sky with her. This was the reason why, despite the distance that spanned between Radha, Rukmini and me, I had never really parted from them. They were always present with me and would spring to life in the sweet music of my flute. Indeed, as long as I had a pure heart and my precious flute with me, how could I ever be separated from Radha or Rukmini...or anyone else for that matter? Understand clearly that there is no place for discontentment in my life, for, I would come to terms with the unavoidable realities of life and accept them as I went along. Rather than dig my heels in and insist on changing the circumstances, I would mould myself according to them and thus remain blissful. This was the very secret behind the ever-present cheerful smile on my face. I had found within myself a self-sustaining happiness that no circumstance, person or time could snatch away. I thus spent the night in the company of these thoughts and memories, barely realising that the morning sun had risen, announcing the arrival of a new day. It was only now that my thoughts had come to a halt, and no sooner had they ceased than I fell asleep. In short, everything was in disarray soon after mother's departure—I stayed awake all night and went to sleep as soon as the sun rose.

Well, I had just fallen asleep when royal messengers arrived with a summons from grandfather. It was the first time he had called for me so early in the day, which meant it must be a matter of great importance. With this thought, my sleep vanished completely and my mind began speculating about the reasons for the summons. In short, the untimely summons from grandfather had plucked my wandering mind from Vrindavan and hurled it back to Mathura once again. Wasting no time, I got ready and rushed to the palace, still wondering why I had been called. With a chariot at my disposal, it wouldn't have taken me long to reach the palace anyway, so I quickly bridged the distance; however, the reason for the summons was shrouded in mystery even now. In fact, the scene that greeted me at the royal palace only took the suspense a notch higher. The royal court was packed to capacity. Grandfather was seated on his throne and the council of ministers had already taken their seats. But surprisingly, there were several visitors and a number of families who seemed to have arrived from another region, seated on the floor, facing grandfather. I looked on in amazement, for, it was the first time I had witnessed such a scene at the palace. Along with the visitors, all the Yadava elite were also present, and to my great astonishment, they all appeared furious. In short, the matter was beyond my comprehension. Well, my understanding of the proceedings of the royal court was limited anyway; after all, it was only recently that I had begun visiting the royal palace. What did I know about politics or the state of affairs at the palace? I was acting important and being treated as such, just for the sake of it. To me, the royal palace was akin to a *gurukul*—a place of learning—offering something new to learn every day. And like a good student, I was always eager to imbibe new learnings. But the present scenario was beyond my grasp. Lost in these thoughts, I took the seat reserved for me, next to grandfather. As soon as I was seated, grandfather advised the Chief Minister to start the proceedings. Oh, so they were all waiting only for me! Indeed, grandfather had accorded great respect to me, and honestly speaking, whatever little prominence I enjoyed at the royal palace could be attributed solely to his love and kindness. My capability certainly had no role to play in it, and as soon as this thought struck me, I resolved that I would make myself worthy of my grandfather's love.

Even as I was thinking this, the Chief Minister rose from his seat and following grandfather's instructions, began to brief the court about the matter at hand. He began, "These outsiders are erstwhile inhabitants of Mathura. They were all affluent and respectable residents, but fearing persecution and harassment at the hands of Kansa, they had fled from Mathura along with their families during his rule. But now that Kansa is dead and the situation has improved, these individuals and their families have returned to Mathura to resettle here. We do not have any objection in granting them residence, but the main issue is, they also want their lands and shops to be returned to them, which they were forced to abandon on leaving the kingdom. Naturally, Kansa had taken control of these properties, making them a part of the royal estate. Besides, the local Yadava elite too are strongly opposed to returning any of their assets, as they feel that doing so might compromise their existing businesses. Most importantly, even the ministers are divided in their opinion over this matter. Thus, this meeting has been called today to invite everyone's views and arrive at a unanimous decision on the issue. The palace has already held discussions with all the affected parties, and I have also clarified everyone's views on the matter." Saying this, the Chief Minister took his seat. After a few minutes of discussion, it became evident that the Yadava elite were still not in favour of the palace giving in to the demands of the Yadavas who had returned. On the other hand, the council too was unable to decide how to make both parties reach a consensus, as the royal palace did not want to displease either party. As for me, not only had I heard the Chief Minister's words attentively, but I had also grasped the essence of all that was being discussed. When the solution remained elusive even after a lengthy discussion, grandfather finally turned to me and asked for my opinion. Well, this was the highest honour he could have bestowed upon me. Indeed, grandfather never lost an opportunity to accord respect to me or increase my stature in the eyes of the courtiers. So, now, it was my duty to live up to his expectations. And today, I had decided that I would honour the respect he had given me. I had already become an expert at evaluating and assessing circumstances, and indeed, with careful analysis, one can easily arrive at the most appropriate solution. Moreover, the issue was also completely clear to me now. It was actually as simple as adding two and two to derive four. It only required a correct analysis of the situation. Now, how difficult was this task for Krishna, who, in the past, had accurately assessed situations on several occasions in Gokula and Vrindavan. Today too, I became deeply absorbed in contemplation, and as a result, all eyes in the court were focused on me. Many people were also laughing inwardly, wondering how a boy like me could contemplate and arrive at a solution. Well, they would soon find out! In fact, you will not believe it, but my brief contemplation had allowed me to grasp the very crux of the problem. In any case, the solution to every problem in this world lies hidden at the root of the problem. The situation had become crystal clear to me, and in accordance with that, the decision was likely to affect three parties: the royal palace, the outsiders and the local Yadavas. Therefore, the proposed solution would have to protect the interests of all three and only then could the matter be considered resolved. Otherwise, the arguments would continue ceaselessly.

Now, the solution I had arrived at was clear in my mind, but how could I bring myself to suggest something so monumental? I was in a dilemma whether to offer my suggestion or remain silent. In Vrindavan, it was easier to advise people and draw plans for them, but this was the royal court of Mathura, packed with seasoned experts and veterans. I wondered, 'What if I end up losing whatever little respect I had gained till now? What if the solution I propose turns out to be childish?' But then, another thought crossed my mind, 'Well, so what? I am, after all, a child. Besides, none of these stalwarts had been able to think of a way to resolve this issue. So, even if my solution turns out to be impractical, it is not as if the sky would come crashing down on me. Moreover, since grandfather had shown such unwavering faith in me, I had to respect his wishes and say something at least. More importantly, I did not see any flaw in the solution I was about to propose. So, why hesitate and lose out on the opportunity to impress those present in the court?'

While I had been given time to cogitate over the problem, the discussions continued among the people assembled in the court. The Yadava elite still appeared quite agitated and in no mood to tolerate an attack on their business interests. Considering all these aspects, I was ready with my solution. Thus, I rose from my seat without a moment's delay and sought grandfather's permission to speak. While doing so, I glanced at the packed court, which comprised around two hundred people, fifty of whom were outsiders, sitting on the floor in front of me. The rest included locals such as the Yadava elite, guards and soldiers and the entire council of ministers. Interestingly, the majority of the people gathered were between fifty to seventy years of age. For someone as young as me, only nineteen, voicing my opinion in this mature gathering was truly a test of my self-confidence. However, I was the epitome of self-confidence, so as soon as grandfather signalled for me to speak, I stood upright, looked everyone in the eye, and spoke with full confidence, "It is widely known that Kansa's reign brought great hardship to Mathura, and during that time, the safety of these Yadava families was certainly in question. However, because of their wealth, they were able to leave Mathura in search of a safe haven. The point worth noting here is that not all affluent Yadavas had left Mathura. Clearly, those who abandoned Mathura in her moment of crisis and only remembered their homeland after the situation had stabilised cannot be called true citizens of Mathura. However, Mathura is a large kingdom, and a large kingdom should have a large heart as well. In light of this, neither can Mathura reject these people today, nor can it welcome them with open arms. Moreover, after staying in foreign lands, these people must have also realised that the respect and regard one is given in one's own homeland can never be gained elsewhere. That being the case, if we return all their lands and shops to them, it would be grossly unfair to those respected Yadavas who had stood by Mathura in her hour of difficulty. On the other hand, if we take a hard stance on this matter and do not return their land, this will be regarded as callous behaviour on the part of Mathura towards its own children. Therefore, I am of the opinion that we should return half their land, but their trade tax should be doubled so that the business interests of the local residents of Mathura remain unaffected by their arrival. The final decision, of course, rests with the court."

Speaking thus, I sat down, but I couldn't help but be astounded by my own analysis and clear articulation. Indeed, in my proposal, I had taken the welfare of all three parties into consideration. On one hand, while I was giving the returning Yadavas the honour of becoming the citizens of Mathura once again by agreeing to return half their lands; on the other hand, the royal palace was earning double the annual tax and retaining half their lands. As for the local Yadavas, their present businesses had been protected by deciding to double the tax on the returning Yadavas. All in all, my analysis and solution were so perfect that not only the entire council of ministers but even the local Yadava elite as well as those who had returned were all completely satisfied. Indeed, it was a well-thought-out and comprehensive solution. For that matter, I had shown my wisdom previously too, when I had shared my opinion on the issue related to the Magadha soldiers, but this matter was much more complicated. And I could clearly see that with this suggestion, I had truly impressed the royal court of Mathura with my wisdom. Grandfather, in fact, was so pleased that setting aside protocol, he embraced me warmly. The assembled Yadava elite as well as the Yadavas who had returned were all astonished to see this display of affection. As for the council of ministers, they were completely enamoured of me. However, I must admit, my heart was unable to handle so much praise and adulation, and this was proven by the fact that feeling vainglorious, I had begun to swell with pride. And although I deserved every right to feel proud at this moment, I realised that it also displayed my immaturity. Well, whatever it was, the fact remained that my suggestion had been accepted in its entirety. And truly, I felt extremely proud of myself.

Basking in all the adulation I was receiving, I was enjoying myself in Mathura in the days that followed. In addition to growing wisdom, I continued to expand my business over time. What made me happier was that, these days, I did not have to suffer the furious glances of my aunts, as they had gone to stay with their father, Jarasandha, in Magadha some time ago. Perhaps, they were finding it difficult to stay in Mathura; and verily, in the absence of their departed husband, what would they do here? Well, as long as the aunts were happy, the nephew could live in peace too. Then, one day, to my great surprise, Uddhava arrived in Mathura. My happiness knew no bounds on seeing him.

But oh, what was this? For some reason, he did not seem too pleased to see me. On the contrary, he wore a look of misery; in fact, I even sensed that he was angry with me. I could more or less gauge that he was upset with me for not returning to Vrindavan, but the reason for his sadness was beyond my comprehension. Still, placating him was not really difficult, for, Uddhava was not Radha—difficult to appease! Thinking that I would soon coax him into revealing the matter, I lovingly enquired about the well-being of everyone in Vrindavan. But what was this? His reaction was completely unexpected, as if he had been waiting for just such an opportunity.

The moment he heard my question, Uddhava unleashed his fury on me and retorted with a sharp barb, "Oh, it appears you still remember Vrindavan!" Needless to mention, this one remark was enough to reveal his state of mind. Well…well! Vrindavan seemed to have progressed in my absence. These days, friends were visiting from afar not to meet me, but to express their indignation. Never mind! I was willing to endure it all, so I remained silent. I was well aware that if I uttered even a single word at this time, I would be subjected to an avalanche of stinging remarks and curt replies. Hence, cunning that I was, I gave up my efforts to glean information about Vrindavan for the time being. Instead, I opted for other means to pacify Uddhava, slowly and progressively, over a period of time. The first strategy I adopted was to take him for a walk around the bustling marketplace. Then, in the evening, I took him on a sightseeing tour of Mathura city in my chariot. Of course, even now, he seemed intent on avoiding any conversation with me. Well, I too wasn't interested in having a conversation with him. After all, my sole motive was to calm him down, and I could clearly see my tactic working and his anger gradually dissipating. After all, how long could anyone remain annoyed with Krishna? By late evening, by the time we had finished our dinner, Uddhava had calmed down considerably, and it was precisely with this clever intention that I had fed him *Chhappan Bhog*!

Well, after dinner, I took him out for a brief stroll, but I still could not work up the nerve to engross him in a long chat. On returning home, instead of retiring for the night, we both sat outside on the swing and began to rock it back and forth. I had also lit a torch so I could clearly see his expressions and gauge if he was still in an angry mood. Although both of us were silent, I could glean from his countenance that he was now ready to speak. Thus, seizing the opportunity, I once again posed the same question for which I had been snubbed in the morning. I ventured, "Is everything alright in Vrindavan?" Hearing the question, this time, Uddhava turned morose and a shadow of grief clouded his face. Dropping his shoulders, he sighed and replied in a dejected tone, "How on earth would everything be alright? Vrindavan has become desolate in your absence. The *gopis* have forgotten to smile, having lost interest in life itself! Even the elders sit for hours staring vacantly into the distance, their aged eyes searching the horizon for a glimpse of you. Believe me, Kanhaiya, every breath they take speaks of just one wish—to see their darling Kanhaiya return home. In fact, they are alive to this day only because they want to see you once again. All that these simple-minded elders are waiting for is to bless you for your great accomplishments. Before breathing their last, these poor elders want to see for themselves how their lovable Kanha has transformed into the mighty Krishna! Even the *gopas* have stopped playing sports and indulging in fun and banter. Where is the fun in playing and cavorting when Kanhaiya is not around? As for River Yamuna, it no longer flows with the same zest and verve that it did in the past. Without you, the waters of the Yamuna no longer bring us relief or peace. Govardhana too has become barren. The fruits and flowers of Vrindavan are so disheartened that they have even forgotten how to bloom! For this very reason, everyone in Vrindavan, especially the *gopis*, have sent me to bring youback."

Although my dear *Brijwasis* were plunged in sorrow, I smiled inwardly on hearing Uddhava's litany of complaints. Truth be told, I was even amused and wanted to laugh out loud. But had I allowed even a chuckle to escape my lips at this moment, it would have landed me in grave trouble. Indeed, if a barely pacified Uddhava became enraged once again, it could spell disaster for me. Therefore, it was in my best interest to simply nod my head and empathise with him. The description he had provided was quite vivid and elaborate. This is the intriguing thing about love: the dreams of the lover, his words, his pain, everything is expressed in a lyrical, poetic manner…always far removed from reality. But the beauty of such musings is that despite being devoid of factual information, they intrinsically appeal to one's heart. Well, at present, though I was able to stop myself from laughing out loud, I could not stop myself from giggling a little. Chuckling with mischief, I said to Uddhava, "You have not given me any news about Radha!"

Hearing this foolish question of mine, Uddhava shot back, "I really thought you were an intelligent person and that you would have gauged Radha's plight after I have so vividly described to you the condition of the others. But if you would rather hear it from me, then listen, she has lost her mind completely. Neither does she laugh or cry, nor does she speak to anyone. All that she does is wander around aimlessly in the by-lanes of Vrindavan like a mad woman. It is as if she is searching for you in every nook and corner of Vrindavan."

Deep in my heart, I mused, 'Perhaps, Radha is not very sincere in her search. For, had she been, she would have surely found me in every nook and cranny of Vrindavan.' I, of course, kept quiet and did not say it aloud, for, today, the talkative Kanhaiya had to listen quietly. This was alright, but Uddhava, having vented all his anger on me, went off to sleep, leaving me alone with the memories of Vrindavan once again. Oh, how enchanting my childhood had been! Indeed, only a childhood spent in a village can be called magical and memorable; likewise, it is also true that one can progress in life only when one spends one's youth in a city. But let us not dwell on this aspect at present. My primary concern was to somehow allay not only Uddhava's sadness but also that of the other inhabitants of Vrindavan, for, I could not bear to see them unhappy. However, the question persisted: how could I alleviate their suffering? They all wanted Kanhaiya, who was in Mathura and could not leave. And without my return to Vrindavan, their unhappiness would surely not abate. Clearly, the matter was complex, so it was necessary to choose a middle path. My mind began to ponder over this, and soon, my deliberations made everything crystal clear. The crux of the matter was that the inhabitants of Vrindavan were despondent because of their attachment to me, and I was unhappy because my own heart was full of love for them. Indeed, these were our personal weaknesses, which had absolutely no connection with the current circumstances. In other words, regardless of our personal difficulties, Nature continued to play its game in its own unique way. And I had no choice but to abide by the circumstances created by Nature. This ultimately meant that we had to assume the responsibility of taking care of ourselves. Well, the moment this thought crossed my mind, I lay down peacefully next to Uddhava and drifted off to sleep.

The next day, I took Uddhava for an early morning stroll. Of course, the walk was just a pretext; my main objective was to explain the ground reality to him. So, after walking for a bit, I addressed him in a serious tone, "Uddhava, it would not be wise for bhaiya and me to shut down our new business venture, which we have set up with great difficulty, just to return to Vrindavan. Besides, I have a duty towards my grandfather as well; he needs me from time to time. So, tell me, how can I come to Vrindavan under such circumstances?"

I had said this with utmost seriousness and I must praise Uddhava, for, he too replied with the same gravity, "Alright, so come along for just a couple of days."

I said, "My dear friend, if I stayed for a few days, neither would I be able to enjoy myself fully, nor would any of you be satisfied. On the contrary, this will aggravate the pain of separation."

Although my reasoning was clear and straightforward, Uddhava was just not ready to listen. I was astounded at this behaviour of his, for, this

had never happened before, and I wondered the reason behind his obdurate stance. It was only after probing him repeatedly that I could coax the truth out of him, and when I learnt the real reason, I was struck amazed, for, his revelation was beyond my wildest imagination! Uddhava had not come here willingly; he had been threatened and forced to come to Mathura. And can you guess who had threatened him? The *gopis*! Honestly, I had never seen Uddhava quake with such fear before. Trembling from head to toe, he said, "Kanhaiya, listen to me carefully. If I return to Vrindavan without you, the *gopis* will surely kill me!"

In my heart of hearts, I wondered, 'What nonsense was this? Punish Kanhaiya if he was not visiting Vrindavan! Why punish poor Uddhava? What has he got to do with it?' Frankly speaking, when I pondered over this a little more, I too was alarmed for a moment—the *gopis* were truly a terror. Seeing me lost in thought, Uddhava went on, "Kanhaiya! They have given me a clear warning that if I fail to bring you back this time around, I should not even dare to set foot in Vrindavan!"

Ah! So, this was the real reason behind his fear. I realised that Uddhava was completely terrorised by the *gopis*. Even otherwise, he had always feared them. Why just Uddhava, everyone was afraid of the *gopis*. Bhaiya too never got along well with them. I was the only person in all of Vrindavan who not only shared a close bond with the *gopis,* but was also greatly cherished by them since childhood. On the contrary, it was the *gopis* who were afraid of me. A voice in my head admonished me, 'Stop boasting and come back to the present, Kanhaiya, for, all that is history! Just think about how domineering the *gopis* have become today. Think about how you will tackle their rebelliousness.' Well, if I could pacify someone like Radha, then what chance did the *gopis* have? But before that, I had to tackle poor Uddhava. And once I decided on a task, how challenging could it be for me? Thus, I somehow managed to sweet-talk Uddhava and convinced him to return to Vrindavan alone. I assured him, "When you convey my personal message to the *gopis*, they will surely calm down and even be delighted. Thereafter, they will not harass you." Honestly, having already experienced the fury of the *gopis*, Uddhava did not fully trust me. But even so, he courageously chose to take my word for it. In his head, he deliberated, 'I am taking back Kanhaiya's message, so they might just spare me!' Well, my message was full of sage advice, the gist of which was, "My dear *gopis*, your Kanhaiya can never be separated from any of you. In spirit, he is still with all of you in Vrindavan, even at this moment. Physical bonds are temporary, whereas mental bonds are everlasting. And with all of you, I share a mental bond, so you can never be apart from me. Grasp this ultimate truth and stay happy."

Now, I am not sure how well Uddhava had fathomed my message, but yes, he had certainly learned it by rote. Surprisingly, although he had memorised the message by heart and I had greatly assured him too, he was still frightened at the thought of returning to Vrindavan alone. This meant that the threat of the *gopis* was still playing on his mind. Honestly speaking, I was breaking into spurts of laughter looking at his condition. Well, what's so surprising about this? It is always easier to laugh at someone else's misery than your own. Nonetheless, the question worth deliberating was, were the *gopis* really capable of terrorising someone to such an extent? Or was Uddhava just suffering the consequences of his own weakness? Well, it no longer mattered, because after extracting the secret from Uddhava, and most importantly, convincing him to return to Vrindavan alone, I had returned home with him.

After staying with me for a few more days, Uddhava finally left for Vrindavan, but not before evoking the golden memories of Vrindavan in my heart. With his departure, he had also set into motion an avalanche of unnecessary curiosities in my mind. How would the *gopis* react to my message? How would they treat Uddhava? Indeed, I found myself in an unusual predicament, for, the sweet memories of Vrindavan and the many curiosities assailing my mind had collectively reduced me to such a plight that my restless mind was unable to focus on anything else. Caught in this dilemma and an endless cycle of thoughts, it had only been a few days when one fine evening, I was once again stunned to find Uddhava waiting for me at home. With great despondency etched on his face, he was pacing around the garden restlessly. But what shocked me even more was that he appeared far more traumatised than before. For a moment, I was dumbfounded to see him in this condition, for, hadn't I sent him back with my message to the *gopis*? But little did I know, there were even more surprises in store for me. This time, he had not arrived alone—my dear sister, Subhadra had also accompanied him. And she was seated on the swing, smiling as she watched Uddhava pace up and down in the garden. Needless to say, the moment I saw Subhadra, all my thoughts shifted from Uddhava's condition to my sister's arrival. Naturally, my happiness knew no bounds on seeing her in Mathura. Meanwhile, bhaiya had also returned and when he saw Subhadra in our presence, he broke into a dance. Mother Devaki, on the other hand, was so happy that she had already scurried to the kitchen to make preparations for a lavish feast. As for Subhadra, she could barely contain her happiness on meeting her brothers after so long. Her face lit up with a radiant smile, and her eyes shimmered with tears of joy as she laid eyes on her dear brothers. It was only much later that I came to know that it was Mother Yashoda's wise decision to send Subhadra to Mathura along with Uddhava. She wanted

Subhadra to take this opportunity to see the great city of Mathura, while also basking in the affection of her brothers.

My mother's decisions were truly wonderful. As was her wont, she would always be concerned about the happiness of her darling son. Subhadra's arrival had, indeed, infused joy and gaiety into our dull, drab lives in Mathura. Naturally, we brothers were thrilled, but Subhadra's joy was beyond description. Her heart was soaring with delight at the sight of the magnificent city. In a couple of strides, bhaiya and I had enveloped our chirpy, little sister in a warm embrace and settled ourselves on the swing, sitting beside her, on either side. Mother Yashoda had sent some fruits and delicacies, which we savoured with great relish while chatting away with our dear sister. The most amusing part of this scenario was that right in front of us, poor Uddhava was still pacing up and down in a foul temper, scratching his head, but none of us were paying attention to him. Well, even though we paid no heed to him, the harried look he wore on his face was certainly dampening the joy we felt on Subhadra's arrival. At the same time, I could not deny that a thousand questions were racing through my mind, as I was curious to know the reason behind his gloomy countenance. For a while, I kept my curiosity in check and both Subhadra and I busied ourselves in reliving the fond memories of Vrindavan, but eventually, I could not contain myself. Jumping off the swing, I walked up to Uddhava, put my arm around his shoulder, and led him for a stroll in the nearby lanes.

Interestingly, although we had set off for a stroll, a wall of silence stood between us. Neither did he reveal anything, nor did I enquire about anything. Moreover, despite my best efforts to ponder over it, I was unable to solve the mystery behind his despondency. In other words, my intelligence had also failed me, unable to fathom the cause of his misery. Finally, exasperated, I gave up and asked him upfront. But when he did divulge the reason, I was left speechless. He began, "As soon as I reached Vrindavan, I asked all the *gopis*, including Radha, to gather around. At first, when they saw that I was alone, they literally pounced on me. But when I told them that I had a message from you, they calmed down a little and led me far away to the banks of River Yamuna. After all, it was their dear Kanha's message, so they wanted to listen to it in peace. Seeing that the mood was set, I rattled off the entire message you had given me in a single breath. I have absolutely no idea what the *gopis* inferred from your fancy little message, but as soon as I delivered it, they began to hurl abuses at me. Not satisfied with this, they began to rain blows on me. They even used derogatory words against me and called me 'wicked' and 'good-for-nothing'. When this too failed to satisfy them, they launched an attack on you. In fact, they spoke of you with nothing but contempt. They said,

'A cruel person's friend is bound to be cruel…what else could he be?' To be honest, they derided you even more, using a host of other disgraceful names."

Even as he finished speaking, poor Uddhava went red in the face with embarrassment. But the rogue that I was, I burst out laughing on hearing about the manner in which the *gopis* had behaved. Well, I couldn't help it, but after my laughter had subsided, still amused, I asked Uddhava with a devilish smile playing on my lips, "Really? Well, tell me frankly, what superlatives did they use to describe me?"

Perhaps, this question was more to Uddhava's liking, so pat came the reply, "Do not even ask! They praised you with several words such as trickster, cheater, betrayer, liar, fraudster, imposter and a selfish person. One of the *gopis* repeatedly cast aspersions on your character, her allegation being, 'Kanhaiya must have fallen for the charm of the city girls. That is why he has forgotten us!' Hearing this, another *gopi* taunted, 'I have heard that, these days, he struts around the city arm in arm with Kubja. So, naturally, he must have lost interest in simple, innocent village girls like us!' And this tirade went on and on. One of them even said, 'It is pride that has gone to his head, all because he has become a great hero after going to the city. But that ungrateful wretch has forgotten that all his heroic deeds have their roots here in Vrindavan!' This was still alright, but another *gopi* went so far as to say, 'He thinks he has become a great businessman after going to Mathura, but has he forgotten that here, he used to steal our butter and eat dollops of it! Would he really find that kind of sweetness over there?'"

Well, what possible reaction could I give after hearing such sweet words spoken in my honour? So, I just kept quiet and continued to listen attentively to their critiques of my character. At times, I even laughed out loud, especially at the hilarious bits. Uddhava, however, did not approve of my shameless laughter, and becoming even more irked, he glared at me as if he was going to swallow me whole. Well, so be it! I couldn't help it. But yes, after wandering around for quite some time, I could hear my stomach growl with hunger, so we turned back towards the house. This was fine, but the problem was, as soon as I had started laughing, Uddhava had fallen silent, whereas I wanted to hear everything he had to say. So, maintaining the same amused expression, I enquired, "The *gopis* spoke so much about me, but what about Radha? Did she not say anything?"

This time, Uddhava lost his cool completely. Pushing my hand off his shoulder, he replied sarcastically, "Oh, why not? She too had quite a few things to say, but I assumed that you would not care about what Radha had to say. Besides, for an intelligent person like you, how difficult would it be to guess what Radha had to say after hearing what the *gopis* said?"

Amazingly, despite his edginess, Uddhava was at his sarcastic best, dipping every word in spite before hurling it at me. However, he was a dear friend, so he quickly gave in to my coaxing and revealed in detail what my dear Radha—the love of my life—had to say. He said, "She remained tight-lipped till the time the *gopis* were venting their ire and thrashing me. In fact, she was the one who instigated them to be violent towards me. It was a good thing that they had dragged me to the banks of River Yamuna and chose to beat me up there. Had I been thrashed in the village, how would I have shown my face to the cowherd boys?" Hearing this, I felt like guffawing, but this time, I managed to keep my laughter in check, otherwise it would have unnecessarily delayed Uddhava's narration of Radha's reaction. As soon as I sympathised with him, Uddhava resumed speaking, "Actually, the *gopis* had just about calmed down, having vented their ire on me, but Radha instigated them once again saying, 'He was always a fraud. Cheating was intrinsic to his nature. Nowhere in his message has he mentioned even once that he would return. Oh, what a scoundrel! From the very beginning, he has believed himself to be smart and the others to be fools!' That's it! Radha's outburst fuelled the rage of the other *gopis* even more. Thereafter, all of them joined hands to pass a resolution of sorts. 'If Kanha does not care for us, then even we know how to discard him from our minds. Let him roam around with the girls of Mathura. No one is missing him here in Brij!' Saying this, not only did they beat me up once again, but also kicked me out of Vrindavan. Speaking in unison, they made their stance clear, 'Neither does Vrindavan need Kanha, nor does it need his stupid 'messengers'!' I was so terrified that I did not dare return to the village, and so I quietly came here."

Frankly speaking, Uddhava's narration shook me up as well, wiping away every trace of laughter that had been on my lips until then. I wondered, 'If I were to go back to Vrindavan, would they greet me too in a similar manner?' The moment this thought crossed my mind, I fell silent for a while and began to imagine Kanhaiya being beaten up by the *gopis* on the banks of the Yamuna. I saw myself hopping about, not because I was dancing, but rather to escape a sound thrashing at the hands of the *gopis*. Oh, what a terrifying scene I had just visualised! However, I soon composed myself and spoke to Uddhava in a soothing tone, "It does not matter. They may not need a 'messenger' but I certainly do. You can stay with me in Mathura." Though I had put forth my proposition in a solemn manner, I chuckled inwardly as I mused, what choice did the poor fellow have anyway? Besides, after successfully delivering two messages to and fro, Uddhava had turned into a seasoned messenger. And indeed, from then onwards, Uddhava became my lifelong messenger, who diligently carried my messages to others and in return conveyed their messages to me. Seen from this perspective, I can very well say that even the ire of the *gopis* had benefitted me greatly.

Well, apart from being blessed with a lifelong, trustworthy messenger, little did I know that a few more good tidings were waiting for me at home as well! By now, father had returned and mother had finished cooking. The mood at home had turned festive with Subhadra's arrival, so instead of the dining chamber, we partook of our dinner sitting on the soft grass in the garden. This too was a one-of-a-kind experience, which was not possible in Vrindavan. For one thing, a meal in Vrindavan did not mean an assortment of delicacies laid out on a platter. There, we would partake of the routine fare of fruits, flowers and curd; besides, we did not have any servants in Vrindavan to wait upon us. All in all, I must say that Subhadra's arrival had changed the very mood at home, as merry sounds of our laughter and chatter rent the air. After dinner, mother and father moved to the swing, while Subhadra sat nearby on a plush seat. The rest of us remained plopped on the soft, velvety grass and sat chatting till the wee hours. Everything was proceeding well so far, but the trouble began later in the night. As soon as we headed to our chamber, Uddhava, having vented his frustration, fell into a sound sleep, but my mind began to replay the outburst of the *gopis*. After much deliberation, I gained clarity on at least one aspect of the situation: the behaviour of the *gopis* had merely brought to light the hidden shortcomings in my own message. The only thing that was acceptable to them was either my arrival in Vrindavan or a definite date of my arrival in the future. Those lovelorn girls were not going to fall for empty words. I have no hesitation in admitting that it was foolish of me to cast pearls of wisdom before those lovesick *gopis*. And it was this very lesson learnt from the *gopis* that day, which I later shared with Arjuna in the Bhagavad Gita. *"Bhakti, or devotion, is complete in itself. There is no need to supplement it with pious deeds or knowledge."* Does a heart full of love need to question or comprehend anything? Love is in itself the key to all truths. It was not as if the *gopis* had failed to comprehend my message; the truth was, the lovelorn *gopis* had fathomed the worthlessness of the message I had sent. Was it any less incredible that they had understood that neither has Kanha come to visit them nor has he given any indication of his arrival in the future?! Therefore, they knew that my message was nothing but pure hogwash. And to be honest, this unexpected behaviour of the *gopis* and the love hidden in it suffused my entire being with an intense yearning to be with them. In fact, I felt an overpowering urge to immediately set off for Vrindavan. But alas, the situation remained unchanged. Considering the present circumstances in Mathura, it was not possible to leave in such haste. And that was the truth that stood before me at present. Surely, I could not shirk my duty to pander to my self-interest. Consoling myself thus, I somehow managed to drift off to sleep.

However, the next morning took me completely by surprise. Uddhava, to whom I had explained the entire situation the night before, fell apart once again and began insisting that I return to Vrindavan. Gathering my wits quickly, I too changed track and instead of a straight refusal, I reassured him saying, "When Subhadra has had her fill of Mathura, we all will go to Vrindavan together. And just wait and see, as soon as I reach Vrindavan, I will set everything right." Needless to say, these words of assurance helped Uddhava regain his composure to some extent. In fact, even bhaiya and Subhadra were happy to hear my decision. Setting Uddhava aside for now, let us talk about our chief guest, meaning, my darling sister, Subhadra. It goes without saying that presently, the attention of both bhaiya and I was focused solely on her. Every day, I would take her on a tour of the marketplace. Sitting beside me in the chariot, she would feel elated. I had even bought her plenty of clothes and jewellery, sparing no effort in taking good care of her. Bhaiya too did not lag behind in taking care of her needs. Every evening, he would take his darling sister to our shop in the marketplace and buy clothes and trinkets for her. But the best news was, over time, even Uddhava had taken a liking to Mathura, embracing it as naturally as a fish embraces water. He had even kept himself occupied by managing all the work at our cowshed. Occasionally, he would even accompany bhaiya to lend a hand to him at the shop. In short, both Subhadra and Uddhava were thrilled to spend their time in Mathura, and along with them, we too were enjoying ourselves to the fullest. But yes, a small problem had arisen—due to Subhadra's arrival, the frequency of my meetings with Kubja had reduced considerably. Ah, but I could not expect to have all the joys of life at once, could I? Still, I must emphasise that our flourishing business and the pleasant company of Subhadra and Uddhava had filled our lives with joy; in fact, the days seemed to pass by in the blink of an eye.

Well, without us realising it, a month had passed in this manner. One night, while we were sitting in the garden and chatting after dinner, a messenger from the royal palace arrived unexpectedly, carrying a summons from grandfather to come to the palace for a meeting of the council of ministers. Immediately, the thought struck my mind, 'Why was the council meeting being held so late into the night? Had some grave trouble befallen Mathura?' Thinking that this was perhaps the case, I hastened to the royal palace. Well, my guess had been correct, for, when I stepped into the courtroom, it was already packed to capacity. Grandfather was lost in contemplation, his entire demeanour cloaked in worry, as he paced around his throne with shoulders hunched and worry lines creasing his brow. A glance at the commander-in-chief revealed that he too displayed a restlessness born out of worry, as he paced up and down. In fact, a look of despair was etched on every face in the court. I was stunned on witnessing this scene. Unable to fathom this strange turn of events, I began to trail behind grandfather. What else could I do? No one was uttering a word and I would have overstepped my limits had I enquired the cause of their worry. It was then that I learnt that we were waiting for the Yadava elite to arrive, for, they too had been summoned to this high-priority meeting. So, I thought, let us wait and watch! As soon as they started trickling in, grandfather took his seat and so did I. Along with the Yadava elite, the *Rajguru*,[4] *Acharya* and other eminent people also started streaming in one by one. Quite frankly, the situation was beyond my comprehension. Of course, the fact that all the important people of Mathura were assembling here at this late hour implied that the matter was indeed quite serious—even a child could gauge this. But to comprehend what exactly was transpiring, my political acuity was proving to be far too weak. The voice within spoke up, 'So, why not admit that?!' Well, alright! I admit it and for this reason, I too wore a serious expression on my face and quietly sat beside grandfather. And while I waited, I could not help but conclude that with new problems looming on the horizon every day, it is never easy to become a king or rule a kingdom. To be honest, at this moment, I silently patted my back for the wise decision I had made to not accept the kingship of Mathura. The grass may seem greener on the other side, and it is very easy to believe that a king enjoys a life of splendour, but the truth is, his responsibilities far outweigh the grand life he is accorded.

Well, after the majority of people had arrived, King Ugrasena began to address the assembly. He began, "As you are all well aware, Kansa's wives have been staying in Magadha for the past several days. We have also seen with our own eyes how grief-stricken they were at the death of their husband. Perhaps, their sorrow and anger must have gotten the better of them and driven by their anguish, they must have instigated their father, King Jarasandha against Mathura. Now, how long would it have taken Jarasandha, a long-standing enemy of Mathura, to get instigated by his daughters?" The king continued in a heavy voice, "The grave consequence of this instigation is that he has decided to launch an immediate attack on Mathura. In fact, our spies have brought the alarming news that a host of other kings and their armies have also joined hands with Jarasandha in this fight against Mathura. That's not all! This gargantuan, collective army is on its way to attack Mathura even as we speak. According to our spies, the army will reach Mathura in a maximum of fifteen days. Jarasandha has given clear orders to his army that

4. *Rajguru* - The royal preceptor.

the two boys, Krishna and Balarama, should be killed on sight, and Mathura should be ground to dust."

Oh, the matter was grave indeed. Naturally, the entire court was stunned into silence as the import of King Ugrasena's words sank in. Shock and trepidation were etched on every face in the gathering. Of course, I had known from the very beginning that my aunts would cause trouble someday, but I had never imagined that their anger would invite such a huge calamity. Although the courtiers were deeply affected by the news, it was I who was shaken to the core of my being. And verily so, for, I was the root cause of the conflict, and I was the main target of Jarasandha's wrath too. With a long face and downcast eyes, I sank lower into my seat. Once again, it was grandfather who broke the silence that seemed to stretch to eternity. While he did not say much, he invited everyone to offer suggestions to resolve the problem at hand. However, no one spoke a word. What could they say? Once again, a heavy silence fell on the court. I was tense and restless. Finally, unable to sit still, I stood up and just like the commander-in-chief, began to pace the courtroom. Of course, my eyes were fixed on the ground, trying to avert everyone's gaze, because after all, it was I who was the root cause of the Sword of Damocles that now hung above their heads! At the same time, I was a bit annoyed with everyone too. When we were certain that Jarasandha was going to attack, then why were we not discussing ways to defend ourselves from his attack? Why did they not understand that it was a question of my life after all? The voice within me interrupted again, 'No, Kanhaiya! Why should anybody be bothered about your life? It is you alone who must try to save your life.' But what could I do? If it was an animal, demon or the devil himself that was arriving, I could deal with it. But an entire battalion was headed our way. The voice retorted, 'So what? Don't you want to become a king sooner or later? Don't you want to prove yourself to Rukmini? And forget all that. Don't you want to live?' Yes, yes! I certainly do! With this thought, I was jolted back to reality, becoming fully aware. First, it was my life that was in peril. Second, it was a question of proving my worth to my dearer-than-life Rukmini. Instantly, I remembered the conclusion I had drawn earlier in life. The path to overcoming any trouble begins only with action. In other words, nothing could be achieved by simply sitting and waiting for Jarasandha to attack; the only solution was to choose the path of action. With this thought, my deliberation kick-started and my confidence soared. And you will not believe it, but after deliberating for some time, it was I who broke the silence in the courtroom. Walking to the centre of the courtroom with great confidence, I turned to address the commander-in-chief saying, "I need to know about the preparations that Mathura has made to deal with this problem."

In a grave voice, the commander-in-chief replied, "Jarasandha's army is more than capable of defeating Mathura single-handedly. Given this, it is clear that Mathura wouldn't be able to withstand a combined army for even seven days. This is mainly because King Kansa had never seen the need to maintain a powerful army. After all, the whole of Aryavarta was well aware that Kansa was Jarasandha's son-in-law. And who in all of Aryavarta would dare to attack Jarasandha's son-in-law?"

My spirits sank further on hearing this. In fact, after this dismal account by the commander-in-chief, the tension in the court intensified and silence once again descended heavily over the gathering. Indeed, what could one say in such circumstances? Most of the people, in fact, felt that it was useless to even contemplate or discuss this matter. They had their reasons, but then, the Yadava elite, who had been waiting for such an opportunity, decided to play a new game. From the very outset, they could not bear the sight of me, and now, this terrible calamity had arrived at their doorstep only because of me. For them, it was plain and simple that had I not killed Kansa, Mathura would not have had to face such grave trouble. So, without considering anything else, they began to glower at me as if saying, "Why wait for Jarasandha to kill this boy?" Their malevolent glances were enough to convey their thoughts, but I deemed it wise not to pay attention to them. They could be dealt with later; first, I had to find a way to save us all from Jarasandha's fury. But I had absolutely no inkling about how to look for a solution to extricate us all from this situation. And this was precisely the problem. Despondency had taken over me so completely that even my mind felt numb. But regardless of the state I found myself in, I just couldn't give up. I couldn't simply embrace death; it wasn't in my nature either. Meaning, I had to fight the circumstances at any cost. Thus, I somehow managed to activate my thought process once again. And once it was activated, my mind began to conceive some small strategies and plans. Indeed, when someone is standing at your door to attack you, you have no option but to fight and defend yourself. Besides, I did not have to contend with Jarasandha's army all by myself. The entire kingdom of Mathura was with me. While all these thoughts were racing through my mind, grandfather suddenly broke the silence in the court. Expressing his faith in me once again, he took a deep breath and asked, "Kanhaiya…tell us what we should do?!"

Oh, there was so much I wanted to say! I even wanted to rally everyone to save my life. Yet, I stood in a dilemma, unsure of whether to speak up or remain silent. After all, Jarasandha's attack was more of a threat to me than to Mathura. That being the case, I wasn't sure how appropriate it would be for me to voice my opinion. However, I had analysed the situation correctly.

And in any case, it was a question of my life, so it did not really matter whether it was 'appropriate' or 'inappropriate'. If I wanted to save my life, I would have to speak. Besides, grandfather had asked for my opinion, so why hesitate? Perhaps, it might open a way out of this dreadful situation. After all, it was not as if solutions were coming forth from anyone else here! And why should they anyway? It was my life that was at stake, so finally, even if it was out of compulsion, I started speaking with full confidence, "In my opinion, questions such as whether Mathura wants a war or not, whether we are in a position to fight or not have become irrelevant now, because Jarasandha has thrust this war upon us. Therefore, I want you all to understand that this war has become inevitable. Having said that, I am well aware that I am still a novice, unable to understand the ramifications of such a huge battle. Until now, the only fighting experiences I have had, had been with wild animals, or at best, with a few wrestlers whom I had defeated in one-on-one combat. This, however, is a battle between two armies and two kingdoms. Even so, I feel it is my duty to share with you the conclusion I have drawn from the discussions so far. If my understanding is flawed, kindly forgive me, for, as I have mentioned earlier, I lack experience in battles of this kind."

Hearing me speak thus, grandfather quickly encouraged me saying, "Yes, yes, go ahead, Kanhaiya! Speak your mind unhesitatingly. You have always given wise counsel and we are all eager to hear your suggestions on this matter as well."

The Yadava elite could not digest this encouragement and respect accorded to me by grandfather, but as I have said before, this was not the time to take offence or even pay attention to them. At present, Jarasandha's imminent attack and the threat to my life were the only two pressing issues that loomed before me. That being the case, the encouragement provided by grandfather was enough to boost my morale. Thus, I continued speaking, "In the present circumstances, it is useless to be idealistic and hope for no damages at all. What I mean is, Mathura will have to bear losses to some degree. Thus, it would be wise for us to focus on solutions that will help us minimise the damage as much as possible. If we decide not to fight, then Jarasandha, that is, the Magadha army will establish a permanent rule over Mathura. And if that were to happen, we will still suffer damage to life and property. Unfortunately, the problem doesn't end there. We should not forget that we have only recently dismissed the Magadha unit from our army and we also know that it was these very soldiers of the Magadha unit who had perpetrated atrocities on the Yadavas during Kansa's reign. Therefore, it is certain that if they assume power in Mathura once again, these infuriated Magadha soldiers will terrorise the people of Mathura with double the ferocity they had shown before. They will vent all their anger over their termination, on the innocent inhabitants of Mathura. Therefore, our duty towards the throne urges us to fight, if not to save the kingdom, then at least to save the inhabitants of Mathura from this terrible backlash."

The matter was crystal clear, hence everyone grasped it at once. And with that, I received praise, and everyone also realised their duty towards their kingdom. The optimist that I was, I could also sense that they were all mentally gearing up for the battle. However, this was my thinking, because the deathly silence from before settled on the court once again. Well, so be it! For now, my enthusiasm had soared due to the praise I had received, making me hopeful that my words would bear a positive outcome. And as you are well aware, once enthusiasm took over, my mind would start racing at an unimaginable speed. And just like that I was reminded of the killing of Kuvalyapeed. Was that mad elephant any less formidable?! But with my unconventional evasive tactics, I had managed to slay him too. My strategy at the time was to hide when he attacked and counterstrike at the first opportunity. So, I thought, why not use the same strategy with Jarasandha? He may be the all-powerful Jarasandha, but Krishna had weapons to battle any kind of storm. The plan had become clear in my mind, and with my self-confidence at its peak, I was eager to share it. However, even now, all this quick thinking was happening only in my head, while outwardly, I still remained silent. My gaze slowly moved across each face seated in the courtroom, waiting for any kind of reaction, but no, the silence dragged on. And I did not want such a perfect plan to be wasted by speaking about it without being asked to. Besides, this was the only idea I could cling on to, hanging precariously as I was on the precipice between life and death. Be that as it may, what could be done about the ominous silence in the courtroom? Well, as always, it was grandfather who broke it. Addressing me directly, he said, "Kanhaiya, we have understood what you have said. We are ready for war too. But can you suggest a strategy for it?"

Aha! This was precisely what I had wanted. Oh, Grandfather, need you even ask? You have, in fact, voiced my heart's desire. I was anyway eager to present my strategy, so before anybody could interject or divert the discussion, I promptly stood up and began addressing the court. I said, "It is a well-known fact that a battle cannot be considered won until the king is defeated or the palace is captured. Therefore, if we shield the proverbial fort by barricading it on all sides, it won't be so easy for Jarasandha to destroy Mathura's stronghold and conquer it. What I mean to say is, we won't allow King Ugrasena to step out of the fort-like palace. He can't be defeated if he doesn't venture out to fight! With this, the possibility of losing the battle will be eliminated. Another important factor to consider is that this war is being fought solely because of Jarasandha's obstinacy. The other kings are obviously not vested in this war. They neither seek revenge from us, nor have any interest in Mathura. Therefore, if we can manage to keep them engaged in battle for a long time, it is certain that they will tire out soon enough. Needless to say, the enemy forces are travelling from quite afar, so the fatigue of the journey will take its toll. Given this, if we can somehow cut off their supply of food and water, they will definitely wear out and retreat quickly. Therefore, as a first step, we must send the elders, women and children to the rear portion of the palace so they can be kept from harm's way for the entire duration of the war. Another strategy we would have to employ is to destock every single item from the marketplace so they don't find a single opportunity to replenish their stock of food supplies and other essentials needed for survival. Additionally, we should also burn down all the forests in the area from where the attacking army plans to enter Mathura. This tactic will deny them the necessary fruits and flowers for consumption. Not just that, we will also have to poison all the water bodies on the enemy's path so that their soldiers do not have access to a drop of drinking water. In fact, we will also have to contaminate each and every well of Mathura. As far as drinking water for ourselves is concerned, we will easily get it from the Yamuna. Since it flows on the rear side of the palace, it is completely safe to go to the river because the enemy cannot reach it without conquering the fort first."

After elaborating my plan, I fell silent for a moment, but in that brief moment, I saw the sparkle return to the eyes of all the courtiers. Grandfather too saw a ray of hope in my plan. Even the commander-in-chief began to regain his lost self-confidence. Within no time, praises for me started pouring in from all corners of the courtroom. Naturally, the nervousness that had gripped the court in its vice-like hold eased considerably. Needless to say, I now had the undivided attention of everyone, all of whom were eager to hear the rest of the plan. That was it! After receiving such a positive response, I was not one to wait. Thus, I began to elaborate on the rest of my plan with double the enthusiasm, "The most important thing is, we will not go out to fight with them; instead, we will wait for them to come to us. In other words, we won't fight face-to-face, but use guerrilla tactics instead. With this objective in mind, all the houses along the path of the attacking army will be converted into cantonments for our regiments to fight, where our soldiers will fight in turn, not all at once. The biggest advantage of this is that we will conserve our energy and strength throughout the battle. I am not only hopeful but certain that by employing this strategy, Jarasandha's army will not only fail to conquer the fort, but due to the paucity of food and water, they will also be unable to survive in Mathura for long. In short, our focus should be solely on tactics to minimise our losses and prolong the battle as much as possible. This way, we will surely be able to save our beloved Mathura and its inhabitants."

Once I had finished presenting my plan, I sat down, but unbelievably, everyone stood up at once and unanimously accorded me a standing ovation for having conceived such a brilliant plan. With no further argument or discussion, it was decided right away that the army would follow my plan to the letter and fight the war. In fact, I too felt quite proud of myself for the brilliant strategy I had proposed and the honour I had received on its acceptance. However, the credit for honing my skills had to be given entirely to grandfather, who never lost an opportunity to encourage me…but having said that, it was I who had honed the skills. By the time dawn broke, everything had been decided. And once all the decisions had been taken, I headed back home in a state of exhilaration. This was certainly the most memorable and successful night of my life. My analysis and awareness had taken such a giant leap today that it would be nearly impossible for anyone to challenge me in the future. I felt a huge wave of confidence surge within me—if anyone had nudged me at that moment, I would have clashed with the skies in an instant! To cut a long story short, my state was indescribable as I returned home. It was early morning by the time I made it home, but I still decided to grab some much-needed rest. I managed to sleep for a while, and honestly, even this short nap reinvigorated me completely.

Naturally, bhaiya, Uddhava, father and all the others were only waiting for me to wake up, for, even they had gauged that a summons from the palace at a late hour could not have been an invitation to celebrate a festival. Moreover, the fact that I had returned at the break of dawn made the gravity of the situation quite evident. All in all, their restlessness was at its peak. Although I was well aware that they were bubbling with curiosity, I thought it prudent to finish my morning routine, freshen up and then explain everything to them in detail. After all, having waited for so long, a little more wait would do no harm! So, as soon as I was ready, I launched into the details of the discussion that had taken place at the palace. Just as I had expected, everyone was worried upon hearing my words. But bhaiya was unaffected. He, on the contrary, was elated at the news of Jarasandha's planned attack, as it would give him an opportunity to fight. Evidently, he was the strongest and most skilled fighter in all of Mathura at present. Perhaps, it was because of this that his valorous spirit longed for an opportunity to impress the people of Mathura. Hence, honouring bhaiya's wishes, I assigned him just one task: to prepare himself both physically and mentally for this war. With a task to his liking, what objection could bhaiya possibly have? He, thus, busied himself with working out vigorously and perfecting his mace-fighting skills. I also decided to send Uddhava and Subhadra back to Vrindavan, as I did not want any harm to befall them in the chaos ahead. And with time running out, I carried out all these tasks as quickly as possible.

Speaking of time, what a strange turn it had taken! Not too long ago, I had been lost in dreams about all of us returning to Vrindavan, and here I was, forced to send back the two people dear to me back home. Oh, what lovely dreams I had woven of all the activities I would indulge myself in once I set foot in Vrindavan! I would swim in the cool waters of River Yamuna with the cowherd boys and indulge in tomfoolery with them, dance the *raasa* with the *gopis* and play all the games that we had played as children. In short, I had dreamt that I would relive my childhood to the fullest. In fact, I had even thought that this time, I would pacify Radha so thoroughly that she would never be angry with me again. But alas, all my dreams had been shattered! Perhaps, this is what life is all about: plans do not always transpire as per your wish. For that matter, who has ever achieved the perfect world of their dreams? In any case, one should clearly comprehend two significant aspects about 'desire'. Firstly, if you desire something, then wish for it firmly with all your heart, and when the opportunities to fulfil those desires present themselves, never miss them. Secondly, if the circumstances are not favourable and your desire cannot be fulfilled for some reason, do not ever lament over it. For, the fulfilment or non-fulfilment of desires, the ebb and flow of trials and tribulations, are all part of the game of life. And this game of life will continue till you breathe your last. Thus, in my opinion, those who lament when their desires remain unfulfilled or those who get frightened of the trials and tribulations in their lives neither have the right to desire, nor the right to live! It is obvious that everyone in this world harbours countless desires, which leads to one person's desires conflicting with another's. And that being the case, it is impossible for everyone's desires to be fulfilled all at once. Consider the present example wherein Jarasandha nursed a desire to kill me, but my desire was to live. Obviously, it's not possible for both these desires to be fulfilled simultaneously. Besides, why do we forget the most important truth that Nature also has its own desire? Man's desires can still be thwarted for once. With the proper use of my intelligence and strength, I may be able to thwart Jarasandha's desire, but what about Nature's desire… which is an amalgamation of millions of desires and actions. In other words, Nature's desire is the final 'justice'. And justice can neither be countered nor altered; it can only be accepted. For instance, I nursed a desire to attain Rukmini. But so what? Would Rukmi and the royal palace of Kundinpur allow their princess to marry a penniless cowherd? Now, the fact that

I am a cowherd is Nature's desire. The fact that she is a princess is also Nature's desire. Along with this, there is also Rukmini's desire, of which I am completely unaware at present. So, in view of all this, what relevance does my desire have? That is why I say, Rukmini is a dream for me, one that encourages me to forge ahead in life; whether I attain her or not is a different matter altogether. Similarly, there are several desires which a person is unable to fulfil because of his innate nature. Let us consider my example to comprehend this matter as well. Now, I hardly need to reiterate that I was yearning to go to Vrindavan. I even had a chariot of my own which could swiftly take me to my village, and believe me, I could have easily visited it for a day or two. But my nature was such that I would never approach anything half-heartedly. In other words, whenever I decided to go, I would go wholeheartedly. What I am saying is, I could not go to Vrindavan with the worries of the royal palace, the responsibility of my business, and the rush and anxiety about returning quickly weighing on my mind. In my opinion, a half-hearted visit is worse than not visiting at all. This being the case, it was better to not go at all than to go with a distracted mind. Instead, wouldn't it be far better to just dream about Vrindavan? Wouldn't it be better to play my flute and lose myself in the memories it evoked? This way, I could at least lose myself in the dreams or thoughts of Vrindavan wholeheartedly. It is also important to understand that Vrindavan, Radha and Rukmini were the sweet pains of my life, not my sorrow. In fact, they had become one with me on such a deep and elemental level that I always felt the sweet pang of separation from them, yet, despite that, I never truly felt separated from them. This is precisely the difference between pain and sorrow. Pain carries a peculiar kind of joy; it has its own special sweetness, whereas sorrow is nothing but self-destruction.

Oh, look at me! Just a moment ago, I was discussing the constraints of time, and just see, how I had veered off track, lost in futile contemplations. So, once again, I focused my entire attention on my tasks, and the most difficult task staring me in the face at present was to send Uddhava to Vrindavan. Indeed, both Uddhava and Subhadra had become despondent on hearing my idea to send them back, but as much as I wished against it, they had to go. So, abandoning all other tasks, I grabbed hold of Uddhava and, in a bid to make him understand, said, "Listen, Uddhava! I know we were planning a trip to Vrindavan together, but trouble has befallen us. Perhaps, Nature has decided this is not the right time for me to visit Vrindavan and revel in its umpteen pleasures. And as you are aware, it is always wise to accept Nature's will, for, there is nothing to be gained by going against it. Just keep one thing in mind: until the situation in Mathura becomes normal again, neither should you return to this city nor let anyone else from Vrindavan come here." Although Uddhava comprehended the import of my advice, he was gripped by despair once again, for, he felt that he had once again failed to take me with him to Vrindavan. However, this time, he had genuine reasons to provide to the *gopis* and the elders of Vrindavan for not being able to bring me along. Indeed, he felt reassured that, at least this time, he would not have to face the wrath of the *gopis*. That left only Subhadra, and there was no question of her going against any idea proposed by bhaiya. Given the long list of tasks I had to attend to, it was crucial to send them off immediately, so I provided them with my chariot and a charioteer.

After seeing them off, I returned to the royal palace late in the afternoon, my mind preoccupied with the battle plan I had chalked out. For, having a viable battle plan was one thing, but executing it was an entirely different matter. Although, after having carefully strategised the slaying of every opponent—from Keshi to Kuvalyapeed—I knew very well that a good strategy, if nothing else, is as good as half the battle won. Upon reaching the palace, I noticed a great deal of commotion, which was well expected. Today, every nook and corner, starting from the main gate to the garden, was abuzz with activity. For that matter, the welcome and attention I was receiving today were also quite special. But the real positive development was that the commander-in-chief had fully committed himself to accomplishing his tasks. When I saw him issue orders to everyone in the garden, I too chose to stay by his side instead of making my way inside the palace. A hundred soldiers and several other skilled warriors were present before us, and as soon as I stood in their midst, the entire atmosphere charged up. To me, this was a completely new experience. So, instead of offering advice, I busied myself with observing the commander's activities. I noticed that he was presently segregating the force into regiments of two hundred soldiers each. Interestingly, he was bellowing out instructions, which a few soldiers nearby were jotting down meticulously. Bhaiya, Satyaki, Chitraka, Shyam, Yuyudhana, Rajadhideva, Mudura, Shavfalak, Satrajit and I along with all the other skilled fighters were made the leaders of these regiments. An extensive regiment of five hundred soldiers was separately formed under the leadership of the commander-in-chief himself. The remaining one thousand soldiers were tasked with the responsibility of protecting the royal palace. Watching the commander-in-chief give a concrete shape to our battle strategy had impressed me greatly. Without wasting time, he had sprung into action and had begun assembling the forces as per the battle plan. This was precisely the strategy that I had suggested wherein half the forces would protect the royal palace, while the other half would be deployed for battle. Engrossed in the preparations, I suddenly realised that it was almost evening and I was still standing outside the palace with the commander. So, taking leave of him, I quickly rushed towards the courtroom, where I found grandfather waiting for me impatiently. Surprisingly, the commander also arrived a few moments later, scurrying behind me. Perhaps, he too had completed his task. So, we both entered the courtroom together.

As expected, the courtroom was filled to capacity on this occasion as well. All the Yadava leaders, the entire council of ministers as well as grandfather were present, along with everyone else who was expected to attend this meeting. The treatment I received this time in the court was also quite exceptional. Indeed, the manner in which they greeted me clearly reflected the powerful impact of my proposed battle strategy on them. Well, who does not like to be respected? Deep in my heart, I was swelling with pride. You cannot even imagine how deeply this respect from the royal court touched the heart of an ordinary cowherd. Now, I could still digest the respect I had received thus far, but my chest swelled further when the commander-in-chief stood before me like an obedient soldier, as if reporting to me: "My task of forming the regiments and segregating the soldiers is complete. Since the battle is being fought as per your strategy, you will not only have to give all the orders from here on, but also suggest all plans of action."

Already bursting with pride from the honour received in the court, I now felt like I was on cloud nine with the respect shown by the commander-in-chief. Truly, my feet refused to touch the ground! At the same time, my self-confidence had also soared high. In any case, this respect was not without reason. Upon careful consideration, the commander-in-chief's statement was both valid and practical, for, it is an indisputable fact that whoever formulates the plan also knows how best to implement it. Nevertheless, before I could get carried away by the respect and adulation I was receiving, I took inspiration from the commander-in-chief and grounded myself. Discarding the veil of arrogance that had descended over me, I prepared myself to shoulder the new responsibilities. Besides, all eyes in the court were already on me, eager to hear my response. So, I stood up at once and addressed everyone with utmost humility, "I am not only grateful for the deep respect and tremendous faith the commander-in-chief has placed in me, but I also accept the responsibility of saving Mathura."

No sooner did grandfather hear these words than he reached up and patted me on my back. The moment he did so, I felt a surge of enthusiasm course through me. Feeling empowered now, I launched into a lengthy speech on the war strategy. I began, "Before engaging in any battle, it is essential to be fully prepared in advance. And for that purpose, as important as it is to delegate responsibilities, it is equally crucial for everyone to carry out their duties responsibly. Taking into consideration the available resources at our disposal, it is obvious that we cannot counter Jarasandha's vast army with Mathura's army alone. Moreover, it is certain that no other kingdom would come to our aid and form an alliance with us at the cost of making an enemy out of Jarasandha. Therefore, obviously, the youth of Mathura will also have to stand shoulder to shoulder with us and assist us in the war. Not only they, but every Yadava leader must also take a keen interest and actively participate in this war…they cannot choose to be mere spectators. We are all well aware that Yadava leaders such as Satrajit, Satyaki, Chitraka, Shyam, Yuyudhana, Rajadhidheva, Mudura, Shavphalak and Prasen have a strong influence on the youth of Mathura. Therefore, with grandfather's permission, I ask these Yadava leaders to not only take command of their regiments starting today, but also mobilise the youth. At any rate, I consider the role of these respected Yadava leaders in this war to be far more important than that of Mathura's army. At the same time, one cannot deny that if the Magadha army ends up capturing Mathura, the loss suffered by these Yadava leaders and their clan will be far greater than that of the other inhabitants of Mathura. After all, it is only from them that Jarasandha will recover the cost of this battle, once he finds the royal treasury empty."

Having stated this final point, I concluded my address and stood quietly, casting a furtive glance at the Yadava leaders. I could very well discern from their shocked expression that my arrow had found its mark. My speech had ensured that everyone was accorded the respect they deserved, and at the same time, it had also instilled the requisite fear in the minds of the Yadava leaders to perform their tasks with sincerity. In short, with this single ploy, I had compelled them to perform their tasks sincerely. Now, whether they liked it or not, they were forced to play an equal part in the war, and this, I felt, was absolutely necessary in view of the current situation. Generally, the elite of the kingdom always distance themselves from any kind of battle being fought by the rulers of their kingdom; no matter whose reign it is, their positions always remain intact. However, I had given my proposal such a clever twist that they had no choice but to fall in line with my suggestion without any protest. In fact, if they distanced themselves from the war, thinking that they would remain safe, the common people would view it as the kingdom's responsibility alone and disassociate from it. But Mathura was in no position to fight the impending war without the collective strength of its entire population. Viewed from this perspective, I had killed two birds with one stone! Enthused by this success and taking their silence to mean acquiescence, I continued with my address. Interestingly, this time, I gave them direct orders saying, "In the next ten days, the Yadava leaders and their group of young men will have to tackle two main tasks. First, with the help of the army regiment assigned to them, they will have to gather all the women, elderly and children and move them to the rear portion of the palace. Second, under the leadership of the Yadava leaders, the youth will also have to look into the food arrangements for everyone including the army. All in all, they will have to make arrangements for at least a month's stock of food and water for everyone. This will undoubtedly boost the army's morale. Freed from the burden of having to organise their meals, the army can, from this moment itself, focus all their energy on making advance preparations for the war. As far as the main battle plan and the deployment of the army regiments is concerned, I will now come to that. As I have mentioned already, our main objective is to harass the opponent and keep them trapped here for as long as possible. They may march all the way here with the aim to rout us in an open battle, but our strategy will be to avoid an open clash with them. This simply means, we will not engage in an open battle with them, but instead, wait for them to come to us, and we will ensure that a horde of obstacles are strewn in their path so that our encounters with them are kept to the bare minimum. All in all, we will wait for them to become harried and retreat. Some principal regiments have already been tasked with the responsibility of amassing food and water and marshalling the youth. As for the rest of the regiments, the first task is assigned to the commander-in-chief's regiment, which will need to constrict the route coming from the direction of Magadha, making it as narrow as possible. Thereafter, they will have to ensure that the entire route is strewn with sludge, rocks and thorns. They will have to repeat this exercise on all the routes that connect to the royal palace so that half the strength of the Magadha army is wasted in just looking for viable pathways and clearing the debris. While they are engaged in this task, bhaiya and I will lead our regiments to destroy all possible sources of food and water the army might have access to. We will pollute and poison all the ponds and wells that lie in the vicinity of the army's path. We will also destroy all the fruits and flowers in the forests that fall on their way to Mathura. In short, postponing the battle for as long as possible and tiring the enemy's army as much as we can by adopting all means possible will be our main strategy. I appeal to everyone that since we are running short on time, we should all gird up our loins and dive into our respective tasks right away. Also, we must keep the council of ministers abreast of our progress at regular intervals. So, in a way, the council of ministers will work as a 'coordination committee'. And exactly ten days from now, we will meet in this assembly hall once again to review our progress."

You will not believe it, but at present, I held such sway over the royal court that my battle plan was being accepted with far greater trust than the determination with which I was outlining it. Nothing could give me greater pride than the realisation that I, an ordinary cowherd who had earlier locked horns with only a few wild animals, was now spearheading a major battle. With this achievement, I also realised that I may not compare to a king where riches and affluence were concerned, but in the context of war, my stature had already risen to that of a 'king'. And I was truly elated at the thought of having acquired this capability, for, this indicated that I had taken a firm step towards making myself worthy of Rukmini... Oh! This was too much! Cursing under my breath, I admonished myself, 'Is this the time to reflect on matters of the heart? Don't you know yourself at all? Don't you realise that if you get lost in thoughts of her, both the battle and the strategy will be reduced to naught?' Shaken out of this reverie, I bid adieu to Rukmini before she could even invade my mind. After all, when I myself never acted at an untimely moment, how could I allow anyone else to intrude my mind at the wrong time?

Coming back to reality, little did I realise that while I was lost in these thoughts, the courtroom had become deserted. Naturally, everyone including me had to gear up and begin executing the assigned tasks without wasting time, so taking leave of grandfather, I left for the wrestling arena in search of bhaiya. When duties were being allocated to all the regiments, bhaiya was entrusted with the task of destroying the fruits and vegetables along the enemy's route, while my task was to poison all the water bodies along their path...both of which were tasks to our liking. As soon as I reached the wrestling arena and conveyed the news to bhaiya, who had been busy wrestling four opponents until then, he jumped for joy. To our good fortune, bhaiya's mace-fighting skills were improving every day, thanks to his daily practice. His progress with the mace held great significance for us, because according to hearsay, Jarasandha was renowned for his phenomenal prowess with the mace. So, viewed from this perspective, bhaiya's formidable mace-fighting skills could prove extremely crucial in this war. However, now that he had finished practising for the day, we set off for home, discussing the allocation of tasks on our way. It was during this discussion that we realised that bhaiya's task was a bit too challenging. This was because before destroying the fruit trees, he had to gather a considerable amount of fruits for our own consumption, because during the war, it was these very fruits that would sustain the inhabitants of Mathura. On realising the importance of bhaiya's task, I quickly turned the chariot in the direction of the palace, instead of heading home. On reaching the palace, I immediately sought the king's permission and made arrangements to sanction ten bullock carts and fifty workers to bhaiya. With this arrangement in place, bhaiya had to now ensure that only the fruits which were of no use to us and could not be gathered were to be destroyed.

That night, bhaiya slept peacefully, but the next morning, he threw himself into his work with great enthusiasm. As a first step, he went to the palace himself and assembled all the bullock carts, workers and other supplies required for the task at hand. I was not one to lag behind either! For, although my task may have been easier, its importance could not be undermined. Under my supervision, I swiftly had every water body contaminated with thorns and bitter leaves of the *Neem* tree. In fact, it was not just us but everyone else too who was engrossed in carrying out their respective tasks. Indeed, the enthusiasm and confidence reflecting on everyone's faces was a sight to behold, and the effect of all these efforts was clearly visible on the royal court as well. The anxiety that had taken hold of everyone so far had diminished considerably; in fact, in the next ten days, everyone had also completed their respective tasks successfully. Most remarkably, even the Yadava leaders had risen to the occasion. With this, it was now time to work out a final, decisive war strategy. The onus of suggesting the final strategy also lay on my shoulders, and needless to say, I was fully prepared with the battle plan. Besides, today was the tenth day since the allocation of tasks and everyone was present in the court. I too had reached well in time along with bhaiya. I had never seen the courtroom so crowded before; in fact, several additional seats had to be squeezed in to accommodate everyone. The atmosphere in the courtroom was charged with both excitement and anticipation; indeed, I was about to reveal the final strategy, while everyone present was eager to hear it.

So, without further ado, I began outlining the battle strategy, "We are all well aware that Jarasandha's army is much stronger than ours in all respects, hence it is a given that we can never defeat it in an open battle. Therefore, our plan is simple—we don't have to defeat them; we merely have to exhaust them. We want them to tire themselves out, and in frustration, give up and return empty-handed. And this, as I have stated earlier, is possible only when the war drags on for a long time. And a long-drawn-out war is possible only when instead of fighting, we invest our time and energy in evading it for as long as we can. With this objective in mind, we have already decided that we will not go to battle. Left with no other option, Jarasandha and his army will be forced to make the first move and approach us. And this will be the most crucial juncture, a testing time for all of us. With that in mind, I am dividing the army into two halves. One half, comprising the regiments of bhaiya and the commander-in-chief, will fight Jarasandha's army face to face, while the other half, which will include our regiments, will engage in guerrilla warfare;

meaning, we will attack from hidden positions while shielding ourselves from their assaults. Our only objective is to prolong this war to the extent that even if the enemy's soldiers try with all their might, no large contingent of theirs should be able to venture anywhere close to the palace. To prevent them from reaching the palace and to unsettle them over and over again, we will keep attacking them from the houses located on their route. This sort of warfare will certainly be an unfamiliar challenge for them, enough to drive them out of their minds. Moreover, starting today, we will toil day and night to ensure that every street leading to the royal palace is made narrow and filthy so that all the energy of the enemy soldiers is expended in finding and clearing the pathway. However, despite all these preparations and obstructions, a thousand soldiers will still stand guard at the palace at all times and protect it from any unexpected attack. With all these preparations in place, our one and only goal will be to ensure that no more than five hundred soldiers of the Magadha army manage to slip through and reach the palace at any given time. This way, every regiment that reaches the palace will be defeated and destroyed by our soldiers who will already be standing there on guard."

Although it was an unconventional battle plan, it was so perfect that everyone was filled with renewed hope and enthusiasm. This was the need of the hour, and an immediate positive outcome of this mood was that everyone was now fully ready for battle. In the meantime, the spies returned with the news that Jarasandha's army would reach the outskirts of Mathura in just a few days. Well, let them come, for, we too had made our preparations and were ready for them. We had already moved the elderly, women and children close to the banks of River Yamuna. The shops had also been emptied and as for soiling the pathways, we had gathered barrels full of mud, sludge, water, thorns and sharp rocks, which only needed to be strewn across the roads. So, as soon as we heard that Jarasandha's army was nearby, we quickly set to work on that task. At any rate, it is creating that takes time; destruction only takes seconds. In just two days, the roads were ravaged to such an extent that it was impossible to even walk on them now.

As soon as we had completed this task, everyone took residence in the palace, in accordance with our plan. Bhaiya and I had taken shelter in the nearby guesthouses along with the council of ministers and the Yadava elite. By way of work, we were just overseeing the tasks accomplished so far, and at the most, bracing ourselves for the war by reassuring one another. But the truth was, everyone was waiting for Jarasandha to arrive. And if there was one person who was finding this wait unbearable, it was bhaiya. He was already known as one of Mathura's top warriors, receiving the respect befitting his rank. So, without thinking about the consequences of the battle, he was eager to prove his fighting prowess. As for Jarasandha, he did not make us wait too long. The setting sun was about to bid us farewell for the day, and as was our routine, we were all sitting in the courtroom, discussing the impending war when a spy brought the news of Jarasandha's arrival. The news turned out to be even more terrifying when we heard that his army comprised ten thousand soldiers, including several stalwarts of the battlefield and valiant warrior kings. Prominent among them were Shalva, Shrutayu, Baadika, Gonarda, Dantvakra, Somaka, Chekitan, Shatdhanva, Viduratha and Jayadratha. Indeed, they were all seasoned warriors and it was evident that Jarasandha had arrived with the best armed regiments from several kingdoms, because only the best regiments accompanied the king. Additionally, the army seemed to be equipped with the most modern weaponry. In contrast to them, all we had were rusty swords and dented maces to fight with. Of course, we did have some small weapons such as lances, bows and arrows and so on, but in comparison to the enemy's arsenal, these were not even worth mentioning. Hearing the names of the kings accompanying Jarasandha had already unsettled me, but when I learnt of the army's strength and advanced weapons, my head began to reel. For a brief moment, all my optimism and enthusiasm dissipated into thin air. Clearly, the weapons of our destruction had arrived at Mathura's gate! It also became increasingly clear that compared to the weapons they were equipped with, we would be as good as unarmed and left with no choice but to dance before them like *gopis*. It wasn't just me who was restless. A deathly silence pervaded the courtroom too, the once-present optimism now overshadowed by fear and dread. Bhaiya was the only odd man out; even though he was aware of the ground reality, his enthusiasm refused to abate. I wasn't sure if this was his courage or immaturity…or just unbounded enthusiasm! Regardless of what it was, if we intended to survive, it was necessary for us to emulate bhaiya's enthusiasm and put our intelligence on the back burner just like him. So, in an instant, Kanhaiya too was filled with excitement! And in this new state of mind, I first composed myself and put on a brave countenance, as if there was nothing extraordinary about Jarasandha's army. In fact, I dispatched ten additional spies to get a minute-by-minute update of the night-time routine of Jarasandha's army. The reason behind sending these spies was simple; our morale would remain high only if the planner of the strategy displayed unbridled enthusiasm. If he himself showed a loss of courage, then it would not take long for the rest to follow suit. So, to keep spirits high, I ordered everyone to conduct a final review of their respective tasks. While everyone else was engaged in reviewing their tasks, I joined grandfather and the commander-in-chief to wait for the next update from our spies.

Meanwhile, soon after Jarasandha's army had set up camp on the outskirts of Mathura, he addressed his troops in a booming voice, "Surround the entire city of Mathura! Station the catapults on high ground and pound the city with boulders the moment the battle begins. Tomorrow morning, as soon as the battle commences, rain spears and arrows on the enemy. Destroy the entire kingdom of Mathura! And the moment you set your eyes on those two scoundrels, Krishna and Balarama, impale their bodies with thousands of arrows—the war must not stop until they are dead!" On this fiery note, Jarasandha concluded his speech. Well, since everyone was exhausted after the long march, they rested the night to recoup their energy. In other words, apart from this speech, nothing special occurred in Jarasandha's camp that night, and this was well expected. We too heaved a sigh of relief that at least the first night had passed with no untoward incident.

But the following day, with the first light of dawn, the enemy camp sprang to life. Riding high on enthusiasm, Jarasandha's army was ready for battle in the morning itself, but Mathura's army was yet to make an appearance. This was still alright, but even after the sun had travelled halfway across the sky, there was no sign of Mathura's army. Jarasandha was baffled! Until now, all the battles in Aryavarta were fought as per the traditional rules of warfare. The army of the kingdom under siege would arrive at the outskirts of the kingdom to protect its inhabitants and the rest of the kingdom from harm. However, this time, Mathura was fighting according to my battle plan, therefore some traditions were bound to be broken! Unaware of this fact, Jarasandha spent the entire day peering into the distance, waiting for the army to show up. But even after the sun had gone down, there was still no sign of it; indeed, how would it show up? This was, after all, a part of my strategy. And as a result, one entire day had been wasted. Now, the enemy had no choice but to retire for the night. Although the rest of the army slept soundly, Jarasandha lay awake, tossing and turning all night. And when he couldn't think of anything, the poor man arrived at the conclusion that perhaps Mathura's army was unprepared for battle the previous day, hence it did not show up. However, feeling confident that it would arrive in the morning, he finally rested his weary mind.

Well, a new dawn was not that far. At the break of dawn, Jarasandha's army promptly formed their battalions and spent hours waiting for Mathura's army to arrive, but today too, there was no sign of the opponent! By now, Jarasandha, who had barely slept the night before, lost his composure. Do you see how my battle plan had worked?! It had pushed Jarasandha, the enemy's crucial driving force, to the edge in the very first days of the war. It had kept him up all night, driving him to the brink of madness. Just like the previous day, Jarasandha faced a similar fate today. His army waited in their heavy armour under the scorching sun all day, while he spent another restless night, tossing and turning in frustration. It was only on the afternoon of the third day that Jarasandha finally came to his senses and ordered his army to march into Mathura. But as you well know, this was easier said than done. For, the moment he and his army set foot in Mathura, a welcome most torturous awaited them. As you already know, all the lanes of Mathura had been narrowed down to treacherous, sludge-strewn, tiny alleys. The roads were covered with rocks and thorns, and the ground was swamped with knee-deep sludge. Meaning, all arrangements had been made to ensure that Jarasandha's army could not enter the kingdom easily. And this strategy began to bear fruit instantaneously. Dusk had set in, and yet, not a single soldier of his massive and well-equipped army had been able to set foot in the city of Mathura.

Meanwhile, we had settled ourselves in the palace, taking note of every piece of information brought in by the spies. Naturally, we had planned to jump into battle only after Jarasandha managed to extricate himself from all the troubles we had strewn in his path. Until then, we simply watched the events unfold. Jarasandha's failed attempt at entering the city had lifted the spirits of the people of Mathura. Overjoyed at this victory, grandfather hugged me in the presence of the entire court. If truth be told, it was only now that grandfather felt confident that Jarasandha's attack could be repulsed and we could save ourselves. On the other hand, the entire city of Mathura was filled with praise for my battle strategy. By night, the mood in the royal palace's garden had become one of jubilation. Praises poured in from all corners, with people queuing up to congratulate me. The atmosphere was so charged that it seemed as if we had already won the battle. The enthusiasm was such that later, a band of youths led by me set off for the banks of the Yamuna, carrying cymbals and kettledrums, to a location where a large number of people, including the elderly and women, had taken shelter. Some had taken shelter under the trees out in the open, while others stayed inside tents. Seeing our enthusiasm, they too couldn't help but feel a rush of happiness and relief. Jarasandha's camp, on the other hand, remained deeply perturbed, engaged in intense discussions that continued late into the night. This is precisely the advantage of doing the unexpected and springing a surprise on the opponent—all their energy is drained in thinking and deliberating. After a long and exhausting march, Jarasandha's army had managed to reach Mathura only to face an all-night vigil for two days. To add to their woes, the third day also culminated in an interminably long wait. Indeed, three days had passed, yet there was no sign of a battle. I was happy, the palace was elated, and the *Mathurawasis* were overjoyed, but the scene in the enemy camp was in stark contrast. Jarasandha was driven to madness, his allies were restless, and their army utterly bewildered!

Well, anyone could have guessed Jarasandha's plan of action for the fourth day. There was no ambiguity about the fact that they had to pour in all their might to enter Mathura. Thus, after a pre-dawn, morale-boosting speech by the mighty Jarasandha, the army engaged itself in the task at hand. But how would that help? They still had scores of nasty surprises awaiting them. To their dismay, they would soon realise that even the tasks that could have otherwise been executed effortlessly had become arduous due to the numerous obstacles we had strewn in their path. In short, they still had to contend with Kanhaiya's strategy. So, even though they did advance with due ceremony and force on the fourth day, the entire army comprising three hundred chariots, scores of bullock carts and thousands of elephants and horses kept struggling all day just to wend their way through Mathura. And before they realised the futility of their efforts, the fourth day had also passed. In other words, all their efforts had come to naught even after striving hard for four days! Seeing the unconventional way in which his army was being harassed, Jarasandha became insane with fury. This became the army's daily routine for the next few days, lasting a total of seven days. While Jarasandha's fury surged with each passing day, voices singing my praises amplified with the same intensity. The roads had been narrowed to such an extent that it was impossible for chariots and bullock carts to ply on them. Therefore, they could now rely only on horses and elephants to help them enter the city. Well, we had made arrangements for that as well. By covering the roads with layers of sludge and clay, they became so slippery that the elephants and horses struggled to get a firm footing, causing them to lose their balance. With every foray ending in a failure, Jarasandha had no choice now but to depend on the foot soldiers. Incredibly, it had taken them a whole week to realise this. But even here, Kanhaiya and his men had made immaculate preparations for their arrival. In addition to making the roads slippery, sharp rocks and thorns had also been strewn on their path to welcome them. All in all, it was not easy for the foot soldiers to enter Mathura either. But whether it was easy or not, the soldiers had commenced their efforts. And after persistent struggle, some had even succeeded in entering the lanes of Mathura. However, here too, they faced misfortune. For, everyone including me lay in wait for them, hidden in the houses along the way. Even though a few daredevils did manage to enter Mathura, the poor men fell prey to our guerrilla tactics. Our soldiers, hidden on the rooftops of houses and in the by-lanes, could easily target them from a distance. All in all, this scene played out for the next three days. Ultimately, even after ten whole days had elapsed, Jarasandha continued to grapple with all these obstructions, unable to invade Mathura!

Ten days had gone by, and Jarasandha hadn't even managed to harm a fly in Mathura, which led to a jubilant atmosphere in the city. There was only one discussion that made the rounds of the city, and that was Kanhaiya and his astute battle plan. Everyone was so overjoyed that they even took out a procession in my honour. But the war was not over yet! We still had to face many difficult and dangerous situations in the days to come. Therefore, instead of being swayed by the adulation, I grounded myself and calmed everybody else too. Just because the first phase of our plan had succeeded, it did not imply that we had scored a victory. Jarasandha had not returned to Magadha yet. He was still lingering around like a predatory leopard, desperate to catch his prey. Well, these were our thoughts at the time. As for Jarasandha, he finally realised that it was impossible to invade Mathura without clearing the streets of the obstacles we had strewn on them. It also dawned on him that this was all part of a clever battle plan devised by us. He thus chalked out a plan whereby his men spent the next two days flooding the streets with water to wash away the debris. These efforts turned out most propitious for us, for, they were wasting their precious supplies of water in the process. Meanwhile, another four regiments of their army had been assigned the task of clearing the rocks and thorns from the roads. We were thoroughly entertained by this sight, as we watched them from afar, hiding on the rooftops of houses, while they continued to toil in earnest. Oh, the joy I felt watching this scene is truly indescribable! How they had come strutting to wage a war against Mathura, but alas, look at what they were doing—clearing and washing the streets of Mathura! I mentally said to myself, 'Brilliant! What an incredible and intelligent strategy you've devised, Kanhaiya! You've cleverly made the mightiest armies of some of the greatest kings of Aryavarta clean the streets of your kingdom!' Well, what can I say? I was so proud of myself that I congratulated myself several times throughout the day.

Well, this game too had run its course after a while. Finally, on the thirteenth day, Jarasandha's army overcame all obstacles and managed to set foot in Mathura. But little did they know that even this effort of theirs would be wasted, and they would soon have to bite the dust, for, bhaiya and the commander-in-chief's regiments were stationed there, ready to give them a bloodthirsty welcome! Although the streets had been widened, the slippery clay still clung to the road, making the chariots veer off dangerously. On many occasions, the foot soldiers were injured by their own chariots which wobbled precariously on the roads. Nevertheless, they had managed to enter the city, and now that they were here, a battle was inevitable. Soon, a fierce fight

ensued on the streets of Mathura, but to our advantage, we were not exactly fighting an open battle, as our army was hidden in various houses. As a result, Jarasandha's army was going berserk trying to locate our soldiers. First, they had to expend their time and energy searching for us and only then could they fight us. Fed up with our tactics, the enemy soldiers started venting their anger on the houses, and in a short while, they had razed several houses to the ground. But as the houses were already abandoned, no lives were lost; but yes, these fiends were certainly damaging the property. All in all, the tactic I had adopted to tackle Jarasandha was severely testing his patience, as well as that of all the kings who had joined forces with him. After all, fighting a three-pronged battle with us was no easy task. Firstly, they were still struggling in the narrow lanes and slippery roads. Secondly, they had to fight a face-to-face battle with bhaiya and the commander-in-chief's regiments, who stood their ground courageously. And thirdly, they had to fight a guerrilla war with an invisible enemy that was attacking them stealthily from vantage points in the houses, rooftops and by-lanes. As a result, their mounting troubles had gradually begun to drive them insane. First, they had reached here after many months of marching, facing countless hardships along the way. The march must have taken much longer than expected due to the large number of elephants and foot soldiers in the army. And to make matters worse, instead of battling a proper army on an open battlefield, they were compelled to engage in menial tasks such as clearing pathways. In short, what they had come here to do and what they were actually doing was a far cry from each other.

Amusingly, they had persevered this far only in the hope that sooner or later, they would get the opportunity to engage us in a face-to-face battle. And seeing their determination, that day didn't seem too far either. Indeed, how long could an animal destined to be slaughtered hope to stay alive? Finally, one day, bhaiya's regiment and Jarasandha's army did clash in a fearsome and pitched battle. And the very next day, the two of them also found themselves in a horrific one-on-one combat. Now, as you are aware, both bhaiya and Jarasandha were masters at mace-fighting.[5] That was it! Whether they won or lost, bhaiya and Jarasandha were truly enjoying the fight, immersed as they were in the battle. With the break of dawn, they would commence their combat and continue fighting through the day, only to stop at sunset with the greatest of reluctance. Interestingly, their fight would take place at a prominent crossroads in the city, where coincidentally, we were hiding in the nearby houses. We would pounce on anyone who passed us by, and whenever we found the opportunity, we would enjoy watching the battle between bhaiya and Jarasandha. Meanwhile, around three hundred soldiers of Jarasandha's army were engaged in a battle with the commander-in-chief's

5. Harivansh Puran, Vishnu Parva, Chapter – 36, Verse – 13-23; Garga Samhita, Part – Dwarka, Chapter – 1, Verse – 41-47; Vishnu Puran, Part – 5, Chapter – 22, Verse – 8-9.

regiment at a parallel crossroads. Meaning, skirmishes had broken out at almost all the crossroads of Mathura. But in comparison to these fights, the battle being fought between bhaiya and Jarasandha was a sight to behold. Truly, both bhaiya and Jarasandha were expert mace fighters, hence no sooner they clashed than everything would come to an abrupt halt and everyone's attention would be invariably drawn towards them. Indeed, even time would come to a standstill, as everyone would become absorbed in watching the clash of the two titans. The fight was even more enjoyable to watch because both opponents adhered to the rules of mace-fighting. And because of this, their fighting style elevated to the level of an art form. What can I say of the others; I myself felt blessed to watch the extraordinary clash of these two expert warriors. Never in my wildest imagination had I thought that a combat with a mace could be so graceful! It seemed as if two mighty mountains were colliding with each other on the heels of a well-thought-out strategy. I considered myself extremely fortunate to have had the opportunity to witness such an epic battle.

However, this prolonged duel between bhaiya and Jarasandha gave rise to another cause for worry. Taking advantage of this duel, Jarasandha's other regiments were now rapidly marching forward. Even the commander-in-chief's regiment could no longer hold its position against them. Gradually, the situation became so grave that even the rest of us had to leave our guerrilla warfare and confront the enemy in the open. The scene was charged with action, with bhaiya engaging Jarasandha in a one-on-one combat, and the rest of us using all our combined forces to battle Jarasandha's huge and powerful army. It was during one such skirmish that I suddenly found myself facing Rukmi's regiment. Seeing him, I was bewildered for a brief moment and wondered what he was doing in this battle. Naturally, a question rose in my mind, 'Why is he fighting from the enemy's side when he is my brother-in-law?' Even as this thought crossed my mind, Rukmi spotted me. And as soon as he caught sight of me, he pounced on me, eyes glowering and face scowling. Clearly, his old wounds were still fresh, but really, what chance did he have against a brave fighter like me? I had defeated him not once but twice, but each time, I'm not sure why I had let him go unharmed. Perhaps, even my old wounds were still fresh. You might recall how displeased Rukmini had been when I had landed just two kicks on Rukmi, which now made me wonder, 'What if I were to wound him this time?' 'Oh no! Never!' At no cost was I willing to displease my Rukmini, who was dearer to me than life itself. But alas! If only Rukmi would understand. The situation had reached a point where, out of consideration for Rukmini's feelings, I was willing to spare Rukmi. Yet, true to his shameless nature, he would return to lock horns with me again. Well, isn't it said that 'what goes around comes around'? That's why Rukmi kept testing my patience, just as I was testing Jarasandha's. Meaning, just like Jarasandha and bhaiya, Rukmi and I were also locked in a long-drawn-out battle. Neither was the battle between Jarasandha and bhaiya coming to a conclusion, nor was it likely that the fight between Rukmi and me would end anytime soon.

For that matter, an end to this huge war was also nowhere in sight! Despite twenty days having passed since the commencement of the battle, there had been no major development. The good news was, the scarcity of food and water had now begun to take its toll on Jarasandha's army. The supplies they had brought with them had all run out, and they had no clue that the water in the nearby wells was poisoned and contained thorns, and that the forests around them had been ruined. Indeed, it was impossible for them to anticipate that the battle would last so long. Although, by now, a few regiments of the allied armies had begun to inch closer to the royal palace of Mathura. But fortunately, their strength wasn't enough to pose a serious threat to the palace. Another good news was that most of the kings accompanying Jarasandha were tired and exasperated with the fight. In any case, they had no real interest in the war to begin with; they had been reluctantly drawn into the fight only because of Jarasandha's immense power and influence over them. So, it was only natural that they would tire soon enough. I was quick to notice these subtle signs, and as a result, my optimism and enthusiasm had reached their peak. And as you know, once I was enthused, my cleverness would also go up a few notches. At the same time, my hopes were rising with each success that came our way. And with our growing morale, a devilish idea struck me all of a sudden. I thought, 'Why not set fire to the carts that carried their remaining supplies?' Then, they would have neither food nor water and would thus be forced to retreat. But there was one hitch in this plan. It was impossible to carry out this sabotage during daytime, and to do so at night went against the principles of war. So, to find a solution to this problem, I discussed the plan with the king and the commander-in-chief. They were both shocked out of their wits. Their horrified expressions on hearing the plan was a clear indication that they did not approve of it at all. In fact, they even strictly forbade me from indulging in acts that violated the principles of warfare. Although I heard them out in silence, deep in my heart, I was incensed and even chided them mentally, 'Oh, then why are you fighting this war according to my strategy? You should have gone to war with Jarasandha following the conventional rules of warfare. Trust me, it wouldn't have taken him more than two days to wipe out your existence along with your ethics and rules of warfare!'

Outwardly, I nodded my head as if I was going to obey their command, but inwardly, my mind was conceiving a different plan. After all, it wasn't in my nature to follow rules or obey orders. You very well know that I was a slave only to my own orders and commands. And the command my mind was giving me was crystal clear—death was staring us in the face and we had to save ourselves at any cost. So, once night rolled in, taking my regiment with me, I reached the ground where the enemy camp had set base. The torches were burning bright, but the enemy soldiers were fast asleep. No more than thirty soldiers were standing guard, and that too, outside the tents of the kings. From a distance, we could see twenty to thirty carts stacked with food and water. Thus, seeing no obstruction, we raced towards them, taking cover in the darkness, and set them ablaze. Within moments, the carts went up in flames, causing a wave of panic in the enemy camp. Needless to say, Jarasandha was infuriated with this unexpected attack on his army's resources. So be it! Getting enraged is, after all, a sign of a helpless person. So, let us not dwell on Jarasandha's mental state; it was far more interesting to note the consternation of the accompanying kings when they witnessed all their supplies going up in flames. After enduring extreme hardships for the past three months, these kings had reached the end of their patience, unable to bear the additional pressure caused by the shortage of food and water. It was a grave matter indeed, if seen from their perspective: they had journeyed for two months under trying circumstances, and for the past one month, were struggling to gain a foothold in Mathura. Moreover, they still had to cover the long and arduous journey homewards. Well, it was not only the kings who seemed worried; even the army was in no condition to be pressurised to fight an extended battle. After all, how long can anyone fight a battle without food and water? Meaning, Jarasandha was harried, the army confounded, and the accompanying kings perplexed! Finally, after twenty-seven days, Jarasandha was compelled to stop the battle and retreat. If I were to draw an analogy, it was as if a grand wedding procession was forced to return without even setting their eyes on the bride! And on this momentous note, the biggest calamity ever to bear down on Mathura was forestalled. And with that, my death, which had seemed almost certain, was also averted.

With Jarasandha turning tail, a festive atmosphere took over Mathura. Sounds of laughter and gaiety rent the air, as every person was relieved to see the clouds of war that had once threatened their existence vanish. The royal palace gleamed like a jewel, its every nook and cranny illuminated by thousands of lamps, casting an ethereal glow. As for the garden adjacent to the palace, it seemed to be taken over by a field of torches. It was even more special to note that people were singing my praises everywhere. My name resounded all over Mathura, so much so that it had become a daily routine for the youths to carry me on their shoulders and lead a procession through the city lanes. At any given time, a hundred youths would arrive for us with kettledrums in hand, perch bhaiya and me on their shoulders and carry us through every street of Mathura, singing and dancing along the way. Wherever our procession went, crowds would gather on both sides of the road, wave excitedly at us and sing our praises. And as for us 'cowherds', we would feel deeply honoured on receiving such immense love and respect.

Putting all this aside, let me share a top secret with you. Although the entire kingdom of Mathura was delighted at this stupendous victory, grandfather was the happiest, and his joy was special indeed. For, it was he who was most afraid of Jarasandha, as the old wounds Jarasandha had inflicted upon him were still fresh in his memory. Indeed, the fact that Jarasandha had to return empty-handed today marked a big accomplishment for grandfather, especially at his age. Moreover, it was certain that after this victory, he would be hailed across Aryavarta for his remarkable comeback. Talking about my state, I felt as if I was living in a dream, the sweetest and most glorious dream from which I had no desire of waking up ever. Everything was transpiring so rapidly in my life after having arrived in Mathura that I often had trouble believing it was all real. However, one cannot deny the truth that after coming to Mathura, this simple-minded cowherd of Vrindavan, 'Kanha' had transformed into 'the supremely valorous Krishna'! My condition was such that on one hand, I was unable to contain the joy resulting from the honour I was receiving, and on the other, I could not resist indulging in a bit of pride. Indeed, I was so overjoyed that it was impossible to rein in my emotions. On many occasions in the past, I had slain beasts and outwitted death disguised as demons; I had even thwarted Nature's will by successfully moving from Gokula to Vrindavan. But this time, I had made the greatest allied army of Aryavarta tuck their tails between their legs and flee! Tell me, who would not be chuffed on achieving such a spectacular feat? At the same time, my self-confidence was growing with each victory I was notching up and every move proving successful. Truth be told, my growing self-confidence was gradually making me invincible. Even otherwise, I enjoyed winning; it was not in my nature to accept defeat at all. And verily, why should I accept defeat? Life, after all, is synonymous with 'victory'. Thus, it was only natural for me to feel this way. However, due to the immense joys my victories brought me, my mind soon started indulging in flights of fancy…and these days, such flights, as you may have guessed, were directed only towards Rukmini. Ah, with my mind engaged thus, I mused, 'Since I have attained so much success in life and did not face defeat even once, sooner or later, I should be able to win over

Rukmini too…my precious Rukmini!' Oh, but why did I say 'should be able to win'? If Rukmini were to actually see the impact of my strategy in this war, she would have instantly agreed to settle down with me in Mathura!

Now, whether I entertained such flights of fancy or not, the truth was that I was discovering ever-new skills and capabilities within me. This, I am sure, was the result of my habit of pushing myself. Truly, if one observes closely, one will find that Nature has endowed man with unimaginable powers and infinite potential. Yet, man takes scant interest in awakening these latent powers. I wonder why! What thoughts prevent him from giving a free rein to his potential and allowing it to bloom? Really, what is it that a person cannot do if he really wants to? Consider me for example. What a fantastic war strategy I had devised! Did I not compel the invincible army of Jarasandha to retreat solely because of the ploy I had formulated?! This is the reason why I say that every human being is born with immense potential and a host of wonderful talents. True, some have more of it than others; some have it in one field while others have it in a different one. But the real question is not about the amount of potential one possesses or the field in which one has potential; it is about recognising one's potential and nurturing it. Then it really does not matter what potential one has, how much of it he has, or in which field it exists. Though I have elucidated all this in the Gita, I do make it a point to reiterate it here while narrating my life story whenever the opportunity arises. My only wish is to see your life brim over with splendour and glory, and to set you on the path of progress.

Well, I seem to have digressed as I have bragged quite a bit about myself and engaged in several lengthy discussions too. So, let me now continue with my story and talk about the current situation in Mathura. The victory scored in the war had become a thing of the past. Taking stock of the situation at present, it became evident that the kingdom would face its real challenge only now. For, most of the houses were damaged, even if partially, while several others were ruined completely. Our foremost priority, therefore, was to build shelters for the people whose homes were ravaged in the war. Our next priority was to repair the roads that were fully damaged. In addition to this, we were faced with an even bigger problem, one that we had brought upon ourselves. With the destruction of the fruit-laden trees and the poisoning of water bodies, we ourselves were faced with scarcity of food and water. Alas, we were caught in the very trap that we had laid for Jarasandha! In any case, this is Nature's way of imparting justice, so how could we be an exception to it? All things considered, it was a bittersweet victory for us, for, although we had saved Mathura's sovereignty, our own lives were now in peril. The problem of housing and food had assumed gigantic proportions,

and to make matters worse, the treasury which had already been scraping the bottom now stood completely empty. To add to its woes, Mathura had also lost around three hundred soldiers in the battle. In such a dire situation, who would step forward to offer a helping hand? Indeed, every person was wounded, every throat parched and thirsting for water, and the hardships were truly beyond description. In short, the euphoria of victory vanished as soon as reality set in.

But I was not like the others. I was a true *karmaveer*—a firm believer in action. Giving up was never an option for me. No matter how grave the problem may be, I considered it my duty to confront it head-on. Naturally then, I assumed the responsibility of bringing Mathura back to normalcy. As a primary step, I rounded up a few young men and began to tackle the problems at hand. We toiled day and night to first clean the wells and then repair the roads as much as possible. Gradually, we also commenced the task of repairing all the damaged houses. Unfortunately, even after toiling day and night for months, we were unable to bring significant improvement in the overall condition of Mathura. In spite of pouring our blood and sweat, the splendour and gaiety of Mathura's marketplaces could just not be restored. Hunger and disease had begun to stalk every home in the kingdom. However, while dealing with all these problems, it had dawned upon me that with a sound battle plan, one can surely win wars, save oneself from defeat, and even minimise the damage resulting from a war, but one cannot fully escape the devastation that a war inevitably brings in its wake. In other words, devastation is the unavoidable outcome of any war—and this is an undeniable 'principle' of war. At present, I could clearly fathom that war is the clash of two egos, the price of which is paid by thousands of innocent soldiers and millions of inhabitants who suffer in its aftermath. Indeed, what is the use of such an ego if it destroys humanity itself? Honestly, seeing the widespread suffering around me, I could feel hatred build up within me for war. Just see how the unreasonable anger of my aunts and the massive ego of Jarasandha had unleashed an avalanche of difficulties on Mathura.

Almost three months had elapsed since we had commenced the reconstruction and rehabilitation activities in Mathura, and yet, there was no significant improvement in sight. The biggest roadblock in our efforts to restore the city to its former glory was the depleted royal treasury. Moreover, local businesses had also collapsed, which meant that no new taxes could be collected. If nothing else, this experience had at least taught me the importance of maintaining a robust royal treasury. I can confidently say that the biggest change I had undergone after coming to Mathura was realising the importance of wealth. Well, be that as it may, in this dull atmosphere of

Mathura, suddenly, one day, good news came knocking on my door—Uddhava had arrived. Amazingly, as soon as I set my eyes on him, the realisation hit me that there still existed a village named Vrindavan somewhere on this earth! Indeed, I had been so immersed in the affairs of Mathura that I had all but forgotten about Vrindavan. Fortunately, Uddhava had brought good tidings with him. With everything running smoothly in Vrindavan, Uddhava was sent specifically to ask after our well-being. Indeed, if not the inhabitants of Vrindavan, who would worry about their dear Kanhaiya? As for the situation in Mathura, what more can I tell you? Uddhava, of course, was elated to see bhaiya and me in fine fettle, but he was shocked to see the condition of Mathura, a kingdom that once stood proud as a splendid city. Verily, this was not the same Mathura that had dazzled him with its magnificence the last time he had visited. Shocked and saddened, Uddhava could not help but compare this visit of his to the previous one. Meaning, all of man's emotions, be it happiness or sorrow, are based on comparisons. This in turn means that if man stops making 'comparisons', then these emotions would cease to exist on their own, and thereafter all that would remain would be a permanent state of 'joy'. However, the conditions in Mathura right now were such that we had all but forgotten the meaning of joy. One need not look far to see what I mean. Our own business, for instance, had been wiped out completely. Bhaiya would toil all day long to bring it back on track, but when the entire city had been wrecked, what could he possibly do? Nevertheless, as a last-ditch effort, I appointed Uddhava to assist bhaiya. As for me, I was so engrossed with the tasks of restoring and rehabilitating the city that I could not spare a moment even to meet Malini. Well, such was the reality of the situation, and since accepting this reality was the need of the hour, I embraced it fully and forged ahead determinedly.

Chapter 3

Education: An Enlightening Phase

After toiling relentlessly for six months, life had just begun to limp back to normalcy when the dark clouds of misfortune cast a shadow over Mathura once again. It was almost as if a peaceful existence and a happy, carefree life were just not meant for the *Mathurawasis*! For that matter, it is a well-known fact that our destiny is shaped by our own *karma* (actions), and I can also say from my own experience that it was difficult to find people as lazy as the *Mathurawasis*. Thus, if you actually think about it, there is no such thing as destiny or luck. It is really a man's *karma* which determines the highs and lows in his life. Oh, I am sure you must be wondering what new trouble had reared its ugly head, which was making me contemplate thus! Well, let me tell you—taking a few youths from my group, I had gone to the marketplace to discuss ways to restore its lost glory, but no sooner had we arrived than a spy came rushing towards me. He led me away from the group and delivered news so terrifying that it sent a chill down my spine—Jarasandha was on his way to attack Mathura yet again, and this time around, he had vowed not to leave Mathura without staining his sword with Krishna's blood! The spies had also ferreted out the information that not only was Jarasandha well prepared to meet any exigencies, but this time, he was arriving with a smaller but stronger army. Moreover, he was bringing along food supplies to last a minimum of three months. The news was alarming indeed! Hearing the despairing news the spy had brought, I could arrive at only one conclusion: Jarasandha would not let Mathura be in peace until he had settled his score with me. Clearly, he had learnt a few lessons from his previous defeat, and that too, in a short span of time. Well, be that as it may! The point worth pondering was, the people of Mathura were idle and lazy, which was why they kept facing hardships over and over; but I was a *karmaveer*, a firm believer in *karma* (action), so why was I facing threats to my life time and again? Perhaps, it was a test of my capacity to perform *karma*. Encouraged by this thought, I instantly prepared myself for the impending war. Now, the first battle hadn't been easy either, but I had found a way out. So, this time too, I was confident that a solution would emerge one way or another.

However, this was my thinking and my reaction to the news. Grandfather's response to this news was disastrous indeed. Lines of worry creased his forehead and his shoulders sagged under the huge weight of the calamitous news. However, he somehow pulled himself out of this state of despondency and promptly called for a meeting of the council of ministers and all the Yadava leaders. I too was asked to attend it. In fact, by the time I reached the palace after hearing the news, grandfather had already convened the meeting. Surprisingly, before he and I could begin discussing the situation, the rest of the attendees had also started arriving, and very soon, the meeting chamber was packed to capacity. Needless to say, the news had driven a shaft of fear through the hearts of all the experts and authorities gathered there, hurling them into an abyss of worry. Well, regardless of everyone's state of mind, the situation was grave and we had all gathered to discuss the same. So, after extensive dialogue and considering all viewpoints, it became amply clear that Mathura was in no condition to withstand another war. Well, so be it. I thought it prudent to maintain my own counsel. After all, I was the root cause of this fracas, which was threatening to wipe out Mathura's very existence! Once or twice, grandfather prodded me to state my opinion on the matter, but I thought it wise to not break my silence. What could I do? What could I say? I would have spoken up if there was actually a solution or battle strategy worth suggesting. But when Mathura was in no condition to go to war, what could I possibly suggest? Seeing their 'saviour' enveloped in a cloak of silence, the unspoken fear which had gripped the court now became palpable. In fact, my silence only exacerbated this fear. But then, I too was quivering with fear from within! But this did not mean that I should open my mouth to utter something ludicrous. Thus, I refused to break my silence. And since I remained tight-lipped, the meeting ended without having reached any conclusion.

Oh, what a strange situation we were caught in! Grave trouble loomed ahead of us, but there was nothing we could do about it. For, Mathura neither had a huge army nor adequate arsenal; and neither did the people have the will to face a war yet again, and that too, so soon. The harsh reality was that Mathura, myself included, had lost the war even before it had begun. I, who had never experienced defeat in my life, could see no way to save myself this time around. In contrast to all of us, the only person who seemed enthusiastic about donning the battle armour was bhaiya. But his enthusiasm stemmed from his own fighting prowess—and a complete lack of sense and sensibility. The reality was that Jarasandha would take no more than three to four days to destroy the whole kingdom. But no matter what the reality was, it just could not be accepted. Though I had spent day and night mulling over the problem, I eventually realised the futility of this exercise, for, what could be gained from simply worrying? It was pointless to take any step until Nature presented a viable solution. This was undoubtedly the biggest challenge of my life, one that even a fierce battle or death itself could not resolve. In other words, the end of Kanhaiya—the lover of life—was very near; it was now just a matter of time. Well, time would decide the outcome, as it always does, but true to my nature, I could not give up hope. So, I continued to think of a way out of this problem. In short, I could not embrace death before it actually snatched away my last breath. My intentions were all good, but alas, Nature did not appear to be satisfied with just this. The problem looming before us was already insurmountable, and it did not seem that it could get any more complex than this—yet, Nature, with its evil intentions, contrived to make it even more menacing. Indeed, it seemed as if Nature had made a firm decision to put an end to Krishna's life—the very Krishna who always wished to remain victorious. Perhaps, that was why I soon received news that not only sealed my fate, but also shook me to the very core of my being.

One night, after dinner, bhaiya and I were conversing with each other, sitting outside in the veranda. Obviously, the sole topic of our discussion was Jarasandha, and we were engaged in an intense conversation, when suddenly, Satyaki dropped by. I was surprised, as it was rare for anyone to visit me so late at night. Let me tell you, Satyaki was the only Yadava leader with whom I had struck up a friendship. As for the other Yadava leaders, they could barely tolerate the sight of me. Well, be that as it may, as soon as Satyaki arrived, he ushered me to a quiet corner and bade me to take a walk with him. Surprised at his sudden arrival, I looked at him carefully; restlessness and worry were etched on his face, hence there was no question of refusing his request. We thus set off for a stroll on the quiet, empty streets. The moment we were out of earshot, he divulged a piece of news that was so painful, it seemed as if someone had inflicted a thousand wounds on my heart all at once! This was the first time I had experienced pain of such magnitude, and one so bitter, it surpassed any suffering I had endured in the past. According to Satyaki, "On the insistence of the Yadava leaders, especially Satrajit, Kritavarma and Shatdhanva, a meeting had been convened at the royal palace yesterday. The agenda of the meeting was to discuss Jarasandha's impending attack. The entire council of ministers, all the Yadava leaders along with your father, Vasudeva, as well as Akrura were invited for this meeting. But you were deliberately kept out of it. Of course, your grandfather wanted to invite you to this meeting, but he was under tremendous pressure from the Yadava leaders who advised him against it. In the meeting, Vikadru[6] spoke on behalf of all the Yadava leaders and put forth a blunt proposal. He said, "We are all aware that presently, Mathura is in no condition to confront Jarasandha once again. We also know that Jarasandha does not harbour any enmity against Mathura; he plans to attack us only because of his rivalry with Krishna. Hence, to save ourselves from this problem, we will have to choose between two alternatives: arrest Krishna and hand him over to Jarasandha, or order Krishna and Balarama to leave Mathura for good. Either of these measures can save us from the impending disaster, for, once these lads leave Mathura, Jarasandha will no longer have a reason to attack us. He will gladly return to his kingdom with his army. If thousands of lives can be saved by trading the

6. Harivansh Puran, Vishnu Parva, Chapter – 37, Verse – 9.

lives of just two individuals, then our duty towards the throne urges us to rise above personal relationships and adopt a more practical stance...even if those two individuals in question are related to the throne!"

I was shocked to hear this news. Indeed, I could feel the blood drain from my body, the only thought pounding in my head was: 'Oh, you ungrateful people! Have you forgotten that it was I who had saved you from Jarasandha the last time? And now, at the first sign of trouble, you want to throw me out like a piece of garbage?' Oh, forget about these Yadava leaders, for, they had always detested me; besides, who would lend them an ear? The entire council of ministers was with me, not to mention father and grandfather as well. Thinking thus, I assured myself. Moreover, Satyaki hadn't finished speaking yet. Of course, I was only trying to reassure myself with these thoughts; in reality, my condition was far worse. I, who normally walked with brisk steps, was finding it difficult to take even a single step at present. However, I somehow managed to regain my composure. Seeing that I had composed myself, Satyaki took a brief pause, then, taking a deep breath, continued, "The proposal stunned everyone in the court and they all fell silent for a while. But unfortunately, since no other solution or suggestion came forth, everyone gradually began to warm up to the idea put forth by the Yadava leaders." Saying this, Satyaki fell completely silent. The import of what he had said and the subsequent silence that stretched between us made my heart race with trepidation, as I realised that along with Jarasandha, Mathura too was slowly turning into my enemy. I stopped in my tracks and stood rooted to the spot like a statue. Even the stream of thoughts racing through my mind had come to a grinding halt, turning my mind numb. Finally, unable to think of anything else, I leaned against a tree trunk for support. Seeing me in this state, Satyaki shifted uncomfortably on his feet and hesitated for a moment.

Well, what recourse did poor Satyaki have? Having already revealed the majority of the narrative, he had no choice but to disclose the rest of it. After a few moments of silence, he placed his hand on my shoulder and continued in a tone laced with great sorrow, "Surprisingly, the first person to support this proposed course of action was your father, Vasudeva. Then, gradually, the entire council of ministers as well as Akrura agreed to the idea. King Ugrasena was the only one who strongly opposed this proposal and stood his ground. Moreover, he was extremely hurt by your father's behaviour. Truly, it was admirable of the king who continued to support you in spite of being the solitary voice of opposition. He even implored the court, 'We should not be ungrateful. This is the same Krishna who, with his bravery, had rid us of the despot, Kansa, and liberated Mathura from his tyrannical rule. This is the same Krishna because of whom Jarasandha had to return empty-handed in the previous war. Do not forget that it was Balarama who stood up bravely against a warrior like Jarasandha and repulsed his attack.'" Taking a pause at this juncture, Satyaki resumed his narrative, "Even though every word King Ugrasena spoke rang true, the fear that had clutched everyone's hearts was far stronger—so strong, in fact, that his words failed to have any impact on them. Not a single person showed any inclination to reconsider the proposal put forth by the Yadava leaders. Finally, seeing no other recourse, your grandfather asserted in no uncertain terms that even if he had to die, he would never hand over the two of you to Jarasandha." In a quieter voice laced with emotion, Satyaki went on, "Towards the end of the meeting, with tears welling in his eyes, the poor king made one last appeal, entreating all those present, 'Just think! These boys have always stood by Mathura whenever trouble struck. Would it be fair to abandon them now, in the face of adversity? Besides, we all know that Jarasandha holds sway over the majority of the kingdoms of Aryavarta. That being the case, just to curry favour with him, the kings of these regions will hunt down these two brothers and kill them on sight. A far better course of action would be for all of us to unite and face Jarasandha. By doing so, we will at least be able to live together or die together!' But alas, Jarasandha's terror had numbed the minds of all those present in the court to such an extent that no one heeded the old king, his pleas falling on deaf ears. On the contrary, everyone was of the firm opinion that the shadow of death was looming large over the heads of Krishna and Balarama, so why should we sacrifice our lives in order to protect them? In the end, buckling under the pressure of the entire assembly, grandfather too had to give in and consent to the proposal. To make matters worse, grandfather was also assigned the unpleasant task of ordering you and Balarama to leave the kingdom of Mathura with immediate effect. However, when and how this court verdict is to be conveyed to you will be decided by your grandfather, who has reserved the right to do so. Essentially, it depends upon his judgment when and how he will issue this order to you. I have informed you about this in advance so that you have ample time to plan the future course of action and decide where to go and how to go about it."

Satyaki fell quiet after speaking, but my legs buckled and I sat down with a thump right where I had been leaning against the tree. Poor Satyaki was equally crushed after sharing this shattering news with me. With his shoulders sagging, he too sat cross-legged in front of me. I felt devastated, as every word uttered by Satyaki had pierced my heart, inflicting a thousand wounds on it. I felt as if my heart was torn into a million pieces, each one drowning in tears. I was not worried about what would happen to us, nor was I bothered about where we would go; it was the behaviour of everyone in the assembly that had shattered me. It was the selfish attitude of these people which had enraged me, pushing me into an abyss of despair. I had faced numerous difficulties in my life and had always confronted them with exemplary courage. I had never felt daunted by any kind of trouble or danger, whether it was in Gokula or Vrindavan; whether I had to battle Kaaliya, the serpent or Keshi, the demon; whether I had to fight a mad elephant or a wrestler like Chanoor; whether it was the challenge of having to rebuild Vrindavan or Mathura or clash with Indra or Jarasandha. I had never been perturbed by any of these adversities, because I firmly believed that as long as you are alive, challenges and difficulties will keep coming your way. If you recall, even when I was trapped on the poisonous hood of Kaaliya and death was about to swallow me whole, all that the cowherd boys did was worry about me from a safe distance on the banks of River Yamuna. In other words, not a single person had even thought of saving me! For a moment, I had even felt distressed by the fact that no one had stepped forward to save me. However, I had quickly consoled myself with the thought that they were quite young and not courageous enough. Why just this, I had endured several other pains too, whether it was the pain of not being able to visit Vrindavan or the pangs of separation from Radha. In fact, I had not just borne them with fortitude, but had also enjoyed them by weaving them into the sweet notes of my flute. They too had never been able to weaken me. Consider the present-day example of Rukmini. She had cast such an entrancing spell on me that without her, life had begun to lose meaning for me. It was natural to harbour such desires at my age, but I also knew that for a cowherd like me, winning her was nothing more than a distant dream. And having realised this, I had transformed the pain resulting from her love into enthusiasm. And as you well know, from that day onwards, I have been striving to make myself worthy of her in every possible way. But, at present, there was a compelling reason behind my sense of devastation. This pain was different and the wounds were deep, for, the people who had inflicted this pain upon me today were grown-ups who were not just competent but wise too. Moreover, they were my own people, my very own father who had acceded to the proposal of handing me over to Jarasandha without even a murmur of protest! This was the sole reason that I, Krishna, who had not felt the exhaustion even after facing a thousand ordeals, the one who had remained unfazed even after encountering death on many occasions, the one who had not broken down in spite of unending sorrows, was shaken to the core today. Not only had I considered every adversity faced by the royal palace as my own, but I had always considered Mathura as my city. But despite all this, they treated me in this manner...why? 'I could tolerate such an attitude from the others, but father, you too...? Had you saved my life as an

infant just so you could hand me over to Jarasandha one day, to be butchered in the prime of my youth?!'

Undoubtedly, the pain was intense, but it wasn't the end of everything, was it? Admittedly, the shadow of death was looming over us brothers, but we couldn't just give up our lives, could we? By now, I'm sure you've come to understand that emotions such as grief, pain, anxiety and fear were not in my nature. Try as they might to bog me down, they could not linger in my mind for more than a few moments. Thus, sidestepping the abyss these emotions were threatening to hurl me into, my consciousness set off in a new direction at once. Whatever these people had chosen to do was their problem; they had acted as per their nature. Why should I suffer the pain resulting from their mistake? It would be far better to contemplate upon finding a solution to the problem staring me in the face. And if I was still unable to come up with a solution, then at the very least, I could focus on enjoying life for the remainder of my days. As soon as this thought struck me, I stood up, pulled Satyaki to his feet, and set off for home. After dropping me off, Satyaki continued on his way. Back home, my carefree brother was fast asleep, while I was the only one who remained awake. I did try to sleep, but alas, it was impossible. One thing was perfectly clear though: I did not want to aggravate my frustration by indulging in the banal exercise of cursing anyone. So, I channelised my thinking in a positive direction, pondering upon where we could go after being sent away from Mathura. Actually, we could head in any direction, but certainly not towards Vrindavan. True, it was situated a mere ten *kosas*[7] away; moreover, everyone in Vrindavan was eagerly waiting for me too. But I did not want the lives of the innocent *Vrindavanwasis* to be put in danger just because of me. God forbid, if I took refuge there, Jarasandha and his army would lose no time in reaching Vrindavan in search of me. But if not Vrindavan, where else could we go? We neither knew of any other place, nor did we have enough money to go elsewhere. Thinking about this with a marked concentration, I suddenly burst out laughing. The voice in my head quipped, 'You don't know where to go, you have no money, and you also lack the resources to face Jarasandha in battle! So, when you have nothing to lose, why are you worrying unnecessarily, you mad fellow?' The voice in my head was right; if there is a solution in sight, one can definitely muster courage and face the problem bravely. But when a problem is devoid of solution, it is wise to leave the matter in Nature's hands and free yourself from worry instantly. Having said that, I must admit that this was the first time I was confronting a problem to which a solution eluded me despite my best efforts. However, since it was not in my nature to worry unnecessarily, leaving this problem to Nature, I freed myself from the shackles of anxiety.

7. *Kosa* - A unit of distance used historically, roughly equivalent to 2 to 3 km.

And the moment I became free of worries, I surrendered myself to the peaceful arms of sleep.

The next morning, I had just stepped out of my chamber after finishing my morning routine, when I saw bhaiya pacing the veranda, worry writ large on his face. As soon as he saw me, he beckoned me over. I walked across to him and took a seat, gazing at the hustle and bustle on the street outside. He peered at me in his unique manner and asked, "Why did Satyaki visit yesterday?" I too, in my peculiar style, cleverly evaded the truth and replied, "Oh, no reason as such! He was feeling bored at home, so he dropped by to join me for a walk." Saying this, I ended the discussion, as I did not think it right to vex or hurt bhaiya. In fact, I could most specifically never reveal to him the truth about father's role in this matter. Knowing bhaiya's nature, it was very likely that if he learnt of it, he would be consumed by ire and bear a lifelong grudge against father and the Yadava leaders. And I did not want such an eventuality under any circumstances. As for me, I no longer held a grudge against anyone. For, my consciousness had once again returned to its balanced state. I believed in learning from every incident in life, and let me tell you, even this incident had taught me an important lesson—*'When a person's life is threatened, he does not care about any relation or individual apart from saving his own skin.'* This being the irrevocable truth, why should I needlessly bear a grudge against anyone? On the contrary, I was grateful to my father and the Yadava leaders for having taught me this invaluable lesson.

Well, after taking a bath, bhaiya left for the wrestling arena. I had freshened up as well, but I was completely clueless about what to do and where to go. I did not want to mull over what had happened in the royal court, but there was nothing else to think about either. The problem was complex indeed with no solution in sight. Death was staring us in the face once again, but alas, my mind could not find a way to escape it, and despite the ample time I had on hand, I was unable to focus on anything! Under the circumstances, my flute was my only solace, the only thing that could help me. Although the idea of playing it was tempting, I'd have to wait until evening to do so. After all, one could not play the flute in the middle of the day, especially when Jarasandha was on his way here, marching with his army, to play the song of my death! That would have only brought me ridicule. People would have mocked me saying, Krishna has lost his mind at the mere news of Jarasandha's arrival. Hence, curbing this desire, I took another route, my feet carrying me in the direction of Kubja. She went delirious with joy the moment she saw me; after all, we were meeting each other after many days. Enjoying each other's company, we chit-chatted till dusk. And eventually, when the setting sun cast its long, languorous rays over the earth, I boarded my chariot and headed for the banks of River Yamuna. Riding to the far end, I brought it to a halt, settled into the backseat and closed my eyes, coaxing a sweet melody from my flute. Now, as you are aware, my flute possessed a special quality. Its melodious notes held the power to rekindle the golden memories of my life, which would act as a soothing balm to instantly erase all my worries. Not just that, its notes would also invoke the golden dreams tucked into the deepest corners of my mind, and in losing myself to them, my present pain would disappear in the blink of an eye. Even today, I had sought refuge in my flute with the very hope that it would steer me down memory lane to the beatific *kunj*[8] that was Vrindavan. But alas, at present, I couldn't produce a melodious note, my flute proving ineffective in transporting me to Vrindavan and allaying the pain that pricked my heart like a thorn. Oh, never mind, I thought, the River Yamuna and its tranquil waters had always been my source of comfort, producing a calming effect on me. So, thinking thus, I alighted from the chariot and took a stroll on the riverbank, looking vacantly at the distant horizon, as the sound of the gurgling water played in my ears. At present, I was anyway craving the company of the flowing waters of the Yamuna, so I walked for a while, wandering far away from the hustle and bustle…so far that no one could see or hear me. Finally, I saw a lone tree standing in a corner, isolated from the rest of the world. This isolation was just what I was looking for, so I sat underneath it and closed my eyes. Suspended in this state, I felt a deep calm envelop my mind. And only when my mind had calmed down completely, I walked to the edge of the riverbank and sat down with my feet dangling in the water. This rejuvenated me thoroughly. At that moment, I was not sure if I was preparing to lose myself in the melody of my flute or simply fooling around due to restlessness. Whatever the reason may be, I pressed the flute to my lips, gazed at the flowing Yamuna before me, and coaxed a melody once again. Soon, I felt myself getting lost in its entrancing spell. Amazingly, this time around, my flute did not fail me, its mellifluous notes transporting me back to Vrindavan. The visual of Mother Yashoda going delirious with joy on catching sight of me flashed before my eyes. Oh, she was an amazing woman, my mother! I was a young man now, but she still wanted to feed me with her own hands. She sat down to feed me fresh butter from the several pots she had kept by her side. Caught under the spell of my mother's love, I polished off every dollop of the scrumptious butter. Within moments, the *gopis* arrived and, grabbing hold of me, they all but physically carried me away to the forest. There, we sang and danced the *raasa* so beautifully that I couldn't help but lose myself in the bliss of it. I was so exhilarated that I refused to stop dancing even after all the *gopis* had surrendered to exhaustion. As for the cowherd boys, the moment they woke

8. *Kunj* - Garden.

up in the morning, they caught hold of me and whisked me all the way to the Govardhana Mountain. There, we started playing a number of games, but this time, they were losing out to me so badly, it was almost as if they had forgotten how to play! And what should I say of Radha! She had not changed one bit since the first day we had met. Sometimes, she would love me, and at other times, quarrel with me. Her love would abruptly turn into a quarrel, and within moments, her quarrelling would inexplicably melt into sweet love. While praising me, she would suddenly start grumbling, and sometimes in the midst of her complaints, she would end up expressing love for me. She would sometimes glare at me, hot embers shooting from her eyes on seeing me dance with the *gopis*, and at other times, she would admonish me for going off to play with the *gopas*. And what should I say about myself, I was madly in love with Radha. I adored both her loving side and her feisty side in equal measure. Ah, how remarkable my flute was, offering me endless peace and solace! I had lived such a wonderful life in Vrindavan that even if Jarasandha were to come and kill me now, I would have no regrets.

As the last notes of my flute drifted away on the gentle breeze, the pleasant thoughts also faded away, and suddenly, I found myself feeling restless again. I felt as if something was left undone; in fact, I was engulfed by sadness in no time. Then, I remembered! I had met everyone in my trance-like state, but I had forgotten to meet my love, my very 'life'. Did you not understand? I'm talking about the love of my life, Rukmini. But how was this the flute's fault? How could I possibly meet Rukmini in Vrindavan? Now, even though it was late in the night, how could this tormented lover leave without meeting his dear Rukmini? The River Yamuna was flowing right before me, so I quickly splashed some water on my face and once again sat down under the tree, losing myself in the sweet melody of my flute. At present, even the flute seemed eager to fulfil every desire of mine. Perhaps, the flute too had sensed the paucity of time. Whatever the reason may be, this time, it immediately evoked thoughts of Rukmini. She arrived to dwell in my consciousness, and today, it was my turn to speak. There was so much I wanted to say to her, so much I needed to explain. However, it was strange of me that instead of explaining, I ended up apologising to her. The apology was for the fact that this grave trouble had arisen between us before I could make myself worthy of her. Indeed, how could I establish my own kingdom when I didn't even have a place to stay? The naïve Rukmini started crying on hearing this and my heart wrenched at the sight of her tears. In this distressed state, I began to pacify her saying, "Do not cry, silly one! Have faith in me. I was born in a dungeon, after all. I had defeated death and escaped prison on the very first day I had set foot in this world. All my life, I have not only worn the cloak of danger with death lurking around me, but I have also been raised under the very shadow of death. Defeating troubles and conquering death has now become a habit for me. So, trust me, I will overcome this danger as well. Any day now, I will conquer death and present myself before you, so do not worry, my dear. As soon as this danger is averted, I will work hard and make myself worthy of you. Have faith in me, for, sooner or later, I will surely marry you." Hearing these reassuring words of mine, she gave a broad smile and laughed her tinkling laughter. Indeed, she was relieved immensely. Seeing a cheerful Rukmini, this cowherd felt so content, it's hard to even describe these feelings to you. Well, immersed in this pleasant game, little did I realise that it was now past midnight. But it mattered little to me; when life itself was engulfed in darkness, who cared whether it was night or day? At present though, I was enjoying myself thoroughly, as I mused, "My dear flute! You are incredible indeed. You helped me visit Vrindavan and you even arranged a meet-up with my dear Rukmini. It is only because of you that I continue to exist." Saying this, I kissed my flute, and in that moment, I felt completely normal. Thereafter, I headed home and as soon as I lay on the bed, I surrendered myself to a deep, peaceful sleep, only to wake up at noon the next day.

Truly, I had become mentally free of the grave danger looming before me after just one day of trying. It was simple really; when there was nothing I could do, why worry unnecessarily? I had thus resolved that in the handful of days I was left with, I would live my life to the fullest. I would worry about the inevitable only when grandfather asked me to leave Mathura. When the next moment itself was uncertain, why worry about the next day? Was I a fool to indulge in such a futile exercise? Well, presently, with no task in hand, all I had to do was wait patiently for grandfather to summon me. In other words, all I had to do was wait to hear the order that would herald my death. Of course, as far as living my life was concerned, I would visit Kubja every day and savour the cool sherbet prepared by her while enjoying the relaxing, rejuvenating massage she administered to me. At other times, I would ride the chariot around the city for some boisterous fun and enjoyment. For peace and solitude, I would steer my chariot towards the Yamuna and sit by the riverside for hours. Interestingly, three days had elapsed amidst all these activities and I had still not received summons from the royal palace. And surprisingly enough, though I met father every day, he behaved normally as if nothing significant had transpired. Perhaps, I had inherited my acting skills from him! However, while I waited, my mind tried to fathom the reason behind the delay in the summons from grandfather. I wondered if he was perhaps finding it difficult to muster the courage to ask me to leave Mathura. For that matter, I was no less astute; I had stopped visiting the royal palace as soon as I had heard the terrifying news. Indeed, why walk into the jaws of death voluntarily? My thinking was clear; it was better to let death approach me rather than march towards it foolishly. In this way, I could at least postpone its arrival.

Now, although my death was being delayed, its arrival was inevitable. And in such a scenario, it was not easy to forget the people who were responsible for these circumstances. One thought that still gnawed at me—even though I tried not to dwell on it—was that the very Mathura, for which I had fought for so long, had not hesitated for a moment to disown me today in order to safeguard its own existence. Oh, how unfair were the ways of the world! And if this was, indeed, the norm, then to remain alive, I would have to elevate my stature to a level higher than that of Mathura. Well, I would surely do that—if I remained alive! For the moment, when death was lurking around the corner, waiting to pounce on me, what was the point of building castles in the air? Besides, regardless of whether there was anything to be gained from it, I could not ignore the reality that it was death I was waiting for, after all. For that matter, I had awaited death's arrival several times in the past too, and gradually, I had even become accustomed to this torturous wait. But the nature of this particular wait was different, for, the people bent on killing me were my own. Be that as it may! Eventually, this wait came to an end too, as I received summons from the royal palace a few days later. I was anyway prepared to hear the order that would herald my death, so I reached the royal palace, free of all worries.

But wait a minute, what was this? Contrary to my expectations, grandfather looked quite happy. Perhaps, he was becoming habituated to springing a surprise on me every now and then. However, on closer observation, I noticed that the happiness on his face suggested some news that could bring a positive development in my life. Had this not been the case, his countenance would have reflected gloom. To be honest, I secretly felt relieved on seeing him in this positive mood. Even so, I reckoned it would be better to hear it from him directly…but that was possible only if he broached the subject. And looking at him, he did not seem inclined to say anything—not yet at least. However, there was another surprise lying in wait for me. Grandfather's throne was occupied by an *Acharya*! This was new to me, and even if I tried to ignore it, it was obvious that grandfather and I couldn't discuss private matters in the presence of such a person. Well, no matter what the situation was, duty beckoned me and obeying its call, I promptly walked up to my grandfather and first touched his feet and then *Acharya's*. Grandfather introduced me to the teacher, *Acharya* Sandipani. Gazing at him with eyes wide in veneration, I could not help but be captivated by his enigmatic personality. For that matter, how much had I really seen in life? This was only the second *Acharya* I was meeting; the first was, of course, *Acharya* Shrutiketu. It was thus natural for me to be impressed. In fact, I found myself impressed by the entire scene as well, because presently, there was not a single soldier or servant in the court. *Acharya* was seated on the throne, while grandfather and I were seated on either side of him. Honestly, this seclusion had sent my curiosity shooting through the roof. At last, after what seemed like an eternity, grandfather broke the silence and addressed me, "*Acharya* Sandipani is currently one of the best teachers in the whole of Aryavarta."

After saying this, he fell silent again. 'All right,' I thought to myself and joined my palms in *pranaam*[9] once again. But deep in my heart, I could feel irritation rise. 'It is evident from *Acharya's* impressive demeanour that he is a learned teacher. But grandfather, have you thought about the impending threat to my life?' I mumbled in my head. Interestingly, while I was lost in my anxieties, grandfather was blissfully lost in his own world, not paying any attention to the expressions playing on my countenance. Instead, addressing *Acharya* with great enthusiasm, he continued, "This is my grandson, Krishna—exceptionally talented and incredibly courageous. In all of Mathura, there is no one more sensible than him; he is as intelligent as he is brave. He is, in fact, the one who brought an end to Kansa's tyranny, and it was his brilliant strategy that saved Mathura from Jarasandha's deadly attack." Argh! I was even more exasperated now. 'What was the point of discussing my bravery and wisdom at present? If I was so brave, why was I being thrown out of Mathura?' I was just beginning to think on these lines when grandfather caught me off guard with yet another surprise. To my amazement, he made a humble request to the venerable *Acharya,* pointing in my direction, and said, "O respected *Acharya*! I know he is past the age for formal education, but this child has been deprived of it due to certain strange circumstances that befell him. Therefore, it would be a great favour to me if you could kindly accept this exceptionally talented boy as your student." Hearing grandfather's words, I was stunned and naturally so. In fact, I'm sure this would have shocked you too. I had come here fully expecting grandfather to ask me to leave Mathura, but he was making plans for my education under the tutelage of the renowned *Acharya* Sandipani. Indeed, I had realised long ago that presuming anything about grandfather was always an exercise in proving oneself wrong.

Well, I had certainly been proven wrong, but you cannot even imagine how happy this illiterate cowherd felt on hearing that he was about to receive education. But alas, my happiness was short-lived as the thought soon dawned on me that I could receive education only if I escaped alive

9. *Pranaam* - Greeting with folded hands.

from Jarasandha's clutches. Grandfather was talking about everything under the sun, but nothing about the sword of death dangling above my head. As I was gradually getting more and more annoyed with him, suddenly, my mind was caught up in another concern. 'Grandfather is quite old! Could it be that he has forgotten all about Jarasandha? Yes, this must be the case; that's why he is looking so happy for no reason at all and daydreaming about providing me with an education. He has most certainly forgotten that he was supposed to banish me from Mathura. It seems as if his love for me has unhinged his mind; perhaps, this threat to my life has rendered him mentally unstable. The very fact that he has seated *Acharya* on the throne in place of him is proof of his insanity!' While all these feverish thoughts were racing through my mind, *Acharya* had begun to scrutinise me in a rather serious and solemn manner. He looked at me carefully, his piercing gaze travelling from head to toe. This meant that he had taken grandfather's words seriously. Sitting before him, I felt a bit uncomfortable. It was a novel experience indeed, for, it was the first time in my life that someone was assessing me. But let me tell you, I was surely floating on cloud nine! For, who would not want to be educated by such a revered teacher? Especially for a cowherd like me, this was akin to realising my dream of marrying Rukmini. Indeed, it was, but just then, I was taken by another surprise. As soon as the thought of Rukmini crossed my mind, all my worries about Jarasandha faded away, and I decided to go along with whatever grandfather and *Acharya* had planned for me. Forgetting the sword of Damocles hanging over my head, I surrendered to the dream of becoming an educated person. For, I reckoned, 'What's the harm in indulging in this madness, if it brings me a few moments of happiness in the present?' Thus, I cast aside all my anxieties and began to feign enthusiasm for the education I was about to receive.

To my amazement, a paradoxical situation had unfolded before me—even as the sword of death hung precariously over my head, grandfather was discussing plans for a brighter future for me. And verily, in such circumstances, it is better to focus on the positive aspect of things because by doing so, one at least gets an opportunity to indulge in pleasant dreams. Well, this was all about me; as for *Acharya*, I wondered what he had seen in me that he became so absorbed in thought. Ignoring the expression on his countenance, I sat before him with expectant eyes, waiting for him to give his consent, as if he was really going to provide me with an education. Fortunately, after thinking for a while, *Acharya* agreed to accept me as a student. I too expressed delight on hearing this and immediately touched his feet, seeking his blessings. Seeing that *Acharya* had agreed, grandfather literally jumped for joy, which was incredible considering his advanced age. Everything was fine until this point, but then in his elation, grandfather accidentally revealed a crucial piece of information. He said, "At the very least, my Kanhaiya will now be safe in your *ashram*[10]!"

Bewildered on hearing this, *Acharya* asked, "What do you mean?"

Grandfather's statement came as a surprise to me too. Meanwhile, he too realised his slip of tongue, but what could he do now? He had to reveal the whole truth by way of an explanation, as trying to hoodwink the astute *Acharya* would be an effort in vain. So, apprising *Acharya* of Jarasandha's impending attack, grandfather said, "There are no two ways about the fact that Kanhaiya is extremely talented. I will also not deny the fact that it is my earnest wish to see him receive proper education. However, my primary concern at present is to save him from Jarasandha, who is baying for his blood and is likely to set foot in Mathura any day now! I'm sure you know that it is forbidden for a king to attack an *ashram,* so this move will ensure that Kanhaiya not only receives education but also remains safe in your *ashram*."

After having explained the crux of the matter to *Acharya*, grandfather fell silent, but continued to look at the venerable *Acharya* with eyes filled with hope. As for *Acharya,* he first looked at grandfather and then fixed his gaze on me. Meanwhile, I could barely contain the surge of emotion that washed over me—a blend of awe and happiness. I had to admit that grandfather had shown great foresight, whereas I, like a fool, had been criticising him all this while. Ah! I felt an outpouring of love for my dear grandfather, but at the same time, I was also angry with myself. How could I harbour such ignoble thoughts about my dear grandfather? Well, this time, I actually looked at *Acharya* with eyes full of hope, for, this great man sitting before me today held the rope of my life in his hands. After mulling over grandfather's request for a while, *Acharya* beckoned me towards him, gently stroked my head as if blessing me, and said, "I consider it my duty to educate the person who has destroyed a terrible sinner like Kansa!"

Ah! With these words, it was sealed at last—I was going to the *ashram*! In other words, the tables had turned. Not only were Jarasandha's evil intentions nipped in the bud and my life saved, but I was also given an opportunity to receive formal education. Naturally, a wave of relief swept over us, making the atmosphere significantly lighter. Once the decision had been made, we chit-chatted for a while, discussing a myriad of topics, but it was in the midst of this conversation that I was suddenly struck by the thought, 'Oh, but what about bhaiya?' The spectre of death, taking the form of Jarasandha, had cast a shadow over him too. And I most certainly could not leave him and go. Did this mean that we were back to square one? Oh no! I really hoped not! If *Acharya* agreed to take Balarama along as well, there

10. *Ashram* - Hermitage.

would be no cause for worry. But how could I bring this up with him? I was so overwhelmed by *Acharya's* personality that I could not muster the courage to ask him. But still, I had to ask him, so finally, I mustered enough courage and requested him, "If you could kindly accept my brother, Balarama, too as your student, it would be a great favour to us. For, I have never been apart from my brother since the moment I was born. He is equally talented, strong and mighty. In fact, he is so skilled with the mace that he had engaged Jarasandha, a renowned mace fighter, in combat for many days, matching him stroke for stroke. He too needs the guidance of a great teacher like you."

After hearing my request, this time, *Acharya* did not ponder for long. A few moments later, he stroked my head and said, "I will grant your request but keep in mind that discipline holds utmost importance in my *ashram*. Until now, the two of you have lived a free, independent life on your own terms, so I don't want you to feel that my *ashram* is like a prison due to the strict discipline practised there." I smiled and said, "*Acharya*! You don't have to worry about that. As for feeling imprisoned in the *ashram,* I was born in a prison!" Hearing this, *Acharya* gave a knowing smile. Clearly, he was impressed with my ready wit. Well, he was bound to, but presently, he spoke in a grave tone, "Most of the students in my *ashram* hail from royal families, and have been studying there for several years. To reach their level, both of you will not only have to work hard, but also overcome any sense of inferiority stemming from the fact that you are cowherds." Of course, what *Acharya* had said was pertinent, but I too had faith in myself, so I spoke with great self-confidence, "With your blessings and guidance, we will endeavour to meet your expectations and not disappoint you."

Saying this, I touched the feet of both the elders and took my leave, for, I sensed that grandfather and *Acharya* had some private matters to discuss. Besides, I was excited to convey this news to bhaiya. Needless to say, my happiness knew no bounds. Today, not just me, even my chariot seemed to have taken flight in the air! It wasn't too long ago that I had been fearing for my life, but look how the wheels of time had turned—Kanhaiya was all set to receive a formal education, and that too, at the *ashram* of *Acharya* Sandipani, where let alone Jarasandha, even his shadow could not dare to set foot! In short, Kanhaiya was completely safe now. Because as per the prevalent tradition in Aryavarta, any kind of attack by a king or any sort of violence in an *ashram* was strictly forbidden. Hence, there was no question of a reputed king like Jarasandha breaking a rule that was prevalent all across Aryavarta. Really, with just one clever move, not only had grandfather managed to save my life, but he had also set me on the path to progress. Oh, how wonderful it would be! I would receive education and take yet another step towards claiming the hand of the princess of my dreams, Rukmini! Suddenly, I felt my life filled with a renewed sense of hope and joy. It is rightly said that the darker the night, the brighter the dawn, as long as one holds on to hope and faith during the dark phase.

I was completely enamoured by grandfather's unwavering love for me. And verily, this is what love is! Showing superficial emotions or merely exchanging sweet or lofty words is not love. Love in its truest sense is an act that is performed considering the highest good of the one you love. Grandfather knew very well that we would have to leave Mathura, but he was worried about where we would go. He was well aware that the whole of Aryavarta was under the sway of Jarasandha, so no matter where we went, the situation would remain unchanged and our lives would still be at risk. Truly, when love stems from the depth of one's heart, a way out from any difficult situation can always be found, just as grandfather's love for me had found a safe haven for us in *Acharya* Sandipani's *ashram*. However, for the first time in my life, I felt like expressing my gratitude to Nature too. For, grandfather had been racking his brains and spending sleepless nights wondering how to save me, but that is when *Acharya* Sandipani coincidentally arrived in Mathura. And verily, the plan to save our lives had emerged in the course of this apparent coincidence.

However, when I conveyed this news to bhaiya, he did not seem particularly pleased. He was not interested in studies anyway, which further made him question why he should be subservient to anyone under the pretext of discipline. However, I could not blame bhaiya, for, he was completely in the dark about the decree to expel us from Mathura; had he been aware of it, I am sure he too would have held an opinion similar to mine. He would have perhaps realised that discipline was far better than death! Well, whether he realised it or not, I had to make him understand. Finally, after enticing him with a number of benefits and painting the picture of a rosy future, I somehow convinced him to come along with me to the *ashram*. I then sent Uddhava back to Vrindavan and we began our preparations to leave Mathura. As preparation, all I had to do was channel my enthusiasm. Kubja, of course, became very sad upon hearing the news, and once again, I had to hear the same old refrain; meaning, her sorrow too was rooted in the pain of separation. I simply could not understand how two lovers could ever be separated. In my opinion, if it is possible to be separated in love, then it is not love but simply a means of satisfying one's ego.

After two days, we were supposed to leave for *Acharya* Sandipani's *ashram* located in Ujjaini. And honestly, I couldn't wait for these two days to pass. Yet, I had to kill time somehow, so I was spending most of my time in grandfather's company. Meanwhile, bhaiya was busy organising all the things he wanted to carry with him to the *ashram*. So, taking a cue from him, I too drew up a long list of things that I wanted to carry with me and handed it to him. Indeed, who knew how long we would have to stay at the *ashram*? However, little did we realise that our ambitious lists would soon be tossed out of the window! Brimming with enthusiasm, we rushed to meet *Acharya*, carrying our lists in hand, but were caught off guard by his response. In fact, a single instruction from him put an end to all our preparations. He specifically instructed us that all we could take with us were two pairs of clothes and two other possessions that we liked. Bhaiya was stunned to hear this. For a moment, I was taken aback too. But we were helpless, because for the first time in our lives, we were forced to obey someone else's orders. Besides, at the very outset, *Acharya* had prepared us mentally by emphasising that if we wanted to stay in the *ashram*, we would have to forsake our independence and embrace discipline. So, I contented myself with the thought that the process of edification had commenced in Mathura itself. Naturally, I decided to take my flute and discus with me, while bhaiya's preference was his mace and plough.

Well, following *Acharya's* instructions, we quietly slinked away from there. At any rate, there were better things to do than feel morose. So, casting our disappointment aside, we engaged ourselves in the pending tasks. With just two days in hand, we barely had time to busy ourselves elsewhere. We still had to make a few preparations for the journey, but more importantly, spend some time with grandfather too. Moreover, I had to console Kubja and seek the blessings of my parents. Most importantly, I had to keep pinching myself to convince myself that we were actually leaving. What can I say? Life would take such unpredictable leaps that it would fling me from one extreme to the other in the span of a moment! Just look at the present scenario. While I was expecting certain death, I was suddenly given the opportunity to receive an education. Indeed, with the pace at which these events were unfolding, I had to convince myself time and again that all of this was really happening.

And talking about the pace at which time was flying, two days passed by in the blink of an eye, whizzing past in farewells and meetings alone. We were scheduled to leave early morning on the third day, and with this, I could say for certain that our departure was now confirmed. As the first rays of the sun hit the ground, we made our way towards the palace with our parents. I was bursting with enthusiasm, while bhaiya wore a long face. On reaching the palace, we were amazed at the sight before us: a large crowd of *Mathurawasis* was already waiting to see us off. Seeing such a huge turnout, I became emotional, recognising it as yet another example of a leap from one extreme to another. Not too long ago, I had been slated to be banished from the kingdom, yet here I was, receiving an emotional farewell. And what a wonderful one it was, with both of us brothers standing at the palace's main entrance, with eight to ten chariots lined up before us. About a hundred-strong crowd had gathered to see us off, which obviously included Kubja and Satyaki along with several friends of bhaiya from the wrestling arena. We were still chatting with everyone when grandfather and *Acharya* emerged from the main entrance of the palace. As soon as they arrived, the fervour of the crowd increased. Indeed, everyone came rushing forward to seek *Acharya's* blessings. Well, after blessing everyone and exchanging a few final words with grandfather, *Acharya* made his way towards the chariot. We too quickly took everyone's blessings, and with our heads bowed, followed *Acharya* to the chariot, before loading our belongings and settling ourselves in the back. This was the first time I was experiencing such nervousness, which made me wonder, 'If this was the state of things with *Acharya* in Mathura, how would we fare once we reached the *ashram*?' Well, this was all about me, but I wondered how bhaiya felt, as he was reluctant to leave Mathura. As these thoughts played in my mind, the chariot lurched ahead, signalling the start of our journey to the *ashram*. And with the first spin of the chariot's wheels, our lives too took a radical turn. We illiterate cowherds were off to receive an education alongside a host of princes, and that too, at the hands of one of the finest teachers in all of Aryavarta.

Our caravan comprised four chariots in all. *Acharya* sat in the first one, while bhaiya and I sat in the second. Preceding and following us were two chariots carrying the servants and various essentials for the journey. In other words, though we were cowherds, grandfather had sent us off with the same pomp and splendour that was typically accorded to princes. This beautiful caravan of ours was now passing through the streets of Mathura, but sadly, since we had left at the crack of dawn, there was no hustle and bustle on the streets. In short, the majority of the *Mathurawasis* had lost out on the chance to witness the splendour of Krishna. Oh, never mind, for, at least the journey was splendid, and our lives had surely taken a step towards progress. Oh! The moment I thought of progress, I, the great Kanhaiya, was lost in contemplation once again. And the crux of this contemplation was that none of this had transpired overnight. Ever since we had arrived in Mathura, our lives had set off on the path of progress. Not only did I own a business in such a large city, but I had also carved an identity of my own and gained a certain influence. Moreover, I was the grandson of the king and also his favourite and most trusted advisor. All these aspects had collectively turned me into a respected citizen of Mathura. And one must admit that my *karma* (actions) and my understanding had played a significant role in this progress.

For that matter, I had made progress in several other areas too after arriving in Mathura. I had especially taken a leap in terms of making new friends as well as exploring a variety of games and sports. Back in Vrindavan, all my friends were of the same age as me, but in Mathura, my closest friend was my grandfather. Meaning, all my friends in Vrindavan were cowherds, but here, the king himself was my friend! Even the games I played in Mathura were different; in Vrindavan, I would play games such as hide-and-seek and catch, but in Mathura, I was enjoying the games of politics and diplomacy. In Vrindavan, my enemies were mad bulls, poisonous snakes and other wild animals, while in Mathura, my enemies were the esteemed Yadava leaders. In fact, it was not just the Yadava elite, but even Jarasandha, the most powerful king of Aryavarta, who had now become my sworn enemy. So, tell me, who would not be pleased after attaining such all-round progress? Well, apart from this all-round progress, I had a few other reasons to feel happy in this journey, the most important being—this was the first time since my birth that I would be leading a safe and secure life. At present, I was completely shielded from the shadow of death; in fact, even if Jarasandha's army were to encounter us face to face, they could not harm us, as we had now taken refuge with *Acharya*. Indeed, it was only because of this journey we had undertaken that we were free from all of life's struggles, at least for the time being. Otherwise, you are well aware that I have always been living in the shadow of death. It had stalked me when I was in Vrindavan and had followed me unrelentingly even in Mathura.

But for now, let me set this contemplation aside. Lost in these thoughts, little did I realise that our chariot had already traversed the streets of Mathura and had now reached the main road. At present, I felt like the proverbial frog-in-the-well who had taken a dive in the great wide ocean to explore it. Indeed, this was the very first time we were getting an opportunity to experience life outside Vrindavan and Mathura. More importantly, this was the most decisive step I had taken to make myself worthy of Rukmini. Think about it; how long would it really take the talented Krishna to become worthy of Rukmini after receiving education from the best *Acharya* in Aryavarta? Oh, let me not hide anything from you; if life accorded me the opportunity, then at this moment too, my greatest happiness revolved around Rukmini alone. Perhaps, this could also be attributed to the fervour of my youth. 'O Krishna, come back! Come back right now! You are lost in a reverie yet again. Now that you have embarked on such a splendid journey, why not enjoy the scenic beauty of the passing countryside instead?' No sooner did this thought cross my mind than my entire attention shifted to my surroundings. Our chariot was now traversing broad roads and narrow by-lanes, snaking through villages and forests and crossing rivers and mountains too. Like a small child, I was engrossed in enjoying the scenic beauty of the landscape, taking in the sights and sounds of Nature. Although I was twenty years old and not a child anymore, I firmly believe that a person does not mature merely with age but through experience. Therefore, as far as this journey was concerned, I had become like a four-year-old, displaying all the curiosity and excitement of a child that age and enjoying every moment of it.

In just two days of travel, we had fallen into a daily routine. Every day after lunch, we would rest for a while, and every night we would set camp in a secure place, while the rest of our time would be spent travelling. Things were proceeding smoothly, but on the third day, *Acharya* shook us out of the intoxication of our princely ways. Although grandfather had ensured there would be no shortage of servants during our journey, *Acharya* suddenly gave orders that we would now have to perform all our tasks ourselves. In other words, our education had commenced even before we had reached the gates of the *ashram*! In the new order of things, we not only had to gather fruits for our meals, but also had to wash our own clothes. This was, indeed, a novel experience for us, for, it was the first time that we were washing our own clothes. Naturally, bhaiya did not take kindly to this new arrangement, which was evident from the frown that had appeared on his brow and the curt manner in which he spoke. Afraid that he would create some sort of trouble on account of this, I would wash his clothes too, away from *Acharya's* gaze. Indeed, if things went awry and *Acharya* grew displeased with us, we would have no choice but to return to Mathura and live with the terror of Jarasandha hounding us night and day. No! Never. It was better to do twice the hard work than live in such fear.

Well, this was a small matter, so I didn't attach too much importance to it. It was worth noting though that *Acharya* commanded great respect in Aryavarta, which was evident from the fact that throughout the journey, kings of every kingdom would come to pay their respects to him without fail. They would also bring with them offerings of sweets, savouries and other delicious foodstuff, much to our delight. However, there was a flip side—*Acharya* would not allow us to eat any of it. We had to curb our cravings and eat only simple fare. Surprisingly, *Acharya* himself would partake of only the simple food. That was still alright, but whenever he distributed the delicious food items among the servants and soldiers right before our eyes, the pain would become unbearable. Indeed, while they would gorge on the goodies, we would sit gaping at them. Perhaps, this was the mark of a good teacher, whose every act had an underlying lesson. Seen from this perspective, it occurred to me that while we would become inmates of the *ashram* eventually, our education had already begun. On the other hand, although we would find plenty of reasons to be upset sooner or later, bhaiya had already started becoming upset. As the saying goes, 'A child's tendencies are displayed while in the cradle,' bhaiya started showing signs of trouble here itself. In short, our future at the *ashram* was already becoming evident. While I found myself becoming increasingly impressed by *Acharya* as the days passed, bhaiya's irritation with him was growing by the day. The key reason for his unhappiness was that he was not able to lay his hands on the delicious food that was being freely distributed to the others. One day, while we were chatting, he even said, "*Acharya* appears a bit unhinged to me. He distributes even his own share of sweets to the servants. Bah! Who would explain to him that delicacies are meant for the master and not the servants?!" Hearing bhaiya speak in this manner, I just smiled, desperate to somehow maintain peace. Under no circumstances did I want a situation which would force *Acharya* to chuck us out halfway through the journey. Although, it was not as if I couldn't empathise with bhaiya's predicament; I knew fully well that food was his biggest weakness. But one also needs to consider timing, fate and circumstances, right? For that matter, I too was fond of food just like bhaiya, but that certainly did not mean that I should go around throwing tantrums! Admittedly, savouries and delicacies were our biggest weakness; true, bhaiya was so fond of food that one could dangle it as bait and make him do anything. But our weakness for good food shouldn't turn us into a meal for Jarasandha, right?

Oh well! Bhaiya's sulking and my efforts at pacifying him would perhaps continue for as long as we stayed at the *ashram*. Speaking about me, I had commenced my learnings in the journey itself by keenly observing *Acharya's* behaviour and every expression that flit across his face. For this reason, I loved spending time with him; in fact, I would often seek his permission and sit with him in his chariot. I had even begun to feel as if his mere presence was enough to induce a transformation in me. In just a few days of my association with *Acharya*, I had surrendered myself completely to him. On the other hand, he too was becoming increasingly impressed with me. As the days passed, he seemed to take pleasure not only in speaking with me, but also in explaining a number of things to me. In short, a fire burnt bright in both our hearts; while one displayed a keen desire to learn, the other displayed a keen interest to impart knowledge. On one such day, while I was sitting with him in his chariot as it traversed through lush forests, all of a sudden, I expressed my curiosity about the education imparted at the *ashram*. In response, *Acharya* satiated my curiosity saying, "The princes studying at the *ashram* are trained in two ways. On one hand, they are taught princely etiquette, the qualities required to be a good king, how one can eventually become an exemplary king and so on. On the other hand, it is my belief that as princes and kings, though they have every right to enjoy opulence and power, their duty as a king lies in serving their subjects to the best of their capability. Seen from this perspective, the king is indeed a servant to his subjects. Thus, even while enjoying the perks of being a king and living in opulence, he has to remain detached from it all. If need be, he should be ready to live a simple and austere life, not just physically but mentally too. For this purpose, apart from the other studies, every student at the *ashram* is also taught how to live a difficult and disciplined life. Similarly, since a king must be adept at wielding weapons, the disciples at the *ashram* are also given training in their use."

Oh! It was only now that I was able to glean the reason behind *Acharya's* strict behaviour towards us and his decree to eat simple food while making us toil hard. But we were not princes; in fact, it was impossible for us to live our lives without working hard. Similarly, we could afford the pleasure of feasting on a large spread only in case of a big event or festival; otherwise, we partook of simple food. Then why were we subjected to such cruelty?! Of course, I was just jesting, but after hearing *Acharya's* explanation, I was reminded of what Rukmini had said to me. She too had described these very three qualities as essential to becoming a good king. She had said that a king must be brave, empathise with his people, and if the need arose, be able to live a tough life. And if I remember correctly, she had also pointed out that I already possessed these three qualities. For that matter, I too had started to believe this. Oh, how accurate Rukmini's words were! Just then, the voice within chided me, 'Well, if what she had said was right, then do not forget that she had also said that you had needlessly thrown away the chance to become the king of Mathura, and that you might never be able to become a king again!' I retorted, 'Well, so what? I had the qualities of a king in me, and one day, I would surely become one.' The voice responded, 'Ah! I do value your resolve, but that would come to pass only if Jarasandha spared your life, right?' I replied in a determined voice, 'I will find a way out of that as well. I have never allowed even Nature's will to stand in my way, then of what consequence are Jarasandha and Rukmini? Besides, I am sitting in *Acharya's* company, so why should I even harbour such negative thoughts?' For now, I was just thinking, in order to become a good king in *Acharya's* opinion, what else was left for me to learn apart from receiving training in the art of combat! I had anyway been living the simple life of a cowherd throughout my childhood. Then, after arriving in Mathura, I had also picked up the qualities of a good king from my grandfather, the king of Mathura. So, it was now only a matter of waiting for the right opportunity. Thus, at present, not only did my confidence soar, but I had also clearly understood the gist of what *Acharya* had said. The clear import of his words was: only a person who loves his people should be allowed to become a king. Only someone who has a burning desire to serve the people—and not just rule over them—should be a king. Only someone who regards royal luxury and splendour as no more than the perks of his duty—and is always mentally prepared to live without them—is fit to be a king. Only someone who can sleep on the bare floor or even go hungry if the need arises can become a good king. Only someone who can remain unattached to the comforts of living in a palace, whilst actually living amidst them, is truly fit to be a king, just like King Janaka.

Oh, I was really strange. Lost in these deliberations, I didn't even realise that it was time for our evening halt. Interestingly, as we were in the midst of a dense forest and there were no rest houses nearby, this time, we set up camp near the edge of a small pond. The pleasant weather and the scenic beauty around us had cast such an enchanting spell on me that it hardly mattered to me that we had to spend the night sleeping on hard, rocky ground. Well, after eating some fruits, we chatted for a while before retiring for the night. Making a bed of leaves on a flat rock, I lay down on it and surrendered to the arms of sleep. Even *Acharya* and bhaiya had put together a heap of leaves for a bed. *Acharya*, in fact, slipped into deep sleep as soon as he lay down. As for bhaiya, he decided to spend the night fuming away in anger. That left me… Well, even if I refused to pay attention to bhaiya's anger, how could I coax myself to sleep? So, naturally, I drifted back into my thoughts. But no matter which point I began my contemplation from, seeing *Acharya* sleep on a rock nearby, it became clear to me why '*Acharya* Sandipani' commanded immense respect in Aryavarta and why he was regarded as the best *Acharya* in this entire expanse. Suddenly, I found myself questioning, 'How did I, a cowherd, receive the opportunity to study under such a great teacher?' You are well aware that once my mind was stimulated, it loved to delve into analysis. And so, I started analysing and trying to find the reason behind this significant development. To begin with, how could one ignore the fact that my aunts' anger and Jarasandha's rage had contributed to the present situation? Had they not considered me an enemy, would I have received the opportunity to be educated under such a great teacher in this lifetime? So, did it mean that whatever had occurred in my life thus far had been for my ultimate benefit? If this was true, then whatever was transpiring at present was also for my ultimate good. And if these two points are true in the case of every human being, then why does he worry? Why does he remain unhappy? For, whatever happens in a person's life is bound to be for his ultimate good. This tentative conclusion sounded good to me, but the truth was, my contemplation at this point in time was not evolved enough to grasp the profundity of such truths. Why should I lie? Presently, my intellect was not so evolved that it could fathom all the mysteries of life. But the conclusion drawn after today's contemplation had certainly fuelled my desire to understand human life and the mysteries of this vast universe. But since today's contemplation was profound and beyond my present level of understanding, I thought it best to pause for now and instead focus on my sleep. It was midnight by the time I drifted off to sleep, but it did not matter. In the morning, after completing my usual routine, I went for a dip in the pond, while bhaiya and *Acharya* bathed sitting on the pond's edge. And with that, we set off on the next leg of our beautiful journey.

All in all, I continued imbibing invaluable lessons from *Acharya* as we progressed on this wonderful journey of ours, feasting our eyes on the passing countryside of Aryavarta. Indeed, was there any aspect of Aryavarta that was devoid of beauty?! Breathtakingly beautiful rivers, lakes, scenic forests, majestic mountains... Ah, the vast expanse was brimming with countless wonders of Nature. In fact, as soon as the chariot would start moving, falling into its rhythmic pattern, I would lose myself in admiring the landscape.

Finally, after journeying for ten days, we reached our destination, Ujjaini. The city, at first glance, appeared quite imposing. Although it was not as vast as Mathura, it seemed far more organised. Interestingly, whichever path our chariot traversed, people would start queuing up to seek *Acharya's* blessings. Indeed, the crowd on the streets and the people swarming towards the chariot had both slackened our chariot considerably. And when our chariot passed through the marketplace, it almost came to a grinding halt. This was just as well, for, it gave us the opportunity to get a better view of the marketplace. Finally, we managed to cross the marketplace too, and it was only by evening that we entered the *ashram*.

Most notably, the *ashram* was situated far away from the hustle and bustle of the city on the banks of the river, Kshipra. Enveloped by lush green mountains at the back and the serene river flowing next to it, the *ashram* made for a picturesque sight. Truly, for *Acharyas* like Sandipani, there couldn't have been a better place than this for an *ashram*! The *ashram* itself was sprawling and well organised, comprising seven chambers, with one reserved for *Acharya* himself. The second chamber was the dining hall and the other five were allocated for housing the students. Meaning, even in terms of facilities, the *ashram* appeared well equipped. Moreover, tall trees encircled it on all sides, giving it the appearance of being nestled in the heart of a forest. Truth be told, as soon as I set my eyes on the *ashram*, vivid images of Vrindavan flashed before my eyes. For, it was just as beautiful...but why just Vrindavan, I wondered. Was it because I had spent my life there? Prior to this,

I would smugly think that Vrindavan had every imaginable attraction, from River Yamuna to Govardhana Mountain and numerous lakes and ponds—could there be any other place as beautiful as Vrindavan? But after this ten-day journey, I realised that every place in the world is a canvas painted with Nature's beauty. It wasn't just Vrindavan that was extraordinarily beautiful; scenic rivers and magnificent mountains abounded everywhere. The whole of Aryavarta boasted ponds and lakes, each more beautiful than the other. In other words, Nature had been generous with its beauty, favouring no particular region. Of course, it's true that every place had its own unique charm. Then why was I so partial to Vrindavan? Just see, we had barely entered the *ashram* and I had already begun educating myself!

After reaching the *ashram*, we first bathed and then partook of dinner. The entire responsibility of food arrangements was being shouldered by *Acharya's* wife, who was '*Acharya-ma*' to all the students. There were a total of fifteen students in the *ashram* including us, but we had not formally met them as yet. Well, our introduction would take place in due course, but presently, having had our dinner, we all went for a stroll. Perhaps, this was part of the daily routine at the *ashram*. After the stroll, we all sat in the open, square-shaped area in the centre of the *ashram*. *Acharya* and his wife sat in front of us on a raised platform built around the trunk of a huge tree. This arrangement also appeared to be part of the daily routine at the *ashram*. You will not believe this but it was only now that *Acharya* introduced us to the other students at the *ashram*. He began by introducing us to his wife, '*Acharya-ma*' and then to all the students. Just as we had been apprised, all the students hailed from royal families. But yes, there was one boy whose name *Acharya* had said was Sudama, the only one without a claim to royalty. They all seemed fine, except for two princes, Vinda and Anuvinda, who appeared rather snobbish—perhaps because both of them were princes of Ujjaini and the *ashram* was functioning solely on the grant given by their father, the king of Ujjaini. Well, so be it...how did it matter to us? We had come here under *Acharya's* care. The rest of the evening passed quietly, without any significant event. Perhaps, *Acharya* was tired. Well, we were tired too, so everyone soon retired for the night. But before turning in, *Acharya* instructed us all to assemble in the same spot at sunrise, after completing our morning routine.

With the first rays of the rising sun, everyone had gathered at the designated place just as instructed. Since we had reached the *ashram* quite late on the previous day, I had not been able to view the surroundings clearly in the fading light, but on this morning, the open area in the centre of the *ashram* appeared quite beautiful. To the right were the chambers, while to the left, lush greenery stretched far into the distance. From our seat, we could see layer upon layer of the mountain range, and behind us, we could hear the gurgling waters of River Kshipra. Taking in these sights, I was convinced that no place could be more splendid than this for receiving education. *Acharya* and *Acharya-ma* sat right in front of us on their designated seat…and on a signal from *Acharya*, Sudama got up, stood next to him and started chanting the *guruvandana.*[11] Perhaps, this was also part of the daily routine. Listening to Sudama sing, I'm not sure why but I too felt a strong urge to play my flute; perhaps, it was my ego that prompted me to flaunt my talent to others. Whatever it was, I stood up at once and sought *Acharya's* permission to play my flute while Sudama sang. *Acharya* gladly consented, and soon, Sudama's mellifluous voice blended with the melody of my flute, creating a symphony so harmonious that everyone sat entranced, listening to us. In fact, from the very next day, this became our daily routine at the *ashram*. Well, it was inevitable! In Krishna's presence, transformation was bound to happen!

At the end of the delightful song and music programme, *Acharya* instructed us to form three groups of five students each. I promptly made Sudama stand with bhaiya and me, and for some reason, Vinda and Anuvinda decided to join our group too. Now, the five of us were required to undertake all activities at the *ashram* together, which also included sharing the sleeping quarters. Interestingly, this marked the beginning of the next chapter in our lives—one I eagerly anticipated, knowing it would shape us in ways we could have never imagined.

11. *Guruvandana* - Obeisance to the guru or teacher.

Chapter 4

Self-realisation

Gazing at the silhouette of the imposing mountain range from the window near my bed, a flurry of thoughts raced through my mind. As unbelievable as it seemed, bhaiya and I were truly at the *ashram* of *Acharya* Sandipani, and after spending a day here, it could most certainly be said that our education had officially commenced. Until now, my only tutor had been the school of life and whatever lessons I had learnt were from the struggles it had thrown in my path. Truly, had I not received the opportunity to learn from *Acharya*, I would have been deprived of many valuable lessons in life! I will forever be grateful to grandfather for granting me this wonderful opportunity. As you are well aware, my childhood had been showered with abundant love from Mother Yashoda, while my youth was spent under the guidance of Grandfather Ugrasena. And now under the tutelage of *Acharya*, my future too seemed to be heading in a promising direction. Even as I was mulling over this, my thoughts suddenly veered in a new direction. I began to wonder how many teachers like *Acharya* Sandipani existed in Aryavarta, and how many students like me longed to learn everything their teacher taught. Perhaps, very few! At any rate, I was always proud of my desire to learn and internalise knowledge from the very outset. And why would I not be? If I had been able to learn so much from life without the guidance of a teacher, you can only imagine the transformation a teacher like *Acharya* Sandipani could bring about in me.

Having woken up at the crack of dawn and gone through the rigours of the routine laid down by the *ashram*, I spent the day mingling with the other students. Even so, I can say that this was one of the most important and unique experiences of my life. Well, it was just the second night at the *ashram*, when suddenly, an unexpected incident occurred. *Acharya* instructed a bunch of us to sleep on the bare floor outside our chambers without any mattress or blanket. And surprisingly, he too settled himself on the bare floor outside his chamber without any bedding. Indeed, what a great personality *Acharya* was! He had set an example by following his own instructions. Really, with teachers like *Acharya* Sandipani and students like me, learning could continue day and night. It was for this very reason that I would keenly observe every little behaviour of *Acharya*. His behaviour at present was teaching me the invaluable lesson that we should ask others to do only that which we ourselves have done, are doing or are capable of doing. I must say, all his actions… even the way he breathed and blinked were worth emulating. Gradually, I was beginning to understand that just by observing *Acharya's* actions, one could learn way more than what he actually taught. And the proof of this was that ever since I had met him, I was continuously learning something or the other by merely observing him.

Well, for now, let me talk about the unique experience that has led me to discuss all of this. Firstly, it was the season of winter, and Ujjaini typically experienced a biting cold weather at this time of the year, as it was located at the foothills of the mountains. Moreover, the *ashram* was situated on the edge of River Kshipra, which meant that cold winds would invariably sweep over the *ashram* and into the open courtyard. You can well imagine how torturous it must have been to sleep without any bedding on the cold, hard floor in these conditions. However, we had no choice but to follow *Acharya*'s instruction, so seeing no way out, I lay down quietly on the bare floor, shivering just a tad bit as my torso touched the ice-cold floor. But bhaiya was extremely uncomfortable as he kept tossing and turning in anger, cursing under his breath. Of course, as cowherd boys hailing from a modest background, we should have been accustomed to such hardships, facing no difficulty in being able to sleep on the floor. But we couldn't help it. This was a first-of-its-kind experience for us, as we had never slept out in the open without bedding before. Besides, we had never experienced such biting cold during the winter season either. Clearly, the climate in Ujjaini was much colder than that of Mathura or Vrindavan. In fact, even I was finding it difficult to sleep, as the discomfort was a bit too much to bear. However, the satisfaction I felt upon obeying *Acharya* and following his instruction kept me composed. So much for bhaiya and me, but the plight of Vinda and Anuvinda, who had been studying in the *ashram* for several years, was no different. In our group, the only person who could be called fortunate was Sudama, as he had no trouble at all slipping into a slumber the moment he lay down on the cold, bare floor. And much to our annoyance, he even managed to snore away happily! Among all of us, *Acharya* and Sudama were the only two who were sleeping blissfully, while the four of us were merely tossing and turning in discomfort. The rest of the students were sleeping peacefully in their respective chambers, as it was our group alone that had been 'blessed' by *Acharya* in this manner.

To make matters worse, our chamber was located in a corner of the *ashram,* with its veranda facing River Kshipra, so you can imagine the extent of our discomfort when the chilly breeze from the river froze us to the bone. Forget about the others, I too was sleeping with my hands clasped between my knees, my teeth chattering and my body shivering. Unable to sleep, I kept stealing glances at the others, who were sleeping some distance away. That's when I noticed that Vinda and Anuvinda had taken their bedding and blankets out of their chamber and were comfortably sleeping in them. I was shocked to see *Acharya* being disobeyed so blatantly. It had only been a few moments since they had committed this transgression, when noticing bhaiya and me tossing and turning, Vinda crawled up to me and whispered, "Why don't you too bring the bedding and blankets from your chamber and sleep comfortably?" Seeing Vinda chat with me, a curious bhaiya slid closer, and Anuvinda followed suit. And just like that, our impromptu conversation had turned into a veritable assembly. Amusingly, while those two had brought out their beddings and were comfortable, we still sat crouched with knees bent to our chests, shivering in the cold. Well, be that as it may, but the idea they were suggesting to protect ourselves from the cold was truly abominable! I frowned on hearing their sympathetic suggestion, which went against *Acharya*'s instructions. As for *Acharya,* he wasn't sleeping too far from us. Despite the darkness, if one looked carefully, one could make out that he was sleeping outside his chamber, enduring the same conditions as we were. This being the case, Vinda's act of flouting *Acharya*'s instructions reflected a poor mentality indeed. If this was Vrindavan, I would have set him straight, but there was no point in unnecessarily getting involved in a scuffle at the *ashram*. So, I replied with great politeness, "Because that would mean disobeying *Acharya*! If it weren't for him, we too could make use of some bedding."

Hearing my answer, Anuvinda butted in and said nonchalantly, "Oh, come on, no one is around to see whether we are following his instructions or not!"

For once, I felt a surge of anger on hearing him speak with such disdain, but then, with great effort, I composed myself and managed to reply in a calm tone, "Whether anyone sees us or not, are we not able to see ourselves? Besides, what we ourselves see is more important than what others see."

Perhaps, Vinda could not digest even these simple words of mine. Snorting with disdain, he retorted sarcastically, "Oh, I had completely forgotten! You two are cowherd boys! You must be accustomed to sleeping like this. Had you hailed from a royal family like ours, you would have understood the difference!"

Even as his barb pricked me, I maintained a calm demeanour knowing fully well that I was being baited, but bhaiya, who was already exasperated by the strict discipline and the simple meals of the *ashram*, lost his composure on hearing Vinda's taunts. With great difficulty, I somehow placated him. Indeed, how did it matter if someone called us cowherd boys? Besides, he was not wrong in calling us so, for, we were cowherds after all, and I was certainly not ashamed of being one. Yes, it was true that they were proud of being princes, but that was their problem. So, why trouble ourselves over it? I was just explaining all this to bhaiya, when suddenly, I saw *Acharya* walking towards us. He had probably overheard the conversation and the resulting altercation between us. The moment he reached us, he asked me, "What is the matter? Are you finding it difficult to fall asleep?" What could I say? I did not utter a word.

Seeing that I had fallen silent, he said, "This is the result of a change in environment. If a person trains his mind to adapt to changing circumstances, he will never face such difficulties. Since these are your initial days at the *ashram*, this transgression can be overlooked. Many students here struggle to adapt even after spending years in practice at the *ashram*."

Hearing these comments, both Vinda and Anuvinda winced as if they had received a stinging slap on their faces. Their uneasiness was evident on their countenance, and in their nervousness, they quickly kicked their bedding off into a corner. But perhaps, *Acharya* wanted to chide them some more, so glaring at them, he said, "What's the matter? Is the discomfort too much to bear?"

Quaking with fear, they both nodded their heads in agreement. Smiling at their discomfort, *Acharya* spoke to them calmly and said, "Then why are you getting rid of your bedding? If you are finding it cumbersome to sleep on the bare floor, then use it. This is an *ashram*, not a religious place where attempts are made to change one by force…or to trouble one unnecessarily. Here, you are taught how to transform your mind. The day you will yourself embrace sleeping on the bare floor, you will no longer feel the need for bedding. The truth is, from that day on, even the cold will not trouble you!"

Saying this, *Acharya* left us alone but not without imparting yet another wonderful lesson—the lesson of 'acceptance'. I quickly imbibed it and from the next moment itself, I accepted sleeping on the floor. That's it! I did not feel cold anymore. There was no need for bedding or blankets now, and in no time, I fell asleep and began to snore. This was incredible indeed! The spirit of 'acceptance' was truly magical. In fact, to call this an ordinary lesson would be an insult. Actually, the spirit of acceptance had been ingrained in me since childhood. Generally speaking, I would quickly embrace whatever came my way, but now, I was completely under the spell of its magic. I had come to realise that if one can change their circumstances, they should; but if not, they should accept it and move on.

And move on I surely did. Thereafter, as the days passed, we gradually began to adjust to the environment of the *ashram*. Meanwhile, my friendship with Sudama was strengthening with the passage of time and one of the main reasons for this was obviously our love for music. But another important reason was that, similar to bhaiya and me, he did not belong to a royal family; therefore, his ego did not clash with ours. However, since he was the son of another *Acharya,* besides being the favourite student of *Acharya-ma*, his arrogance would sometimes reflect in his behaviour. But fortunately, his condescending attitude was tolerable and did not bother us much. Meanwhile, our lives had become quite disciplined after arriving at the *ashram*. We were responsible for all our daily tasks, from washing our own clothes to making our own beds. Additionally, we had to step out to procure supplies needed to run the *ashram*. We were also required to exercise regularly and follow a strict schedule for sleeping and waking. Now, you are well aware that we were not accustomed to a disciplined lifestyle. And while I had come to accept it as a part of life in the *ashram*, bhaiya faced a huge problem in toeing the line, which often left him irritated. He especially hated the idea of waking up at the crack of dawn. Nonetheless, I continued my attempts to help him adapt to the life we were living at the *ashram*; sometimes by explaining things to him, and other times, by enticing him. But the problem was, bhaiya had not one but a thousand grievances. To make matters worse, trouble would come our way on a daily basis, in one form or the other. Consider this particular instance. One day, the royal palace sent delicious food items to the *ashram*, and naturally, bhaiya and I were thrilled. While I kept my happiness in check, bhaiya's mood changed completely, his face lighting up with a wide smile. Now, as you know, both of us had a great love for food, and after coming to Mathura, we had developed a fondness for delicacies, enjoying a wide variety of sweets and savouries. Besides, bhaiya and I were capable of wolfing down food meant for four people all by ourselves! In contrast to all this, the food at the *ashram* was quite simple and the portions meagre. How could we ever satiate ourselves with just this? Hence, considering our craving for good food, it was only natural for us gluttons to go delirious with joy seeing all the delicious foodstuff that had arrived at the *ashram*. But as they say, not everything you wish for in life comes true…and perhaps, this is what makes life interesting too. And as if to prove this point, *Acharya* permitted us to eat only the fruits and curd from all the delicious food sent by the palace. Needless to say, we were deflated on hearing this. *Acharya* gave his instructions and left, but bhaiya was truly devastated. A frown appeared on his face as he fumed from within. Indeed, he looked as if someone had snatched away the very morsel from his mouth!

In other words, trouble had come knocking at our door once again, and it was only a matter of time before it assumed a terrifying form. Well, we did not have to wait long for that either. With long faces, we had just begun to pick at the simple food when Vinda and Anuvinda lost all control. The moment they saw the delicious food, they began to drool, and ignoring *Acharya*'s instructions, they pounced on it and started gorging. This, of course, was like rubbing salt into our wounds! We were already troubled at the sight of such a delicious spread, and now, standing there watching these two brothers feast right before our eyes was too much to bear! This too was an entirely new experience for us—a delectable spread lay before us and we desperately wanted to gorge on it, but all we could do was eye the food with longing. Seen from this perspective, on this day, I was introduced to a new character trait within me, which was perhaps the result of voluntarily agreeing to follow *Acharya*'s instructions. It can be said that *Acharya's* influence over me had a greater role to play in this than my own special ability. What I mean to say is, had any ordinary *Acharya* given these instructions, I would have probably brushed off his command myself and devoured all the delicious spread that lay before me.

But for the moment, the scene at the *ashram* had become quite amusing. While Sudama and I were quietly eating the fruits and curd, bhaiya was attacking the same simple food, venting his frustration on it. On the other hand, sitting right across us, Vinda and Anuvinda were still gorging on all the scrumptious food. Having had our fill, Sudama and I got up, but bhaiya refused to get up from his seat. No, no, it was not as if he was busy eating; he was only staring at all the delicious food! He was in fact glaring at it, as if he wanted to devour it all with his eyes, and believe me, he had already gobbled up as much as he could with his eyes! What tormented us the most was that Vinda and Anuvinda were still gorging on the food, as though they hadn't eaten in months! By now, the other students had gathered around as well. Everyone stood silently, witnessing the spectacle before them. Though I had gotten up, having eaten my fill, I still stood there, taking great pleasure in seeing the two brothers eat. When Anuvinda saw us staring at the food, he asked bhaiya and me, "Don't you wish to eat this food?"

Bah! What sort of a question was that? There were others too who were watching them with an unflinching gaze, yet he had addressed only us. So be it! I did not want to encourage any further exchange on this issue, so in order to put an end to the matter, I replied, "Of course, we do. Why should I lie? To some extent, the desire is still there, but I have a greater desire to follow *Acharya*'s orders."

Vinda, it seemed, was just waiting for an opportunity like this, and without a moment's hesitation, he repeated his previous sarcastic comment, "Both of you are cowherds after all, and that too, hailing from the godforsaken forests of Vrindavan! Had you ever tasted good food, you would have known what you are missing out on!"

Hearing this, bhaiya went livid and seeing him in this state, I became tense and shot nervous glances at him. For, what if bhaiya, unable to consume this scrumptious food, took out all his frustration on Vinda? Believe me, I had to beg, beseech and plead with bhaiya to calm him down. Still, glowering

at Vinda, bhaiya warned him, "Beware, I am not used to hearing sarcastic comments!"

To this, Vinda replied with calm arrogance, "Oh, but I excel at making sarcastic comments!"

Alarmed that the matter was getting out of hand, I intervened once again to diffuse the situation. With great humility, I said, "All right, my friend, you may continue to pass sarcastic comments. Over time, we shall learn to tolerate them too. We are learning some lessons from *Acharya* and we will learn some from you as well." Meanwhile, Sudama, who had been standing in a corner, was deriving immense pleasure from our squabbling. Perhaps, in addition to being accustomed to following *Acharya*'s rules, he was immune to the jibes of the snobbish princes too. After all, he was one of the older students of this *ashram*. But just then, for no apparent reason, Anuvinda jumped into the fray, perhaps not wanting to lag behind in hurling taunts at us. While he did not address us directly, he turned to Vinda and spoke sarcastically, "I wonder where *Acharya* found these two wild pigeons! They have certainly ruined the good name of this fine *ashram*."

Uh-oh! The moment he heard this comment, bhaiya stood up, ready to explode. I was afraid he might just smash these two brothers to a pulp! The situation was quickly spiralling out of control. The harder I tried to douse the fire, the more Vinda and Anuvinda seemed determined to stoke it. And unfortunately, they appeared to be winning. Of course, I was not one to accept defeat easily, but as we all know, it's far easier to keep tempers flaring than to calm them down. So, naturally, Vinda and Anuvinda were overpowering us.

Well, just when the situation was about to explode, *Acharya* appeared out of nowhere. Seeing him, I was relieved immensely. Perhaps, it was the clatter of our arguments that had caught his attention. No sooner he came, he shot a stern look at Vinda and Anuvinda and said, "The prestige of the *ashram* does not hinge upon who comes here to seek knowledge. The *ashram's* glory and reputation are based on what the students who pass out from here go on to achieve in life. But how can arrogant students like you ever understand these things? Let me make it clear that you two brothers do not have to follow my orders from today onwards. For, it is not my task to stifle your desires, but to refine them; suppressing desires only ends up fuelling them, causing them to resurface with twice the intensity. Well, I do not need to explain any of this to you. But yes, in return for absolving you both from following my orders, it is expected that you two will no longer interfere in the matters of other students at the *ashram*." After a few moments of silence, he added in a sterner voice, "Otherwise, be prepared to face grave consequences!"

The manner in which *Acharya* spoke made Vinda and Anuvinda's faces go pale with fear. Even I was amazed by the authority he commanded. Well, *Acharya* had left after saying this, but once again he had taught me an invaluable lesson before leaving. The essence of his teaching was clear: 'To renounce something physically is of little worth; what actually holds importance is to renounce it from your mind.' And this teaching became etched in my mind forever. After this incident, I never felt the urge to eat forbidden foodstuff at the *ashram*. And as far as the stifling of desires is concerned, I had always vehemently opposed all forms of it, from the very beginning. I was always an advocate of complete independence. The most fortunate aspect of this entire incident was that *Acharya* had managed to appear in the nick of time; otherwise a fight between bhaiya and Vinda-Anuvinda would have become inevitable. And had this happened, God only knows what bhaiya would have done to them! Well, they would have met their fate, but I shudder to imagine what would have happened to us after that. They were both princes of Ujjaini and the *ashram* was sustained solely by the largesse of Ujjaini's ruler. So, if we were to offend them and be expelled from the *ashram*, our death at the hands of Jarasandha would have been certain. Well, do you see what I mean? The *ashram* had definitely shielded us from the menace called Jarasandha, but we were still not free from his terror. And this was only because I had a problem named bhaiya tagging along with me at all times, and this problem ensured that the looming shadow of Jarasandha always hovered above our heads.

Well, as soon as this matter was resolved, all of us retired to our chambers. Interestingly, we had just been involved in a fight with Vinda and Anuvinda, and now, we had to sleep in the same chamber as them! This meant that I had to stay awake to ensure that bhaiya and the two brothers did not pick a fight again. And in my heart of hearts, I was even cursing Vinda-Anuvinda for this. You would recall how I enjoyed seeing the many princes as they rode in their splendid chariots in Mathura. Oftentimes, I would be lost in admiration, looking at their royal finery, as if they had just descended from heaven! However, my admiration for them had vanished into thin air after close encounters with these princes at the *ashram*. Thinking about the princes, my thoughts veered off in an entirely new direction. I wondered, these very individuals will one day become kings and rule their kingdoms. What will become of the future of Aryavarta in such a scenario? How will the common people ever lead a peaceful life under their reign? In light of this, was it not essential to change the age-old tradition of crowning the prince as the new king? In order to secure a bright future for the common people, shouldn't the most deserving person in the kingdom be made king instead of the prince?

There are, in fact, many other matters worth considering, but nothing can be done about them, and this line of thought fell into the same category. As I continued to mull over these thoughts, little did I realise that the night had passed, ushering the golden rays of the rising sun.

Well, let us put aside these thoughts and talk about what we were learning at the *ashram*. It had only been a few days since our arrival, and we had already commenced our training in the art of wielding weapons. Though the students were trained to wield all kinds of weapons, *Acharya*'s training laid more emphasis on the use of the mace and the sword. Needless to mention, this was the first time we were formally learning to use weapons, which was undoubtedly a crucial experience. Well, the training programme would take its own course, but a positive outcome of this exercise was that with the commencement of the weapons training, bhaiya had started to enjoy his stay at the *ashram*. And because of this, I had been relieved of the arduous task of pacifying him every now and then. As for me, I was so impressed by everything *Acharya* did that I had completely fallen in love with his enigmatic personality. In fact, not once did I think of Mathura or Jarasandha. Most surprisingly, I had even forgotten Vrindavan and Rukmini! *Acharya* had replaced everything else, holding complete sway over my mind. And an even more gratifying aspect was that *Acharya* was genuinely pleased to have me as his disciple at the *ashram*. Perhaps, that is why he had commenced the evening classes too—a very useful and novel experiment indeed. In these classes, *Acharya* encouraged us to ask questions that crossed our minds, which he would then answer. You would not believe it, but the moment I heard about it, a thousand questions had started racing in my mind from that moment itself.

Well, today was the first day of this experiment and I had spent the entire morning waiting for the evening class to begin…in fact, I was waiting ever since the announcement was made! After the evening meal, we all gathered around *Acharya* in the courtyard and took our respective seats. Bursting with enthusiasm, I sat next to bhaiya and Sudama in the very first row. Indeed, sitting on the grass in Ujjaini's cool climate was a unique pleasure in itself. Soon, *Acharya* arrived along with *Acharya-ma*. We all stood up and greeted them with a *pranaam* and took our seats again after they were seated on their designated platform next to the tree. I can't say how anyone else felt but my heart was thumping with excitement, as I mused, if one could get the answers to all the questions in one's mind, what better education could there be? But surprisingly, even after *Acharya* had repeatedly invited all of us to ask our questions, no one came forth. However, I, who had been waiting eagerly since morning, needed no prodding. In other words, the discussion commenced with the very question I asked. And I opened my question with a well-thought-out preamble, “Respected *Acharya*, as a new student here, I kindly request your pardon if there is any error in my question. What I would like to understand is, what connection does abstaining from eating tasty food or sleeping on the bare floor have with our future? What is the objective behind this exercise? Why should we renounce that which is coming to us of its own accord? If something does not harm us, why abstain from it?”

As soon as I had finished my question, *Acharya* motioned me to take my seat. Then, he spoke in an encouraging tone, “Dear student! Your question is excellent. Actually, there are two objectives behind this exercise. First, consider this: if something you’re fond of is placed in front of you, but following my instructions, you are able to abstain from it—not only physically but also mentally—it means that you respect me. And one can gain education only from a teacher one respects. Otherwise, all your learning will be reduced to naught. Secondly, life, even if it is that of a king, is not always a bed of roses. New problems and challenges come up every day. In this *ashram*, we prepare you to face any exigencies that may arise in the future. Remember, even a king has to leave all his comforts behind when he steps into the battlefield. And if he is defeated, he has to face imprisonment too. So, consider all of this as both a mental and physical preparation for such eventualities.”

But I wasn’t content with just this! So, as soon as *Acharya* finished speaking, I stood up again and shot another question at him, “So, does it mean that you have no objection otherwise to good food and the comforts of life?”

A smile lit up on *Acharya*’s face on hearing my naïve question. He replied, “That’s right! After passing out from the *ashram*, everyone will enjoy royal comforts anyway. Remember, a person who does not have wealth and yet wishes to enjoy luxuries is a fool. But a man who has wealth but still does not enjoy it is a bigger fool!”

Oh, how wise *Acharya* was! He had answered my query in such a simple and lucid manner, dispelling all my doubts in an instant. And with these few lines of wisdom, the day’s session was concluded. However, gradually, I had begun to enjoy these question-and-answer sessions so much that I would look forward to these evening sessions from the morning itself. Well, this was the case as far as I was concerned, but I wondered why bhaiya was still not completely happy at the *ashram*. I was well aware that adhering to discipline or pursuing education was something that never really agreed with him. In fact, over time, his restlessness grew so much that to kill time, he would sneak out of the *ashram,* perhaps to take a stroll. Truth be told, every time bhaiya sneaked out, I would turn into a ball of nerves, anxious at the repercussions in case he were caught. I even tried to dissuade him a couple of times, but all my pleas went unheeded. I feared only one thing: what if *Acharya* learnt about this and took disciplinary action by expelling bhaiya from the *ashram*? And if that were to happen, I too could be considered expelled along with him. After all, I could never leave bhaiya alone, could I? And once we were thrown out of the *ashram*, the demon called Jarasandha would begin stalking us once again. This would not only end our education, but also put our lives in jeopardy! But was my obdurate bhaiya ever going to pay heed to this? In short, while I was experiencing peace and happiness at the *ashram*, I also had to endure mental torment.

Bhaiya, however, refused to heed the voice of reason. By now, his escapades had turned into a daily affair. One day, during one of his secretive outings, he had inadvertently wandered quite far into the forest. Actually, the *ashram* shared its boundary with the forest, but on that day, bhaiya had strayed deep into the forest. Loitering aimlessly all afternoon, he was enjoying himself, breathing in the fresh air of freedom, when all of a sudden, a tiger leapt out of the bushes right in front of him. Of course, bhaiya was not one to get frightened by a tiger. Besides, staying at the *ashram*, he had been deprived of action for far too many days. So, it was only natural that his hands were itching to pick a fight. In short, there was no question of him letting this golden opportunity slip by. The dense forest and eerie silence were enough to send a chill down anyone's spine, but not bhaiya's. He stood his ground, glaring at the wild beast standing fifty yards away! Instead of fleeing or moving away from the tiger's path, bhaiya started inching closer towards the tiger with slow, measured steps. The tiger, noticing its prey walk towards him, was not one to turn tail either, hence both continued to advance towards each other and finally stood face to face. In a split second, both bhaiya and the tiger lurched at each other. Interestingly, Vrindavan did not have such huge tigers, and this was probably why bhaiya underestimated the tiger and had kept his plough aside before leaping into the fight. But the tiger was quite agile, strong and huge, almost twice the size of bhaiya. Bhaiya was locked in a duel with the beast for quite some time, but when he realised that the tiger would not be overpowered easily even after a spirited tussle, he lost his patience. Now, there was no way the tiger could escape bhaiya's plough! So, taking a few steps backwards, bhaiya snatched his plough and in one swift movement, he lodged it firmly in the tiger's chest. Before the tiger could react or defend itself, the plough had found its mark. Now, finishing off the wounded tiger was akin to killing a goat, so within moments, the tiger lay slain at bhaiya's feet. Now, although bhaiya had shown courage by killing the huge beast single-handedly with his weapon, he mused, 'Why not narrate this tale of bravery to everyone at the *ashram*?' There were two reasons behind this line of thought. Firstly, bhaiya wanted to flaunt his bravery in front of everyone; secondly, he wanted to do something that would make *Acharya* proud of him, as he would always feel unsettled whenever *Acharya* praised me. And I am not saying this without reason. For, during one of our conversations, he had even expressed this grievance to me. Finding the right moment when we were alone, he had posed his question in a very helpless tone, "Kanhaiya, how much longer do we have to stay at the *ashram*?"

I had enquired, "Why do you ask?"

And he had replied, "I am not enjoying myself here."

I had said, "But *Acharya* is teaching us such valuable lessons. And these lessons can transform our lives. Then, why are you not enjoying yourself?"

He had replied, "Pfft! You are able to effortlessly grasp whatever he teaches, while I cannot remember even one of his teachings."

Assuaging his feelings of helplessness and despair, I had spoken to him in an encouraging tone, "Oh, but this is very easy. Whenever he is explaining something to us, you should listen with such rapt attention that you forget your very existence. That's it! Then, even you will be able to imbibe *Acharya's* teachings with ease."

Responding to this, bhaiya had said, "That is true, I suppose, but *Acharya* keeps scolding me all the time. He has repeatedly told me, 'You cannot remember anything, but your brother only needs to hear something once and he remembers it word for word!'"

Hearing bhaiya's grievance, I had realised what the real problem was! It was not about his inability to memorise or *Acharya*'s chiding. The real problem was *Acharya*'s constant comparison between him and me, which had pricked his ego. However, this was not the only blow to his ego; living in close proximity with the princes and witnessing their royal ways had instilled a feeling of inferiority complex in him. Actually, the fact that he hailed from an ordinary family was gnawing at him from within. Interestingly, in contrast to bhaiya's line of thinking, I considered myself better than a thousand princes! Such silly problems never bothered me; besides, you are well aware that I have always been quite taken with myself since childhood. However, putting my thoughts aside, let us focus on bhaiya at present. He certainly did not want to miss out on the golden opportunity of blowing his own trumpet. But to do so, he had to drag the carcass of the tiger all the way to the *ashram*. Now, ego is also a form of the all-powerful consciousness, which can make man perform even the most challenging tasks with ease. Thus, in spite of encountering great difficulty in lugging the huge beast, which was twice his size, bhaiya huffed and puffed and somehow managed to drag the tiger to the *ashram*'s gate.

Everything was fine up to this point, but then, leaving the carcass at the entrance, he came inside in search of me. At the time, I was seated in the courtyard with everyone else. Seeing bhaiya sweating and panting, I gaped at him in bewilderment. Without uttering a word, he escorted me towards the entrance, while everyone else followed us out of curiosity. Seeing a tiger lying on the ground near the entrance, I was stunned and stopped short in my tracks, as did those who were trailing behind us. But as soon as bhaiya landed a punch on the lifeless tiger's body, I realised what must have transpired. Oh, what a huge beast it was! I had never laid my eyes on a tiger of this size and magnitude in Vrindavan. Incredibly, the dead tiger had made bhaiya sweat profusely even in this cold weather! Seeing what bhaiya had done, I recalled our childhood days, when he had once killed a huge crane and had kept bragging about it for days. His habit of blowing his own trumpet was an old one. And this time, it was a tiger after all! On the other hand, the *ashram* was teeming with princes, which meant this was the perfect opportunity for bhaiya to flaunt his prowess in front of a distinguished audience. Now all that was left to see was when bhaiya would open his mouth to sing his own praises! However, it was only I who was waiting for bhaiya to open his mouth; the others looked on perplexed at the sight before them. Indeed, it was beyond the princes to even imagine that a person could single-handedly kill such a huge tiger! However, I was sure that all their doubts would be cleared once bhaiya opened his mouth to brag. I was very happy for bhaiya though, because at least now, everyone would glorify him and sing his praises. This also meant that now, there was no need for me to worry about him leaving the *ashram*. Meanwhile, hearing all the commotion, *Acharya* too rushed to the main entrance and froze when he saw a tiger lying dead at the *ashram's* gate. His gaze slowly travelled over bhaiya, whose one foot was placed proudly on the tiger's back. He then glanced at the rest of us who were watching this spectacle. Bhaiya's pride soared the moment *Acharya* arrived, while I went and stood close to bhaiya. True to his nature, as soon as bhaiya noticed that everyone was present and the stage had been set, he started bragging, "I was just taking a stroll in the forest when this tiger dared to approach me. Oh, the temerity he had to cross my path! Naturally, this incensed me and I put it to death in just a couple of blows."

Hearing this, everyone broke into applause, singing praises of bhaiya's bravery. Brimming with pride, bhaiya puffed up his chest even more and, looking at *Acharya,* said, "I dragged the carcass here only to present it as a gift to you."

Acharya had been absolutely quiet until now, his countenance devoid of expression. I found this very surprising, for, I could not fathom what was going on in his mind. Then I reasoned, 'It is impossible to discern what's going on in his mind, which is precisely why he is a *guru* (teacher)!' On the other hand, it was quite obvious why bhaiya had killed the tiger and dragged it to the *ashram*, and this is precisely what makes bhaiya who he is!

Well, be that as it may! For now, realising it was futile to try and fathom what was going on in *Acharya's* mind, I decided to steer my contemplation in a direction that was well within my comprehension. And as soon as my thought process kicked into action, I couldn't help but chuckle to myself, recalling *Acharya*'s sneering comment, which had ultimately led to this innocent tiger losing its life. Well, this thought faded away soon, but not before rattling my entire line of thought, as I wondered, 'Can other people's words and behaviour really influence a person to such an extent? Can a person really be turned into a puppet?' The connection between *Acharya*'s jibe and bhaiya's killing of the tiger was obvious. And if what I was thinking was indeed possible, this would be the best game ever. In fact, in this way, one could easily use people like toys. Ah, this game was very much to my liking, and from that point onwards, throughout my life, I used people like toys. That said, I never used them for selfish gain. Incidentally, learning this game of influencing people had an added benefit: no one could upset me or influence me. After all, it's fun to play with toys, not to become one in someone else's hands! It was incredible how I had fathomed such a profound truth...but I still couldn't comprehend what was going on in *Acharya*'s mind. Finally, I gave up, thinking that this was probably why he was the *guru* and I, the disciple.

Even more remarkable was the fact that, after such deep contemplation, I had returned to my usual state of mind, while *Acharya* continued to remain tight-lipped. I shot a nervous glance at bhaiya, who was still standing with his foot on the dead tiger, and then at *Acharya,* who stood among the other students. But no matter what I did, I still couldn't work up the courage to break the silence. Then suddenly, *Acharya*'s expression changed. Wearing a look of anger, he moved a few steps closer to us. Then, unleashing his fury on bhaiya, he bellowed, "You have committed two transgressions! First, you stepped out of the *ashram* without my permission, and second, by killing this tiger, you have unnecessarily killed a living being. The reason you have been able to simultaneously commit these two transgressions is because until now, you have only seen your *guru*'s kindness...not his ire!"

Bhaiya was badly shaken on hearing *Acharya*'s words, which now echoed in the silence around us. This was the first time I had seen bhaiya look terrified. Why just bhaiya, even I was quaking with fear. How stern and harsh *Acharya*'s tone was! How frightening his demeanour was! Fortunately, the situation did not worsen, but yes, before departing, *Acharya* did issue a final warning to bhaiya. In the same reprimanding tone as before, he said, "This was your first offence, so I am condoning it. But bear in mind, eating flesh or bringing it in this *ashram* is strictly forbidden." With these curt words, *Acharya* turned on his heels and left, while the rest of us followed suit. Naturally, bhaiya had fallen into a deep, despairing gloom. The whole episode was upsetting indeed. *Acharya* had reprimanded him in front of everyone at a time when bhaiya was expecting nothing less than accolades. Consequently, everyone in the class was unusually quiet this evening. Bhaiya hung his head low, refusing to look up. Everyone else was frightened too, worried that if they committed any mistake, it might just invoke *Acharya*'s wrath. My condition was the strangest—while my heart went out to bhaiya, who was caught in this embarrassing situation, a storm of thoughts raged through my mind. And, of course, it would, because this was the first time I had heard of the concept of violence against animals, and naturally, a number of questions related to it were swirling in my mind. But nervous that I was, I could not muster the courage to open my mouth this evening. In the past, I had killed several wild animals myself, so did that mean I had done something wrong? Only *Acharya* could answer this, but for that, I would have to pose the question to him first. However, I still could not work up the courage to do that, and when I was so scared myself, there was absolutely no question of anyone else daring to pose questions to *Acharya*. Even otherwise, no one ever showed much interest in asking questions. Noticing that the gathering was unusually quiet today, *Acharya* finally enquired of me, "What's the matter, Kanhaiya? Even you don't want to ask any questions today?"

Hearing *Acharya* address me, I could feel my courage build up. And that being the case, I reckoned, why wait for another opportune moment? Thus, I promptly shot off a question, "Respected *Acharya*, if a wild animal attacks us, should we not kill it even in self-defence?"

Acharya explained, "To defend yourself, you can resort to any measures, but remember, even animals reserve this right. The way you have the right to kill an animal to defend yourself, even the animal has the right to kill you to defend itself. But the truth is, an animal will never attack you unless it feels threatened by you. Of course, if it has gone feral or is inherently violent, then it is a different matter. Let me give you my own example: tigers and lions very often sleep next to me. But till today, even their nails have never touched me, not even by accident."

Having fathomed what *Acharya* said, I felt a wave of relief wash over me, for, my actions so far had been aimed in the right direction. Forget self-defence, I had killed wild animals only for the greater good! Well, my first question was answered, but *Acharya*'s explanation had given birth to another question. And now that my courage had returned, I felt bold enough to pose the question that was lingering in my mind. Indeed, why suppress curiosity? So, I posed the next question to *Acharya*, "Then why is this quality not present in humans? They make enemies for no reason."

Hearing my question, *Acharya* smiled and said, "This is because, instead of focusing on his inner self and spiritual growth, man has placed more emphasis on developing his intellect. As a result, he has gradually become accustomed to relying solely on his brain to navigate life. He began searching for causes and reasons behind every task and phenomenon, and that is why, he became involved in trying to measure the infinite with his limited capability. Consequently, he has become disconnected from Nature's supreme energy and has become unnatural. And this is precisely the reason why the man living in today's age has become so despondent and unsuccessful. Actually, in the present times, man has made phenomenal intellectual progress, but at the psychological level, he has actually become worse than animals in many respects. This is proven by the fact that animals can sense the approaching seasons and impending dangers in advance, whereas man remains clueless about the dangers lurking around him even when his own life is at stake! The unfortunate outcome of this is, today, he resorts to violence not just to protect his selfish interests, but even when his ego is hurt due to some reason."

Oh, how simply and beautifully *Acharya* had explained all this! But now, my curiosity was piqued further, giving birth to a unique query. Besides, I reckoned, if the person providing the answers is not tired of answering my questions, why should I hesitate in posing questions? Thus, I asked, "So, don't religious scriptures and codes of ethics help man in this regard?"

Hearing this, *Acharya* laughed and said, "All religious scriptures are filled with theoretical complexities! At best, they can guide the ignorant to some extent, but in reality, a man's soul and consciousness are his true guides. In other words, without awakening them, there is no salvation."

Well, my curiosity was stoked even further on hearing this response and I couldn't stop myself now. After all, if the well does not shy away from quenching one's thirst, why should the thirsty hesitate in asking for water? Thinking thus, I stood up once again and shot off another question. I said, "*Acharya*, why is it that man continues to indulge in misdeeds when the soul is present in his body? Why does he remain sorrowful? Does the soul not help him in addressing such matters?"

Acharya said, "Since man has given more prominence to his mind, intelligence and ego; the soul, despite being present in the body, is always relegated to being in a dormant state. And because one's consciousness is clouded by selfishness and ego, very few, say, one in a hundred thousand, gain enlightenment."

I then asked, "So, how does one know if one's consciousness is in an awakened state?" Naturally, I wanted to get an idea of my own state of consciousness.

Acharya laughed again and said, "Having no interest in religious texts, moral codes and traditions is a definite sign of an awakened consciousness."

Well, this sounded like good news! For, I had never studied religious texts, so there was no question of being interested or uninterested in them. And neither did I believe in moral codes and ethics to begin with. As for traditions, I was a rebel who habitually disregarded them. Considering all this, I was convinced that my consciousness was indeed in an awakened state. And that was certainly a powerful reassurance for my future. But now, my curiosity regarding this subject had been ignited completely, and in this excited state, I could not stop myself from asking another question, "How can a man awaken his soul?"

Acharya smiled and replied, "If a man's nature is one of concentration and he performs every task and duty, big or small, with focus, gradually increasing his concentration, he will eventually find that it has reached such a level that he has forgotten not only his body, mind, intelligence and ego but his very existence too. It is at that very instant that his soul is awakened. However, this moment of enlightenment is rarely attained. Only one in a million attains this state of being. And that moment of enlightenment is important not just for that person or humankind at large, but for the entire universe as well. For, the moment he forgets his existence, he merges and becomes one with Nature."

You will not believe it, but today I was enjoying myself so much that my growing curiosity compelled me to ask one final question. I said, "So, do *gurukuls* not assist one in attaining this state?"

Acharya replied, "*Gurukuls* will, of course, guide you in this matter. However, it depends on both the *guru*'s love and the student's grasping ability." As he finished saying this, his face clouded over unexpectedly. Becoming a little irked, he continued, "But forget it! These days, the standards of both *gurus* and *gurukuls* are degrading. Take Hastinapur, for example, where *Acharya* Drona runs a *gurukul* that trains students in archery. A tribal boy, with no direct help from Drona, managed to imbibe his teachings and became an exceptional archer, simply by devoutly installing Drona's statue. This accomplishment was remarkable indeed, but it ended up pricking the ego of the fiend, Drona, who believed that if people could master archery merely by placing statues and without the guidance of a *guru*, what would become of the *Acharyas*? In fact, he was greatly distressed by this foolish thought. As for that boy, he had learnt archery due to his incredible grasping ability; certainly, Drona had made no tangible contribution towards it. But how was that innocent boy supposed to know this? Abiding by the prevalent custom, he offered to pay Drona his *gurudakshina.*[12] However, the depraved Drona, filled with conceit and ego, exploited this opportunity and demanded the boy's right thumb as his fee! The poor tribal boy! Having chopped off his thumb, how will he ever be able to hold the bow and shoot his arrows? And the most horrifying aspect of this sordid episode is that Drona accepted this appalling *gurudakshina* for a teaching he had never even imparted! This makes one wonder, if even *Acharya*s stoop to the level of beasts, then what is the use of *gurus* and *gurukuls*?" Saying this, *Acharya* Sandipani's brows creased in a deep frown, his entire countenance turning sombre. Then, he suddenly rose to his feet and walked off to his chamber without speaking any further. As for us, realising that today's session had concluded, we too returned to our respective chambers.

Lying on my bed, I cogitated on *Acharya's* words. Truly, I felt blessed after coming to this *ashram* and associating with a great personality like *Acharya* Sandipani. With each passing day, my personality was blossoming and growing by leaps and bounds. Even my contemplation had now surpassed the calculations of the mind, and had started focusing on the mysteries of this world. In short, my inner self was developing so rapidly that my consciousness had begun to soar to newer heights every day. Meanwhile, everything was peaceful in the *ashram* too. The confrontations of the earlier days were now a thing of the past. All of us co-existed in peace and harmony; even Vinda and Anuvinda had discarded their snobbish behaviour and become friends with us, while Sudama, Shwetketu and the others were already our close companions. As for me, I had always enjoyed the company of friends from the very beginning. Thus, on one hand, while my personality was evolving after coming to the *ashram*, on the other, my mischievous nature had resurfaced on finding a close set of friends. We would now enjoy ourselves in our chamber as well, playing all kinds of games and causing mischief. Meanwhile, bhaiya's cowherd-like nature had all but disappeared due to his blossoming friendship with the princes. And speaking of myself, I was so happy that my entire life now revolved only around the *ashram*.

One night, all five of us were asleep in our chamber. I had also gone to sleep on time, but woke up around midnight. And once awake, there was no question of my going back to sleep immediately. So, my mind began to ponder over our playful antics and mischief at the *ashram*. Needless to say, we had indulged in great fun and frolic on this night as well. But coming back

12. *Gurudakshina* - An offering made to a guru (teacher) to acknowledge, respect and thank him after a period of study.

to my contemplation, I realised that being accorded an opportunity to study under *Acharya* had proven to be the most progressive step in my life. With this thought, my contemplation took off in a different direction. Now, on the face of it, my arrival at the *ashram* seemed like just another incident, but if one were to actually reflect on it, one would realise that it had taken several years for it to culminate into this. Upon further reflection, one would see that several smaller incidents had led to my arrival at *Acharya*'s *ashram*. For instance, had Kansa not tried to kill me as soon as I was born, I would have never reached Gokula and subsequently Vrindavan. Had we not encountered threats from wild animals and demons in Vrindavan, I would have never had the opportunity to become so strong and capable. Similarly, had Kansa not devised the ploy to kill me in Mathura, I wouldn't have come across the opportunity to go to Mathura. And had Kansa not unleashed his fury on the innocent *gopas* and father on that fateful day at the festival, I certainly wouldn't have killed him. Perhaps, I would have returned to Vrindavan without incident. Most importantly, had my aunts not become so enraged and agitated, I wouldn't have had to fear Jarasandha at all. And had Jarasandha not dangled the sword of death over my head, grandfather would have never sent me to *Acharya* Sandipani's *ashram*. Meaning, I would have never been able to set foot in this *ashram*. All in all, the gist of my deliberation was that every event that transpires in our lives is actually a culmination of a number of smaller events that have occurred previously. This also means that the current highs and lows in one's life are merely harbingers of a major event that will occur in one's future. While this remains the irreversible truth, on analysing all the preceding events, the most startling fact that emerged was that my enemies had a big hand in moulding my future. Delving deeper, it dawned on me that it was the culmination of all these events that had led me to the *ashram* to receive my education under the tutelage of *Acharya* Sandipani. This also implied that my enemies had played a major role in whatever good I had achieved in life! And if one's enemies were benefactors in an indirect sense, then who can actually be called an enemy in this world? This being the case, whom should one consider an enemy? Perhaps, no one. Consider my own example: all my biggest foes had ultimately proven to be my greatest benefactors. They were, in fact, the ones who had become the guiding light in my life. The moment this thought struck me, my entire being was suffused with gratitude towards these so-called enemies of mine, so much so that I began to thank not just the troubles that had come my way in Vrindavan, Kansa or my aunts, but even Jarasandha, whom I truly thanked from the bottom of my heart. For, I had reached this stage today entirely due to their intervention.

Although I had arrived at this conclusion after an in-depth analysis of the various occurrences in my life, it seemed as if my contemplation was not satiated yet, and was in fact eager to delve deeper. After tossing and turning some more, yet another thought struck me, as I wondered, 'Does this also mean that whatever is transpiring in a person's life is only leading him towards a specific destination?' And I had a valid reason for thinking so. Indeed, it was the confluence of all the events that had occurred in my life so far that had led me to *Acharya* Sandipani's *ashram*. With one successful analysis after another, my mind began to glide unfettered, and finding the opportunity, it soared on new flights of deliberation. Now, my contemplation had nothing to lose by doing so, but it was my sleep that had to pay the price. Oh well, what choice did I have at present other than to comply with my thoughts? So, given the free rein, my contemplation sought to dig deeper into the mysteries of Nature. But considering my current level of intelligence, this was not an easy task. Still, I was confident that sooner or later, my analytical mind would get to the bottom of all the mysteries of the universe. And indeed, this confidence stemmed from trusting my grasping ability and my determination to learn.

Speaking of learning, my desire for it was so strong that during our trip from Mathura to Ujjaini, I had learnt how to pack and prepare for a long journey. I had carefully observed the smallest of details that needed to be taken care of, tucking away the information for future use. And the result was that I had automatically learnt about all the articles and supplies that needed to be taken on a long journey, how to keep a chariot well-maintained, how to repair its wheels, and so on. Additionally, it had not taken me long to understand that a night halt is the most important aspect of a long journey. In fact, in that single journey, I had realised that it is always best to take a night halt in the vicinity of a settlement, preferably in a temple compound, rest house or inn. Speaking of night halts, I recalled how, while crossing the desolate forests of Chambal, we could not find a suitable place for a night halt. I vividly remember that we had to spend an entire night on a rocky outcrop, with a few of us standing guard all night long to protect our caravan from attacks by wild animals. This meant that in addition to being alert and brave, one also has to be prepared for an all-night vigil when undertaking a long journey. Moreover, one must ensure that the horses are regularly provided with sufficient water to drink. Feeding them on time and giving them adequate rest in the afternoon may seem like small details, but they are actually crucial to the journey. You must be wondering why I am telling you all this. Well, the reason is simple...I had learnt all this on my own; neither had anyone taught me these things nor had anyone emphasised their importance. I had imbibed all this on my own simply because I was fond of learning.

Oh! I was truly one of a kind. Thinking of long journeys, I suddenly felt an urge to embark on one…but unlike the previous one, I wanted to embark on a trip with only my friends for company, much like a lark soaring on the wings of freedom. Indeed, you would recall that during our most recent journey to the *ashram*, we had to adhere to strict discipline since *Acharya* was travelling with us. And this discipline had certainly drained the fun out of that journey. While we wished to bathe in a scenic lake, *Acharya* would instruct us to gather fruit, and when we wanted to lie down and relax, he would order us to get up and exercise. Naturally, all these strictures gave birth to the idea of embarking on a long journey without the encumbrances of a disciplinarian. Truly, how wonderful it would be to set off on a long journey in the boisterous company of friends! Every stream, mountain, settlement, village, town, and the myriad flora and fauna along the way would bring us endless joy. Oh, how wonderful it would be to indulge ourselves uninhibitedly, to stop at our will to eat and drink, and enjoy to our heart's content. We would quarrel and argue, romp and play, swim and bathe in the rivers and lakes, and enjoy a thrilling and memorable journey!

Oh! My thoughts were definitely running wild today. My contemplation had begun with an attempt to understand the mysteries of the universe, but here I was, thinking of a long, enjoyable journey with my friends. For that matter, whether in life or contemplation, the highs and lows we experience do carry their own charm. Speaking of highs and lows, we were faced with a sudden upheaval in our smooth-sailing life at the *ashram*. It had only been a few days since this night of contemplation, when I unexpectedly fell victim to a few more sleepless nights. The incident which precipitated this state of mine occurred when Rukmi, of all people, arrived at the *ashram* one fine day. He had come to meet Vinda and Anuvinda, who were perhaps his friends. However, his arrival flooded my mind with sweet memories of Rukmini, and naturally, I lost my mental peace. It was possible that he failed to recognise me, dressed as I was in my *ashram* garb; but just to observe caution, I thought it prudent to stay out of sight. In fact, I did not step out of my chamber till he left the premises of the *ashram*. Fortunately, he did not stay for long. Taking *Acharya's* permission, he soon departed with Vinda and Anuvinda, perhaps to attend a function at the royal palace. Now, although he had left the *ashram*, his presence had once again reminded me of a menace called Jarasandha which continued to rear its head in my life. Seeing the friendship between Rukmi, Vinda and Anuvinda, I also realised that Aryavarta had many kings who were friends and allies of Jarasandha. This meant that it would be well-nigh impossible to steer clear of Jarasandha for long. The only thing that could save me from his wrath—standing like an armour and shielding me until this day—was my determination to stay alive. Without it, left to my own devices, this story of my life would have ended long ago.

To cut a long story short, let me confess, just one sight of Rukmi had shaken me to the core of my being. I, who had made the *ashram* my home and was enjoying myself thoroughly, living completely in the present, found this sweetness in my life soured by Rukmi's, meaning, my would-be brother-in-law's arrival. My mind had once again begun to vacillate between the memories of the past and the anxieties of the future. The first transgression Rukmi had committed was to refresh the memories of my dear Rukmini; secondly, he had inadvertently reminded me of the menace named Jarasandha. At the same time, Rukmi's friendship with the Ujjaini princes, Vinda and Anuvinda, had proved that even Ujjaini was well within the sphere of Jarasandha's influence. This meant that sooner or later, Jarasandha would learn of our presence at the *ashram,* and the moment we crossed the threshold of the *ashram*, he would swoop down on us like a hawk waiting to pounce on its prey. Did you see how the mere arrival of Rukmi had entangled my mind in such futile thoughts! Well, this was only natural, for, setting eyes on a worthless person only brings worthless thoughts to the mind. I was spending my days so peacefully in the *ashram,* but my future brother-in-law's arrival had revived unpleasant memories of the demon Jarasandha, while also triggering a bittersweet pain in my heart by invoking memories of the love of my life, Rukmini. Of course, the reality at present was vastly different. Neither could Rukmini set foot in the *ashram* at this point in time, nor could the menace named Jarasandha dare to even peek into this safe haven. Prudence, therefore, suggested that it would be best to free myself from these worthless contemplations as soon as possible.

Well, I did manage to break free of them. But how would that have helped? Nature seemed intent on devising new methods to torment me. It had become Nature's habit to ensure that I was steeped in a constant state of restlessness, if not through the ever-present shadow of death than the no less deadly sword of love! It so happened that the next day, an incident occurred which, for the first time since I had arrived here, compelled me to think about the world that existed outside the *ashram*. On this day, it was my turn to go outside the *ashram* and beg for alms. And so, I had set out. I do not know what came over me, but I soon found myself walking along the path that led towards the royal palace. Now, as the *ashram* was situated outside the city, the road leading from the *ashram* was devoid of the hustle and bustle of the city. With lush green trees lining both sides of the road, this was certainly a peaceful and pleasant way to tread on foot. As the long road stretched ahead, not a wayfarer or even a stray animal could be seen. Lost in my own thoughts, humming a fine tune, I was majestically strutting towards the city. This was alright, but I have still not apprised you of one thing; perhaps because it was not that important at the time, but in the context of what I am about to tell you, it assumes great significance. Actually, on the third day after bhaiya and I had arrived at the *ashram*, our shiny, curly locks had suffered a casualty. Yes, our heads had been shaved leaving just a tuft of hair at the back. Moreover, like everyone else, we too had to wear the simple clothes provided by the *ashram*. This was not just a part of the discipline we had to adhere to, but was also the identity of *Acharya* Sandipani's students in Ujjaini. In the beginning, bhaiya and I would find the new pig-tailed look amusing, but over time, we had grown accustomed to it. Besides, how long does it take for hair to grow? Oh, I was about to tell you something else, but look where this discussion has strayed instead! Well, coming back to the point, I was still walking on the desolate road, clad in my *ashram* garb, begging for alms. It had only been a while since I had left the gates of the *ashram,* when suddenly, I heard the sound of a chariot approaching. I turned my head and saw a splendid chariot hurtling down the path, as if tearing through my very being. Although I was lost in my thoughts, my sharp eyes had not missed it; and when I peered inside, I was stunned. The passenger was none other than Rukmini! She appeared so poised, dignified, and oh, so beautiful! Even her attire was as attractive as she was. The queen of my dreams had passed by, her very glimpse tearing through me like a knife, and I had just stood there, too dumbfounded to even react. Oh, what can I say? The chariot had passed by in a flash, but the image of Rukmini did not escape my eyes. I just stood there, immobile like a statue. The thought that she had not stopped saddened me a little too. Dejectedly, I stood on the lonely road when another thought struck me; perhaps, she had not recognised me. Oh, how could she, for, my head was shaved! Indeed, my bald pate was bereft of its identity—the peacock feather—that was always tucked in my curly hair. Moreover, I was wearing the garb of a celibate. Perhaps, all of this had collectively made it difficult for her to recognise me. Argh! The thought made me curse my attire, making me wish that I was dressed like the Krishna I had been not so long ago. I am sure she would have recognised me then and stopped the chariot. Of course, this was nothing but wishful thinking on my part, as my attraction towards Rukmini was a secret shared only between my love-struck heart and me. Neither bhaiya nor Uddhava, and not even Rukmini herself knew anything about it. Indeed, how could I put into words the attraction that I, an ordinary cowherd, felt for a princess? Would everyone not ridicule me and call me a madman?

Well, wearing a forlorn look, I stood in the middle of the road, with all these thoughts working up a storm in my mind, when I noticed that the chariot

had suddenly halted some distance away. In fact, it had not just stopped, but taking a turn, it was heading towards me. I jumped for joy. Perhaps, my Rukmini had recognised me despite the attire I had donned, and if she had, then I could certainly say that she too was attracted to me. The mere thought was enough to make this cowherd go weak in the knees. The spectacle playing out in the middle of the road was strange indeed: I stood dazed, staring at the chariot with hopeful eyes, as it gradually came closer towards me. In fact, in that single instant, I lived a thousand beautiful dreams! The chariot too had come to a halt where I was standing, so it had obviously returned because of me. Noticing this, I nearly lost control as a thrill ran down my spine. As soon as the chariot stopped near me, Rukmini daintily alighted from it, while I just stood there and watched her step down from the chariot and walk towards me. The nearer she approached, the louder my heart thumped, making me fear that it would burst out of my chest any moment now. Oh, but what was this? Without so much as glancing at me, she dropped a bunch of fruits in my begging bowl. Oh no, this single act on her part shattered all the wonderful notions I had held until this moment! My condition had become strange, for, one moment, I was in the throes of happiness, and in the very next instant, all my dreams lay shattered, as I stared at the begging bowl in my hand. In it, I could almost see my sad little heart too, as if it had been wrenched from my body and tossed in with the fruits! However, I immediately shifted my glance from the bowl and looked at the smiling Rukmini. Surprisingly, my very life was standing before me, while I was standing like a lifeless corpse before her. The very person who could make my heart skip a beat with just a thought of her, now stood in front of me, but alas, she had failed to recognise me. If nothing else, this behaviour of hers was a harsh reminder that she was a princess and I, an ordinary cowherd. The voice within seemed to mock me saying, 'Dream all you like, Krishna, but she won't even acknowledge your existence!'

Oh, but this meant that I had lost in love...and what a terrible defeat it was! In fact, it wasn't just a defeat for me; it was a defeat for every love-struck cowherd who longed to soar on the wings of love. No, this just wouldn't do! Besides, you know all too well that defeat was never an option for me, and now, it was a question of all the poor lovers too, who had ever pined for their beloved. Still, what could I do? This was not a battle that could be won by force or deceit. Well, so what? A beloved's heart could be won by employing other methods too, so let me try those. After all, efforts will have to be made to win; I could not let my dreams be shattered in this manner. Thus, I took immediate control of myself, steeled my mind and consoled my heart that perhaps she was angry with me for some reason. 'Why do you worry? Is anger not the first step towards love?' So, I glanced at her with eyes filled with hope and flashed my most famous, disarming smile. But just look at the attitude of this princess! She neither paid heed to it nor offered any acknowledgement. Oh, this was too much! She could have at least shown some consideration for the feelings of a poor lover. She could have at least given some sort of a response, even if it was not a genuine one. But no, her attention was focused elsewhere. While I stood before her with love-filled eyes, her gaze was fixed on her chariot. Oh, I could feel my life forsaking my body in that instant! As for Rukmini, her deed was done after offering alms. 'But oh, my love! It is not these fruits that I crave; it is your heart that I want!' For a moment, I felt irked by the thought that this princess, intoxicated by the power of wealth, had made a fool of this poor lover. But as these thoughts raced through my mind, she had already turned around and started walking towards her chariot, while I stood there, gazing fixedly at her, watching my life walk away. Then suddenly, she turned around and hope flickered within me once again. Any moment now, I expected her to say, "Ha! I was just pulling your leg!" But unfortunately, nothing of that sort happened. Oh, the air these princesses put on! She had paid no attention to my charming smile; instead, in her own way, she had put me in my place—that of a poor cowherd boy. Well, folding both her hands, she spoke with great humility, "Forgive me, our carriage was moving swiftly and we couldn't stop sooner. We know it is improper to pass by a celibate without giving him something."

Hearing this, my consciousness reawakened, and with it all the hopes I had pinned on Rukmini! Mentally slapping my hand on my forehead, I realised only now that she had not recognised me. Argh! I was annoyed at myself, for, I had unnecessarily heaped all kinds of allegations upon her. Well, perhaps, this is what happens in love. The fault may be yours, but it is the other person who is invariably blamed for it. Just then, another thought struck me. Agreed, she mistook me because of my attire, which was perfectly fine... but what about my smile? Had she forgotten that as well? Clearly, this was no longer a question of just ignoring me but a matter that pertained to my very identity and existence. And I certainly did not like a question mark to be put on my existence! So, I thought, why not flash my trademark smile again? Perhaps, it might ring a bell. In fact, adding a dash of wit wouldn't hurt either. This time, she'd definitely recall this poor lover! Besides, my self-confidence and enthusiasm had returned on realising that she was not deliberately ignoring me; she simply hadn't recognised me. So, with a majestic air, I took two steps towards her and said with a smile, "Everybody gives alms to a celibate and unsolicited advice to others! In that case, how should I express my gratitude to you?"

Perhaps, she liked the way I spoke…or maybe she did not expect such wit from a celibate; whatever the reason may be, for the first time, she looked intently at me, paying close attention to my smile. That's not all! She even proceeded to examine me from head to toe, as if trying to jog her memory. My hopes were soaring now, while a thousand wishes stemmed forth from my heart. Luckily, as she continued to peer at me with marked concentration, her gaze fell on my flute. A flicker of recognition spread across her face and she literally jumped in surprise. However, the look of surprise on her face reflected more of innocence and less of love. Whatever it was, as far as I was concerned, she had recognised me and even this little bit sufficed to make my heart sing with joy. Indeed, I could feel my life-force return, and with it, my consciousness too. This poor lover's fate had changed dramatically, and on this note, I quickly resumed my natural self. As for Rukmini, as soon as the realisation dawned on her, she spoke in a chirpy voice that rang with sweet familiarity, "Oh, it is you! Krishna! You look so different; your appearance has changed completely!"

This time, I too smiled and replied jauntily, "It is not just my attire; my life too has changed completely!"

She said, "But your nature has not changed at all. It is, after all, the nature of a person that keeps his past connected to his future."

I said, "For that matter, my flute has not changed either, as it always helps me revive the golden memories nestled deep in my heart." Then, taking a deep breath, I added, "It also helps my friends recognise me."

Hearing this, Rukmini smiled and walked back to her chariot. Oh, what was this? Why was she walking away? I mentally pleaded with her, "Don't go! Let us talk for a while longer. This is so much fun." Then, another thought flashed in my mind, 'But what sort of a princess would she be if she obeyed you?!' Meanwhile, throughout this exchange of ours, her charioteer was staring at us, perhaps trying to fathom how the princess of Kundinpur was familiar with a mendicant from Ujjaini. I thought, 'Do not even try to understand, my dear fellow. This is the magic of Krishna!' Oh, but let us ignore him and instead focus on the magic that Rukmini was conjuring up. She had now stepped into her chariot, while I stood on the road beside it, my gaze unwilling to leave her face even for a moment. I was sad to see her go, but all of a sudden, I saw her beckon me over. My face lit up with joy and I dashed towards her chariot, as if she had invited me to accompany her to Kundinpur. Oh, but what do I say about Rukmini's charm! I had just started to smile at her, leaning against her chariot, when she spoke in a sombre tone, "I wonder what this man—the valorous hero who had slain Kansa, and the saint who refused a kingdom—has come to learn at the *ashram*? Courage and renunciation are the only two things worth learning in human life. And you have already demonstrated that you have learnt them well."

Speaking thus, her voice trailed off in the air, as the chariot kicked off a cloud of dust and sped off. And on this fateful note, our beautiful encounter came to an end as far as she was concerned; but for me, it lingered on. Yes, I was still standing right there in the middle of the road, looking at the disappearing chariot and the dust rising from it. Finally, when the chariot disappeared from sight and the dust had settled too, I returned to my senses. And as soon as I came to my senses, I reflected on the words she had spoken. Once again, the depth of her words struck me, revealing the profundity of her thoughts. Truly, in the form of my beloved, I had found a teacher who would invariably teach me a valuable lesson every time I met her.

Well, Rukmini had departed, but not without suffusing my being with her vivacious presence. Indeed, I could feel her presence in every pore of my body—it was not just my heart and mind but even my bones, flesh, marrow and blood that were calling out her name. Once again, Rukmini had left me speechless, her eyes and words working their magic, and once again, I was left staring after her. Indeed, I was so intoxicated by her charm that I found it difficult to shake it off. But the question was, did I even want to? Truly, what would be left of my life if I didn't let this intoxication permeate me? Oh, what an enchanting moment it was! Could she not have stayed a while longer? But how could she have stayed? Why would she have stayed? It was I who was wounded by the excruciating pain of love, not she. That was why she had laughed in amusement and disappeared from sight. At any rate, it is futile to expect heartbreakers to show mercy. Besides, when she herself had laughed it off, what was the need for me to stand here like a statue cloaked in gloom? When the one who had made me lovesick did not wish to cure me, it was best that I find the cure myself. Rukmini was long gone, but the fruits she had given me as alms lay innocuously in my bowl. Oddly, I felt a great affection for them. Although they had been given to me as alms and thus belonged to the whole *ashram*, I still couldn't bring myself to share them with anyone. How could I? They were fruits given to Krishna for being Krishna. Indeed, Krishna alone had a right to them. Thus, setting propriety aside, I partook of all the fruits, savouring them with love right then and there. To a lover like me, could anything taste sweeter and more ambrosial than these fruits?

But then I thought, 'What next…? Am I supposed to keep standing here till the cows come home?' Well, no, but the great Krishna could no longer proceed with begging for alms either. So, with slow steps, I started making my way back to the *ashram*. As I neared the gate, thoughts of Rukmini automatically receded from my mind. And as soon as I set my eyes on *Acharya*, every intoxicating thought of Rukmini vanished completely. I was back to being a dutiful student who had taken refuge at *Acharya's* feet. Truly, this was a unique gift I possessed. In Rukmini's presence, my entire being was absorbed in her. Had I been cut into a million small pieces, each and every one of them would have called out her name...and her name alone! But now, in the *ashram*, my whole being was devoted to *Acharya*. Rukmini had vanished, and no matter how hard you searched, you would not find her within me. It was simple, really: Rukmini was the truth of that moment, and *Acharya* is the truth of this moment. This was nothing but my habit of living in entirety, due to which whatever my mind focused on, it did so completely, and whatever I let go of was discarded totally from my being. To tell you the truth, this was one of my most prized qualities, and to have cultivated this quality was in itself an admirable achievement. Unfortunately, I had also gained a bad reputation because of this very trait. This ability to live completely in the present moment was a character trait that should be greatly respected, but due to people's misunderstanding, it managed to earn me monikers such as trickster, fraud, liar, bewitcher and cheat. Understand well that when Radha was in my life, there was only Radha; similarly, when I was with Kubja, I was wholly present with her. Just as I was with Rukmini a few moments ago, I am now in *Acharya's* presence. But most importantly, wherever I was, I was fully present, in my entirety. But I wonder why this completeness of mine had become a problem for everyone. Ah, but then, it is not very difficult to fathom the reason behind it. For, whenever I was with someone, I was present with them with all my being, wholeheartedly and with complete sincerity. And naturally, it is difficult for a human being to forget the moments he has spent with someone in entirety. Really, tell me, in this world filled with deceit and lies, who is ever present with anyone completely? And if someone has stayed with you completely for even a second, would you not hold that moment to be the most beautiful moment of your life? This was the reason why everyone wanted to possess me fully for themselves. But little did they know that my life was akin to a flowing stream, and this being the case, how could anyone hold me down? If one could be tied down, can he really be complete? So, in this game of 'catch', everyone started parting from me one after the other. And naturally, whoever parted from me would curse me. They would not admit that they could not live without me or that they harboured sweet memories of me which were now pricking them like thorns due to my absence! Hence, the only recourse they were left with was to find faults with me and curse me.

But let us not dwell on this anymore. Instead, let me describe to you the wonderful days I was spending at the *ashram*. Whether it was *Acharya*'s lessons, the art of combat, the company of friends, or the discipline at the *ashram*, I was enjoying it all. Then, all of a sudden, something happened that, though completely unexpected, turned out to be the most significant event of my life. One afternoon, after lunch, all of us students were gathered beneath a cluster of trees behind the *ashram*, chatting casually, when *Acharya-ma* called for Sudama. On impulse, I followed him. Actually, we had run out of firewood, so as soon as we reached *Acharya-ma,* she said to Sudama, "We have no firewood today."

Before I could react, Sudama promptly looked for an axe and a bunch of rope and prepared to go to the forest to collect firewood.

Seeing this, the concerned *Acharya-ma* called out, "Please take someone with you!"

Sudama answered, "Krishna…he is already here with me."

When I heard this, I too grabbed an axe and some rope. As we were about to leave, *Acharya-ma* beckoned Sudama over. She then quietly led him inside the kitchen, and when he stepped out a few minutes later, I saw from a distance that he was carrying a small bundle, which he was trying to tuck into his waistband. I couldn't understand what the matter was, so as soon as Sudama came within earshot, I asked him, "What did *Acharya-ma* give you, my friend?"

He said, "Oh nothing! She just called to warn me to be cautious in the forest."

"Be cautious of what?" I asked in surprise.

He said, "Uh, she just said we shouldn't mess with wild animals."

I realised then that Sudama was lying. I could clearly see that he was hiding something from me. However, I thought it best to not pursue the matter further, noticing his reluctance. We thus set off quietly, the pair of us making for a peculiar sight, with ropes hanging from our shoulders and axes in our hands. We took the path that snaked into the forest, which wasn't very far. Soon, we entered the forest, but even after walking for a while, we had not come across any dead tree that could be chopped for firewood. It was the monsoon season and the forest, having soaked up all the rainwater, seemed content, joyfully swaying and proudly showing off its lush greenery. The weather was indeed pleasant, but the rains were making it problematic for us to find dry firewood. Walking on soft earth, our feet sinking in the mud, we had walked a long distance without finding even a single dead tree. Frustrated by our failure, Sudama scowled, "Green trees can also be chopped, and their wood can be dried. So, why has *Acharya-ma* instructed us to gather wood only from a dead tree?" I, however, deemed it best to not reply, hence he himself answered his query, "Perhaps, deadwood is easier to burn." I still

remained silent. Honestly, I was so lost in the lovely weather that I did not feel like conversing about anything else. We thus kept walking in this manner, crossing one mountain after another, but still could not find a single dead tree! Soon, it was evening and the sky started to darken. Although tired to the bone, we still had to abide by the rules of the *ashram*. If we had been sent to fetch dry firewood, then that was all we could bring with us. And there was no question of us returning without the firewood. But now, with dusk approaching, we were compelled to stop our search for firewood. We had no choice but to wait till the next morning. I did not mind waiting, but Sudama was quite irritated by the situation we found ourselves in. Well, to each his own!

To settle for the night, we took shelter near a waterfall. Flowing from behind a large boulder, this waterfall was picturesque, with three huge trees standing guard around it. It was an enchanting sight indeed, as the water gushed from a considerable height. Just behind the waterfall, one could see a range of mountains spreading far and wide, and right in front of it lay the forest in all its natural glory. Honestly, I was entranced by the waterfall's beauty the moment I laid my eyes on it. Sudama, who was exhausted, sat down immediately, but I, an ardent lover of Nature's beauty, stood on a tall rock and craned my neck to feast my eyes on the scenic beauty all around. Once satisfied, I drank some of the cool, crystalline water and quenched my thirst. But what do we do next? The atmosphere was not conducive to idle conversation due to the deafening roar of the waterfall. Besides, we were exhausted from the long trek we had undertaken, so we quietly lay down on a large rock next to the waterfall. Incredibly, Sudama fell asleep as soon as he lay down, but I could not. It was probably because I was hungry; I hadn't eaten anything since afternoon, and this was my first experience of being completely famished. Sudama was perhaps accustomed to it. Although I tried my best to fall asleep, my efforts were in vain.

Then suddenly, flashes of lightning tore through the inky sky. Sudama woke up with a start. And even as we watched, strong winds began to lash the forest, and with them came torrential rain. In fact, the rain quickly started pouring down in sheets. Desperately, I looked around for shelter, but there was no cave in sight that would protect us from the rain lashing down on us. It was then that I caught sight of a huge rock, with enough room underneath for three people to stand comfortably. I nudged Sudama and urged him to make a dash for it. At the very least, we would not get soaked. Within seconds, both of us ran towards the rock and seated ourselves underneath it. Thankfully, we were saved from getting soaked, but the rain showed no signs of abating. The relentless sound of the rain accompanied by the crash of thunder reverberated all around us. It was so dark now that one could not even see one's hands.

It was only the intermittent flashes of lightning that helped us get a fleeting glimpse of our surroundings. To our misfortune, the downpour only worsened, manifesting into a full-fledged storm. It seemed as if the sky would burst any moment now, as strong winds lashed through the mountainside. Lightning flashed, while tiny waterfalls sprang up across the hills, their gentle trickle gradually swelling into sizeable streams. By now, Sudama was a quivering picture of fright. Trying to speak over the din, he could only manage to let out a whimper, "What will happen now, Kanhaiya? Oh God! When will this rain stop?"

I smiled with amusement and said, "Do not worry, Sudama. The stormier the night, the sunnier the morning will be!"

Oh, do not think that I was preaching useless philosophy. The words were culled from my own experience in life. Until now, my life had been eclipsed by darkness in the form of Jarasandha, but today, a bright morning had dawned in the form of *Acharya* Sandipani. Thus, with full confidence, I continued to reassure Sudama saying, "If the rain expends all its fury tonight, it will have no energy left to continue the next day. Therefore, there is no need to worry unnecessarily."

"But what will happen tonight?" asked Sudama in a trembling voice.

"This night shall pass too, just like all the others in our lives," I continued. "Don't worry, there's no reason to be frightened. Tell me this, my friend: what is the difference between fear and death itself?" But alas, all my assurances fell on deaf ears as Sudama's fear remained resolute. In the flash of lightning, I could see that he had actually become pale with anxiety. I made one more effort to change his mood saying, "What is the use of sitting quietly like this?"

"What do you want me to do then? Cry?" he asked irritably.

"No, sing," I replied. "This rain is breathtakingly beautiful. Would it not be wonderful if you sang and I played the flute?"

"You really are a strange fellow," retorted Sudama, "You want me to sit in the lap of death and sing? Have you gone insane?"

I said, "Had we been at the *ashram* right now, with a storm raging outside, what would we be doing? Certainly, you would be singing and I would be playing the flute. Come now, we have always done this when it rains…and this is verily the art of living."

Indeed, it is sheer foolishness to ruin your future by worrying about the present, and ruin your present by worrying about the future. In any case, I had a strong dislike for fear, worry and sorrow. I was a seeker of joy and merriment. So, why ruin such a priceless night of my small but precious life by worrying unnecessarily? But this was my thinking and understanding;

Sudama was still overcome with fear. However, I was not one to quit easily. Once again, I tried to allay his fear and bring him back to normalcy. I said, "We may not be at the *ashram* at present, but here we are...in the forest. And the rain is beautiful and the weather so lovely! So, why not sing and play? If circumstances can force a human being to change his nature, what kind of a human being is he?"

However, after uttering these words, I too plunged into self-reflection. Ever since I had become associated with *Acharya*, I had begun speaking many enlightening truths, as if I were a sage myself. Nonetheless, when I sensed that my wisdom was not producing the desired effect, I quickly resorted to discussing practical needs. Changing the subject, I said, "I am famished! If you have something to eat with you, bring it out."

Shocked a little, Sudama replied a bit embarrassingly, "What do you mean? Where could I have gotten anything from?"

Astonished at his response, I asked him, "When we were leaving, did *Acharya-ma* not give you something to eat?"

"No, she did not!" Sudama lied blatantly.

But his lie could not remain hidden for long. Soon, I sensed that he was nibbling on some food which he had kept hidden in his waistband. Unable to restrain myself, I asked him, "What are you eating, my friend?"

He replied, "Why, nothing at all!"

"Then how come I can hear you chewing?" I asked again.

He said, "Maybe it is the cold. It is making my teeth chatter. Can you not feel the strong lashes of wind?"

I knew at once that the more I questioned him, the more he would spout lies. For, to conceal one lie, it often becomes necessary to continue telling more lies. And who knew this better than me? I would often have butter smeared on my face, yet I would still try to convince Mother Yashoda saying, "I did not eat the butter." And then, I would answer every question she asked with increasingly inventive lies. This is precisely what Sudama was doing at present. In the stark lightning, I had clearly seen him eating roasted gram fished out of a small bundle. But I decided to be patient. In other words, I did not think it appropriate to expose his lies. Well, I had spared Sudama, but frankly speaking, I was surprised at *Acharya-ma's* mindset. She was *Acharya-ma*, meaning, the mother to all the students at the *ashram*. She should have treated all of us equally. If she had given Sudama a handful of gram, she ought to have given some to me as well. Such behaviour certainly did not befit the wife of *Acharya* Sandipani. Besides, Sudama was a dear friend of mine. He seemed so simple-minded. But having said that, I also knew from experience that when the opportunity arises, it is these very simple people who behave strangely. Did you not see how frightened Sudama was? Indeed, what can you expect from such a terrified person? It is rightly said that great deeds can only be performed by the fearless!

After stewing over my anger for a while, I thought, 'Why should I spoil my night with such worthless thoughts?' It would be far wiser to discard all thoughts of *Acharya-ma*, Sudama and the roasted gram from my mind. However, at present, I could not focus much on myself either. While torrential rain lashed all around us, the gnawing pangs of hunger were tormenting me within. The hunger was also making me unusually cold. Well, these circumstances were unavoidable at present. So, I consoled myself with the thought that when a problem has no solution, why dwell on it? I would eat food when food was available; the rain would cease when it was meant to. Dawn too would arrive at its designated hour. When none of these things were in my control, why worry unnecessarily? Why not accept the situation as it were and instead enjoy this beautiful night? Isn't it obvious; withdrawing one's mind from the problem is the best solution! Ironically, here I was, the wise one, struggling with myself, while the fearful Sudama had eaten his fill and peacefully nodded off to sleep. Truly, a stomach that is full makes it easy to drift off to sleep. Well, the spectacle was certainly interesting. Sudama was sleeping in the shelter of the rock, while I sat crouched on my knees, near his head, rubbing my hands together to ward off the cold. It was then that my hand brushed against my flute. Oh! How did I forget my flute—my closest companion in the crests and troughs of my life! The entire world may betray me, but my faithful flute would never abandon me. Now, I no longer cared about my hunger or anything else. I immediately pulled out the flute from my waistband and touched it to my lips.

All thoughts of cold and hunger vanished as I sat down cross-legged, making myself comfortable as if I was sitting on a plush seat. Gradually, I became absorbed in playing my flute, and as my absorption increased, my hunger faded away and I stopped noticing the rain as well. I could only sense the notes of my flute mingling and becoming one with my being. Truly, my flute had never sounded so heart-wrenchingly sweet before, enrapturing me completely in its mellifluous notes.

By now, I had forgotten my hunger and the biting cold, but you will not believe this; as the music gradually pulled me into its deep spell, I became so immersed in it that I was forgetting my physical existence too. It was surprising indeed! Losing myself in the melody of the flute, I found my memories fading away too. One after the other, all my memories including those of Vrindavan, Mother Yashoda, Radha, Govardhana and Yamuna trickled out of my mind, as if riding away on the notes of the flute. I neither remembered Mathura nor

Jarasandha; even the memory of bhaiya had become a distant blur as his face slowly disappeared in the darkness of the night. The only event taking place was my lips playing the flute and with it, my existence slowly melting away. At this point, even my mind, my intelligence and my all-powerful ego were being drawn out in the melody of the flute. I was not sure what exactly had transpired, for, my flute was taking everything away with it. Gradually, it had made me forget even Rukmini and my teacher, *Acharya* Sandipani. Now, neither did I exist nor my own people or anything that belonged to me. Only Nature remained; only consciousness in a vibrant, pristine state remained. And even as I remained immersed in this state, the night melted away in the bright rays of the morning sun, welcoming a new dawn. The first rays of the sun were now caressing my body with their golden warmth. And all of a sudden, my hand slipped away from the flute, and with that, I became aware of my surroundings once again. The moment this awareness returned, I raised my head and looked up at the rising sun. The sunrays in all their resplendence made me go delirious with joy. In an instant, I jumped to my feet and leapt towards the open ground. For a while, I continued to gaze at the sun with both my hands raised above my head. Then I began dancing, almost in a trance, lost in my own world. It was incredible! I was the sun! I was its rays too! This pleasant morning, this lovely forest, the cascading waterfall, all of it was just me...me! The flying birds, these lush, verdant trees, the open sky, the wind, the moon, the earth, the rain, the fire...I was everything! Why just this, I was Sudama and *Acharya-ma* too. Radha and Rukmini were also my forms. Jarasandha and Kansa had emanated from me, and I was *Acharya* as well. Oh yes! I was Time too! The past, the future and the present, everything functioned because of me. Was there anything in this entire universe that was not a part of me?

I was immersed in this wondrous realisation when my attention was suddenly drawn back to the flute in my hand. And just like that, in a snap, I was jolted back to my senses. My mind now felt like becoming one with itself, as I thought, 'Let me just take a peek within and see if everything is alright.' So, I sat beneath a tree, my back against its trunk and my legs stretched out in front of me. And as soon as I was seated, I remembered that along with all of these, I was also Krishna, a cowherd of Vrindavan, trapped in this human body. Oh yes! This body too is mine! But if I am the all-pervading Soul, if I am everything, then why did I have a separate body? Why did I have this human birth? Ah, this was incredible. The question was mine and the answer too had to be provided by me. However, the answer was present in the Soul itself—this fleeting, ephemeral human life, despite being an illusion, is real. Although it is a drama, it is nonetheless the reality. This human life has

been created to enjoy its own creation. Not just the body, but even the mind, senses, brain and ego have been made available for this very purpose. Yes! This is verily the truth. I am the master of these five elements. In fact, I am *Parmatma*, the all-pervading Supreme Soul!

Oh, this was absolutely marvellous! *Acharya* had blessed me with such a wonderful education that it had led me towards 'self-realisation'. He had rightly said, 'If a person can lose his entire existence even for a moment, then in that very instant, he can realise his Soul!' Ah, my flute was remarkable, for, it had helped me enter this incredible state of meditation. What does not transpire even after a hundred lifetimes had come about so easily to me in this lifetime! I had neither made any effort, nor taken any actions, and I had certainly not desired the realisation of the Soul. Everything had transpired on its own. Undoubtedly, at present, I was firmly established in my body; however, the ebb and flow of emotions had stopped completely. All that remained was the realisation that I was the Supreme Soul.

I do not know why, but I suddenly resumed playing my flute. As soon as the notes of the flute wafted through the air, my focus began to sharpen. My mind and senses became active once again. I could feel my body in its entirety. Even my brain and ego were now making their presence felt. Gradually, I started recalling everything. Gokula, Vrindavan, Malini, bhaiya, my cowherd friends, Mother Yashoda, the *gopis*, Mathura, my maternal grandfather, Rukmini, *Acharya* Sandipani; they all rushed back to my mind with perfect clarity. And yes, Radha too had arrived to dwell in my consciousness. The feeling that was predominant at this point in time was a sense of gratitude. Then, gradually, that feeling intensified and I was suddenly transported back to my past birth. I thanked Nature for the fact that I had been born such an innocent fool in my previous birth. After all, that was why I had been able to make a resolution at the time of my death to always be victorious. I was also grateful for Kansa's cruelty and Narada's compassion, because of which I had received the opportunity to be born in Devaki's house. I was extremely grateful to Nanda too, for, had he not sacrificed his daughter, I would not have been alive today. And mother...had I not received her love, I would have never been able to reach where I was today. I was also thankful to the cowherd boys and *gopis,* who had been my companions and had played with me in my childhood. I was grateful for Radha's love, which had instilled in me immeasurable self-confidence. I was thankful to bhaiya who had always stood by me like a rock. I had to especially thank Kansa's paranoid and scheming mind, compelled by which he had become desperate to kill me. Had it not been for that fervent desire, he would not have summoned me to Mathura, and perhaps, I would have then spent my whole life as an ordinary cowherd in Vrindavan. I was also grateful to the Yadava leaders of Mathura who had pressured grandfather to banish me from the kingdom; truly, it was because of them that I had gained the wonderful opportunity to associate with *Acharya* Sandipani. And as for *Acharya-ma* and Sudama, I could not thank them enough. Had she not been partial to Sudama and had he not lied to me, my flute wouldn't have played the way it did, making me forget my existence. How could I not thank *Acharya* Shrutiketu, who had taught me to play my flute...and *Acharya* Sandipani! In fact, the feeling of gratitude was too inadequate for all that they had done for me. Today, through my own experience, I became keenly aware that great teachers were truly greater than Nature. Verily, many people had played a part in this fascinating flight of self-realisation I had taken today. Each one of them had been instrumental through the role they had played. But was this enough in itself? Did I not play a part in it too? Indeed, my own intelligence had played the most important role in helping me reach this stage. Thus, from my own experience, I can assert that if a human being develops his qualities and flows along with Nature, then he too can transform himself from an ordinary cowherd into the 'self-realised Krishna'.

Just see the effect of self-realisation! My mischievousness, my dancing the *raasa* with the *gopis*, breaking their butter pots, stealing their clothes, watching them bathe, Radha's love for me, Rukmini's influence on me—everything was now bringing me twice the pleasure. In other words, on one hand, I was experiencing the exhilaration of having attained self-realisation, and on the other, my mind and ego were giving me immense pleasure as well. And both these joys were unique in their own way. You are well aware of my nature; deriving 'joy' had always held utmost importance to me. I could never live a life that was devoid of vibrancy; no, never...a drab and dull life was not to Krishna's liking at all! Hence, unlike other self-realised people, I did not weaken my mind, brain and ego in any way. I did not consider them my enemies but rather the source of my joy. This was why once my mind, brain and ego were back, I immediately resumed my normal self, in other words, the same Kanhaiya who had left the *ashram* the previous day to fetch firewood from the forest. The only difference was, I had now become self-realised. The difference was subtle yet significant. At this point, let me tell you one more thing. I agree that the Bhagavad Gita was the ultimate height of my consciousness and concentration. I also agree that it was aligned with Nature's flowing energy, but even so, my role in it cannot be overlooked. For, its foundation was rooted in my own experiences in life. Through the Bhagavad Gita, I had conveyed to Arjuna all that I had ever learnt, all that I had experienced or contemplated upon, and all that I had repeatedly been saying and doing in life. Along with the consciousness of Nature, my experiences were also encompassed in the Bhagavad Gita in equal measure. I'm sure you'd recall that when I had told Arjuna that "I am the Sun, Earth, water, wind, sky and they are all the same as me," it was verily my first experience after my self-realisation. With great ease, I had been able to tell him to consider me the mind, brain and ego as well, simply because this was the experience of my entire life. Indeed, I had lived my whole life with them; the only difference was, I had full control over all of them.

That is why, truth be told, I attribute my success as much to my own qualities as to Nature and to those who had become instrumental to my achievements. Frankly speaking, and at the risk of sounding conceited, I would say that my qualities were even more instrumental to my self-realisation than the other factors mentioned here. I am not one of those who in my humility to acknowledge the favours done by others, forget the contribution that I myself have made towards my own success. But unfortunately, because of this very reason, many people started considering me as supremely egoistic, whereas in reality, I was devoid of ego. Well, they were free to think so. As I have said before, the extent to which I had surrendered myself to my Soul was the same extent to which I had surrendered myself to the ego. At any rate, the Soul is imperceptible; it is the ego that is meant to be visible. So, to negate its importance is akin to killing life itself. No, never! Krishna is that peak of exuberance which is all-encompassing. Hence, even after attaining self-realisation, I did not forsake my ego, instead, I became its charioteer, just as, during the Mahabharata war, I had become the charioteer of Arjuna, who can be called a personification of ego. That is why, as far as religiousness is concerned, the wise call me the 'one and only complete *avatar*'[13] in all of mankind's history. And they are not wrong; my awareness is supreme. Ordinarily, self-realisation is such a major milestone in a person's life that it becomes evident whenever one attains it. At the very least, the people around the self-realised person can certainly discern it. But my mind and ego were exactly the same as before, so how would anyone recognise it? This was my very state of awareness which was praiseworthy and which would forever set me apart from the others. Just see for yourself; no one knew at what point I had become self-realised. Most remarkably, no one ever came to know that I had become self-realised. For, unlike other wise men, I did not make any effort to disseminate this knowledge. I did not open an *ashram*, nor did I wear the attire of a mendicant or leave home. On the contrary, after attaining self-realisation, I got married and settled down. Another point worth noting is that I had attained self-realisation effortlessly. I had attained it without studying the scriptures, without performing fire sacrifices, without meditation or even

13. *Avatar* - Incarnation or embodiment.

ritualistic worship. For that matter, enlightenment can never be attained by performing any of these acts. Throughout the enunciation of the Gita, it is this very 'effortless yoga' that I had endeavoured to elucidate. I had explained to Arjuna, "I cannot be attained by studying the *vedas* or by performing penances, sacrifices, meditation or even worship. One attains me naturally."[14] Just let whatever is happening, happen. You will reach where you have to, just like I have.

At present, however, let me discuss the realisation that had dawned on me just now. This entire visible creation is pervaded by one 'Supreme Soul'. The entire universe, the earth, and all the human beings and animals are suffused with that 'Supreme Soul'. And just see, how easily I had realised that very 'Supreme Soul' within myself! The point worth pondering is that when everything is that Supreme Soul, when all the emotions are also that one Soul, then why should one harbour enmity against anyone or hate anyone? This is what I had said to Arjuna in the Gita, "Know, O Arjuna, I am not just everything that you consider good in this world, but I am also all that you consider bad. The Supreme Soul is present in all of them as well. I am the gamble. I am the ego as well. It is I who is war too." Moreover, I had also said, "Consider me to be sex for bearing progeny."[15] Now, I had become 'God'; I was the Supreme One. But I wanted to become the God of all gods. Why just this, I also wanted to enjoy my life a thousand times more. I wanted to enjoy my own creation. In other words, I had to give a fresh beginning to the cycle of *karmas* (deeds) in life. Agreed, having the knowledge of the Soul is the ultimate knowledge. I also accept that the Soul is all-knowing and is the sole witness to the creation and destruction of this world. But even so, as it is tied to a body, one has to live. And if one has to live, then one must live by enjoying oneself, while also taking care of one's actions and duties. So, I decided that I would now live my life with much greater enjoyment than before. I would accept each and every aspect of myself, embracing even the tiniest bit of myself. And let me tell you, this was the very knowledge I had attained; and that is why this Soul is the knower of everything. That is why I had said in the Gita that knowledge of the self is the most supreme knowledge. For that matter, I had also said to Arjuna that this 'supreme knowledge' is hidden within the self. "Just like a womb is covered by a sheath, just like fire is covered by smoke, this knowledge remains concealed because of one's attempts to obtain other unnecessary knowledge."[16] However, Arjuna displayed scant interest in self-realisation. Throughout the Gita, he remained mired in the very scriptures and morality which I had staunchly opposed.

Well, for now, let me discuss my experience of self-realisation... which vastly differed from that of the others because of the existence of the

14. Shrimad Bhagavad Gita, Chapter – 11, Verse – 53-54. **15.** Shrimad Bhagavad Gita, Chapter – 9, Verse – 32-33, Chapter – 10, Verse – 28, 36. **16.** Shrimad Bhagavad Gita, Chapter – 3, Verse – 38.

ego in its complete form. Until now, the knowledge of the self was believed to be the ultimate goal of human life. But how could a *karmaveer* like me content himself with this achievement alone? I wanted to soar higher on a new, incredible and unprecedented flight. In other words, instead of turning life into a dull journey by walking the barren lanes of knowledge, I wanted to make the remaining years of my life even more beautiful by painting them with the vibrant hues of love. However, this was no easy task. I had to ensure that both my 'Soul' and my 'ego' were firmly grounded in my personality. Interestingly, neither had anyone thought of doing something like this before, nor had anyone even imagined it was possible. It has been observed until now that a person's Soul lies in slumber because his ego has become much stronger; and as soon as the ego dissolves into nothingness, 'the Soul becomes apparent'. What I mean to say is that, until this moment, the ego and the Soul had never coexisted within anyone. But I wanted to demonstrate that this wonderful feat was indeed possible. In this respect, I can say that I wanted to challenge the handiwork of Nature itself. In fact, I firmly believed that life, until death intervened, was an endless chain of actions (*karma*). If one has attained self-realisation, then one must think further. At any rate, once the Soul becomes apparent, it will never disappear; and with this thought, the ego too had manifested itself fully. What I mean to say is, for the present, both the Soul and the ego stood side by side, strong and determined. Still, it would be better if this could be proven true. And in any case, truth is always self-evident. So, I stood up and walked back to the rock where Sudama was resting. If I could bewilder him, the truth would be proven beyond doubt. So, restless as I was, I shook him awake as soon as I reached him. This was my moment of truth. If he was able to suspect even slightly that such a great event had transpired in my life, then it would mean that there was some imperfection in my act. If not, then it would prove beyond a doubt that both my forms—my pure Soul and Krishna, a real-life character at play—were established firmly in my personality.

As soon as I nudged Sudama, he woke up with a start. Seeing that the sun had risen, his happiness knew no bounds. It was at this moment that I enacted the first scene of my drama. With great haste, we dunked our faces in the flowing water of the spring, washed ourselves, and set off in search of firewood. Fallen branches lay scattered everywhere, as the fierce storm and rain had wreaked havoc, uprooting many trees during the night. We quickly gathered firewood and made our way back to the *ashram*. I had scored my first victory. Krishna had proven himself to be his former self, just as he had been when he had left the *ashram*. Sudama had not noticed anything different in me. Perhaps, my theatrics since childhood had played a crucial role in this.

This was surely the case, because the event of self-realisation, which typically occurs in the life of perhaps one in a million people, had transpired in my life; and given its nature, such an event immediately becomes known to everyone, whereas I had succeeded in easily concealing even this fact from the world. And surely, this second achievement was far greater than the first. That is why I say, there may have been many other self-realised people, but none like me. It is possible to hide the sun, they say, but it is impossible to hide a self-realised Soul. But just see! What was once considered impossible was made possible by me. Sudama had not suspected the slightest transformation in me! Of course, he shouldn't have noticed, for, if he had, how could I call myself a great actor?

Well, at present, we were proceeding towards the *ashram,* carrying bundles of firewood tied with rope on our heads. Truly, with an axe in one hand and the other supporting the bundle of firewood, we looked quite strange as we walked. Naturally, this made it difficult for us to even converse casually. So, we quietly trudged along with the load on our heads, feasting our eyes on the lush greenery, before finally reaching the *ashram.* As we neared the gate, we saw everyone waiting for us, a look of anxiety etched on their faces. Of course, the torrential downpour the previous night and our failure to return had worried them greatly. When the news of our arrival reached *Acharya* and *Acharya-ma,* they too rushed out. Seeing that no harm had befallen us, everyone heaved a sigh of relief. As for bhaiya, it appeared as though life had returned to his body only now. Even our friends appeared relieved, and the same could be said of *Acharya* and *Acharya-ma* as well. We were promptly freed of our bundles of firewood and escorted inside. On the other hand, seeing that we were exhausted, *Acharya* came straight to the point saying, "You must be famished!"

This was my chance! In a tone laced with sarcasm, I said, "I am really hungry. I do not know about Sudama; that is between him and *Acharya-ma*!"

As soon as Sudama and *Acharya-ma* heard this, both their faces fell. This was my second victory. After all, I was the Soul, whereas the reply had been given by my ego. What I mean to say is, I had now become the 'witness' of not only Nature and all human beings, but also of my own ego. This was truly a remarkable achievement. Now, I wanted to take this game further. Lost in these thoughts, little did I realise that I had reached the open ground along with everyone else. Though I had taken my seat on the ground with the others, I was still lost in my ruminations. Today, *Acharya* too had sat down with us. Well, so be it! At present, my mind wanted to scale greater spiritual heights. In a way, it could be said that I wanted to ensure the presence of my ego. I wanted to fly in a manner that I could use the Soul which I had realised through this life, to discover life itself. Had I desired, after attaining self-realisation, I could have protected myself from the dangerous deeds that life would subject me to. But I wanted to choose the path of *karma*, because in my opinion, to accept life as it comes is the only form of 'non-violence'. In fact, I would like to advise all those who will attain self-realisation in the future that they too should accept everything that life has to offer naturally. It is true that after realising the self, there is nothing in this world that is worth obtaining and that cannot be obtained. This is because you are in everything and you have already attained yourself. This is what I had explained to Arjuna in the Gita, "There is no object worth attaining which I have not attained. Still, my specialty is that I am engaged in *karma*. For, if I ever fail to engage in *karma* because of being cautious, then the whole of mankind would accept passivity as their *dharma*[17] and I would become the cause of confusion.[18] We all know that everyone follows in the footsteps of great men. Whatever standards they set, that becomes the standard."[19] For this reason, it is essential for the self-realised too, to be careful about their *karma*. The crux of what I want to say is simple yet profound. If all the common people were to follow the path of the self-realised, there would be no kings and no warriors. There would be no love and no children either. Because of this, the world will first turn into a dreary place devoid of joy, and ultimately, all of humankind will perish. In other words, due to this, not only will the hard work of billions of years be rendered futile, but the journey of man through millions of births—from the microscopic germ to the human form—will also come to a grinding halt. And this being the case, what purpose will this universe serve? For, it is only the human being in whom the Soul can manifest itself fully. So, tell me, if human beings cease to exist, won't this vast universe become irrelevant? Won't the Soul have to unnecessarily wait for billions of years again to manifest in its entirety? It will take eons to be born in the form of tiny micro-organisms and then complete the journey of evolution till they assume the form of a human being. And it will take ages to be able to enjoy this vast universe again! No. Why should I wait? Why should I lose that which is easily available in this present moment? Remember, the advice of non-violence and celibacy given by ignorant people can prove to be the greatest act of violence. For, it can ultimately cause the extinction of the human race itself. Whereas, I want to preserve both humans and humanity so that they can enjoy this creation called the universe. This is why I had been able to advise Arjuna so easily in the Gita, "It is me that you should consider 'sex' for bearing progeny."[20] And you are well aware that I have never uttered empty words. You are also aware that I have never objected to violence or sex. That was why I was able to say to Arjuna, "No one can kill or be killed. Life is eternal."[21]

17. *Dharma* - Duty. **18.** Shrimad Bhagavad Gita, Chapter – 3, Verse – 22-24.
19. Shrimad Bhagavad Gita, Chapter – 3, Verse – 21. **20.** Shrimad Bhagavad Gita, Chapter – 10, Verse – 28.
21. Shrimad Bhagavad Gita, Chapter – 2, Verse – 20.

At present, however, let me tell you one more secret; this advice which I had given when I enunciated the Gita much later was not so much for Arjuna as it was for the self-realised. This is the reason why I proclaim, I am the only 'complete incarnation' in all of mankind's history, for, I had advised even those who had attained self-realisation. Indeed, when I enunciated the Bhagavad Gita, my knowledge and my consciousness were at their peak. This is why, in the Gita, I had instructed those very self-realised individuals who go around instructing everyone in the world. Hadn't I said, "O self-realised people! After attaining self-realisation, do not renounce the world; neither wear a monk's garb nor oppose violence or sex. Instead, direct people onto the path of progress. Discover new facets of glory, live like ordinary human beings, because in actuality, self-realisation is a person's own achievement.[22] Do not unnecessarily renounce or oppose violence, sex, progress or prosperity, thus creating misconceptions in the minds of ordinary people. Human beings have so much potential for advancement hidden within themselves that they can rule over the moon and the stars, provided you, the self-realised people, do not develop distaste for action by unnecessarily recommending renunciation of action!"[23] To tell you the truth, it is verily my knowledge, awareness and vision that collectively make me the 'complete incarnation' as compared to all other 'partial incarnations'. However, it is also true that because of these views of mine, many ignorant people consider me to be the ultimate egoist. So be it! Returning to the present, even *Acharya* had not sensed that something had transpired within me, and this was certainly a unique achievement for me. For, if *Acharya* himself had not been able to sense that I had attained self-realisation, then there was no question of anyone else ever learning of it. I was elated! And why should I not be, for, it was because of my 'supreme consciousness' that I was getting an opportunity to lead an ordinary life in spite of becoming self-realised. In other words, I was getting a chance to begin a new game of *karma*. Oh! Lost in these thoughts, little did I realise that *Acharya-ma* had called us for the meal. I was famished anyway, so leaving the company of all those present, I scurried inside to partake of my meal.

22. Shrimad Bhagavad Gita, Chapter – 3, Verse – 26.
23. Shrimad Bhagavad Gita, Chapter – 3, Verse – 26.

Chapter 5

Killing the Pirate King Panchajanya to Honour Gurudakshina

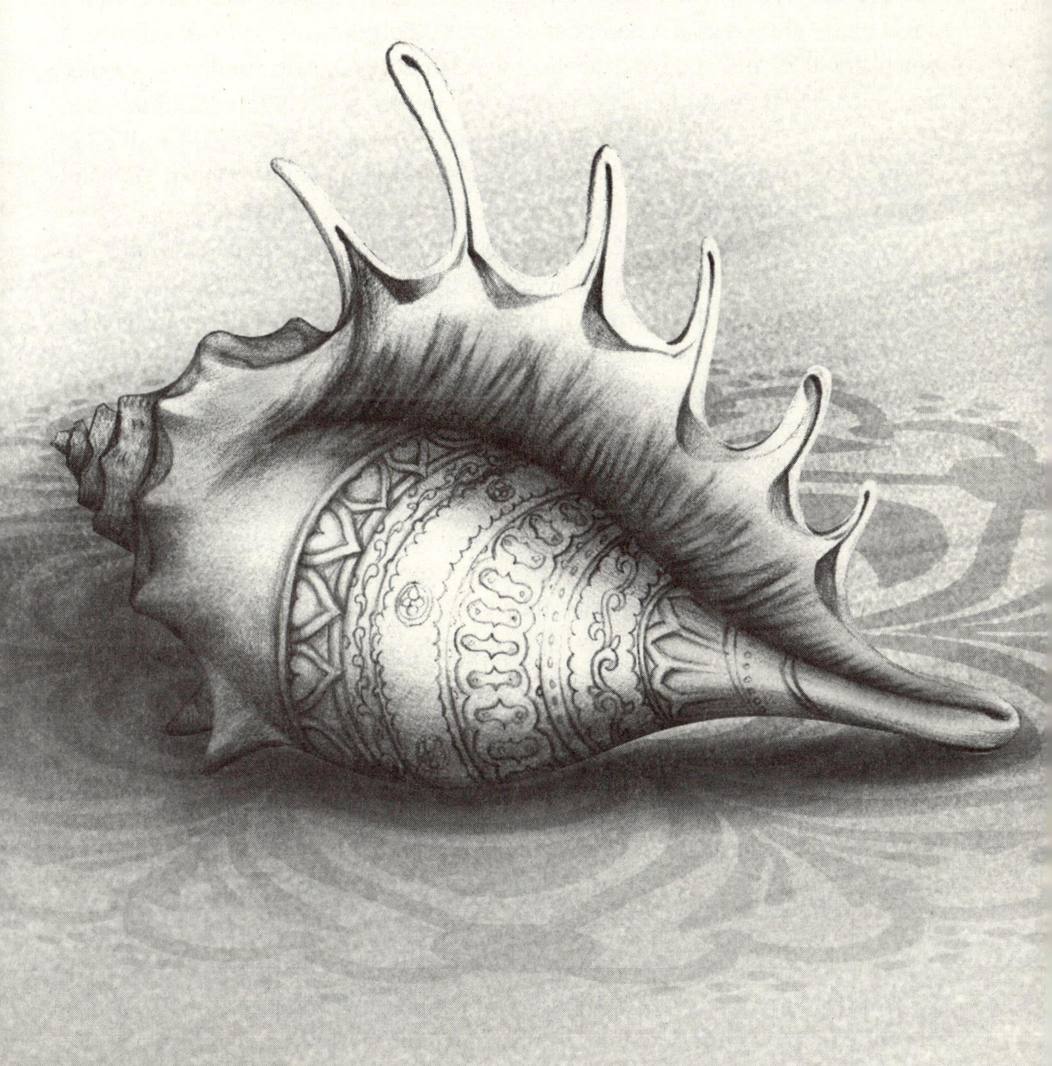

All the secrets of the world had now been revealed to me. This made me wonder, what was left to be learnt now at the *ashram*? But amazingly, my curiosity for learning did not abate, and I continued to pose questions to *Acharya* with the same fervour as before. To state it differently, I had easily managed to balance both my personalities—the Supreme Soul Krishna and Vrindavan's Kanha—within myself. And frankly speaking, because of this, my stay at the *ashram* had become several times more enjoyable. Of course, the credit for this went to my witness more than me. Meaning, everything at the *ashram* continued in the same manner as before, the only difference being, I was now enjoying myself more. It had only been a few days since the momentous event, when one morning, something occurred that rendered me speechless, almost as if I had been struck by lightning. It was early morning when *Acharya* took me for a stroll. It was a quiet path, surrounded by woods, and not a person in sight as far as the eye could see. I had to admit that even at his age, *Acharya* was easily matching my brisk pace. We mostly walked in silence, but on the way back, to my utter surprise, he gently placed his hand on my head and said, "Krishna, your education is now complete."

Hearing these words, I stopped in my tracks, stunned. I failed to understand what he meant by that statement. Barely six months had elapsed since our arrival at the *ashram* and my education was already complete?! I felt as if I had been struck by a thousand bolts of lightning. For, there were many students who had been studying at the *ashram* for several years, yet their education was far from complete. I wondered, was I being asked to leave due to the pressure exerted by Jarasandha? No, no! How could I even think of *Acharya* in this manner? He was not the sort of man to buckle under pressure. Then what could the matter be? Even as I was mulling over this, my legs had stopped moving, and I stood rooted to the spot for a moment. Noticing the look of bewilderment on my face and the fact that I had been rendered immobile because of the effect of his words, *Acharya* stopped walking as well. Indeed, how could the turmoil in my mind remain hidden from him? Immediately, he came close and, patting my back, said, "I have imparted all my knowledge to you. Actually, it's your ability to grasp the knowledge that was more significant than my imparting it. Just as the earth soaks up the rainwater that pours down on it, you too have absorbed all the knowledge I could impart. Indeed, you have learnt not just everything I had to teach you, but also that which I have not taught. Truly, I am blessed to have a student like you!"

Oh, what is this I'm hearing? This accolade was completely unexpected. In fact, I had just received the highest honour possible for my competence and grasping ability. Elated by this, I quickly resumed walking, and as I did, my contemplation kickstarted too. *Acharya* was right; I deserved this recognition. Truly, my determination to learn and my grasping ability were incomparable. I was always eager to learn from every incident and every moment. Then, another thought struck me, 'Wait! My education was complete, but what about bhaiya?' As soon as this thought struck me, I promptly posed the question to *Acharya*, "And what about bhaiya?"

"He too has learnt all that he can possibly learn, and I too have taught him all that I can possibly teach him," *Acharya* said.

In short, both of us were being discharged from the *ashram* together. In any case, after leaving the *ashram,* what would I have done without bhaiya? And as for bhaiya, it was impossible for him to even imagine spending a few minutes at the *ashram* without me. It was good that the matter had been resolved without us having to disobey *Acharya*. Well, we had reached the *ashram* but it was only now that the real trouble began. My mind was drawn to solitude, eager to wander in a thousand different directions. And, of course, the *ashram* had no dearth of such places where one could sit alone. So, descending a few steps from the backyard, I found a quiet spot beneath a tree, facing River Kshipra. The most important point worth contemplating was that bhaiya and I were back to square one. In short, we had returned to the same point from where we had commenced this journey of ours. What I mean to say is, since our education was complete, we obviously couldn't continue staying at the *ashram*, and as soon as we stepped outside, the threat of Jarasandha would begin to haunt us once again. In fact, just a few days ago, grandfather's spies had come to the *ashram* with the latest news of the state of affairs in Mathura. According to them, Jarasandha had indeed come to Mathura to launch an attack, but when he learnt that bhaiya and I were no longer there, he had returned without waging a war. But the trouble did not end there. Furious, he had instructed all the kings who were his allies to imprison us on sight and immediately inform him. This meant that we had been safe until now only because we were staying at the *ashram*. In other words, we would have to gird up our loins once again to live a life without shelter or protection. For, considering the present circumstances, Mathura would no longer give us refuge and no matter where we went, the fear of being captured by Jarasandha would continue to haunt us. To make matters worse, we barely had any money to sustain us and help us travel far. So, the question looming before us was, where would we go and how would we live? Agreed, we were accustomed to living in small houses in both Gokula and Vrindavan, and the *ashram* had taught us everything we needed to know about leading an austere life. What I mean to say is, *Acharya* had taught us how to sleep on the hard ground, even in the most deplorable conditions, be it in freezing weather or torrential rain, and that too, without blankets or bedding. So, even if I were to not consider this a major impediment, the question of saving ourselves from Jarasandha's wrath and finding a place to stay still remained unresolved. Well, so be it, for, when had I ever decided any of these things myself? I had always waited for Nature to show me the path I had to take, because I firmly believed that the one who has created us is also prepared to take on our responsibility, provided we surrender ourselves to him.

Besides, merely thinking about the problem would not conjure up a solution. So, I spent some time calming my restless mind and enjoying the view of the river flowing by. Once calmed, I returned to the *ashram* with slow but determined steps. According to *Acharya*'s instructions, we were slated to leave the *ashram* after three days, so what was the need to trouble myself from now itself? Would it not be better to live my life to the fullest and make the most of these last three days? We could deliberate on the future once we crossed the gates of the *ashram*. Incidentally, even *Acharya* was engaged in making these three days memorable for us, so much so that in my honour, he had relaxed all the rules of the *ashram* during this period. Surprisingly, not just us, but the rest of the students were also exempted from all rules and regulations of the *ashram* during these three days. And that's not all! Even the daily classes had been put on hold temporarily. Meaning, our last three days at the *ashram* were exclusively reserved for us to indulge in fun and feasting! As a result, my flute and Sudama's songs resonated in every nook and corner of the *ashram* every morning, noon and evening over the next three days. Moreover, we were also served sweets and savouries at dinnertime, which thrilled us beyond words. Bhaiya and I, actually bhaiya in particular, would gorge on all the delicious food without reserve. Now, although there was a general atmosphere of festivity in the *ashram*, it was not without an undercurrent of sadness. Our friends were happy that the rules had been relaxed, but at the same time, they were sad that we were leaving the *ashram*. Strangely, the unhappiest of us all was *Acharya* himself, for, he had grown quite fond of me during the short time we had spent at the *ashram*.

The only exception to these bittersweet emotions was bhaiya, who experienced just one emotion—joy! He was, in fact, delighted beyond words and danced with glee at the prospect of leaving the *ashram* and returning to Mathura. Honestly speaking, the excitement on his face was making me anxious, because the present circumstances in Mathura were not conducive to our return. Thus, before a bolt of lightning struck his cheerfulness, turning delight into despondency, I decided it was best not to reveal the entire truth to him. However, I was compelled to share a part of the truth regarding the conditions in Mathura and the opinion of the royal court. Of course, I did lie about one thing: I placed the blame for the situation squarely on the shoulders of the Yadava leaders. I told bhaiya that although grandfather and father had strongly opposed this decision, they had to acquiesce to the demands of these leaders. By doing so, I had hidden the truth about father's stance on this matter, and the reason was simple: I did not want bhaiya to harbour a grudge against father. Really, what a beautiful weapon lies can be—provided they are not used for selfish purposes.

But bhaiya was truly one of a kind. He was not going to let me be at peace. Instead of worrying after hearing the entire narrative of what had transpired in Mathura, he was filled with rage towards Jarasandha. Bellowing at the top of his voice, he declared, "Bah! I will not wait for him to find me. I will myself go and kill him!" Oh no! This was a new problem that had reared its head. Agreed that bhaiya was brave and courageous, but he did not possess the intelligence to temper such raw courage. Obviously, Jarasandha would not march in alone and say, "Come, Balarama, let us fight one-on-one!" His army would obliterate us in an instant! But it was pointless trying to explain all this to bhaiya. For now, the most important thing was that he was free of worries. I had to content myself with the fact that, at least, he had accepted the reality that we were not going back to Mathura. However, the difficulties did not end here. I had visualised myself enjoying these last three days at the *ashram*, but here I was, caught up in the problems of the future! It was certain that we could not return to Mathura, but where else could we go if not Mathura? The problem was becoming even more complicated because I could not discuss with bhaiya which kingdom we should go to, given his fiery temperament. Of course, the need of the hour was to seek refuge in a kingdom that was inimical to Jarasandha; and verily, only someone who respects the need of the hour is truly wise. However, had I suggested this to bhaiya, he would have become furious and, in his typical brash manner, declared that he feared no one, not even Jarasandha. But when the need of the hour is to be cautious and one chooses instead to show bravado, it is not bravery but sheer foolishness. Alas! Who could make bhaiya see that every such act of recklessness by a human being has ultimately proved to be suicidal?

In short, we were currently left to our own devices—we had no money, no shelter and no one to help us. Moreover, the most powerful king of Aryavarta, Jarasandha, was baying for our blood. This being the case, where could we possibly go? How could we save ourselves from his wrath? The problem was so complicated that there appeared no solution in sight. We had neither money nor resources to go anywhere, nor a place to stay, nor anyone who could offer us shelter. We had been to no other place except Mathura and Ujjaini, so even if we were to travel on foot, where and how far could we go? In short, we poor brothers were left with no recourse, tossed around like driftwood in the vast ocean of the world. So be it! When there is truly nothing that one can do, then it is wise to leave it to Nature's justice, and that is precisely what I did too. I was well versed with Nature's *leela*.[24] If Nature wished to protect us from Jarasandha, then it would surely direct us to a safe destination. Meaning, if we were meant to be saved, we would find a safe haven, just like the last time when we had found refuge in *Acharya* Sandipani's *ashram*; otherwise we would go along with whatever Nature chose for us. After all, the plan or thought of seeking shelter in *Acharya* Sandipani's *ashram* wasn't my own, was it? I had not even met *Acharya* until that point. In other words, if Nature finds a new secure shelter for us, then we can rest assured that it wants to save us at present. If not, then it wouldn't be wrong to assume that our time to depart from this world had arrived. How difficult could it be for a self-realised person to understand this simple truth? If understood correctly, it is only because of his stubbornness to go against Nature's will that a human being's life is mired in complications. He wants to make all decisions using his own intellect, but the truth is, many important decisions of life must be left to Nature's discretion. And this trust of mine was not unfounded; it had stemmed forth from my own life experiences which proclaimed it loud and clear. Indeed, in the past, I had courted death on several occasions, and yet, here I was, alive and kicking! Wasn't this enough to prove the point made above? Reasoning thus, I quickly freed myself from worry and anxiety. For, I also knew the truth that Nature does not lend a helping hand to worriers. Moreover, even the experiences of my life so far proved that irrespective of whatever had happened with me, the final outcome had always been positive, so why would it be any different this time around? Nature, with its farsightedness, often sends us trouble for our own good; however, due to our short-sightedness, we consider it an ordeal and become entangled in it.

Well, barring these worries and ruminations of mine, the last three days spent at the *ashram* were truly splendid. Now, the time had come to put this peaceful and secure life behind us, for, we had to leave this morning. As for our luggage, we did not have many possessions to pack. Let alone luggage, we did not even have a chariot for the journey ahead. So, after getting ready early in the morning, bhaiya and I stepped out of our chamber—me in a state of worry and bhaiya in a state of cheerfulness. Indeed, his mood was in complete contrast to mine, excited as he was to step out of the *ashram* and breathe the fresh air of freedom. Everyone was waiting for us in the open ground outside our chamber, and we too headed straight to meet them. The mood was one of despondency. Forget about *Acharya-ma* and our friends,

24. *Leela* - Play.

Acharya too looked unhappy. For a while, we chatted with everyone, relished the fruits that *Acharya-ma* had cut for us, and then set off for the main gate. I was walking ahead with *Acharya,* while bhaiya walked behind with the others. Interestingly, grandfather had no inkling that our education at the *ashram* would be completed in such a short time. Had he been aware, he would have surely sent a chariot for us. Well, no matter what the reason was, we had to begin the next phase of our journey on foot. And that didn't bother me in the least. For, I was always ready to face any eventuality that came my way. Thus, crossing the entrance and embracing all our friends, including Sudama, Shwetketu, Vinda, Anuvinda and the others, we proceeded towards *Acharya* and *Acharya-ma.* With great reverence, we touched their feet, received their blessings and braced ourselves for the most arduous journey of our lives. It was then that Vinda and Anuvinda realised that we did not have a chariot at our disposal and offered to arrange one for us. But I found this offer fraught with risk. They were, after all, Rukmi's friends, and Rukmi was under the influence of Jarasandha. Therefore, taking a chariot from them would entail leaving a trail. No! That would be suicidal. So, rather than getting caught and slaughtered by Jarasandha, we preferred to undertake this journey on foot. Well, even as we were leaving, *Acharya* placed a hand on my head and spoke words that provided great solace to my heart. He said, "Krishna, you have become more of a friend to me than a student. Whenever you pass this way, please do come and stay with us without hesitation. You are like my son; therefore, from today, I would like you to consider this *ashram* as your home." Needless to say, *Acharya*'s words, spoken at this difficult juncture in life, touched my heart. My eyes glistened with unshed tears and a warm smile played on my lips. In our current situation, we were in dire need of such reassuring words and good wishes. Indeed, I felt proud to have received as much love from *Acharya* as I had received knowledge.

However, for some reason, the moment *Acharya* referred to me as a son, *Acharya-ma's* eyes welled up with tears. And within moments, she lost control of her emotions and began crying inconsolably. Alarmed on seeing this emotional outburst, *Acharya* tried to console her, while I looked on perplexed, unable to fathom the reason behind it. Not just me, everyone else was dumbfounded too on seeing *Acharya-ma* cry in *Acharya's* arms. The scene only added to the gloom hanging heavily around us. Well, after a long time had passed and *Acharya-ma* still couldn't control her emotions, I could no longer hold myself back. Indeed, how could I stand there like a silent spectator and watch her weep so bitterly? So, mustering courage, I asked her in a slow, halting voice, "What is the matter, mother? Is there anything I can do to ease your sorrow?"

Hearing my voice, she composed herself. Then, quickly wiping her tears, she replied, "No, no, it is nothing. It is just that I was reminded of my son."

Surprised, I exclaimed, "Your son! Where is he?"

This time, *Acharya* replied, "Our only son, Punardutta, was kidnapped twelve years ago when he was just five, by a demon named Panchajanya."

"But why?" I asked in bewilderment.

Acharya said, "Because the demon wanted me to educate his son at my *ashram*."

Hearing this, I concluded the rest of the story and said to *Acharya*, "And you were not ready to take his son as your student!"

He replied, "Krishna, how could I? If a teacher himself is compelled to take decisions under pressure or fear, what teaching can he possibly impart to his students? Think about it, Krishna, if the *Acharya* of an *ashram* himself gets caught up in attachment towards his children, how can he teach the students of the *ashram* to become free of attachment?"

Truly, both *Acharya* and his teachings were incomparable! I was really fortunate to have had the opportunity to receive my education from such a great teacher. Even though I had become knowledgeable after my self-realisation, my learning had not stopped. For, it was the Soul that was knowledgeable, but I wanted to elevate my mind, intelligence and ego too, to that level so they too could attain knowledge. I wanted every pore of my being to be enlightened. And verily, by the time the Mahabharata war took place, I had already attained this wonderful state. That is why, throughout the Gita, I had been able to use the terms 'me' and 'I' to represent Nature. Who else has been able to accomplish this till today? No one! Who will be able to do this in the future? Perhaps, no one. This is why I, Krishna, am unique!

Well, I may be unique, but I was certainly not alone, surrounded as I was by *Acharya-ma* and the others. Presently, looking deep into *Acharya-ma's* eyes, I could clearly see the suffering she was undergoing. Indeed, her eyes seemed to express whatever was left unsaid. And for me, her helplessness was akin to a command. I asked myself, what had I not obtained after coming to this *ashram*? I had not only gained love and knowledge from *Acharya*, but with his blessings, I had attained self-realisation too. Hence, it was my duty to dedicate the rest of my life to his happiness. Indeed, had *Acharya* not accepted me as a student, I wouldn't have been alive to see this day... Jarasandha would have ensured it! Besides, once we left the *ashram*, our lives would be under threat anyway. We could not go to Mathura and no matter where we went, Jarasandha and his spies were bound to ferret us out. So, if we were destined to be pursued by the shadow of death, why not embrace it while trying to wipe away *Acharya-ma's* tears? In fact, what greater happiness could there be for me than getting the opportunity to eliminate the sorrow of my great teacher? After all, an opportunity like this—one that allowed me to express my gratitude to a great teacher—was rare indeed. Furthermore, we were already facing a dilemma about where to go. So, when this mission presented itself, I took it as a sign from Nature. Without a second thought, I consoled *Acharya-ma* saying, "I promise that if your son, Punardutta, is alive, I will surely bring him back to you. This will be my *gurudakshina* to our great *Acharya*."[25]

Hearing this, *Acharya-ma* rushed forward and pulled me into an embrace. With her loving arms around me, I became emotional too. As for *Acharya,* he stood beside us, while this entire scene unfolded at the main gate of the *ashram,* with all our friends in attendance. Hearing me utter these words, a smile of delight spread on the faces of some of the students, while a few looked astonished, and some even looked worried. As for bhaiya, he was unbothered with whatever was transpiring before him, lost as he was in the feeling of unbridled happiness, his spirits soaring high at the very thought of securing release from the *ashram*. But curiously, there was still no response from *Acharya*. Well, regardless of the reason behind his silence, one thing was certain; he seemed far from happy after hearing my proposal. And verily, after a few moments, he did express his objection saying, "No, Krishna. Panchajanya is an extremely powerful demon. He is, in fact, the ruler of the Dasyus, with a huge army at his disposal. For the sake of one son of mine, whose present condition I am unaware of and whose abilities I am clueless about, I cannot risk the life of another son whom I know to be highly promising."

Acharya's equanimity, completely free from any attachment, left me deeply impressed. Indeed, one who is bound by attachment can never maintain true equanimity. Well, *Acharya* may have expressed his concern for my safety, but I was fully aware of my duty. Therefore, I questioned his worry itself by saying, "O *Acharya*, by expressing worry and concern for my well-being, you are doubting my capabilities. Kansa too had an army; Keshi too was extremely powerful, but I had slayed both of them with my bare hands. The real question is, whether your goal is right or not, and how resolute you are towards achieving that goal. At any rate, I will be indebted to you for the rest of my life for the knowledge you have imparted to me. Therefore, please grant me the opportunity to express my gratitude to you by bringing back your son, Punardutta."

Although it took some convincing on my part, *Acharya* finally relented and gave his consent, and consequently, our departure from the *ashram* was

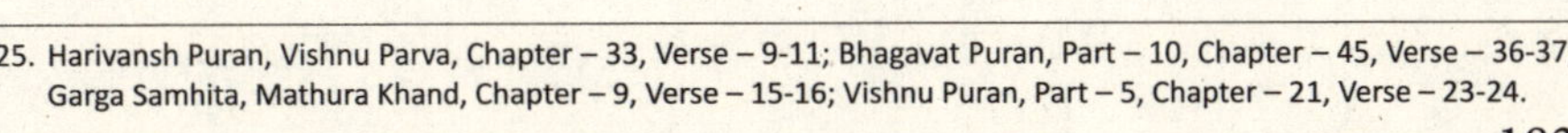

25. Harivansh Puran, Vishnu Parva, Chapter – 33, Verse – 9-11; Bhagavat Puran, Part – 10, Chapter – 45, Verse – 36-37; Garga Samhita, Mathura Khand, Chapter – 9, Verse – 15-16; Vishnu Puran, Part – 5, Chapter – 21, Verse – 23-24.

postponed, as it was essential for us to gather every bit of information about Panchajanya. Moreover, we had to make special provisions for this unique journey too. In the next two days, *Acharya* gave us all the information which he had gleaned about Panchajanya. The crux of his findings was that Panchajanya was a demon who sailed the high seas. His kingdom was located near Kushasthali and its capital was Vaivasvatpur. But that's not all! Panchajanya also ruled the entire coastal region. Considering all of this, the enemy appeared so powerful that rescuing Punardutta from his clutches seemed nearly impossible.

However, I did not care, for, once I became resolute about doing something, nothing could hold me back. Besides, of what use was this life of mine if it could not be employed in the service of *Acharya*? At any rate, it was far better to embrace death while trying to rescue Punardutta than to be hunted down by Jarasandha while fleeing from him. In short, my decision was made! Fortunately, we no longer had to worry about a lack of resources, as *Acharya* had placed his own chariot at our disposal. The chariot was old, yet in good working condition. As a first step, *Acharya* had instructed us to head directly to Kushasthali, where we would meet Jaivik, a well-wisher of *Acharya*, who would provide us with additional information about Panchajanya. He was also likely to have more information about Punardutta. Moreover, he was expected to help us with all our requirements as well. This meant that all of *Acharya's* preparations were complete, and now, both bhaiya and I were ready, mentally and physically, for the journey. Although, let me tell you, the main reason behind bhaiya's willingness to go with me was the 'freedom' he was about to experience. For, bhaiya never bothered to think, analyse or fathom the nitty-gritty of any matter. As far as he was concerned, leave alone Panchajanya, there was no question of him being scared of anyone's might. This was all fine, but ever since I had offered to rescue *Acharya's* son, my mind had latched on to a curious thought. A number of princes from several powerful kingdoms were under *Acharya's* tutelage, so why had none of them ever stepped forward to rescue his son? Actually, the answer was quite simple: perhaps, it is not in human nature to exhibit courage when it comes to helping others selflessly.

Well, amidst all these musings of mine, we were now ready to embark on this unique journey, powered by *Acharya*'s blessings, *Acharya-ma's* prayers, and an emotional farewell from all our friends. My enthusiasm knew no bounds. Bhaiya was happy too, because to him, if not Jarasandha, he would fight Panchajanya! All that mattered to him was securing an opportunity to display his valour. Moreover, he was also pleased because as soon as the chariot left the *ashram*, he would be freed from the shackles of discipline.

Well, we were touched by the warm farewell we received—our second in just three days! Meanwhile, *Acharya*'s old, battered chariot stood ready outside the *ashram,* with the condition of the horse not much different from that of the chariot. By now, we had reached the entrance amidst much noise and fanfare. Our belongings had already been placed inside the chariot. Thus, embracing everyone, we sought blessings from *Acharya* and *Acharya-ma* once again. The same scene had unfolded two days ago; the only difference was the chariot, into which we jumped after bidding farewell to everyone. For that matter, there was yet another change that I could discern. Last time, while everyone had worn long faces, despondent as they were to see us go, this time, their emotions reflected hope and enthusiasm. Of course, it made scant difference whether they were despondent or enthused, because although we did not have to face Jarasandha, we now had to deal with Panchajanya; thus, either way, we would be walking straight into the jaws of death! But yes, there was definitely a marked difference; while earlier, we would have been put to death for no reason, we were now getting a chance to die fighting while performing our duty.

Well, for now, let me remind you that ever since we had taken the long journey from Mathura to Ujjaini with *Acharya*, a desire had kindled in me to experience such a journey again. A journey in which the reins of the chariot would be in my hands, and I wouldn't have to worry about *Acharya* or his discipline. Well, as it is rightly said, if your desire is strong enough, then it definitely finds fulfilment; of course, how soon it is fulfilled depends entirely on how strong it is. And as you well know, everything I did in life, I did wholeheartedly. Therefore, it was only natural for my desire to be fulfilled immediately. At the same time, let me tell you, a lesson I had learnt from my life so far was that in order to succeed in your endeavours, it does not matter whether you are good, bad, sinful or pious; the real question is about 'one' or 'many'. One strong desire can make you reach your goal, whereas too many desires can distract you and lead you astray. Oftentimes, a single desire, a single reason for harbouring ego, a single lie, or even a single act of stealing can prove to be a virtue; meaning, it can fetch you the desired result. Whereas, at times, too many desires, too much pride, too many lies… or even too many truths, too many altruistic acts and too much service at one time could ultimately prove to be sins. Doing so will inevitably bring failure, much against one's wishes. Remember, focused attention is the Soul, whereas divided attention is the ego. Then, it makes no difference what names you give to glorify these actions. To do one thing at a time is *yoga,* whereas doing several things at once is *kaam* (greed). Consequently, a *yogi* will always be successful and happy, whereas a *kaami*[26] will remain unsuccessful and

26. *Kaami* - One who is driven solely by his greed.

unhappy. And I was a *yogi* not only in Soul but also in mind, which is why this beautiful dream of mine had turned into reality in such a short time.

And now that the dream had come true, it was obvious that I would enjoy it to the hilt. Although the chariot was rickety, groaning and squeaking now and then, its reins were in my hands; and with bhaiya sitting beside me, how long could it have taken us to cross Ujjaini? Once we had crossed the city, it seemed as if the two of us had suddenly sprouted wings and were flying in the air. Travelling on long, winding roads, we revelled in the beautiful scenery passing us by and the cool breeze that rejuvenated every pore of our being. By afternoon, we had entered the forest. Feeling ravenous at the sight of the lush, fruit-laden trees in the jungle, we put to use our practice of pelting stones at the fruits and satiated our hunger. Oh, what fun it was! Seeing the poor, emaciated condition of the horse, we fed it armfuls of grass and gave it plenty of water to drink. Naturally, the horse had now become our companion through thick and thin. In fact, our entire journey depended on the horse being in the best condition, for, if the animal fell sick, it would be well-nigh impossible for us to reach Kushasthali. So, not only did we tie the horse in the shade of a clump of trees to let it rest, but we too decided to relax on a flat rock for a while. Indeed, the scene had transformed into a beautiful picture: the two brothers lying supine, with the rock as our pillow, tall trees with thick foliage serving as a canopy, our horse tethered to one of the trees munching on soft grass, and the open chariot standing in front of us. I became so lost in this enchanting scene that in that fleeting moment, I attained *yoga*.[27] At present, this was my *karma* as well as the fruits of having performed my *karma*. In any case, when one is in a state of *yoga,* how can *karma* (action) ever be separated from its fruits? Actually, man has gone astray only because he considers *karma* and its fruits separate from each other. This is precisely what I had said to Arjuna much later in the Gita. *"Perform your karma, but never worry about its fruits."* Truth be told, there can be no greater aphorism than this for the upliftment of human beings. But just see, in spite of this, Arjuna kept discussing the fruits of action throughout the Gita, whereas I was repeatedly explaining to him that this inevitable war was his *karma,* and the joy he would experience on demonstrating his bravery in the war is the very fruit of that *karma.* Just as my *karma* at present was to take in this beautiful scene, the fruits of which I was receiving instantly in the form of bliss. Had Arjuna been in my place, he would have perhaps not undertaken this journey at all. And even if he had managed to embark on this journey, he would have barraged me with a slew of questions such as, "Why go to Panchajanya?", "How powerful the demon must be?", "How will we fight this battle?", "Will we be able to find Punardutta or not?", "Will I survive this battle or not?",

27. *Yoga* - Union with the entire creation.

"Who will win ultimately?" I'm sure you'd recall the kind of nonsensical questions Arjuna had posed in the Gita! And I had responded to each one of them with just one answer, "The Mahabharata war is a journey and you are a valorous hero, so just enjoy demonstrating your valour. The pleasure you will derive from displaying your prowess is the very fruit of your actions. Thereafter, questions such as 'Who will win?', 'How to kill?', 'Why to kill?', 'Is it correct to kill one's kith and kin?', 'Will the war result in a kingdom or a place in heaven?', 'What do the scriptures have to say about all this?' and so on and so forth will be of no consequence."

Well, let us put all this aside, for, it was almost afternoon now. Having rested well, both man and beast were ready to resume their journey. After harnessing the horse to the chariot, we set off. Oh, what fun it was to ride the chariot! Manoeuvring the reins in my hands, I was able to race it with dexterity, sending it flying in the air, while bhaiya sat beside me and enjoyed this 'flight' under the open sky. The excitement and joy were clearly visible on his countenance as he revelled in the freedom of being liberated from the confined existence of the *ashram*; verily, the happiness had permeated his whole being. As our chariot moved forward, we passed imposing mountains, gurgling streams flowing down to merge into rivers, and small towns with their cluster of dwellings. On seeing the towns, bhaiya and I would jump for joy, as we would invariably find shops selling savouries and delicacies. Now, being cowherd boys who were fond of good food, how could we miss out on such opportunities? Besides, we had been eating extremely simple fare for the past six months and were really fed up with it. Fortunately, at the time of leaving, *Acharya* had given me a bunch of coins to help us along the way. Though not enough to buy clothes or jewellery, they were sufficient to satisfy our hunger with good food. If we really enjoyed the food we ate, we would get an extra portion of it packed to carry along with us. Indeed, as the journey progressed, we satisfied both our aesthetic and gastronomic senses, feasting our body and mind on all the beautiful things we encountered on our way. We had even stopped at numerous lakes and streams, refreshing ourselves with a dip in the cool water to wash away the tiredness of the journey. That's not all! Whenever a new variety of fruit caught our eye, we would halt our chariot, pluck the fruit and taste it; and if it pleased our taste buds, we would gather heaps of it and carry with us on our onward journey. However, I could not deny the fact that riding the chariot all day was exhausting. As a result, I would fall fast asleep as soon as I lay down at night. Being considerate of my fatigue, bhaiya had voluntarily taken up the duty of keeping the night vigil as well as some other duties such as washing our clothes. Of course, watering the horse, preparing the chariot in the morning, making repairs when needed, tethering the horse and unharnessing the chariot at night were still my responsibility, as bhaiya had yet to learn these tasks.

Did you see how my careful examination of everything during our journey from Mathura to the *ashram* with *Acharya* was proving so useful today? Nobody had taught me how to carry out repairs on the chariot or how to harness and unharness the horse, nor had anyone outlined the importance of having knowledge of such things. This implies, if you have a strong observational power and the desire to learn and grasp things, there is so much you can learn without being taught. Conversely, if you lack these two abilities, you can end up spending your entire life trying to learn just one thing. Consider me for instance; if like the others, I too had depended on a formal education instead of relying on my ability to observe and grasp, then at best, I would have learnt just ten to twenty things in my life. Lessons like riding a chariot, looking after horses, repairing a chariot, undertaking long journeys and so on would have taken me months to master; whereas I had learnt all this myself, without wasting a moment, in a single long journey, only because of my keen observational power. To sum it up, how much you learn in life depends on how fast you can learn things. Otherwise, looking at the princes studying at the *ashram* and gauging how much or how little they had learnt, I can say with conviction that without serious application on the part of the student, the education imparted to him is of no use. Honestly, such teachings end up being nothing more than a waste of time!

However, let me stop lecturing you about education and instead describe our journey. This being a long journey for us, bhaiya would often head to the rear seat of the chariot and take a nap during daytime. Of course, this was the consequence of him staying up all night to keep vigil. And naturally, when he was asleep, I would immerse myself in contemplations to pass the time; but once he was awake, we would mostly chit-chat. Even now, bhaiya was sleeping while I revelled in the solitude of the serene surroundings, with the reins of the chariot firmly held in my hands. The only unfortunate aspect of this journey was that we did not have enough money with us. How much could *Acharya* have given us anyway, as he himself had never accepted anything from anyone! Whatever he had given us was enough to demonstrate his strong and unwavering sense of duty. Of course, I understood everything, yet the lack of money bothered me, because there were marketplaces teeming with beautiful objects in all the towns we passed through. While some of the things available in these markets were essential, others were just objects of desire. But poor us, we could only admire them from a distance. At the most, we could gaze at them longingly, but we definitely could not purchase them. However, since we were extremely fond of eating, all our money was being spent on delicious food. From my current experience, I can definitely say that there is no greater feeling of helplessness in this world than to be without sufficient money. For, prosperity is another name for life, or one could even say that prosperity is the key to fulfilling one's needs. But neither is everyone able to enjoy prosperity nor is everyone able to fulfil their needs as per their desire. So, does that mean that a person who is not prosperous is doomed to remain unhappy all his life? No, certainly not! Human life is intended only for enjoyment. But how can a penniless person enjoy himself? With these thoughts assailing my mind, all of a sudden, my contemplation picked up speed, racing faster than the chariot. At any rate, these reflections were the only things keeping me company during the journey today, for, bhaiya was resting, and I was riding the chariot in silence. In other words, I had the time as well as the opportunity to ponder at length. My analytical mind thus began to contemplate on how one could strike the perfect balance between wealth and enjoyment in life. If wealth and enjoyment are the primary goals of human life, then why is it that they are not available to everyone simultaneously? So, does that mean that attaining both of these simultaneously is verily one's *'dharma'*? As soon as this thought struck me, I found my contemplation soaring higher and higher. Remember, self-realisation simply means recognising your inner self. And while I agree that attaining self-realisation is a great achievement, it is not the final goal of life. With this in mind, I embarked on a mental journey to seek 'completeness' even in that which is already 'complete'.

Well, in the present situation, I was already experiencing how a paucity of wealth could make a person feel utterly helpless. Therefore, there was no need to dwell on this further. In the *ashram,* I had also seen how the princes studying with me were living with an abundance of wealth, but at the same time, their behaviour had made it evident that they were completely ignorant about the art of enjoying life. In fact, I had always seen them being irked or frustrated. And with so much unhappiness within, what was the point of having all the wealth of the world? Moreover, from my own experiences, I knew that living in a constant state of happiness is an art in itself, one that must be learnt. On the other hand, attaining prosperity requires an entirely different set of skills. So, the question prodding my mind was, is it not possible for a human being to cultivate both these skills simultaneously? Pondering over this question, my mind set off in a different direction altogether. These princes had done nothing to earn their wealth…so, was it Nature that decided who would be bestowed with riches and who would remain bereft of it? If Nature desires someone to be wealthy, does it orchestrate their birth in a king's palace? No, wait! That can't be the case. Why would Nature be partial? Could it be that Nature grants them wealth, but withholds the art of being happy, leaving them miserable all their lives? But that seemed impossible too, for, this would also imply partiality on Nature's part.

Well, for the time being, without delving into a deeper analysis, it was evident that *Acharya* had joy, while the princes had wealth and prosperity. And seen from my perspective, both were incomplete. So, was *Acharya* teaching them the art of being happy in life by making them sleep on the bare floor? However, as far as bhaiya and I were concerned, we had always lived like this, so what was the need for us to learn this lesson? Oh, the matter was becoming convoluted! Even so, I wanted my contemplation to get to the bottom of this mystery. My analysis so far had revealed that while the wealthy must learn the art of being happy, it is the compulsion of the poor to learn the skills that could help them attain wealth. Mulling over these issues, I doubted whether the matter could be resolved in an instant, but deep within, I was determined to solve this mystery—even if it meant challenging Nature itself. If Nature believed that only its chosen ones would receive wealth, I would shatter that belief. I would discover art that could bring prosperity to every individual in this world. And I wouldn't stop there! To prove this to Nature, I would one day scale the highest peak of grandeur myself. No sooner did I make this resolve than everything became crystal clear. Actually, the teachings doled out for enjoying life or renouncing this world are meant only for the wealthy; whereas, the poor and penniless ought to be joyful and content by nature, just the way I was. This was verily my philosophy and also my formula for turning the poor into the rich. Let me elaborate on it: if any person with simple means continuously endeavours to perform every single duty of his joyously while keeping the objective of prosperity in mind, then surely, sooner or later, his very nature of being happy will help him scale the peaks of prosperity and grandeur. However, bear in mind that one should not harbour a desire for grandeur or feel jealous of others' grandeur; one simply needs to be aware of it within. For, as soon as you desire grandeur, joy disappears, and once joy vanishes from life, the possibility of attaining grandeur is greatly reduced. Therefore, while performing one's *karma* and enjoying it fully, if one comes across an opportunity to become wealthy and takes full advantage of it, then such a person will surely scale the peaks of grandeur. The voice within spoke up, "So, are you implying that you too will scale the peaks of joy and grandeur one day? After all, you have been performing every *karma* of yours with a smile on your lips, while enjoying life to the fullest." Yes, absolutely! If this formula of mine truly works, then one day, even an ordinary cowherd like me must reach the highest peak of prosperity and grandeur.

Well, only time would tell whether this formula was truly efficacious. However, it is worth understanding here that to be successful in this world, even a self-realised person needs to acquire practical knowledge of the material world. I agree that the Soul is the knower of itself and experiences all the mysteries of this world. However, the art of emerging a winner in this world can only be learnt through practical knowledge of the material world. In other words, despite their self-realisation, even the greatest individuals cannot reach the peaks of grandeur or achieve success in this world without practical knowledge. Here, it is also worth noting that while it is easy to reject wealth and prosperity, earning it is very difficult. Therefore, in my opinion, a person can be called 'complete' only if he is a king on the outside and a sage within. If one must abdicate the throne to embrace renunciation, then the result is the same, and he would once again remain incomplete. Similarly, despite being a king, if a person is unable to enjoy life, then his kingship is rather pointless. To sum it up, a person can be considered 'complete' only if he is happy and blissful within, while also enjoying riches and grandeur externally. And once I understood this, I made up my mind to become complete. I'm sure you know that I've always valued completeness. In other words, I was already on the summit of joy; now, all that remained was to scale the pinnacle of prosperity.

The voice within exclaimed, 'Well, isn't that just brilliant, Krishna! This is verily an outstanding quality of yours. You no doubt want to aim for the sky, but at present, your very life hangs in uncertainty!' Well, so what? This is precisely the sign of a resolute person. And when one's resolve is strong, one can expect complete support from Nature too. If nothing else, this ideology had at least given me a purpose for leading a life in this material world. And for a *karmaveer* like me, the current situation provided both the opportunity and the circumstances. For, at this point in time, I was penniless and entirely without means. And with Jarasandha's ominous shadow trailing behind me, I couldn't possibly find any shelter or refuge. And if this was not enough, I was on my way to clash with Panchajanya—the very personification of death. Really, seen from this perspective, our lives could not have been any gloomier than they were now; we did not even know when death would swoop down on us and gobble us whole. But this was precisely the time to dream big, to dream of ruling the world. This is why I say that everyone should learn from me the art of indulging in flights of fancy.

Well, this is how we continued with our journey, passing through numerous towns, villages and marketplaces and enjoying ourselves to the hilt. With the reins of the chariot in my hands, the verdant countryside all around us, and bhaiya sitting next to me, what could be more enjoyable than this? In fact, we were so immersed in our enjoyment that we barely realised the passage of time; much to our surprise, twelve days had passed since we had embarked on this journey. Actually, the journey wasn't long; the distance could have easily been covered in a week. But since we were travelling at our own leisurely pace, enjoying the sights and sounds and indulging in delicious food, it took us an additional five days. Besides, the condition of the chariot and the horse were also partially responsible for this delay in our arrival. However, we finally made it to Prabhasa on the twelfth day. Prabhasa did not seem to be a thriving or highly developed town, but it stood out for its location. Situated along the seashore, this town made for a pretty sight. Well, this was the first time we had the opportunity to view the sea, and frankly speaking, its vastness was something we could never have imagined had we not seen it for ourselves! A huge body of water stretched far into the horizon as far as the eyes could see. When we first caught sight of it, both bhaiya and I were dumbstruck. In fact, so enchanted were we that instead of taking the path leading towards the town, we turned our chariot onto the path that led us to the seaside and brought it to a halt on the shore. Alighting from the chariot, we stretched our limbs and made our way towards the sea, watching the waves gently roll in and deposit their foam on the rocks. Perched on a rock, bhaiya and I spent hours gazing at this enchanting and idyllic view. After a while, we walked along the shore as far as our feet would carry us, leaving the horse unharnessed to roam freely. I have, in fact, no recollection of how many times I must have sat down and jumped to my feet again just to catch a better view of the waves and their playfulness. We just couldn't believe that there existed such a vast body of water in one place! Incredible, isn't it? I had even taken a sip of the water, but astonishingly, it was salty and did not seem potable. Perhaps, we couldn't drink it, but we could at least satiate our desire for bathing. With this in mind, bhaiya and I jumped into the sea. I cannot even begin to describe what fun it was to splash around in the water! By now, it was late afternoon and the sun was about to set too, yet we were reluctant to step out of the water, wanting to play around a little longer. It was natural, wasn't it? We cowherds, who could barely control our excitement at the sight of small ponds and lakes, were certainly not going to step out of the sea so easily. However, we had to put a stop to our fun as we were on a mission to rescue *Acharya's* son; this was definitely not a pleasure trip. So, finally, with great reluctance, we stepped out of the water and set off to meet Jaivik at the address *Acharya* had given us.

As we were nearing the city, we saw signs of habitation, with people moving about on some errand or the other. Everyone in this region appeared to have a dark complexion, which needless to say, pleased me. In comparison to them, my dusky complexion appeared glowing, and for the first time in my life, I felt a surge of pride at being fairer than others. Well, as soon as we entered the city, we were met with narrow streets and pathways with houses stacked next to each other due to lack of space. This too was our first experience of seeing such tightly squeezed houses, but yes, every house had its own veranda made of stone. In fact, the houses were so close to each other that one could roam the entire city just by hopping from one veranda to the other. The streets, in fact, were so narrow that it had become impossible to manoeuvre the chariot. So, we brought our chariot to a halt in an open space and set off on foot in search of the address. At last, we found the house! It looked quite ordinary in its appearance, but my eyes looked past it and settled on the man we had come to meet. The good news was, as soon as we met Jaivik and told him that we had been sent by *Acharya*, he greeted us respectfully. Moreover, he promptly made living arrangements for us, providing a private chamber to stay in. We were anyway exhausted from the journey—it was no small feat to have travelled so far over the course of twelve days—so putting all our questions about Punardutta on hold until the next day, we were compelled to take rest.

The next day, we partook of our meal with Jaivik, who lived with his wife and two children in this tiny house comprising two living quarters and one meeting chamber. After finishing our meal, we headed to the meeting chamber and sat down on a couple of mats that had been rolled out for us. At present, my attention was focused entirely on my goal of paying my *gurudakshina*, and that too, to such an extent that even while having a casual conversation, I had collected quite a bit of information about Panchajanya from Jaivik. According to the latter, not only was Panchajanya a demon king but also a notorious bandit and pirate who had several warships in his possession. Apart from this, he had a modern and well-equipped army. Due to all these factors, he was able to plunder numerous coastal towns such as Prabhasa at his will. Many a time, his soldiers would even carry off girls from the village, while no one could raise a murmur of protest, leave alone challenge them. Finally, seeing no way out, the inhabitants of Prabhasa came up with the best solution possible to tackle this problem. They began to pay a monthly tax to Panchajanya to rid themselves of the sword of terror hanging above their heads. And to ensure their prolonged safety and security, the inhabitants were still paying this tax. This was all the information Jaivik could provide about Panchajanya, but it was enough for me. Do you not comprehend? Jaivik's narrative had made it clear that I had unknowingly set off on the most difficult journey of my life! Certainly, the goal was far-fetched, but there was no alternative; because it was not in my nature to turn tail and flee midway. Hence, I could move in only one direction—forward. However, the path ahead remained elusive, as I was unsure of how to proceed from here. Viewed from this perspective, Jarasandha seemed a far better opponent, for, we could at least flee from him. And in any case, we had not chosen to take up a fight with him; it was my aunts who had sent him chasing after us. But taking up the cudgels against Panchajanya was my own choice. I had gotten carried away by the idea that I had to offer to pay my *gurudakshina*. Suddenly, the voice in my head chided, 'What do you mean you got carried away? Is it not your responsibility to wipe away *Acharya-ma's* tears?' I instantly stilled the voice, saying that it most definitely was. Besides, who would pass up the wonderful opportunity to repay such a great *Acharya*? It was just that my ego had become fearful for a brief moment. Now, although I had quietened the voice within, I was still at sea not knowing the direction I needed to take to reach my destination. The enemy was so powerful and alert that not even a wisp of breeze could waft through his territory without his knowledge. This being the case, how were we to accomplish the mission we had set out to achieve? Well, regardless of how impossible the task seemed, I had to gird up my loins and accomplish it at any cost. Thus, after much deliberation, I posed a question to Jaivik, "What if a person is unable to pay the tax?"

Jaivik said, "Then he has to arrange for a guarantor. They take the guarantor with them and release him only after all the dues are paid."

That was it! I had found a way in. I would become the collateral or guarantor that Jaivik would arrange, and this would pave the way for me to reach Panchajanya's capital without having to fight or lock horns with him. Once we reached the capital, we would see what steps had to be taken next. Thinking on these lines, I said to Jaivik, "Do not pay your tax this time. In return, we will go with them as your guarantor."

"No, how can I agree to this?" replied an alarmed Jaivik, "First of all, you are my guests; I cannot let you become my guarantor. Secondly, Panchajanya, as ruthless as he is, subjects all the guarantors to immense hardships. I have even heard that his men torture them as well. How can I knowingly push you two—my guests—into the gates of hell?"

He was absolutely right and hearing him speak with so much concern for our safety had touched my heart. Indeed, nothing could make me happier than knowing that a person realises his duty and puts it before his self-interest. But even though he was right, I had to enter the lion's den, come hell or high water. And when I had already put my life at risk, why should I be scared of what Panchajanya may do to us? 'Let him torture us; let him turn us into slaves. We will endure everything.' Thinking thus, I explained my viewpoint to Jaivik saying, "Do not worry, Jaivik. Actually, we have made a promise to *Acharya* Sandipani that we will rescue his son, Punardutta, from Panchajanya's clutches to repay our *gurudakshina* to him. So, we will have to

reach Panchajanya at any cost. You will actually be helping us by allowing us to become your guarantor."

When Jaivik realised that our intention was to rescue Punardutta, he did not argue further. I could gauge from his demeanour that *Acharya*'s pain was no secret to him and he too wanted to see Punardutta set free. As for me, I was glad to have found a way to enter Panchajanya's kingdom. However, there were still seven days before Panchajanya's ship would arrive at Prabhasa. Until then, there was not much to do except spend those days in the town. So, even in this new place, we set up a daily routine…and yes, you have guessed it right, visiting the seashore every morning and evening became a significant part of our routine. We would partake of the evening meal at Jaivik's house and if we had time to spare, we would loiter around Prabhasa or visit the market; otherwise we spent most of our time at the seashore, where we would also take our evening bath. Sitting for hours by the sea, we would gaze at the vast body of water spread like a sheet of shimmering silver. At any rate, what else could we do in this place? It was already decided that we would go as guarantors in lieu of Jaivik's non-payment of taxes. We did not know what the future held in store for us, but for now, we could at least enjoy the enchanting sea to our hearts' content. Of course, I also utilised the time available to glean as much information about Punardutta as possible. Unfortunately, the only information Jaivik had was that Panchajanya had abducted Punardutta, but he had no clue about where he was held as a prisoner…or whether he was even alive or dead.

Whiling away our time in this manner, I noticed a peculiar trait in the inhabitants of Prabhasa. Everyone here was fond of wine. Although the inhabitants of Mathura also drank wine, in Prabhasa, people were habituated to partaking of wine with every meal. This was fine, but the interesting part was that bhaiya had developed a taste for it and had even begun to enjoy it. Though I was saved from its influence, bhaiya was caught under its spell and had, in fact, become addicted to it. Now, every evening, as per our daily routine, we would head to the seashore where he would relax and sip his wine, while I would give him company by playing my flute. Here, in Prabhasa, I had learnt a lot of new words too. I also noticed that the style of dressing, dietary habits and the customs and traditions of the region were vastly different from what we were accustomed to. This fascinated me immensely, and I found myself keenly observing the diversity of this region, paying attention to the minutest details.

The difference in our tastes and needs could also be seen in the commodities available in the marketplace. Everything was different here, from the clothes and jewellery to the eating habits and the food consumed in this region. The people here wore *dhotis*[28] and garments in a wide range of vibrant colours. In places like Mathura and Ujjaini, I had seen clothes mostly in white, yellow, pink and saffron hues. However, the inhabitants of Prabhasa wore bold and vibrant colours such as red, green, blue and purple. Most notably, these clothes of myriad hues looked outlandish on the dark-complexioned inhabitants, perhaps because I was seeing these colour combinations for the first time. The marketplace in this region was also completely different from the one in Mathura. Here, the shops selling clothes, jewellery and foodstuff were few in number. In contrast to them, huge shops catering to other businesses were in majority. As I explored the place, I noticed that they specialised in ironmongery and carpentry, and one could hear the sound of metal clanging all day long from the shops on either side of the road. Well, be that as it may! At present, I realised this was our seventh day in Prabhasa and Panchajanya's ships were expected to arrive any time.

Even on the day the ships were due, bhaiya and I were loitering in the marketplace. As daily visitors and guests of Jaivik, we had become acquainted with quite a few locals. Although we faced challenges in communicating with them due to our languages being different, we were still able to understand each other. Presently, bhaiya was trying to comprehend the workmanship required in the making of iron wheels in a big shop, while I sat in a small clothes shop, trying to understand how they made the garments. Then, all of a sudden, I could sense commotion all around, and I turned to see people run helter-skelter. The shops too hastened to close down their shutters. Indeed, it seemed as if an earthquake had struck Prabhasa, as everyone started racing towards their homes. The girls in the marketplace disappeared in a flash, the way a deluge wipes out crops in a field. Even as we stood and watched perplexed, an atmosphere of fear and terror gripped Prabhasa. Then all of a sudden, I heard a searing gust of wind sounding the warning, "The ships are coming! The ships are coming!" It was then that I realised what the commotion was all about. Panchajanya's ships were spotted nearing the shoreline. Well, I expected it, but seeing the terror on the faces of the people, I was filled with deep apprehension, as I thought to myself, 'What have you gotten yourself into, Krishna! If a person could inject terror in the hearts of the people in other kingdoms, how powerful must he be in his own kingdom?!' Well, I should have thought of all this before embarking on this journey. Now, we had to face whatever came our way. Besides, even if we breathed our last on this mission, we would have died trying to pay *gurudakshina* to our teacher. At the very least, we wouldn't have died in vain!

With these thoughts surging through my mind, we raced towards Jaivik's house. Today, Jaivik seemed busier than usual and quite worried too.

28. *Dhoti* - A garment worn by men around the lower half of the body.

Moreover, his entire family had gathered in the kitchen, preparing a variety of dishes, each more delicious than the other. Perhaps, Jaivik wanted to feed us well before sending us to Panchajanya to get slaughtered. Bhaiya and I were delighted, thinking that we would at least get to enjoy a hearty meal. However, our beautiful dream was short-lived, as the reality was far from what we imagined. It turned out that it was Jaivik's turn to feed the soldiers of Panchajanya, and the entire family was therefore busy preparing a meal for them.

No matter, but seeing us stand at the threshold of the kitchen, we were instructed to go and wait in our chamber and stay quiet. Abiding by their instruction, we went to our chamber and sat on the bed. But our restless state would not allow us to sit still. So, we started peeping outside the tiny window. Argh! We were stuck in a strange situation. We had already been told not to leave the chamber, and Jaivik and his family had no interest in attending to us. Moreover, the delicious aroma wafting from the kitchen only aggravated our hunger. Besides, it was mealtime for us gluttons! Now, I had managed to stay calm, but bhaiya began to seethe with anger. You are already aware that it was impossible for him to control his hunger; besides, the aroma of good food and the fact that we were being ignored was too much for him to bear. He thus turned to me and exploded, "Do you see how cruel Jaivik is? He has not called us for lunch yet. He feeds us simple fare every day, and for these demons, he is preparing a splendid feast. Oh, just look at the hospitality they are extending to their enemies! I think it's time to teach this scoundrel a lesson."

Clearly, it was the hunger pangs that had driven bhaiya berserk, his ego taking the affront too strongly. Firstly, he was ravenous, and to add fuel to the fire, he felt humiliated. These were the two things in the world that angered bhaiya the most. Now, his ego and his hunger may have been his weaknesses, but how would teaching Jaivik a lesson help? Fortunately, I was adept at pacifying bhaiya; else, he would have really brought the roof down with his outburst. At once, I began pacifying him saying, "Bhaiya, you are getting worked up unnecessarily. This hospitality is being accorded not to please the demons, but to ward off the terror wreaked by them." However, driven mad by hunger, bhaiya was in no mood to listen; instead, he now directed his fury at me. Oh, wasn't this incredible! I had to pay the price just because he was hungry. Come to think of it, I too was fond of eating, but despite my hunger, I managed to control myself. And the credit for this went to the unique quality I possessed: the awareness that our journey to repay *Acharya* had begun the very moment we had set foot in Prabhasa. To me, whatever we had to endure was simply the next step in our endeavour to offer *gurudakshin*a to *Acharya*.

Seated on the bed in our chamber, gazing out the window for what felt like an eternity, I was finally relieved that the trying period had come to an end. Soon after the demons had departed, Jaivik called us. As soon as the summons came, bhaiya calmed down a little, and as soon as he was served the delicious food, his anger dissipated instantly. Needless to add, both of us devoured our meals with great relish. Jaivik was amazed at our appetite. Having partaken our meal, bhaiya quickly nodded off to sleep, but I tossed and turned in bed, knowing fully well that this was our last day as free men. The following day, we would be shackled and branded as slaves of Panchajanya. I was not concerned about myself, but I was definitely worried about bhaiya. One way or the other, he was bound to vent his anger at me. If just a delayed meal could upset him so much, I could well imagine how distressed he would become by the atrocities our captors would inflict on us from the next day onwards. Well, do I really need to wonder about his reaction? Whatever atrocities he would be subjected to, he would surely vent it out on me a hundredfold. It was this very trepidation that had gripped me, robbing me of my sleep. Really, after reaching Panchajanya's lair, should I be concentrating on placating bhaiya or focusing on trying to free Punardutta? I thus spent the entire night preparing myself for the avalanche of troubles I was wont to face.

Well, with the dawn of a new day, a fresh chapter of *karma* was about to commence in my life. I was about to take a decisive step in my journey to repay my great teacher. After lunch, bhaiya and I set off with Jaivik. On reaching the seaside, we were struck by the scene that met our eyes. Bordering the sea, a large platform—a flattened surface of rocks and boulders—had been erected. Two massive ships were anchored to it. Now, we had certainly seen small boats in Mathura and Ujjaini which could seat two to four people. But these ships were so gigantic that twenty-five such small boats could easily fit into them. On the other side, the port was bustling with hundreds of people and goods. Around two hundred people were present at the port at this time, and verily, bhaiya and I stood apart in the crowd. Looking into the distance, we could see a serpentine queue waiting outside a ship. Clearly, these were the people who would stand as guarantors, and with that in mind, Jaivik guided us towards them. Though I stood in the queue, my eyes were fixed on the ship, filled with awe and wonder. As for Jaivik, seeing us join the queue of people who had stepped forth as guarantors, he looked crestfallen. Naturally, he did not find it agreeable to hand us over as guarantors. Well, it was not as if we were fond of the idea ourselves, but the satisfaction of having the opportunity to repay *Acharya* far outweighed the distress. However, the same could not be said for bhaiya, who was growing restless from standing in the queue. Well,

I thought it best to leave him alone. Why let his restlessness affect me? So, I turned my attention to the activities of the soldiers who were streaming in and out of the ship. At that moment, I felt as if I had mentally entered into a battle with Panchajanya!

The individuals whose names were being called out stepped forward and handed over their belongings as payment to the soldiers. Those who couldn't pay up were handing over the individuals they had brought along as guarantors. Inside the ship, the soldiers were housing both the people and the belongings, and judging by the manner in which they were doing it, it was clear that for them, there was no difference between the goods and the people. In short, it was crystal clear how our time would be spent from this point onwards. After a long wait, it was finally Jaivik's turn. As per our plan, Jaivik folded his hands and pleaded his inability to pay the tax. The officer in charge gave him an icy stare before barking at him to present his guarantor.

While Jaivik did not say anything, he nudged us towards the officer. With that, the soldiers shoved us onto the ship and ordered us to sit on the deck. This area of the ship was teeming with guarantors. Being pushed around so unceremoniously, bhaiya was beside himself with anger; naturally, his ego could not tolerate this affront. In contrast to him, I quietly sat cross-legged on the floor, as if nothing untoward had happened. For me, every incident was a step in my journey to pay my *gurudakshina* to my teacher. And that being the case, what difference does honour or dishonour make? We were made to sit at the aft of the ship, away from the hull. Oh, and I mustn't forget to mention that we were surrounded by soldiers, seated comfortably on wooden benches in front of us, armed with the most modern weapons. Looking at them, I began to wonder, if the ship had such well-armed soldiers, what must be the level of security in the capital city? Another question followed close on the heels of the first one. Would this really be the last journey of our lives? For a brief moment, I was surprised that self-doubt had crept in. So, shaking it off, I took a firm grip on myself and reassured my mind. After all, it is our own vibrations of self-doubt that spoil the results, while our confidence helps us emerge victorious. With this thought, I focused on building my self-confidence. I told myself, 'So what if Panchajanya has a huge army? I too am a mastermind!'

By evening, the ships finally weighed anchor and hoisted their sails. I found this quite enjoyable, and like an inquisitive child, I kept craning my neck to peer outside. Oh, how I wished I could sit where the soldiers were. Surely, the view outside would be much clearer from those seats. Unfortunately, we were not destined to partake in this pleasure as we were slaves. This was also my first experience as a slave, and after this experience, I can say with certainty that there is no suffering worse than that of a slave. Each ship carried around fifty guarantors, and I must confess, I found some comfort in the large number, knowing we weren't alone. Indeed, it is always better to be in a large group when walking into the jaws of danger. On the other hand, by my estimates, there were about twenty soldiers in each of the ships. As for the ship, it was constructed entirely out of wood and housed a cabin in the centre, with enough space outside the cabin to seat us slaves. Along the sides of the ship, across the entire length, long wooden benches were built for seating the soldiers. On either side of the ship, there were around eight people who were rowing it with wooden oars. In front of us was a huge net made of ropes, on top of which hung a massive pennant. Though we found ourselves in a tricky situation, the cool breeze that wafted in as the ship sailed brought us some relief.

It wasn't for too long that we had been sailing in this manner when the soldiers decided to give us a taste of what it really meant to be slaves. They went around tying everyone's hands with rope, and although this was uncalled for, I quietly fell into line and allowed myself to be bound. However, when it was bhaiya's turn to be tied, he shot a glaring look at me, which spoke volumes of the rage he suppressed within. His anger was justified, for, I was the culprit. It was my ardent wish to pay *gurudakshina* to *Acharya*. And admittedly, every human being has to bear the consequences of his actions. But the matter did not end there. Not content with merely tying us, the soldiers were bent on snatching away bhaiya's plough and mace as well. This action of theirs made matters worse. Fury spouting from his eyes, bhaiya began to protest against this move. Seeing the situation deteriorate, I jumped into the fray and tried my best to placate him. I explained, "Bhaiya, we are no longer free men; we are slaves. Just think, are slaves allowed to carry weapons?" Well, he relented and handed over his weapons to the soldiers, albeit reluctantly. Now, although he had given up his weapons, it was clear from his expression that he was extremely annoyed with me. Firstly, it was not in his nature to be subservient to anyone; secondly, if anyone were to even lay a finger on his mace, he would turn it into the war of wars! This was the very difference between my way of thinking and that of others. In my understanding, if bhaiya did not accept being enslaved now, then it implied that he did not want to rescue Punardutta either. And in my thinking, by doing so, he was shying away from paying his *gurudakshina*. Contrary to him, paying *gurudakshina* was a duty for me; and once I accepted something as my duty, I would surrender myself to it completely. Admittedly, rescuing Punardutta from Panchajanya's clutches was a formidable task—a long and onerous process, if you will. It was akin to climbing a steep mountain, and the only way to do that was to take one step

at a time. For me, enduring humiliation, having my hands tied, convincing bhaiya to give up the mace and so on were merely steps that constituted that climb. And I knew that only after taking many such steps would we finally complete our mission.

It was good that I was well acquainted with bhaiya's nature; similarly, I was no stranger to the challenges this journey posed. I had, of course, anticipated that I would have to face two major hurdles—bhaiya's ego and Panchajanya's power. And verily, I had prepared myself to face both before setting out on this mission. At any rate, what difference would any of this have made to me? I had become accustomed to living in a constant state of struggle—tackling them and even enjoying these very struggles, considering them to be a *raasa.*[29] For, had I relied on Nature or circumstances for my happiness and joy, I would have long forgotten how to even smile! For that matter, I had to contend with another struggle—a struggle with myself. I had to keep my self-confidence intact under all circumstances, for, how else would I emerge victorious? And since winning had become a habit with me, I obviously could not fall out of habit. Besides, I had to win this battle to pay my *gurudakshina* to my great teacher as well. And to emerge victorious in a great war, it is imperative to work on several fronts simultaneously, and this was precisely what I was doing. On one hand, my mind was busy assessing Panchajanya's might, while on the other, it was keenly observing the soldiers' activities on the ship. However, I was not overly worried about any of this; my real worry was bhaiya. Needless to say, a considerable amount of my energy was being spent in keeping him in check. Fortunately for me, I viewed all of life's struggles as nothing but a game. And if one were to truly examine their struggles, they too would seem like nothing more than a game! I'm telling you the truth. In fact, at that moment, I was playing a game with both bhaiya and Panchajanya's soldiers. The soldiers had tried to make bhaiya furious by tying his hands together, after which I had somehow managed to calm him down thus winning this game. Thereafter, the soldiers had annoyed bhaiya once again by taking away his mace, but I beat them yet again by succeeding in pacifying bhaiya. So, tell me, was this not a game played out between Panchajanya's soldiers and me? The only unfortunate aspect of this game was that bhaiya had ended up becoming a pawn. But then, the ego is bound to be used as a plaything by others. This is because the ego has no existence of its own; it gauges its worth based on others' opinion of it. People generally say that two heads are better than one, but from my current experience, I can say that one is definitely better, unless of course the two in question are perfectly in sync with each other. But if the second person is of an arrogant and adamant disposition, then a lot of energy is expended in managing that person.

29. *Raasa* - Game or play.

Well, this game continued all day long, and finally, as the sun dipped on the horizon, dusk came rolling in, enveloping us all in a shroud of darkness. Our hands had become stiff and numb due to being tied up, but it did not matter, because soon enough, the moon emerged from behind the clouds. It was the night of *Poornima*[30] and the moon shining brightly overhead had cast its radiance all around us. As you are aware, the moon always held a special place in my heart, especially the full moon! And at any rate, in view of our current situation, it was far better to shift our attention elsewhere. So, forgetting all discomfort, I immersed myself in marvelling at the sight of the moon illuminating the night sky. So lost was I in the mystical charm of the soft, white moon that I began to weave dreams of taking up residence there! Wasn't I a little crazy? I was dreaming of residing on the moon when I had no place of my own on Earth! Plonked on the floor with my hands bound in rope, sailing into the jaws of death, and yet, weaving dreams of settling on the moon…tell me, could there be a person more optimistic than me? However, there was yet another aspect to indulging in such thoughts. If the poor and the enslaved don't dream, who will? I was already poor, and now, I had become a slave too. So, why not act as per the dictates of one's circumstances? Weave beautiful dreams and enjoy them thoroughly! Another point worth noting was that instead of spinning dreams and losing himself in them, if a slave turned his attention to the harsh reality, wouldn't his condition be the same as bhaiya's? In fact, it is in these very moments of life that it becomes essential to dream. Well, it was dinner time now, made evident by the pangs of hunger which had begun to gnaw at us. The soldiers had already started eating, but wait a moment…why were we not being served? Alas, there was no dinner for us, as we were slaves! It appeared that we would have to go to sleep on an empty stomach. Argh! The hunger was slowly becoming unbearable, driving us mad, and to make matters worse, the soldiers were devouring their meal right in front of us. Now, I could bear with this situation, but I'm sure you can imagine the torment bhaiya must have been going through. That's right! Trouble had knocked on Kanhaiya's door yet again. It would certainly be difficult to control him now. But no matter, this was all a game for me anyway, the only difference being, the opponent was different this time. First, it was the soldiers who were aggravating bhaiya's anger, and now it was his hunger that was making him furious. As for me, I had to somehow find a way to pacify him and win this game too.

For that matter, I was hungry too, but I was not one to fret over problems that had no solution. In fact, I had elucidated this to Arjuna in the Gita, *'In life, one shouldn't unnecessarily worry about matters that are unalterable.'*[31] However, at present, bhaiya's hunger was gradually taking on a monstrous form. His fury had reached its peak and before he became

30. *Poornima* - Full moon night.
31. Shrimad Bhagavad Gita, Chapter – 2, Verse – 27.

uncontrollable, it was imperative to calm him down; else he could become violent and create havoc. So, redoubling my effort, I said to him very calmly, “Bhaiya, why are you getting angry for no reason? The fire of your anger will burn only you!”

Hearing this, bhaiya lashed out at me, “Shut up! You are the root cause of this fracas. If only I had burst open the head of the soldier when he was trying to take my mace away...” Saying this, bhaiya lapsed into silence. Hearing his outburst, I was just about to open my mouth when he exploded once again, “Oh, spare me your nonsense! It is easy for you to give advice when you haven’t had to part with your discus; nor have they taken away your precious flute!”

Oh, will you look at that! First, bhaiya was unhappy because his hands were tied, then he was outraged because he had lost his mace and plough. Later, he became furious on account of his hunger, and his present grouse was: why had they not taken away my flute and discus? Bah! Who would explain to bhaiya that discus and flute are not weapons? Why did he have to get irritated unnecessarily by comparing himself to me? But I suppose it was good in a way, for, at least his anger had finally found an outlet. For, suppressed anger often takes a more frightening form when it is released.

However, let us put this aside, for, all of a sudden, we saw giant waves rising in the sea and lashing the ship. Needless to say, the sight was terrifying. In fact, the ship started rocking so violently that even the soldiers were alarmed. Tamas, the captain of the ship, could be seen running helter-skelter on the deck. The apprehension on his face indicated that something terrible was afoot. Soon, a sense of panic took over everyone on the ship, each heart palpitating with fear. My gaze was fixed on Tamas, my eyes following him in whichever direction he darted, hoping that I’d be able to comprehend the problem at hand. But there was no question of me understanding anything, for, this was the first time I had seen a ship in my life, let alone travel in one. Besides, we were not being apprised of the calamity that had struck us. In fact, even the soldiers’ condition wasn’t very different from ours. They too seemed to have been kept in the dark. But even so, one of them worked up the courage to ask Tamas, who was still darting around the ship, about what was going on.

A bewildered Tamas scratched his head and replied, “I’ve made a blunder. I forgot that it’s a full moon night and hence the high tide, and today, the sea is quite rough too. Now, there is very little hope of our survival. It looks like the ship will come to rest only after drowning us all.” Saying this, he handed a bunch of oars to a few soldiers standing nearby and barked at them to start rowing. But honestly, the ship was being tossed around so violently that I didn’t think merely rowing hard would make any difference.

Oh, just see! Even before Panchajanya could lay his hands on us, his ship was conspiring to put us to death. Really, death and I were inseparable! It would suddenly spring out of nowhere, catching me unawares. Having said that, I had clashed with death on so many occasions that I had become habituated to defeating it. Indeed, how could I surrender such a precious life in the hands of death without putting up a fight! If you think about it, difficulties storm into one's life to test one's abilities; that being the case, if a person does not take action in such times of distress, when will he? It is verily in times of trouble that a person has to employ not just the strength of his body and mind, but also the power of his Soul. So, thinking thus, I began to keenly observe the flurry of activities on the ship in order to gauge what was going on.

But oh, what could I possibly understand? It was only now that I had learnt that a full moon night triggers a high tide in the sea. And verily, how could I have known this before? After all, this was the first time I had set my eyes on the sea and seafaring ships. Even so, I had to make every effort to avert death. It's simple really—hope is alive as long as you are alive. Moreover, all my experiences in life had shown me that 'action' is the magic that can ward off even the most certain death! Finally, after watching the drama play out for some time and still failing to comprehend anything, I mustered the courage to ask the captain directly, "Is there no way we can save the ship?"

Hearing my question, Tamas glared balefully at me, but the very next moment, he was baffled to see a serene smile play on my lips. Astonished by my calmness, he was thrown off guard. I can say that, all of a sudden, my confidence stood out like a beacon among all the frightened people, making me seem unique. And this was precisely the difference between the others and me. Everyone knew how to fear and panic in the smallest of instances, but no one believed in taking action. Contrary to them, I believed in action. If something can be done, then it should be done; if not, one must accept the consequences, but no matter what, one should always remain cheerful. And at present, this very calm and unperturbed nature of mine was beginning to pay off. My assured demeanour finally compelled Tamas to provide an answer. Speaking without much hope, he said, "There is only one solution. If we can somehow cut the rope holding up the main sail, we can be saved."

Instantly, I looked at the mast and then at the rope that was holding the sail. The rope was indeed tied at a great height. Considering the jerky motion of the ship, it seemed almost impossible for someone to climb up the mast, cut the rope and release the sail. So, did that mean there was no way to save ourselves now? But all of a sudden, I was struck by another thought, 'If death was afoot, it was far better to die attempting to untie the sail than wait for the ship to sink.' I was lost in this thought, when suddenly, my hand brushed against my discus. Aha! I had found the solution. In fact, I now had the upper hand in this game. The predicament we were faced with was not a difficult task for my discus at all. Perhaps, the soldiers' mistake in not taking it away allowed me the opportunity to make an impression on Panchajanya's soldiers. At any rate, death had always opened the path for me to remain alive. So, naturally, as soon as the thought of using the discus struck me, a wave of zest washed over me. The future of Panchajanya's ship was in my hands now. So, continuing in the same flow, I asked Tamas airily, "What if I bring the sail down?"

He replied, "Then I will do whatever you say."

I asked, "Will our hands be untied then?"

Before he could respond, bhaiya jumped in and said, "And while you are at it, you will also have to return my mace and plough!"

Hearing this, I smiled and added, "Not only this, you will have to serve him a meal as well!"

What would a drowning man not do in order to survive?! All our conditions were accepted without question. However, only my shackles were removed at first. Since I was the one who had promised to deliver, naturally, it was my chains that needed to be removed. In any case, I had merely said I will do the needful; the rope had not been untied yet. So, obviously, bhaiya couldn't be freed right away. Well, as soon as my hands were free, I became the centre of attention, with all eyes now riveted on me. The only thought racing through everyone's minds was, how would I manage to climb the mast in such stormy conditions? But little did they know that I did not have to climb the rope to cut it; I simply had to stand on the deck and demonstrate the magic of my discus. So, fishing the discus out, I immediately aimed at the ropes and hurled my discus at it. In a split second, the discus sliced through the ropes, and as soon as they were cut, the sail fell down and landed with a thud on the deck. Seeing the sail come down, a roar of applause rent the air. Tamas was beside himself with joy, while the soldiers were elated too. Bhaiya's hands were untied instantly, and as soon as he was freed, he puffed up his chest and stood tall with pride. It was, of course, a matter of great pride for him—after all, it was his own brother who had just saved the doomed ship. On this momentous note, the two of us quickly began to hold sway over the entire ship.

This was all great, but my attention was caught by something even more exciting. In two long steps, I hopped over to the wooden benches and plopped down with a sigh and a smile. It was a wish I had clung to since the moment I first set foot on this ship. Watching the huge waves lash against the ship and the resounding splash they created, I sat mesmerised, and not to mention the radiance of the full moon. Oh, what an enchanting scene it was, enough to put anyone in a blissful state! However, despite my joy, I glanced at the other slaves, who were clearly in great discomfort with their hands tied. Of course, at present, everyone did seem relieved at having been saved from certain death. It was then that I noticed, Tamas' face had suddenly turned pale. He walked with slow, heavy steps and silently stood in a corner. I could not fathom this sudden change. The ship had been saved, yet the captain seemed unhappy; the matter was beyond comprehension. Well, since there were no restrictions on my movements now, I walked over to him out of curiosity. He was so engrossed in his thoughts that even when I went and stood by his side, he did not react. But from his expression, I could clearly make out that he was troubled. On prodding a little, the matter became apparent. With great humility, he asked me, "Can you release the sail of the ship that is following us too?"

Ah! It was only then that I understood the cause of his anxiety. The issue was simple and straightforward. The ship trailing us must also be facing the same problem that our ship had run into, so the captain's anxiety was justified. Considering the precarious nature of the situation, instead of putting on airs, I nodded in assent without hesitation. As soon as I agreed, he jumped for joy. Then, with folded hands, he gestured to me as if to say, "So, what are you waiting for, mister? Kindly cut the ropes."

Well, alright! I won't put on airs. But I could help the other ship only if we could spot it, right? We began scanning the surroundings, but saw no sign of it. Tamas was terrified, as the thought that perhaps the other ship had capsized gripped him. But although he was worried, he was extremely grateful to me. For, I had not only saved his life but also his ship. So, even though he was worried about the other ship, he did not forget the mores of hospitality and respectfully led bhaiya and me towards his cabin, where we were served food as well as wine. Ah! It was only now that I realised that this section in the centre of the ship which looked like a house was actually the sitting chamber of the captain. Though the chamber was tiny, it was magnificent. Seating arrangements were made on three sides, and there were three windows to the right, through which one could clearly see the sea. Whatever the case may be, I could not deny that the circumstances had taken a complete volte-face. While bhaiya and I were beginning to enjoy ourselves, Tamas, on the other hand, was becoming increasingly restless. Not long before the storm hit, we were shackled in chains, while he seemed completely carefree. Indeed, it doesn't take long for the tables to turn! Still, to establish a rapport with him, I asked, "Why are you so anxious? At least our ship is safe now."

He replied unhappily, "That's alright, but due to my oversight, the other ship has sunk. For this loss, King Panchajanya will never spare me. He will surely put me to death."

Oh, this was a matter of grave concern…not just for him but for me too. After all, I had just become friends with an important official. If he were to be put to death, how would I accomplish the formidable task I had set out to do? Seen from another perspective, it was also a bit frightening to think about how terrifying Panchajanya must be, if even his ministers quaked at the thought of displeasing him. This implied that the adversary was exceptionally strong, making it clear that any attempt to rescue Punardutta could only be initiated through Tamas. Indeed, in such a strange and dangerous place, it was necessary to garner both the support and assistance of an amiable official. Thus, it had become necessary to save Tamas. But how could I save him from Panchajanya? How could I interfere in the proceedings of a royal court in an unfamiliar kingdom? It was not as if Panchajanya was at my beck and call, and if I asked him to release Tamas, he would gladly do so. Whereas according to Tamas, the reality was that Panchajanya would not spare him, and I would have to become a mute spectator and watch him die. If that were to happen, I would not only lose an influential friend whom I had gained with much effort, but all my hopes of rescuing Punardutta would also be shattered. In short, no matter which way I looked at the situation, I needed both Tamas' friendship and influence. Now, a person may have a thousand needs, but what really counts is how he goes about fulfilling them. This was the issue here as well. Tamas had made a mistake, the punishment for which would be decided by King Panchajanya…what could I do about it? I couldn't change anything, but the need of the hour was such that it demanded some effort on my part. Basically, I not only had to come up with a plan, but also put it into action.

Oblivious to the hindrance in our mission, bhaiya was busy gorging on food and drinks. In any case, he had only two responsibilities: one, to love me ardently, and two, to use his strength when needed. As for thinking and decision-making, he had handed over that responsibility to me ever since we were children. And, at present, that was exactly what I was trying to do. I was constantly thinking of a way to save Tamas' life. It was certainly the most peculiar scene: three people were sitting in the chamber and the emotional state of each one was starkly different. While Tamas was worried, I was lost in thought, and bhaiya was relishing the food laid out before him. But as they say, if you ponder over a problem at length and in the right direction, you often come up with a brilliant solution. And that is exactly what transpired with me as well. An ingenious thought crossed my mind; when there are so many officials on board, why should the noose be tightened around Tamas' head only? Perhaps, because he was the senior-most officer on this ship. This meant that if I could find another officer on board who was at a higher position than Tamas and put the blame on him, then Tamas and my hopes could both be saved. With this thought, I enquired of him, "Tell me, friend, is there a minister or officer who is senior to you on board this ship?"

He replied, "Yes, General Chandak is aboard this ship. In fact, the king has also appointed him the Chief Minister. He is resting in the cabin next door."

I lit up with joy on hearing this. Addressing Tamas confidently, I said, "There is no need for you to worry now! Take me to his cabin and inform him about the ship that has sunk. At the same time, introduce me to him and tell him that it was I who saved this ship. Then, just wait and watch how I save you from Panchajanya's wrath!"

Well, do I really need to tell you about his reaction? He was already impressed with the impressive feat I had performed in saving his ship, and now, I had given him the hope that his life could also be saved. So, there was no question of him refusing the idea I had proposed. He shot up from his seat and leaving bhaiya behind, the two of us proceeded towards the cabin which was adjacent to Tamas' and knocked on the door. Stepping into the cabin, at first glance, I could see that it was not only bigger than Tamas' cabin, but also equipped with many more amenities. Chandak was reclining with his legs stretched out, sipping wine, while I stood behind Tamas near the door. Now, if I were to compare the physique of these two men, Tamas was of medium build, but Chandak was extremely tall and well-built. His face was rather long, and he had small, close-set eyes and a swarthy complexion. Interestingly, though not good-looking, he still had a very attractive and imposing personality. So, there was no question of directly confronting him. Well, the moment Tamas informed him about the sinking of the ship, he glared at him threateningly. Then, after a few seconds of silence, he asked with a fierce growl, "How?"

Hearing the ominous implication in his tone, Tamas began to tremble. In a voice quivering with fright, he replied, "Actually, it skipped my mind that it is a full moon night."

This time, Chandak spoke in a chilling tone, "Then be ready to receive the death sentence!"

Standing behind Tamas, I remained silent like a spectator, listening to their exchange of words. Unfortunately, in his nervousness, Tamas made another blunder by forgetting to introduce me. Hence, seeing no alternative, I jumped into the conversation without any introduction and, addressing Chandak directly, said, "Can I say something, please?"

It was only now that Chandak noticed my presence. Looking at me with disdain, he asked Tamas, "Who is he? And why have you brought him here?"

Realising that he had not introduced me, Tamas immediately corrected his mistake and said, "Oh! He is Jaivik's guarantor. He is very brave and clever. Actually, he is the one who saved our ship from capsizing!"

When he heard this, Chandak's piercing gaze bore into me as it travelled from head to toe, trying to gauge whether I could really save a huge ship from sinking. From his expression, it was evident that he found this hard to believe, but because Tamas had said so, he had to believe it. After a moment's silence, he addressed me directly, "Alright. What do you have to say?"

Thinking on my feet, I reckoned that a direct attack was far better than beating around the bush, for, I may not get a second chance. In fact, the man might just throw me out of his cabin if he became enraged! Thus, wearing a worried expression, I said, "I've been standing here all this while, listening to your conversation. Do forgive me for saying this, but I think that you too will receive the death sentence."

Hearing these ominous words, Chandak was taken aback and stammered, "W...w...why? Why me?"

His shocked expression was proof that my arrow had found its mark. So, why wait now! I had brought along the trump card with me, so employing it at the right moment, I launched into an explanation, "As a rule, if a junior officer takes a wrong decision, it is the responsibility of the senior officer to rectify it. I reckon the king will consider you equally guilty in this case."

Hearing this, Chandak looked at me in stunned disbelief. He realised that every word spoken by me was absolutely true. Silence took over the cabin as Chandak sat lost in thought. But yes, Tamas appeared somewhat relieved. Of course, he must have thought that two people sharing the blame was better than one! Well, this was between them. For me, I reckoned that Chandak's nervousness was the very ladder that would lead to the successful completion of my mission. Because now, along with Tamas, even Chandak had started quaking with fear, and it is always easy to manipulate and control a person who is terrified. Nevertheless, it was I who finally broke the silence in the cabin. After all, who else could? Neither of them was in a condition to react or do anything, staring as they were at the spectre of death; whereas for me, this was the perfect opportunity to strike. So, coming straight to the point, I spoke with great confidence, "But I can save you both!"

In unison, they asked, "How? Oh, please save us. We will be indebted to you forever!"

This was precisely the assurance I was looking for. So, this time, speaking with an air of self-importance, I said, "Alright. Here's what you need to do: when you are called to stand trial in Panchajanya's court, simply insist that I be summoned there as well. Once I am presented in court, I will handle everything." Seeing the confident manner in which I spoke, they both felt reassured. Indeed, it is an undeniable fact that in times of crisis, a strong assurance sounds no less than magic. And my reassuring words had indeed worked like magic, soothing their jangled nerves. Besides, it was not difficult for them to place their faith in me, for, they had already seen my intelligence and power at work. In fact, why just them, I too was beginning to believe that if given an opportunity to speak to their king, I could definitely turn the tables. Just see! I hadn't even spent one night on this ship, and I already had the ship's captain and a minister of Panchajanya's court under my control. Indeed, a goal may appear unattainable from a distance, but once you set marching towards it with determination, it never turns out to be that difficult. As soon as they were assured of their safety, both Tamas and Chandak became even more eager to extend hospitality to us. Bhaiya and I were now given the treatment reserved for the most important guests. Additionally, we were provided a separate cabin so that we could rest comfortably. Most importantly, bhaiya's anger—my bane in this mission—had all but dissipated. The special treatment, especially the food and wine, had won him over. Just look at how, in such a short span of time, the entire scenario has changed. Both of us were resting in a small, private cabin with an aide appointed specifically to tend to our needs. Indeed, it wasn't too long ago that we were shackled and herded like animals when we had set foot on the ship, but now, we were enjoying the finest hospitality the ship had to offer. Peering out of the little window of our cabin, we could see the faint light of the rising sun emerge on the horizon. However, we were so exhausted that we slept soundly and woke up only by late afternoon. After waking up and having a meal, I stepped out of the cabin to enjoy a stroll on the deck. Wherever I ventured on the ship, I was met with immense respect. In short, our journey was now marked by warm hospitality, great respect, and the joy of travelling aboard a sailing ship. The splendid treatment we received made it feel as if we were the owners of the ship! And indeed, when the journey becomes pleasurable, one hardly notices the passage of time. Thus, after two days of sailing, we reached Vaivasvatpur, the capital of Panchajanya's kingdom, at the crack of dawn.

Standing in a corner of the ship's deck, bhaiya and I marvelled at the enchanting scenery that met our eyes, as the ship neared the shore. On the horizon, we could see the sky shed its dark cloak as the early rays of the morning sun began to peek through the night sky. As we neared the port, the

hustle and bustle of the soldiers on board the ship had gained momentum. Behind us, the poor slaves who had come on board as guarantors were still tied up. Not so long ago, I too had been one of them; however, at present, I stood like royalty, with one foot placed on the wooden bench, as I gazed at the distant fort of Vaivasvatpur. Engrossed in admiring the view, I was jolted from my reverie when Tamas and Chandak approached me and, with folded hands, requested that I sit with the slaves. Of course, there was nothing wrong in this, for, we were about to enter Panchajanya's stronghold, and for him, we were mere guarantors. So, we quietly sat among the slaves—I with a smile on my countenance and bhaiya with a scowl on his face. Soon, the ship anchored at the port of Vaivasvatpur. Interestingly, the kingdom was situated just a hundred yards away from the shore. Surrounded by high stone walls and ramparts, it seemed invincible at first glance. Additionally, Vaivasvatpur had a single main gate, made of iron and appearing extremely strong. Despite that, a battalion of soldiers could be seen patrolling at the gate. This in itself was a strong indication of the kind of danger we had landed ourselves in. As soon as the ship anchored at the port, the slaves were the first to be herded out. Needless to say, bhaiya and I were also part of this group. On the ship, it was a different matter, but here in the city, we were slaves of Panchajanya and not the guests of Tamas and Chandak. And verily, our 'welcome ceremony' took place accordingly! As soon as we alighted from the ship, all of us were made to stand in a queue. Even the soldiers who had disembarked from the ship were made to stand in a tight formation under Tamas and Chandak's command. This concerned me deeply. With even the kingdom's soldiers subjected to such strict treatment, we could only brace ourselves for the worst. And if such a situation came to pass, would bhaiya ever spare me? Then, I thought, 'Krishna, life is another name for trouble.' 'That's right! Bring on the troubles; Krishna is prepared to face them all.' I was lost in these thoughts when, on the instructions of Tamas and Chandak, we were made to enter the gateway under the tight security of soldiers. I did not dare look at bhaiya, who was moving ahead in the queue with his hands tied, for, I definitely did not want to invite his wrath. Once inside, we were lined up in a huge open square. Looking around, I realised we had become the centre of attention of a huge crowd that had gathered to watch the proceedings. Just then, ten to twelve soldiers marched in carrying a metal cage. A sudden silence enveloped the square with the arrival of the cage. To my astonishment, the cage was placed on a high throne, and about twenty soldiers quickly formed a circle around it—and seated within the cage was Panchajanya! I was amazed by his personal security, and the first thought that struck me was, 'My dear Krishna! From whose clutches have you come to rescue Punardutta? Forget you, even the mightiest king of Aryavarta cannot defeat this man. In fact, even if all the kingdoms of Aryavarta were to join forces, they would still not be able to defeat him! Oh, you are badly trapped, Krishna!' Well, so be it. Coming back to Panchajanya, he seemed almost twice the size of Kansa as far as his height and build were concerned. His neck was thin and long, and his face was rather small. And if I were to describe his overall physique, it most certainly was strange. His stomach was large and weighty, while his legs were thin and long. In other words, both his upper and lower body appeared thin, whereas the middle portion of his body was huge. His body structure seemed bizarre to say the least. Honestly, from a distance, he appeared less like a man and more like a giant fish! Meanwhile, Tamas and Chandak had begun trembling with Panchajanya's arrival. Despite the cool breeze blowing in from the sea, I could see beads of sweat trickling down their foreheads. The only 'action' they engaged in was glancing back at me, with hope writ large on their faces. Frankly speaking, seeing Panchajanya's power and influence, I too was terrified. Yet, considering it my duty, I maintained a buoyant smile on my face to reassure them that I would honour my word.

But what could mere assurances do? As soon as Panchajanya was informed that one of his ships had sunk, he roared in a thunderous voice and ordered the immediate arrest of Tamas and Chandak. His authority was absolute. With no regard for their positions, both were arrested instantly. Within moments, the smile vanished from my face and I quietly watched the drama unfold in front of me. What else could I do? Forget about doing something, after the two officers, it was now our turn to be arrested. Well, we were all herded into a prison. Scores of people who had come as guarantors were packed into every cell. Around seven to eight such cells were built adjacent to each other. For light and air to enter, there were just two vents in each of these cells. With walls made of stone, the cells had strong iron doors, with two soldiers standing guard outside. The bleak, cold, stone-walled cells were a vivid reminder that our stay here would be a long and torturous one. But what recourse did we have? We managed to spend the day somehow, but as night descended, the situation turned even more ominous. The dinner served to us was disgusting to say the least. Our plight was such that although our stomachs were aching with hunger, we could not even swallow the food, for, we had been served raw flesh! Needless to say, there was no question of us falling asleep in these cramped quarters, and that too, on an empty stomach. There was no bedding either. The only relief—if you could call it one—was that all our fellow prisoners were the ones who had travelled with us on the ship, so the poor men were according respect to us while also trying to partake in our sorrow. As night progressed, everyone lay down on the floor, and soon, the cell resounded with their snores. Bhaiya and I, on the other hand, could not bring ourselves to sleep in such a situation. So, we stood quietly, holding onto the cold iron door, nodding off every now and then. Now, although I was trying to think of ways to pass the night somehow, I deliberately kept my gaze averted from bhaiya, for, I did not want to shrivel under his piercing glare. We thus spent the entire night on our feet. Meaning, in a single night, Panchajanya had made us experience a living hell. You can easily imagine how much bhaiya must have 'entertained' me all night long, without even meaning to!

Well, like all things good or bad, this terrible night ended too. However, it was not as if we could expect the situation to change for the better with the dawn of a new day. The change would come only once we were summoned to the royal court, but even that depended on the prudence of Tamas and Chandak, that is, whether they could convince Panchajanya. In the eventuality that they failed in their efforts, they would have to meet their fate at the gallows, while we too would slowly rot in this hell and perish away! If I may confess, considering the high-level security and the sordid conditions we found ourselves in, not only did our mission to rescue Punardutta seem impossible, but so did our own escape from this hellhole. Fortunately, my despondent thoughts held sway only briefly, for, we were summoned to the royal palace by afternoon. With this summons, I could also see a ray of hope for our escape. The soldiers promptly escorted us to the royal court. Clearly, it was judgement day for both us and Tamas and Chandak. My condition was quite peculiar. Surrounded by soldiers, I was overwhelmed by a storm of thoughts and a vortex of emotions. This was, after all, our last chance. Very soon, my communication skills would be put to the ultimate test. And if I failed to outsmart Panchajanya, the story of our life would see its end at that very moment. But how could I outsmart him? The ship had sunk because of Tamas and Chandak's mistake, and the penalty for such a disaster was death. This being the case, how could I possibly save them? Lost in contemplation, we had already crossed the distance to the royal palace. Once inside, I was taken straight to the royal court, where King Panchajanya was present. Silence prevailed in the courtroom. Tamas and Chandak were already there, bound in chains, as expected. But surprisingly, Panchajanya was seated in his iron cage, even in the courtroom, with a troop of soldiers positioned around him. Argh! The matter appeared far more serious than I had imagined.

Well, so be it! As soon as I arrived, Panchajanya commenced the trial. Perhaps, they were waiting for me. Meaning, I had been summoned even before the trial had begun, which all things considered, was a good sign. Nonetheless, as soon as Panchajanya gave the go-ahead for the trial, the court announcer called out, "Tamas and Chandak! The guarantor that you wanted brought as a witness is here. Thus, I formally announce the commencement of the trial." Then, turning to the king and addressing him, he said, "O King! Tamas and Chandak are accused of negligence of duty. Because of their carelessness, we have lost one of our ships at sea."

Hearing this, the king bellowed, "Tamas and Chandak! Do you accept that the ship in question has sunk because of your carelessness?" Out of fear, both nodded their heads in admission. This time, adopting a dramatic tone, Panchajanya continued, "And it is due to your negligence that close to a hundred people have lost their lives. Do you admit to this as well?"

Both of them meekly nodded their heads once again. However, this time, they turned their heads slightly towards me, looking at me with eyes full of hope. I too reassured them with my charming smile. But honestly, considering the terse and straightforward manner in which the trial was being conducted, I did not see any chance of them being saved. And this is exactly what happened. Before I could even think of making a move, Panchajanya pronounced the judgement. For him, it was a simple and straightforward trial anyway. Speaking in a harsh tone, he declared, "Both of you have been found guilty of dereliction of duty, because of which our ship has sunk and a hundred people have lost their lives. Thus, as per the law of the land, I hereby sentence you both to death. You shall be put to death in front of everyone in the open square."

There was no hearing, no appeal. The death sentence had been announced straightaway. Alarmed at this, I roused myself thinking, 'Wake up, Kanhaiya! It is now or never. The time has come to work a miracle!' With great difficulty, I had made these two senior officers my friends, and now, if they were put to death, how would I pay my *gurudakshina*? Thus, without thinking further, I interjected somewhat hesitatingly, "O K…k…king, with your permission, may I make an appeal on their behalf?"

Panchajanya looked condescendingly at me and said, "In my court, collateral slaves have no permission to speak!"

I said, "It is true that I have been brought here as a collateral. Nevertheless, I come from Aryavarta, a land far beyond your borders. Throughout Aryavarta, you are regarded as a king of great wisdom and strength as well as a deliverer of exemplary justice. If you do not hear me out today, you may commit an injustice, and your name could be tarnished all over Aryavarta."

This was, of course, a desperate bid on my part; seeing no way out, I had decided to appeal to his ego. Fortunately, it seemed to work. Panchajanya appeared to be gradually falling into my trap. Indeed, it is rightly said that while all other weapons may fail, the weapon that assuages the ego is always effective. This was exactly what was happening here. Rather than see his great name sullied, Panchajanya wisely decided to hear me out. Granting me permission, he spoke in a stern voice, "Alright! Since you come from a distant kingdom, I will grant you the permission to speak. But keep it brief!"

Perfect! This was the opportunity I had been waiting for. You know very well that once I'm given a chance, I can convince even the devil himself! Hearing the great Panchajanya accede to my request, a ray of hope kindled in the heart of Chandak and Tamas as well. Taking a deep breath and focusing my entire consciousness, I began to speak. "O King! By pronouncing the death sentence on your ship captain, Tamas, and Chief Minister, Chandak, you have shown that when it comes to justice and wisdom, there is no one in this world superior to you. For, it is an indisputable fact that your ship has sunk because of the carelessness of these two senior officers of your kingdom. And by imposing the most severe punishment of the death sentence without any regard for their position or designation, you have proved that your justice does not discriminate between the common citizens and the influential."

Hearing this flamboyant, little speech from me, the faces of the two condemned men fell, as they felt they had been backstabbed. They quickly assumed that, with complete disregard for them, I was now trying to flatter the king. Well, they were not wrong in thinking so, because on the face of it, this is what it looked like. However, I knew exactly what I was doing. My target was Panchajanya only, and my arrow had found its mark. The litany of praises I had sung had trapped his ego to such an extent that his chest puffed up with pride, and he seemed to sit up even straighter in his seat. And why would he not? He had just discovered that tales of his justice resounded all over Aryavarta. Seeing that he had fallen for my bait, I grew more confident and continued, "But, O King, a small question has arisen in my mind regarding this matter. If you permit, I shall present it before you for your wise counsel."

Panchajanya was already swayed by my sweet talk, hence speaking in a calm voice, he said, "Certainly, you may."

Adopting a tone of utmost humility, I spoke, "O King, I understand that the punishment for drowning a ship is the death sentence. But I wonder, what is the punishment in your kingdom for saving a ship from drowning?"

Hearing this, Panchajanya let out a loud guffaw and exclaimed, "Punishment! If someone saves my ship from sinking, he will be awarded immeasurably. He will be gifted scores of precious stones, ornaments, and six, no, seven beautiful women to serve and satisfy his whims!"

I replied, "O King! The ship in which we have sailed here would have also capsized had it not been for the intelligence and courage displayed by Tamas and Chandak."

Poor man! Panchajanya did not know what hit him when he heard this. His intelligence appeared to have abandoned him, and he was caught in a vortex of conflicting thoughts. Failing to fathom the meaning of this double-sided argument, he sat in deep thought. I was thrilled to see him in this plight. I was sure that if given the opportunity to speak, I could bewilder anyone. Here too, within a few moments, I had turned a seemingly simple and straightforward matter into a complex one. Much to his annoyance, Panchajanya could not understand how a simple sum of two plus two had yielded an inexplicable 'five'. And while I was elated from within, I had somehow managed to keep a straight face on the outside. But Tamas and Chandak could hardly contain their happiness, their faces clearly reflecting the hope that had resurfaced. However, the expressions on the faces of these people were of no consequence. Panchajanya was the one who mattered, and his condition was such that he was still trying to fathom what I had said. When even after racking his brain for a while, he could not reach a conclusion, I decided to assist him. I reckoned, why not offer him some wise counsel? So, putting on an elaborate act, I spoke with great humility, "O King! You have already punished them for letting a ship drown. Now, you only need to reward them for saving the other ship!"

Hearing this, Panchajanya's face lit up. He liked my suggestion. He had to, of course. After all, you well know that I had no ill-intentions towards him; I merely wanted to help him arrive at a solution. And fortunately, he had arrived at it. He immediately declared, "Alright then. Keeping the previous sentence valid, I reward them with jewels, precious stones and seven beautiful maidservants for saving my ship!"

This time, it was the courtroom that was left bewildered. In fact, hearing this pronouncement, even I felt like laughing out loud, but with immense restraint, I managed to control myself and remained silent. After a brief moment, Panchajanya too seemed to realise that he had passed a verdict that was anything but intelligent! Tamas and Chandak also stood poker-faced, unable to fathom whether to be elated at their king's justice or lament the implications of it. The situation had become so complicated that everybody was flummoxed, while I was the only person in the courtroom who was not confused. How could I be? After all, I was the one who had created this web of confusion! And it was not a trivial one, as its effects were evident in the silence that hung over the courtroom. No one could make sense of what was going on. As for Panchajanya, he was trying his best to dispel his own confusion, but all in vain. How could he, when I had subverted his intelligence, rendering it useless! Consequently, he found himself totally confounded, and needless to say, the entire court was in the same state. Seeing the bewilderment I had caused, I felt a deep sense of pride in the move I had played. I was also enjoying myself to the hilt, watching with glee the perplexed faces in the courtroom.

Finally, Chandak could no longer contain himself. Speaking in a vexed voice, he asked, "O King! Of what use are jewels and women to us when the gallows await us?"

The king also realised that Chandak's argument was valid, and as a result, he fell into deeper contemplation, scratching his head and wondering how a muddle like this had never occurred in his courtroom before! How could it? After all, I had never been here before! Poor Panchajanya! Already at his wits' end after hearing Chandak's question, he held his head in his hands, still trying to rack his brain. Feeling defeated and unable to think of anything, he finally asked me, "What should be done now?"

Aha! I was already waiting, eager to help him. And now that the fish had jumped into the net of its own will, there was no question of letting it slip away. Thus, putting on a sombre expression, I said, "O King! In my opinion, their punishment should be cancelled, and so should their rewards. This is because they have drowned one ship and saved the other...the matter is thus settled."

My suggestion found favour with the king and he promptly ordered the release of Tamas and Chandak. Then, turning to me, he said, "Today, you have saved me from committing injustice. Therefore, from now on, you will stay here not as a slave, but as a guest."

Hearing him speak so, my heart burst with joy. Indeed, I felt as if I had conquered both heaven and earth! Of course, outwardly, I spoke in a tone dripping with gratitude. I said, "Ah! This is nothing but your generosity. As it is, I'm already more than impressed with your sense of justice. Until now, I had only heard of it, but today, I have witnessed it with my own eyes!"

Hearing this, his ego surged to the fore once again. He lifted his head and looked all around, as if to say to his courtiers, 'Do you see how famous I am in Aryavarta!' In fact, he was so thrilled that he fished out the conch shell tied to his waist. Oh, how beautiful the conch shell was! And when he blew into the conch shell, its sound reverberated in deep, booming echoes. The sound had such a resonant and haunting quality that it penetrated the very depth of my being, captivating me thoroughly. Tamas and Chandak, on the other hand, could not contain their elation. And as far as I was concerned, I felt I was inches away from accomplishing my goal. The favour I had done to the two senior officials was bound to produce the desired effect. Moreover, I had also won favour in the eyes of the king. The situation was now looking extremely favourable. As soon as the court proceedings came to an end, we were moved to the royal guest house. Now, we were no longer watched by the guards, free as we were to roam around the kingdom. Meaning, we had access to everything—the best accommodation, the best food, and much-desired freedom too. Amazingly, this journey from being a slave to becoming an important guest of the king had taken just three nights, a feat that was certainly beyond bhaiya's comprehension. Although he was in awe of my clever ploys, he could not fathom my tricks.

Well, be that as it may! We had not come here to gallivant and enjoy ourselves—our sole objective was to free Punardutta. And although Tamas and Chandak were deeply indebted to me, accomplishing this task was not going to be easy considering Panchajanya's iron hold on his kingdom. Indeed, the enemy was both cunning and powerful. It was also obvious that if Panchajanya were to catch even the slightest hint that I had come to his kingdom to rescue Punardutta, he would ensure that I never left Vaivasvatpur alive. In such a scenario, Tamas and Chandak would be rendered useless and I would surely meet my end. Meaning, the sooner we accomplished our mission, the better it would be for us. So, I began to wander around the kingdom, trying to come up with a foolproof plan. It was worth noting that Panchajanya alone reigned supreme in this kingdom, and no one else had any say whatsoever. The kingdom consisted of only two classes of people—soldiers and servants. The soldiers helped in ruling the kingdom, while the servants served their masters. As unbelievable as it may sound, there was no marketplace in Vaivasvatpur. Even the total strength of the population was a mere four to five thousand. This could hardly be called a kingdom; these people were pirates who terrorised neighbouring kingdoms, plundered them, and sustained themselves on the wealth and resources they looted. Nothing was produced here, nor was any business conducted here. Meaning, everything was functioning solely on the power and might of the army. Well, so be it! At present, it seemed unlikely that I would be able to either find Punardutta or escape from here on my own. In short, I could accomplish my task only with the assistance of Tamas and Chandak. So, as soon as I found the opportunity, I grabbed hold of Chandak and tried to glean information about Punardutta in the course of our conversation. On hearing me enquire about him, Chandak was surprised. Ah! This was certainly a good sign for me, for, this meant that he was at least aware of Punardatta. By now, Chandak had already become my trusted confidant; besides, why keep secrets from friends? So, without hesitation, I told him everything about our education at *Acharya* Sandipani's *ashram* and our intention to pay him *gurudakshina*. For, in my opinion, if you want anyone, especially friends, to help you accomplish your task to the best of their ability, you must not hide anything. They should always know the real

reason behind the task entrusted to them; otherwise, most of their energy is expended in trying to fathom the reason behind it. What I mean is, concealing facts or prevaricating is a strategy used with enemies, not friends.

Chandak, on the other hand, appreciated the manner in which I opened my heart to him, and in return, he too divulged all the information he had about Punardutta. Even better was the fact that all the details he shared were very encouraging. The most important fact was that Punardutta was not only alive, but Panchajanya had handed him over to Chandak after kidnapping him from the *ashram*. And even more significantly, Chandak was more than willing to help me rescue Punardutta from the soldiers who guarded him. I was thrilled to hear this. The goal which had seemed almost impossible until now had suddenly become attainable. However, there were still some difficulties to overcome, the biggest being extricating Punardutta from the cordon of soldiers surrounding him. Chandak and I discussed in great detail the strategy we could adopt, but even after deliberating over it at great length, we still could not formulate a definite plan of action. All our deliberations ran into a dead end, as it seemed impossible to extricate Punardutta from this fortress-like city without this information reaching Panchajanya's ears. It was not as if Chandak was acting pricey; no, the poor man was trying his best to find a way to help me, but the problem was, we could not reveal the matter of Punardutta to anyone else. For, in doing so, my own life could fall into jeopardy. So, all in all, even with Chandak's support, the idea of rescuing Punardutta single-handedly and freeing him from such tight security seemed unthinkable. The kingdom was so well guarded that even a tiny bird could not fly out of its own free will without being noticed by the hawk-like vigilantes. In this scenario, how was it possible for three people to escape in a boat unscathed?

But as they say, every problem is born with its solution! The issue is, we panic and become so mired in the problem that the solution escapes our notice altogether. I, for one, had always believed that just as there is a way to climb even the tallest of mountains, just as some path can surely be carved to cross even the densest of forests, a solution to every problem can also be found. Although this problem was fraught with complications, a viable solution did finally present itself after much deliberation. By now, it was evident that all our efforts would be reduced to naught as long as Panchajanya was alive. Truly, without eliminating him, it would be impossible to expect even a leaf to flutter in this kingdom, considering the immense power he wielded! All in all, assassinating him emerged as the only solution to our problem. But then it was easier said than done, for, it was well-nigh impossible for me to kill him single-handedly. Apart from Chandak, I needed the support of a multitude of soldiers too; but the question arose, why would they kill their king? Why would they put their own lives at stake in an attempt to do so? At the very least, they would not do this just to rescue Punardutta. Well, so what? By weaving a web of ambition, I could make my mission appear as if it was their own. If I could make Chandak aspire to become king, he would surely mobilise his trusted soldiers to accomplish this mission.

However, this was merely a one-sided plan taking shape in my mind. In reality, killing Panchajanya was no easy task, and the plan could very well backfire. Having said that, it could still work, especially if I could convince Chandak and Tamas to lend their assistance in accomplishing it. Meaning, the problem seemed on the verge of being solved. Initially, the challenge was—how to rescue Punardutta, and the solution appeared to lie in Panchajanya's death. The next problem that arose was—how to kill Panchajanya. The answer to that was clear: by convincing Chandak and Tamas to lend their support. And how could they be convinced to assist in the killing of their own king? Well, as I mentioned earlier, by fuelling their ambition...and I was fully prepared to do that. Chandak was already my well-wisher, offering all the help he could. In fact, seeing that we were unable to come up with a solution, he had even made arrangements for us to escape unscathed from here, keeping our safety in mind. But since I could not leave without Punardutta, I resolved to stay put in Vaivasvatpur until I completed my mission. For that matter, Chandak had even promised me that in the eventuality that we could not rescue Punardutta, he would attempt to free him later when the opportunity arose and personally bring him to *Acharya* Sandipani's *ashram.* Oh well! Looking at the delicate situation we were in, it was better to content ourselves with the fact that at least Punardutta was alive. But having said that, who knew what the future held? Moreover, how could Krishna return empty-handed? Thus, seeing no way out, Chandak too was trying his best to find a solution along with me.

Having decided what needed to be done, there was no point in wasting any more time. So, setting all past discussions aside, I immediately went to see Chandak. After some polite conversation, I came straight to the point. I said, "I understand that you too are saddened by your inability to assist me in rescuing Punardutta. But let's forget that for now. More importantly, if I'm being honest, we have grown so close that I must express how shocked I was by Panchajanya's insult towards someone as wise and loyal as you in front of the entire court. Does any king humiliate his own chief minister like this and sentence him to death?" Having spoken thus, I knew I had touched a raw nerve and hit him where it hurt the most. I could clearly see from his expression the pain and anger it was bringing to the fore. Seeing my plan work, I deliberately began to lure him further into the trap. This time, setting aside all sympathy, I adopted the stance of a seer and said, "Ideally, only a wise and brave warrior like you ought to be the ruler of this kingdom. A king who insults his army general in front of an entire assembly is certainly not fit to sit on the throne. Before insulting you, Panchajanya should have at least considered the fact that the army is always under the control of the general. Moreover, you are the respected chief minister of Vaivasvatpur. The king should have thought at least a hundred times before insulting someone like you!"

Although my intention was to trap just one fish, the net I had cast was so wide that it could easily ensnare every fish in the sea. And this being the case, what chance did poor Chandak have? The political manoeuvring I had learnt in Mathura and the experience of slaying Kansa were both proving extremely useful at present. Although Chandak did not say anything, from his changed demeanour, I could see that he was in agreement with me. It was evident from the look on his face that in his heart of hearts, he had already begun to dream of becoming king. Great! My arrow had found its mark. Now, I did not have to do much. With my expression, I indicated to him that in Krishna's presence, nothing was impossible. Indeed, when he had resorted to using expressions as a way of communication, how could I be left behind? However, not everything could be discussed through expressions alone. Besides, expressions aren't all that reliable; they can always be twisted around. One could always say, "No, I never meant that. Why would I speak against my own king?" But words once spoken cannot be taken back. Thus, it was essential to verbalise all that I had conveyed so far by way of expressions. If words also reflected the same determination, then one could be sure of the intention. So, I spoke earnestly, "Why do you not become the king of Vaivasvatpur?"

Hearing this, he blurted out, "As long as Panchajanya is alive, this is not possible."

'Ah! That is precisely what I have come here to make you understand,' I mused. And just see how his heartfelt desire had surfaced to the fore in a matter of moments! Indeed, in Krishna's presence, it was impossible for even the cleverest of the clever to hide his thoughts. Nevertheless, as soon as the words escaped Chandak's lips, he realised the blunder he had committed. But what could be done now? His intention had been revealed. At any rate, the ego and self-importance that grips a person at the thought of becoming a king does make him lose his mind. Besides, Chandak never stood a chance when dealing with Kanhaiya, who could make even the *gopis* lose their senses! However, the task was not finished yet, hence it was not right to indulge in self-praise prematurely. Seeing that the iron was hot, I thought it best to strike my final blow. For, what if he changed his mind altogether? So, this time, I posed a question in a rather dramatic tone, "What if I kill him?"

Chandak nearly jumped out of his skin upon hearing this and asked, “Is that possible?”

I replied with quiet confidence, “Of course, it is…but only if you help me.”

Speaking in the humblest tone, he said, “You have my unflinching support. In any case, I have committed the rest of my life to you. Moreover, it is through your endeavours that I shall be made king, hence all you have to do is command this slave of yours.”

With Chandak’s assent to the conspiracy, my success and Panchajanya’s death became even more certain. And now that the goal was set, we quickly began discussing the tasks ahead. First and foremost, I obtained complete information about all of Panchajanya’s friends and enemies from Chandak. Unfortunately, this information was of no use to us. There was just one demon named Punyajan who was known to be Panchajanya’s arch enemy. At one time, he and Panchajanya had been bosom friends; and as it is well known, an enmity between former friends runs much deeper than enmity between strangers. However, despite this, Punyajan was of no use to us. Because presently, we did not need an enemy who was an outsider but one who was close to Panchajanya. We merely wanted to rescue Punardutta, not take over the kingdom. Well, it did not matter if Panchajanya had no enemies within the kingdom; I could easily create them for him. Given that I had already turned Chandak against him, I could easily turn a few more people into his enemies. Besides, Panchajanya could not be defeated by mere strength alone. In fact, no king in Aryavarta had the power to defeat him. The only way to bring him down was through political manoeuvring. And needless to say, I was quickly becoming adept at devising such strategies. However, there was one problem here as well—I could not do anything directly. Whatever move I played, I needed to do it through Chandak alone. He was my only pawn as well as my sole support. In other words, I was still bound by the limitation of having to rely on others to execute my plans.

But how could Krishna’s firm resolve ever bite the dust? If the task was difficult, I would apply more intelligence and work harder with greater sharpness and vigour. Enthusiasm and confidence would also be increased as required; in fact, as these thoughts crossed my mind, I could already feel a marked surge in both. Thus, pushing aside all obstacles, I dove headlong in accomplishing my goal by assigning three tasks to Chandak. First, he had to secure the trust of the senior army officers. Next, he had to persuade Tamas to join him in this mission. And lastly, he had to somehow convince Panchajanya to step out of the cage, even if it was just for a short while. As far as Tamas was concerned, I was confident about his support, for, not only had

I saved his life, but he was also promised the post of chief minister in the new regime. And verily, everything transpired exactly as I had predicted. As soon as Chandak revealed to him that I was the mastermind behind this ploy, Tamas agreed to lend his support without hesitation. And with him on our side, I had automatically gained control over the army as well as the navy. As for the third step in my plan to get Panchajanya to step out of his cage, this good news was also brought by Chandak. He had scheduled a grand festival in Vaivasvatpur on the next new moon night, complete with dance programmes and wrestling matches. Panchajanya would be invited to preside over the ceremony, and the plan was to arrange for him to step out of the cage during the welcoming ceremony. In short, Chandak's plan seemed not just promising but effective as well. That's not all! Chandak had even organised a regiment of soldiers loyal to him to be present at the festival venue. In short, while he had carried out his task diligently, the strategy had also taken shape in my mind fully. Honestly, it was only now that victory appeared in sight, ready to welcome me with open arms. All we had to do was wait for the new moon day. As for bhaiya, he was a happy man, engrossed in his own world, too busy to bother about these matters. He was content with the fine hospitality extended to him and the great care taken to serve him his favourite food and drinks. Of course, seeing me engaged in a flurry of activities, he knew that I was in the process of executing some devious plan, but so far, he had not enquired even once about what new ploy I was involved in. It wouldn't be wrong to say that living with a happy person like bhaiya was nothing short of experiencing ultimate happiness!

Finally, the fateful new moon night arrived. The festival was arranged in the open ground, which I had to admit, had been decorated beautifully. By the time we arrived, the venue was lit up with scores of torches lining the entire length of the ground. Truly, Chandak had made elaborate arrangements for this 'event'—the slaying of Panchajanya! If nothing else, he was bidding farewell to his king with great pomp and splendour. Well, so be it! For now, let me return to describing the festival ground, which was a huge, rectangular area. From where I stood, I could see a huge podium, perhaps built as a seating arrangement for Panchajanya. An open space spread out just below the towering stage, which was obviously meant for conducting dance performances and wrestling bouts. At the far end of the ground, seating arrangements had been made for the members of the council of ministers, senior officials and important guests. As a mark of respect, our seats were also reserved next to theirs. After all, we were now honoured guests of the king himself. All this was fine, but at present, I was quite alarmed to see a battalion of soldiers stationed all around the ground. This made me wonder, had Chandak really made foolproof arrangements or was he just making empty promises? Well, we would find out by the end of the festival. At present, enthusiasm abounded among the audience standing on both sides of the podium. My eyes were keenly observing all the arrangements when Tamas came to fetch us and we set off with him. Leaving the podium, we sped across the festival ground and arrived at the designated area for our seats. Once seated comfortably, I let my eyes wander all over the ground, noticing every movement; after all, I had nothing else to do. Presently, I was just a spectator whose job was to watch the tug of war between Chandak's diligence and Panchajanya's alertness. I would jump into the fray only after Chandak's success in this particular battle. Meanwhile, unaware of the conspiracy being hatched by us, poor bhaiya was waiting impatiently for the wrestling matches to begin. Had I not told you earlier that bhaiya was a happy-go-lucky person; he could never understand why a plan was required to kill someone. The only strategy he believed in was to pick up the mace and engage your opponent in combat—that's all! Thinking about consequences and indulging in mental gymnastics was just not his forte.

Meanwhile, Chandak walked up to me and shared the encouraging news, which not only boosted my confidence but also set my pulse racing with excitement. He whispered in my ear that, according to the plan, he was stationed right behind us with three hundred of his loyal, armed soldiers. What more could I ask for? I swelled with confidence. Everything was falling into place as per the plan; our seats too had been arranged right in front of Panchajanya's cage. Of course, my senses were on high alert and I could feel my heart pounding against my chest, experiencing the nervousness one typically feels before the execution of an ambitious plan. Now, all we had to do was wait for Panchajanya to arrive. Honestly, even the short wait now seemed to stretch to eternity, because if the plan failed, it would mean certain death for all of us involved. In other words, the next few moments were most crucial, as they would decide whether we would live or die. And under such circumstances, we certainly needed to be in control of our faculties in order to execute such a dangerous plan. On one hand, we had to keep a sharp eye on every activity and movement, while on the other, we also couldn't deny that these were possibly the last few moments of our lives. Of course, I had experienced several such tense moments before. Truth be told, no matter what task I undertook, my life would always be at risk. In fact, I had spent my entire life walking on the sharp edge of a sword. For that matter, a person born under the spectre of death, especially in a prison, should expect nothing more from life. If observed closely, it was this very deep understanding on my part that allowed me to maintain a unique sense of joy within me despite all adverse circumstances. Consider the present situation for instance. A momentous and decisive event was afoot. My strategy, along with Chandak's diligence, was about to be put to the test. The foremost question was: Would he succeed in making Panchajanya step out of the cage? Once he did, it would be up to me to finish him off. Even assuming the killing went smoothly, the loyalty of the soldiers who, as Chandak claimed, swore allegiance to him, would still be tested. In other words, we could very well be arrested for assassinating Panchajanya. Yet, the unique trait of my personality was that, despite all these complications, I remained alert, not frightened at all.

Well, the moment of truth had finally arrived. The distinct sound of Panchajanya's conch reverberated across the ground, heralding his arrival. Everyone stood in obeisance to welcome the king, and I quickly rose from my seat as well. His faithful soldiers trotted up to the platform and placed his cage on it, instantly sharpening my senses. Just then, a group of young girls came forward with garlands to welcome him. I stood in preparedness, all my senses alert, acutely aware that it was now or never. If I missed this chance, the game would be over. Then let alone Punardutta, I too would find it impossible to escape from here. Naturally, Tamas and Chandak were far more anxious than me, for, the stakes were really high. As soon as Panchajanya stepped out of the cage to accept the garlands, I aimed my discus at his exposed neck and sent it flying. The discus soared above the arena, flew inches above the top of the flower girls' heads and struck Panchajanya's neck with precision. In the blink of an eye, his severed head fell off with a thud and rolled onto the edge of the podium. There was no question of my discus missing its target at such a precarious moment, and on that momentous note, my mission was accomplished.

Pandemonium broke loose in the festival ground, as people scrambled in sheer panic. Panchajanya's guards stood frozen in shock, not having the faintest idea of what had just unfolded. As for me, I didn't even have the time to taste the joy of my victory, for, it was essential to gain control over the situation immediately. I quickly signalled Chandak to eliminate all of Panchajanya's loyal bodyguards, not letting any of them escape. His soldiers were prepared already, and within moments, they pounced on the bodyguards and slaughtered them all. I heaved a sigh of relief, as I could now see that Chandak had not been over-optimistic at all. However, time did not allow me to savour this sense of relief. I bounded up to the stage with Chandak, heading straight for the spot where Panchajanya lay dead. Amid the pandemonium, I pressed forward, shielded by Chandak's soldiers. My feet seemed to take on a life of their own, racing ahead, with bhaiya, Chandak and Tamas following close behind. Clearly, there was only one way to control the mayhem all around, and that was to proclaim a new king with immediate effect. But just see my childishness; the moment I noticed Panchajanya's conch lying by his side, I could not stop myself from picking it up. Any sane person would have questioned whether this was really the time to be enamoured by a conch? I wasn't sure whether to call this my childishness or immaturity…or my keen aesthetic sense! Well, no matter what term I used, my childishness did not stop there. As soon as I had the shell in my hands, I blew into it. Oh, what a magnificent sound it produced! And let me tell you, it was because of its deep, resonant sound that the 'Panchajanya conch' was famous all across Aryavarta. As for me, I was so enamoured with the conch that it remained with me lifelong. You would remember that much later in life, I had blown this very conch to signal the commencement of the Mahabharata war.

Well, returning to the present, let me clarify that it wasn't my fascination with the conch shell that had led me to assassinate Panchajanya. It was just a temporary distraction. My actual mission was to free Punardutta and to accomplish that task, it was necessary to quickly declare Chandak the new king. Upon hearing the familiar sound of the conch, the mayhem subsided to some extent. Everyone felt that perhaps Panchajanya was still alive and this was all just a game. Regardless, I grabbed the opportunity to bring the situation under control. As a first step, I asked Chandak to address the crowd immediately. He climbed up the stage, but amusingly enough, I too bounded up behind him to make use of my political skills. I advised him that whilst he was declaring himself king, he should also make grand promises of bringing peace and prosperity to his subjects. He was a chief minister, so I knew he would not take long to understand the gist of what I was saying. Thus, as soon as he took the stage, the commotion died down. And why would it not? He was, after all, the chief minister as well as the commander-in-chief of Vaivasvatpur. Naturally, his address at such a delicate moment held great significance. Although, seeing the gravity of the situation, his self-confidence wavered a little, but irrespective of how he felt, it was he who had to make the announcement. An outsider, especially someone who had assassinated Panchajanya, could not be expected to make such an announcement. Therefore, even though his speech began on a nervous note, Chandak addressed the people and declared himself the new king of Vaivasvatpur. In the same breath, he also elaborated on why it had become necessary to eliminate Panchajanya. Even as he was addressing the masses, he saw several people nodding their heads in agreement, and taking this as a positive sign, he continued with greater confidence. He promised that under his regime, the subjects would not be terrorised and special care would be taken to improve the common man's standard of living. He also promised that there would be no discrimination

between a servant and a soldier. Reassuring the assembled crowd with several such promises, he thus concluded his speech.

With this declaration, it was now confirmed that Chandak had become the new king. The situation that had unravelled here was similar to the one that had transpired in Mathura; after Chandak's speech, there did not seem to be any major opposition from the subjects to the killing of Panchajanya. On the contrary, everyone seemed to wholeheartedly welcome the idea of Chandak being crowned the king. In fact, I had not expected everything to get resolved so easily. For that matter, even Chandak was finding it hard to believe that Panchajanya had actually been killed and that the people had accepted him as their new king. To him, it all seemed like a vivid dream, which he was seeing with his eyes wide open. Of course, he could not help it, and neither could I. After all, everything had transpired in a fraction of a second. This is the very *leela* of Krishna—the wondrous drama orchestrated by Krishna, which ensures that even the most daunting tasks are executed effortlessly. Well, now that I had achieved this stupendous victory, I thought, why not take a moment to bask in pride? Actually, I could've let myself soar higher, but the circumstances simply wouldn't allow it. My task was far from complete, and the threat hadn't been fully averted. For that matter, I did not expect any fresh opposition, but it was necessary to stay alert and cautious. So, signalling Chandak to bring Punardutta, I hopped off the podium. Then, grabbing bhaiya's hand, we made a dash towards the ship with Tamas in tow. You cannot even imagine how fast these developments were taking place one after the other. Striding forth with quick, large steps, bhaiya, Tamas and I headed towards the shore, flanked by soldiers. Although the cacophony of the crowd had subsided by now, they all looked perplexed at the sudden turn of events and were certainly taking their time to digest the occurrences so far. Well, taking care of this situation fell under the purview of King Chandak; my mind was now fully focused on reaching the shore without any mishap, for, only then could I say that my mission was successful. We crossed the threshold of Vaivasvatpur without any hurdles, and on seeing the ship ashore, a wave of renewed vigour washed over me. And when the soldiers saluted me as I boarded, I felt certain that I had escaped unscathed. However, as a precautionary measure, I still did not send Tamas off. On the other hand, my heart was pounding hard in anticipation, waiting for Chandak to arrive. To be honest, though I had slayed Panchajanya and the deed was done, it was only now that I could feel the reverberations of the enormity of this deed, which was still making me feel jittery. After all, killing such a powerful king of the pirates was no laughing matter. Now, whether it was a joke or reality, the deed had been done. My heart was truly racing with apprehension over the potential consequences of my act, and Chandak's arrival alone could restore my confidence. Fortunately, I did not have to wait long. Very soon, Chandak arrived with Punardutta and a battalion of soldiers guarding him. Surprisingly, he had brought with him a heap full of gifts such as diamonds and other precious stones as well as fifty dancing girls. I accepted the jewels but sent back the girls. Dancing girls were the adornment of a kingdom, and we had no kingdom of our own. Forget a kingdom, we did not even have a place to call home! Forget about home, we did not have even a single safe refuge on this vast earth. For, as soon as we left these shores, the devil named Jarasandha would begin hounding us once more.

But what was the point in worrying about Jarasandha now? At present, I wanted to celebrate the fact that we had saved Punardutta, and in doing so, were able to pay our *gurudakshina* to our great guru. I would lament about Jarasandha after fulfilling my *gurudakshina*. Well, this was how I saw the situation, but looking at bhaiya, he seemed to have frozen, unable to comprehend the events that had transpired at such a fast pace. Neither had he understood anything earlier, nor was he able to comprehend anything now. In fact, he still could not believe that Punardutta had been rescued and Panchajanya had been slayed. But, of course, bhaiya was not at fault. I had worked my magic so swiftly, and the events too had occurred at a rapid pace. Well, Punardutta had finally taken a firm step towards freedom by boarding the ship, but even now, it was essential to maintain the pace of our activities. For, our mission was still not over! Until we managed to take Punardutta beyond the boundaries of Vaivasvatpur, let alone Punardutta, even we could not consider ourselves safe. With this in mind, I hastily took leave of Tamas and Chandak, who bid us an emotional farewell. Additionally, they sent ten of their loyal soldiers with us. This was all fine, but I, like a truly conscientious person, extracted a strong assurance from King Chandak that he would not commit any atrocities on his people and that he would not raid the coastal settlements unnecessarily. And so, after securing a splendid victory, our ship finally set sail for Prabhasa. Strangely, I was in such a tearing hurry to leave Panchajanya's kingdom that, even after the ship had set sail, I had not glanced at Punardutta even once!

Chapter 6

Deserting the Battlefield

With Punardutta on board, our ship weighed anchor and set sailing on the vast ocean. Standing on the deck, we waved out to Chandak and Tamas, and soon, they became a speck in the distance as we sailed towards the horizon. Heaving a sigh of relief, it was only now that I felt a sense of having come back to reality. However, I still could not believe that Punardutta—my *gurudakshina*—was standing right before my eyes. But he was very much present—in blood and flesh—right in front of me, in the open part of the ship. And you may find this hard to believe, but it was only now that I looked at him properly. Honestly, I could not stop looking at him. Taking in the sight of the young boy standing in front of me, I could feel my eyes moisten with unshed tears. We were still standing on the starboard side of the ship, where I stood watching Punardutta, who was immersed in gazing at the limitless ocean and the huge ship, his wonderstruck eyes flitting from one to the other. Of course, his curiosity was only natural; besides, he had no clue about who we were or why he had been brought here after being released from the dungeon. His face mirrored a sea of expressions, which I kept observing affectionately. I felt as if all of a sudden, *Acharya* Sandipani had entered my being and was admiring his dear son. No matter how long I stared at his innocent face and the eyes which looked around with child-like curiosity, it still did not suffice. Seeing him stand before me in flesh and blood, I felt a deep sense of gratitude towards Chandak, giving him full credit for taking such good care of the boy. Even bhaiya kept looking at him in a peculiar manner for quite some time. However, this game also came to an end. The journey ahead was a long one, so taking Punardutta by the hand, I led him to the cabin, with bhaiya following behind. And let me tell you, this gesture on my part was enough for Punardutta to feel the warmth of our friendship. Once inside the cabin, he took his seat opposite me. As we began conversing, I was surprised to learn that Punardutta was totally unaware of his past. Perhaps, Chandak had deemed it unwise to reveal anything, to avoid upsetting him. Well, never mind! I decided to fill in the missing pieces of his past and gradually explained in detail about his father, Sandipani and *Acharya-ma*. Naturally, upon hearing all this, tears welled up in his eyes, and he became so overwhelmed that he fell at my feet. Fortunately, he soon calmed down, and in no time, we developed a friendly rapport. But yes, he was deeply pained by the fact that despite being the son of such a great teacher, he was brought up by a demoniac king and had remained uneducated. Another reason he felt distressed was that he had absolutely no knowledge of the world outside, having spent his entire life within four walls. Not only were ships and the sea new to him, the poor boy was witnessing everything in the outside world for the very first time. As for me, the mission's success had marked a tremendous political victory in my life. In fact, I must

confess, I had developed a taste for politics. No war between two armies, no unnecessary violence and no pointless devastation! All it required was some clever manoeuvring, hatching a plot, killing a king, that is, severing the very root of the problem…and the matter was resolved.

Well, presently, the mood in the cabin was one of cheer and bonhomie. And in such a pleasant atmosphere, how long does it take for time to pass? By the morning of the third day, we reached Prabhasa. Alighting from the ship with Punardutta and the treasure in tow, we rushed towards Jaivik's house. Seeing us return hale and hearty from the jaws of hell, he could not believe his eyes or the fact that we had slain the powerful King Panchajanya and freed Punardutta. Truly, his happiness knew no bounds and in this very elated state, he shared the good tidings with everyone in Prabhasa. As the news of Panchajanya's death spread like wildfire, all the inhabitants of Prabhasa thronged his house to meet us and express their gratitude. Of course, this respect was more for the 'slayer of Panchajanya' and less for me, but even so, I could not deny that it was ultimately I who was being honoured. Besides, who does not like being honoured? However, this was not the time to be side-tracked by praise. The danger had still not been averted completely; moreover, Jaivik's foolish act of spreading the news had only escalated it. So, without a moment's delay, we set off for the marketplace in our chariot. We already had the treasure that Chandak had gifted us, so we bought clothes, jewellery and several essentials for the journey. Needless to say, while purchasing clothes and accessories, Punardutta's needs were attended to with utmost care. After all, he was our prince now—our *gurudakshina*—who had also become a close friend of ours. And you can only imagine how someone who was forced to take on the garb of a demon all his life, would feel on being decked out in proper clothes and accessories. In fact, he looked dashing in his new attire! Honestly, draped in these clothes, he emanated a royal air and looked no less than a prince to me. Oh well, I had the whole journey and the rest of my life to keep admiring him. At present, as soon as we had finished purchasing everything we needed, we loaded our luggage onto the chariot and without inviting any more trouble, left forthwith for Ujjaini. My haste in speeding up our departure from Prabhasa was not without reason. Assassinating Panchajanya was undoubtedly a major event, and if any of his loyal supporters or well-wishers got even a whiff of our whereabouts, they would surely come after us to avenge his death. Not that I feared them; it was just that I believed in always being cautious. I wouldn't have hesitated in giving up my valuable life in battle, but losing it on account of carelessness was unacceptable to me. Besides, I believed it was best to move on quickly after completing a mission successfully.

After taking leave of Jaivik, we crossed Prabhasa in a flash. I had made Punardutta sit in the front with me, while the treasure had been entrusted in the strong and able hands of bhaiya. Needless to say, journeying in a chariot in the company of friends was making Punardutta go delirious with joy; moreover, he was feeling mighty proud of his new clothes too! Oh, you should have seen the joy and excitement on his face as he watched the passing scenery with wide eyes! This was a positive sign, which indicated that he was quickly adapting to his new surroundings. Punardutta's presence had made the journey even more enjoyable for us, as we now stopped at all the marketplaces that fell on our way and shopped to our hearts' delight. Punardutta was thrilled at the sight and taste of so many delicacies. As for bhaiya and me, what can I really say? I had to admit that a little bit of wealth and the company of good friends truly infuse your life with colour, elevating your enjoyment to a whole new level! And at present, I was experiencing this truth to the fullest. We were thoroughly enjoying our journey, eating and drinking to our heart's content and shopping all the fascinating goods we saw in the markets. This was the first time we had earned money and were deriving immense pleasure in spending it as well. Really, I could not imagine a journey more pleasurable than this!

Riding the chariot swiftly, enjoying the scenery and chatting with Punardutta, we reached Ujjaini after twelve days of travel. My enthusiasm and Punardutta's curiosity were at their peak, but as we reached closer to the *ashram*, Punardutta's eyes welled up with tears. Seeing us arrive, *Acharya*, *Acharya-ma* and all our friends came running to the entrance. We too stopped the chariot at the gate and jumped down. I took the blessings of *Acharya* and *Acharya-ma,* but surprisingly, no one had noticed Punardutta except for *Acharya-ma*. As for Punardutta, he could not hold back his emotions on seeing his parents. The tears that had welled up in his eyes now streamed down his cheeks. Realising the significance of the moment, I promptly nudged him to stand in front of *Acharya* and, very humbly, said, "Kindly accept my *gurudakshina*!"

Hearing me say these words, *Acharya* was astonished, while *Acharya-ma* burst into tears of joy. As for Punardutta, he felt blessed, embraced in the loving arms of his mother and receiving his father's blessings. Our friends, on the other hand, could not believe that the two of us, all by ourselves, had rescued Punardutta from a powerful demon like Panchajanya, and that too, in just four months. For that matter, even *Acharya* and *Acharya-ma* could hardly believe it. And let me confess, it was not just them; I too had to pinch myself repeatedly to make sure this was not a dream or fantasy!

Exhausted from the long journey, we first took an invigorating bath to wash away our tiredness. In the meantime, *Acharya-ma*, with the help of

a servant, had prepared the meal and also cooked some *kheer*.[32] She had, of course, prepared this *kheer* to celebrate the return of her darling son. After partaking of the meal, all of us gathered in the open square, and within no time, this gathering was transformed into a festival. Once again, Sudama and I enraptured everyone in the *ashram* with our singing and flute-playing. This time around, the sweet melody of my flute also seemed to reflect the satisfaction I felt on having offered my *gurudakshina*. The atmosphere was so charged that even *Acharya* could not stop himself from singing some hymns. And surprisingly, mother too sang a couple of hymns today. This in itself reflected the happiness that both *Acharya* and *Acharya-ma* felt. And as for Punardutta, who was the chief guest of the celebration as well as its main audience, he was enjoying himself immensely, his face emanating the joy he felt within. Indeed, for a boy who had spent his entire childhood confined in the cold walls of a dungeon, a celebration was indeed a novel concept. Coming back to *Acharya-ma*, she seemed to have gained a new lease of life, happiness pouring forth from every pore of her being. All her actions were marked with the unbridled joy she felt in her heart, and all along, she held on to the hand of her dear son while also quietly crying tears of joy. Truly, the pleasure I had experienced after defeating Panchajanya or after receiving heaps of wealth as a gift paled in comparison to the bliss I was experiencing on seeing *Acharya-ma's* elation. Truly, there is no greater joy on this earth than seeing happiness and bliss light up the face of another person; and especially if it is borne out of your actions, then it is all the more pleasurable.

I was thinking about this when my contemplation took a sudden turn and I began to wonder, is it not the duty of every human being to remain happy under all circumstances? Could *Acharya-ma* not derive the same joy she was experiencing on getting Punardutta back, from the very act of breathing in and out? Is breathing any less important? In fact, this game called life lasts only as long as one is able to breathe. Look at me, I would always be as happy as possible in every situation and circumstance. Throughout my life, I had immersed myself fully in every emotion and every situation. For, I believed, if a situation has presented itself, it means it has already fallen to your lot. Whatever is happening has become inevitable, then whether it is the mighty Jarasandha looming before you or the vicious serpent Kaaliya. So, if it has already fallen in your path, why bemoan it? Why not welcome it with open arms as if it were Radha? Why not make the ensuing struggle a celebration of sorts? Whether it was the serpent Kaaliya or the demon Keshi, this was precisely how I had welcomed trials and tribulations in my life. And just see the result: despite having grown up and lived under the spectre of death at all times, I had never stopped enjoying my life. Oh well, immersed in these

32. *Kheer* - A sweet dish made with milk, rice and sugar.

thoughts of self-appreciation, little did I realise that the evening's festivities had already come to an end.

Well, it did not matter, because every day at the *ashram* had now turned into a festival. Celebration, joy and cheer abounded in every nook and corner. But even in this atmosphere of happiness, a shadow of gloom lurked on *Acharya*'s expressions, which somehow gave me the impression that he was deeply troubled by something. No matter how much I racked my brain, I just could not fathom the reason behind his grave demeanour in such a joyful atmosphere. Nevertheless, seeing him in a sombre mood time and again, my mind kept returning to it, yet I couldn't understand why. However, I could fully trust the play of expressions on his face. If he was sombre, then there was definitely something worth worrying about. Actually, it was my naivety that was at fault; because this clearly meant that although I considered myself sharp and astute, there was still so much I had to learn from life. Indeed, a person must continue to learn as long as he is alive. Knowledge of the self may be attained in a fraction of a second, but as for the knowledge of this world, even if a person were to continue learning lifelong, there would still be an immense amount left to be gained. However, since I couldn't comprehend what the matter was, I decided to go with the flow. After all, the depth of *Acharya*'s feelings seemed beyond my understanding at that moment.

Well, today was Punardutta's first day at the *ashram* in a practical sense, hence all the existing rules had been relaxed to celebrate the occasion. We were served delicacies in both meals, and we celebrated on this night as well. Once again, my flute and Sudama's singing mesmerised everyone. Meaning, everything was proceeding well, but *Acharya* was still engrossed in his thoughts, unable to enjoy any of the festivities. Therefore, whether I liked it or not, my attention would invariably get drawn to him. Well, that was bound to happen, but a special feature of today's celebration was that I concluded the day's festivities by blowing into the Panchajanya conch. The deep, sonorous sound reverberated all around, enthralling everyone so much that, going forward, just like my flute, I would play the conch on various occasions as well. And that's not all! Just like my discus and flute, the conch too became an inseparable part of my identity for life.

However, it was only after the festivities had come to an end that trouble came knocking on my door. With the conclusion of the festival, everyone retired for the night. I was exhausted and sleepy too; after all, riding the chariot for twelve whole days was no small feat! But what can I say, *Acharya*'s solemn demeanour had robbed me of my sleep. Despite my fatigue, my consciousness was engaged in trying to fathom the secret behind *Acharya*'s sombre mood. The trouble was, even though I was trying my best, I was still unable to fathom it. And how could I uncover the secret anyway? After all, not only had Punardutta been rescued from the clutches of Panchajanya, but I had also returned to the *ashram* safely. Indeed, there was not even a scratch on my body, so why did he seem so troubled? Caught in these thoughts, I tossed and turned in bed all night.

Finally, after lunch the next day, the secret behind *Acharya*'s grave demeanour was revealed to me. And no, not because of my intelligence or smartness, but due to *Acharya's* kindness when he made me sit in his chamber and spoke gravely, "Jarasandha's messengers had come to the *ashram* a couple of times. Like a madman, he is searching for you everywhere. I don't know why, but this time, he seems bent on putting an end to you. Not only that, he has also issued a warning to all his allies that if any one of them provides refuge to Krishna and Balarama, then that individual would be put right at the top of Jarasandha's list of enemies. I see your life besieged by grave troubles!"

Oh! So, this was the reason behind *Acharya's* serious demeanour. Interestingly, it was not *Acharya* who was worrying unnecessarily; it was I who was being careless in my foolishness. Well, my careless attitude vanished into thin air the moment *Acharya* conveyed this news to me. Certainly, I needed to ponder the next course of action. Although I had never been free of the ominous shadow of Jarasandha, the fact that such a reputed king had nothing better to do than hatch a plot to kill me was certainly a cause for concern. Moreover, none of the kings of Aryavarta would grant us refuge now. Naturally, at present, there was no king in Aryavarta who was brave enough to defy Jarasandha. And as for Mathura, it was already planning to have us banished out of fear of Jarasandha. In short, we were once again left with no refuge. Neither did we have a home, nor a place to call our own. In a matter of moments, we poor brothers were left with no recourse.

It was a peculiar situation indeed. An air of tension pervaded the chamber. *Acharya*, who was sitting opposite me, was trying to gauge my expressions, while I was lost in deep thought. But then, he said something which kindled hope in me once again. In the course of our conversation, he informed me that after we had departed for Vaivasvatpur, grandfather had sent a messenger inviting us back to Mathura. Oh, this was great news indeed! This meant that the situation in Mathura had stabilised; at the very least, it had improved enough for grandfather to consider inviting us. I had just begun contemplating on these lines when *Acharya* advised me against going back to Mathura, because according to him, we would not remain safe there for long.

Before I could ponder upon this new information or analyse the situation properly, *Acharya* put forth a unique idea. He said, "In my opinion, it would be better for you to stay here a while longer. Believe me, you will find no place safer than this in all of Aryavarta. I say this because Jarasandha's ambition to become the emperor of Aryavarta would never allow him to attack an *ashram*—especially not one like mine."

Hearing *Acharya's* proposal, my thoughts veered off in a new direction as I mused, 'I could always go back to Chandak if I want to.' In fact, with great emotion, he had extended an invitation to me to return anytime I wished. Besides, considering the remote location of his kingdom, Jarasandha would never be able to make it that far...at least not in this lifetime. On giving it some more thought, I realised that we were not completely without shelter. Incredibly, just a few moments ago, it seemed as if we had no refuge, and now, there suddenly appeared to be several safe havens for us. In fact, we could now choose where we wanted to go. However, despite this, arriving at a decision was not as easy as it appeared. But yes, it had certainly become necessary to make a decision in a day or two. At present, I had understood both what *Acharya* had said and the cause of his worry. Honestly, his offer to let us stay at the *ashram* made me emotional. But for now, I asked him for some time to decide and took my leave.

However, even as I stepped out of his chamber, I became immersed in deep thought. All day long, I paced about the *ashram* from one end to the other, carefully considering all possible scenarios. But instead of getting resolved, the situation seemed to grow even more complicated. Because if safety was given top priority, then there was definitely no place safer than the *ashram*. But taking refuge here did not bode well for the *ashram's* reputation. Secondly, if we did so, it was certain that the *ashram* would become a permanent annoyance for Jarasandha. Moreover, we had to consider the fact that the *ashram* was supported by the royal palace of Ujjaini. Certainly, King Jaisen would never want us taking shelter in an *ashram* within his kingdom. After all, Jarasandha could not be trusted at all—what if he took out his anger on Jaisen? Another point to consider was that we could not live in the *ashram* forever. Life is akin to a flowing stream, and staying at the *ashram* would bring it to a standstill. Thus, after much deliberation, I reached the conclusion that instead of obstructing the flow of life and becoming stagnant, it was better to move forward and let life flow freely. It was definitely not acceptable if *Acharya* Sandipani or the *ashram* were to run into trouble because of me. As far as Vaivasvatpur was concerned, we could certainly take refuge in Chandak's kingdom, for, Jarasandha could not even imagine attacking Vaivasvatpur, at least not in this lifetime. But going there was problematic too; after all, security is not the only goal of life. Living in a kingdom of demons was akin to throwing one's life in the abyss of ruin. It was better to live in the shadow of death rather than live interminably in a kingdom of demonic pirates. So, in the end, the only alternative left was Mathura. In the present circumstances, returning to Mathura and confronting Jarasandha seemed to be the best option. At any rate, considering the extent of Jarasandha's desperation for revenge, the matter could be resolved either with the death of either of us or after elevating life to a stage whereby our safety and security would be guaranteed. Besides, if someone like Panchajanya could be slayed, then why couldn't Jarasandha be confronted? In the latter's case, we would at least have Mathura's army and its strength on our side. When I had slayed a demon king like Panchajanya single-handedly, of what consequence was Jarasandha? Thinking thus, I felt my confidence soar, and with that, I could clearly discern Mathura emerging as the best alternative. Even otherwise, it is always better to die in your homeland than lead the life of a fugitive, forever on the run. Thus, after considering all the options, I finally decided to return to Mathura.

Later that night, after dinner, when I announced my decision to *Acharya*, he was, of course, not too happy. For, he still held the opinion that we would be safe only at the *ashram*. It was heartening to know that our *guru-shishya*[33] relationship was based on a deep sense of selflessness. He was worrying himself sick, thinking about my safety, while I was caught up thinking about his safety and security. Indeed, if a relationship reflects even a hint of selfishness, can it truly be considered a relationship? Well, we were still discussing the matter when Anuvinda arrived. He had likely overheard part of our conversation, so sympathising with me, he offered his opinion, "Why don't we go to my father. Perhaps, by seeking his counsel, he might offer a solution." I could see that Anuvinda's suggestion had its merits. Jaisen, the king of Ujjaini, was the father of Vinda and Anuvinda. But how could I forget that he was completely under the influence of Jarasandha? Vinda and Anuvinda were still not well versed with the politics of the land, hence I could see that their suggestion had merely sprung forth from their immature love for their friends. Nevertheless, what did I stand to lose? There was no harm in asking, especially when there were no expectations. In any case, it is expectations that lie at the root of all losses and disappointments. It was then that a thought crossed my mind which made it necessary for us to go to King Jaisen. I began to wonder, 'If King Jaisen is under the influence of Jarasandha, then it is quite possible that he is displeased with our growing proximity to *Acharya*.' And if this were indeed the case, it could result in a strained relationship between the *ashram* and the royal palace, which was certainly not what I desired. Thus, it had become imperative for us to go to the palace and seek an audience with the king, to at least ensure that this relationship is never strained.

33. *Guru-shishya* - Teacher-student.

And now that the decision was made, there was no point in wasting time. So, we immediately set off with Vinda and Anuvinda to meet King Jaisen. On reaching the palace, I could see that it was quite magnificent. But at the moment, my mind was not interested in taking in the beauty of the palace; our priority was to seek a roof over our own heads. Sensing our impatience, Vinda and Anuvinda set aside all protocol and formalities and took us straight to the king's chamber. This was one of the benefits of receiving education at a reputed *ashram*. The more reputed the *ashram*, the more the number of princes you manage to befriend. Otherwise, who would have allowed a bunch of cowherds from Vrindavan to set foot in the palace of King Jaisen? Well, as soon as Vinda and Anuvinda introduced us to their father, his face fell. The king's handsome visage was creased with anxiety, making it evident that he was not pleased with our visit to his palace. I had foreseen this eventuality and was prepared for it too. But Vinda, unaware of all this, put forth to his father the idea of providing us shelter in his kingdom. The moment he heard this, a variety of emotions flitted across King Jaisen's countenance. After a few moments of unease, when he did regain his composure, he spoke in a serious tone, "You are a brave hero. You have killed two powerful kings, Kansa and Panchajanya. You are a friend to my sons and the best student of the greatest *Acharya* in our kingdom. It would be an honour for any king to provide shelter to a promising individual such as yourself. But please forgive me, the fear of Jarasandha is holding me back from extending this honour to you. However, if *Acharya* is willing, you can certainly continue to stay at his *ashram*. The *ashram* is forever free from any kind of political pressure."

Saying this, he let out a long sigh. Hearing their father speak thus, Vinda and Anuvinda were deeply disappointed. They had never imagined that their father would decline such a simple request. Well, one cannot gain practical knowledge just by studying in an *ashram*, can they? Such knowledge is attained only in the school of life, facing the harsh realities of life. As for me, hearing the king's pronouncement, I was neither surprised nor concerned, for, I had expected this response. Besides, the suggestion of providing us refuge was made by his own son. Therefore, it was not appropriate for me to give a reaction…and so, I remained silent. Seeing me lost in thought, King Jaisen broke the silence and spoke with a heavy heart, "Even if you stay at the *ashram,* it could still create challenges for us. If nothing else, we will surely face Jarasandha's ire because of it. You are wise enough to decide on the best course of action."

I was impressed by the eloquence with which King Jaisen had voiced his concerns. Even unpleasant facts had been communicated with finesse to soften the blow of the words. But this time, since he had spoken directly to me, I had to give an appropriate response. After all, it was necessary for me too, to maintain the high standard of the conversation. So, speaking in a calm tone, I said, "You are right. Actually, neither do we desire a safe haven in your kingdom, nor do we wish to put you or the *ashram* in trouble by continuing to stay there."

Hearing this, King Jaisen breathed a sigh of relief, and for the first time, the sombre look was replaced with a cheerful smile. I too did not miss the opportunity to take advantage of this smile. Since it was I who had brought the smile to his lips, I decided to call in the favour. So, continuing in the same vein, I said, "However, I do have a small request. At present, we do not have any means of transport to go to Mathura. If you can kindly provide us two chariots and charioteers, we shall be extremely grateful to you."

The moment he heard this, the king piped up, "Why just two; I will give you four chariots and horses. Kindly wait for a few days, as I am expecting my brand-new chariots to be delivered any day now!"

Honestly, I thought it was my right to demand the chariots. After all, we were doing him a favour by leaving his kingdom. Besides, I was no longer an ordinary cowherd. After slaying Kansa and Panchajanya, I was swiftly emerging as a valorous hero across the span of Aryavarta. Thus, by giving him an opportunity to do me a good turn, I was only doing him a favour. For, given a chance to accomplish a few more feats of valour, my standing in Aryavarta would indeed be beyond compare. In such a scenario, why would anyone pass up the opportunity to increase their proximity to me by refusing to provide a couple of chariots? After staying in Mathura for so long, I had become well versed in politics enough to understand at least this much. Also, let me share a secret with you. I had come here specifically to arrange for the chariots; and seeing the opportunity present itself, I had grabbed it with both hands. We needed chariots to safely carry to Mathura the treasure Chandak had given us. *Acharya* had only one chariot, so we couldn't possibly take that. And to be very honest, the other reason I wanted to return to Mathura was to keep the treasure Chandak had given me in a secure place at home. So, the treasure Chandak had gifted us had also played an important part in my decision to return to Mathura. Also, after the many accolades the king had showered upon me, it had become all the more necessary to ask for a chariot. I had to find out whether I had really become a valorous hero or whether the king's utterances of praise were just empty words to serve his selfish goals and wriggle out of a tricky situation. What if the thought of having become a hero was just a misconception on my part? For, after slaying Panchajanya and receiving the treasure, I was definitely filled with pride at having become a gallant hero. But now that King Jaisen had agreed to gift me chariots, I was sure that I had indeed become an eminent person on the map of Aryavarta. And the indisputable proof of this came on the fifth day when four brand-new chariots arrived at the *ashram* and were parked outside its main gate. As soon as the chariots arrived, bhaiya and I began our preparations to leave for Mathura. To be honest, we had puffed up a little on seeing four new chariots. Well, our plan was to depart the *ashram* the very next day; however, a mood of despondency had descended over the *ashram* with everyone wearing long faces now that the time had come for us to leave. Punardutta was the most affected, unable to control his tears on hearing that we would have to part ways. In contrast, *Acharya* looked more worried than sad, and undoubtedly, the cause of his worry was our safety. This made me wonder, were we making a wrong decision by choosing to go to Mathura? Well, whatever it was, tonight, all of us sat together and chit-chatted till the wee hours, despite a gloomy mood pervading the atmosphere.

Finally, with the dawn of a new day, it was time for us to bid farewell to the *ashram.* Early in the morning, mother had arranged for baskets of fruit to be packed in the chariots for our journey. Perhaps, everyone had woken up early today. I lost count of how many times we had embraced our friends and said our goodbyes. Poor Punardutta had still not given up on his pleas, trying to convince us to stay back at the *ashram.* I could well understand his emotions, but circumstances demanded that we leave. You will not believe it, but this 'farewell ceremony' continued for quite some time at the entrance of the *ashram*. Finally, embracing Punardutta and our friends one last time and taking the blessings of *Acharya-ma* and *Acharya,* we boarded the chariot. Everyone's eyes glistened with tears. The condition of *Acharya-ma* and Punardutta was the worst. Well, bidding farewell to everyone, bhaiya and I boarded the same chariot, and I handed over the reins to the charioteer. For some reason, I did not feel like riding the chariot myself. Instead, I sat majestically in the back seat, as if I were an esteemed king. Well, if I wasn't one now, I would soon become one; at the very least, this journey felt like one taken by wealthy travellers. Indeed, the chariot following us was loaded with the treasure that Chandak had gifted us. Moreover, one chariot preceded ours, while another followed the chariot carrying the treasure. So, it was only natural for this cowherd to sit a little smugly. The chariots were ours, and so was the wealth in them. And with me sitting regally, you can only imagine how bhaiya, an expert at being pompous, must have seated himself! We were no longer ordinary cowherds, and now that we had taken this leap of progress, what was the harm in dreaming big? Unbelievably, I soon drifted into a reverie where I pictured myself draped in royal clothes with a peacock feather tucked in my curls, strutting around like a prince! Oh, we hadn't even crossed Ujjaini yet, but here I was, already lost in flights of fancy!

However, this journey was not spent in daydreaming alone. Let me tell you that I kept thinking of the emotional farewell accorded to us by *Acharya*, *Acharya-ma*, Punardutta and all our friends. The look of gratitude in *Acharya-ma* and Punardutta's eyes was a sight that would stay with me for life. I had seen the very same look of gratitude in Chandak and Tamas' eyes as well when we had parted from them. And this made me think, 'How heartwarming it is to see gratitude in the eyes of others at the time of parting!' But only someone who has helped another person selflessly can experience this feeling. Well, putting this aside, let me draw your attention to another interesting fact. The chariots and charioteers gifted to us by King Jaisen were both a testament to Jarasandha's terror. Neither did the chariots bear the royal insignia of Ujjaini, nor were the charioteers dressed in royal uniforms. This meant that while Jaisen had certainly helped us, he had also ensured that Jarasandha remained unaware of his assistance. As far as I was concerned, this was fine, and I did not take offence at it. At any rate, our influence at present was not greater than that of Jarasandha. Indeed, there is a basic principle in this world: if you want respect, you must expand your sphere of influence.

Well, I would do that as well…if I managed to survive. At the moment, to lighten my mood, I engaged in some light-hearted banter with myself, cursing Uncle Kansa in my mind. I said to him, 'Were Jarasandha's daughters the only women you could find to marry? Had you married the daughters of some ordinary king, I swear on Mother Yashoda, I would have put an end to that king in no time!' Oh, when will this dark, looming shadow of Kansa vanish from my life, I wondered. His presence had started haunting me from the moment I was born, continuing until his death. And now, even after his death, he had unleashed this terrible, bloodthirsty fiend, Jarasandha, to chase after me. 'Wow, Uncle! You are truly one of a kind!' Indeed, now that we had set off for Mathura, it was only natural that all my thoughts would revolve around Kansa and Jarasandha.

But as our journey progressed, my mind drifted away from these worthless musings and began focusing on Mathura. For, it was crucial to contemplate over the situation prevailing in Mathura too. Speaking of Mathura, I found my mind returning to the same question time and again. Despite the fact that grandfather had invited us to come to Mathura, would the Yadava leaders respect his wishes? Even if they gave refuge to us on account of grandfather's insistence, how would they tackle the menace of Jarasandha? Because after hearing the news that I had returned to Mathura, he would definitely attack the city. In other words, as soon as we reached Mathura, a clash with Jarasandha was inevitable. Well, when a clash was certain and death unavoidable, what was the point in entertaining futile thoughts and ruining the pleasure of this journey? Besides, this was the first time we were travelling in royal comfort, with servants to tend to all our needs, so I reckoned, why not enjoy it to the fullest? Thus, pushing aside dismal thoughts, I became absorbed in enjoying our journey. Time and again, I would turn around to look at our magnificent caravan of four chariots. The journey, as we travelled during the day, was no doubt pleasurable, but at night, one of us brothers had to stay awake. Well, we couldn't help it, for, the treasure we were carrying along had made the nightly vigil a must for at least one of us. Apart from this sole concern, our journey was splendid in every sense of the word. Really, was there anything lacking in this journey? Nothing at all! We had everything we needed! We had four magnificent chariots in addition to charioteers and servants too. For the first time, we were experiencing the luxurious life of a prince. Travelling thus, time flew by as if on wings, and we didn't even realise when the journey came to an end.

After ten days of travel, our chariots rolled into Mathura. I cannot even describe the joy I felt on returning home after a span of one year. After all, there is no place like home. The first thing we needed to do was tuck away our treasure in a secure place. We thus headed towards Father Vasudeva's mansion. Had the circumstances been different, we would have surely gone straight to the palace. Interestingly, as our chariots moved ahead, I noticed that the inhabitants of Mathura appeared quite excited to see us return. However, I soon realised that their curiosity about our four chariots was far greater than their excitement on our return. Now, irrespective of whether the people were curious about us or our caravan, the news was sure to spread. So, by the time we reached father's mansion, the news of our arrival had spread all over Mathura. The moment our parents saw us, they were elated. The pride on seeing their children return after completing their education was clearly visible in their eyes. But my attention was focused solely on securing the treasure. Hence, the first thing I did was move all the treasure given by Chandak safely into my room. Indeed, it was for this very purpose that I had come to father's house before visiting the palace. You know very well that in Krishna's life, duty always took precedence over emotions. But yes, once I had taken care of the treasure, I chatted with mother and father to my heart's content. Amazingly, no sooner had I arrived in Mathura than my political brain became active once again. And accordingly, I first instructed bhaiya not to disclose any information about 'Mission Panchajanya' to anyone. Because in my opinion, the killing of Panchajanya carried powerful leverage that could be used to impress the Yadava leaders when the need arose. And a well-known fact about leverage is that it is essential to deploy it at the right moment, else it often fails to bring about the desired result.

Well, no sooner had I put away the treasure than I set off for the palace, leaving bhaiya at our parents' house. I was eager to meet my beloved grandfather, as I wanted to learn about Mathura's situation as soon as possible. At first glance, the condition of the palace seemed poor; it appeared to have deteriorated since our departure. In fact, even the soldiers of Magadha, whom we had dismissed earlier, had resumed their positions…and this was definitely not a positive sign. This implied that although Jarasandha had not invaded Mathura yet, he certainly had a strong hold over the royal palace. Meaning, the prey had walked straight into the death trap! Nonetheless, I had to seek solace in the fact that even though Jarasandha had tightened his grip over Mathura, it was my grandfather who still reigned as the king. For the time being, this was the only reassurance I could content myself with. So, it was with this feeling of reassurance that I entered grandfather's chamber. The news of our arrival had already reached him, so naturally, he was ecstatic to see me. However, his joy at my arrival could not conceal the despair he was trying to hide. And the warning sign for me was that his despondency ran deep, proven by the fact that he was guzzling wine in broad daylight! Never mind! Seeing grandfather's condition, I braced myself for the tidings he would give me regarding the current situation of the kingdom.

For a while, the two of us sat in silence, facing each other. While there was nothing that grandfather could say to me, I had grasped everything after observing the state of affairs at the palace. The situation was so delicate that it had become difficult for us to even speak a few reassuring words to each other. In any case, a smart person only needs a hint to understand what's going on around him. Another fact that became apparent to me was that inviting us to return to Mathura must have been grandfather's personal decision; the Yadava leaders could not have been in favour of it. Thus, if I wanted to stay on in Mathura, I had to impress these Yadavas thoroughly, otherwise the situation would slide back to its previous state. They would once again pressurise grandfather to banish us from Mathura, and we would once again be left with no refuge whatsoever. And verily, there are many battles in life which require one to launch an attack first; and the battle between the Yadava elders and us seemed to be of a similar kind. In short, there seemed to be only one way out of this situation. Before the Yadava leaders voiced their protest and demanded our banishment from Mathura yet again, I had to impress them to such an extent that they would feel compelled to welcome us instead. The idea seemed favourable, so I acted on it immediately. Breaking my silence, I asked grandfather to arrange a meeting of the Yadava leaders, and insisted that he invite the inhabitants of Mathura as well. Indeed, when the time had come to beard the lion in its den, why not do it in front of the common people? My grandfather was incredible! Once he knew he had my support, he would become so enthusiastic as if all his troubles had vanished already, and proof of this was the fact that as soon as I suggested a meeting with the Yadava leaders, he agreed to it instantly. You would not believe this, but grandfather had not even enquired about the agenda of the meeting. Of course, there was no cause for alarm, as I had already analysed the situation carefully and had even chalked out the battle strategy down to its last detail. Now, our future depended entirely on its implementation. Well, I would do that when the time came, but at present, the good news was that grandfather quickly fixed the date of the meeting and instructed the chief minister to make the necessary arrangements. The meeting was scheduled to be held in a week's time at Mathura's main ground. Fully aware of the significance of the matter, I too immersed myself in preparing for the meeting with immediate effect, and as a first step, I took grandfather's leave and set off from the palace. Naturally, I needed to think in solitude about every move I would make from here on.

Unaware of all these developments, bhaiya had begun enjoying himself as soon as we had returned to Mathura. Generally, during the day, he and I would keep each other company, but at night, he would unfailingly go to the royal palace while I would return to father's house. The free-flowing wine at the royal palace had certainly played a big role in separating the two brothers! Nevertheless, at present, I had to concentrate on the meeting, and in that regard, my objective was absolutely clear. I wanted the meeting to be attended by as many *Mathurawasis* as possible. My intention was clear—the larger the number of common people who attended, the greater my chances of dominating the Yadava leaders. For, even though the Yadava leaders were completely against me, my standing and stature among the inhabitants remained intact. Leaving political matters aside, if I were to speak about Mathura's condition, it was quite pitiable even now. Neither had the task of repairing the houses progressed, nor was there any proper arrangement made for food or water. In short, Mathura had deteriorated from bad to worse. Well, talking about the meeting, its sudden announcement by the royal palace after my arrival in Mathura had sparked great curiosity among the Yadava leaders. This was definitely a good sign for me, as their curiosity would ensure that they would all be present at the meeting. Besides, several other factors were fast emerging in my favour too. For one, the battle that we had won against Jarasandha was still fresh in the minds of the common people. This meant that I would no longer need to impress them by demonstrating another instance of my bravery. More importantly, the fact that I had been sent away from

Mathura due to the threat of Jarasandha was known only to grandfather and the Yadava leaders. The common people of Mathura were completely in the dark about this. What I mean to say is, the factors which were in my favour were known to all, and those that were against me had remained hidden behind closed doors.

Well, engrossed in all these deliberations and lengthy discussions with grandfather, we did not even realise when an entire week had passed. The day of the meeting had finally dawned. I woke up early and promptly reached the palace. In the past, I had witnessed many nights that were crucial for me; this however was a decisive day. And since I had scheduled this meeting as part of a strategy, the success of the meeting depended entirely on my own preparations. Naturally, as I was fully aware of the significance of this meeting, I had not spared any effort in contemplating over it. I had carefully considered every minute detail from a strategic viewpoint. In fact, grandfather and I had decided to reach the meeting venue at different times. As per the plan, I had sent him on his way well in advance, while I decided to make a late entry to emphasise my importance; but now, it was time for me to leave too. My caravan was ready, so bhaiya and I sat regally in one of the chariots, with three empty chariots following us. You could say we had made this trip to the meeting venue look like a veritable procession. On our way, we crossed paths with many people who were still heading towards the main ground. Meaning, we were reaching well in time. The Yadava leaders were already present at the venue, and as soon as they saw bhaiya and me alight from our chariot with pomp and style, they stood stupefied. It was precisely for this purpose—to make a powerful impression on the Yadava leaders—that I had arrived at the meeting with all four chariots in tow. Well, moving on, grandfather had already taken his seat on the throne, with all the Yadava leaders seated around him. Unfortunately though, the inhabitants of Mathura had not displayed much enthusiasm; a maximum of five hundred people had gathered at the ground. But oh, they couldn't help it, as Mathura's economy was all but destroyed, and most of the inhabitants were reduced to a penurious state, barely able to eke out a living. Overwhelmed by their own problems and the struggle for survival, who would want to embroil themselves in this political game? Well, if that's the way they felt, then so be it. At present, just as I had expected, there was an uproar in the assembly the moment we arrived. While some people began applauding and demonstrating their solidarity with us, others began shouting out their denouncements. And this was the biggest proof of my incredible personality—a person could either love me or hate me, but no one could remain indifferent towards me. Pray tell me, how could anyone ignore a personality like me? In short, the crowd had split into two factions upon my arrival. On one hand, the Yadava leaders and their sycophants were bristling with anger upon seeing me, and on the other, the common people of Mathura were responding to them by shouting slogans in my praise. And in my heart of hearts, I was quietly enjoying this tug of war between the two groups. Well, this was how I felt, but poor grandfather, despite his age, had to expend a lot of energy in silencing the crowd. Well, he was bound to do at least this much out of love for his grandson. Nonetheless, after much effort, when the assembly finally calmed down, grandfather commenced the meeting and announced, "Krishna has something important to say to all of you. I, therefore, invite him to come forward and speak." As soon as my name was announced, I, who was sitting behind everyone on the stage, jumped up and, tearing through the group of Yadava leaders, went up and stood next to grandfather. The crowd sitting below was now directly in front of me. As soon as I smiled and welcomed them by waving my hand, the entire ground resonated with slogans in my praise. Oh, but you should have seen the look of displeasure on the faces of the Yadava leaders sitting on either side of me! Unable to bear the love and respect being accorded to me, they rallied together, openly shouting slogans against me. In fact, they seemed determined to not let me speak. Seeing this, the fervour of the crowd scaled even more, while I stood watching this drama in great style, arms akimbo and legs spread slightly apart. Did you see how the mere announcement of my name had created such an uproar! Well, my personality had always been controversial; the very mention of my name could raise even the dead from their grave…this was, after all, just a meeting of the Yadavas.

Well, no matter how amused I was at this spectacle—which was actually orchestrated by me as a part of a strategy—the chaos and pandemonium had begun to make grandfather a bit jittery. Still, he rose to the occasion and did not shirk from doing what had to be done; he once again made an earnest effort to quell the uproar. Undoubtedly, the Yadava leaders were the loudest in their opposition. Actually, they were all clamouring to speak first, and I did not want to give them the opportunity at any cost. For, I feared they would stoke the *Mathurawasis*' fear of Jarasandha and turn them against me. And in case they succeeded, all my efforts would be in vain, because gripped with fear, whatever I said to them next would fall on deaf ears. So, I continued to stand determined in my place, firm as a rock. Grandfather, of course, wanted to hold the meeting in accordance with my wishes, granting me the right to speak first. Therefore, he too refused to budge and continued to stand in my favour. Now, how long could the old king be ignored? Soon enough, everyone calmed down. And that was my cue. I did not want to waste any time presenting my views before yet another outburst from the Yadavas spoiled my plans or caused the meeting to be sidelined. Hence, without hesitation, I blew the Panchajanya conch and began addressing the crowd. The conch and the sound that emanated from it were so impressive that an astonished silence fell over everyone present in the gathering. The conch had done its work, and now, it was my turn to grab the attention of the audience. Dressed in splendid attire and adorned with ornaments, I was anyway set to make an impression, and verily, making a good impression in this meeting was fundamental to my plan. So, I commenced my address by waving the Panchajanya conch, which I had held aloft in my right hand. Speaking haughtily, I began, "This is the famous Panchajanya conch, which we have obtained after slaying the demon king, Panchajanya. When we heard that our *guru*, *Acharya* Sandipani's only son had been kidnapped in his childhood by Panchajanya, we resolved to rescue the poor boy and present him to our *Acharya* as *gurudakshina*. We were well aware that Panchajanya was many times more powerful than Jarasandha, but we were still obliged to pay our *gurudakshina*. Besides, we also had complete faith in our own strength and might. In any case, when your resolve is unshakeable and is supported by the requisite strength and power, the desired results are bound to follow. You will not believe it, but not only did bhaiya and I defeat the entire army of Panchajanya on our own, but we also assassinated him. However, since we are deeply attached to Mathura, we did not accept the opportunity of kingship and establish our rule over that kingdom."

Hearing this, the assembly broke into a thunderous applause, and with this, the poor Yadava leaders were silenced, as if struck by a thunderbolt. They could not even begin to comprehend what Krishna had done! Grandfather was so elated that tears started streaming down his face. And how do I even begin to describe the enthusiasm of the masses! The commander and the chief minister were delighted as well. In any case, given the imminent attack by Jarasandha, what Mathura needed was a hero, and I fit the bill in every respect. Hence, it was only a matter of time before the crowd accepted me as their hero. Seeing that my plan had worked, I became enthusiastic and, driven by that enthusiasm, continued, "And instead of ascending the throne ourselves, we instated Chandak, the former chief minister, as the king of Vaivasvatpur. I'm pleased to inform you that he has now pledged loyalty to us. That's not all! In his elation at being crowned king, he showered us with many gifts and immense wealth. It gives me great pleasure to tell you that we too have become affluent Yadavas now. Honestly, it was to share these good tidings with you that I had requested grandfather to arrange this meeting. Having said that, we were also anxious about Mathura's welfare, for, as you are well aware, Mathura is facing turmoil, both internally as well as externally. On one hand, the economy is stumbling, and on the other, the fear of an attack by Jarasandha still haunts us. Of course, Jarasandha is not a big problem in my opinion; when we can defeat a powerful demon like Panchajanya, of what consequence is Jarasandha? I strongly believe that instead of infighting, if all of us Yadavas stand united, we can permanently rid ourselves of Jarasandha. Besides, the united force of the Yadavas will also help lift the sagging fortunes of Mathura and pull it out of its current abysmal condition. In my opinion, to accomplish all this, it is imperative that we now choose a Yadava Chief from amongst ourselves, someone who is not only capable of saving us from Jarasandha but is also committed to improving Mathura's deplorable state!"

This was verily my trump card, which I had played cleverly. For, I knew I was the only one who fit this role. Well, regardless of whether I fit the bill or not, I had surely hinted at this possibility through my address. And just as I had expected, my efforts paid off! My name echoed from all corners of the ground, leaving the Yadava leaders stunned. Not a single person from the crowd was suggesting their name. Well, do you see, this is what happens when you come to wrangle with Krishna...the artful Krishna! Needless to say, I was elected the leader of the Yadavas, and with this, the objective behind convening the meeting had also been achieved. The cowherd boy who had arrived in Mathura from the small village of Vrindavan not too long ago, had now become the leader of the Yadavas! Well, as soon as the *Mathurawasis* made their decision clear, the Yadava elite beat a hasty retreat. So be it! I turned to look at grandfather, who had gone delirious with joy. And as for the inhabitants of Mathura, they had lifted me on their shoulders and, beating their drums and cymbals, paraded around the ground a couple of times. Seeing this, tears welled up in the eyes of my tender-hearted brother. He was deeply moved by the respect shown to his younger sibling. He did not care about the political manoeuvrings; he was simply overwhelmed by the fact that I had been made the Chief of the Yadavas. But how long could this drama and celebration continue? Eventually, it came to an end and we departed from the ground with grandfather in tow.

Truly, this was the biggest personal achievement of my life. I could not contain my happiness. Most importantly, I felt assured that no one could now pressurise grandfather to banish us from Mathura. For, how could the leader himself be ordered to leave the kingdom? Secondly, we no longer had to prove that we were Yadavas and not just cowherds, since I had now been appointed the Yadava Chief. However, if I were to express what I really felt, none of this made any difference to my worry and anxiety. For, I still did not have a permanent solution to the recurring problem of Jarasandha. To impress the people of Mathura, I had boasted at the meeting that we had defeated Panchajanya in battle. However, I could not deny the truth that I had assassinated him through political manoeuvring. I could not use the same strategy with Jarasandha; with him, it would be a one-on-one combat. And by now, even you must have understood that it was impossible to defeat Jarasandha in a one-on-one combat.

Ah, but for now, let us cast aside these worries. I had become the leader of the Yadavas, and a leader never worries himself sick. So, let me talk about something positive. Grandfather had become absolutely free of worries after this entire episode. For that matter, even the lost confidence of the *Mathurawasis* had been restored to a great extent. Seeing all this, I felt like patting my back and congratulating myself time and again. Oh, what a fabulous trick I had played! Now, who would dare ask us to leave Mathura? Grandfather was the king, and I, his dear grandson, was the leader of the Yadavas. Meaning, the reins of Mathura were now completely in our hands. Indeed, lies, politics, diplomacy, theatrics, deception were all suiting me perfectly. In fact, they were not just suiting me; day by day, I was fully imbibing these qualities too. And why should I not? After all, it was because of these very qualities that this leader of a small troop of cowherd boys had now risen to become the leader of thousands of Yadavas. And interestingly, as soon as I became the leader, I also began to feel proud of my prominent position. Now, I would take my caravan of four chariots even on routine trips to the marketplace, sitting so haughtily that my very demeanour reflected the authority of being the chief of the Yadavas. On the other hand, the condition of the Yadava elite had become pitiable. They were finding it hard to digest that an ordinary cowherd from Vrindavan had become their leader. You would not believe it, but for a few days, none of them even dared to step out on the streets of Mathura.

However, this sense of joy did not last long. I, the new Yadava Chief, had barely begun to enjoy my life, having met Malini just a couple of times, when suddenly, I found myself besieged by a new set of worries. And the reason for it was bhaiya, who seemed unusually happy these days. His joy over me becoming the Yadava Chief had long subsided; he was now excited about the prospect of locking horns with Jarasandha! Great! His happiness had unnecessarily reminded me of Jarasandha and the danger that still loomed large over our heads. Ironically, the very thought which had robbed me of my sleep, had filled him with excitement. And the sole reason for this was that he took great pride in his prowess with the mace. But in truth, his confidence was far removed from the ground reality. It was not as if he would get an opportunity to fight Jarasandha in a one-on-one combat. For that matter, even grandfather's faith and that of the *Mathurawasis* was misplaced. Forget

saving them from Jarasandha; I was incapable of saving them even from his shadow! Little did these naïve people realise that I had used all those political manoeuvres just to secure our stay in Mathura.

But now, the real question was—what good was securing refuge if it would only last until Jarasandha launched his attack? On his arrival, we were doomed to be either homeless or lifeless! Meaning, I, the one who had been strutting around as the Yadava Chief, was now steeped in anxiety day and night. Meanwhile, unaware of the turmoil brewing in my mind, everyone else was filled with delight, seeing me strut around Mathura with swagger. And this led to a humorous outcome in the coming days. After the dramatic, boastful speech I had delivered at the meeting of the Yadavas, grandfather and the rest of Mathura had become completely relaxed, free of worries...as if Jarasandha was of no consequence at all! And in contrast to them, I, the one in whom they had so happily reposed their faith, allowing them to sleep peacefully, had lost his own sleep! Even if I were to ignore them, my problem was that I couldn't think of a concrete battle strategy against Jarasandha, nor did it seem likely that he would fall for any plan or plot I might devise. Moreover, I did not know how to wield a sword or mace or even shoot an arrow. The only weapons I knew how to use were cunningness, trickery and deception; but at present, even those seemed useless against Jarasandha. Caught in this conundrum, it was only natural for this poor cowherd to lose his sleep.

But the question was, what would I gain by losing sleep over it? Besides, it was not as if Jarasandha was already on his way to Mathura. We still had some time, so I was hopeful that some strategy would soon present itself. Oh, what can I say to you? Reassuring myself with such false assurances, I would somehow manage to get some sleep. But to add to my woes, no sooner I freed myself from anxiety than the behaviour of the *Mathurawasis* would make me restless all over again. Interestingly, the more worried I was, the more relaxed and assured they were becoming due to the faith they had vested in me. Oh, it seemed I had boasted a bit too much at the meeting of the Yadavas! Indeed, I was angry with myself for having bitten more than I could chew. After all, there is a limit to lying and boasting too! Well, while I spent my time grappling with these thoughts, the news of our arrival finally reached Jarasandha, and with this, our fate was sealed. All he needed was this news, for, he was anyway ready to launch his attack. This time, no special preparations were needed, so he promptly set off for Mathura with full force. Here in Mathura, when grandfather's spies brought him the news of Jarasandha's imminent attack, he quickly summoned me. And much to my irritation, he conveyed this grave news to me in so cheerful a manner, as if Jarasandha was coming to invite us for a feast. He said, "Krishna! My spies tell me that Jarasandha and his army have set off for Mathura. Oh, I pity the poor fool! He is coming of his own accord, playing right into your hands!"

Hearing grandfather's cheerful tone, my heart sank, for, what frightened me even more was the manner in which he had disclosed the news. He was perhaps the first king in history who was delighted to hear that his kingdom was about to be attacked by a king who was several times more powerful than him. But alas, I could not blame him, as the fault was entirely mine for weaving grandiose tales of my valour. Indeed, I had been such a braggart at the meeting of the Yadavas. Oh, what could I possibly say to grandfather now? But then, I reckoned, since the fault was mine, why unnecessarily spoil his mood? Thus, with a smile, I quietly left the palace, as though confirming that his thoughts were right. As for myself, what was I supposed to do with the avalanche of worries that had laid claim to both my heart and mind? To whom could I turn to, to share this burden of mine? I considered telling bhaiya, thinking that a serious discussion with him would help in some way. But bhaiya was really strange, because the moment he heard the news that Jarasandha was on his way, he reached for his mace and began brandishing it in the air, as if he was going to smash Jarasandha's skull right away. Exasperated at his foolhardiness, I slapped my palm against my forehead in sheer frustration. Really, I was caught in a mad circus. No one was willing to understand the gravity of the situation. Bhaiya was capricious to begin with, and now, grandfather too seemed to have gone senile due to his advanced age. Honestly, at this point in time, I was far more worried seeing bhaiya happily swinging his mace in the air and grandfather cheerfully delivering the dreadful news than I was about Jarasandha's imminent arrival. I thought, 'There is no doubt that bhaiya is naïve, but grandfather, you are experienced, aren't you? You are a seasoned king with decades of experience behind you. So, why aren't you serious even after hearing the news that Jarasandha has set out to attack us? Oh, dear grandfather! If Jarasandha is on his way here, kindly convene an urgent meeting of the council of ministers. Summon the commander of the army. Why are you conveying this news only to me, a poor cowherd? Wake up, dear grandfather, wake up! Jarasandha isn't playing into Krishna's hands; he is coming to chop off the very hands of your dear grandson!' But, poor grandfather, could you really blame him? I had given such a melodramatic account of Panchajanya's slaying at the meeting of the Yadavas that anyone would fall under its spell. Argh! I was furious at myself for the rabble-rousing speech I had given at the meeting. In my mind, I said to grandfather, 'I am immature but at least you, grandfather…you are mature. So what if I spoke childishly? Will you put me to the test by pitting me against Jarasandha? Will you get your beloved grandchild killed?' Driven by anxiety, I spent all day babbling to myself like this. I rued the fact that my own bragging had made the problem so much worse, turning it into something I couldn't fix. Ah, my boasting was proving to be my own undoing!

Well, the die was cast, but what now? Finally, I came to the conclusion that when the king is not serious about the impending attack on his kingdom, and when no one else is preparing for the forthcoming battle, then why should I, who always wore a happy countenance, worry unnecessarily? It was better if I too became part of the foolishness that now prevailed everywhere. But to do so, I would have to be a little foolish myself. So, casting aside intelligence, I began to act foolish; and naturally, I started with my grandfather. One day, I said to him in a rather casual manner, "Do you see the suicidal mindset of Jarasandha? Disregarding my presence in Mathura, he has set out to attack us! But don't you worry. I am here!" Although while speaking this, I did feel a bit odd. Though the words I had used sounded reassuring, I actually wanted him to worry, at least a little. In fact, I couldn't help but feel angry that a destructive war was right around the corner, but he, the king, was just sitting there, smiling, as if all of this was of little consequence. But, of course, this one-sided conversation was playing only in my head; as for grandfather, my bravery had made him so ecstatic that I had to reluctantly assume a carefree attitude in front of him. What can I say! The situation was pitiable indeed. I couldn't come up with any battle strategy, and worse still, I had to bear everyone's strangely laidback demeanour. You could say that these days, I was paying the price for being a sensible person. The worst part was that despite being overwhelmed with anxiety inside, I had to fake a happy demeanour on the outside. And amazingly, the more I smiled, the more relaxed people became. Oh, what a ludicrous situation I had gotten myself into! I wasn't sure what to do. Should I just continue to smile or be prepared to embrace death? If I wore a serious demeanour, nobody would take me seriously, and if I smiled, everyone became even more carefree. And the end result of this was, just as time had earlier taught me to live with all my sorrows and desires hidden within, it had now taught me to live without revealing my anxieties as well.

Never mind! At least I was getting the opportunity to enter the jaws of death with a smile on my face. Gradually, the news of Jarasandha's impending attack spread all over Mathura, but despite this, no fear or nervousness could be seen on the faces of the inhabitants this time around. After all, I, their hero, saviour and leader of the Yadavas, was standing shoulder to shoulder with them! On seeing this maddening nonchalance all around me, my brain had ceased to function. An intelligent person like me could no longer think of a solution. Neither was anyone talking about preparing for the war, nor did anyone seem worried about the danger looming before us. These foolish people were no doubt destined to die, but it seemed that they had decided to get me—the sensible one—killed too. Someone has rightly said, choose the company you keep wisely, for, befriending fools can put your very life in danger. After much deliberation, there seemed to be only one way to stop this insanity—to convene another meeting of the Yadavas and make certain clarifications about my bravery. Taking a step back, I needed to apprise everyone of the reality of the battle we had to face. Perhaps, they will then come to their senses and view the impending battle with the seriousness it deserved. Indeed, the mad, carefree attitude had become so widespread now, that everyone was happily discussing the news of Jarasandha's arrival as if he was coming to Mathura bearing gifts for the *Mathurawasis*.

Oh well! Presently, I was the leader of the Yadavas, so it was I who had to convene the meeting and address it as well. As for the speech, it didn't amount to much. After having praised myself to the skies in the previous meeting, this time, I had to tone it down and clear the air. In fact, I reminded myself repeatedly, 'Kanhaiya, do not boast this time around. Tread with caution and kindly stay grounded.' Interestingly, everyone including grandfather was surprised to hear about another Yadava meeting. They then reasoned that I had perhaps convened the meeting to explain the war strategy or to tell them not to panic. In other words, the gravity of the situation had not dawned upon any of them, nor did they deem it necessary to discuss or chalk out a strategy for the war. But it did not matter; I would soon make them see reason. After all, it was with this very objective that I had convened the meeting. Finally, the day of the meeting arrived. This was a new day and the strategy I had adopted was brand new as well; meaning, I, Krishna, was fully prepared with the new strategy.

This time, I went to the meeting dressed ordinarily; after all, once bitten twice shy! However, I had sent grandfather before me on this occasion as well. In fact, I had asked him to take bhaiya along too. Needless to say, I set off with just one chariot and was also riding it myself. The strategy for this meeting did not permit any flashy or flamboyant displays. Fortunately, the number of people attending this meeting was quite high. Grandfather and bhaiya were already seated on the dais with the Yadava elite and the council of ministers. On arriving at the venue, I, like a poor boy with his head bowed down, began walking towards the stage with slow, heavy steps. This time, I had left the chariot at the entrance. And as for my smile, I had kept it tightly guarded, so much so that I wouldn't have smiled even if I heard the funniest joke! I had even left my Panchajanya conch at home. I realised that it was because of the thrill of blowing into it that I had gotten carried away last time and bragged a bit too much. All in all, the message was clear. I had already boasted too much in the previous meeting, so this time, I had to tone things down. Indeed, the sole objective of holding a second meeting was to curb the insanity that had gripped the palace and the inhabitants of Mathura. I had to shake them out of their complacency and get them to prepare for war. But alas! What transpired was exactly the opposite! Before the meeting could even begin, the situation slipped right out of my hands. Those present at the meeting were suddenly caught in a frenzy, bordering on insanity. I had not even reached the dais when I received a standing ovation from all around. And if this was not enough, the gathering had begun cracking jokes about Jarasandha. The worst part was, I saw grandfather and the responsible ministers also laughing along. And the less said about the jokes, the better! It was as if they were not talking about Jarasandha, but an inconsequential, tiny bird that Kanhaiya would capture and lock into a cage in a flash! Unbelievably, the majority of people began likening me to a lion and Jarasandha to a goat. Only I knew what the reality was, my mind screaming, 'Oh, ask me! Ask me who the lion is and who the goat is!' Honestly, these demented people did not seem half as dangerous when they roamed the streets alone as they now appeared in the grip of collective insanity.

Well, tearing my way through the din, I somehow reached the podium in the midst of this raucous behaviour. My face was still downcast and my ears did catch a few good jokes, but because of the problem that weighed on my mind, I was not laughing at all. On the contrary, once I stood on the stage, I looked all around with a sombre expression, thinking that maybe my serious demeanour would produce the desired effect on the gathering. But alas, this was not to be! Even the sorry plight of their Yadava leader made no difference to them. They perhaps reckoned that even this was a dramatic scene that I was enacting. At least a thousand Yadavas were seated in front of me, but not a single one of them appeared serious. On the contrary, their laughter and tomfoolery echoed loudly in the air. What could I say? No one was ready to listen. As soon as I opened my mouth to speak, the words were drowned in the slogans eulogising me. I could perhaps deal with these insane people one at a time, but dealing with a group of them appeared next to impossible. I did try to put forth my views a couple of times, but when collective stupidity grips a crowd, no one listens to anything remotely sensible. Besides, could I really blame them? For, I alone was largely responsible for their present state of insanity. Oh, I had trapped myself badly by painting such a grand picture of Panchajanya's assassination at the Yadava meeting! These fools were ecstatic for no reason, and it seemed that even Nature was not in favour of my speaking the truth, as I couldn't find a single opportunity to do so.

Oh well! If that was Nature's wish, then so be it. Finally, exasperated from trying to get my message across, I too joined the crowd of fools. The purpose of the meeting was ruined anyway, so I reckoned, it was better to indulge in some madness with these featherbrained men. For, there was only one topic being discussed here, "When our Yadava Chief has single-handedly defeated Panchajanya's vast army, of what consequence is Jarasandha?" Oh, what do I say about the emotions I was experiencing on hearing them speak so! Indeed, I was caught in the web of my own lies, which was proving to be an expensive blunder on my part. And what a pack of lies it was! It was only a matter of time before Jarasandha arrived and all this bravado would vanish into thin air. Well, so be it. Presently, seeing no way out, I thought it best to join in the revelry of these fools. At any rate, there was no point in worrying now, for, I could not devise any strategy, and Mathura was not interested in preparing for war. Forget preparing for it, no one even wanted to discuss the war, even though Jarasandha was due to arrive in ten to twelve days. This was my last chance, yet nothing seemed to be falling into place. Mulling over all this, I was about to give up when a wise, elderly Yadava lifted my spirits by posing a question, "Kanhaiya, what is your battle strategy this time around?" Naturally, on hearing this, my heart was filled with hope. But before I could answer, everyone shut him down saying, "What battle plans? As soon as Jarasandha shows up, he will be ground to dust. Are you not aware of our Yadava Chief's incredible strength and prowess?" Now, could a lone voice ever be heard above the din of a noisy meeting? Unfortunately, that's exactly what happened with the elderly person—his voice of reason was drowned in the hysteria, and he was forced to sit down quietly. In short, the one intelligent person who had dared to speak was silenced, which led me to wonder if I was actually the leader of Yadavas or a bunch of fools! Really, considering the incredible yarn I had spun at the previous meeting, the only role I remained capable of playing now was that of the leader of fools. And at present, that was precisely the position I held.

In a way, it was for the best. For, after seeing this prolonged bout of insanity, it had become difficult for me to remain detached from it. Gradually, I too became somewhat convinced of my bravery, as if the world was ruled by none other than my father, Vasudeva! This was still alright, but with this newly acquired faith in myself, I concluded the meeting by speaking reassuringly, "It is best to reveal the war strategy when the time is right. I am going to meet the commander today itself and discuss all plans with him. There is no need for you to worry; just sit back and relax. Your leader is here to take care of everything. I am here!" My parting words were met with a resounding applause and everyone returned home in high spirits. I asked bhaiya and grandfather to leave too. In a short while, the entire ground stood desolate, reflecting my mood as I walked with heavy steps towards my chariot. My mind was swirling in a whirlpool of emotions. Although I had participated in the madness, I had certainly not lost my wits or gone insane. Really, I am finding it difficult to even describe how painful everyone's dancing and cavorting was for me! The behaviour of the *Mathurawasis* had, in fact, given me such a jolt that I had returned to my senses. Time was running out, and if we didn't act swiftly, death would come knocking on our door. Contemplating in this manner, I reached the chariot and boarded it. But as soon as I held the reins of the chariot in my hands, I was assailed by a sudden, strange whim, which made me race the chariot towards the distant forest near River Yamuna. I thought, perhaps if I could distance myself a little from Mathura, my brain would begin to function again. And that is exactly what happened. After riding through the forest for a while, I saw a ray of hope emerge in the form of the commander of the army. For, in the assembly of fools, he was the only one who had appeared somewhat serious. Besides, wars and battles fell under his purview anyway, so I reckoned, why not discuss the war preparations with him. Akin to a drowning man who had found a straw to clutch on to, I turned my chariot in the direction of the royal palace, with the flame of hope burning bright in my heart. Of course, by the time I had reached the palace, evening had set in, but never mind; I had to somehow save myself from the dusk that was threatening to set on my life.

Oh, but I was in for a rude shock! My conversation with the commander left me in a worse state than before, his revelation shaking me to my core. He informed me that the majority of weapons in Mathura's armoury were rusted. Moreover, one-fourth of the kingdom's army comprised soldiers from Magadha, and naturally, they would never take up arms against Jarasandha. The treasury too was all but empty, so the army was being paid only half its wages for the past several months. As a result, it was possible that even our army would not readily agree to die without a cause. Oh! So, this was why the commander appeared so grave. This meant that he too had no battle plan—he was simply worried because no war strategy could be devised. Essentially, this hope was dashed too, but it did not matter. After getting an overview of the situation, I assured him with the same words, "Why do you worry? I am here!" With this, it was amply clear that I was there for everyone, and for me, there was Jarasandha! In other words, Mathura was feeling assured on account of me, and once Jarasandha arrived, he would ensure that I would be put to rest forever. No one was willing to understand that they were expecting nothing less than a miracle from me. And miracles are not possible in Nature! Everything transpires in accordance with specific laws. To obtain the desired results, one has to act, but alas, no one was willing to do so. And now, even that opportunity had been lost. As for me, I certainly did not wish to die unnecessarily and that is why I was desperately trying to find a way out of this problem. It was not that I was afraid of death; as a matter of fact, I had stared it in the face several times before and fought it each time. But in this situation, there seemed to be no way to fight the problem. And to die without fighting...the mere thought was galling! There was no problem in locking horns with Panchajanya, because the objective had been clear—I had to pay my *gurudakshina.* I was willing to walk into the jaws of death, but I had done so after careful consideration. Even otherwise, life and death pale in comparison to the honour of paying one's *gurudakshina.* But here, I was being primed to die without any reason. Mathura was on the verge of ruin, yet no one wanted to comprehend the gravity of the situation, nor was anyone willing to do anything about it. Of course, bhaiya was there for me, but even he was of no use in this situation. I could not discuss anything with him either. All that he understood was the language of might and mace; on the contrary, he was waiting impatiently for Jarasandha to arrive, as if he would meekly offer his head to him and say, "O Brother Balarama, please crush my head!" Oh, I can't begin to describe how furious I was! There's a limit to how delusional one can be. And it wasn't just about my survival—it was the lives of everyone in Mathura that were at stake. It was certain that after this devastation, Mathura, which was already fighting for survival, would be destroyed completely.

Well, with no solution in sight, how long could I continue to give vent to my fury? So, I reckoned, why not spend the last few days of my life in peace? And under such circumstances, I had just one recourse—my flute. Perhaps, it would provide me some measure of happiness in my final days and allow me to spend these few days in peace, just like everyone else. Surprisingly, till date, I had always seen others fret and fume, while I, regardless of the situation, had maintained my equanimity. But this time, the opposite was true. Everyone was relaxed, oblivious to the danger, while I was the only one caught in a vortex of worry. Of course, it goes without saying that I was the root cause of this as well. The trouble about to descend on Mathura was on account of me, and everyone's carefree attitude was also the result of my loud mouth. It was worth noting that at present, everyone except me was bent on indulging in foolishness, and surprisingly, they all looked happy. I had never thought that, at times, even foolishness can be a wonderful state to be in—it certainly helps a person live a life free of worries. In a way, this was a unique experience for me. But let us forget about these matters, for, there was no end to them. Presently, I had to act upon what I had decided. So, taking my chariot, I headed alone to the banks of River Yamuna to play my flute in peace. The sky was already changing its hues as dusk came rolling in; in other words, I already had a reason to play my flute, and now, the time was perfect too. Finding a secluded spot, I sat under a tree and began playing… but on this occasion, my flute betrayed me too. Indeed, why would it support me when the rest of my world was falling apart? It couldn't transport me to Vrindavan, evoke sweet memories of Radha, or even arrange a meeting with Rukmini. And this being the case, how could it help me find a solution to avert the imminent danger? With my flute failing me, there was little left to do, so I quietly went home and turned in for the night.

With my flute's betrayal, I returned to my senses the next morning. Thereafter, I too began to roam the streets of Mathura with bhaiya all day long, thinking that I might never get another chance to wander around so carefree. There was only one topic being discussed in Mathura—Jarasandha—so whenever anyone asked me about him, I would furnish them with a reply that I had learnt by rote, "Don't worry! I am here!" As for bhaiya, he would proudly swing his mace in the air whenever Jarasandha's name was mentioned. This made me wonder, of what use was one's intelligence in a city of fools? Now, it had become our daily routine to give this reply to all the people we encountered throughout the day. Well, this routine went on for a day or two, but then I began to think, 'Is this a way to end one's life? Besides, why should anyone end their life? Only because Jarasandha wanted them dead? No, never! Wake up, Kanhaiya, wake up!' Oh, what a strange dilemma I was caught in! Neither could I spend these precious days wallowing in misery, nor could I surrender my life to death in this manner. I'm not sure why I was caught up in such nonsensical thoughts instead of realising such an important fact. Perhaps, the atmosphere of insanity prevailing in Mathura had affected me as well. But enough was enough! The voice within piped up, 'O Krishna! You are a *karmaveer*, a man of action—you cannot simply surrender to death! Besides, Mathura is in trouble because of you, so you have to save it at all costs. So what if Mathura is betraying you? So what if your flute has let you down? It is not the end of the world. No, Krishna, no! Come on! Think seriously! Think of a solution!' With this positive thought, my soul, meaning the 'Universal Benefactor' pushed me into deep contemplation. Interestingly, the strategy I had employed just a few months ago to kill Panchajanya had been rendered useless here. I wonder how people are able to use scriptures that are thousands of years old when I couldn't reuse a strategy that was just a few months old! Perhaps, they keep waiting all their lives for a miracle to occur. For that matter, those who shirk action can do nothing except this.

This was the problem with me! Once I immersed myself in contemplation, I tended to flit from one thought to another. Many a time, the primary issue itself would get lost in the labyrinth of these thoughts. This was precisely the predicament I found myself in. I had set out to find a solution, but here, my thoughts were leading me on an entirely different path. I was thinking, why not write a book—a scripture of sorts—offering solutions to every problem of every era! Indeed, there was nothing wrong in desiring something like this. But I was someone who dreamt, someone who resolved to do things. And if the idea was good, then why wait at all? Thus, I instantly made a resolve that, one day, I would surely write a book that will contain solutions to all kinds of problems. Oh, just look at me! At present, I was not able to think of even a semblance of a solution to my current problem, yet here I was, dreaming of writing an extraordinary tome offering solutions to every problem in the world. The voice within me quipped, 'O Krishna! Has Jarasandha's impending attack unhinged you?' I replied, 'No, my friend. I am perfectly sane. Besides, when I was already dreaming of attaining the peak of glory and grandeur as well as marrying Rukmini, what was the harm in harbouring yet another big dream?' It was then that I shook myself out of this reverie and reprimanded myself saying, 'Is this really the time to dream? Thousands of lives are at stake, and time is slipping away. Jarasandha could storm into Mathura any moment and shatter your reputation to smithereens. Yet, here you are, lost in dreams of writing a book with solutions to all problems for all time. Clearly, you have slipped over the edge. First, tackle the threat of Jarasandha. Once that's done, you can write not one but thousands of books and chase as many dreams as you like.' Indeed, it was only if I survived that I could give shape to a million dreams. But, at present, I had to first concentrate on finding a solution to save ourselves from Jarasandha.

Ah, but before that, let me share a truth with you. Only someone who can dream of ruling the entire universe, despite death hounding him, is a dreamer in the truest sense of the word. In my opinion, he alone is a true optimist. Indeed, who can be a greater optimist than the one who never gives up hope, regardless of circumstances? And while we are on this subject, let me also shed light on one more thing. The culmination of this dream of mine is present before the entire world now. 'Bhagavad Gita' is the very scripture that I had enunciated much later in life—one that encompasses solutions to all the problems faced by humankind down the ages. Undoubtedly, this book was the result of Nature's grace and my fervent desire. Of course, Arjuna's contribution to it could not be undermined, for, he alone had served as the instrument through which this book had found expression. And now that we are on this subject, let me also tell you something about the secrets hidden within the Gita. The essence of the Bhagavad Gita is that a human being's Soul invariably finds a solution to every problem at any given time and in every circumstance. And the Bhagavad Gita is the key that activates that Soul within. And believe me, once the Soul takes charge of a person, no harm can ever befall him. The voice within quipped, 'Isn't it incredible, Krishna, that on one hand, your mind is soaring to ever-new heights of contemplation; you are even claiming that the Bhagavad Gita will have solutions for every problem of humankind hidden within itself. But on the other hand, you are still not able to find a solution to address your current problem named Jarasandha!' 'Oh, but what could I do? I have channelled my thoughts in that very direction, but unfortunately, no one is taking the battle seriously. To make matters worse, both the weapons and the soldiers of Mathura are not fit for battle. So, what am I supposed to do? Play my flute for Jarasandha…or invite him for a flute-playing competition? Or should I hand over my list of grand dreams to Jarasandha in the hope of tugging at his heartstrings; perhaps, his heart would melt, he would take pity on me and thus spare me!' A point worth noting is that I did not know how to wield weapons, which could have otherwise given me some hope of displaying my bravery on the battlefield and increase my chances of survival. All I knew was politics and it would be of no use against Jarasandha. Meaning, I wanted to act but I just could not think of any action that could lead to a positive outcome. The voice piped up yet again, 'So, dive deep into your Soul. Moments ago, weren't you talking about the essence of the Gita, which says that all the solutions lay hidden in the Soul? Then what are you waiting for? Show me that you can save yourself as well as Mathura. Only then will I believe the claims you make about the essence of the Gita.' Did you see how my own mind was bent on instigating me? Well, what can I say; the mind did not want to die either. It could see all its dreams being shattered. Forget becoming a king or marrying Rukmini, all that my poor mind could visualise was death inching closer by the day! All in all, the situation had reached a stage where the present hung in a limbo, while the strings of my future lay in Jarasandha's hands, to be manipulated as per his whims. In such a bleak scenario, I reckoned it was best to seek refuge in the golden memories of my past. Indeed, in Vrindavan, in spite of the myriad problems, I could at least find solace in my mother's lap or in Radha's sweet company. At present though, neither Yashoda nor Radha were by my side, which left only bhaiya. But he, instead of helping me, was bent on pestering me with his foolhardy actions, wielding his mace at every opportunity. Do you see how even the golden memories lose their warmth and turn bitingly cold when time is not in your favour? In any case, when death is close at hand, both the past and the future lose their significance.

Eventually, exhaustion caught up with me. For, how much could a person think and rack his brain? At such times, it is better to resort to the *Brahmastra*—the ultimate weapon. Meaning, when you cannot come up with a solution, then leave everything to Nature's justice. So, that is exactly what I did. I said to Nature, 'If you think we need to be saved, then show me a way out…else do as you please.' I was not sure about the future, but in the present, this little appeal made to Nature instantly brought a positive outcome. I became relaxed, casting all worries aside. But yes, it definitely saddened me that circumstances had knocked down even a man of action like me, compelling me to meekly walk into the arms of death. They had not given me any scope even to take action to save myself. Perhaps, no one else in the history of mankind must have waited for death in the manner that I was waiting. Well, when my entire life as well as my actions had made history, this wait for death was bound to make history too. For that matter, every previous wait of mine had been unique, whether it was waiting for Radha or waiting to go to Vrindavan; whether it was my wait to become a king or waiting to win Rukmini's heart. Well, I was thinking about such nonsensical things only because I found myself going through a period of inaction. I had done everything that was in my power. I had contemplated upon the issue as much as I could and had taken whatever action I could. I had lived in the memories of the past and the dreams of the future as well. Now, neither was there anything left for me to do, nor was there anything I could relive. I had fully accepted death and had completely surrendered myself to Nature. That being the case, I just wanted to spend these last few days with myself. And there was surely no better way of doing this than by immersing myself in the melody of my flute. Yes, it had left me in the lurch just a few days ago, but there was no harm in trying once again. Besides, how did it matter, for, Jarasandha would arrive any day now. When time had run out and I had also exhausted myself thinking of a solution, what was the harm in going back to my old, faithful friend?

At the time this thought crossed my mind, I was at Malini's house. So, from there, I raced my chariot till the farthest end of River Yamuna. Finding the perfect opportunity, place and solitude, I coaxed a melody out of my flute. Oh, but this was just incredible! Now that I had surrendered myself to Nature's sense of justice, my flute began to respond to me. And now that I had gained my flute's sublime approval, of what consequence was emotion or action? I thus kept playing for hours, long into the night, so much so that I had even managed to bid a final farewell to Mother Yashoda, Radha and

Rukmini. However, I did not give up my dream of becoming a king, nor did I forsake my resolve of giving birth to a great scripture. In short, I had held on to my desire to perform great deeds, but I had fulfilled my worldly obligations and duties. Now, with such a beautiful melody springing forth from the lips of a fighter who had surrendered himself to Nature, was it possible that a solution would not present itself? It definitely would, and a plan did flash in my mind. A smile played on my lips as I realised that now, Jarasandha would not be able to harm me in any way. And not just me, my dear flute had found a foolproof solution to save the inhabitants of Mathura as well. Really, no harm can ever befall a person whom Nature wants to save; just leave your problem to Nature's sense of justice and watch what happens! Having said all that, if I were to give all the credit to Nature alone, then what about my own contribution to it? Within moments, my ego reared its head saying, 'Bah! Is it a joke to kill Krishna, equipped as he is with thousands of psychological weapons? No, not at all.' Well, expressing my gratitude to Nature, I even kissed my flute a number of times. In fact, in my euphoric state, I felt like dancing with wild abandon. But time did not permit me to celebrate just yet. Once I managed to survive, I would have all my life to celebrate. So, leaving everything aside, I dove headlong into implementing my plan, as I raced my chariot straight towards home.

Back home, the first thing I did was to prepare my chariot for a long journey. And as soon as the chariot was ready, I prepared myself as well. For, my plan was such that it was necessary to prepare myself mentally too. Half the night had elapsed by the time I had finished the preparations. I was aware of the paucity of time, and accordingly, I was charged up as well. Well, no sooner was I ready than I quickly roused bhaiya from his sleep. Strangely, in spite of having woken up from a deep sleep, he instantly reached for his mace and began enquiring, "Has the fiend, Jarasandha, arrived? Come, let us go and crack his head open!" Slapping my palm on my forehead, I grabbed hold of him and led him out of our chamber. For, God forbid, if our parents woke up due to the noise and commotion, my plan would fall to pieces. This was fine but what next? Because, right now, gauging bhaiya's mood, I could clearly see that trouble had still not left my side completely—it had merely changed its form. First, it was Jarasandha and now it was bhaiya! Perhaps, being embroiled in one mess or the other had become my fate. Indeed, when it was certain that we were in no position to win a battle against Jarasandha, and it was also certain that even if we surrendered to him, he would not spare our lives, why was he displaying such enthusiasm? Well, I ignored it because time was scarce and the task had to be accomplished as soon as possible. So, coming straight to the point, I said to him, "My dear brother! Jarasandha has not arrived yet, but he certainly will. So, please get ready and board the chariot. And yes, do carry an extra set of clothes with you!"

Bhaiya shot me a puzzled look that clearly said, 'If Jarasandha has not arrived yet, why are we boarding a chariot?' His confusion was understandable, and I reckoned it was better to just tell him where we were going and why. With time running out, I thought it best to talk directly than beat around the bush. So, I said, "Neither has Jarasandha reached Mathura yet, nor are we going to battle!"

This time, bhaiya verbalised his thoughts. With great surprise, he asked, "Then where are we going so late at night carrying extra clothes?"

Letting out a sigh of frustration, I replied, "Bhaiya, we are going far away from Mathura."

He asked firmly, "Why?"

I replied, "Because I do not think we are capable of fighting Jarasandha."[34]

Hearing these words, his demeanour changed completely. Speaking in a loud and firm voice, he said, "Then don't say that we are going far from Mathura. Say that we are fleeing Mathura in fear of Jarasandha! Why are you mincing your words? Why don't you just say that we are tucking our tails and running away from Jarasandha?"

This time, I lost my cool too. Death was looming large above our heads, and here, we were locked in a duel of words. I snapped, "As you wish!"

Bhaiya retorted, "And what about the fake assurances you have been throwing in people's faces since the past several days, strutting about and saying, 'I am here! I am here!' What about that?"

With a small smile playing on my lips, I lovingly took hold of his hand and answered, "That was a mistake, I admit. But now I am telling you, 'I am not there. I am not there!'"

Seeing the shamelessness with which I had responded to him, bhaiya exploded and snatched his hand away from mine. Then, he stated emphatically, "You can run away if you wish. I cannot flee from a battle!"

I knew only too well that bhaiya would not readily agree to flee from a battle. He staunchly believed that one should always fight to the finish. But I had never imagined that it would be such a herculean task to make him see reason. Nonetheless, seeing the precarious situation we were in, I had to make him see reason come what may. Thus, adopting a patient approach, I said to him humbly, "We are merely leaving the battlefield, not the war itself! Remember, lifting a sword against a sword is not the only kind of bravery. To save oneself from falling prey to a sword is also a sign of bravery—bravery coupled with intelligence."

34. Harivansh Puran, Vishnu Parva, Chapter – 39, Verse – 8; Vishnu Puran, Part – 5, Chapter – 22, Verse – 17.

Hearing this somewhat philosophical explanation, this time, bhaiya cocked his head to the side and spoke a bit pompously, "Very well then! Go ahead and exhibit your bravery coupled with intelligence; I am comfortable with bravery displayed with a mace!"

Oh no! Convincing bhaiya to flee from a battle was turning out to be far more challenging than I had thought. But I had to persevere, come hell or high water. Otherwise, neither would bhaiya survive, nor would I. For that matter, the math was very simple. If I wanted to avoid a war with Jarasandha, I would have to battle with bhaiya till the end. And presently, fighting bhaiya was an easier challenge. Hence, despite time running out, I had to explain everything to him in detail. In fact, I tried to explain the situation to him in many ways. I elaborated on Jarasandha's power and might, Mathura's lack of preparedness for the battle and several other factors. After much effort, I managed to take the sting out of bhaiya's anger. Somewhat calmer now, he began to mull over everything I had said. Thereafter, he enquired thoughtfully, "Rest is all fine, but if we leave the battle and perform a disappearing act, what will the *Mathurawasis* say?"

Hearing his childish query, I was irked. Thus, replying in an annoyed tone, I said, "To even hear what they have to say, it is necessary for us to be alive, isn't it?"

And with that, it disheartens me to say that we had taken two steps forward and four steps back! All my explanations lost their significance, for, as soon as bhaiya's mind veered off the war, his ego came to the fore. This is the problem with human beings; they can deal with just about anything, but they do not know how to tackle their ego. Whereas the simple truth is that a person who cannot deal with his own ego perishes away bit by bit. However, I let it pass, because now was not the time to delve into contemplations. All I wanted was to quickly flee from Mathura taking bhaiya along with me. But oh, if only he agreed! Well, I was not one to give in so easily, for, I had a range of *Brahmastras* to counter bhaiya's reluctance. Indeed, wherever love abounds, there is no dearth of such weapons. And it had become clear to me now that without wielding a *Brahmastra,* I would not be able to achieve my objective. So, resorting to the ultimate weapon, I feigned as if I was about to leave and enquired of bhaiya, "Are you coming along or should I go alone?"

But lo and behold, bhaiya gave a nod of his head, signalling me to go. So, did this mean that my *Brahmastra* had failed? My own brother, who could not live without me even for a single day, was being so adamant. Well, I thought, 'Let me set things right by using my *Maha Brahmastra,* the supreme weapon.' So, putting on an act as if I was actually leaving, I placed my luggage in the chariot. But even this did not have any effect on bhaiya. Fine! I

boarded the chariot, but bhaiya was still resolute in his stance, watching every action of mine with a stubborn expression on his face. Never mind! I knew I could bring him down from the lofty stance he had taken by making him emotional. So, taking hold of the chariot's reins, I turned my head towards him and spoke melodramatically, "Bhaiya, my childhood has been blessed by your love. You were the one who held my hand and taught me how to take my first steps. You have protected me from every imaginable danger. And today, when I am left with no refuge, you are leaving me alone. You do not even want to accompany me."

I could see my *Brahmastra* beginning to show its effect. Bhaiya seemed to thaw a little. Sensing an opportunity, I summoned an even more sorrowful expression and spoke haltingly, almost in tears, "In the event that Jarasandha captures me, I will embrace death. I will tell him, 'Kill me if you want to, but remember, had my brother been here, standing by my side, he would have cracked your head open!'"

Saying this, I nudged the chariot forward a few feet. Once again, I turned to bhaiya and locked eyes with him. My words had struck home; I could see it in his eyes that he had broken down completely. This is what makes the *Brahmastra* unique—it never misses its mark. The weapon I had used at present was, of course, the emotional *Brahmastra,* and let me tell you, I had a variety of such weapons in my arsenal like the *Brahmastras* of 'ego', 'theatrics', 'fear' and 'self-confidence'. I knew that bhaiya could tolerate anything, but he could never bear to see me in trouble. After all, I was his younger brother, so it was only natural that I would have some petulant demands and would play-act a little. Besides, I considered it my right too! Well, all that remained now was to enact the final scene of this act. Bhaiya seemed all set to capitulate. Thus, I alighted from the chariot, forced tears into my eyes, bent down and touched his feet to take his blessings. Then, I embarked the chariot once again and sat with a forlorn look on my face. For a while, silence prevailed. Naturally, it was I who had to make the final move too. So, taking the reins of the chariot in my hands, as if I was all set to go away from his life forever, I said, "Alright, bhaiya, I am leaving. Perhaps, we will never cross paths again!" Saying this, I rode the chariot a few feet further. Then, halting once again, I looked at him. His soft heart had melted completely. Poor bhaiya! Despite his reluctance, he quickly bundled up his belongings and sat down in the chariot with me, without uttering a word. This meant that although he had acquiesced to accompany me, his anger was still intact. In short, he had come with me out of compulsion. Well, whether it was out of compulsion or of his own accord, my mission was accomplished.

As soon as bhaiya took seat, I breathed a huge sigh of relief. In my heart of hearts, I was delighted, but of course, I did not let this happiness reflect on my face. I was no fool to lose my precious life by letting my actual emotions show! If bhaiya were to catch even a hint of the elation I felt, he would instantly jump off the chariot. Indeed, he would realise that I had played a trick on him. Well, do you see Krishna's *leela*? The whole of Mathura was asleep and their leader was making his escape! I am not sure why people found this *rannchhod*[35] form of mine so endearing. In fact, the name *rannchhod* was lovingly added to the long list of monikers that I had acquired thus far. However, in stark contrast to this, you would recall, when Arjuna wanted to become a *rannchhod* at the onset of the Mahabharata war, I had strongly dissuaded him. As a matter of fact, I had enunciated the entire Bhagavad Gita to him so that he would not desert the battlefield. Really, how could history bear testimony to two *rannchhods*? Ha! I am just joking. In actuality, Arjuna wanted to flee the battlefield because of fear and attachment, which was not acceptable to me at all. There was negativity behind his intention to flee the battlefield, whereas the sole reason behind my escaping the battlefield was *ahimsa* (non-violence). Neither did I want to die, nor did I want bhaiya to lose his life. I also did not want the *Mathurawasis* to be slaughtered unnecessarily. If considered carefully, there was nothing but positivity in my fleeing from the battlefield. And if I were to explain this in detail, then truth is nothing but the midpoint between two contradictions. Throughout my life, I was able to stand with the truth because I very well knew how to maintain a balance between two contradictions. Are you able to fathom this point or are you still flummoxed? Alright, let me explain it in greater detail. No one in this world is more deceitful than me; therefore, there is no one in this world who is as innocent as me either. Because I was supremely egoistical, it would be difficult to find someone who is as devoid of ego as me. And it was because of this egoless nature that this *rannchhod* was able to vehemently oppose Arjuna's decision to flee from the battlefield. In the scenario that an egoistical person leaves the battlefield, he would never be able to muster the courage to stop another person from doing the same. For, he would always be assailed with the doubt: what if the person he was stopping from fleeing the battlefield turned around and questioned him as to why he had beaten a hasty retreat from the battle?!

In a nutshell, there is a time and place for everything in life. There is a time to be egoistical and angry; there is a time to confront the enemy in a war, and a time to flee from it too. It is time that decides when and what a man must do. For instance, this was the time for me to abandon the battlefield, and this was the sole reason why I was running away. However, when Arjuna wanted

35. *Rannchhod* - One who flees the battlefield.

to flee, it was actually the time to stand and fight. He was caught in the grip of attachment at the wrong time, which was why I had opposed his decision. Otherwise, I was not one to flee from the battlefield and had never done so either. I had never been scared and no one could ever instil fear in me either. But yes, in my opinion, killing someone or giving up one's life should be the last resort. Similarly, even if one chooses to fight as a last resort, one must not fight to lose. Because life is synonymous with victory. Giving in easily or surrendering one's life are the traits of a loser. At present, time favoured Jarasandha, and to respect time is a sign of intelligence. To challenge it, however, is akin to inviting death. Since time favoured Jarasandha presently, it was best to flee. One day, when the tide of time turned in our favour, we would either have an army bigger than his or an opportunity to engage him in a one-on-one combat; or perhaps, one of my political manoeuvres would do the trick. What I mean to say is, when time changes, everything else will change too. But one must definitely be patient for it to change.

Well, presently, we, the deserters, had set off on our journey. Needless to say, I was racing the chariot at top speed. I had no idea which way we were going; all I knew was that we were heading in the opposite direction of where Jarasandha and his army would arrive. What made the trip pleasant from the very beginning was the fact that although bhaiya was sitting beside me, I was actually enveloped in my own solitude, engrossed in deep reverie. There was no conversation taking place between the two of us. Since bhaiya had accompanied me in the chariot only because he was compelled to, it was natural for his resentment to reflect in his behaviour towards me. You know very well that bhaiya was present in the chariot only because he was countered by my *Brahmastra;* otherwise, he would still be waiting in Mathura, mace in hand for Jarasandha to arrive. Unable to protest much, he was displaying his irritation at being made to flee by refusing to talk to me. Well, so be it! For now, I left him alone, but while riding the chariot, I did throw a few furtive glances at him, naturally to check whether his anger was subsiding; but alas, there was no question of it abating anytime soon. A brave hero like Balarama had fled from the battlefield! So, how could his ego allow his anger to subside so easily? Well, let him remain angry. If he was performing his *karma*, I too was honouring its dictates, and my *karma* was asking me to continue riding the chariot and move as further away from Jarasandha as possible. It was nearly dawn now, but there was no question of stopping the chariot. The fear of Jarasandha was so perceptible that I continued to race the chariot as swiftly as possible. For, what if Jarasandha learnt that the two boys had fled in a chariot and he then dispatched twenty chariots in pursuit of us? Meaning, if our lives were to fall in danger even after being disgraced for fleeing the battlefield, then our loss would have doubled indeed. And you very well know that Krishna would never entertain a loss-making deal.

Well, the light of the sun had torn through the night sky, but the light of peace was still refusing to shine through bhaiya's dark mood. Of course, I did not dare talk to him while he was upset, especially since I was the cause of his fury. Therefore, I continued to ride the chariot in silence. Soon, my eyes spotted a lake! This seemed to be the perfect halt, so stopping the chariot near its edge, I alighted in silence and washed my face and hands. I also unharnessed the horses and took them to the lake to drink water. After that, I sat down on a rock to rest. Eventually, bhaiya got down too and refreshed himself. However, he chose to sit on a rock some distance away from me, the frown refusing to leave his brow. In fact, it seemed as though it had etched itself permanently onto bhaiya's visage! To me, this behaviour of his was enough to indicate the extent of his resentment. But even so, like a good brother, I mustered up courage and threw him my most disarming smile. But what was this? Giving a snort of displeasure, he turned his face away. No matter, I decided to be brazen and tried to speak to him a couple of times, but he remained adamant and refused to engage in conversation. Whenever I addressed him, remarking on sundry things, he would resolutely turn his face away. In short, I realised that his anger would not subside easily. We did not even know where we were presently or where we were headed; and to add to my woes, I had to deal with bhaiya's childish behaviour as well. Our current location did not matter much, but we definitely needed to think about where we could go. And to deliberate over it, we needed to talk. But my dear brother wouldn't even look at me. Oh well, never mind! I decided to think it over myself.

Now, in my opinion, it would be safe to seek refuge in any of the kingdoms ruled by Jarasandha's enemies. But even so, it would have been better if I could have bhaiya's opinion on the matter. However, looking at his foul mood, it did not seem likely that he would give his opinion anytime soon. Finally, seeing no way out, I began consoling myself, 'Kanhaiya, just smile and endure every difficulty that comes your way. Sooner or later, these dark clouds will surely dissipate. But first, allow them time to become darker, denser, gloomier! For, until the sky is completely dark, how can a ray of hope break through? Have faith that sooner or later, bhaiya will calm down.' Besides, I had to attend to other matters too, other than placating my upset bhaiya. Thus, I quietly busied myself in tackling them. First of all, I fed the horses and then plucked some fruits for us. We also had some food in the chariot, so as a final attempt to appease bhaiya, I set it all on a platter and served him. My goal was simple: I wanted him to view it as a delicious spread, partaking which he would hopefully cool down. Thankfully, after showing some reluctance, bhaiya did finally eat. This was a peculiar trait of his; he would never vent out his anger on his stomach. This boded well for me and I certainly took it as a good sign. Once he had his fill, there was a good chance that he might start talking too. And just as I had expected, his mood seemed to improve a little after the meal, and he surely appeared to have calmed down to some extent. I reckoned, this was the right time to muster courage and try striking a conversation with him once again. Moreover, speaking to him about our current situation would appear more natural; at the very least, it would not appear as if I was trying to appease him. So, with this thought in mind, I asked him, "Where do you reckon we should head to?"

As soon as he heard the question, he retorted in a dramatic manner, "Where else can we go except on a pilgrimage? After all, those who flee from a battlefield are left with no choice but to embark on a pilgrimage!"

Hearing bhaiya's jibe, it became clear to me that he was still seething with fury. But so what? Even the hardest of rocks eventually breaks down if water is constantly poured on it. At present, I took solace in the fact that he was at least responding, even though his replies were curt and dripping with sarcasm. Taking this as a positive sign, I took our conversation forward and asked, "Why don't we go to Chandak's in Vaivasvatpur?"

Hearing this, bhaiya became even more furious and, in his rage, lashed out, "And what will you tell him? 'Look, Chandak! We, the heroes who had killed Panchajanya, have come running to you to seek refuge because we are frightened of Jarasandha!' You know, Kanhaiya, frankly speaking, running after the *gopis* and fooling around with girls has rusted your bravery. But bear in mind—I am still a brave hero!"

Well, bhaiya could be as sarcastic as he wanted to, but I had to keep the conversation going. Thus, I continued with great humility, "Alright then, we will not go to Chandak, but tell me, where should we go?"

This time, he replied with irritation, "The decision to flee was yours. So, you decide where we must go. I will simply sit in the chariot, just like I did while fleeing from the battlefield!"

With this final statement, bhaiya lapsed into a stony silence once again. Clearly, his anger was not going to abate easily. I would have to jump through many more hoops before I won him over. But presently, seeing the mood he was in, I decided to give up trying to pacify him. For, I feared, what if he lost his temper again after taking so long to calm down? I would no doubt suffer the consequences! Thus, without wasting any time, I prepared the chariot and we set off in an unknown direction. The only calculation I made was, if we travelled on a familiar path, Jarasandha would find it easy to locate us. So, for four days, we continued travelling in an unfamiliar direction without any concrete thought in mind. There was no question of entering or travelling through towns, for, if we were recognised, Jarasandha would surely get to hear of it. All in all, I was bound by just one routine during these four days: getting the chariot ready in the morning, riding it all day, unharnessing the horses for our night halts, trying to converse with bhaiya after dinner, only to throw up my hands in exasperation when my efforts yielded no results—and finally, playing my flute to drive away my fatigue. However, my sustained efforts did bear some fruit; bhaiya's anger seemed to abate with each passing day, albeit at a painfully slow pace. From my end, I had spared no effort to allay his anger, and at this point, there was nothing more that I could do. The situation was such that to act was in my hands, but the fruits of the action depended solely on bhaiya.

Well, during this period, unbeknownst to us, we had landed ourselves in a dense and desolate forest for two days. There was no sign of human habitation as far as we could see. In this period, we had to sustain ourselves on raw and semi-ripe fruits, much to bhaiya's chagrin. And naturally, this scarce and fitful supply of barely edible food completely ruined whatever progress I had made in assuaging bhaiya's anger. Oh, have you not understood? With an assault made on his stomach, how could bhaiya not explode with anger? Fortunately, on the third day, we stumbled upon a settlement; seeing it, I breathed a sigh of relief and straightaway parked the chariot in front of a sweetshop. Since we no longer faced a shortage of money, we not only devoured all kinds of delicacies, but even packed a load of them to sustain us on our onward journey. Once our hunger was satiated, the situation began to stabilise and the grim look on bhaiya's face seemed to lift. And with bhaiya looking a bit satisfied, it was necessary to satisfy the horses as well, for, they needed rest too. While the horses rested, we took the opportunity to rest as well. As we lay under a tree, I kept throwing furtive glances at bhaiya, trying to establish eye contact with him. Oh, but it was all in vain. Well, that was fine by me! For now, our journey resumed with the hope that bhaiya's anger would subside eventually. However, where we were headed and where we would halt for the night were questions that still begged for an answer. For that matter, whether bhaiya's anger would subside or not also begged for an answer, but whether he was inclined to speak with me or not, the time had come for us to seriously give a thought to where we could seek refuge. After all, we could not wander around aimlessly in the forest! Lost in these thoughts, I was riding the chariot as usual when I saw an ascetic walking towards us. I immediately stopped the chariot, jumped down from it and greeted him. Bhaiya too alighted and stood next to me. We were standing beside the chariot, while the ascetic stood in front of us. Nothing seemed out of the ordinary, but for some reason, I felt compelled to ask him his name to start a conversation.

However, my request for his introduction proved to be a grave mistake. Turning angry, he spoke in an irked tone, "An ascetic is an ascetic! He does not have an identity. Why don't you tell me who you are?"

For a moment, I was badly shaken by his stern voice. However, composing myself, I introduced myself saying,[36] "I am Krishna, and this is my brother, Balarama. We are inhabitants of Mathura. Compelled by circumstances beyond our control, we had to kill Kansa, the king of Mathura. And as Kansa was the son-in-law of the king of Magadha, Jarasandha, the latter seeks revenge by wanting to kill us. We are thus trying to save ourselves from Jarasandha and are searching for a safe haven. But unfortunately, we do not even know where we are exactly."

The ascetic replied, "Oh, so you are Krishna. I have heard of you. Aren't you the one who slayed Panchajanya to pay your *gurudakshina*?"

I was secretly pleased, delighted in fact to hear that stories of my valour had spread far and wide. Still, I controlled my emotions and merely nodded my head in acknowledgment. It was enough for me that his attitude towards me had suddenly changed for the better on knowing who I was. Adopting a courteous tone, he now spoke in a calm voice, "Since you have been tutored by the great *Acharya* Sandipani, you do not require any additional knowledge. However, do not mind my saying this, but the fact is, Sandipani is not very well versed with the art of politics and warfare. Therefore, I will definitely give you some advice: anyone who seeks refuge is weak, and no one likes to give shelter to a weakling. A hero, who has slain the likes of Kansa and Panchajanya, ought to be his own refuge. So, become your own refuge. In other words, give up the idea of looking for refuge and focus on increasing your strength and might. Regardless of how far you run or how well you conceal your identity, Jarasandha will ultimately find you. Do not forget that the majority of kings in Aryavarta are under his influence. Admittedly, by slaying Kansa and Panchajanya, you have not only proved your valour but have also destroyed two vile sinners. This feat in itself makes you great, but remember, a hero's life must reflect a harmony between his self-interest and the interest of humankind at large. Meaning, you should ensure that what is in your interest is also in the interest of all. In my opinion, gaining wealth and becoming a king is not only good for you but beneficial for everyone else too. For, common people can remain happy only when wealth and power are vested in the hands of worthy individuals. Remember, wealth and power support one another. Therefore, my advice to you is to focus on increasing your wealth, gaining power and becoming stronger and

36. Harivansh Puran, Vishnu Parva, Chapter – 39, Verse – 20-70.

mightier. For, only then will you be able to permanently keep Jarasandha at bay. And yes, while advising you, I almost forgot to answer your primary question. At present, you are very far from Mathura, on the border of the kingdom of Vidarbha."

The advice given by the ascetic shook the very foundation of my knowledge. Indeed, he was a great and knowledgeable sage! I must admit that by giving us the right advice at the right time, he had shown us the right direction. For that matter, giving the right knowledge at the right time is verily the sign of a great ascetic. I began to wonder, was this ascetic an instrument sent by Nature? Had Nature's wish become one with my dream of scaling the heights of glory and grandeur? Perhaps, yes. That was why, in just a few moments, I had gained knowledge which would have otherwise taken years to learn, and that too, when it was least expected. And if that's the case, has this aimless wandering come about only to open the doors to my becoming powerful and mighty?

Ah, but these were all matters pertaining to the future. At present, it was imperative to tackle the problem that loomed large before me. So, before the ascetic walked away on seeing me lost in thought, I pulled myself back to reality and, folding my hands together in humility, said, "Truly, your suggestion that I should become stronger and mightier has given my life a new direction. This single advice of yours has saved us from wandering aimlessly…but I beg your pardon, until we reach the stage where we gain power and might, we would certainly need to seek refuge. And since we do not hail from a royal family, we are totally unfamiliar with the politics of Aryavarta. Frankly speaking, we are ignorant even about who Jarasandha's allies are and who his enemies are. But if my estimation is correct, Karvirpur is not very far from Vidarbha. And I think that King Shringlava of Karvirpur is a Yadava and also a distant relative of ours. I reckon we will definitely find refuge in his kingdom. I would like to know your opinion on this."

As soon as he heard this, the ascetic laughed out loud. Then, sobering a little, he said, "Truly, you are ignorant of the politics of Aryavarta! Shringlava is extremely selfish, cruel and arrogant. He does not care for caste, clan or relationships. He is intoxicated with power and in its heady stupor, he has imprisoned many priests and *Acharyas* of his kingdom. Yes, it is possible that he might grant you refuge, but he may also just strike a deal with Jarasandha in exchange for your life. It is also quite likely that after spending one night in his kingdom, you may just wake up to find that you have become Jarasandha's prisoner!"

Hearing the sage's words, I was shaken to the very core of my being. This meant that under the present circumstances, we desperately needed to familiarise ourselves with the political scenario in Aryavarta and all the kings in this region. Indeed, our ignorance could get us killed at any moment. It was verily Nature's grace that it had sent this ascetic as an instrument to save us; had I paid heed to my intellect, I would have gone straight to King Shringlava's kingdom to seek refuge. And had we done that, we would have perhaps found ourselves rotting in Jarasandha's prison all our lives, or maybe, he would have killed us long before that! The consequences would have been disastrous to say the least. Oh, but let us forget about what could have happened; why think about something that has not come to pass? And going by what had actually happened, I had begun to believe that Nature was bent on saving me under all circumstances. Had this not been the case, the idea to flee from the battlefield would not have occurred to me at all. Well, even if I were to not think on these lines, at the very least, I wouldn't have chanced upon this great ascetic who had shown us the right path at the right time. At any rate, I had already seen how knowledgeable I was about political matters! Besides, each passing day was revealing a new chapter on the extent of Jarasandha's influence and dominance over Aryavarta. Neither could we set foot in a kingdom that was friendly to Jarasandha, nor could we rely on our intellect to seek refuge with a king we were familiar with. And now, I was afraid to seek shelter even in a kingdom that was inimical to Jarasandha. Who knew when such a king might change his stance influenced by the fiend, Jarasandha? Honestly, at this critical juncture, I had begun to feel as if no place on this earth could provide us a safe haven. But even so, we had to find a way to survive. Since my intelligence was failing to provide a solution, I thought, why not ask the ascetic for help? Thus, with a voice laden with helplessness, I asked him, "So, where do you suggest we go?"

The ascetic promptly replied, "To the Gomanta Mountain! Given your current situation, Gomanta would be safe and secure in every way. The sprawling mountain range and the dense forest cover will ensconce you safely, much like a mother nestling her child in her lap. The mountain is so huge that it is impossible to climb! I have also heard that about two thousand years ago, there used to be a thriving settlement on it. However, it was ravaged by a natural disaster and has since transformed into a mountain. Currently, there are no settlements anywhere close to it, and no one ventures there either. Nonetheless, there is a settlement of tribal people a short distance from the mountain, and that is as far as your chariot can go. Beyond that, you will need to walk a considerable distance to reach the mountain and climb it. And as I have said, the climb will certainly not be easy."

Ah! The ascetic's words filled me with enthusiasm, as a ray of hope had now appeared. In fact, the second piece of advice he gave was equally excellent. All of a sudden, I felt a surge of confidence within me and in that same confident state, I assured the ascetic, "Do not worry. We are cowherds. We are used to roaming in dense forests and climbing high mountains."

Hearing me, the ascetic replied gravely, "Alright, but there is one more thing you need to be careful about. This mountain falls within the boundaries of Karvirpur, so you will not only have to be on guard at all times, but also be careful not to reveal your identities to anyone."

Touching the ascetic's feet, I said, "O revered sage, you have shown us the right path in life. By cautioning us not to go to Shringlava, you have given us a new lease of life. You have even directed us to a safe hideout. At present, you are the Supreme Soul who has appeared before me in the form of a *guru*. Thus, if you do not mind, I would like to know more about you."

The ascetic replied in a gruff tone, "It is enough for you to know that I am Parshuram."

Hearing the ascetic's curt reply, my curiosity to ask further questions was quelled automatically. Truly, more than the name or whereabouts of ascetics, it is their knowledge that holds significance. And he had already given us much more than a glimpse of that. Having taken his blessings, I was about to turn away when I noticed that his water pot was empty. I reckoned, it would be my good fortune if I could be of some small service to this ascetic, so thinking thus, I humbly said, "O great sage! Give your water pot to me; I will fetch water for you."

He replied brusquely, "No. I am the one who is thirsty, so I will fetch the water myself."

Hearing this, I was silenced at once. Could anyone ever stand against great *Acharyas* and ascetics? Besides, even though I had attained self-realisation, I was still leading the life of an ordinary person. And of what consequence was a common man in the presence of a true ascetic? So, quietly, I touched his feet and we took our leave. I felt truly blessed to have met such a great saint. In just a few moments, this great ascetic, in the form of a teacher, had imparted to me everything I still needed to learn, beyond the knowledge we had gained at *Acharya* Sandipani's *ashram*. First, it was *Acharya* Shrutiketu, then *Acharya* Sandipani, and now, this great ascetic, Parshuram! I considered myself highly fortunate that even though I was a mere cowherd, I had received the opportunity to meet such great souls. Well, having shown us the right path, the ascetic went on his way, while I watched him walk away for quite some time. In fact, I kept gazing at him with admiration until he was out of sight. Now, there was no ambiguity about where we had to go. Bhaiya had already taken his seat in the chariot, and I too jumped in and took the reins in my hands. Now, the manner in which I was riding the chariot was marked by fresh enthusiasm, as we headed towards the settlement of the tribal people. In fact, I was so elated that I had completely forgotten that bhaiya was still annoyed with me. So, without thinking, in great excitement, I gushed, "Did you see, bhaiya? What a great ascetic he was! His teachings were truly enlightening. When I asked him for his water pot, did you hear what he said? 'No, I am the one who is thirsty; I will fetch water myself!' Wow!"

Bhaiya snorted and replied, "No, Kanhaiya, I was there and I saw it all. It was just an excuse to avoid giving you the water pot. He was wary of you because he must have wondered—if you could flee from the battlefield, you could certainly run away with his water pot too! And what did the poor man have in his possession except that pot? Had you taken even that one possession, he would have surely died of thirst and attained instant salvation!"

Argh! Bhaiya's biting sarcasm made me bite my tongue in frustration. It was a harsh reminder that his anger still simmered beneath the surface. I had no idea when, or if, it would ever subside, and now, he had even perfected the art of throwing sarcastic barbs at me. But it did not matter—I too had learnt to adapt to every situation. And so, our journey began anew...but this time, with a clear destination in mind.

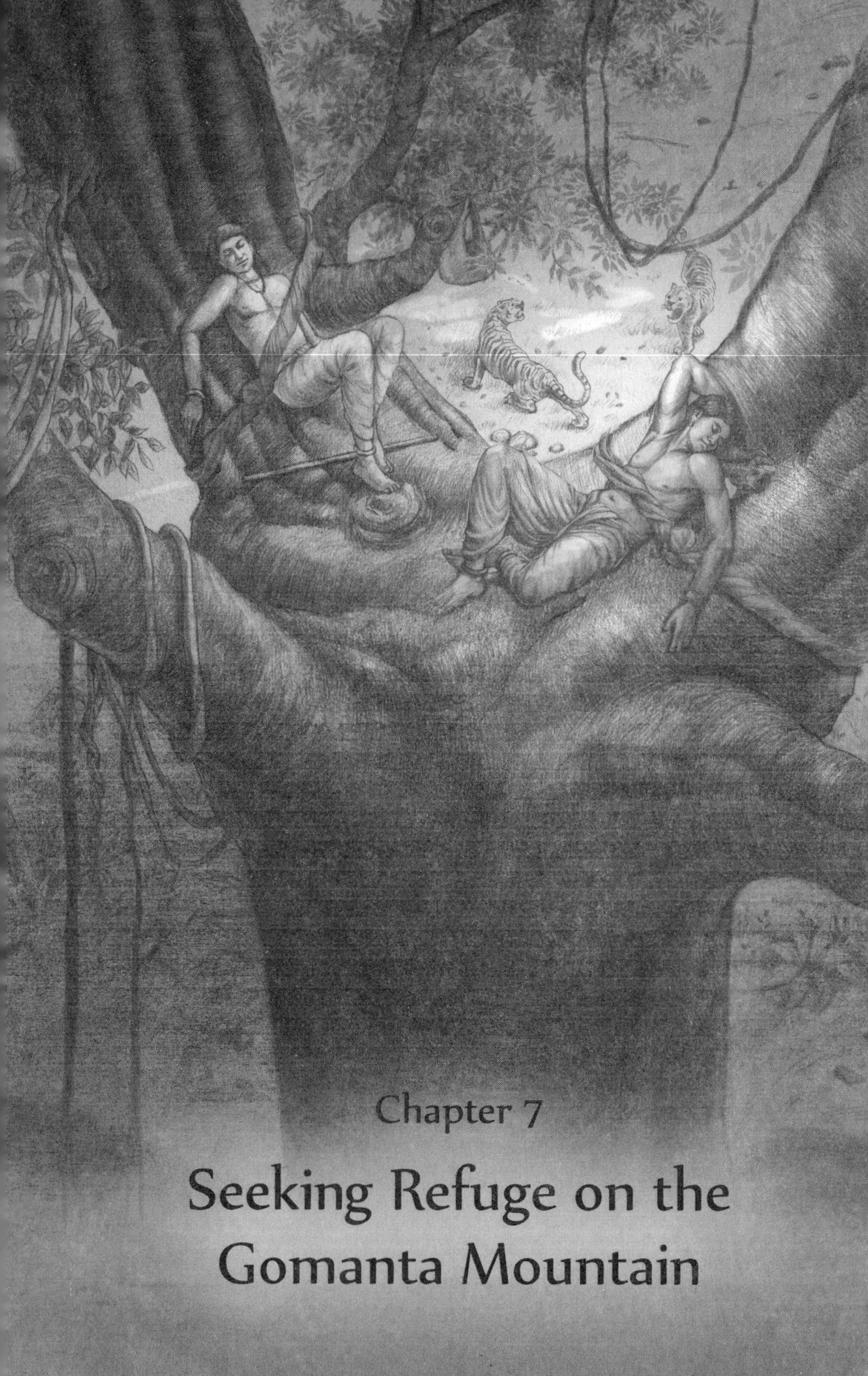

Chapter 7

Seeking Refuge on the Gomanta Mountain

With the words of the ascetic resounding in my ears, I steered the chariot in the direction of the Gomanta Mountain. We were passing through dense forests, with not a settlement or house in sight as far as the eye could see. Bhaiya sat with a grim face and still refused to speak with me. Hence, riding the chariot in silence, I began to contemplate upon the ascetic's words. His advice that I should increase my power and earn wealth was truly inspirational. But the question was, how would all of this come to pass? The voice within interjected, 'Oh, leave it, Krishna! Why have you engaged yourself in thinking about the future, forgetting the present?' The voice was right, for, who knew when my power would increase, when I would become king, and when I would win Rukmini over?! The voice continued, 'So, why not set aside these dreams and return to reality? Right now, you and your brother are fighting a lone battle for survival. Your sole objective at present is to save yourselves from Jarasandha, and to ensure your survival, the Gomanta Mountain is the only safe destination. So, just keep riding the chariot in that direction.' Well, I couldn't argue with that. So, pushing aside all thoughts of the future, I focused on the journey once again. Bhaiya was still sulking, and I had to rein in my meandering thoughts. So, I kept myself occupied by gazing at the dense forest cover.

Finally, by afternoon the next day, we reached the tribal settlement. And truth be told, the moment I entered it, I felt a sense of security envelop me. The village was small but picturesque. There were barely two hundred people living in the twenty or so huts made of mud and stone. To me, that still seemed quite a lot, for, ever since we had crossed the border of Mathura, we had longed to see other humans. So, we were happy to have come across even this small settlement. I had just halted the chariot on entering the settlement when a few tribal people gathered around us. We quickly jumped down from the chariot. Naturally, since we were strangers who had set foot in an unfamiliar settlement, the tribal people escorted us straight to their leader, Adeshwar. To my relief, he appeared to be a very pleasant and wise man. He first enquired the reason for our visiting this area and also wanted to know who we were. Heeding the advice of the ascetic to hide our identities, we introduced ourselves with false names; however, you well know that bhaiya could not bring himself to tell even a simple lie! It was I who had to do it, as I was the one responsible for landing us in this situation. At any rate, I was an expert in this art right from childhood and remained one throughout my life. So, I immediately replied, "We have come from Vidarbha. Sage Parshuram had suggested that we go to the Gomanta Mountain to perform austerities, and we have come here following his instructions."

Hearing this, Adeshwar said, "Ah! Then you are our guests. We have great respect for Sage Parshuram and his followers. Please accept our hospitality and allow us to serve you."

We were anyway in dire need of rest, and if one gets what one's heart desires, there is absolutely no question of refusing it. Surprisingly, Adeshwar proved to be the perfect host, who even allotted us a hut to stay. This was just what we needed, because after only a short period of rest, we felt reinvigorated. However, you may find it hard to believe, but there were no sleeping mats or blankets in the hut; we had to sleep on a bed of leaves! But despite that, bhaiya and I had slipped into a deep slumber and had begun snoring as soon as we lay down. Our fatigue was obviously the result of our non-stop journey. Come to think of it, it is perhaps only those who do not work hard that require comfortable, cushioned beds. Well, as soon as I woke up, I took a walk around the settlement. I was amazed to see that it had been built in such a way that, from the outside, it blended seamlessly with the forest. We were fortunate that Sage Parshuram had informed us about this habitation, else we would have missed it completely. After taking a stroll for some time, I returned to our hut. Bhaiya had woken up already and was sitting outside the hut on the ground, so I too took a seat next to him. It had only been a short while since we had been sitting here when Adeshwar arrived and invited us to partake in the evening's celebration. Hearing the word 'celebration', our faces lit up. Naturally, for two poor boys who had been wandering around the forest aimlessly, being invited to a celebration felt like a blessing! My happiness was of no great consequence, but bhaiya becoming happy surely boded well for my future.

As soon as dusk came rolling in, drums and cymbals began resounding all around. Enthused, bhaiya and I dashed off to participate in the celebration. Everyone had gathered in an open square situated at one end of the settlement. The torches tucked in the tree trunks illuminated the entire square, lending it a surreal appearance. It was worth noting that we were given the place of honour, our seats arranged next to Adeshwar. A short distance away, four women were busy preparing food for everyone. Meanwhile, cups of wine had started arriving for the men. Seeing wine being served, bhaiya's face lit up. As for me, I sipped a little out of courtesy, but bhaiya attacked it with gusto, guzzling goblets full of it. I was not sure whether to marvel at bhaiya, who looked truly happy after what seemed like ages, or admire the wonderful atmosphere all around me. Seated in style on the ground beside Adeshwar, I gave equal attention to both. About twenty people sat with us, and right before us, children were playing and running about. Further in the distance, the women were still busy preparing meals for the entire community, while several groups of men and women sauntered across the ground. A warm sense of cheer and bonhomie filled the air, and I committed this beautiful moment to memory forever.

Not long after, the song and dance programme commenced. Several women had begun singing and dancing, with the men accompanying them with their drums. As the night progressed, people began to drink excessively, including bhaiya, who showed no signs of stopping. However, it was good to note that with the wine settled in his system, his anger had vanished. This was definitely a positive development, as he appeared happy after so many days of sullenness. And for this reason, there was no question of my holding him back from overdrinking. With one knee raised up and reclining against a tree trunk, he was sitting as if he had no intention of getting up anytime soon. All this was fine but seeing everyone sing and dance, a peculiar feeling began to stir within me, an urge actually to join the dancing men and women; my lips too were longing to play the flute. But despite this urge, I stifled my desire and sat quietly, for, hiding my identity was of prime importance at present. Honestly speaking, the experience of stifling my desire was also a new one in my life. Do you see how the wheels of time had changed, landing me in a situation where I had to stifle even the desire to play the flute! However, this time around, it was easy to console myself because considering our present situation, I at least had the chance to enjoy some song and dance as a spectator. However, the festivities now appeared to be dragging on endlessly, with no end in sight. I was famished, but the food was supposed to be served only once the festivities concluded. Finally, after what seemed like an eternity to me, the song and dance came to an end and the meal was served. Oh, but what was this? The main dish was raw meat, which was totally unappealing. In the end, we had no choice but to go to bed hungry. It is true, I suppose, that when you are going through a bad phase, nothing goes right. But then, this too was a one-of-a-kind experience.

The next day, I woke up early and went out for a stroll. The walk was just an excuse; the truth was that my stomach was growling, and I was hoping to find some fruit in the forest to eat and bring back with me. Hungry as a bear, I began grumbling in my mind, 'What strange hospitality is this, where guests must arrange their own food!' Fortunately, the forest was laden with fruits and flowers, so I ate to my heart's content and brought back an armful for bhaiya. My brother, the happy soul that he was, had just woken up when I stepped into the hut with the fruits. Unexpectedly finding fresh fruits for breakfast, he jumped for joy and ate heartily. Coincidentally, Adeshwar too entered the hut to invite us for the afternoon meal. Fortunately, on seeing us devour the fruits with such relish, he understood our preference and quickly dispatched a few men to the forest to gather fresh fruits. All of a sudden, seeing the promptness with which Adeshwar had acted and given instructions, I couldn't help but be impressed with his wisdom and hospitality. Truly, how swiftly self-interest can change a person's perspective! This was alright, but interestingly, in just a few days, bhaiya had grown so fond of the forest dwellers' company that it seemed he had almost settled down here. I too was enjoying myself immensely, but I still had to observe caution, and presently it advised me to seek refuge in the Gomanta Mountain as soon as possible. However, I did not want to disrupt bhaiya's merrymaking, especially since he seemed to be returning to his normal self so quickly. It was important for me that he resumed his normal state of mind, for, I did not know how many days, months or even years I would have to spend alone with him at the top of the mountain. Moreover, after the long and stressful journey, I too was enjoying some much-needed rest, living with these tribal people. Besides, the chances of Jarasandha finding us here anytime soon seemed minimal. So, considering all these factors, there was no harm in letting bhaiya enjoy himself for a few more days.

Now, although bhaiya had nothing to worry about, I was faced with a peculiar problem. No, Jarasandha hadn't dropped in for a visit, and he was unlikely to for two reasons: first, we had fled Mathura overnight; second, the distance we had covered was so vast that locating us or reaching here would be a tall order. The problem I was facing was unique in the sense that the daily festivities were reminding me of Vrindavan. To make matters worse, I could not play my flute either. For that matter, not just the settlement or the nature of the festivities, but even the love and camaraderie that this close-knit community shared was strongly reminiscent of Vrindavan. Honestly speaking, it was only such people who truly knew the art of living. Even though they had not progressed much, the life they led here was stress-free, akin to the one I had lived in Vrindavan in the not too distant past. Well, so be it! For now, surrendering to bhaiya's wishes and Adeshwar's entreaties, we spent another eight days in this forest settlement. And in this period, not just Adeshwar but his entire community became very attached to us. Every night, we would partake in their festivities and bhaiya especially would join their drinking sessions. Finally, on the ninth day, I managed to convince bhaiya that it was time to go, and with this, we took Adeshwar's and the entire community's permission to leave. But no one wished to part ways with us. Hearing of our decision to leave, their eyes moistened with tears. Despite our short stay together, we had become so fond of them, it felt as if we had been living with them for years. In fact, I was receiving the same love and affection here that I had received in Vrindavan. Adeshwar must have been forty years of age, but despite the age gap between us, he had become my friend. Indeed, living with such simple-hearted, loving people—who would want to leave? Yet, the need of the hour was that we had to go. It was highly reassuring though that Adeshwar had asked us to reach out to him whenever we required his assistance, no matter the task or circumstances. All in all, due to these sentimental reasons, we could take our leave only by afternoon after bidding everyone an emotional farewell. About fifty men and women had accompanied us to the outskirts of the habitation. As for my chariot, I had handed it over to Adeshwar, asking him to look after it. When the situation improved, it was this very chariot that would help us return. And now, of course, we had to continue the journey ahead on foot.

We thus embarked on yet another perilous journey of our life. The passage ahead seemed daunting. Once we left the settlement, it felt as if two birds flying freely had suddenly lost their wings. Travelling on foot through such a dense forest was not going to be a pleasant experience. Moreover, the problem was, as we ventured deeper into the jungle, it became all the more impenetrable. Honestly, I had never seen such a dense forest before! You will not believe it, but the thick foliage was gradually making every step laborious, and as a result, we had to tear through the branches and bushes to carve a path for ourselves. Very soon, our hands became bloodied from being pierced and slashed by thorns. To add to our misery, we could constantly hear the calls of wild animals and the sound of their movements in the thick undergrowth. Fearing an attack, we had kept the mace and discus ready in case an animal lunged at us out of the blue. Truly, I had no idea that our journey would be so gruelling. It was a good thing that we were carrying only one tiny bundle of treasure and two sets of clothes; else it would have been difficult to even trek up the mountain. However, despite our minimal luggage, the journey was not without hardships. The biggest problem was that to satiate our hunger, we had to make do with whatever fruits we could find in the forest, whether ripe or raw. The only heartening aspect was that our destination, meaning, the Gomanta Mountain, loomed right in front of us. And naturally, as we approached closer to the mountain, it appeared even more colossal. To me, it seemed as if the Gomanta Mountain, surrounded by several hills, big and small, was the king of the range. To tell you the truth, I had never seen such a massive mountain before. All things considered, our experience of grazing cows and climbing the Govardhana Mountain was proving invaluable today. Otherwise, we wouldn't have even imagined being able to climb such a vast mountain and navigate through such dense forests.

Actually, the treacherous path and the thick foliage were not the only difficulties; I had one more problem that I was taking along with me. Yes, you guessed it right—bhaiya! He was already troubled by the difficult terrain, and to make matters worse, as soon as evening set in, he would start missing his wine. You can well imagine what a trying time I must have had in dealing with him! Although I had spent my entire life with him and was well acquainted with his temperament, I was presently being put to the most vigorous test.

Coming to the forest, it was so dense that, even during the day, sunlight could barely filter through. But look at our perseverance! We were still clearing out our path and forging ahead, stumbling over uneven ground and treading with caution in the dim light. And once evening rolled in, we would climb up a large tree to rest our weary limbs. We would eat whatever fruits we could lay our hands on and spend the night on the tree, sleeping fitfully in the fear of either slipping off the branch we were resting on or becoming a meal for some wild animal. Truly, our nights spent in this forest were frightening and fraught with danger. Spending even one frightening night like this would have been a tough—or rather impossible—task for the uninitiated. Catching even a wink was next to impossible amid the sound of the wind whooshing through the trees and the bloodcurdling calls of wild animals. Leave alone sleep, as a precaution, we had to wake ourselves up even if we did manage to fall asleep, fearing that a dangerous animal might attack us. One slip and we could find ourselves becoming the meal of a wild beast! For that matter, we had to encounter many wild animals during the day too. In fact, our short journey through the forest had already seen many animals falling target to bhaiya's mace. All in all, the journey we had undertaken to reach our destination, the Gomanta Mountain, was truly arduous.

Finally, after trekking non-stop for five days, we reached the base of the mountain. The vastness of the mountain was astonishing and well beyond our imagination. However, after the harrowing trek through the forest, we had no strength left to climb the mountain on this day. So, finding a huge tree, we made ourselves comfortable on its branches and fell asleep. Overtaken by fatigue and feeling a bit reassured with the fact that we were almost free from the danger of wild animals here, we slipped into a deep slumber and woke up only the next afternoon. Just imagine! We had managed to sleep for so long even on the branch of a tree! Well, now that we had rested well, we were full of vim and vigour. After hungrily devouring fruits, we began our trek up the mountain. Covered by numerous trees, big and small, this mountain also appeared densely forested. In fact, the shrubs were so thick that it made it difficult for us to find a path ahead. Even after toiling hard all day, it felt as though we had barely made any progress. And believe me, this was not the end but just the beginning of a series of seemingly endless difficulties. Though there was hardly any danger from wild animals on the mountain, it was home to all kinds of snakes. Fortunately, both bhaiya and I were adept

at handling snakes. Besides, I also had the experience of killing the savage serpent, *Kaaliya*. Actually, it was our past experiences that were helping us overcome the many hurdles we were facing, ensuring our journey progressed safely.

Well, even after moving to the mountain from the plains, there had been no change in our daily routine. We would climb the mountain all day long, sleep on the branches of trees at night, and resume our climb the next day. But our troubles, instead of abating, were only burgeoning as we moved ahead. What can I say? The climb had become so steep that we had to struggle really hard to move ahead. Gripping rocks and outgrowths with both hands, we would push ourselves up, while small pebbles and loose stones tumbled down the slope beneath our feet. In fact, several times, we had to hold each other's hands to climb. Often, when one of us slipped, we would quickly grab hold of each other to help regain our footing.

After trekking laboriously for eight days, we managed to reach the first flat surface of the mountain. Needless to say, we jumped for joy on seeing this place, never imagining that such a vast plain existed at such a great height. Another positive aspect was that we could not spot any snakes or predatory animals here. Instead, we saw several dense trees growing close together, and fortunately, most of them were laden with fruits and flowers. Oh, what a relief it was, as this meant we wouldn't face any shortage of food! More importantly, I wouldn't have to endure Bhaiya's ire over hunger anymore.

Looking all around us, we could see that the mountain was habitable in every respect. And even more delightful was the fact that there was a small pond on the other end of the clearing. The sight of this pond, nestled among tall trees, made me feel as if I had attained both heaven and earth! After encountering innumerable difficulties on our way up, discovering a plateau with fruit-laden trees and an enchanting pond...indeed, this mountain seemed no less beautiful than heaven itself...and perhaps it wasn't. So, we decided to set up camp here, because even from a security point of view, this place was unmatchable. The reason was clear: if we had taken all of eight days to climb to the summit of this mountain, after crossing thick and dense forests, then without a doubt, no one else would be able to scale this height in less than thirty-forty days. After all, we had the experience of wandering in the forests of Vrindavan and climbing the Govardhana Mountain, which kings and their armies most certainly did not. It is for this reason it is said that whenever life gives us a chance to learn anything, we must learn, for, who knows when an experience or lesson might come in handy?! My own experiences so far had made it evident that whatever one learns from life invariably proves useful later on. Unfortunately, it is the fake ascetics and mediocre *gurukuls* that propagate useless knowledge, which has no connection with life whatsoever. Whereas, life gives us opportunities to learn only those things which prove useful in the future.

However, putting aside these contemplations, let me tell you that we had fled Mathura in search of a safe haven, and I can confidently say that we had found one. Even if Jarasandha were to learn that we were up here, it would take his troops months to climb the steep mountain and reach us. This meant that we were safe for the next three to four months at least. For that matter, by taking refuge on this mountain, not only had the threat of Jarasandha been averted, but we had also stumbled upon a scenic place. Neither was there any shortage of food and water, nor a dearth of natural beauty. Oh, I was thrilled to the core! The atmosphere was so serene that I had begun to enjoy myself from the very first day. As for the place itself, tall trees laden with a variety of fruits and flowers abounded everywhere as far as the eye could see. Towards the right-hand corner of the mountain stood the lovely, little pond that would naturally take care of our drinking and bathing needs. Peering down the mountain, all one could see was dense, lush forest, while strong breezes swirled around us, cooling the air. In fact, in just two days of our arrival, my routine had been set. Twice a day, I would roam around the mountain and pluck and eat all kinds of fruit. Amazingly, not only was I humming a tune of peace and harmony here, but there was actually no danger even if I were to play my flute here. Every evening, I would lose myself in its mellifluous strains, and the flute in turn would transport me to the by-lanes of Vrindavan or in the midst of Radha and the *gopis* to perform the *raasa*. Oh, but it would be torturous when my dear flute would invoke the memories of the princess of my dreams, Rukmini, leaving me with no choice but to pine for her like a hopeless lover! The inner voice surfaced, 'Well, why are you so troubled over this? You haven't stopped dreaming of Rukmini, have you? Don't be upset! If today, your life has been saved; tomorrow, you may also live your dreams with her.'

Now, although this thought was reassuring, one could not ignore the ground reality. What could we accomplish by merely saving our lives? In reality, the situation had deteriorated further. I wanted to earn wealth and build my own kingdom so that I could marry Rukmini. But here I was, a deserter, hiding on top of this huge mountain without a roof over my head, no utensils or even a bed! At present, the earth was my bed and the open sky my blanket. Certainly, to even imagine being worthy of Rukmini or winning her hand in marriage seemed nothing short of foolishness. At the same time, it was well-nigh impossible for me to cast her from my mind. In short, my evenings would be spent lamenting how far my dreams were from reality.

And speaking of my poor heart, though I was prepared to suffer this inner turmoil, I was not willing to give up dreaming about Rukmini. You might think that a penniless cowherd, with no home to call his own and whose very life was at the mercy of Jarasandha, must be either insane or foolish to dream of winning the hand of a princess like Rukmini or becoming a king himself. But I can say with utmost certainty that I was neither insane nor foolish; but yes, I was certainly a dreamer, living with the hope that, sooner or later, just like all dreamers, I too would carve the perfect world of my dreams.

Well, it remained to be seen whether my dreams would ever turn into reality, but for now, thanks to the grace of my flute, I was surely living the most splendid dream, experiencing the bliss of two worlds! For that matter, my flute had always been dear to me, but it had never seemed as precious as it did now. Because, at present, my flute alone was my Radha and my Rukmini; it was my flute that was my wealth and my kingdom! That is why I say, if you have a love for art, in any form, you can survive even the most adverse circumstances by immersing yourself in it. Now, this was true for me, but bhaiya's condition, in stark contrast to mine, had become pitiable indeed. As the day drew to a close, he would begin craving the wine he had recently come to enjoy. Besides, art was anathema to him! Let alone art, he was not interested in even the most essential activities of life which directly affected its quality. He neither exercised nor showed any interest in going for a stroll. As a result, in the evenings, when he began to crave his wine, he would grow increasingly aggressive, making it hard for him to spend his time productively. All day long, he would loiter around aimlessly, dragging his feet from one spot to another, only to plonk himself under a tree for hours due to exhaustion. The problem was that his restlessness had gradually ensnared him in its web. Moreover, his crazed behaviour had now started creating hurdles in my way of life as well, so much so that he had stopped talking to me once again. He held a deep grouse against me, believing that he had to endure all these hardships because of my decision to flee from the battlefield. From his perspective, his anger was justified as well. But unfortunately, I did not have an immediate solution to this problem. And in my opinion, a problem that cannot be resolved must be accepted. So, ignoring bhaiya's behaviour, I continued to enjoy myself. But yes, I would frequently cast a wary, sidelong glance at bhaiya's sad demeanour and the bitterness that spilled from it. Watching the frown on his forehead deepen with each passing day, I could clearly see that this could not continue for long. Sooner or later, he would lose his patience and the anger he had held on a tight leash would snap violently. Oh, this was a huge predicament indeed! Here atop the mountain, bhaiya was not letting me live in peace, and if we stepped down from this safe haven, Jarasandha would pounce on us, ready to take our lives. However, considering both scenarios, I reckoned I was better off with bhaiya, for, I would at least remain alive. Thus, for now, I deemed it wise to put up with his antics.

Now, whether I considered this to be the best course of action or not, bhaiya's rancour and tantrums were growing dreadful by the day. It had only been ten days since we took refuge on this mountain, but bhaiya's disposition made it seem as though we had been suffering here for years! Honestly, his growing restlessness had compelled even me to question, 'What kind of a life was this? How long could we continue living this way?' Well, surely not the rest of our lives. On the other hand, it was difficult to determine when and how the threat of Jarasandha could be eliminated. By now, he must have arrived in Mathura, but it was anyone's guess how he would react on hearing that we had escaped from there. Also, sitting cooped up over here, it was not easy to ascertain what his future strategy would be. Most importantly, how will any news reach us here? So, even though our lives had been saved, we couldn't consider ourselves safe. Indeed, it was difficult to imagine a more arduous life than this! And this being the case, if bhaiya were to lose his patience and go berserk, and I were to make some wrong decision under pressure, it would certainly spell our doom.

In other words, before all my apprehensions turned into reality, it had become necessary to create an atmosphere wherein bhaiya could enjoy his stay on this mountain. It was afternoon and I was sitting under a tree, pondering this, while bhaiya was resting under another tree a little farther away. Honestly, just by looking at him, I grew anxious. Then, suddenly, a scene flashed through my mind and a chuckle escaped my lips. The scene had me telling bhaiya that I would teach him how to play the flute and dance so that he would start enjoying his stay in the mountains. But on hearing my outlandish proposal, he became so enraged that beating me up, he dragged me all the way to Magadha and left me at the mercy of Jarasandha, asking me to now give him lessons on how to dance! The scene I had imagined was so hilarious that anyone would have burst out laughing. However, as I glanced at bhaiya with a smile still on my lips, my mirth vanished instantly. Shaken from my reverie, my mind snapped back to the present problem. I let out a sigh and thought to myself that life should, indeed, be punctuated with some interests, some fun and some goals; otherwise, how different is the life of a human from that of an animal? That may be so, but the important question was, how could life be filled with zest? How could it be turned into a fun-filled ride? What could I do on this mountain which would breathe life back into it? Alas, even after racking my brain over these questions for quite some time, I was unable to come up with any concrete idea. Gradually, this anxiety occupied my mind to such an extent that neither did I feel like exercising, nor could I derive pleasure from my evening stroll. In vain, I tried to play my flute too, but restlessness held me in such a vice-like grip that the notes emanating from my flute sounded discordant, almost as if my flute had disowned me! Perhaps, the flute too had lost interest in leading such a drab existence. Neither did it invoke Radha, nor did it invite Rukmini. Even the *gopis* seemed to shy away from its magic. It was understandable, for, how long could anyone while away their life in a place like this? And when nothing else seemed to help, why would sleep be any different? All night long, I kept tossing and turning, but sleep had abandoned me completely. Meaning, the day had been ruined by depressing thoughts, and now, even the night offered no respite.

Well, never mind! I reasoned that since I could not sleep, I might as well analyse the situation. Lying on my back, looking upwards towards the starlit sky, I let my mind wander into its deepest recesses to pluck out a solution that would infuse colour into this dreary life and bring a smile to our lips. Actually, it was not just bhaiya; I too could not endure this drab existence anymore. How long could I, a seeker of love, celebration and joy, lead such a dull life? So, as I watched the moon shine bright in the dark night sky, I once again lost myself in deep contemplation, digging into the problem layer after layer. I began to look for the tiniest possibility of a solution. Finally, my contemplation bore fruit! As it is aptly said, if you try with all your heart, results are bound to follow. I too began to see a ray of light emerge in this labyrinth of darkness. In fact, I could see life and celebration galloping their way onto this mountain. Now, there was no question of my going to sleep. I waited impatiently for the sun to rise and for bhaiya to wake up. I wanted to share my plan with him as soon as possible and watch his face light up with hope and happiness. However, the night dragged on endlessly, making my wait even more intolerable. Besides, it was difficult to even toss and turn, resting as I was on a cold stone strewn with leaves. Finally, in exasperation, I got up and began to pace up and down. Bhaiya was lying in a regal pose on a nearby rock, having strewn it with leaves. The light of the rising sun had already dispelled the darkness, but bhaiya continued to sleep, his snores carrying in the clear morning breeze. It was funny really; while bhaiya was snoring like a bear, I was pacing to and fro like an impatient squirrel waiting for him to wake. Finally, fed up, I started making loud noises. Soon, my efforts paid off, and bhaiya woke up with a start. Excited, I immediately urged him to listen to my plan. All he had to do was trouble his ears a little. So, nodding his head, he gave me permission to speak. As soon as I had his consent, I began, "Bhaiya, if you notice, this mountain is very beautiful. There is no fear of predatory animals here, and we are safe from Jarasandha as well. There is no problem as far as food and water are concerned. If there is anything this place lacks, it is life, and certainly, everything is worthless without life. Moreover, the weather is pleasant right now, considering it is summer. However, during monsoon and winter, it will not be possible to live here without a proper house. We will have to make some arrangements for that too." It was true that bhaiya was not paying attention to me, but it was enough for me that he was not completely ignoring me either. At any rate, whatever I was saying tallied with his own thoughts, so how could he disregard it completely? Enthused thus, I continued with my idea, "Bhaiya, do you remember, the ascetic had said that this mountain used to be an old, prosperous city? Going by that story, there could indeed be plenty of treasure buried underneath this mountain. We already have the treasure given to us by Chandak; why don't we use that to bring life back to this mountain and try to hunt for the buried treasure as well? In other words, we will invest our wealth to earn more wealth. Secondly, Adeshwar has already become a good friend of ours. His village keeps facing threats from wild animals, implying that they too are in need of a safe haven. I'm certain they would not be able to find a safer place than this mountain, and that too, so close to their present settlement. So, I am wondering, why don't we ask these tribal people to come and live with us on this mountain? This will infuse this place with both life and celebration."

Hearing this, bhaiya jumped for joy. And why wouldn't he, because now, he would have access to all the things he desired—festivities, drinking, singing and dancing. He had just begun to weave pleasant dreams when he became despondent all of a sudden, as if something had derailed his train of thought. I could not understand what the matter was, but very soon, the suspense was lifted by bhaiya himself. After all, he could never hide his thoughts from me for long. In a quiet voice, he asked, "But will Adeshwar and the tribal people agree to relocate to this mountain?"

I said, "Of course, they will. Why would they refuse? It is in their interest as well." That's it! With a firm assurance from me, bhaiya's mood brightened again. For the first time in ten days, he looked happy. Seeing him so delighted, I felt a fresh surge of energy and enthusiasm. Did you see what a brilliant solution I had come up with! I was happy, bhaiya was thrilled, and the tribal people...they would obviously be elated too! It was the perfect solution to one of our most persistent problems. Life would improve for both us and the tribal people, and the relocation would be mutually beneficial as well. Instantly, I began to feel a sense of pride and thought to myself, 'Wow, Krishna! Regardless of the problem that comes your way, you do seem to tear through it and come up with a solution!' Well, I couldn't help but feel proud, as this had become a habit for me. Oh! Please do not think that I'm being conceited. In fact, let me leave it to you to decide whether I was merely strutting around, feeling as proud as a peacock, or if my actions were truly praiseworthy.

Well, bhaiya, in his excitement, sprang to his feet, and we almost raced down to the tribal settlement below. This time, we had to descend the mountain, not climb it. Moreover, the path was familiar, and we were enthused too. So, by the afternoon of the next day, we reached the settlement. Adeshwar and the entire community went wild with joy on seeing us in their midst again. And what can I say about the happiness of my innocent brother? He couldn't wait for the evening to set in and for the festivities to begin. Thinking about the dance and wine that would follow shortly, he was already feeling intoxicated. I could clearly see that these two interests were gradually becoming his weaknesses. For that matter, I was restless too, but the reason for my restlessness was completely different from his. I was restless because I wanted to ensure that I presented my grand scheme to Adeshwar in a manner that he would find acceptable. So, in a bid to quell this restlessness, I took the first opportunity I could find and led Adeshwar to a quiet corner, where I discussed my proposal with him in great detail. Adeshwar was undoubtedly wise, not because he agreed to my proposal at once, but because he was a straightforward man with a sensible head on his shoulders. Agreed, I often praise people when I want to get something done by them, but why do you forget that I never use such tricks with innocent and honest people. On the contrary, I go out of my way to help them. Besides, in my opinion, acting smart is fun only when you are dealing with oversmart people.

Well, just as I had expected, in the course of the evening celebrations, Adeshwar amply proved that my assessment of him was correct. He effortlessly convinced all the tribal people of my plan and obtained a unanimous consent from them to migrate. Bhaiya was filled with twice the joy, firstly due to the wine, and secondly, because the tribal people had agreed to relocate. I was thrilled as well, for, I too could not lead a drab existence for long and lay to waste this precious human birth obtained with great difficulty. Well, now that the decision was made, there was no point in wasting time. Since we already had a chariot at our disposal, early the next morning, Adeshwar, a few tribal people and I headed to a small marketplace on the outskirts of Karvirpur. From there, we purchased the supplies needed to build houses. We also bought several tools and implements for digging. That's not all! I also bought clothes for bhaiya and myself so that we could start living like human beings again. Additionally, I did not forget to gift some modern clothes to Adeshwar as well. After all, he was our prince of the hour! And since we did not face a shortage of wealth now, I could not resist buying two cows and buffaloes in

addition to everything else. After all, why should a cowherd go without curd and milk unnecessarily? These purchases of ours fuelled our enthusiasm even more. So, without wasting a moment, everyone threw themselves into their respective tasks with such fervour that the entire village was cleared out in just four days. Now, there was no need to wait for an auspicious moment to set out. A positive task should be initiated as soon as possible, because that is precisely the auspicious moment for it. As for negative deeds, there is neither an auspicious time for them, nor has Nature determined a favourable period for them.

So, early the next day, we loaded all the goods on our shoulders and began our trek up the mountain. Happiness and good cheer accompanied us on this long trek. Be it the youth, the elderly, the women or the children, all of them moved with agility, their faces wreathed in smiles. Everyone carried loads in accordance with their capacity. And despite repeated requests by Adeshwar not to do so, bhaiya and I were also carrying heavy loads on our shoulders. Meaning, while steering the chariot with one hand, I was holding luggage with the other. And since bhaiya and I knew the way, we naturally took the lead with Adeshwar and a few youths accompanying us. Thus, I, who used to lead Mathura, was now leading a caravan of two hundred tribal people. Every time I looked over my shoulder, the sight of the vast caravan following us would take my breath away. However, due to the weight we were now carrying and the fact that there were old people and women with us, this time, it took us twelve days to reach the mountain top. Needless to say, we were all exhausted by the end of the journey. Well, there's a saying that to achieve greater comfort and happiness, one must first endure small struggles. And so, everyone faced these hardships with a smile. Having said that, the moment everyone saw the plateau and the glistening pond on one side of it, the entire mood was transformed. Every vestige of fatigue vanished from their faces as the pristine beauty of the mountain captivated their hearts. Consequently, despite having laboured for hours up the mountain slope, no one was in a mood to rest; instead, they all began to wander around, curiously peeking into every nook of the mountain. They all wanted to imprint the beauty of the mountain in their hearts in a single glance! And what should I say about bhaiya? He was bubbling over with joy, showing every nook and corner of the mountain to the curious audience. He was so enthused that he had even plucked plenty of fruits with the help of the young boys. For the evening's celebration, everyone satiated themselves with these fruits. Needless to say, they also found comfortable spots and went to sleep early. Oh, what a wonderful sight it was to see two hundred people, resting on the mountaintop, making themselves as comfortable as possible on the stones and grass!

It goes without saying that the excitement of the previous day had exhausted everyone, and the majority of people woke up only by afternoon the next day. This day was not very different from the previous one. Now that everyone was well rested, I decided to initiate the process of establishing the settlement. And accordingly, I engaged everyone in this task from the very next day. Of course, it was I who had taken charge of this entire operation. After all, I had ample experience in building settlements, and was also the most eager to see this mountain throbbing with life as soon as possible. And as they say, 'self-interest is the noblest of all virtues', so, first and foremost, I taught two tribal women how to bathe the cows, milk them, and make curd and butter. For, this *Gopala*[37] could not accomplish great tasks on an empty stomach. To take care of the rest of the work, I segregated the men and women into groups. The first group comprised ten men and twenty women who had to dig out stones and mud. The second group was bigger, with thirty men and as many women, who were assigned with the task of building the houses with stones and mud. I had also drawn up a blueprint of the settlement, keeping Vrindavan, Vaivasvatpur and *Acharya* Sandipani's *ashram* in mind. I had deliberately excluded Mathura from this list because its town-planning was not to my liking at all. I also kept a large space near the pond, adjacent to the settlement, completely vacant, with no construction planned. Yes, you guessed it right! This area was reserved for holding festivities or conducting assemblies. For that matter, with everyone now here, there was no need to wait for the groundwork to be finished before organising celebrations. Because without festivities and celebrations, work can feel burdensome, but when work is combined with merrymaking, it becomes a sacred duty.

As per my plan, a total of fifteen homes were being constructed for the tribal people, positioned along the two sides of the mountain. Our house was being constructed right opposite the pond, and it was planned to be a little bigger than the others. In fact, it was being built on the lines of Nanda's house in Vrindavan. You know how deeply I loved that house and how much I missed it along with the charming lanes. However, I had not lost sight of my duty while fulfilling these dreams of mine. I made sure that the largest house was built for Adeshwar to live in. Well, all this was taken care of, but what pleased me the most was seeing everyone completely engrossed in their tasks. Indeed, their enthusiasm was worth watching as they busied themselves in their respective tasks. Even I was busy, enthusiastically giving directions for the construction of the houses and the festival ground. Now, I did not have any means to write down the instructions, and even if I did, they would have been of no use to me, for, I had no formal training in house construction. All I would do was draw a few stray lines on the ground and impress the tribal

37. *Gopala* - Cowherd.

people. Amusingly, I would sit all day long on a large stone, with three or four big sticks by my side. Seeing me as the epitome of wisdom, the poor tribal people would queue up all day with their teams, eager to know what needed to be done next. A bit puffed up with all the attention, I would draw some lines on the ground and assign them their next task. I was really enjoying this work! Frankly, it gave me the thrill of being a leader.

As for everyone's diligence at work, you could gauge it from the fact that the first good tidings came in just a week later, when work on the communal kitchen near the pond was completed. In any case, there was no dearth of stones and mud in this place, for, it was lying in abundance everywhere. And now, with the kitchen ready, everyone's enthusiasm increased manifold. Actually, these forest dwellers did not have the custom of cooking separately in their individual homes. And honestly, even I was greatly impressed by the custom of cooking community meals. And now, along with their food, I had made arrangements for my food as well. A team of four men was permanently assigned to pick fruits and firewood, while two women were engaged in making curd and butter. At any rate, I considered the fondness for good food as one of the best passions a human being could cultivate in life.

Well, now that everyone's food requirements were taken care of, let me return to discussing the progress of the various tasks at hand. By now, a team of men had fashioned several torches, which helped light up the entire dining area and the festival ground, which shone brightly as we sat down and partook our meals together. These torches placed atop the mountain, casting their glow on the slopes and the thick foliage below, made for a truly ethereal sight! Indeed, they had cast an enchanting spell on me. As a matter of fact, many such joys were gradually becoming a part of my life. I remember being similarly captivated when I had first partaken *Chhappan Bhog*. For that matter, I was ecstatic even when I had first laid eyes on the marketplace of Mathura. And yes, I had experienced the same thrill when I had taken the reins of the chariot in my hands for the first time, and also when I had first set my eyes on Rukmini… Oh, but let us leave that aside for now, for, this wasn't the time to lose myself in reveries. Let me instead narrate an interesting incident to you. Isn't it often said that man invariably finds his way to what truly interests him? So, just as I had made provisions for my curd and butter, the tribal people had also made arrangements for their liquor. Apparently, there were a number of trees of *Varuna*—the three-leaved caper—in the forests here. And within a few days, the tribal people had started making wine from its juice, which was called *Varuni*. Enthused by this, Adeshwar had himself assigned four men to this task. With this development, bhaiya's needs, along with everyone else's, were also well taken care of. In short, no one was going hungry or thirsty on this mountain anymore—everyone was satisfied. Actually, executing a task becomes enjoyable only when there are content people around you. And to be honest, work can only be extracted from those who are content.

Well, the once-silent mountain was now abuzz with life. Sounds of laughing children and the humming of a merry tune reverberated all around as men and women went about their tasks. While the days were spent toiling hard, the nights were enlivened by fun and festivities. Speaking of celebration, the glow of the burning torches had added an ethereal touch to the festivities, transporting me to the quaint by-lanes of Vrindavan. And the entire credit for my state of happiness went to these simple, honest forest dwellers, whose affection was no less than the love showered on me by the inhabitants of Vrindavan. And now that I was comparing this settlement with Vrindavan, I reckoned, why not go all the way? The abundant vegetation on this mountain ensured that we did not have to venture far to pluck fruits. Most importantly, we did not have to contend with the menace of wild animals. Seen from this perspective, the living conditions here were far superior to those in Vrindavan. Now, tell me, was it wrong to congratulate myself for this stupendous achievement? If I refrained from doing so, it would be a grave injustice to me. And if I did bask in the accomplishment, you will blame me for continually patting myself on the back. Well, regardless of what I did, you will have to admit that just a few days ago, this mountain was as silent as death. And now, the same place had started throbbing with life, with such vibrancy that even great, reputed kings would feel envious on witnessing it. What can I say? Whether it was intentional or not, I would invariably achieve such feats that would make me proud of myself. Why just me, even you wouldn't have been able to stop yourself from saying, "Krishna! What an exceptional *karmaveer*[38] you were!"

Ah, but enough about me. The happiest person on the mountain was bhaiya. And you all know how much his happiness meant to me. However, with time, a sad aspect to his happiness was fast becoming evident. Bhaiya was gradually becoming addicted to the festivities and wine.[39] Not only that, with the passage of time, these addictions were taking a turn for the worse, for, he had now begun drinking during the day as well. Along with that, I do not know what had come over him, but he had now started mingling with the tribal women. All his life, women had been anathema to him, but now, it was the demand of his age; moreover, the wine and the atmosphere of this place had perhaps fuelled it too. In a way, it was good that bhaiya was now getting along with women, but considering the place and the circumstances under which this fondness was blooming, it certainly couldn't be regarded as a positive sign. I strongly believe that no deed is inherently good or bad;

38. *Karmaveer* - Man of action.
39. Harivansh Puran, Vishnu Parva, Chapter – 41, Verse – 8-30.

whether it is right or wrong depends entirely on the time and circumstances in which it is performed. Seen from this perspective, the love and affection blossoming in bhaiya's heart could only be described as ill-timed.

Well, leaving bhaiya and his interests aside, the good news was that after a month of toil, the construction work was finally over. And certainly, the entire credit for it went to the diligence and hard work put in by the tribal people. They had completed several weeks' work in a matter of days. Well, it was not as if we had to build mansions on this mountain; all that needed to be constructed were walls of mud and stone to shield us from wind and rain. Once the village was established, all the tribal people, including Adeshwar, were thrilled to the core. Looking at their radiant faces, I was delighted as well. Standing on a huge boulder, I cast a glance all around, taking in the enchanting scene—a small settlement of fifteen houses surrounded by lush greenery as far as the eye could see! Oh, what a sight it made! This made me wonder, what is destiny after all? Nothing! It is *karma* (action) that actually matters. This is why I had never accepted any adversity that came my way as my destiny, but instead fought it off with *karma*. This is why I say that I was, I am and I will always remain a *karmaveer*—a man of action. Why just me, every person must become a *karmaveer*, or else they will amount to nothing. If man wants to live happily in this world, he must carve a great life on the strength of his *karma* (actions). Nature's design is such that, apart from man's intelligence and his *karma* (actions), nothing in this world will come to his aid.

Ah, but let me stop philosophising and come back to the settlement. Once the village was built, a new change had come over all the tribal people including Adeshwar. Their unbounded love for me was now transformed into worship and reverence. Strangely, this expression of reverence was new for me, and if I must confess, it was fuelling my ego. For that matter, I had received immense love and respect since childhood, but this reverence seemed dangerous. Because of this, I had to now unnecessarily expend all my energy in keeping my arrogance in check. I had never worshipped anyone, and I did not want anyone to worship me either. I had accorded respect to worthy individuals and learnt from them. So, all I wanted was for people to respect me and learn valuable lessons from me.

Well, putting this aside, let me return to the settlement. The deep, earthy hues of stone and mud blended with the vibrant greenery made this habitation a beautiful sight to behold. Spread across the entire plateau high up on the mountain, with the open ground in front of it, the settlement evoked pleasant memories of Vrindavan. But having said that, the small pond sparkling in the sunlight, coupled with lush mountains and forests surrounding it, definitely placed this settlement a few notches higher than

Vrindavan in terms of natural beauty. Oh, it felt as if I had reached the pinnacle of grandeur! Moreover, the regular evening festivities had turned this mountain into a veritable paradise. Indeed, I could not praise this settlement enough; it was because of its presence that the mountain which had stood in silence for so long had suddenly come alive, pulsating with vibrant energy. On the other hand, bhaiya, Adeshwar and the rest of the tribal men had turned into inebriated elephants. And why wouldn't they? After all, there couldn't be a more beautiful place to live than this, nor a safer one. Just a month ago, this mountain seemed like the playground of death, and today, heaven-like life had descended on it. That is why I implore you to think, what can man not achieve on the strength of his intelligence, willpower and diligence?!

Digressing a little from the topic, let me tell you that just like the others, I was thrilled too but far from intoxicated, because for me, the task had just begun. Surely, life had stabilised, but I still had to ensure it remained secure and was nurtured as well. And this was possible only if I prepared this mountain for a war against Jarasandha. Indubitably, this was a difficult task. On one hand was Jarasandha's large, well-trained army, equipped with the latest weaponry, and here I was, with just a handful of tribal people. Well, I'm sure you must have realised why I was not intoxicated. Ordinarily, when a person gets intoxicated, he throws caution to the winds, but observing caution was an integral part of my personality. Admittedly, the mountain was safe and there was no immediate threat from Jarasandha, but the threat had not been totally averted yet. How could I turn a blind eye to the reality that, sooner or later, Jarasandha would surely charge up the mountain and stand before me in the form of death? Indeed, I must be commended for keeping this thought alive at the back of my mind. You will not believe it, but even when I was engrossed in the task of establishing the settlement, my mind kept pondering over how to get rid of Jarasandha. After all, death and Jarasandha were not going to seek my permission before making their entrance. They were not going to ask me, "Krishna, are you ready; shall we come now?" I had also discerned that my next battle with Jarasandha would take place on this very mountain. For, sooner or later, he was bound to arrive here, sniffing us out. It was also certain that we could not leave this mountain and go anywhere else. After all, we had reached here after being on the run for so long! Where else could we go now? So, just as there was no choice but to enter into a battle with Jarasandha, I had no option but to keep thinking of a strategy for this inevitable battle. And whether I liked it or not, my thoughts kept revolving around it. All said and done, I could see only two possibilities playing out on this mountain: either we would be killed in battle or we would have to repulse

Jarasandha's army by launching a counter-attack. Naturally, my focus was entirely on the second possibility.

Finally, one day, my deliberation bore fruit. I devised a battle strategy that, though not enough to defeat Jarasandha, could certainly harass him and force him to flee. And verily, what more did I want? Our lives would be spared if he fled. After being harassed a couple of times, he would surely forget all about me and busy himself with other matters. The idea was so encouraging that I promptly began implementing it. First and foremost, I instructed ten well-built men to collect small, medium-sized and giant boulders and strategically place them on all sides of the mountain. This exercise took about ten days to complete; once this task was accomplished, I got the stones and boulders stacked in a sequence. Closest to the border were the small stones, then came the medium-sized rocks, followed by the giant boulders. Now, you might think, 'Krishna has definitely lost his mind. What is he planning to do with all these boulders? Is he dreaming of defeating Jarasandha's army with a bunch of stones and rocks?!' Alright then, pay close attention to what I am saying—truly wise are those who believe they have sufficient resources and make the best use of them, not those who blame their defeat on a lack of resources. This approach applies not just to an armed war but to all struggles of life as well. And now that we are on the subject, let me reveal one more secret to you. It is owing to this very formula that Krishna is hailed as *Jai Shri Krishna*![40] Funnily, just like you, neither Adeshwar nor the other tribal people could fathom what purpose these boulders would serve in the future. But thankfully, the objective did not matter to them; my command alone was enough. All said and done, a crucial task of mine had been completed. Even otherwise, from a security point of view, there was nothing more that could be done at present. Besides, it was not as if Jarasandha would launch an attack right away. What I mean to say is, the first obstacle in Jarasandha's path had been put in place. There was nothing more to be done or thought about on this front. A full-fledged army or weapons would not spring up on the mountain overnight; I had to keep my spirits up with the resources that were available to me. Thus, once these preparations were made, I pushed all thoughts of Jarasandha to the back of my mind.

No sooner had I done that than my mind began to dwell on my interaction with the great sage, Parshuram. Had he not said that a prosperous city lay buried on this mountain?[41] Oh, just look at my carelessness; engrossed in thoughts of Jarasandha, I had all but forgotten this important point. But now that I had remembered, I did not want to waste a second. I wanted to start looking for the hidden treasure right away. Besides, I had clearly understood

40. *Jai Shri Krishna* - The victorious Krishna.

41. Harivansh Puran, Vishnu Parva, Chapter – 39, Verse – 80.

the import of Sage Parshuram's words when he had emphasised that I should become my own refuge; and for that, he had advised me to increase both my wealth and power. Therefore, I did not want to miss this opportunity under any circumstances. Now, I do not wish to hide anything from you; I certainly did not want to spend the rest of my life as an ordinary cowherd. I wanted to scale the peaks of prosperity and grandeur. You could even say that I wanted all this to win over my dear Rukmini. So, in view of this and other factors, it had become imperative for *karmaveer* Krishna to unearth this treasure as soon as possible. The next step was to take Adeshwar into confidence. Well, he had become my devotee anyway, but still, I needed a seal of approval on my proposal. Thus, during the evening festivities, while everyone else was busy singing and dancing, I led him to the far end of the pond. That is to say, I led him away from the noise; otherwise, honestly, the sight of the settlement and everyone singing and dancing appeared even more beautiful from over here. Well, putting the festivities aside for now, I frankly shared with him the legend of a prosperous city buried underneath. Hearing about the treasure, he was not only delighted but he also promised me that all the tribal people would be available to assist in unearthing it. Now, although I had promised Adeshwar a share in the find, the simple man that he was, he seemed hungrier for my love than for the treasure! It was this simplicity of his which had captured my heart. Well, after sharing my proposal with him, we quickly made our way back to the festival ground. The singing and dancing continued with great gusto, accompanied by numerous rounds of drinks. Bhaiya too was enjoying his drink near the pond with a band of young tribal men. As soon as we returned, Adeshwar made me sit on a large rock near the communal kitchen, while he himself stood next to me and gave a loud clap. As soon as he clapped, the singing and dancing stopped abruptly. Once he had everyone's attention, he informed them about the hidden treasure in detail, sparking a wave of enthusiasm in the assembled crowd. Thereafter, everyone became so enthused that the singing, dancing and drinking were flavoured with greater zest and vigour than before, winding down only in the wee hours. On that occasion, Adeshwar and I were also pulled into the centre of the ground and made to dance. This not only gave me an excuse to indulge in one of my favourite activities, but everyone's enthusiasm also convinced me—the dreamer—that I would soon become a wealthy man.

Well, by afternoon the next day, we even held a meeting at the festival ground. Naturally, I wanted to begin hunting for the treasure without wasting time, and accordingly, once again, it was I who took command of the operation. To begin with, I divided all the tribal people into two teams; I took charge of one team, while Adeshwar led the other. Furthermore, it was decided that both teams will start working from the next day itself. By evening, we had also piled up all the materials required for the excavation on the ground itself. Seeing everyone's enthusiasm, I was on cloud nine. Perhaps, they too had realised that if there was indeed a prosperous city hidden underground, then the possibility of finding an enormous amount of treasure could not be ruled out. This was all fine, however, bhaiya's conspicuous absence even during the execution of such an important task had me worried. He was the only one amongst the youth who did not take an active interest in anything. He was busy enjoying himself with his friends—the tribal women—in the settlement. And honestly, bhaiya's ill-timed amorous adventures had started to become a major cause of concern for me. For, I knew that if there arose a misunderstanding owing to bhaiya's antics, all would be lost. We were wholly dependent on these tribal people on this isolated mountain, and this being the case, if Adeshwar or anyone else were to get even slightly miffed about something, or if there was even a hint of conflict between us, we would find ourselves in deep trouble once again. Indeed, what if bhaiya's bubble of love, which had taken a flight of fancy at the wrong time and in the wrong place, ruined our very lives?

Immersed in these thoughts, I found myself worrying about bhaiya instead of focusing on the tasks ahead. I really wonder why man wants to indulge in everything at the wrong time. In both Vrindavan and Mathura, the time and the place were just right for love and romance, so I wonder why bhaiya never got along with the *gopis* then. Remember, one is always in one's senses when doing things at the right time, but if something is done at the wrong time, it is a sign of unawareness. To state it differently, it is only because man is unaware that he does the wrong things at the wrong time. This was precisely what I had said to Arjuna in the Gita, *"Why are you gripped by this ill-timed attachment?"*[42] Throughout his life, Arjuna never thought of taking up renunciation, for which any time would have been appropriate—but no, he thought of it only on the battlefield. Tell me, standing in the battlefield, what was this sudden desire to renounce the world, if not fear? Similarly, in my opinion, ill-timed love is not love but merely lust. Therefore, to put it in plain words, bhaiya, at present, was a victim of lust. Of course, I had no intention of picking a quarrel with him; on the contrary, I would gladly lay down my life for his happiness. But his ill-timed mischief could pose a danger not just to us, but to everyone else too. In short, it had become necessary to rein him in. Hence, without wasting time, I mustered up courage and decided to have a word with him. As soon as the meeting ended, I caught hold of him and explained to him that these tribal people were our only support now and if there was even a hint of a misunderstanding between us, our lives would

42. Shrimad Bhagavad Gita, Chapter – 2, Verse – 2.

turn into a living hell all over again. Therefore, it was best that he maintained distance from the tribal women.

Now, my concern was genuine, but I do not know why bhaiya took umbrage at it and became incensed. Perhaps, he was slightly drunk and I suppose I was spoiling his fun too. Consequently, he almost scolded me saying, "You're one to talk! You, the one who loitered with the *gopis* of Vrindavan day and night, and the one who used to spend all his time with Malini in Mathura, are here to give me lessons on propriety?! You better keep your preaching to yourself!"

Hearing his outburst, I became angry too. I could not help it, and for the first time in my life, I spoke to him with a voice full of indignation. I said, "Oh, do not talk about me! Even my indulgences are nothing but a form of devotion. Mark my words, bhaiya, if wine and lust take control of a person and overpower him, he is bound to lose his way in the darkness."

But bhaiya was bhaiya, after all. He was not one to be subdued by my loud and angry voice. On the contrary, he became even more furious and, shaking with rage, shot back, "Affliction, indulgence, devotion! Keep your fancy ideologies and lofty words to yourself. Don't you dare trap me in words! Your tricks are not going to work on me."

Well, that was the end of the matter. I realised there was no use trying to explain anything to him, inebriated as he was. So, I gave up and stomped away in exasperation. Really, what else could I do? Bhaiya could do as he wished; I would deal with the consequences when the time came. Indeed, issues that cannot be resolved are best left to Nature's justice. In any case, I had far too many matters to attend to, so I quietly walked away from there. Surprisingly, after our altercation, bhaiya kept me at arm's length for the rest of the evening's festivities. Well, so be it! On this day, however, the celebration ended much sooner, as everyone had to start work early the next morning.

The following morning, everyone assembled at the ground on time. Spades, pickaxes and long iron rods were already piled on the ground, so taking these, around fifty of us set off on our mission. I had carried a pickaxe on my shoulder, while Adeshwar walked alongside me with a spade; and we were followed by fifty women and men carrying shovels and spades. Soon, we reached the tip of the mountain—the starting point of our excavation. Without wasting time, my team began digging the ground from one end, while Adeshwar's group began working at the other. Excitement and enthusiasm ran high as everyone became engaged in feverishly digging up the mountain. Truly, the fervour with which they were working had to be seen to be believed! We continued digging all day long and returned home only in the evening when our bodies began to cry out in weariness. This became our daily routine for the next several days. In the morning, we would have a light meal before setting off in search of the lost treasure. We would toil throughout the day and return to the settlement only by dusk, just in time for the evening meal, freshly prepared for us by the tribal women. We would partake of the meal and indulge in a bit of singing and dancing before retiring to bed. The next day, we would set off once again at the break of dawn to continue the excavation work. However, even after ten days of continuous digging, we found nothing! Let alone the ancient township, we couldn't even find traces of its ruins. Naturally, after the passage of a few days, everyone's enthusiasm began to wane and doubts started to creep in about whether the story of a prosperous township on the mountain was just a fable! Well, quite often, such popular tales are nothing more than myths, but even so, I wanted to put in my best effort. I was anyway enthusiastic by nature, so I did not allow disappointment to dampen my fervour. Besides, there was no other important work to be done on this mountain that would discourage us from continuing our treasure hunt. Consider me for instance. I knew that Jarasandha could arrive on this mountain any day and stand before me in the form of death. But did that mean that driven by fear, I should give up the very hope of living? Thinking about the possibility of death, I cannot give up the hope of living a good life and stop making attempts towards that end. In my opinion, regardless of the darkness that has engulfed one's life, one must strive to tear through the shadows and move towards the light without losing hope. Thus, I encouraged everyone by lifting their sagging spirits and pushed them to resume their digging with twice the enthusiasm. Along with that, I also modified the search strategy a little. This time, I formed ten teams of five diggers each and spread them across the length and breadth of the mountain. All of them were instructed to inform me the moment they found anything. Truly, it was impossible to shirk action in Krishna's presence!

Well, you will not believe this, but the new search strategy paid rich dividends on the third day itself, when one of the teams reported a startling find. Verily, positive thinking brings positive results! It so happened that I was busy digging with my team near the tip of the mountain when one of the teams rushed to me bearing good tidings. Some remnants of the ancient town were discovered at the rear end of the settlement. I jumped for joy as soon as I heard this and raced off in that direction. Indeed, the remnants of a township lay buried in the rubble. And even as we were expressing our elation on this discovery, another team came running towards us. They were ecstatic too. And why wouldn't they be? For, they too had found remnants of the township near the other incline of the mountain. In great excitement, I ran to the other spot too, and sure enough, there were signs of an ancient town buried here as well. These findings now decided my future course of action. Instead of the evening celebration, I held a meeting with everyone wherein we decided on two most vital things. One, we would set off early in the morning, and two, we would now continue digging only at these two sites. So, from the next day onwards, we poured all our strength into digging feverishly at these two sites. I too had enthusiastically joined the digging at the rear end of the mountain. Under Adeshwar's leadership, the digging at the tip of the mountain had also started in earnest. With the discovery of the ancient town's remnants, everyone was filled with zest once again. Based on this new experience, I realised that nothing else can boost one's enthusiasm as much as success. But remember, success is attained only by those who can sustain their enthusiasm even in moments of despair. In my opinion, a person who does not forsake his enthusiasm even when caught in a whirlpool of failures is truly entitled to success. And who else could know this better than me? After all, I had been shadowed by despair all my life. You are well aware that my birth itself had taken place in a dark, dreary dungeon. What I mean to say is, Nature had left no stone unturned in ensuring that my life would be steeped in darkness. But it was because of my tenacity and other qualities that I was always able to bring light into this darkness. Today, let me tell you with every bit of conviction that life is just another name for working rigorously and enjoying oneself wholeheartedly whenever one finds the opportunity. There is no third purpose of life!

Well, let me stop philosophising and return to the present endeavour, which I was pursuing diligently. After digging non-stop for three days, we unearthed some rusted, worthless weapons. This discovery was indubitable proof that a town once flourished here. We were now moving closer to our goal—not just me, everyone else was bubbling over with enthusiasm too. We simply had to continue digging for a few more days and we would find the treasure! Needless to say, this sense of exhilaration pervaded the evening festivities as well. I could clearly see big dreams reflecting in everyone's eyes. But these simple people were no match for my imagination! For, I was an expert in spinning dreams. In my mind, I had already become wealthy and had even managed to impress Rukmini. But alas, in Nature's presence, how could anything in my life be accomplished so easily? Just when our boat of hope was nearing the shore, we could see signs of a storm approaching. Nature had already vowed to hurl obstacles in my path, and it did not fail this time either. Of course, I had never held any grudge against Nature for this. On the contrary, I had always taken it as a game being played between the two of us. Nature continued to test my resolve of being a man of action, and I always rose to the challenge and forged ahead.

Speaking of the latest challenge Nature had hurled in my path, one night, all of a sudden, silver streaks of lightning illuminated the dark sky, accompanied by thunder, heralding the arrival of monsoon. At the time when Nature was busy orchestrating this phenomenon, I was resting in my chamber, dreaming of cuddling up next to Rukmini, seated as we were on a swing. The booming sound of thunder not only disrupted my pleasant dream, but also jolted me out of my sleep. I rushed outside and was dumbstruck to see sheets of rain lashing down on us. Now, you all know how difficult it is to dig in the rain due to the slush. So, abandoning my sweet dreams, I returned to reality and spent the night brooding in the veranda, watching the rain vent its fury on the earth.

Well, the dark, stormy night finally came to an end, heralding a fresh, new morning...but this made no difference to the unrelenting downpour. Never mind, I reached the ground well on time after completing my morning chores, but I noticed that no one had turned up so far. Well, I sat under a tree and began enjoying getting drenched in the rain. After considerable time had passed, Adeshwar arrived with four men in tow. A while later, twenty people arrived, albeit feeling compelled by their sense of obligation. From their demeanour, I could gauge that none of them seemed keen to continue digging. Now, whether they were excited or not, I could not let my dreams be shattered. Besides, there was no question of Krishna turning his back on action. I, therefore, pepped up those who had come and set off with them to resume digging. Unbelievably, just a single downpour had ruined all the efforts we had made thus far. Firstly, we had set off late on this day; secondly, the slush had reduced our walking pace even further. So, by the time we reached our excavation spot, half the afternoon had already elapsed. But it couldn't be helped as we had to tread with caution, carefully watching every step we took. This was alright but after a point, the mud had become so slippery that we faced the danger of losing our footing from such a great height. In short, while it was difficult to dig on this mountain even in ordinary circumstances, now, because of the soft, slushy mud, our very lives were in peril. As a result, we were compelled to return to the settlement without accomplishing anything, our drooping shoulders and weary faces reflecting our disheartened mood.

Well, since it was the first day of monsoon, the situation was quite understandable, but this could not go on endlessly. With the onset of the monsoon season, rain was inevitable, which meant that our task would become even more challenging with each passing day. And that being the case, we obviously could not wait for months for the rains to subside. Besides, we did not even have that much time on hand! Don't you remember? By the end of monsoon, there was every possibility of the menace called Jarasandha descending upon us. In short, we had no choice but to keep digging despite the challenging circumstances. And I was well aware that I alone would have to take the lead in this matter. Thus, later in the evening, I assembled everyone once again and delivered an empowering speech, painting a rosy picture of how beautiful their life could become in the future if they put in the effort today. Charged up thus, the next morning, they all gathered at the ground, brimming with enthusiasm, and that too, well before time. Seeing their cheerful faces, I administered one more dose of enthusiasm and ensured that the digging operation resumed in earnest. Of course, the rains had considerably slowed down our speed, but on the bright side, the work had at least begun. And as they say, any task performed wholeheartedly invariably yields the desired result, and this was precisely what happened in this case as well. In the next one week, despite the pouring rain, the results were quite encouraging. Gold, silver and jewellery studded with diamonds and other precious stones were unearthed. And once this treasure was discovered, everyone's enthusiasm skyrocketed! Now I did not have to make any special efforts to motivate these people. The lashing rains, the slippery mud, and the risk to life and property were no longer obstacles for them.

Cheer and exhilaration marked the actions of the tribal people as they went about the task of digging deeper into the bowels of the earth. Loud chatter accompanied each strike to the ground, their hearts beating in anticipation of discovering more precious stones and gems. However, while they had become engrossed in their task, I found myself straying from the path of action, losing myself in dreams of my precious princess, Rukmini. In fact, my mind had veered off to such an extent that in my delusionary state, I started seeing Rukmini's face in the heaps of diamonds and pearls. I had gone crazy indeed, slipping into a romantic mood. And why would I not? Why else do you think I was looking for the treasure in the first place? It was only to become worthy of Rukmini that I had willingly endured so much trouble. And just see, boxes upon boxes of treasure were emerging from the lap of earth. In no time, it seemed as if gems and precious stones were spurting from the mountain. Needless to say, in the joyous state I found myself in, I even began to see my dream come to life with every chunk of treasure that was being unearthed. However, let me clarify one thing: though I had lost my mind in sheer delight, I had not strayed from my duty or the strategy I had devised. I ensured that all the treasure chests were kept safely in Adeshwar's house, reassuring the forest dwellers that it was their wealth, which also helped sustain their enthusiasm. In any case, they did have a legitimate share in it. Well, after twenty days of excavation, we had managed to dig out a sizeable amount of treasure; and digging any further now seemed impossible, with the strong winds and heavy rainfall that were continuing to wreak havoc. Thus, casting greed aside, I decided to bring the efforts to a stop. As it is, the quantity of treasure we had found was by no means small; and at least for a cowherd, it was more than enough! So, instead of risking the lives of the villagers, I thought it wise to content ourselves with what we had found.

Needless to say, everyone was ecstatic on finding these riches. However, my happiness surpassed all of theirs put together! In my heart of hearts, I was jumping for joy, because overnight, I, a penniless cowherd, had become affluent, and now, nothing could stop me from dreaming big. But oh, the menace called Jarasandha would invariably besiege my mind and make this euphoria vanish into thin air! Indeed, his ominous shadow would never leave my side, not even allowing me to dream in peace. Really, once this menace was done away with, my life would become so beautiful and carefree. But how could this threat be averted? For, the threat wasn't small—it was the equivalent of a thousand threats combined! Certainly, this wasn't something that could be warded off easily. But then, what else could I do except perform my *karma*? And I was doing that diligently. At any rate, as time flitted by, Jarasandha's attack was drawing closer. I well knew that it was impossible to stay hidden for long from the extensive spy network of his allies. Sooner or later, Jarasandha would surely come knocking at my door.

But if we were to forget about Jarasandha for a moment and take a look around this mountain, what did it really lack? It was a beautiful spot with such fine weather, delicious food, daily festivities…and the rain! You already know that monsoon was my favourite season. So, consoling myself somehow and pushing the menace called Jarasandha out of my mind, I focused my attention on enjoying the rain! Now, obviously, I could not play my flute for fear of being identified, so I contented myself with wandering around the mountain and enjoying getting drenched in the rain, or sitting for hours on a large rock and gazing far into the distance. Since we were staying on the summit of the mountain, we were always cocooned by soft, sublime clouds; and to add to it, the joy of gazing at the dense forest all around us while it continued to rain was simply indescribable. Indeed, surrounded as I was with so much beauty, who would want to sit and brood about Jarasandha? So, casting dreadful thoughts aside, I wandered around happily. As for bhaiya, he had found a unique way to enjoy the monsoon. He would start drinking in the morning, joined by a few of his companions. As for his physique, he had always been stouter than me since childhood; and now, due to his regular drinking and lack of exercise, he appeared twice my size. Frankly speaking, my handsome brother had started looking ungainly. But of course, I did not want to invite his wrath by showing him the mirror, so to speak. For that matter, I too had been quite chubby since childhood, but owing to regular exercise and a balanced diet, I was becoming quite athletic and attractive with age.

Oh well, let me stop praising myself by making such comparisons and instead apprise you of the current state of affairs—the torrential downpour had completely washed away my worries about Jarasandha, giving me a sense of relief at least for the time being. For, he was surely not insane to set off in search of me in the midst of such heavy rain. Still, one could never be too sure—he was Jarasandha, after all. In his frenzy, he could very well come charging up the mountain and pounce on us with a surprise attack. Thus, even though it was merely a precautionary measure, I felt it was necessary to prepare Adeshwar for a possible war. However, I could not reveal to him that Jarasandha was my arch enemy and that he might launch an attack anytime. For, if I revealed the truth to him, Adeshwar and the rest of the tribal people might consider this to be my personal matter and thereby distance themselves from the war. I, therefore, had to talk to him in an indirect manner...and this simply meant that I had to spin a yarn. And verily, how difficult would that be for me! My fertile mind quickly came up with a convincing story which I narrated to Adeshwar expertly. Adopting a tone of caution, I told him that it is a well-known fact that wherever one finds treasure, sooner or later, thieves do come sniffing it out. Therefore, we must be prepared to face such bandits. Well, has it ever happened that Krishna played a trick and the target didn't fall for it? Indeed, who would want to lose such a precious bounty, earned with such great effort? Adeshwar was bound to take the bait! He thus promptly convened a meeting and cautioned all the tribal people to beware of thieves who could come in search of the treasure. This was precisely what I wanted. My task had now become easy. Under Adeshwar's leadership, the entire army of tribal people was ready to pick up arms to protect their treasure. And why would they not? After all, this had now become their personal war. They had to protect their hard-earned treasure from the bandits. Well, this was all fine and necessary too, but I must praise Adeshwar for one thing. He never asserted his right over the treasure even though I had repeatedly told him that he and his tribe had as much right to it as we did. And it was this very simplicity of his that endeared him to me. Besides, practically speaking, even if we had the chance, we would not have been able to carry all the treasure with us. Keeping this in mind, I had already set aside two large chests filled with diamonds, pearls and other priceless jewellery from the very beginning. After all, it was highly unlikely that we would spend the rest of our lives on this mountain. Either Jarasandha would kill us or he would grow tired and abandon the fight. If he retreated, we would enjoy our wealth, and if he killed us, he would take the treasure with him.

Oh, I was incredible, wasn't I? I had already thought things through to the extent of carrying the treasure with us when the time came; not just that, I had even gotten it stuffed in two large chests and placed in our chamber, as if we would definitely get the opportunity to make our exit! Well, there's nothing wrong in nursing such optimism in life. But taking it a step further, I had even started thinking about the arrangements for taking the treasure with us. And in this regard, the first thing that needed to be considered was that both bhaiya and I as well as the treasure would have to travel by chariot...whereas we had just one chariot. And to me, it did not seem likely that both we and the treasure could be accommodated in a single chariot. Call it my optimism or height of foolishness, but since the matter pertained to the treasure, it was necessary for me to take prompt action. Thus, taking Adeshwar along, I set off for Karvirpur and purchased a brand-new chariot. This, however, meant that we had to face extreme hardships in bringing the chariot to the top of the mountain, navigating it through dense forest and heavy rain, the entire activity taking a whole of fifteen days. But so what? How could one hope to enjoy such a priceless treasure without incurring a few hardships? Having taken care of all eventualities, it was only now that I felt that all my tasks had been accomplished. The treasure had been found and packed into boxes. Meanwhile, with Adeshwar's help, I had also prepared the tribal people for the impending war. And now, the chariots were also ready, in case we needed to flee if the situation demanded.

Well, once a person is freed from all the tasks that need to be completed, his capacity to enjoy increases manifold. Besides, I was a fun-loving person anyway, so I let my senses feast on the lush verdant landscape, making the most of the monsoon season. Oh, what an enchanting sight it was! And if this was not enough, we also revelled in the daily celebrations with much fervour and enthusiasm. There was no dearth of love or food, and no adversities or struggles to mar the pleasant atmosphere either. Naturally, I was ecstatic. And what can I say about my state of mind? Pleasure, joy, life and peace had all scaled their peak. Truly, one experiences a unique kind of happiness when one is mentally free. And this was precisely what I was experiencing at this moment. It is rightly said that the joy of becoming free after having performed one's duty is beyond comparison. This joy can neither be experienced nor understood by those who shirk their duties. You will not believe it, but I was so overjoyed that I would regularly join the tribal people in their song and dance programmes. The beautiful mountain and the daily celebrations had compelled me to lose myself in the sweet memories of Vrindavan once again. In my flights of fancy, I fervently wished for Yashoda, Radha, the *gopas* and *gopis* to be here with me. Oh, wouldn't that be fabulous! If that were to really happen and the danger of Jarasandha could somehow be averted, then I would never leave this mountain! Indeed, I would settle here forever.

But alas, was it possible for so much happiness and peace to descend upon my life, and that too, with the keen eye of Nature trained on me at all times? It was simply impossible! Many a time, I would even wonder if Nature had anything better to do than keep sending troubles and struggles my way! And just see how I was proven right! Monsoon passed us by in the blink of an eye, as we celebrated and cavorted around happily, but once the season ended, we were back to where we had started. The rains had washed away the boulders that we had so painstakingly stacked for security, and this highlighted Jarasandha's threat once again, throwing my mind into a spin. On one hand, overwhelmed by the joy of obtaining the treasure, I was yearning to attain Rukmini, and on the other, I was worried if I would even survive long enough to savour this pleasure, especially when death in the form of Jarasandha was close on my heels. Meaning, my life had come to such a crossroads that both eventualities seemed equally possible in spite of being diametrically opposite to each other. There was the possibility of Jarasandha wiping me from the face of the earth; but if I survived, there was also the opportunity to live life to its fullest with the woman of my dreams, Rukmini. And trapped between these two possibilities, finding a way to live in the present was certainly not easy. At the same time, one could not deny that the future always takes birth from the present. This meant that if I could find a cure for the disease called Jarasandha in the present, then everything would be all right. But how could I save myself from this menace? After all, we did not have any means to tackle him. But no matter what the situation was, it was better to prepare myself for a confrontation with him rather than just wait for him to attack. So, as soon as the monsoon bid us goodbye, my mind became focused on finding a solution, even as everyone else was still immersed in fun and celebrations. Wandering far away in the heart of the forest in search of solitude, I would spend hours lost in contemplation. But no matter how deeply I mulled over it, the reality was that the only weapon we had on this mountain were boulders, and even they were washed away by the rain. In fact, it had become even more difficult to put them back in their place at strategic vantage points, for, the rains had washed away not just the boulders that we had stacked carefully, but also most of the other stones and rocks on the mountain. This meant that we would first have to find new rocks and boulders and then restack them. For that matter, this wasn't the only problem we faced. The grass on the mountain had also overgrown, becoming taller and denser, due to which finding the requisite stones and rocks was not easy either. However, I could also see an advantage in this. The lush undergrowth and the prickly shrubs were bound to create hurdles for Jarasandha's army; besides, the slippery slope would not make it easy for them to climb up. As for us, we could hardly complain, for, we cowherds and our friends, the tribal people, were used to hard work. So, we immediately engaged ourselves in hard labour. It took us ten days to locate the rocks and boulders and another four to make a secure boundary by stacking them. In short, we were able to reverse the damage. As for our war strategy, it was the same one that I had used previously—exhaust Jarasandha and force him to flee. I had to somehow drain that scoundrel's energy so much that he would be forced to turn tail and return empty-handed. Now, according to the strategy, we had already stacked the stones and boulders to create hurdles. The second obstruction had been created by the rain in the form of the dense undergrowth, ensuring that Jarasandha's army would take at least a month to climb the mountain. It was also certain that without scaling the steep slope, he could not reach us. And it was even more certain that we would never approach him to fight. He was the one who had to climb up, no matter how hard the struggle.

All in all, with a little help from me and some assistance from Nature, the strategy to exhaust Jarasandha was taking shape, but this in itself would not suffice. Based on his earlier experience with me, he would come fully prepared this time around. And he would come with enough resources to last him for at least three to four months. It was also a foregone conclusion that after being thwarted twice, his fury would be at its zenith. This meant that I would have to think of some other tactic too. I had just begun pondering over this when the possibility of a diametrically opposite scenario emerged out of nowhere. It crossed my mind that to make his climb easier, Jarasandha might burn the very undergrowth, which I thought would work as an obstruction in his path. And if he did so, we would face a whole new kind of trouble, perched as we were on top of the mountain. This meant that I had not covered all contingencies yet. The dense undergrowth could prove to be either a boon or a bane! It could become a blessing, if the idea of setting it on fire does not occur to Jarasandha. But if it were set on fire, the same undergrowth could burn us alive. Now, the question that needed serious consideration was, how do we solve the problem of the undergrowth? It was no doubt complicated, but it was necessary to arrive at a solution as quickly as possible. Well, after a little bit of deliberation, I came up with the perfect solution. I decided to get the undergrowth removed from the top to approximately halfway down the mountain. There were two reasons for this. The obstacle in Jarasandha's path would remain intact, and even if he set fire to it, the smoke and flames would not reach us because there would be no grass on the top portion to fuel the fire. With the partial removal of the undergrowth, I had now taken all the measures I could possibly take to fight and save our lives with the materials and manpower that were available at our disposal. Meaning, I had taken care of all the contingencies we were likely to face and carried out the tasks within my control. Moreover, at no point did I stop thinking of additional ways to create obstructions in Jarasandha's path. After all, who knew what brilliant idea might strike my crafty mind!

Well, the idea would come to me in its own time. For now, let me tell you that six months had elapsed since we had sought refuge on the Gomanta Mountain. And these six months had been spent amid varied experiences of hard toil, fun and enjoyment and a few personal achievements. But now, it appeared that the wheel of time was about to turn. Jarasandha would come knocking at our door any day now. For, considering the efficiency of Jarasandha's spies and the spy networks of his allies, it was quite unlikely that he would remain unaware of our refuge on the Gomanta Mountain, especially after the passage of such a long period. And verily, my assessment was correct. Just as every wait comes to an end, so did my wait for Jarasandha. Eventually, his army arrived in search of us. Naturally, I was the first to catch a glimpse of the army; after all, I was the one expecting an attack, constantly on the lookout, and most importantly, the one the army was coming for. In that sense, I alone had the right to see it first.

In the next two days, everyone else had the privilege of witnessing the breathtakingly beautiful sight of Jarasandha's massive army![43] The approaching army was clearly visible from the summit. Naturally, Adeshwar and the other tribal people were terrified on seeing the mighty army of elephants, horses and numerous chariots approaching the mountain. Their initial fear was well expected, but as the army advanced, panic set in among the tribal people. Argh! This was not a good sign. Theirs was the only army I had, and if their courage failed, then all would be in vain. So, I had to jump in to lift their sagging spirits. I thus gathered everyone and explained in a philosophical manner, "It is never easy to amass wealth, so of course, the plunderers were bound to come. But why worry? We will unite and fight them, and our collective strength will surely drive them away!" For good measure, I even narrated to them a few tales of my valour, embellished with exaggerations. At any rate, by now, everyone had vested enough trust in me that they were convinced at least for the time being.

Well, I might have convinced the others with my speech, but I could not fool myself; the irrevocable truth was that death had spread its claws around us. By now, not only the pennants flying high on their chariots, but even the chariots and the army itself were clearly visible. How much time would it take now? It was only a matter of days, and before we knew it, the army had

43. Harivansh Puran, Vishnu Parva, Chapter – 41, Verse – 51-53.

reached extremely close to the mountain. Meaning, the one I had been waiting for had arrived with great pomp and show. However, this time, Jarasandha's army seemed quite small—perhaps a result of their past experiences. From his previous experiences, Jarasandha was bound to realise that a big army cannot fight a battle for longer durations; besides, he was here just to capture two boys. That may have been so, but the view of the approaching army was quite intimidating from the top of the mountain. As it advanced, it appeared to grow in size too, and now, it had come so close that not just the chariots and carts, even the horses and elephants could be seen clearly. As for the army itself, it had about two hundred chariots, as many horses and about fifty elephants. Accompanying them were about three to four hundred foot soldiers. Jarasandha's previous experience had taught him such a valuable lesson that even to sustain such a small army, there were about twenty-five bullock carts carrying food and other supplies. Meaning, this time, he had come well prepared. He seemed to have made a firm decision not to return without my severed head raised high atop his sword, displayed as his trophy! This was the reason why he had come well equipped with all the instruments of death. Jarasandha's thirst for revenge was truly peculiar, making me wonder if such a great king had nothing better to do than chase after me. Or perhaps Nature had chosen him specifically to torment me on its behalf!

'Oh, Kanhaiya, what will you do now? How will you escape death? Once Jarasandha's army climbs the mountain, escaping to safety will become well-nigh impossible. And look at the height of your delusion! You even have chariots standing by to carry your treasure. Well, you can rest assured that along with your head, your treasure will also be claimed by Jarasandha!' Then, another voice snivelled, 'I... I...can understand that, but what about Rukmini?' The first voice replied, 'Oh, poor her, what can you do when it is not in her destiny to find happiness? You fool! Rukmini will easily find the best of princes. You just worry about your own fate!' The whimpering voice retorted, 'Worry? What is left for me to worry about now? Jarasandha is already here to put an end to my worries!' In this manner, I had suddenly started babbling to myself, as if I had lost my mind. Perhaps, I had! Anyone in my position would lose his mind on seeing such a strong, robust army marching its way up. Oh, I was a lover of life and a seeker of joy, but just see the predicament Nature had put me into! Forget living in peace, it was not willing to even let me die in peace. Just then, the voice spoke, 'Oh, come on now! How can you lose hope like this? You are a true *karmaveer*—a man of action. How can you drop to your knees and surrender to defeat? Stand up, square your shoulders and face it resolutely. Awaken your intelligence! You are the one who had danced merrily on the hood of Kaaliya, the serpent. It

is not in your nature to accept defeat before being defeated, or to forsake life before you actually breathe your last. For you, every struggle is a game. So, get up and get ready to play this game too!'

The voice was right! And just like that, I, Kanhaiya, was all set to play this game. Oh, have you not understood? Jarasandha's army would try to climb the mountain and I would try to stop it. He would try to kill me and I would devise ever-new ways to make him tuck tail and flee. Was this not a fine game then? Surely, it would be great fun to play such a game and see who emerges the winner. Did you see? It was this very positive thinking of mine that would never let me be despondent and hopeless for long; indeed, feelings of despair and depression could never make a nest in my mind. When life itself is a game, then every adversity in life is also a game. So, why not enjoy this game, regardless of the circumstances, and live happily? I had just managed to compose myself with these thoughts and regain my enthusiasm when another problem cropped up. Oh, how do I even begin to describe it? My dear bhaiya was also present with me, and you are well aware of his enthusiasm in such situations. While I was alarmed and at my wits' end, he was raring to fight the moment he saw Jarasandha's army approach! Now, tell me, wasn't his enthusiasm another pain in my neck? I was quietly sitting on a boulder and observing the approaching army, when bhaiya arrived on the scene brandishing his mace. Seeing Jarasandha's army, he jumped with delight as if Jarasandha had come bearing gifts for him. The way he swung his mace in the air time and again, it seemed as if he would rest only after breaking Jarasandha's skull this time around. The height of his enthusiasm was such that had I not stopped him, he would have bounded down the mountain by now, as if Jarasandha would fight him single-handedly, and the massive army he had brought along with him were here just for sightseeing! Argh! Who could make bhaiya understand that enthusiasm is beneficial only when it is tempered with good sense! This ill-timed haste to turn into a *rannveer* (a hero of the battle) from a *rannchhod* (a deserter of the battle) was nothing but pure insanity. I too wanted to be a *rannveer,* but only after carefully considering all aspects of the situation. For, you cannot win a war without a sound strategy. When it was clear that bhaiya and I couldn't defeat such a huge army, tiring them out was the only viable strategy. And the only way to exhaust the army was by prolonging the war as much as possible. This was my plan, but not comprehending this simple fact, bhaiya was repeatedly causing hindrances in its execution. Bah! Was this really the time to make him see sense or plan the next phase of my strategy? All in all, before clashing with Jarasandha, I had to constantly reason with bhaiya, and no matter how many times I tried to knock sense into him, he would return inevitably, swinging his mace in the air.

However, setting bhaiya aside, let me speak of Jarasandha's army. Though the army was small, it included many kings, several of whom were prominent such as Shalva and Damghosha. This meant that, despite its size, the army was filled with formidable warriors. And as for Jarasandha's enthusiasm, it was indescribable. The moment they reached the base of the mountain, he began addressing all the kings and the army in a thunderous voice, "At the break of dawn tomorrow, we will approach the mountain from the front and start ascending it. Once you reach the summit, you will ferret out those two boys and behead them without any hesitation, and stay put on the mountain until they are dead!" This meant that Jarasandha had allocated only one night for the army to rest. That was fine by me, as I could peacefully sleep tonight.

And you will not believe this, but I really slept well that night. The next morning, after finishing my daily routine, I headed to the edge of the mountain and perched myself on a boulder. Honestly, I had not even bothered to bathe today. After all, Jarasandha had arrived to give me a royal bath in my own blood! Well, he repeated his rousing speech from the previous night, and soon after, everyone forged ahead as per his plan. Seeing their enthusiasm, I went numb. Not only Jarasandha's fervour, but even the ardour of the kings accompanying him was at its peak. But how could fervour alone help? It soon became clear to Jarasandha that it was impossible to ride the chariots up the mountain. And when chariots could not be used on this terrain, bringing the elephants along after trudging such long distances naturally turned out to be a futile exercise. In the morning, while I was the only one watching this spectacle, by afternoon, Adeshwar and about twenty more people joined me, perching themselves on boulders placed along the edge of the mountain. To them, the frustration of the 'bandit chieftain' was evident and they were thoroughly enjoying this sight. As for Jarasandha, he was still trying to motivate the charioteers to steer the chariots up, but how could the chariots be made to climb such a steep incline? Every time they tried, they would slip down to the base. By now, not only I but everyone else was enjoying this spectacle too.

Well, the army spent the entire day in these futile efforts, while I was thoroughly delighted. In any case, I firmly believe that all battles of life are more mental than physical. And since Jarasandha had suffered the first mental blow, it could be said that we had won the first round. Now, although I had nothing to do with the struggle happening down there, I did have my own mental struggle to contend with at the top of the mountain. That's right! By night-time, bhaiya was truly charged up, and as a result, he kept persuading me to go down and attack them while they were struggling to climb uphill.

And I was engaged in the utterly arduous task of dissuading him instead of focusing on more pressing issues. He kept harping on just one point, "Today, I will smash Jarasandha's skull," while I had to repeatedly calm him down and tell him that it was not the time to fight yet. "You will never get the opportunity to fight Jarasandha in a one-on-one duel. He has not only come with a well-equipped army, but is also accompanied by numerous great warriors. We will be ground to dust within moments! So, let the enemy exhaust itself—let some of their energy get drained, let some of their soldiers die. We are anyway sitting on top of the mountain; let them climb up first. Once they climb up, there will surely be a war, whether we want it or not." You will not believe it, but even at this crucial hour, more than half my energy was being expended in reining in bhaiya. I really could not understand which side he was on!

The next morning, several other people joined me at the edge of the mountain, just like the previous day. This entire, unexpected drama had become a form of entertainment for them, and as the day progressed, the number of spectators also increased steadily. Indeed, who would miss such an opportunity? After all, the drama unfolding below was too entertaining to pass up, unlike anything they had ever seen. Funnily enough, Jarasandha had spent two whole days just to realise that the chariots could not be made to climb the mountain! Thereafter, he tried to make the horses climb the steep incline. All the horses were unharnessed and set free, leaving the poor chariots rudderless. In short, with each passing day, the enemy's time was being frittered away in futile pursuits. Fortunately for us, since the mountain was steep and slippery, not a single horse from Jarasandha's army was able to climb even after trying relentlessly for a week. And the most fortunate aspect was, the kings accompanying the army had soon become disillusioned in the face of these impediments. They had reached here after a long and tiring journey; moreover, the elephants must have made the journey extremely slow and cumbersome. And now, to add to their woes, this steep mountain had emerged as a fresh nuisance. Interestingly, none of these kings had any personal grudge against me; it was only Jarasandha who was burning in the fire of revenge. And it goes without saying that if a person has no personal interest in the task he is involved in, he experiences exhaustion very easily. In short, even before the war had begun, this was the sorry plight of the kings who had accompanied Jarasandha. After a few more days of strenuous efforts, it became clear to them that even the horses would not be able to carry the soldiers up the mountain. This meant that, if they wanted to reach us, everyone would have to climb the mountain on foot, alongside the soldiers. Now, how could the kings who were not accustomed to walking even on flat ground ever scale such a steep mountain? But King Jarasandha had commanded, so they had to obey his decree. For us, this turned out to be an even more entertaining sight. Oh, poor kings, they were reduced to a pitiable plight! They would somehow climb a little way up, only to come slithering down. As for us, perched on our seats, we were enjoying this fine spectacle. A steep mountain covered by a dense forest and no clear path to follow—you can only imagine the chaos below. The situation was such that even after five days of relentless efforts, they had managed to make only a wee bit of progress. However, I could not deny that the distance they had covered had brought them that much closer to us.

Now, as far as their daily routine was concerned, the entire army would be washed out by evening, and as soon as night fell, they would all drop off to sleep. But one must admit that as the days passed, they were gradually beginning to get accustomed to climbing this terrain, which did not bode well for us. In other words, if we did not act quickly, they would succeed in climbing higher and faster. The most commendable aspect was the determination displayed by Jarasandha, who was stomping his way up, ahead of everyone, even at such an advanced age. As for his age, you can gauge it from the fact that he was the father-in-law of my uncle! Nonetheless, the time for idle musings and merely watching the fun as spectators was over. The army was now slowly but steadily gaining upon us. If we did not act quickly, then instead of being a bunch of spectators watching the drama, we would soon become a spectacle ourselves! Oh, but how do I think clearly? Bhaiya's enthusiasm was proving to be a hindrance, wasting all my precious time and energy; and to add to my woes, a new problem had surfaced. Seeing the army advance steadily towards the top, panic had set in amongst Adeshwar and the other tribal people. Meaning, along with the task of controlling bhaiya, I was now saddled with the new task of allaying the fear of these people. But these were minor problems; the one and only major problem we faced was to think of a strategy to stop the approaching army from reaching us. Essentially, we had to stop them in their tracks at any cost. But how? Well, I continued to ponder over this issue…when suddenly, a brilliant idea struck me. And as soon as this thought crossed my mind, I cheered up. 'Oh yes! What was Jarasandha's weapon until yesterday could very well become ours today! Why not burn the grass downhill and take his army by surprise?' And if executed at night, it would prove to be even more effective. This would not only ensure their retreat, but also spread panic in the enemy camp. Actually, it was against the prevailing rules of warfare to attack or cause any trouble at night. But considering the situation we were in, was I going to be constrained by any rule? I knew only one rule of warfare—victory must come at all costs!

So, at night, with the help of the tribal people, I set fire to the grass from the top. Though not a big conflagration, it soon reached Jarasandha and his soldiers. And fire is fire, after all! Besides, the terror and commotion it causes on a pitch-dark night is on an entirely different level. Just as I had expected, the moment the fire reached Jarasandha's camp, it caused pandemonium among the soldiers with everyone running helter-skelter. Chased by the roaring flames, the petrified army fled right back to the base of the mountain, while I, standing atop the mountain, watched this spectacle with glee. After fifteen days of tireless effort, they had managed to climb to some extent, but due to my ploy, it all ended in vain. And what can I say about the reaction of Adeshwar and the tribal people? They started playing drums and cymbals in the middle of the night! This was the mood among us, but a huge setback for all kings accompanying Jarasandha, which naturally upset them. Even Jarasandha himself was deeply perturbed. But his determination was his strongest ally, not allowing him to break down. This time, he did not want to return empty-handed at any cost. Thus, for the next two days, Jarasandha's camp was engaged in intense discussions. In one of the meetings, Shalva suggested that the whole mountain be set on fire. This would ensure that the two boys are burnt to ashes, and if not, it would at least serve to clear the mountain of the remaining grass and make it easier for them to ascend. Jarasandha approved Shalva's idea and they spent the next two days preparing to set fire to the mountain. I was taken aback. We had merely ignited a small fire, but they were bent on burning up the whole mountain! Oh, but what could I do? Clearly, it was my turn now to become a spectator.

As per their plan, on the third day, they set fire to the whole mountain. Bit by bit, the mountain was engulfed in flames, but fortunately, we were completely safe. Today, I was feeling proud of my farsightedness, as we had already cleared all the undergrowth near the top. As a result, the fire couldn't reach us. But yes, although it was quite far from us, we could still feel its heat. This was alright, but soon, an event transpired that even I had not anticipated. By evening, the enemy was ensnared in a trap of their own making. It so happened that because of the fire, all the big, poisonous snakes on the mountain began to rapidly slither down towards the forest to escape the flames. And on their way down, they caused utter mayhem in the army camp below, biting Jarasandha's elephants, horses and men. Meaning, the snakes vented all their fury on Jarasandha's army. And if that was not enough, by night-time, the fire too began to spread downwards. Due to the two-pronged attack of the fleeing snakes and the leaping flames, pandemonium broke loose in Jarasandha's camp. Frightened noises of the animals tore through the silence of the night, while screams and loud voices reverberated in an eerie echo all around the mountainside. The entire army along with the kings fled in the opposite direction and took cover in the distant forest. This was the peak of misery for the army; they had come to climb the mountain but were instead forced to flee miles away from it. Moreover, several soldiers had suffered burns in the fire, while many were injured by snakebite. Indeed, to all of them, the mountain now seemed to possess some kind of magical power! The spectre of death loomed large over their heads now. Their spirit broken, none of them were willing to fight anymore. For, even after twenty days of constant struggle, they were miles away from their goal. On the contrary, they were needlessly suffering losses of life and property.

As for me, I was elated, as this possibility had never even occurred to me. Indeed, aside from our own efforts, we had also received Nature's support. Honestly, seeing the situation below, I could feel my dreams coming to fruition. Now, it did not seem likely that Jarasandha would attempt to climb the mountain all over again. Meanwhile, Adeshwar and the tribal people shared the same feelings as mine. The plunderers who had come to steal the treasure were defeated, and seeing this, they too had begun to spin grand dreams. Oh, but what can I say? Our wishful thinking did not last long. Surely, the forest fire had abated, but the metaphorical fire that this failure had ignited in Jarasandha's heart only served to fuel the simmering embers of his revenge. Now, he was in no mood to back down. Once again, he seemed determined for a fight to the finish, so much so that he gathered everyone, and after a rousing, fiery speech, bolstered their confidence and prepared them to fight the final war. Jarasandha's energy and enthusiasm, even at his age, were truly admirable. For that matter, if one has taken birth as a human being, one must remain enthusiastic till the last breath, and Jarasandha's fervour and energy exemplified this in every way. However, the state of the other kings stood in stark contrast to that of their leader. Though they felt helpless, they could not refuse Jarasandha's commands without a concrete reason. Consequently, they had to reluctantly prepare themselves for war once again. And this was not a good sign for us. As you are well aware, the grass on the mountainside had burned completely, leaving nothing to obstruct their climb. Sigh! It seemed as though my dreams were about to die a premature death!

Never mind, I thought, we would cross that bridge when we came to it. Now, as the grass had been burnt, Jarasandha shrewdly seized the opportunity to boost the army's morale once again, urging them to scale the mountain and finish us off. After his speech, everyone began to ascend the mountain, taking various routes—albeit reluctantly. It was a half-hearted attempt, as no one had any strength left, nor did they have the will to continue this war. But they were all helpless, faced with Jarasandha's obduracy. And as you know, the pace of any task that is performed unwillingly is bound to slacken. But on the other hand, the climb was no longer that difficult since the undergrowth was all but eliminated. Consequently, after just a week of steady climbing, we could see Jarasandha's massive army ominously threading its way up the mountain. Naturally, on seeing this, panic gripped the tribal people once again. But since I had one final weapon in my arsenal, I was more or less calm. In fact, the time had come to use that weapon. But yes, if this too did not work, then there was no way I could stop the enemy from advancing. However, for now, it was far more important to concentrate on the final alternative than think about all that. The enemy had made its move, and now, it was my turn to retaliate. You may have forgotten about this, but I had piled boulders and large rocks on the edge of the mountain for precisely an eventuality like this. However, I was not satisfied with this alone. So, I spoke to Adeshwar and asked him to make arrangements for our escape as well. I had the chariots stationed at the back of the mountain. That's not all! I also made sure our share of the treasure was stashed in the chariots. And this crucial task had not been left to some irresponsible person; Adeshwar himself had been assigned the responsibility of guarding the chariots and the treasure. In short, while Jarasandha and his army had climbed halfway up the mountain, I did not lag behind in making all-round preparations either. Now, it was a fight to the finish anyway. I no longer had to sit back and wait for him to ascend the summit, so as soon as I was satisfied with the arrangements for our escape with the treasure, I gathered everyone and motivated them. For, naturally, the outcome of the next set of events depended entirely on the impact of this final attack.

As soon as I disclosed my plan to the tribal people, everyone jumped for joy and we decided to implement the plan that night itself. As for Jarasandha, he continued to scale the mountain until evening, and once evening set in, he set up camp at a point on the mountainside with his army of two hundred men, including all the kings who were climbing the mountain just to finish us off. I was, in fact, astonished to see these kings, accustomed as they were to sleeping on soft, plush beds, lying scattered on the mountainside, trying to sleep on the hard ground. Indeed, the poor kings were facing extreme hardships only because of Jarasandha's thirst for revenge. But the one who surprised me the most was Jarasandha himself. I wondered, even if he managed to finish me off after enduring so much trouble, what would he gain ultimately—just the satisfaction of revenge? Does one really need to suffer so much for something like that?

Well, the sun had set behind the mountain, and with the approaching dusk, most of the soldiers had retired for the night after partaking of their evening meal. But I was in no hurry. I wanted them to slip into a deep slumber, and only then would I work my magic. I was stationed at the edge of the mountain with about fifty tribal men, waiting to put my plan into action. Everyone stood in attention, waiting for me to give the signal to charge. But clever that I was, I gave the signal only around midnight. And with that, we began to push the stones and rocks down the mountain. In no time, there was an avalanche coursing down the mountain. First, the smaller stones went rolling down, which was enough to wake them up. The unexpected shower of stones bewildered everyone, as they jumped to their feet in an instant, scratching their heads in trying to fathom how the mountain could suddenly start hurtling stones. Aha! But they had forgotten that anything was possible when Krishna was around. Although everyone was still holding their ground due to Jarasandha's insistence, panic set in quickly. At the same time, they kept asking each other frantically what their next move should be. Oh, I cannot tell you the glee I felt, the laughter rising from my belly and shaking my entire body, while I stood watching their pitiable condition! I was amused, wondering how long they'd be able to continue holding their positions. When the smaller stones had reduced them to such a state of panic, how on earth would they be able to bear the avalanche of the huge boulders? Well, there was no need to wait, so we started pushing down the boulders, which were verily our *Brahmastra*—our strongest weapon. It required three to four well-built, tribal men to use all their strength to push down a single boulder. With this, I'm sure you can gauge the colossal size of the boulders. Well, with a thunderous sound that only added to the cacophony emerging from the camp below, these boulders went crashing down the mountainside, causing death and devastation. Pandemonium reigned everywhere, as the boulders crushed not only the horses, but many soldiers too, claiming their lives. Now how could anyone bear such an onslaught in the middle of the night when they had been fast asleep? There was bedlam in the army camp below. The soldiers raced downhill with such speed that, in the blink of an eye, they were at the base of the mountain once again. That was not all; everyone was so panicked that they continued running even after reaching the foot of the mountain. Some had grabbed chariots, racing away in them, while others sped off on horseback. The less fortunate, unable to find either a chariot or a horse, were scurrying away on foot. Funnily enough, even while scampering off, they were shrieking on top of their voice saying, "Run! Run for your lives! This mountain has the devil upon it! Run! It is haunted! Save your lives! There is an evil presence on this mountain!" Exasperated on hearing this, poor Jarasandha kept shouting, "There is no devil here! This is just a trick played by those two infernal boys!" But his voice was lost in the darkness, for, there was no one around to pay heed to him. The poor king shouted himself hoarse. "Why are you fleeing from the battlefield? We cannot leave until we have eliminated those two boys!" But no one was willing to stay back even a second longer. Jarasandha's orders no longer carried weight. It was perfectly understandable too, for, how can a person gripped by terror ever be made to obey someone's command? Well, you could say that with this frenzied, ignominious departure, the biggest menace in Krishna's life had fled, bidding him a hasty farewell.

Success, grand and glorious, bowed before me once again. Jarasandha's might was crushed by my craftiness yet again. But this was not the time to gloat over our victory. Until we escaped safely from here, we could not call it a victory. And now that everyone was scurrying away, why would I not do the same? At any rate, I was an old hand at it. Besides, the time had come for us to flee, for, with the passage of time, it was possible that Jarasandha might manage to regroup his forces. No! Never! My mind spurred me on saying, 'Run, Krishna, run! An auspicious task must be done post-haste.' So, I quickly bade farewell to the singing and dancing tribal people, and with bhaiya in tow, I took the path that led to the rear side of the mountain and reached the spot where the chariots stood with our treasure. Adeshwar was already waiting for us with the chariots and the treasure, all the while keeping an eye for any suspicious movements. We were ready to scamper off as well. Indeed, while wasting time on other pursuits may be fine, one must not waste time when on the run. For, the consequences of dilly-dallying while escaping are invariably grave. Thinking thus, we hastily thanked Adeshwar, and with repeated promises that we would meet again soon, we hopped into our chariots and sped off.

Once we reached the base of the mountain, I thought, since all our problems had been dealt with in the most splendid manner, why not give bhaiya an opportunity to fulfil his ardent desire? After all, bhaiya's satisfaction was crucial for my mental peace. Even though Jarasandha was retreating from the battlefield, we could not ignore the fact that we were escaping as well. What if bhaiya felt that I had once again forced him to abandon the fight? I was afraid that if he perceived it this way, he would make my life extremely miserable this time around. So, with this thought, I gave him the go-ahead to launch an attack on the fleeing army. Hearing this, bhaiya was overjoyed. Bursting with unbounded energy, he charged ahead with his chariot. Within moments, he had reached the fleeing enemy soldiers. So thrilled was he that he did not miss a single opportunity to vent his anger and make full use of his mace. In no time, he had burst open the heads of several soldiers. You can gauge his enthusiasm from the fact that despite my skill at riding the chariot, bhaiya, in his enthusiasm, had left my chariot far behind. In other words, I could only admire this beautiful scene from afar. But then, how long could I allow myself to be a spectator either? After all, I also wanted to experience that feeling of satisfaction. So, along with bhaiya, I too felled a couple of fleeing soldiers; indeed, we had to leave the impression that we had chased Jarasandha off. In any case, this battle was pointless as the enemy was already fleeing. At the most, it was merely a question of assuring ourselves and creating an impression that we had chased Jarasandha away. Hence, there was no sense in engaging in unreasonable violence anymore, for, we had established what we wanted to. The news that would spread across Aryavarta was that the army of Jarasandha and his allies had fled in fear of two boys. Indeed, these two boys had proven to be incredibly powerful. Well, no one knew of the strategies we had used to defeat Jarasandha, and neither would anyone find out that we were not alone on top of the mountain. Meaning, it was just us brothers who would be credited with this valorous deed. And certainly, this validation as valorous men would prove useful all our lives. Thus, the violence we had engaged in presently could not be termed useless from any perspective.

However, we had wreaked enough havoc on Jarasandha's army, and I did not think it was appropriate to engage in further violence unnecessarily. So, I called out to bhaiya time and again, but he was enjoying himself so much that he was in no mood to return. Really, I could not understand what had overcome him; perhaps, he was planning to escort Jarasandha all the way to Magadha?! I wondered what pleasure he was deriving out of chasing soldiers who were already on the run, fleeing in terror…but no, he continued to chase them, brandishing his mace high in the air. And you know very well that I would forget everything when I saw bhaiya in a happy mood, so there was no question of my forcing him to return and spoiling his fun. I thus quietly parked my chariot under a tree and gladly watched him enjoy himself as he decimated the retreating army.

It was then that my attention was diverted on noticing a king approach me. I instantly became alert, but curiously, his demeanour did not reflect hostility. Besides, there was no question of a threat because he had come alone; his chariot and soldiers were standing a little further away. Even so, I remained alert, not wanting to fall for any clever tricks. In fact, not only did I jump down from my chariot, but just to be cautious, I also grabbed the discus. By now, he had come within speaking distance and before I could fathom anything, he greeted me with folded hands. With this single gesture, I was now assured that he meant no harm. So, I too greeted him in return and let my guard down. He then introduced himself saying, "I am your father's sister's husband, meaning, your uncle, Chhediraj Damghosha."[44] The moment I heard who he was, I bowed and paid my respects. I had heard a lot about

44. Harivansh Puran, Vishnu Parva, Chapter – 43, Verse – 79-80.

him from my mother, but had met him for the first time today. Funnily, I was under the impression that this cowherd had become so important that even mighty kings were now offering their respects; however, it turned out to be just a meeting of two relatives. Ah, the perils of false pride! Well, such things do occur from time to time, and they happen especially with someone who likes to feel conceited about every little thing.

Nonetheless, striking up a conversation, Chhediraj spoke in a grave voice, "I was waiting back all this while just to meet you. Actually, witnessing the destruction that you two brothers have wreaked, I too wanted to flee, but it was important to give you some information…so I waited. Let me state clearly that I staunchly oppose Jarasandha from the bottom of my heart, but what do I say…my son and your cousin, Shishupala, is completely swayed by Jarasandha. I had to come here because of him. In fact, Shishupala wanted to join Jarasandha in this battle, but I did not want one brother to fight the other. Therefore, out of compulsion, I accompanied Jarasandha instead. There were two main reasons for this: first, I wanted to help you if the need arose, and second, I came to prevent two brothers from fighting each other. I must say, you have performed a valorous deed by defeating Jarasandha."

Well, he was right! We had single-handedly defeated the one whose name sent shivers across Aryavarta! Certainly, it was a matter of great pride. And why should I lie to you, I was truly filled with pride the moment Jarasandha had fled. For that matter, I was not one to miss such an opportunity, and one should not even think of missing a chance like this. When you have accomplished a great feat, you are certainly entitled to feel proud of it. And mind you, this was no ordinary feat. My arch enemy, the very person who had forced me to flee the battlefield, had now himself fled, cowering in fear of me, despite having a well-equipped army. A smile of pride curved at the corner of my lips…but then I thought, forget it, I had the rest of my life to revel in this feeling. Right now, circumstances demanded that I focus on the urgent message which uncle was keen to deliver after encountering a number of hardships himself. Incidentally, he appeared even more eager to convey the message than I was to hear it, and his grave demeanour clearly indicated that the message was of utmost importance. Perhaps, it was because of the gravity of the message that uncle had fallen silent for a moment. Looking at his puzzled face, I waited patiently for him to speak. As far as I was concerned, the only significant news could be one related to Jarasandha, whom I had defeated right in front of my uncle's eyes.

Well, seeing that I was keen…impatient even to hear the news, he began in a sombre tone, "I have some bad news for you. Your grandfather, King Ugrasena, had sent out spies in search of you. And along with the spies, he had sent your friend, Uddhava, because your grandfather believes he is the only one who can recognise you in any disguise. But unfortunately, Jarasandha's spies were extremely vigilant. They followed Uddhava, and it was only by following him that they learnt about your hideout."

That's alright, but what about Uddhava? For, he was not here. My brow creased with worry, because after all, this was my friend, Uddhava, he was talking about. But before I could enquire about him, Uncle Damghosha, on seeing me become grave, took a deep breath and continued, "Unfortunately, Uddhava went to Karvirpur in search of you. There, he hunted high and low, but while he was looking for you, he landed himself in deep trouble. Shringlava, the king of Karvirpur, made him his prisoner for some unknown reason. Consequently, Uddhava is trapped there, while Jarasandha showed up here. This news has been able to reach you only because your grandfather used all his experience while sending Uddhava on his quest. Actually, he had asked many of the kings who are friendly to him, such as me, to help Uddhava in his quest and find you using our own spy networks. And as my kingdom is close to Karvirpur, our spies promptly received the news of his capture."

I was dumbstruck! My dear friend, Uddhava, was in grave trouble and that too because of me. Naturally, all my pleasure and pride at having defeated Jarasandha and acquiring so much wealth vanished in a trice. Seeing me in a state of shock, uncle tried to console me by speaking in a comforting tone, "I do not know for certain what Uddhava has been charged with, but now, it is your duty to save him from the clutches of Shringlava." Of course, there was no doubt that I would drop everything and rescue my friend. In fact, with this news, our next destination was confirmed too. Without losing time, we would have to steer our chariots towards Karvirpur and rescue Uddhava. Argh! We had barely breathed a sigh of relief when another dangerous task had loomed before us. Really, my life was a bizarre, topsy-turvy ride. Honestly, it had turned into an unending series of perilous missions. Peace and happiness were never given a chance to linger in my life for long. Well, uncle had finished speaking and I had just started thinking of the next course of action when bhaiya returned from the battlefield. I promptly introduced him to uncle, but bhaiya barely paid heed to him, lost as he was in his own world of bravado. Swinging his mace in front of us, he intoned, "I chased Jarasandha off. Ha! The nerve he had to come and clash with me. You should have seen him run away with his tail tucked in!"

Seeing bhaiya charged up, I momentarily forgot all about Uddhava. I was relieved to see that this battle had at least allowed bhaiya to regain his composure. And this was precisely why I had sent him to chase Jarasandha's retreating army. I knew my brother well; if we had left without fighting at

all, he would have considered even this an act of cowardly desertion. And as you would remember, the last time we had fled from the battlefield, he had been furious with me for seven whole months! Had I repeated this mistake, he would have probably remained angry with me for the next seven years! All things considered, this decision of mine had boded well for both of us. However, this joy was short-lived. My mind was once again gripped by the worry and anxiety arising out of Uddhava's imprisonment. I was really shaken up by this news. But oblivious to it all, bhaiya was still prattling away, so intoxicated by his victory and sense of achievement that he failed to notice our grave demeanour and the lines of worry etched on our faces. But now, enough was enough. How long could I wait for him to sober down? So, in a bid to bring him back to his senses, I told him about Uddhava, to which he replied airily, "So what? When we have defeated Jarasandha successfully, of what consequence is Shringlava?" Now, how was I to explain to him that we had been able to defeat Jarasandha only because of a clever strategy? In Shringlava's case, we might have to engage in a full-fledged battle. However, it was futile to explain all this to bhaiya, especially when he was so intoxicated by success. It was a strange scene indeed. The three of us were standing near our chariots, but each of us was caught in a vastly different state of mind. While bhaiya's head was in the clouds, gloating over his victory, I was gripped with worry. And poor uncle was darting looks between bhaiya and me. Seeing bhaiya's mood, my mind went completely blank, unable to come up with a solution to help rescue Uddhava.

Fortunately, uncle rescued me from the conundrum I found myself in. Indeed, he seemed not only simple, straightforward and loving but wise and sensible too. Understanding our present requirements, he promptly made arrangements for five chariots and a small coterie of soldiers to accompany us. Even better was the fact that these soldiers were familiar with every nook and cranny of Karvirpur, and also acquainted with the political situation in the kingdom. Indeed, many people do extend their help, but help that is offered at the right time, right place, and most importantly, without having to ask for it, can only be offered by a farsighted, wise person.

Well, now that I had my uncle's support, my mind became active once again. Firstly, I thanked him profusely for bringing me the news about Uddhava and also for his generous gift of chariots and soldiers. Actually, he was Uddhava's uncle as well. Oh, this reminds me! I have not mentioned before that Uddhava was a distant cousin of mine. But more than that, we were good friends, and perhaps that is why I forgot to mention it earlier. Well, be that as it may! For now, we took uncle's blessings and set off for Karvirpur post-haste. This time, bhaiya and I rode the same chariot. Naturally, the treasure too was kept in the same chariot so that I would not have to worry about it and could focus on rescuing Uddhava instead. Who knew what condition the poor boy was in—what trials and tribulations he must be suffering! Thinking about his plight was enough to put me in a vortex of worry. Well, our caravan of seven chariots was moving at a slow but steady pace towards Karvirpur. As for bhaiya, he was still suspended in his bubble of happiness, not realising the gravity of the matter. He was so ecstatic about our victory over Jarasandha that he remained in high spirits throughout the journey to Karvirpur. Well, no matter! But I sincerely hoped that good sense would prevail and he would step out of his ebullient state before we set foot in Karvirpur.

Chapter 8
Rescuing Uddhava from Shringlava's Clutches

Navigating our way through the dense forest, I was gripped with countless thoughts about how to rescue Uddhava. The journey to Karvirpur was only a day long, but since night had fallen by the time we reached, we had no choice but to stop at an *ashram* on the outskirts of the city. As soon as we were allotted chambers, I first arranged for our treasure chests to be moved in. As a precautionary measure, we also got the chariots parked behind the *ashram*. Indeed, it would look suspicious if someone were to spot them. Fortunately, bhaiya had sobered down by now, which meant that he too had begun to worry about Uddhava. Incidentally, this overnight halt was a compulsion due to the late hour of our arrival; otherwise, there was no chance of us falling asleep in the face of such news. We thus tossed and turned, worrying about poor Uddhava and waiting impatiently for dawn to arrive.

As soon as the first rays of the sun lit up the sky, we sprang out of bed and got ready. Without wasting time, I headed into the city with bhaiya, dressed like locals. The disguise was necessary as it would make it easier for us to understand the workings of this kingdom. Naturally, before attacking an enemy, it is crucial for a warrior to understand the enemy's psyche. I may not have been a great warrior, but I certainly was a very good strategist. After two days of moving around in the city in disguise, my findings indicated that danger lurked in every nook and corner of this kingdom. The situation was even more frightening than what we had been told. King Shringlava was perhaps mentally unsound, for, he harboured the delusion that he was Lord Vishnu himself! But that was not all! The real problem was that whoever refused to accept him as the Supreme Lord was subjected to severe punishments including torture. The height of his insanity was that he had created a special 'hell'—a place of torture—where non-believers were taken and persecuted in an inhumane manner. And even more shocking was that he had dumped most of the *Acharyas* of his kingdom into this 'hell', for, they were the ones who were most vocal in their protest against this preposterous idea. Needless to say, this act of his had spread a wave of terror in the hearts and minds of the inhabitants of Karvirpur. And that being the case, these poor, frightened people had no choice but to accept Shringlava as Lord Vishnu. The most unfortunate aspect of this brutality was that he was making the *Acharyas* and *Brahmins* pull his chariot in lieu of horses. Indeed, it was distressing to note that in order to maintain his supremacy, he was forcing venerable *Acharyas* to perform tasks that were carried out by animals! Things had come to such a pass that Shringlava, living under this false sense of superiority, had crossed all levels of atrocity—he would mercilessly whip the poor *Acharyas* who, due to exhaustion, slackened the pace of the chariot even a wee bit. Even Kansa had never engaged in such acts of cruelty! Could any ruler torture his innocent subjects in such a manner? Really, it is nothing but the ego of man which makes him stoop to subhuman levels.

Coming back to the current problem, I was now convinced that even Uddhava must have been hurled into this hell. I was familiar with his nature; he would have never accepted such a cruel king as God. And this was probably why he must have been punished and thrown in the hellhole. Certainly, considering the prevailing situation and Shringlava's sway over his kingdom, rescuing Uddhava seemed extremely difficult. However, it was pointless to think about this now, because I had to first ascertain whether Uddhava was actually in 'hell' or not. Once I confirmed his whereabouts, I would decide the next course of action. This made perfect sense, but the real predicament was, how could I find out if Uddhava was really languishing in this hell without entering the place myself? Gaining entry into such a prison was not an easy task, but come to think of it, it was not that difficult either. All I had to do was to deny that Shringlava was God. But the problem was, this would not help free Uddhava; on the contrary, we ourselves might have to rot in that hell. In short, it was far more crucial to return from that 'hell' safe and sound than it was to gain entry into it. The situation was extremely complex, but honestly, I no longer enjoyed easy challenges either. Playing simple and straightforward moves did not satisfy my crafty mind anymore. Perhaps, that was why I soon found a solution to this conundrum too. However, I needed bhaiya's help to execute the plan. And you are well aware of bhaiya's nature, especially when it comes to forsaking his pride. Bhaiya could fight heroically, but humility was not his strongest trait. Indeed, convincing and coaxing him to act modest was a huge challenge in itself. But well, since the matter involved Uddhava, who was very close to bhaiya as well, my dear brother did relent after a few attempts on my part. And on that note, I could very well say that I had won a big battle already!

Early next day, as per my plan, we reached the royal palace close to prayer time. As soon as I stepped into the palace premises, I began to chant loudly, "Glory to Lord Vishnu! Glory to Lord Vishnu!" Don't be surprised with this action of mine; devotees could move around freely in the palace without any restrictions, and that being the case, how long would it have taken me to pose as a devotee? And this move of mine proved advantageous at once. Despite the tight security, we had secured entry into the palace with no hurdles whatsoever. The courtroom was turned into a veritable temple, and right in front of us, seated regally on a high throne, was King Shringlava, pretending to be Lord Vishnu! The dark-complexioned, short-statured king looked very strange because of his pudgy frame. For that matter, his courtroom too had a strange appearance. Behind the courtiers, arrangements were made for the devotees to sit and stand amidst tight security. Funnily enough, not only was the court filled to capacity with 'devotees', but it also resounded with chants glorifying Lord Vishnu. If my estimate was correct, then presently, there were about five hundred devotees in the palace…oh, I meant…in the temple of 'Lord Vishnu'! Shocked at this sight, I stopped short at the entrance itself for a brief moment. Even bhaiya stood stupefied beside me. What do I say; I was stunned beyond words. Truly, ego makes people do such strange things! Moreover, if one is gripped by the ego of being holy or divine, then one can truly be considered a lost cause.

Still dazed, I remained standing like a statue, and soon enough, it was time for the 'lord's worship'. Everyone stood up from their seats to make offerings and prayers. The prayers too were offered in loud voices. We too stood in the crowd, deriving great enjoyment from the prayers that were being offered to the 'lord'. And as soon as the ceremony was over, I resumed my loud chant: "Glory to Lord Vishnu! Glory to Lord Vishnu!" And while I was chanting, I started inching close to Shringlava, exactly as per my plan. You will not believe it, I was chanting so loudly that everyone's attention was now fixed on me. Even Shringlava could not help but turn his head towards me. After all, it was to grab his attention that I had been shouting myself hoarse. Bhaiya, of course, did not approve of this drama, but since it was a question of saving Uddhava's life, he quietly walked behind me, sulking all the while. Fortunately, a few other devotees had also joined us. This was fine, but tearing through the crowd, I now dashed ahead of everyone and stood in front of the king. Surprisingly, it was only now that I saw an extraordinarily beautiful woman sitting beside him, which I learnt was his sister, Shaivya. Great! This meant that she too was an accomplice in this wicked game. Well, like a humble devotee, I touched Shringlava's feet and respectfully stood in front of him with folded hands. As for bhaiya, his ego was unable to tolerate this excessive devotion of mine, and for a brief moment, he was close to losing his cool. Honestly, every time we had to use our wits instead of brute strength, bhaiya would prove to be a living, breathing bundle of trouble. As a result, I would often find myself fighting on two fronts simultaneously. I certainly wasn't as strong as bhaiya, and to make matters worse, I would invariably have to face opponents who were several times stronger than me. Given that, I had no choice but to use my intelligence, whether I liked it or not. And believe me, necessity often turns a person into an expert! At any rate, it is impossible to fight an entire army using only physical might; such a task can only be accomplished through a proper strategy. Thus, as soon as the opportunity presented itself, I bowed to the king and, like an ardent devotee, with folded hands, I said to him, "My Lord! I have a humble request to make."

He was already impressed by my devotion, so with a proud gleam in his eye, he said, "Oh, surely, my dear man!"

Pointing to bhaiya, I said, "O King, my friend here hails from a faraway land, and is therefore unaware of your extraordinary feats. The young man, naïve as he is, refuses to accept you as God! I feel he should be given a glimpse of hell once, which I'm sure will set his mind right."

Saying this, I had played my first move, putting the king in deep thought. Certainly, no one must have asked to be shown 'hell' until that day. I did not mind that he was thinking about it, but on hearing my request, bhaiya had lost all control, and I most certainly had a problem with that! The silly man that he was, he even mumbled in my ear, "What are you doing? Let us kill this cruel king right away. Let us make him cry out to his God in his own court!" You will not believe it, but even in such a delicate situation, I had to patiently explain the foolhardiness of making such a move. "We are surrounded by guards," I hissed, "The moment we utter something stupid or make an aggressive move, we will be as good as dead! Our primary objective is to locate Uddhava, after which you can gladly smash the king's head." However, I was also aware that bhaiya could not be made to stay calm for long, no matter how hard I tried to trick him. This only meant that I had to act quickly. This is the problem with the ego: it knows how to kill or be killed, but it fails to understand the gravity of the situation, remain humble and make an escape. It just does not know how to accomplish the task at hand. On the other hand, look at me; I was ready to stoop down to any level and become as humble as possible to achieve my goal. Case in point, I had stooped down to such a level that I even touched Shringlava's feet in feigned reverence. Indeed, why leave any stone unturned to accomplish one's goal? This is precisely the 'egoless state'.

Finally, my feigned devotion bore fruit and my plan succeeded. Shringlava accepted my request and magnanimously allowed bhaiya and me to take a tour of his hell, escorted by a few soldiers. My goodness! This 'hell' turned out to be even worse than the one so vividly described in religious texts! Prisoners were being tortured in the most unimaginable ways possible. I was livid at the sight before me. About thirty to forty prisoners were crammed into one cell, and scores of such cells were lined one after the other. In an open space in the front, some prisoners were being whipped mercilessly, their bare bodies showing nasty gashes brought on by the whip, while some were thrown on the rocky ground and kicked brutally. Loud cries of the prisoners being beaten rent the air, while battered and bloodied bodies lay scattered everywhere. How could human beings be subjected to such barbaric treatment? Looking at all this, I felt a shudder course through my being. I could clearly see that Shringlava had

extracted various methods of torture from useless religious texts. Well, whoever wrote such texts could not have been any less vile themselves. Returning to the present, the soldiers proudly escorted us, giving us a tour of 'hell'. As for me, I kept my emotions in check, focusing entirely on spotting Uddhava among the inmates. As we passed yet another chamber, my gaze fell on the familiar form of my dear friend—unfortunately, he too was being tortured. Uddhava's beard was overgrown, while the sunken eyes and hollow cheekbones bore the tale of trauma he was undergoing. Truth be told, his face was the colour of death itself! Seeing him in this condition was nothing less than torture for me. As for Uddhava, naïve that he was, he nearly shouted with joy when he saw us, but I instantly signalled to him to keep quiet. He shut up at once, but when I turned to look at bhaiya, he almost screamed, unable to bear the sight of his friend in this appalling condition. In fact, distressed at the sight before him, he shouted in anger. Now, this was verily bhaiya's drawback: he appeared tough and spoke harshly, but deep down, he was soft-hearted and innocent. On the other hand, I was adept at keeping a tight leash on my emotions, which meant there was no chance of me losing control at the wrong moment, in the wrong place or for the wrong person. That was why, when the soldiers demanded to know why bhaiya had screamed, I was able to defuse the situation with ease. I smoothly told them that he was simply frightened by the sight of the torture being meted out in this 'hell'.

For now, it was enough to know that Uddhava was detained here. A plan to rescue him could only be devised once we got out of here unharmed. And even that seemed like a daunting challenge! Because for us to walk out of here safely, bhaiya's cooperation was essential, but seeing his emotional outburst, he did not seem to be in a position to cooperate. Normally, bhaiya would have complied, but after witnessing Uddhava's plight, securing his support had become even more difficult. Well, regardless of whether it was difficult or easy, we had to get out of here, and for that, I had to convince bhaiya somehow. Just as we were stepping out, I folded my hands in a silent plea and, in a quiet whisper, asked him to praise Lord Vishnu on our way out. I told him that the king should be convinced that bhaiya had come to his senses on witnessing this hell, as this was the only way we could safely leave the courtroom. Now, you can very well imagine what bhaiya would have liked to do to me on hearing such a request. But I was no fool; I convinced him by pleading with him to do it for Uddhava's sake. And with that, victory bowed to me once more, as we walked out of the royal court unharmed, gleefully chanting, "Glory to Lord Vishnu! Glory to Lord Vishnu!"

Now, although we had returned to the *ashram* safe and sound, we had completely lost our peace of mind. Even after racking my brain a thousand times over, I could not come up with a plan to save Uddhava. The matter was grave and we had to find a solution quickly. As for bhaiya, seeing Uddhava's condition, he seemed to have slipped into despondency. Every now and then, his sorrow would boil over in the form of burning rage. I was deeply disturbed too and definitely angrier than bhaiya, but that did not mean I would start thinking of hare-brained solutions like crushing Shringlava's head in his own courtroom! The problem required a deeper analysis, but bhaiya was not interested in wasting time on planning or discussion. He believed in immediate action and the power of his mace, as if the moment bhaiya marched into the courtroom, Shringlava would bow his head and say, "Here, Brother Balarama, please crack my skull open!" Oh well! After much deliberation, I found my compassion overtaking my anger, as I yearned to free not just Uddhava but all the others too, who were being tortured in this 'hell' designed by Shringlava. Why just them, I wanted to liberate all the inhabitants of Karvirpur and give them their lost freedom and happiness. But how could I do that? I could not fight Shringlava with just four soldiers under my command. Neither could I hope to reason with him. What was the solution to this problem then? Finally, after analysing the situation from every angle, I could see only one clear solution—Shringlava's assassination. For, nothing could be resolved unless the root of the problem was eliminated first. In my opinion, the commoners and the soldiers would be under duress only as long as their king was alive. Once the king was slain, who would bother? There was no question of the masses and the soldiers supporting such a despotic king. In short, I decided to put Shringlava to death. But simply deciding would not yield the desired outcome. It was not as if I could take bhaiya's oft-repeated advice and rush to the palace and smash Shringlava's head. To display such audacity in the courtroom could, in fact, put our own lives in peril. Thus, a strategy had to be devised and the task had to be accomplished using intelligence and shrewdness. In other words, Shringlava had to be slayed in a place with lax security. And obviously, such a place could only be found outside the palace. However, given the tight security everywhere, finding such a spot was no easy task.

Nonetheless, once the course of action was decided, I devoted all my time and energy to come up with a plan that would bring it to fruition. After much investigation, I found the opportunity I was looking for. I learnt that every full moon night, the king would leave his palace and sit atop a ceremonial chariot, leading a procession of his devout followers. During this procession, a large crowd would gather on either side of the street. And needless to say, in such a crowd, it would not be difficult to find a chink in the security arrangements. Fortunately, a full moon night was due in just three days, which meant that we did not even have to wait that long to execute our plan. Incidentally, our stay in Karvirpur had revealed one more crucial aspect—the inhabitants were completely fed up with Shringlava. It was just that their fear of him far outweighed their discontent. To tell you the truth, even the majority of the soldiers seemed opposed to him. For that matter, who in their right mind would support such a despot, except for his own sins? In fact, many of my own experiences stand as a testament to this truth. You would recall that when I had killed Kansa, the circumstances were similar to those in Karvirpur. Even during the killing of Panchajanya, a similar situation prevailed. You would remember that neither the subjects nor the soldiers had retaliated after their king's death. So, obviously, who would oppose Shringlava's killing? The logic is simple—it is impossible to escape after assassinating a king who is well respected by his subjects and whose soldiers are truly devoted to him. But in that case, why would I ever feel the need to kill such a noble king in the first place? Ah, we shall delve into this another time; for now, with the plan of action finalised, all that remained was to wait patiently for the full moon night.

The decisive day was not far either, and before long, it arrived. I woke up early in the morning in anticipation of the big day; however, nothing much could be accomplished by waking up early, for, the ceremonial procession would commence only in the evening. And evening couldn't come soon enough, despite the fact that I had been ready since morning. As for being ready, I did not have to prepare much; I just had to carry my discus with me. Thus, all day long, I paced the chamber from one end to the other, my restlessness soaring with every passing hour. Finally, dusk arrived, bringing an end to the interminably long wait. Eagerly, bhaiya and I made our way to the main square of Karvirpur, just before the scheduled time of the procession. We only had to wait a little longer, yet the wait seemed to stretch forever, perhaps because the matter involved our dear friend, Uddhava.

Well, fully alert, bhaiya and I stationed ourselves near a tree. As this tree was on higher ground, the main square could easily be seen from here. On the other side, a huge crowd had already gathered on the roads, with people crowding near us too. Everyone had assembled to catch a glimpse of their God. Speaking about me, I could not bear this wait any longer. With my patience wearing thin, I shifted restlessly from one foot to the other. Fortunately, it was just then that I spotted four chariots clattering down the road from the direction of the royal palace. The soldiers riding in them were raising their whips at random to push the crowd aside. Just see, this was how they were making way for their God! This also meant that 'God's chariot' was expected to arrive any moment now. And finally, this wait came to an end too. 'Lord Vishnu's'...I mean, King Shringlava's chariot, pulled by twelve *Acharyas,* finally arrived at the square. Around two hundred devotees followed it, singing, dancing and chanting his name. About a thousand-strong crowd stood waiting on either side of the road. The scene was really frightening, but my focus was entirely on Shringlava. Surprisingly, his sister, Shaivya had accompanied him this time as well. People were queuing up to offer prayers and garland their God, while I stood quietly, watching this elaborate drama put up by the fearful subjects of a demoniac king. Despite all these theatrics, my eyes were fixed on Shringlava's neck. All my senses were on complete alert, ready to strike as the king's chariot inched closer to us. By now, I had stealthily fixed the discus on my finger too. And as soon as his chariot came close, I took a careful aim and hurled my discus at his neck. Obviously, there was no question of my discus missing its target at such a crucial moment. In an instant, Shringlava's head was severed from his body and fell with a sickening thud on the chariot floor.

Seeing their God's severed head, the crowd was momentarily shocked into silence, but the very next moment, pandemonium broke loose as loud shrieks rent the air. Realising how delicate the situation was, I immediately began shouting loudly to divert the people's attention. I said, "This is how a sinner's life ends. This is how a sinner must be punished!" Hearing my slogans, bhaiya was not one to be left behind. I had only used my intelligence, but he did not hesitate to use his might. With mace ready in hand, he swung it and, in one fell swoop, brought down four to five soldiers who were standing close by. And before anyone could wrap their heads around what was happening or even step forward in Shringlava's favour, we began creating an atmosphere against him. Bhaiya's 'mace swinging' was certainly helping the situation. His act of killing the soldiers had such a powerful effect that everyone else backed off. No one dared to stand in support of Shringlava now. They were anyway fed up with the king's cruelty. In their heart of hearts, they must have even prayed a number of times for deliverance from his atrocities. This being the case, how long would it have taken them to calm down? In fact, as soon as everyone was certain of Shringlava's death, the situation turned completely in my favour. Even the soldiers bowed down to me. Within moments, slogans in my praise resounded all across the square. The only exception was Shringlava's sister, Shaivya, who was trembling with uncontrollable rage at her brother's killing. It was clear that she was unable to reconcile herself to the fact that her brother was dead. In fact, she was glowering at me from inside the chariot. So intense was her anger that I was not able to look her in the eye! Well, she could not help it; her brother's head and decapitated body were still lying in a pool of blood on the chariot's floor.

Well, before her anger could create problems for us, I thought it best to quickly tend to the tasks that lay ahead. At present, I had the support of the masses, but swayed by emotions, they could just as quickly switch loyalties and turn against me. No, no! If that were to happen, all our efforts would come to naught. We could even end up losing our lives! Thus, I instantly took action and, tearing through the crowd, forged ahead. In any case, half the people had already fled the scene, fearing that something untoward might happen, so it was not difficult to cover the distance. I thus strode ahead and hopped onto Shringlava's chariot. Bhaiya climbed in behind me, brandishing his mace. Shaivya, in the meanwhile, looked bewildered and could not fathom why we had climbed into her chariot. Ah, she would soon find out! Touching the raw nerve of the crowd, I called upon the people to join us in the task of releasing the innocent prisoners from 'hell'. Hearing this, a wave of delight swept over the crowd, and within moments, loud cries singing my praise echoed everywhere. Even the soldiers were no less ecstatic. This was bound to happen; the prisoners, after all, were relatives of the subjects and the soldiers.

Well, now that I had the support of the people, I felt a surge of happiness and excitement course through me, and riding on that wave of excitement, bhaiya and I jumped off the chariot and set off towards the 'hell'. A crowd of about four hundred people and around twenty soldiers followed us. Meaning, His Majesty, Krishna, had already donned the mantle of the leader of Karvirpur as soon as he had arrived! Surprisingly, we were moving ahead without any obstructions, with no one opposing us anywhere. In the blink of an eye, our procession had reached the main entrance of 'hell'. News of Shringlava's death had reached here as well, and the rest of the task was now made easy by the soldiers accompanying us, who apprised the guards stationed in the 'hell'. Thereafter, not only was the main entrance opened immediately, but the doors of all the cells were unlocked too. Within moments, a horde of people including Uddhava came pouring out from this inhuman 'hell'. Seeing Uddhava stand in front of us, unshackled and freed, both bhaiya and I wept with joy. Uddhava too clung to us and cried his poor, unsullied heart out. It was surprising to see that even after going through such a terrible ordeal, he still had tears left to shed. Well, what could he do? The poor fellow must have given up all hope of us ever reaching this place to rescue him. Perhaps, he had mentally prepared himself to rot here for the rest of his life. So, it was only natural that he would cry after being unexpectedly rescued from this hellhole.

Shouts and cries of joy rang through the air as all the rescued prisoners poured onto the streets. And with their release, the fervour of the crowd intensified as well. Such was the zeal of the people that a crowd of about five hundred accompanied us to the *ashram*, shouting our praises all along. That was not all; they even stood outside the *ashram* for quite some time and continued to shout slogans glorifying us. Seeing the joy reflect on their

faces and the respect and honour they were according to me, I was sure that we were no longer in danger. And I felt even more reassured after receiving the support of the soldiers. To be honest, it was only because of this sense of security that I was still present in the *ashram;* otherwise, I would have fled right after the deed was accomplished. I'm sure you are aware of my habit of scampering off on sensing the slightest hint of danger.

This was all about us, but as darkness fell, the entire kingdom broke into a celebration. It seemed as if the inhabitants of Karvirpur were celebrating the death of their king. And why would they not; they did have a reason to be happy, after all. For, not just the prisoners, but in a way, the whole of Karvirpur was breathing the air of freedom after a very long time. Hence, the celebration of their freedom was bound to be grand. People thronged the streets, and all night long, they congratulated one another, expressing their relief and happiness, and shouting our praises. Watching the people in such a celebratory mood, I wondered, how unfortunate must be the king whose death was making his subjects rejoice! Whether it was Kansa or Shringlava, what did they gain by nursing a massive ego? Looking at this situation keeping the ultimate truth in mind, I realised that all of this had become possible only because of Uddhava. He was the sole instrument of liberation for the people of Karvirpur from the torturous reign of King Shringlava. Speaking of Uddhava, the poor fellow was still in a grave condition. Actually, he appeared to be in a far worse state than I had imagined, and therefore needed a strong dose of reassurance. Thus, shifting our focus away from Karvirpur and its people, we concentrated entirely on helping Uddhava restore his physical and mental well-being. However, even after spending the whole night attending to him, he showed little sign of improvement. Clearly, the torture he had undergone in 'hell' had wreaked tremendous damage on his psyche.

Well, all of that would be dealt with in time. But on waking up the next morning, before we could think of our next move, a guard from the royal palace delivered the message that Queen Padmavati had arrived to meet us. I was startled momentarily, for, this was completely unexpected. I couldn't think of any clear-cut reason why she had come to meet me, but whether I understood her intentions or not, I had to meet her. Thus, trying to guess a plausible reason for her arrival, I promptly accompanied the soldier who took me to meet her. Seeing her stand at the *ashram's* entrance, I was dumbstruck. Shringlava's wife, meaning Queen Padmavati, was remarkably beautiful and impressive even at the age of sixty-five. Not only this, she appeared totally composed and extremely confident. She had not come alone though; Shaivya had accompanied her along with a young boy. She had arrived with a procession of six chariots, guarded by scores of soldiers. About a hundred-strong crowd had also come to see us. But I could not focus on them right now. I touched the queen's feet respectfully, but to my surprise, neither did she extend her hand out to bless me, nor did she say a word in response. She did, however, examine me from head to toe, as if she was trying to assess me or glean something about me. At once, I became alert on noticing this behaviour, for, I too was completely clueless about the reason behind her arrival. Moreover, she was Shringlava's wife, who had just lost her husband. So, not only was I curious to see her reaction, but it had also become necessary for me to know her reaction. It was a strange scene indeed; while she was trying to assess me, I was trying to fathom what she wanted from me. Unaware of this silent little exchange between us, the crowd stood outside, still shouting slogans of praise for both the queen and me.

Fortunately, the suspense underlying her visit was lifted soon. After assessing me for a while, the queen finally broke the silence saying, "This is Shringlava's sister, Shaivya." Then, she nudged the boy forward and said, "And this is his son, Shakradeva." After making the introductions, she heaved a deep sigh and continued, "It is obvious that the inhabitants of Karvirpur are very happy with you, singing your glories all over the kingdom. But the reason I have come here is to ask you—have you killed my husband, Shringlava, to take over the throne of Karvirpur?"

The queen's arrival itself was unexpected for me, and now, her straightforward question shattered all the possibilities I had conjured up in my mind. I continued to remain silent and looked keenly at her. She appeared absolutely calm, and I could not detect any grief in her eyes for her slain husband. For a moment or two, I stood spellbound, impressed by her equanimity and maturity. Perhaps, these are the very qualities that are a distinctive mark of great queens and kings. For that matter, the ability to regain your composure and return to normalcy after any incident is the best quality a human being can possess. And as far as kings and queens are concerned, they should certainly possess this quality, because in my opinion, an emotionally weak king can turn out to be as dangerous as a cruel and arrogant one.

Well, coming back to the queen, her serene eyes had quelled the storm brewing in my mind. There was no malice in those eyes and this brought peace to my heart, at least for the time being. Ah, now that I have touched upon the topic of satisfaction, let me also tell you the reason behind my dissatisfaction, which I was simultaneously feeling at this moment. Shaivya, dressed in white clothes, appeared far more furious than before. Seeing her simmering anger, I felt a shiver course through me, and honestly, I even felt a little intimidated by her demeanour. However, I quickly regained my composure. But now what? I even asked myself, why did I feel this way? It was the first time in my life that I had felt any kind of tremor within me. And based on this experience, I can say that there is no difference between trembling with fear and dying. In a manner of speaking, the very moment in which I had trembled with fear was also the moment in which I had died. Perhaps, I had experienced this shiver so that I could understand its terror. Otherwise, would I ever shake with fear? I had not trembled even when I faced the serpent Kaaliya or the demon Keshi. I had not shivered when I had faced Kansa or Jarasandha. So, it was strange that Shaivya's anger had made me tremble. Perhaps, the bitter experience of my aunts' anger was still fresh in my mind. And why would it not be? It was only because of the fallout of that anger that I was running from pillar to post at present, and it was that very fury which had sent the fiend, Jarasandha chasing after me. Whatever it may be, I can now say with certainty that trembling in fear is the biggest sin man can commit. If you remember, I had shared this experience with Arjuna in the Bhagavad Gita when I had said to him, *"O Arjuna! Why are you shaking with fear on seeing the vast army of the Kauravas? It is this trembling which is a sin. Be it happiness or sorrow, man should always live in equanimity. Whether you tremble because of happiness or sorrow, both are akin to a living hell."*[45]

Well, we have discussed enough about Shaivya. Let me now tell you something about Shringlava's son, Shakradeva, a ten-year-old lad. He was quite attractive and impressive, but curiously, he too did not seem very affected by his father's death. Coming back to the queen's question, I had completely prepared my answer to her unexpected query. Interestingly, not only the queen, but even the assembled crowd was impatiently waiting to hear my response. Some of the people were even shouting slogans and urging me to stake a claim on the throne. But I was not one to be trapped like this. I had to move forward on the basis of my decision alone. Thus, with folded hands and a calm and humble look upon my face, I replied, "No, Mother! I did not kill Shringlava with the intention of becoming the king.[46] The only thing I had in mind when I slayed him was his oppression as well as the interests of the subjects he ruled over. The truth is, the king's death was a culmination of his own actions; I was merely the instrument. But even so, I beg your forgiveness if I have hurt you knowingly or unknowingly."

Queen Padmavati was listening to every word with rapt attention. I too was equally attentive as I stood before her, trying to gauge her reaction to my words. In short, both of us were trying to glean each other's motives. Fortunately, everything I had said so far seemed to have had a positive impact on her. It was bound to, for, my words and intentions were both clear. I had faced similar circumstances when I had killed Kansa too, meaning, that experience was still fresh in my mind. Hence, showing a sense of maturity, I

45. Shrimad Bhagavad Gita, Chapter – 2, Verse – 12-15.
46. Harivansh Puran, Vishnu Parva, Chapter – 44, Verse – 55-58.

continued to speak with a quiet confidence, "I wish that King Shringlava be given a royal funeral. I too will be present to pay homage to him. Moreover, I want Prince Shakradeva to be crowned the new king. I am just an outsider; I will return to my homeland after the coronation of Prince Shakradeva."

Hearing my decision, the crowd enthusiastically raised slogans and shouted, "Glory to Krishna! Glory to Queen Mother! Glory to Prince Shakradeva!" Naturally, on hearing me out and realising my intent, the queen became much more calm, composed and happy. This was clearly evident in her expression and eyes, which were still fixed on me. In any case, I had said what I had to; it was the queen's turn now.

And what do I say about her regal manner? She first greeted the gathered crowd and waved out to them. Then, asking the people to remain quiet, she turned to me and said, "I am satisfied with your intentions and all that you have said. But before I continue, I want to know your identity."

I spoke at once with great humility, "I am Krishna, son of Vasudeva of Mathura."

For some reason, as soon as I gave her my introduction, she became completely calm. Not only that, she even blessed me! Honestly speaking, I felt honoured upon receiving her blessings, for, the danger had been completely averted now. However, the cordiality did not stop here, because as soon as the decision to crown Shakradeva was made, the queen asked the prince to touch my feet and seek my blessings. Needless to say, I was bursting with pride. Krishna had become so eminent that even princes were now seeking his blessings! Well, now that normalcy was fast being restored, I looked across at Shaivya with hopeful eyes. Perhaps, the hatred simmering in her eyes had quelled by now. But no, the fire still burned bright in her eyes, spewing embers. I was astounded! Here, I was ensuring that Shakradeva be crowned the king; I was not even trying to gain control over Karvirpur, then why was she still seething with rage? In fact, consumed by anger, she had not even bothered to respond to my greeting. I thus set everything aside and focused completely on pacifying her. For, I had seen fury of a similar kind in the eyes of my aunts after I had killed Kansa. And it was because I hadn't paid attention to their anger at the time that I was suffering the menace called Jarasandha even at present. Surely, I did not want to repeat the same mistake. The love and affection of women is beautiful, but their fury...oh goodness! What if I failed to calm Shaivya's rage and she created a new problem for me? Thus, after the bitter experience with my aunts and subsequently running from pillar to post for several months, I wanted to save myself from the fury of a woman's revenge at any cost. Even otherwise, being cautious was in my nature; moreover, it is a sign of intelligence to foresee a problem and avert it before it manifests and assumes epic proportions. Shaivya was a princess, and she was extremely beautiful as well. To win her love, a thousand kings and princes could very well compete to claim my head and present it to her on a platter. Therefore, I did not want to leave without pacifying her.

While I was occupied in these thoughts, the queen's caravan had departed already. I too greeted the crowd and quietly returned to my chamber. Now, the only task at hand was to calm Shaivya's rage. And with this intent, I went to Shringlava's funeral and also attended Shakradeva's coronation. I reckoned, perhaps her anger would subside on seeing me take such keen interest in these proceedings. Besides, whenever and wherever I ran into her, I greeted her unfailingly and even flashed my trademark smile at her at every opportunity. In other words, I was leaving no stone unturned to mend bridges from my end. Fortunately, my efforts began to bear fruit soon enough. After Shakradeva's coronation, her demeanour towards me did undergo a slight change and she certainly seemed to have softened a little. For me, this was a positive sign, and with hope springing in my heart, I stepped up my efforts to pacify her further. To be honest, Queen Padmavati also offered support in this. Consequently, I soon succeeded in making Shaivya my sister, while she too was glad to have found an affectionate brother in me in place of the one she had lost.

On this encouraging note, my task in Karvirpur was accomplished and a grave trouble was averted too. The time had now come for us to depart. The uncertainty of our next destination had also been laid to rest. I had fled from Mathura as a deserter in fear of Jarasandha and now that I had chased him away, I had become a hero; so obviously, I wanted to return to Mathura only. Frankly speaking, I was yearning to go to Mathura and flaunt myself as a hero. Oh, how I wished I could sprout wings right this instant so that I could close the distance to Mathura in a flash! However, when I apprised the queen of my decision, she was unwilling to let me leave so soon. Even Shaivya expressed her wish that I delay my departure and stay with them for a few more days. If the situation had been different, I wouldn't have declined Shaivya's request, but what could I do? As mentioned before, my heart was eager to go to Mathura. Perhaps, my ego too was impatient to impress the *Mathurawasis* with tales of my valorous feats. So, I decided to set off for Mathura and managed to convince everyone to grant us permission to leave.

The queen was so pleased with me that during our farewell, she gifted us a glut of diamonds and other precious stones, twenty chariots and about thirty orderlies. I felt honoured upon receiving this generous gift. Moreover, it wasn't just the royal palace but all of Karvirpur that bid us an emotional farewell. Many of them even walked all the way to the outskirts of the kingdom to see us off. Receiving so much love and respect, and that too, in an unfamiliar kingdom, was certainly a matter of great honour. As for me, I truly believed that I deserved it. I was accorded this respect because of my great accomplishment. Our journey thus began with this burst of self-energising pride. Amidst great fanfare, we departed the kingdom of Karvirpur with our grand caravan comprising twenty-five chariots and several orderlies. Naturally, bhaiya, Uddhava and I were seated in different chariots, handing the reins over to the charioteers. After all, now that we had both the opportunity and the means, why wouldn't we travel in style?!

This was all great but what do I say about my nature? The headiness of the honour I had received in Karvirpur had barely abated when I began to feel intoxicated at the very thought of the hero's welcome we would receive on reaching Mathura. Indeed, the recognition and respect one receives in one's homeland has a different charm altogether. Besides, Krishna was no longer an ordinary cowherd. First, I had killed Kansa followed by Panchajanya, after which I had forced Jarasandha to retreat from the battlefield, and now, I was also instrumental in the elimination of the evil king, Shringlava. This ordinary Kanha from Vrindavan had become the supremely valorous Krishna of Aryavarta! And that's not all! We were no longer Vrindavan's penniless cowherds; we were now affluent gentlemen of Mathura. And although I did not know much about wealth, I could roughly estimate that there was perhaps no one in Mathura who possessed as much wealth as we did. You might remember that we already had the boundless wealth given to us by Chandak. Then, we had discovered gems and precious stones on the Gomanta Mountain, and now we also had the treasure gifted to us by Queen Padmavati. Meaning, we had become affluent in the truest sense of the word, and were also currently travelling in a regal manner, with a caravan of chariots riding with us. Surely, Mathura would not chase off such valorous and wealthy gentlemen from its gates; on the contrary, it would feel honoured to provide us with refuge. In fact, it would feel compelled to give us a grand welcome. This being the case, how could I keep my ego in check? And why should I? When I had performed one extraordinary feat after another, what was the harm in indulging in a little pride over it? In short, for the first time in my life, my ego was divided between the past and the future. On one hand, I was rejoicing in the honour I had received in Karvirpur, and on the other, I was dreaming about the hero's welcome I would receive upon reaching Mathura. Honestly speaking, today, I was experiencing first-hand how honour inflates a person's ego. And what is 'ego' after all? To describe it in one sentence, it is nothing but moving away from the present. And just see, at present, my mind was vacillating between the honour accorded to me in the past and the anticipatory welcome of the future. The present moment comprised only this journey, but my mind was not paying any attention to it.

This prompted me to question, if my mind was really not inclined to focus on the present moment, then why not reminisce about the memorable moments of the past? And so, I immersed myself in thoughts of Vrindavan. The love and honour I had received there was no less! Oh, how do I even begin to describe it? The love I had received in Vrindavan was of a different kind altogether. My dear *Vrindavanwasis* had given me as many names as there were facets to my life. It was because of them that I had such a long list of names—I had been called Kanha, Kanhaiya and Krishna since childhood. Because of my swarthy complexion, some people would lovingly call me Shyam, while a few would call me Nandakishore since I was Nanda's son. Breaking their butter pots had earned me the title of Matkiphod, and as I stole their butter, they called me Maakhanchor! What I mean to say is, there had been no dearth of love and respect in my life right from my childhood days. But surprisingly, my ego had never been as inflated as it was right now. Perhaps, it couldn't quite digest the series of unexpected triumphs I had notched up in such a short span of time. First, the killing of Panchajanya, then chasing off Jarasandha and earning boundless wealth, and finally, the slaying of Shringlava. Just think, how could an ordinary cowherd's pride digest such great achievements?!

But how long could this go on? What was the point of feeling proud over what I had achieved through my own actions? Thus, I awakened my consciousness at once. 'Oh, come now, you are merely an instrument through which these great feats were accomplished, and who knows this better than you? And why should an instrument feel proud? Of what consequence is the past and the future for an instrument? So, save yourself from getting trapped between these two dangerous grinding stones, and focus on the present at once.' Well, I did just that...but there was a hitch here as well. As soon as I became conscious of the present, I first cast my eye over my caravan. And lo and behold, the sight of the long procession of twenty-five chariots and about fifty orderlies filled me with pride even in the present moment. Not so long ago, we had fled from Mathura bereft of a refuge, and here we were, returning to Mathura in a magnificent caravan that would put even a prince to shame! However, the pride that exists in the present moment does not last very long. So, my mind soon focused itself on the journey, and accordingly, I first took the reins of the chariot in my own hands and asked bhaiya and Uddhava to sit next to me. Indeed, travelling in style and comfort is all well and good, but a journey is best enjoyed when you're riding in the same chariot as your friends, reins in hand. And how do I even describe this journey? As I let my gaze wander over my surroundings, I realised that the passing countryside, rivers, mountains, forests and lakes appeared a million times more beautiful than before. And then began a long session of banter and a riot of laughter among us that simply refused to end. Indeed, the joy of living in the present is beyond compare. The truth is, joy is just another name for the present. Truly, carried away by my ego, I was unnecessarily vacillating between the past and the future, and spoiling the pleasure of this beautiful journey.

And oh, what a long and wonderful journey it was! Scores of chariots, a bevy of servants and soldiers at our beck and call, and most importantly, the company of friends! Neither did we have to stay awake for a night vigil, nor did we have to lead the horses to the water to quench their thirst. Moreover, we did not even have to arrange for our own food. All in all, this was the first journey of our lives that allowed us to travel in a manner befitting princes. In fact, this was the first time we had realised how wonderful a life of comfort was. While we were floating on a cloud of happiness, poor Uddhava could not even begin to comprehend how we had become so wealthy! The poor fellow had set out in search of us, worrying that we were perhaps starving and languishing in some forsaken place, but here we were, rejoicing in the lap of comfort and luxury. Well, this is nothing but Krishna's *karmaleela*—the play of *karma* (deeds), which changes everything in the blink of an eye! Consider this journey for instance; even the manner in which we were travelling had changed so much. At times, all three of us would sit in one chariot, and when we felt the need to relax, we would head to our respective chariots. And yes, wherever we halted for the night, I would unfailingly play my flute out of pure joy. And when the melodious tune reverberated in the cold, night air, it would invariably awaken fond memories of Vrindavan. Indeed, how was it possible to not miss Vrindavan during such a peaceful and enjoyable journey? Amazingly, with the mellifluous notes of the flute, I could recall Vrindavan so vividly that it felt as if I was reliving it in the present moment. What a carefree and happy life we had lived there! Oh, I wished I could fly off to Vrindavan that very instant!

But the question was, should I listen to my mind or pay heed to the dictates of Nature? Of course, Nature! At any rate, I had never imposed my will and desires upon Nature, so why would I do it now? However, Nature only has the power to determine where we must live or what we must do, but it is entirely in our power whom we keep ensconced in our heart. And you very well know that taking advantage of this fact, I had never let the memories of Vrindavan fade away from my mind; I had never allowed them to become my past. Besides, the mind of an action-oriented man like me could discern no difference between Vrindavan, Mathura or Gomanta Mountain. Whether it was

Radha or Malini, I accepted whoever was with me in the present moment. I did not get caught up in likes and dislikes, but wholeheartedly enjoyed everything that came my way. I never complained to Nature why it repeatedly pushed a fun-loving, colourful artist like me, who was fond of music and dance, to fight battles one after another. I never complained why it was forcing this soft-hearted artist to live a life of strife and struggle. No! I embraced life fully in all its hues. I never differentiated between my flute and my weapon, the discus; I never made a choice between the two. When Nature granted me the opportunity to play the flute, I gladly took it, playing joyfully and expressing my gratitude for the same. When Nature compelled me to use the discus, I did so with the same degree of love, considering it my duty. Despite the fact that I was a simple-hearted man, Nature created circumstances in which I had to become cunning, so I effortlessly embraced craftiness as well, accepting it as Nature's will. This is because I had firm, unwavering faith in Nature, which governs this colossal universe with absolute perfection. It understands our lives and what is in our best interest far better than we do. From its divine perspective, Vrindavan was Nature's own and so was Mathura. Radha was its creation and so was Malini. Similarly, simplicity and cunningness are two attributes which have also been created by Nature. Then who was I to choose? Who was I to be partial to one or the other? It was Nature's will and the task of implementing it was mine. It was neither good nor bad. This is precisely what I had said to Arjuna repeatedly while enunciating the Bhagavad Gita, *"Rise above sin and virtue. Discard both while you are still alive and just surrender to Nature's will."*[47]

Oh well, let us leave Arjuna aside and return to the journey, which we were enjoying to the fullest. When we were in the same chariot, we would chit-chat endlessly, and when we were in separate ones, I would lose myself in contemplation. Our pomp and pride was such that we just had to point towards a fruit and the servants would make haste and collect an armful for us. Sometimes, when we could not find a rest house and had to sleep in the forest, it was the servants who would make our bedding, strewing piles of leaves on the hard ground to make our rest comfortable. Of course, as far as shopping was concerned, we ourselves bought whatever we wished from every new market that we passed through. After all, I wasn't going to wear clothes and jewellery chosen by the servants! In fact, due to my love for fine attire and jewellery, I would buy a couple of *pitambars* from every market we passed. Now that we were well off, why would I suppress my desire to purchase things I liked? And when I was not holding back in any respect, why would I be stingy with my dreams either? One such day, in the midst of my musings, I fell asleep in my chariot after having partaken a heavy meal in the

47. Shrimad Bhagavad Gita, Chapter – 2, Verse – 50.

afternoon. I had barely nodded off to sleep when Rukmini appeared before my eyes. And with her arrival, her presence overwhelmed my entire being. I have no qualms in telling you that her effect was so overpowering that I could feel tingles all over my body; and within moments, she took over my thoughts completely. Well, there was no harm in indulging in such fantasies. After all, I had now become worthy enough to dream about her. Not only was I a great warrior who had chased off Jarasandha, but I was affluent too. Moreover, I was now loved not only by the inhabitants of Mathura and Vrindavan, but also by the people of Karvirpur and many other kingdoms. Honestly, it was for the first time today that I felt my dream of attaining Rukmini was inching closer to reality.

And even if this was just wishful thinking on my part, it was nonetheless amazing. Just the thought of her had filled me with enthusiasm, making this regal journey even more enjoyable. It was on one such day when we had stopped to rest for the night that an odd but significant incident took place. Bhaiya and I were engaged in idle conversation, while Uddhava had retired for the night. During a lull in our conversation, we heard the whispering of the soldiers. The soldiers of Queen Padmavati and those of my uncle were conversing with one another, when one of them spoke sadly, "We are soldiers but we do not belong to any unit."

A second one said, "You are absolutely right, my friend. But what can we do, this is our fate!"

A third added, "Our situation is disgraceful. If someone were to ask us which kingdom we belonged to or what the name of our king was, we would not have an answer."

Hearing their conversation, bhaiya and I were shaken up. All of a sudden, I felt numb. They were absolutely right. The realisation dawned upon me that we still had a lot more to achieve, and in that one instant, all the heady intoxication of our success evaporated. Nevertheless, I considered every incident to be a sign from Nature. Just think about it, the fact that we were awake and had overheard the soldiers' conversation could not have been just a coincidence. So, after deliberating on this for a while, I concluded that Nature was signalling to us that the time had come to establish our own kingdom. I immediately shared this insight with bhaiya saying, "Perhaps, this is a sign from Nature that we must establish our own kingdom."

Hearing this, bhaiya began to laugh at what he considered to be a preposterous idea. However, when his laughter subsided, he spoke in a serious tone, "Kanhaiya, establishing a new kingdom is no laughing matter. The main aspects of a kingdom are: land, subjects, soldiers, and finally, wealth. Besides, if you really harboured the desire to be a king, why did you refuse the throne of Mathura? We had the opportunity to sit on the throne of Karvirpur as well, so why did you not accept that?"

I said, "No, bhaiya. To capture another's kingdom or to snatch away someone else's right to become king is not in our nature. And as for hard work, my experiences so far tell me that to attain something, a human being does not need to break his back as much as he needs to be in sync with the flow of Nature. For, events will always unfold according to Nature's plan; the question is whether you can flow with the events or not. Just think, bhaiya! In Vrindavan, we were spending our lives as illiterate and ignorant boys, but look where we have reached today! Tell me, what efforts did we make to achieve any of this? What role did our intentions play in it or how hard did we work for it? Kansa invited us to Mathura and we complied. Nature orchestrated the circumstances, and we became instrumental in killing Kansa. To pay our *gurudakshina* to our teacher, we ended up killing Panchajanya. And no sooner did we kill Kansa and Panchajanya than we shot into prominence. We not only made Chandak a king, but we were also responsible for the coronation of Shakradeva. Meanwhile, we also managed to accumulate immense wealth. And to cap our achievements, we also chased away Jarasandha, the most powerful king of Aryavarta, and overnight, became the greatest heroes in this region! If observed carefully, our progress has been the result of events unfolding one after another. But what exactly did we do to achieve this? We merely went along with the flow of the events. What I mean to say is, if our own kingdom is slated to be established sometime in the future, the events leading to its inception would also take place accordingly. We will just have to become the medium through which these events would unfold. Besides, bhaiya, why do you forget that the people of as many as three kingdoms—Mathura, Vaivasvatpur and Karvirpur—now revere us. We are the ones who have liberated them from their former cruel rulers: Kansa, Panchajanya and Shringlava. The blessings we continue to receive from these people day and night will also help us greatly. Indeed, you will see that these very blessings will prove enough for us to establish our own kingdom one day."

Well, I was not sure whether bhaiya had truly comprehended the import of my words, but I want you to grasp this principle clearly if you wish to make great strides in life. If you are still unclear, read it over repeatedly, but pray, do not live under any delusion. And from now on, allow whatever is happening in your life to just happen. Go along with whatever is happening, and trust me, one day, you will surely reach where you are supposed to.

Engrossed in this contemplation, little did I realise that we had already traversed the distance to Mathura and were now very close to its border. If we wanted to, we could have continued our journey and entered

Mathura by late night. But one does not enter a city so late at night with such a large entourage! Indeed, how could I lose the opportunity of stunning all of Mathura by making a grand entry in the middle of the day? So, we entered the city the next day, not early in the morning but just before noon. I was riding my chariot with bhaiya next to me and Uddhava sitting in the rear seat. And this chariot of ours was followed by scores of chariots. Bhaiya and I were sitting in a royal stance, pride emanating from our countenance. After all, the victorious heroes were stepping into their own city in the manner of princes. Needless to add, the news of our arrival spread like wildfire. In the beginning, whoever saw us was stunned, as if a bolt of lightning had struck them. But gradually, the astonishment turned into a warm welcome. As the news of our arrival spread, a large crowd gathered to welcome us. Actually, the news of our routing of Jarasandha's army had already reached Mathura, and consequently, our valorous feat was the most discussed topic, even among children. So, people naturally hastened, abandoning all tasks to crowd around us. Additionally, our large caravan was attracting curious onlookers, who were peering at it inquisitively. About two hundred people had already joined us, and as the procession moved ahead, the crowd following it also swelled in size. Gradually, the situation had come to such a pass that it had become difficult for our caravan to move even an inch ahead. Well, I was in no hurry either, as I basked in all the attention and adulation I was receiving. Honestly, I did not want this welcome to end anytime soon. We had left Mathura in a state of sheer dishonour, so it was only natural for us to crave this respect—in fact, the more, the better. And the swelling crowd seemed bent on fulfilling this need of ours to the fullest. The air was rent with loud chants praising us. Flowers and garlands of many hues and fragrances were being showered upon us. We were enveloped in a rainbow of colours as *gulal*[48] and flowers intermingled with each other turning the entire scene into a rich, vibrant tapestry. Women vied with each other to mark our foreheads with vermillion to welcome us. Oh, how do I describe how elated I was on being welcomed in my own city! And if I were to confess, this was precisely the moment that my ego had been waiting for. It had been longing to receive this honour, and I must say, it deserved it too. Thus, with the accolades pouring in, I had set it free to revel in all the praise it received. After all, the poor thing seldom got such opportunities in my presence.

Meanwhile, bhaiya's happiness had to be seen to be believed. His ego soared skywards, as he looked around with eyes filled with pride and joy. It was natural for him to feel so; after all, he had been protesting against fleeing from the battle only because he was worried about us losing our reputation. But today, on receiving such a grand welcome, he felt truly blessed. You know how

48. *Gulal* - Coloured powder thrown into the air and on to others as a mark of celebration.

my heart would dance with joy whenever bhaiya's ego was satiated; meaning, my happiness had now doubled on its own. This was our state of mind, but in contrast to us, Uddhava found himself in a strange plight. Ever since we were reunited, the poor boy was dumbfounded on seeing our grandeur, the bevy of servants, the contingent of soldiers and our huge caravan of chariots. And now, seeing the grand welcome being accorded to us, his head started to spin with bewilderment. Interestingly, on seeing our grand reception, the complaints of our coterie of soldiers had all but vanished. Indeed, they too were bursting with pride on seeing the manner in which we were being welcomed. They had realised that though their masters were no kings, they were no less than any king as far as honour and grandeur were concerned. And they were not wrong either. Although I did not have a kingdom of my own, I certainly ruled the hearts of scores of people across several kingdoms.

Gradually, our arrival in Mathura took on the form of a victory march. About five hundred people walked alongside our chariots as we proceeded through the streets of Mathura. And as the chariots passed through my favourite haunt—the main marketplace—a generous shower of flowers and garlands greeted us. People had even climbed atop the verandas of shops to get a better view of their heroes. The crowd had swelled so much that whichever way we looked, all that we could see was a sea of people craning their necks to catch a glimpse of us. In fact, there was no place now to even stand, and as a result, our caravan had all but stopped. It was at this point that my heart skipped a beat, when I espied Malini making her way through the crowd, dressed in finery. I was elated to see her. She applied the mark of victory on my forehead and garlanded me, after which I jumped down from my chariot and walked up to her veranda. This pleased her no end, making her puff with pride. And why would she not feel so? Her friend had returned after accomplishing several feats of valour, and upon his return, it was she who received the highest regard from him. Besides, her friend, meaning I, was himself perched on the peak of glory. Truly, the welcome Mathura had given us remained etched in my mind forever. Having said that, we had received a similar reception in Karvirpur too, but my ego had not inflated to this extent. Perhaps, the ego swells more when it is accorded respect among one's own people.

Well, our welcome ceremony finally ended, but this had slowed down our pace so much that we could reach the palace only by evening. Naturally, grandfather was waiting for us impatiently, for, he too had made splendid arrangements for our reception, and it was only after this official, royal reception was over that we entered the palace. As soon as we were inside, grandfather first congratulated us on our stupendous victory. But the very next moment, for some reason, his eyes welled up with tears. After all, he loved me a lot, and considering the circumstances in which I had left Mathura, the past year must have been very hard on him. Hence, seeing me hale and hearty, and on hearing about my progress and valorous feats, he was bound to become emotional. For that matter, I too had become misty-eyed on seeing him after a whole year. And in any case, how could I forget that the entire credit for my bravery and progress went to the encouragement he had given me from time to time? Coming back to the present, it goes without saying that both grandfather and grandson partook of dinner together. We spoke for a long time; in fact, I wanted to chit-chat with him all night long, but the treasure stashed in the chariots did not permit this. Moreover, my eyelids were growing heavy due to exhaustion. Thus, after talking with him for a while, I sought his permission to leave. But yes, I must mention that bhaiya had chosen to stay back at the palace on grandfather's insistence. That was fine by us, so Uddhava and I soon headed home.

The moment we reached home, we found that the reception was not over yet, for, mother and father also welcomed us, greeting their brave son with great warmth and affection. Mother could not contain the pride she felt at her son's achievements. Certainly, having a valorous son like me had minimised the pain of losing her seven children. However, at present, my top priority was to take care of the treasure I had brought along. So, as a first step, Uddhava and I hauled the treasure chests inside the house and placed them safely in my chamber. At the same time, I selected four of the most diligent soldiers who had come with us and instructed them to guard the house with immediate effect, while I sent the remaining chariots and soldiers back to the royal palace. I had not even freed myself from all these tasks when mother called us for dinner. Now, I had already feasted with grandfather, but I did not think it right to refuse mother and hurt her feelings. Moreover, she had not eaten yet, having waited for me all this while. Besides, it barely made a difference to a glutton like me if I had two meals back to back! But let me tell you one thing: this was my first experience of having a meal at this late hour. Actually, no matter how many delicious meals you've had, they can never match the food prepared and served by your mother. Now, just imagine my plight after feasting twice in my utterly exhausted state! Of course, I fell asleep as soon as my head hit the pillow.

Naturally, after the excitement and celebrations of the previous day, I woke up only by late afternoon. After a good night's sleep, not only was my mind refreshed, but physically too, I felt ready to take on the world. Thus, I quickly got ready and went to meet grandfather at the royal palace. I shared an extremely close rapport with grandfather, and like I had said earlier, I had reached this position in life solely because of him. So, I was longing to have a deep, intimate conversation with him. But when I reached there, I was dumbfounded. Grandfather's, meaning, King Ugrasena's expression bore no semblance to the happy visage I had seen yesterday. On the contrary, his brow was furrowed with lines of worry. Perhaps, he had other concerns apart from Jarasandha, so I felt it was my duty to ask about them. Upon enquiring, he revealed the cause of his anxiety in great detail. He told me that business in Mathura was in complete shambles, as a result of which Mathura's coffers were now empty. The situation had deteriorated so much that for the past three months, the palace staff had not even been paid their wages. Moreover, most of the Yadava leaders were busy squabbling with each other, and to make matters worse, Satrajit had permanently moved to Mathura. And for some strange reason, he was instigating the Yadavas against the royal palace. It was alright to have ignored this in the beginning, but now, he was actually making headway with his malicious plans. He had instigated many powerful Yadavas, including Satyaki, and turned them against the royal palace. And since he had been vehemently opposing me right from the beginning, grandfather feared, now that I was back in Mathura, he might create serious trouble for the palace.

However, honestly, I did not find the situation to be as grave as grandfather believed it to be...or perhaps I felt this way because I had very little knowledge of administrative affairs. Nevertheless, after giving it some thought, I asked grandfather, "If things are as you say they are, why do you not counterattack these rebelling factions of Yadavas, especially Satrajit? Why don't you ask for their help in replenishing the treasury?" Grandfather shook his head sadly and replied, "What do I say, Kanhaiya? Satrajit is the most influential of all Yadavas. He has in his possession a magical gem called Syamantaka, which gives him several grams of gold every day. This continuous inflow of gold has made him so wealthy that he has even set up a small kingdom somewhere near Saurashtra. Not only does he have abundant wealth, but he also has a small army comprising hundreds of soldiers. It is on the power of his wealth and position that he exerts tremendous influence over all the Yadavas. However, I fail to fathom his intentions and the interest he is evincing in Mathura despite having his own kingdom. Incidentally, not only in Mathura but in many other kingdoms, the Yadavas regard him as their leader. Of course, the main reason behind this is that he is the richest Yadava in Aryavarta. All in all, his malicious meddling in the affairs of Mathura can lead to grave consequences. You are suggesting that I take his help to replenish the treasury, while he has been instigating everyone not to pay their taxes! He keeps telling everyone that neither is the royal palace capable of protecting Mathura, nor are any of the businesses prospering in this kingdom.

He is also telling them that no new construction is taking place in Mathura, and all the parks and gardens have become barren. So, why pay taxes to the royal palace?"

After listening to what grandfather had to say and sympathising with him, I left the royal palace mulling over the situation. In fact, my mind continued to mull over this problem for the next several days. Leave alone living peacefully, I now found myself drowning in restlessness. For, I had fathomed the matter completely after grandfather had explained the situation to me in detail. Not only was Satrajit the most powerful Yadava, he had no dearth of wealth either. But perhaps, he is not content with his small kingdom; therefore, he is increasing his influence in Mathura and creating these conflicts to further his ambitions. And clearly, he had succeeded in creating a parallel kingdom of his own in Mathura. Perhaps, he intended to hand over the reins of Mathura to an acolyte of his. In such a case, I would certainly prove to be an obstruction to his evil intentions. For, not only was I loyal to grandfather, but I was powerful as well. This meant that his opposition was not personal; it was all part of an elaborate strategy. It was only now that I had understood why he had always opposed me. And seen from this perspective, Satrajit's intentions were dangerous indeed. For, this could not only lead to Mathura's downfall, but also compel me to once again run helter-skelter without refuge. Admittedly, the troubles brewing at this stage were not that alarming, but their long-term consequences could be extremely grave. Indeed, if the reins of Mathura were to slip from grandfather's hands, it would become impossible for me to withstand Jarasandha's onslaughts. After mulling over the situation at length, I realised there was only one solution to this problem. I had to confront Satrajit head-on and increase my influence over the Yadavas.

Of course, this would be accomplished in due course, but what about the immediate crisis that had plagued the royal palace? What about the pathetic condition of the royal coffers? Actually, I too possessed enough wealth now to help the royal palace. But if I did that, it would weaken my own financial position, and with that, my long-term goal of becoming wealthier and more powerful than Satrajit would remain a pipe dream, whereas my main goal was to win over the Yadavas and foil Satrajit's evil designs. Did you see how Nature would invariably hurl one trouble after another in my path? It had only been a day since I had arrived in Mathura. I had thought that, this time, I would enjoy my days in peace since neither did I have to deal with the menace called Jarasandha, nor did I have a shortage of wealth and honour. In fact, I had even thought that I would now carve out time to visit Vrindavan and bring everyone along for a tour of Mathura. But I had forgotten that Nature would just not let me be at peace. Bah! I did not care! Nature could throw as many hurdles in my path as it wished. As for me, I could discern a positive aspect in this bleak scenario as well. I had learnt today that if one possessed wealth, one could verily become a king like Satrajit. Meaning, it was not necessary to have a royal lineage in order to become a king. And if this was true, it meant that my beloved Rukmini was just a few steps away from stepping into my life. Now, tell me, what better news could I hope for than this?

As soon as this thought took root in my mind, I became lost in weaving dreams of owning a kingdom of my own…but that in turn gave birth to fresh anxiety. We no doubt possessed a good amount of wealth now, but it did not seem enough to establish a kingdom of our own. So then, how will I acquire this additional wealth? Neither did we have a permanent, income-generating business, nor did we have a gem like the Syamantaka, which could magically conjure a heap of gold every day. Whatever wealth we had was given to us in recognition of my valourous deeds. Meaning, even today, it was one thing to weave grand dreams, but to turn these dreams into reality was a huge challenge. So, I wisely set myself free from these worries for the present. Setting up a kingdom and gaining wealth was a matter that pertained to the future, and the future has never been under anyone's control. At present, I could only worry about Satrajit and the problems created by him. So, it was better to focus on the problem looming before us in the present. In any case, the future is not carved from thinking, planning or dreaming about it; it is the present that shapes the future. And the present was crystal clear—if Satrajit succeeded in his political plans, then forget about establishing our own kingdom, we would not be able to find refuge in any other kingdom either. So, I snapped out of my reverie and determinedly busied myself with the tasks ahead. Indeed, what choice did I have? Not only my dreams, but even my life now depended on the outcome of this new struggle.

And this fresh struggle, if seen from a different perspective, was vastly different from all the previous ones I had encountered. This time, neither did I have to fight Satrajit nor kill him. I simply needed to make a better impression on the Yadavas than the one he had created. And as far as the Yadavas were concerned, it was clear that given the condition in which we had left Mathura and the valorous feats we had achieved thereafter, our influence had already increased many times over. Chasing Jarasandha off had established the fact that we were valorous, and whatever else was lacking could be accomplished by announcing that we were now wealthy. Why just the Yadavas, the entire world bows down before wealth and power! The fact was, Satrajit could not compete with us as far as power was concerned; and as for his wealth, well, we too had become quite affluent now. Ah! We are back to where we had started. Meaning, whatever was in the interest of Mathura was in our interest too. Just as it was in Mathura's as well as my interest that power remained in the hands of grandfather, it was in both our interests that I remained wealthy and powerful. Is it not said that in the benefit of everyone lies one's own benefit? For that matter, how could the two be different from each other? After all, 'we' too are a part of 'all'. Consider my example: I have always risen above selfish interest and thought of the larger interest, whether it was killing the serpent, Kaaliya or vanquishing the demon, Keshi; whether it was stopping the worship of Indra or starting the practice of worshipping the Govardhana Mountain. All of this was in the interest of Vrindavan. There was not even a hint of self-interest in any of these actions of mine. And just see, all these actions not only benefitted Vrindavan, but also laid the foundation of my becoming valorous, establishing my reputation as a brave warrior across the entire span of Aryavarta. Similarly, whether it was the elimination of Panchajanya or Shringlava, what selfish interest did I have in slaying them? On the contrary, I had risked my life while executing both these deeds, but in the end, they both led to us acquiring immense wealth. What I mean to say is, if I had focused only on my self-interest, I would probably still be playing hide-and-seek and tag with the cowherd boys in Vrindavan. So, why don't you too rise above your self-interest and start thinking in the interest of all?

Well, what you do is up to you; for now, let me move ahead with my story. Since the past several years, I had anyway been nurturing the desire to become wealthy; moreover, amassing wealth was extremely important for attaining the love of my life, Rukmini, too. Fortunately, there were clear signs that Nature too was willing to grant me my desire. This was because what was earlier only in my interest or that of my love, was now in the interest of Mathura too. And when self-interest aligns with the greater good, it is, without a doubt, Nature's will. And now that my self-interest was aligned with the greater good, there was no reason to waste any time. My mind immediately engaged itself in an undeclared confrontation with Satrajit. And the first thought that occurred to me was, if I was anathema to Satrajit, it meant that he was certainly displeased with my valorous deeds, such as my recent routing of Jarasandha's army and my killing of Shringlava. Hence, I reckoned, why not launch a formal battle against him by provoking him to react to my recent heroics? In any case, to defeat an opponent, it is important to get to know him well, especially for people like me who fought strategic battles.

Thinking on these lines, one day, for no apparent reason, I hopped onto my chariot and steered it in the direction of Satrajit's mansion. Even otherwise, under normal circumstances, the two ends of the earth do not meet easily; one of the two invariably has to take the initiative and make the first move. So, I thought, I might as well go and give it a try. Even from a distance,

Satrajit's mansion resembled a royal palace, and for a moment, I was stunned by its opulence. But my surprise did not end here, for, as soon as the door to the mansion was opened, I was met with another surprise...albeit a rather pleasant one. The door was opened by a beautiful maiden who was about thirteen years old. I certainly did not expect to receive such a beautiful welcome at my enemy's door! Actually, she was Satrajit's daughter, Satyabhama. She was stunningly beautiful, exuding calm and dignity, yet there was a playful, vivacious spark in her demeanour. Let me not lie; compelled by my romantic nature, I could not help but be bowled over by her. To impress her, I instantly turned on my enigmatic charm and introduced myself, flashing my most magical smile. Surprisingly, even now, I was standing on the threshold, while she stood inside, holding the door open. What came as a bigger surprise was that when she realised who I was, a flurry of expressions swept across her attractive face. I was astonished, for, this meant that she had heard about me. But even more surprisingly, in her effusiveness and excitement, she took me straight to the meeting chamber. I followed her, admiring the grace with which she walked. And when my gaze moved away from her, I could not help but admire the interior of the mansion, which also mirrored a grand palace. Every object reflected opulence; in fact, the luxurious interiors made me realise that no matter how much I praised myself, there was still a gaping difference between Satrajit and me as far as wealth was concerned. Funnily enough, Satyabhama was as astonished to see me as I was in taking in the splendour of the mansion. But soon, she composed herself and in a calm and refined manner, offered me a seat. Thereafter, she served me a cool, refreshing drink made from rose petals, which I relished with great pleasure. Soon after she served me, she sat down on a seat opposite to me, with her legs crossed. Out of sheer habit, even while sipping the sherbet, I could not resist looking up and stealing glances at her. Well, she was no less; she kept gazing at me intently. We exchanged these furtive gazes for quite some time. Finally, it was Satyabhama who broke the silence. In a soft, demure voice, she said, "I have heard a lot about your valorous deeds. I always imagined you as a middle-aged man, but I'm quite surprised how you managed to accomplish all those extraordinary feats at such a young age! To be honest, I am in awe of you."

Listening to her soft, lilting voice as she spoke, I too found myself being impressed with her. There was demureness as well as confidence in the manner in which she spoke. Interestingly, Satyabhama was about ten years younger than me, and her demeanour made it evident that her condition was quite similar to the plight I was in when I had first seen Radha. The only difference was, Radha was much older than me, and I was much older than Satyabhama. So what? The roles had changed, but the story was the same. In the current situation, Satyabhama had stepped into Krishna's shoes, while I was playing the role of Radha. After chatting for a while, Satyabhama enquired the reason behind my visit. Oh! I was so stupefied by her beauty that I had all but forgotten the reason why I had visited the mansion. I had even forgotten Satrajit, mesmerised by his beautiful daughter. The voice within chided, 'O Krishna! Learn to behave yourself. Be serious for once!' But why should I be serious? Tell me, is there a greater curse than to be serious and solemn in this world? Can there be a greater boon for a human being than pure, unbridled joy? Actually, our heart is like an exotic garden, one that we must adorn with the flowers of joy whenever the opportunity arises. The truth is, to lead a dull, drab life, devoid of pleasure, is the biggest disgrace to human existence. Consider me for instance; I would make the most of even the smallest moments of joy offered by life. Actually, no one could surpass me in terms of seizing every opportunity to celebrate life. No matter the life one leads, it is necessary to savour every chance one gets to live fully. This especially holds true for someone like me, whose life was an unending series of strife, struggle and pain, with fleeting moments of peace and pleasure. If I were to let even those precious moments slip away, what would be left to live for?

Well, in the midst of these musings, I became aware that Satyabhama was still waiting to know the reason behind my visit. So, as soon as my thought process ended, I disclosed the reason saying, "I have come to meet your father, Satrajit."

"But he is not at home," she replied.

"Oh! Well, it does not matter. I can come later," I replied. "I had no particular business with him; I had simply come to offer a courtesy visit."

After this brief exchange of words, there was a momentary lull in our conversation, but from Satyabhama's conduct, it was obvious that she was as captivated on seeing me as I had been on seeing Radha. Yet, there was a fundamental difference between the two situations. I had lost control over myself upon seeing Radha, whereas Satyabhama appeared in complete charge of her emotions. Perhaps, this was the difference between a blundering cowherd boy and a sophisticated city girl. That is why when I got up to leave, she spoke in a calm tone, "Very well! Do visit us again."

The manner in which she spoke stopped me midway for a moment, and I could not help but turn my head and flash her a smile, before proceeding towards the door. Now, I wonder what spell this act of mine cast on her that she not only came to see me off till the door, but she even stood there for a long time, gazing at me till my chariot was well out of sight. This was my first, short and sweet encounter with Satyabhama, but a memorable meeting nonetheless. Oh well! Let me now turn my attention to Satrajit, who had already begun his campaign against me, and now, with my memorable meeting with Satyabhama, I too had shown my readiness. Now, I was waiting for his reaction.

Satrajit, however, turned out to be a seasoned player. Even after a week had passed, there was complete silence from his side; not even once did he try to enquire about the purpose of my visit. But yes, after my visit, he had certainly intensified his political attacks on me and the royal palace. In turn, I too had begun playing my own strange manoeuvres against him, under the aegis of the palace. Needless to say, within a month, this undeclared battle between Satrajit and me had created a tense atmosphere in Mathura. While most of the Yadava elite and Yadava leaders sided with Satrajit, it was I who remained dearer to the *Mathurawasis*. As a result, this tug-of-war promised to be quite entertaining.

However, this new activity I was involved in had a downside to it—it had upset my daily routine. Nonetheless, I would unfailingly go for a morning walk every day and later head to the palace to partake in grandfather's sorrows. The rest of the time, I would wander on my own. Poor Uddhava would occasionally accompany me, or sometimes, it would be bhaiya. As for my dear brother, he lived in a world of his own, unmindful and unconcerned about the prevailing situation in Mathura. Contrary to him, Uddhava would try to understand the situation after listening to the discussions between grandfather and me. Seeing his receptiveness regarding these matters, I would sometimes discuss this issue with him too. And yes, whenever I got the chance, I would go over to Malini's house to spend a few moments of peace in her company. However, even amidst all these activities, my mind remained preoccupied with Satrajit. And the only conclusion I could draw after much deliberation was that Satrajit held sway over the Yadavas only on the strength of the Syamantaka gem. The truth of the matter was that he himself had no significant part to play in his meteoric rise. He had not earned it, but had acquired it by sheer chance. It was definitely not the fruits of his own labour which warranted such respect and honour. As soon as this thought crossed my mind, a thousand questions arose concerning the rightful ownership of the Syamantaka gem. In short, after thinking over it for a while, I couldn't come to terms with the idea that Satrajit had the sole right to this gem. Just as no one could stake a claim over the sun, moon, air, rivers and mountains, no one could claim their sole right to the Syamantaka gem either, because the gem was also a gift of Nature. This logic was crystal clear in my mind. Just as all the inhabitants of Mathura had an equal right to the River Yamuna, they should have an equal right to the Syamantaka gem as well. And this could happen only if the gem was officially declared as the kingdom's property.

To sum it up, these days, my contemplation had picked the right direction on its own. For, if the thread of my reasoning was accepted and could be put into action, all of Mathura's problems would be solved in no time. Firstly, this would improve the pitiable state of the royal treasury overnight. Secondly, although it would take time for me to match Satrajit's affluence and power, this single move could diminish his status drastically. Once the gem was prised away from him, he would instantly lose his status. After all, his influence over the Yadavas was not due to his own power or nature; it was solely due to the Syamantaka gem. Thus, if the gem was taken away from him, who would even spare him a second glance? And once he was booted out, the Yadavas would remain under my influence only. In short, with a single arrow shot from my bow, I could take down several targets. In other words, I had to use this arrow, come what may! But how would I do it? Prising the gem away from Satrajit was like extricating his soul out of his body. Well, so what? When the task was aligned with the greater good, a way to carry it out would inevitably be found. Thus, deep within, I was becoming increasingly determined to somehow wrest the gem from Satrajit's hands.

Determination had always been my forte, but finding a solution to this problem was not as easy as it sounded. Thus, my visits to the banks of River Yamuna and immersing myself in playing the flute had become more frequent. Indulging in this activity was harmless, but due to the repeated visits to the Yamuna, a desire to live close to the river took root in my heart. Well, this was a great wish indeed, and now that we had a sufficient amount of wealth, I reckoned, why not live fully and enjoy freely? Life, after all, is not just about struggling and toiling hard—naturally, pleasure, joy, rest and recreation are its primary needs. With this thought in mind, I decided to build a house on the banks of River Yamuna. The decision was a propitious one and I felt good about it...but that's when a new problem surfaced. My dear friend, Uddhava was no longer enjoying his stay in Mathura. He would repeatedly badger bhaiya and me to return to Vrindavan. Well, I wanted to go to Vrindavan too, but not half-heartedly. But how do I solve Uddhava's problem? So, I patiently sat him down and apprised him of Satrajit's evil designs and the sad state of affairs at the royal palace. I explained to him that if I left Mathura, Satrajit's accomplices would tighten their grip on the palace. I also told him that Satrajit's burgeoning influence over the palace did not bode well for the future of Mathura. Besides, it wasn't right to leave grandfather alone in such troubling circumstances. Moreover, it did not portend well for my future either. Finally, in order to convince Uddhava and to reassure the *Vrindavanwasis*, I decided to send both bhaiya and Uddhava to Vrindavan. This, I was sure, would enrage the *gopis*, for, they would naturally question that if Balarama could return, why not Krishna? Perhaps, this would even reinforce my image as a trickster and a selfish person, but you know very well that I scarcely bothered about such attacks, accusations or complaints. So, I quickly apprised bhaiya and Uddhava of my decision. Needless to say, both of them jumped for joy on hearing it and hastened to make preparations. As for me, I took solace in the thought that they would bring me news about everyone in Vrindavan, and at the same time, tell them about my great, valorous deeds…yes, yes, especially to Radha.

But then, something truly extraordinary happened! As soon as they busied themselves in packing their things, I was lost in thoughts of Vrindavan. In fact, I even imagined everyone's reactions to my valorous deeds. Radha… she could barely contain her pride when she heard about her Kanhaiya's exploits. As for my parents, the *gopas* and the *gopis,* they were all dancing with joy on hearing about my feats. Yet, beneath their cheerfulness, a sense of sadness lingered, reminding them of my absence. However, Uddhava was trying his best to explain my helplessness to them. While everyone else was satisfied with the explanation, Radha and the *gopis* refused to listen to any reason whatsoever. Poor Uddhava! I burst out laughing on imagining his condition…and that shattered my beautiful dream, jolting me back to reality. Once again, I found myself in Mathura with Uddhava and bhaiya standing before me, ready to depart for Vrindavan. Well, so be it. For now, they had said their goodbyes and left, and no sooner did they leave than my mind was lost in thinking about Uddhava. At present, he was the only bridge between Vrindavan and me. Did you see how the very thought of Vrindavan thrilled me to the core? Oh, how my heart wished that I could once again roam barefoot on the quaint streets of Vrindavan, the winding pathways, the banks of River Yamuna, the Govardhana Mountain and so many other places where I had spent my time. But every single wish is not destined to find fulfilment. After all, time, place and circumstances do play a major role in it. Well, I comforted myself in this manner, but thoughts of Vrindavan refused to let go of me. Indeed, Uddhava was highly fortunate that he could travel to Vrindavan whenever he wanted and return to Mathura whenever he wished. These thoughts were flitting through my mind, because this time, I was truly yearning to visit Vrindavan. Honestly, I had never felt such a deep longing to go there before. If it were up to me, I would race to Vrindavan at once, taking scores of chariots teeming with gifts for everyone. I would show them their Kanhaiya's current status and leave a lasting impression. Perhaps, this intense desire to go was driven by a need to flaunt my grandeur. But whatever the reason may be, the reality was, I couldn't go to Vrindavan.

You won't believe this, but after Uddhava and bhaiya's departure, the memories of Vrindavan started tormenting me so much that I began to cherish solitude. Every day, I would sit by the banks of the Yamuna, gazing for hours at our house which was under construction; and as soon as I found a moment of solitude, I would start playing my flute. But oh, how long could this last? I soon overcame this sadness too, but the memories of Vrindavan still lingered around me. In fact, a sense of curiosity had now replaced the pangs of sorrow, with me yearning to know how Radha and Mother Yashoda were as well as their actual reaction to my heroic feats. As you know, Radha's reaction mattered to me greatly, for, it was her love that had turned me into a valorous hero. Whatever I was today, was only because of her. So, it was only natural that I was keen to know her reaction. And this eagerness led me to feel a different kind of impatience—my mind was now awaiting the return of bhaiya and Uddhava. Fortunately, around the same time, another wait came to an end. The house being built on the banks of River Yamuna was finally ready. It had a lovely garden right next to the river—truly, an outstanding feature—as the soothing sounds of the flowing river would bring peace to my heart. Set against such a beautiful backdrop, with the river flowing by its side, this was truly the house of my dreams.

And now, to take my happiness several notches higher, bhaiya had returned from Vrindavan. However, Uddhava had not returned with him. No matter, I could wait a little longer to know the reactions of the inhabitants of Vrindavan, especially the *gopis*. I had to wait because I could not ask bhaiya about the *gopis'* reaction, could I? But yes, I was definitely glad to hear that my parents were well. So, relegating Vrindavan to the back of my mind, I lost myself in enjoying our riverside house. Every evening, bhaiya and I would go to the house, and while I would lose myself in the sweet melody of my flute, bhaiya would busy himself with sipping wine. On several occasions, we even spent the night there. Once we took residence in this house, our mundane and drab existence in Mathura suddenly sprang to life. Really, I felt proud of my decision to build this house. Many times, father and mother visited us too. I even had the privilege of welcoming grandfather in this house a couple of times. Now, although we were having fun here, it did not mean that the looming threat of Satrajit had been averted. He did not seem inclined to stop his machinations and political manoeuvrings, creating ever-new problems for the royal palace. Well, how did it matter? I may have been engrossed in fun and frolic, but I too had hatched a plan to effectively silence him. Now, I was simply waiting for the right moment to strike!

Chapter 9

My First-Ever Meeting with the Pandavas

Time moved at its own pace, as I patiently waited for the right moment to strike at Satrajit. But do things ever transpire as per one's wishes? Before I could trap him in a tight spot, I was caught up in another task. No, not a dangerous task; on the contrary, it turned out to be one of life's unexpected joys. It so happened that just a few days after Uddhava had departed for Vrindavan, my aunt, Kunti from Hastinapur came to visit father, accompanied by her five sons, the Pandavas. They were all the same age as me. Now, since bhaiya and I had guests at home, and more importantly, boys of our age, I was obviously thrilled. You know well that I, in particular, was quite fond of striking up friendships with people my age. And ever since I had left Vrindavan, I had been yearning to enjoy the company of friends, for, I had not been able to make even a single close friend in Mathura. Here, it was only grandfather who was my friend, mentor and guide. Yes, at the *ashram*, I had surely enjoyed the company of friends, but only for a short while. Honestly speaking, friendship was as important to me as love; it was perhaps for this very reason that I missed Vrindavan time and again. Thus, with the arrival of these five brothers, I felt my life infused with vibrancy all of a sudden. All five of them appeared very refined, educated and talented. And with such friends around, tell me, why would I even bother myself with the likes of Satrajit?

Well, let me give you an introduction of these new friends. The eldest was Yudhishthira, who seemed reserved and serious. He was about four to five years older than me. The second was Bhima, a muscular and incredibly strong man. The third was Arjuna, roughly my age, with a bow slung over his shoulder. And finally, Sahadeva and Nakula, both of whom were younger than me and quite intelligent and poised. After just a day or two, we had forged a close bond with each other. Actually, most of the conversations were taking place between Bhima, Arjuna and me; the others would just respond in monosyllables of 'yes' or 'no'. Nevertheless, in just a few days, we had all become close friends. We were of course cousins, but since we were all of a similar age, naturally, we became good friends too. This was all fine but I noticed one thing which was proving to be a hindrance in our fun. Because of the presence of the elders in the house, we, and especially bhaiya, was unable to fully enjoy the company of our new friends. I had already started getting along well with the Pandavas, but bhaiya was finding it difficult to strike a rapport with them. He obviously liked their company, but he enjoyed his glass of wine even more! This was the only reason why he would keep to himself most of the time. It was only because the Pandavas had come to visit father that bhaiya was forced to stay at home, else he would have been staying at the royal palace, and yes, the reason was apparent—he could indulge in drinking without inhibition. Thus, to resolve bhaiya's problem and to make the most of the company of our new friends, I took all of them to stay at our house on the banks of River Yamuna. Presently, there was no dearth of servants and neither did we lack chariots. Come to think of it, it was only now that the chariots and servants gifted to us by Queen Padmavati were utilised well.

So, loading our luggage in five chariots, we set off for our riverside home. But when we arrived with our caravan of servants, soldiers and chariots, we realised that the house was actually small and ill-equipped in terms of amenities. We had never imagined we would stay here for a sleepover with friends. The house consisted of two spaces: one was a large chamber and the other was a small veranda with two swings facing the garden. But well, what difference did it make? The freedom we had here was much more desirable than a few creature comforts. Needless to say, bhaiya was thrilled with the decision of coming to the riverside home. By evening, he had even arranged for the wine. Now, there was no point in waiting! As soon as evening set in, we settled down in the garden, with the soft grass beneath us serving as a cushion. Indeed, when one is in the company of friends, what difference does it make whether one sits on the ground or on a luxurious settee? Besides, with the Yamuna flowing right past the garden, we could hear its gurgling sounds, carried forth on the breeze, making the surroundings cool and pleasant as we relaxed and chatted to our heart's content. Indeed, there could not have been a better place than this to spend time with friends. But the mood really caught on when, on a signal from bhaiya, the servants began to serve us wine. Seeing the pitchers of wine, even Bhima and Arjuna's faces lit up; from their countenance, I could clearly see that the two brothers were also quite fond of their drink. In contrast, Yudhishthira, Nakula, Sahadeva were content with taking just a sip every now and then. This was all fine, but interestingly, as soon as the food was served, Bhima quit drinking, while Arjuna and bhaiya continued to drink, taking a sip or two along with their food; in fact, they continued to drink even after having partaken their meal. To my great delight, after consuming a few glasses of wine, bhaiya had found his voice and was now interested in the conversation. Earlier, I was the only one leading the conversation, but now bhaiya, Bhima and Arjuna had also taken equal charge. Obviously, the credit for this went more to the wine than to them. But yes, Yudhishthira, Nakula and Sahadeva had been quiet since the beginning and continued to remain silent even now. All in all, though some were reserved and others talkative, everyone was thoroughly enjoying themselves on this evening.

Really, as long as one feels free, it makes no difference whether one is in a palace or a modest hut. After all, what is joy? It is just another name for the unfettered flights of the mind; and naturally, discipline and rules impede

such flights of freedom. And just see, once we tasted this freedom, we started enjoying ourselves so much that the cheerful atmosphere lasted well into the night, even after dinner. Amidst this mood of light-hearted banter, I do not know what thought suddenly struck Arjuna that he gave the conversation a serious turn by addressing me directly. He said, "You are truly a great hero, having slain powerful kings like Kansa, Panchajanya and Shringlava."

I responded by saying, "Well, none of you appear any less heroic to me."

Now, I had just said a simple thing, but on hearing me, Bhima boiled over with anger. In a loud pitch, he began, "What heroism are you talking about? The whole world knows we're cousins to the Kauravas. We're princes too, yet we—*we*—are the true heirs to the throne of Hastinapur. But look at us, we are nothing more than dependents in our own kingdom!"

When I heard this, I was taken by surprise and asked, "Why is that?"

And what surprised me more was Yudhishthira silencing Bhima before he could continue. Frankly speaking, I did not like Yudhishthira silencing Bhima in this manner, for, this meant that he was still considering bhaiya and me as outsiders. For that matter, Arjuna had already told us a lot about Yudhishthira's nature, and I had especially become uneasy hearing about his rigidity. In any case, I was always suspicious of people who were strict about adhering to ethics and principles; it is a proven fact that they are never close or loyal to anyone. Besides, I disliked moral codes and principles anyway, thus it did not seem likely that I would get along well with Yudhishthira. So, I did not encourage this topic further and the matter ended there. It was anyway time for us to retire to bed and sleep had announced its presence too. Thus, this beautiful session concluded for the day. Arjuna and I slept in the veranda; I liked sleeping in the open anyway. Bhaiya and Bhima slept in one of the bedchambers, while Yudhishthira, Nakula and Sahadeva slept in the other. So, although the house was small, it had accommodated all of us comfortably.

From the very next day, our fun and frolic took on a whole new level, quickly turning into a daily routine. We would wake up in the morning and first make a dash for the Yamuna for a refreshing bath. After an invigorating bath, we would perform our daily exercises and then go out for a leisurely stroll. Later, with the sun shining bright overhead, we would head to the marketplaces of Mathura and relish a variety of savouries. Here, I must mention that Bhima's prodigious appetite had impressed me no end. He ate as much as all of us combined! Bhaiya, Arjuna and I had healthy appetites too, but they paled in comparison to Bhima's. That's not all! Bhima also seemed to be the most simple-minded and straightforward among all the Pandava brothers, whereas Arjuna's oratory skills were far more superior to the rest of them. As for Yudhishthira, he and I had almost nothing in common. In fact, even gauging from the manner in which he ate, it seemed as if he was doing us a favour by eating! I wonder if these purist types are the ones who eventually become egoistic…or is it that the egoists themselves are purists!

Well, for now, let me talk about our fun-filled days a little more. One day, while we were casually lounging in the garden, Bhima started bragging about his valour in a good-natured manner. Bhima, bhaiya, Nakula and Sahadeva were seated on the grass, while Arjuna and I had taken a seat on the swing. Seeing us, Yudhishthira occupied the other swing and made himself comfortable. Honestly, the mood at present seemed even more cheerful than what it had been the previous day. Bhima seemed a bit too chirpy, for, without any prompting or provocation, he was boasting about his prowess with the mace and narrating slightly exaggerated tales of his heroism. We did not mind this, but bhaiya could not tolerate these tall tales for long. Firstly, like Bhima, he too was adept with the mace; besides, you are well acquainted with bhaiya's ego. So, how long could he have tolerated such boastful stories? As a result, he jumped into the fray to give vent to his irritation. Needless to say, the argument turned intense and the accompanying wine only made it worse. We, of course, did not intervene; on the contrary, we were enjoying the heated debate. However, there was a fundamental difference in the manner in which the two were speaking. While Bhima still spoke naturally, bhaiya's words were tainted with ego. It was indeed this simplicity of Bhima that instantly won me over and made me his fan. However, coming back to the present situation, the discussion had taken such an interesting turn that both were trying to recollect incidents of their valour and narrate them with great passion. It was then that all of a sudden bhaiya lost his patience and challenged Bhima to a fight. Bhima was only too glad to accept the challenge. And once it was decided that they would demonstrate their prowess, why would they wait even a moment longer? Both sprang to their feet, ready to engage in a duel. The rest of us were merely spectators, and you know that it is the spectators who enjoy themselves the most in such situations. However, this new development had a flip side to it as well. Actually, it was now time for dinner. Our stomachs were growling with hunger, and honestly, if this friendly tussle had not erupted, dinner would have already been served. But how did it matter, the spectacle before us was far too interesting and enjoyable to heed the voice of our poor stomach!

So, this tinge of resentment was only momentary. While I was lost in thinking about food, the duo had already stepped out, clad in loincloth, maces in hand. Naturally, the fight was to take place in the garden. Seeing that the mood was set, we too jumped off our swings and settled ourselves in the adjoining veranda. Surprisingly, Bhima and bhaiya's enthusiasm in displaying their valour was so high that we had not even managed to fold our knees and sit comfortably, and the fight had already begun. I cannot tell you how thrilling the scene was! On one hand, the cool weather had made the atmosphere quite pleasant, and on the other, the flowing Yamuna was adding to the beauty. And in this idyllic location between the Yamuna and us, the glorious duel with the mace had begun. We were all enjoying ourselves thoroughly. The warriors were evenly matched and the fight was proceeding well. The mood was such that whenever either of them made a good move, we cheered for them. The duel, however, showed no signs of ending anytime soon and neither could we see a clear winner. Well, regardless of the outcome, the fight surely brought one benefit in its wake—bhaiya and Bhima became good friends by the end of it. This was the second time in my life that I had the privilege of watching an excellent duel with the mace. You might recall that earlier, I had the good fortune of watching a mace-fight between bhaiya and Jarasandha as well. Actually, bhaiya's adeptness and agility were both marginally better than Bhima's. At any rate, I had always been proud of bhaiya's skills and his unbridled courage. For now, more importantly, since the two opponents had become good friends, the enjoyment was bound to increase too; and the biggest proof of this was that after the fight had ended, everyone gorged on the food, eating to their heart's delight.

Needless to say, the next day was filled with even more fun and laughter. All day long, we rode our chariots around Mathura and feasted on delicious food from numerous shops in the marketplace. By evening, we had stuffed ourselves so much that we had to look for ways to digest the massive quantity of food we had wolfed down. And the only recourse we could see was to take a dip in the Yamuna and swim vigorously. We also played a variety of water sports, challenging and competing with each other, all the while splashing water and making merry. Oh, what great fun it was! You won't believe it, but it was only after this that we were able to return to our normal selves as decent human beings, and by the time that happened, the sun had melted away giving way to dusk. Once the sky darkened, bhaiya and Arjuna commenced their drinking session. It was the same assembly, the same garden, and the same conversation, revolving around the mace-fight from the day before. Everyone praised the impressive duel between bhaiya and Bhima. Everything was fine for a while, but when the litany of praises refused to abate, it pricked Arjuna's ego. Consequently, he too started narrating his deeds of valour. He told us that not only was he an expert archer, but he could also hit a target without seeing, even in pitch-black darkness. This bit of information stunned both bhaiya and me. Actually, neither of us had any

knowledge of archery and when Arjuna described his skill in glowing terms, we couldn't help but be impressed. Seeing that he had made an impression on us, Arjuna's ego was satiated and he stopped blowing his own trumpet.

The drinking session was nearing its end, and the servants had already begun to serve us the meal. The mood was such that everyone had sat down for dinner in the veranda itself. All of us were so famished that we began gorging on the food as soon as we were served. But then all of a sudden, a strong gust of wind blew out the torches, throwing us all in complete darkness. Everyone automatically stopped eating, and I promptly ordered the servants to light up the torches again. However, because of this impediment, we gluttons were briefly in a pitiable state. The food was spread out in front of us, its aroma gently wafting around us, yet we could not eat. This was no doubt a unique predicament. But it was then that I realised that not only were there clinking sounds near me, but I could also distinctly hear someone busily munching on food. I was surprised; Bhima had not stopped eating even in total darkness! We considered ourselves to be big gluttons, but Bhima had proved us wrong. Funnily, this also turned into an opportunity to crack a brilliant joke. Seeing Bhima wolfing down the food in this manner, Arjuna reprimanded him saying, "Brother Bhima, can you even see the food in this pitch-black darkness, or are you just eating whatever comes into your hand?"

To this, Bhima laughed and replied, "Absolutely! No matter how dark it is, I never lose sight of my food. Tell me, brother, what is the use of learning to hit an arrow in the dark? Instead, had you learnt to take an aim at your food even in the dark, you would not be sitting hungry now!"

Hearing this brilliant jibe, everyone burst out laughing. Oh, we were all having such a lovely time! All in all, with the arrival of the Pandava brothers, it felt as though time was flying by. However, having stayed with these five brothers for the past so many days, I had observed that all of them greatly respected Yudhishthira and paid heed to him without exception. Just a signal from him or a nod of his head was a command for them. Truth be told, this perturbed me deeply. Gauging from the manner in which they obeyed Yudhishthira's orders, I could foresee a dark and dreary future for them. But I let the thought pass, realising I was thinking too far ahead for no reason. Instead, let me talk of the fun and frolic we were indulging in presently. One evening, as we were lounging around in the garden, our casual conversation drifted towards the subject of education. The Pandavas narrated some interesting anecdotes from their days spent at *Acharya* Drona's *ashram*. You know very well that just like the memories of Vrindavan, the days I had spent at the *ashram* had also become etched in my memory. Thus, naturally, when they narrated the anecdotes about their *ashram,* I found them quite interesting. Indeed, I was listening to their tales with rapt attention. Seeing my eyes light up with interest, Arjuna enquired about our education. We too had anecdotes, but compared to their bright and sparkling ones, ours did not seem as fascinating. Nonetheless, since Arjuna had asked, I had to say something to him. So, I replied casually, "Unfortunately, Nature did not permit us too many opportunities to be formally educated and so the knowledge we have gleaned has been culled from the school of life. But yes, after the age for education was well past, we did spend six months in the *ashram* of the great *Acharya* Sandipani in Ujjaini. And it was our good fortune that *Acharya* Sandipani did not behave like *Acharya* Drona who, without imparting any education, had asked for Eklavya's thumb as *gurudakshina*."

My story concluded here, but I do not know why my sarcastic comment about *Acharya* Drona did not go down well with Arjuna. It surprised me that he could not tolerate a word against his teacher, even when the latter was in the wrong. All of a sudden, the atmosphere became serious. Thus, in a bid to change the subject, I quickly added, "Oh yes, I just remembered! In my childhood, I had also received training in music from *Acharya* Shrutiketu. He was the one who taught me how to play the flute."

On this, Bhima piped up, "Play the flute for us then. How are we supposed to believe that you can actually play the flute?"

Hearing this, everyone erupted in laughter. Naturally, this comment of his lightened the mood once again. But for some reason, this time, Yudhishthira did not seem to approve of Bhima's remark. He instantly reprimanded Bhima saying, "That's not the way to speak; think twice before you open your mouth!"

Hearing Yudhishthira admonish Bhima for a harmless joke, I was rankled. Nevertheless, I brushed the feeling aside, for, everything about Yudhishthira was beyond my understanding. So, ignoring him, I complied with Bhima's request and mesmerised everyone, coaxing a beautiful melody from my flute. Bhima was delighted with my music and, in his enthusiasm, spontaneously declared, "Kanhaiya, my friend, you seem to be an exceptional artist!"

Hearing the word 'artist', bhaiya pounced on it, for, surely, he was not about to let such an opportunity slip by! With measured sarcasm, he spoke, "Ah, my friend, our Kanhaiya is endowed with many other artistic talents as well. If you want to acquaint yourself with the various talents of this 'artist', take him with you to Hastinapur!"

Hearing this, everyone burst out laughing except Bhima, who surprisingly wore a puzzled look on his face. I looked at him with quizzical eyes, but soon my confusion was cleared; when the laughter subsided, Bhima

enquired very innocently, "What other talents do you have, Kanhaiya?" That is when I realised that the innocent Bhima had taken even a joke seriously. This was alright, but Bhima's innocence had allowed bhaiya to seize the opportunity once again. It was as if he had just been waiting for the chance to rib me. And my brother was not about to let me off the hook so easily. He said, "Ah! Do you not know? Our dear Kanhaiya is an expert at spinning webs!"

I actually heaved a sigh of relief, for, the Pandava brothers failed to catch bhaiya's jibe. As a result, the matter lost its steam and soon, we became busy chatting about other things. That was when Arjuna brought up a peculiar question, posing it to me in a serious tone, "What other interests do you have, Kanhaiya?"

I blurted out, "My sole interest is in destroying sinners while working towards my own progress."

Although I had spoken these words, I was momentarily puzzled too, for, even I had not understood what I had just uttered. But Bhima was quite impressed with my answer and instantly said, "Then, you are a very useful person to know, Kanhaiya. For, even in Hastinapur, we have two big sinners, Duryodhana and Dushasana. Why don't you come along with us and destroy them as well? We will be rid of the evil plaguing our lives, and you too will have notched up two more evil-doers on your list."

Hearing Bhima speak thus, Yudhishthira's brow creased with a frown and he rebuked him saying, "Brother, have you taken an oath to always speak without thinking?"

This time, I lost my patience. After all, how long could I tolerate Yudhishthira's unwarranted and unnecessary nitpicking? So, I replied to Yudhishthira sharply, "Bhima has not said anything wrong!"

Naturally, Yudhishthira did not like what I said, nor did he approve of the manner in which I had spoken. He thus became red with rage. Seeing the matter take a dangerous turn, Arjuna jumped into the fray. Trying to defuse the situation, the poor boy said, "Actually, our brother is upset because both Duryodhana and Dushasana are our cousins."

But this inane explanation by Arjuna made me even more furious. In a loud voice, I retorted, "A sinner…is a sinner! He is a curse upon this earth, no matter the circumstances. How can a sinner be considered kith and kin? Kansa too was my uncle, and you are well aware that he was the first person I slayed!"

Bhima fully subscribed to my argument. In a happy voice, he said, "That is exactly what I have been telling them since we were children!"

Hearing this, Yudhishthira's face fell. He did not say anything, but his expression spoke volumes. Bhima's open endorsement of all that I said was too much for his wounded ego to bear. Regardless, I had said what I had to say, and before the situation could deteriorate further, I laughed the matter off. I surely did not want to pick a fight, and so the matter ended with me jesting and fooling around for some time; and on this joyous note, the evening session came to an end.

Truly, life had become much more enjoyable with the arrival of these five brothers. The days were flying by so fast that even if my entire life had flitted by in spending time with them, I perhaps wouldn't have realised it! Really, I was enjoying myself to the core! Interestingly, there was not a single game or sport which we hadn't played. Throwing a ball in the waters of the Yamuna and then jumping in to retrieve it was my favourite game. Being an expert swimmer, I was always the first to grab the ball. Besides, you are well aware of how much I loved winning ever since I was a child. Thus, it was only natural for me to take a liking to this game. For that matter, there were many other games too wherein no one could beat me. It was I who would always win at chariot-racing too. Also, no one could hit a target with a stone better than me. That was perhaps because I was a skilled marksman when it came to aiming with my discus. But yes, there were a few games in which my skills were extremely lacking such as throwing a heavy stone as far as possible and matches of wrestling. Actually, it was only bhaiya and Bhima who would compete in these games. The rest of us were mere spectators, enjoying the games to the fullest. In fact, you will not believe it, but we even ended up playing really childish games such as chase and hide-and-seek. I was all of twenty-one years old and just look at the games I played! Oh, but leaving the fun and frolic aside, let me tell you something interesting. During this visit of the Pandavas, Arjuna and I had struck up a close friendship. Apart from his boastful nature and his habit of drinking wine, Arjuna had other peculiar traits too such as asking a plethora of questions and engaging in prolonged debates. Except for these two traits, many of his other habits were similar to mine. But his best trait was that he was extremely disciplined when it came to waking up early in the morning. We would often greet the rising sun by taking long walks by the Yamuna. In contrast, bhaiya and Bhima had to be shaken up from their slumber every morning.

Well, we were all different by nature, but we were still enjoying ourselves to the hilt. Verily, life had taken a radical turn. Not too long ago, we had been isolated from the world, compelled to spend a drab life on the Gomanta Mountain, and now, in the blink of an eye, our days were marked with joy and festivities once again. I have no idea whether good days follow the bad ones or whether bad days follow the good. Whatever the case may be, the truth is that human life is a tapestry woven with both good and bad days as well as good and bad times. No matter the person or the kind of life he leads, the cycle of sunshine and storms is ever-present in his life. Thus, only a person who knows how to face the bad days and bad times with grace, can actually be happy in life. And this can only be learnt by someone who is willing to understand that if one has been given a human life, then bad phases will also announce their arrival from time to time. In short, only a person who accepts the bad times and learns the art of finding joy and cheer even in such times, can truly make his life meaningful. Otherwise, man is destined to lead a miserable life.

Oh well! Let us put aside these contemplations as there is no end to them. Instead, let me tell you about an interesting incident. One day, while on our morning walk along the banks of the Yamuna, Arjuna apprised me of the situation in Hastinapur. The gist of his narrative was that despite the Pandavas' right to the throne of Hastinapur, Duryodhana's stubbornness prevented them from claiming it or gaining any importance at the palace. Although Duryodhana's father, that is, King Dhritarashtra as well as *Pitamah*[49] Bhishma had their best interests at heart, the poor men were helpless when confronted with Duryodhana. In fact, the sole reason Arjuna had spoken to me about all this was that he wanted my advice on how they should tackle the situation. Now, I am not sure about Arjuna, but I was pleased with the opportunity given to me. For, you very well know that I was always eager to explain such things to others. So, I began, "If you ask me, all of you need to reconsider your way of thinking. You believe that *Pitamah* Bhishma and King Dhritarashtra are wholly in support of you, but because of Duryodhana's overbearing nature and stubbornness, they are unable to make the right decision. Even if this were true, in my opinion, sentiments that don't yield results are worthless. The truth is that all three—the perpetrators of injustice, the ones who tolerate injustice, and the ones who watch silently and do nothing to prevent it—are equally at fault. Duryodhana and Dushasana are the perpetrators, you are the ones tolerating their wrongdoings, and *Pitamah* Bhishma and King Dhritarashtra are silently watching this injustice being done to you and your brothers. So, if understood correctly, all three parties are sinners in equal measure. All said and done, until you reform yourself, you do not have any right to complain about others." Hearing my frank opinion, Arjuna fell into deep contemplation, as if he was trying to reflect on the import of what I had just said. Now, whatever he may have grasped, I was satisfied with having given my frank opinion. Thus, there was no question of my interrupting his thought process. So, we continued walking, all the while admiring the beauty of the Yamuna. I am not sure how much Arjuna agreed with me or to what extent he understood my point of view, but he suddenly came up with a

49. *Pitamah* - Grandsire.

ridiculous question. He said, "Do you know the difference between *dharma* (right conduct) and *adharma* (wrong conduct)?"

I was surprised, nay, stunned to hear this question. Of course, at this point in time, I had no idea that one day, Arjuna would ask me the same question once again, standing on the battlefield of the Mahabharata war. Well, at present, I have to say, this was the first time I had such a big opportunity to speak my mind. Under no circumstances was I going to let go of this chance! Interestingly, whether by coincidence or not, it was Arjuna who gave me the opportunity to express my thoughts for the first time today; and it was he again who became the instrument for the greatest flight my contemplation had taken—the Bhagavad Gita. But that would come much later. At present though, in very practical terms, I replied, "Arjuna! It is actually an individual's Soul which decides what is right or wrong conduct. This Soul knows everything! Thus, the one who heeds the voice of his Soul adheres to right conduct and whoever ignores it indulges in wrong conduct. But the sad reality is, an individual rarely takes refuge in his Soul. Instead, he ponders upon countless other things, allowing him to not only live with wrong conduct being perpetrated around him, but also indulge in wrong conduct himself."

I, of course, had no idea that this definition of right and wrong conduct which I had stated to Arjuna in just four sentences at this point in time, would have to be delivered to him once again in seven hundred verses in the Bhagavad Gita! Well, at present, it did not seem as though Arjuna had comprehended much of what I had said. Actually, he believed more in making others understand rather than comprehending something himself. This is precisely what he had done throughout my enunciation of the Gita. Leaving that aside, let me narrate another incident to you which shocked me greatly. One day, while Bhima, Arjuna and I were sitting idly and chit-chatting, Bhima mentioned that Yudhishthira had taken a vow to always speak the truth. What?! Did I hear that right? I was shocked to the core of my being, for, I had never expected to hear anything of this sort. However, this did offer an explanation for his egoistic attitude. How can anyone take such an absurd vow and decide about the future, when everything in Nature always exists in the present? Well, only an extremely arrogant person would do so. Seeing me in a deeply reflective mood, Arjuna enquired, "What are you thinking about, my friend?"

I said, "I fail to understand why Yudhishthira has taken a vow to always speak the truth. To that end, it is necessary for him to first know what is truth and untruth himself."

Hearing such a frank and straightforward response, Arjuna was taken aback a little, but he decided to keep his own counsel and instead just shook his head thus ending the discussion. But it was evident from his expression that he did not like my speaking in this manner about his elder brother. Well, it hardly mattered to me whether Arjuna approved of my stance or not; I wanted a closure on this matter today itself. I was just thinking about this when bhaiya joined us. The three of us were seated facing the River Yamuna; and watching us immersed in deep conversation, bhaiya sat down with us. I was happy to see him participate in our conversation, for, this had set the mood to put forth my argument even more determinedly. Thus, despite Arjuna's reluctance to continue the discussion, I said to him, "Perhaps, you failed to understand what I said about having knowledge of truth and untruth." With his head bowed low, Arjuna nodded in agreement. This was exactly what I was waiting for. Now, the opportunity to take my argument forward was readily available to me. So, taking advantage of it, I began, "Arjuna! Great religious deeds cannot be performed on the basis of what we discern to be the truth with our limited understanding. Consider my own example. All the great deeds that I have performed—or should I say all the great religious deeds that I have accomplished—have been achieved either by telling lies or by resorting to untruth."

Hearing this bold statement, both Bhima and Arjuna were shocked. Only bhaiya remained unperturbed. Well, not only was he undisturbed, he even passed a sarcastic remark at my expense by quickly adding, "Actually, even Kanhaiya has taken a vow to speak the truth at least once a day!" And with this ill-timed but splendidly sarcastic comment by bhaiya, the topic lost its gravity once again. And once the discussion lost its seriousness, all of us started cracking jokes. Well, in this atmosphere of fun and laughter, today's meeting came to an end too. In short, the single hindrance created by bhaiya had robbed me of the opportunity to express my profound thoughts on the subject of truth and untruth. Well, so be it! For the rest of the time, we indulged in great fun, realising little that an entire month had flitted by in this joyful atmosphere. Then, just as the time comes for every traveller to pack his bags and leave, it was time for the Pandavas to depart too. I had become so engrossed in their company that I had forgotten the fact that they would not be staying here with us forever. Naturally, when the realisation dawned upon me that it was time for them to leave, I became sad...but well, has anyone ever been able to stop those who are meant to part ways? I thus consoled myself in this manner and when the time came for them to depart, I also took them to meet grandfather, as is customary. You will find it hard to believe, but I was meeting grandfather after an interval of one whole month. And now that I stood before him with the Pandava brothers by my side, I noticed that he appeared greatly worried. Really, I had become so absorbed in merriment that I had not even enquired after him for an entire month! Seeing him so grim, I was rudely reminded of the menace called Satrajit which threatened Mathura's existence. But then, this was a formal courtesy call; besides, we could not discuss such matters in the presence of the Pandavas, hence neither was there any conversation between grandfather and me on this issue, nor did we exchange sympathies as was our wont. So, our formal meeting soon came to an end and we made our way home, where Aunt Kunti was already waiting for us. Bhaiya and I took her blessings, and on that note, the Pandavas' caravan comprising five chariots and four orderlies and soldiers set off for Hastinapur by mid-morning. Seeing them leave, both mother and I felt sad as we watched the last chariot of their caravan disappear in the far distance. For that matter, even Bhima and Arjuna had become very emotional. But time demanded that we parted, and so we did.

Well, the Pandavas were gone but not without leaving me with wonderful memories of our happy times together. Truly, the days I had spent with the Pandavas were the happiest since leaving Vrindavan. All this while, I had not bothered to ask for news of the royal palace, nor had I enquired about grandfather; even thoughts of the malevolent Satrajit had been relegated to the back of my mind. That's not all! Even Radha, Vrindavan and Rukmini had slipped into oblivion during this period. Naturally, when life was offering its best fare, why would I pay attention to other matters? But there are many fools who lose out on the opportunity to live a beautiful life by getting caught up in useless worries. Well, since I was fond of living life to the fullest, I did not squander this opportunity. However, in the process, I found myself becoming highly concerned. Although the Pandavas had departed, thoughts of Bhima and Arjuna constantly played on my mind. Even Yudhishthira and his silly vow of always speaking the truth kept niggling at the back of my mind. Actually, in just a few days' time, I had become very attached to the Pandavas, and because of this, whenever I recalled Yudhishthira's vow, my mind was besieged with worry and misgivings, making me doubtful about the future of the Pandavas. I failed to understand, when Nature itself is completely 'the present', and lives every moment as it happens, bringing ever-new phases and circumstances in our lives...how can a person take a vow to always speak the truth in every circumstance and situation? If ever there arose a situation wherein Yudhishthira was compelled to become the agent of lies, untruth and deception for the sake of the greater good, would he tell the truth even then? Would he end up committing such a grave misconduct only because he considers always speaking the truth to be the right conduct? If that were to happen, he would destroy the lives of all his brothers along with his own. For, all those fools humbly obeyed every one of Yudhishthira's commands.

This would be a sin made worse by an even bigger sin! Meaning, first, there would be the sin of Yudhishthira speaking the truth when he was meant to be an agent of untruth, and then there would be the bigger sin of the implicit acceptance of his orders by all his brothers, without even evaluating them. What if these obedient brothers landed themselves in great peril someday because of Yudhishthira's vow? But I suppose these thoughts belonged to the future and it was best to leave them where they belonged. With this thought, I once again shifted my focus away from the Pandavas and their peculiarities, and instead concentrated on understanding the situation brewing in Mathura. Thus, I immersed myself completely in grasping the political ploys at play in Mathura.

Chapter 10

Swayamvar of the Love of My Life - Rukmini

Karma beckoned me once again now that the month-long revelry with the Pandavas had come to an end. *'Karma'* is a task, or a set of tasks, executed as per the demands of time and circumstances. But remember, actions alone cannot effect a change. However, by consistently performing actions in line with the demands of time, bad times can surely be warded off. And, at present, time demanded an analysis of the situation brewing in Mathura. It demanded that I foil Satrajit's evil designs and break the burgeoning unity of the Yadava leaders against the royal palace. Thus, by night-time, I had moulded myself as per the demands of time. In other words, I pushed the Pandavas out of my mind and tried to focus on the current situation in Mathura. However, since I was delving into contemplation after so many days, I was finding it hard to focus and sleep too was eluding me. Perhaps, I was sorely missing my dear friends, the Pandavas, having become used to their company night and day for almost a month. I found myself in a strange situation indeed; if I tried to fall asleep pushing away thoughts of the Pandavas, Satrajit's conspiracy would rear its head and drive my sleep away. But when I tried to focus on Satrajit's evil machinations, memories of the good times spent with the Pandavas would flood my mind. Oscillating between these two, I ended up lying wide awake, tossing and turning all night in the vain hope of catching some sleep!

Oh well, one sleepless night does not cause much harm. But I could not go on like this on a daily basis. The solution was right in front of me: once I immersed myself in Mathura's situation completely, I would automatically quit thinking about the Pandavas. Actually, there is only one way to forget a problem that has no solution—losing oneself in a problem which has a solution! So, even though I was still groggy from a sleepless night, I got out of bed, made my way to my chariot and steered it in the direction of the royal palace. Grandfather was resting in his bedchamber, but upon seeing me, he sat up immediately. I touched his feet as a mark of respect, took his blessings and sat beside him on the bed. It was pointless to enquire about anything, for, the state of affairs at the palace was evident from grandfather's expression. Even so, I needed to understand the actual situation in detail. On enquiring, grandfather heaved a deep sigh and unburdened his worries to me. Perhaps, he had been waiting for this opportunity all month long. Indeed, my absence had made him lonely. But no matter…now that I had come back refreshed, I would soon set everything right.

Well, this was all about reassuring myself; coming to the gist of what grandfather told me, Mathura's coffers had run dry. The fiscal condition was so pathetic that it was becoming difficult to cover even the daily expenses of the palace. This deterioration was worsened by the fact that people had stopped paying taxes due to Satrajit's incitement. And going a step further,

Satrajit had now started a new campaign demanding that Brihaddal be made the crown prince. To make matters worse, not only the Yadava leaders, but even the common people had gradually begun to support his demand. But the most dangerous aspect of this problem was, grandfather firmly believed that Satrajit had been able to make a rapid headway with his campaign because he had succeeded in convincing everyone that Krishna's ulterior motive was to stake a claim to Mathura's throne. In fact, Satrajit even went around instilling the idea in their minds that Krishna was trying to sidle up to King Ugrasena and claim the title of crown prince, and if he were to really become the crown prince, then Jarasandha, who was waiting in the wings like a wounded serpent, would not think twice before attacking Mathura. And if that were to happen, Mathura would be wiped off the face of Aryavarta. However, Jarasandha has promised that if Brihaddal is made the crown prince, he would never attack Mathura.

Even as grandfather narrated all this, each word uttered by him shocked me to the core. I had been busy enjoying myself with the Pandavas, and meanwhile, Satrajit had made all arrangements to pack me off from Mathura. The scoundrel had put forth a strong argument, twisting the facts in such a manner that the entire kingdom was bound to support him. But the question was, what difference did it make to me if Brihaddal was made the crown prince? I had never harboured the ambition of being crowned the prince of Mathura anyway. But even as I was thinking this, the inner voice piped up, 'Kanhaiya, what are you saying? Understand the real issue here! Once Satrajit gets a hold of Mathura's reins, will he allow you to stay here? All said and done, the very intention behind this move is to uproot your well-entrenched position in Mathura. Do you see it now?' Oh yes, I do. But see what was happening with me...the situation had become so dire that I had begun talking to myself! Well, I could completely understand Satrajit's intentions, but what had come over the *Mathurawasis*? How did they get alienated from me? How did they forget the hero who had chased away Jarasandha twice? Come to think of it, I wasn't really surprised that they had forgotten me; after all, what could be expected of them? Their condition was even worse than that of the royal palace. Neither did they have any trade or business, nor was anyone encouraging them to work. Moreover, the brothels were now in business all day long. The Yadavas had been addicted to meat-eating and drinking from the very outset; and to make matters worse, the gambling they indulged in all day long had completely destroyed their competence. This being the case, their excessive indulgence and fondness for dance and music had pushed them to the brink of destruction. And it is a well-known fact that an idle mind is the devil's playground. Honestly, until now, I had never witnessed such a widespread consumption of meat and wine, nor such a heavy addiction to prostitutes in any other kingdom. Actually, not just Mathura, but many Yadava kingdoms of Aryavarta suffered the same fate. The Yadavas had truly etched their name in the book of notoriety. But even so, Mathura aced all the other kingdoms where indulging in vices was concerned. In such a scenario, it was useless to hope for loyalty or even truth and justice from such good-for-nothing subjects. It can be said that when I could not think of anything else, I was venting the frustration I felt over Satrajit on the inhabitants of Mathura. But how long could I continue venting? So, grandfather and I partook of some fruits, and after reassuring him that I would take care of Satrajit, I hurried out of the palace.

But where could I head next? The gravity of the situation was such that there was no respite no matter where I went. Still, taking a chance, I quietly left for my house on the banks of River Yamuna to spend some time alone. Actually, I first wanted to carefully analyse the situation from every perspective. For, once the actual gravity of the problem is known, it becomes easy to find a solution. Thus, lost in thought, I would sometimes sit on the swing, or at times, take a stroll in the garden, still deliberating over the issue. To avoid any disturbance while I contemplated, I hadn't brought along any orderlies with me. When my mind grew tired, I would walk along the riverbank, pluck fruits from nearby trees and live off them for the day. This became my daily routine until very soon, my contemplation bore fruit. I had arrived at several important conclusions. The most dangerous realisation that had dawned upon me was that now, more than ever, Jarasandha had become my greatest enemy. I had been under the impression that by chasing him away from Gomanta, I would be rid of him at least for the time being. But perhaps, the disgrace of having to flee from the Gomanta Mountain had wounded his ego so badly that finishing me off had now become the single most important mission of his life. But since he was not in a position to attack at the moment and surely did not want to repeat his previous mistake, he was first creating a tense situation for me in Mathura. And most dangerously, to achieve this, he was cleverly using Satrajit as a pawn. Now, just think, what news could be worse for me than knowing that Jarasandha and Satrajit, my two long-standing enemies, had joined hands against me? The inner voice returned, 'Kanhaiya, this time, you are in serious trouble!' Truly, if Satrajit had been operating all by himself without the backing of Jarasandha, I could have tackled the situation somehow. And even though I had dealt with Jarasandha on two previous occasions, how could I tackle the combined force of these two? For, a person can either deal with the enemy at home or with the one outside. But when one has to face enemies on both fronts, the situation becomes grave indeed.

The situation had become even more challenging because this time, Jarasandha had kept his temper on a tight leash, contrary to his nature. I'm sure you too must have understood the point I am making at present. Both his previous attacks were outbursts of anger, which blinded his judgement and led to defeat on both occasions. But this time around, since he had kept his temper under control, he had succeeded in making a good strategic move. As a first step, by enlisting Satrajit's help, he wanted to make Brihaddal the crown prince of Mathura. Then, he wanted to have me removed from Mathura by sowing the seeds of hatred in the minds of the *Mathurawasis* against me. In short, he was trying his best to get me thrown out of Mathura, either by inciting the people against me or by forcing me to leave the kingdom by creating insurmountable problems for me. Do you see now? As long as Jarasandha was burning with the desire for revenge, he was not that dangerous...but as is often said, cold anger can be even more dangerous and effective. My brain had stopped functioning, as the enormity of the problem loomed before me. For, how could I ever forget the days, nay months, spent in exile on the Gomanta Mountain? Indeed, the very thought of undergoing a similar experience all over again made my heart quiver. But enough about me; even if I were to think about Mathura's welfare, I knew that Brihaddal was totally incapable of being crowned the prince. Yes, when it came to misconduct and offensive behaviour, he was indeed the 'leader of the Yadavas'! Actually, Brihaddal was closely related to me; he was, in fact, my cousin. But how could someone who wasted all his time in debauchery be made the crown prince? Mathura was already floundering in darkness, so how could a man who himself remained intoxicated all day be put in charge of its destiny?

It was really one of the most critical situations I had ever faced in my life. Let alone mine, even Mathura's future appeared bleak. The path ahead was shrouded in darkness and I could see no way of surviving this crisis; in fact, it did not seem that Mathura would survive either. It was already tottering on the brink of starvation, and to make matters worse, shirking work had become a part of its inhabitants' psyche. In such a scenario, Mathura needed a guide, and I was certainly capable of fulfilling that role. I could even save them by applying my diligence and showing them the right way. But just see the game played by Nature—my own existence in Mathura was now in question. But regardless of my situation, I could not bear to see so many lives being ruined in this manner. I had to try to save them. In fact, they had to be saved! But how could I do it? The great *karmaveer* Krishna had become completely powerless. The situation was such that I could not orchestrate a discord between Satrajit and Jarasandha, and as long as the nexus between these two existed, it was not possible to save either Mathura or myself.

Looking at the situation from another perspective, neither could I stop the wave of opposition gathering strength against me in Mathura, nor could I stay here much longer if this campaign against me continued to gain momentum. Truly, this was a grave and precarious situation from which I could see no means of salvaging either myself or Mathura.

So, did that mean that I, *karmaveer* Krishna, would give up and do nothing? Never! That was just not possible. Once again, I seriously meditated on the problem. After deliberating for just a few days, I arrived at the conclusion that Mathura and I were not only afflicted with the same problem, but we shared a common enemy too. And when the greater good included my benefit as well, what was the harm in tackling this difficult task by trying to save Mathura first? Perhaps, a way to save myself would also emerge in the process. Actually, I had only two enemies, Jarasandha and Satrajit, whereas Mathura had a third one as well—Mathura itself.

Having arrived at this conclusion, I returned to my father's house, and needless to say, I also carried the worries concerning Mathura with me. Truly, these foolish Yadavas had pushed themselves so close to ruination that it was indeed very difficult to save them. And as long as the conditions in Mathura did not improve, their thinking could not be changed. And as long as their opinion of the royal palace and me remained unchanged, it would be well-nigh impossible for me to clip Satrajit's wings. The matter was quite simple: if I wanted to save myself, there was only one solution, and that was to rein in Satrajit's devious moves. And considering the current situation, this was not something that grandfather and I could do on our own. But yes, if the inhabitants of Mathura supported us, then we could easily tackle this menace too. As for the common people, they would not come to their senses until their situation improved. Only those who were gainfully employed would worry about the palace, whereas an idle person would only enjoy creating a ruckus. And verily, both the situation as well as the inhabitants of Mathura had deteriorated to such an extent that just thinking about them made my head spin. Mathura's economy was already gasping for breath, and with everyone's savings depleted, there was no money to revive dead or dying businesses and none to start new ventures either. Moreover, Mathura could not boast of a product that was exclusively produced here, one that would help us generate income. The royal treasury was wiped clean, which meant that even the palace was in no position to help its subjects. All in all, Satrajit's political manoeuvres and the vices of the people had clearly set the stage for a civil war to erupt on the streets of Mathura. This was precisely why I had pointedly refused the gift of scores of courtesans from Chandak as well as Queen Padmavati. Good courtesans were certainly a necessity of every kingdom, provided a hard-working person visited them once or twice a week to enjoy their song and dance performance. But in Mathura, these courtesans had become the bane of society, threatening to wipe out the very existence of the kingdom. Here, they were no longer just a means of relaxation after hard work; instead, they had become the epitome of debauchery.

Well, at present, I could see no solution to save myself, so what was the use of thinking about such things? The only recourse left for me at this point in time was to keep a keen eye on the situation unfolding in Mathura and wait for the right opportunity. And as far as saving Mathura was concerned, its foremost need was money. If money could be pumped in, businesses could be revived. Once businesses were revived, there would be employment. If there was employment, people would focus on work and move away from debauchery. And if that were to happen, the royal palace would begin to receive an inflow of taxes once again. However, for this entire cycle to kickstart, the masses had to be motivated to work hard. Even if a single person from each household worked as a cowherd, it would solve the current problem of starvation in Mathura. But as simple as these tasks appeared to be, they were just as difficult to accomplish in reality. To establish business in these miserable conditions and to engage these indolent people in gainful work was no child's play, especially when Satrajit was busy instigating them to do exactly the opposite with his counter propaganda. Now, whichever way one looked at the situation, the conclusion remained the same. As long as Satrajit remained powerful, Mathura could not return to prosperity. At the same time, I could not stay here for long unless Mathura regained its affluence.

As far as my survival was concerned, it did not matter, because at the most, it was a question of just two people's lives. The fight between Satrajit, Jarasandha and me would continue endlessly, but was it justifiable to make the whole of Mathura bear the brunt of this? As soon as this noble thought concerning everyone's welfare crossed my mind, I thought, why not deposit a portion of my wealth in the royal treasury? Forget about me, this would at least improve Mathura's condition to some extent. But then I realised that this would significantly weaken my own financial position. And frankly speaking, if my position weakened, it would not bode well for Mathura's well-being either. So, I had to come up with a solution that would bring my influence and Satrajit's to the same level. So, why don't I put forth the idea that if all the Yadava leaders contributed to the treasury, then I too would willingly aid the royal palace? Yes, this was the right thing to do. Really, once the financial condition of the palace improved, then by taking several measures to benefit its inhabitants, at least Mathura could be saved from ruin. In addition to this, the condition of the royal palace would improve too. And since I had taken on the onus of making the royal palace prosperous, what was the point in settling for half measures? In other words, casting my own interests aside, I was gradually channelling all my thoughts and efforts towards solving the problem that had gripped Mathura. It is rightly said that when you think of the good of others, you find a way that leads to your own benefit as well. And sure enough, by constantly thinking about the betterment of Mathura, a brilliant idea struck me...an idea so perfect, it could kill several birds with one stone! In fact, it could solve all the problems in a single masterstroke. The menace hovering over my head could be warded off, and Mathura's condition could improve as well.

Now, I am sure you would ask, "Krishna, what miracle cure did you stumble upon? Please tell us!" So, here it is. I was thinking that the precious Syamantaka gem was a gift of Nature. And that being the case, ideally, it belonged to the kingdom of Mathura. So, why not ask Satrajit to donate the Syamantaka gem to Mathura's coffers? If this magical gem was deposited in the royal treasury, all of Mathura's woes would be chased away in the blink of an eye. Not only that, this could also help clip Satrajit's wings, for, his dominance was solely due to this gem. And when the gem itself would no longer be in his possession, the Yadava leaders would desert him and naturally return to the fold of the royal palace. The inner voice resurfaced, 'Well, you have thought of the perfect solution, Krishna. But you're speaking as if Satrajit eagerly listens to you and will hand over the gem to the royal palace on a platter! He has to agree to give up the gem in the first place! Until then, all your brilliant ideas are nothing more than wishful thinking.' Yes, you are right! It would be far easier to wrest a prey from a lion's mouth than to make Satrajit part with the gem. Of course, I am fully aware of this impediment, but this is the only solution and also the right thing to do. But what if he does not agree? Well, in that case, he would be made to part with it by hook or by crook. But what if he still refuses to part with it? Then I would conclude that Nature does not want Mathura's situation to improve. Thereafter, I too would not go out of my way to help the royal palace. The voice within instantly reprimanded me, 'Now, what is this? You are reneging on your word. Why don't you deposit your own wealth in the royal treasury as planned earlier?' I retorted, 'Now, wait a minute. We were talking about Satrajit, weren't we? When did this conversation shift to me? Believe me, I do sincerely care about Mathura.' But neither was I stupid nor an emotional fool to obstinately stick to what I had said earlier even after knowing the ground reality.

Let me explain in detail. The truth of the matter was that I had already embraced Mathura as my own a long time ago. But these Yadava leaders had always orchestrated situations whereby Mathura had still not accepted me fully as one of its own. So, how could I sacrifice all my personal wealth for its upliftment, especially considering the fact that Satrajit's evil designs would gain strength with my bankruptcy? And as far as motivating the people of Mathura was concerned, I had no doubt about my ability to do so. With my untiring efforts and power of persuasion, I could free the *Mathurawasis* from all their addictions and steer them onto the path of honest, hard work. Meaning, I had the ability to turn them into diligent and productive citizens, and I had nothing to lose in doing so. Besides, as you well know, I was always ready to work for the greater good. 'So, do not bother me with talk of wealth,' I told the voice within. I had understood that if Mathura had to be saved in earnest, it was crucial for me to survive as well. Besides, a *karmavadi*[50] like me would always take into consideration all the factors while arriving at a decision. Thus, I came to the conclusion that I would save myself and Mathura as well. However, the voice within me continued with its questions, 'But how will you improve Mathura's condition without wealth? And who will let you improve it in the first place?' Well, the voice was right yet again; Satrajit and the other Yadava leaders would leave no stone unturned in hurling obstacles in my path to stall my efforts. For, their very purpose was to worsen Mathura's condition and thereby pressurise grandfather into making Brihaddal the crown prince. On the other hand, it was also true that grandfather would never allow this to happen and put Mathura on the path of destruction. Under no circumstances would he agree to this, no matter how much he was pressured. Meaning, this would only lead to a conflagration and ignite a civil war in the kingdom.

No, I would certainly not allow the situation to reach this point. I would deliberate upon this issue some more, but I would surely find a solution to save both Mathura and myself. So, leaving this topic aside for now, let me introduce another aspect of this problem to you. In his heart of hearts, grandfather harboured the dream of seeing me being coronated as the crown prince of Mathura. And as far as I was concerned, neither did I want to become the prince nor were the circumstances conducive to me becoming one. How could the very Yadavas who hated the sight of me and could not even bear my presence in Mathura, allow me to become their crown prince? On the other hand, how long could grandfather tolerate this kind of power tussle at such an advanced age? And if grandfather's power was eroded, I would be kicked out of Mathura in no time. What I mean to say is, the problem was complicated in not one but a thousand ways. All said and done, considering the need of the hour, it was better to resolve these issues one at a time instead of indulging in over-the-top flights of fancy. So, other issues such as changing the mindset of the Yadavas or reviving Mathura's flagging economy would have to wait. The foremost task was to increase my influence over the Yadavas so that the

50. *Karmavadi* - The one who believes in *karma* (action).

pressure on grandfather could be eased; this would ensure a safe haven for me and I would not be forced to leave Mathura under any circumstances. The matter was plain and simple—only if I stayed in Mathura could I help improve its condition. So, once again, the entire issue was tied to my own survival. Now, even to take action, it is necessary for one to be alive, is it not? And to ensure my safety, the only alternative before me was to cut Satrajit and his cohorts down to size. Thus, I would spend long, sleepless nights trying to think of ways to establish my influence on Satrajit and the other Yadava leaders. However, when I could not come up with anything even after giving the matter considerable thought, I decided to pay a visit to Satrajit. For, time was running out, and with the passage of time, Satrajit was tightening the noose around the royal palace. So, before he could make his final strike and destroy both Mathura and me, I thought, why not find out exactly what was on his mind?

So, the very next afternoon, I paid Satrajit a visit at his house. Now, although I had gone there to glean Satrajit's intentions, I myself was in danger of losing my path. For, once again, it was Satyabhama who opened the door, and as soon as I saw her innocent face, I recalled my first meeting with her. On seeing me, a look of sheer delight lit up her face, but then just as quickly, her demeanour changed and she froze. It was not difficult for me to understand why her mood had switched all of a sudden. I could clearly see that she was not her normal self. Well, what do I say, it was usually difficult for young girls to maintain their composure on seeing me. Now, let me not hide this from you: Satyabhama's demeanour reminded me of Radha once again. You would remember that whenever I chanced upon Radha, I would react in a similar manner. But this was not the time to think about such things or pay too much attention to them. So, I straightaway asked her if I could meet her father. Hearing my curt, formal query, Satyabhama responded accordingly. In a tone devoid of emotion, she replied that he had gone to the chamber which housed the gem and might take a while to return. And verily, why would she not respond in a cold, curt manner? My question, after all, was terse in itself. But I couldn't help it. I was so caught up in my problems that despite wanting to, I could not be more loving in my interaction with her. Well, so be it! My work was done as I now had valuable information with me. The Syamantaka gem was kept here, in the house, and there was no doubt that at this very moment, Satrajit was extracting gold from it to fill his coffers. Meaning, not just the hunter but even the prey was present right here in Mathura. Now, after having obtained this significant information, I decided it was futile to wait for Satrajit. Since I had accomplished my task, it was better to slink away. But just as I was about to leave, a sudden thought struck me. Now that my work was done, why should I leave the innocent Satyabhama unhappy? How would I have felt if Radha had done the same to me? So, I immediately changed my demeanour. Stepping inside the house, I lovingly asked Satyabhama if she would be so kind as to bring me a glass of that divine sherbet she had offered me on my previous visit. As soon as I changed the manner in which I spoke to her, her mood changed as well. She made haste and in no time waltzed back with my drink. Seeing her face light up with joy, I was pleased too. Well, having completed this task as well, there was no reason for me to stay here any longer. So, I smiled and asked for her permission to leave. Hearing this, she replied with a slight air of surprise, "Will you not wait to meet father?"

Well, her question was valid, but since I had discovered such a big secret, what was the point in meeting Satrajit now? So, turning the conversation on its head, I said, "Oh, it was nothing important. I had come here just to pay him a courtesy call. Kindly let him know that I had visited."

Saying this, I rose to leave, but Satyabhama was not willing to let me go so easily. Well, when did I ever let Radha go either? So, in order to stop me from leaving, the innocent girl asked in a voice laden with emotion, "Well, since you are already here, why not stay a little longer?"

I did not mind spending some time with Satyabhama, but my political strategy forbade me from meeting Satrajit at this point of time. In fact, taking advantage of the opportunity at hand, I wanted to unsettle him. I believed that, at the very least, he would be occupied for a while, trying to decipher the purpose of my visit. The advantage of such a move is that, while your enemy is preoccupied with finding something about you, he definitely won't attack. Meaning, you earn some respite from his attack at least for a short while. Besides, this is between you and me, whereas I myself was at a loss as to why I had gone to his house! And when I was unsure myself, there was no chance of Satrajit making sense of it. It was possible that his failure to understand the purpose of my visit might lead him to make a mistake that would unwittingly show me a way forward. Nursing this hope and the secret that the gem was housed in Mathura itself, I bade farewell to Satyabhama, despite her reluctance to see me leave so soon.

But what can I say? Satrajit was a devious old hand at politics. I kept waiting for him to make some move, but neither did he try to contact me, nor did he make enquiries about me. I had visited him to catch him unawares, but it can be said that it was he who had stumped me instead! Oh well, it did not matter. I would wait for another opportunity and think of some other tactic. Thus, once again, I immersed myself in contemplation, but no matter how hard I tried, I could not come up with a new strategy. It was on one such day, while I was relaxing at home, that grandfather sent for me. Wondering what fresh problem had surfaced now, I quickly set off for the palace. Despite it being afternoon, grandfather was seated in his bedchamber, appearing more perturbed than usual. Looking at the deep worry lines etched on his forehead, I could not fathom what exactly the trouble was. There was already a mountain of troubles looming before us, and here, one more issue had surfaced! I began to wonder whether this was really Mathura or the 'city of troubles'. Well, I didn't think much about it; I simply went up to him and plonked myself by his side, with my slouched shoulders and long face to match his mood. Then, after what seemed like an eternity, grandfather broke his silence and, with a deep sigh, enlightened me on the new problem at hand. In a dejected tone, he said, "Kanhaiya, I am sure you already know that these unruly Yadava leaders have made my condition so miserable that despite being the king of Mathura, the kingdom is no longer under my rule. I am just a titular king."

Indeed, what grandfather had said was true and honestly, I too could not bear to see him reduced to such a pitiable state. But, at present, I was sailing in troubled waters myself. What help could I offer to him under these circumstances? What consolation could I give? Truly, at this moment, we were like two drowning men clutching at each other to save ourselves. As a result, the shore seemed the farthest from where we stood, as both of us were just flailing our arms around to stay afloat. Caught in this bleak scenario, there wasn't much to say or do. So, this time, unlike my usual practice, I didn't even try to understand what the matter was; I just sympathised with grandfather as best as I could and got up to leave. In fact, of late, this had become a weekly ritual between us. Grandfather would send for me, pour his woes to me and unburden his heart, while I would offer a few words of consolation and return home. But what was this! Just as I was about to leave, grandfather reached out and stopped me. Suddenly, his face turned graver, and before I could fathom what was going on, he broke the silence and spoke in a morose tone, "And that's not all, Krishna! Even Mathura's sovereignty is now being threatened in Aryavarta. On one hand, I am no longer being accepted as a king in Mathura, and on the other, Aryavarta is not considering Mathura as a kingdom. I can no longer endure such humiliation. I am thinking of abandoning everything and surrendering to this situation."

Uh-oh! This cannot be! My main pawn, the king himself, was being trumped. The inner voice sounded concerned, 'Kanhaiya, if grandfather surrendered out of dejection or fear, then you, my friend, can bid farewell to Mathura forever. Indeed, you might as well start pounding the doors of every kingdom in Aryavarta in search of another 'Gomanta Mountain'!' Although I could not comprehend the import of grandfather's words, I could certainly understand that this time around, his worries ran very deep. And I was also well aware of the fact that if I did not tackle this situation quickly, everything would be lost. It was also crystal clear to me that considering the circumstances and the age at which he was holding on to the throne, every moment for him was no different from dying. I could also understand that this time, I could not leave him without giving him a strong assurance and a definite plan to resolve the situation at hand. And to reassure him, it was necessary for me to get to the bottom of the issue. I was familiar with the situation in Mathura, but completely clueless about the new trouble that had come to us from Aryavarta. Thus, I asked grandfather to explain the matter to me in its entirety. I could think of a way out only if I knew what the problem was, right? The poor man was eager to unburden himself, so he began to paint a clear and detailed picture. It so happened that grandfather's spies brought news that, in a month's time, a grand *swayamvar*[51] would be arranged for Rukmini, the princess of Kundinpur. Through their report, it came to light that the entire *swayamvar* has been planned under Jarasandha's supervision.[52]

Hearing these words from grandfather, I could feel my head reel. Each word that he spoke pierced my heart like a dagger, searing it mercilessly. However, I quickly regained my composure, as grandfather had not finished speaking yet. And since the matter concerned Rukmini, it was necessary to pay close attention to every single word of his. The gist of his narration was that in order to please Jarasandha, Rukmini's brother, Rukmi, had plans to forcefully marry his sister off to Shishupala. Actually, this was their personal matter, but our concern was that Mathura was not going to be invited to the *swayamvar*—clearly on Jarasandha's orders. This was not only a huge insult to Mathura, but on a personal level, it was a grave affront to grandfather too, as he was the king of Mathura. After revealing this, grandfather lapsed into silence once again, but then, suddenly, overcome by a fresh wave of emotions, he burst forth, "Tell me, Kanhaiya! Am I not being humiliated both within and outside the kingdom? How much humiliation can I endure after all? How many more insults must I swallow in silence? And after all this suffering, why should I continue sitting on the throne of Mathura and tolerate insults at my age?"

Well, he was right, but not entirely. It was evident that grandfather was so exhausted that if he was pressured any further, he would certainly abdicate the throne. Besides, why should he suffer so much stress at such an advanced age? But on the other hand, if he did abdicate the throne, I would be debarred from Mathura in no time. Meaning, from this perspective, succumbing to pressure and breaking down was not in my favour at all. The problem was grave and it demanded a solution immediately. But what could I do? The moment I heard Rukmini's name, forgetting everything else, I became immersed in thoughts of her. Indeed, how could my poor mind function? It

51. *Swayamvar* - A ceremony wherein a princess chooses her bridegroom from a large number of assembled princes.
52. Harivansh Puran, Vishnu Parva, Chapter – 47, Verse – 1-11.

was helpless when confronted with my desperate heart. Oh, just see! Here, I was drowning in my own worries, while a *swayamvar* was being held for the queen of my dreams, and an even more worrisome aspect was, she was being forced to marry a rascal like Shishupala! Meaning, while I would continue to weave beautiful dreams of her, she would become Shishupala's wife. Oh, what do I tell you…a flurry of such thoughts flitted through my mind in a split second! While the problem of Jarasandha and Satrajit remained as is, grandfather's condition had complicated it further. In such a situation, when all my heart sought was solace, the news of Rukmini's *swayamvar* had instead inflicted a thousand wounds upon it, tearing it to shreds. Now, tell me, how could this poor Kanhaiya, whose heart was mortally wounded and bleeding, fight battles on all these fronts? Struggling to stay afloat, how could he even think of a solution?

Oh well! My life and my very existence had been under attack ever since I had taken my first breath. But this time, it was Rukmini, the queen of my dreams, who was in great peril, so you cannot even imagine the turmoil I was going through. I had to save both my life and my dream; I had to save Rukmini, come what may. My love aside, even from a humanitarian point of view, a girl being forced to marry someone against her wishes was a punishment worse than death. It did not matter if I could not attain her, but how could I bear to see her living a hellish life? Now, regardless of whether I could tolerate it or not, the truth of the matter was that there was nothing else that I could do. Obviously, when one's own existence was in question, what can one possibly do? 'O Krishna, how can you be so despondent? How can you surrender to despair like this?!' I thus roused my entire being. For, surrounded by troubles, the only support I had was of my consciousness. After all, even for my consciousness, it was a question of 'now or never'. And you won't believe this, but an idea did spring forth in my consciousness almost immediately. Indeed, when the matter concerned Rukmini, my mind had no option but to muster all its strength and come up with a solution. And amazingly, the news of the *swayamvar* which had shaken me to my very core had turned into a blessing after just one flight of my contemplation. If the plan I had in mind were put into action effectively, the present problem could be resolved completely. The plan was clear, but first and foremost, I had to take care of grandfather. For, he was the one I needed to implement the plan perfectly. Actually, no sooner had the plan crystallised in my mind than my self-confidence surged forth. And speaking with that same confidence, I addressed grandfather in a tone laced with optimism, "It is clear that we are faced with two problems. The first, and more important, is the internal situation in Mathura. In my opinion, the king must respect the wishes of his subjects. When all the Yadava leaders want Brihaddal to be made the crown prince, why do you object? You are being unnecessarily stubborn."

Taken aback at my statement, Grandfather replied haltingly, "Kanhaiya, what are you saying? Are you not well acquainted with his vices? He is your cousin, after all. Who knows him better than you?"

I said, "Grandfather, why don't you think of it this way...once he shoulders the responsibility that comes with being the crown prince, he will automatically come to his senses. I suggest you call a meeting of all the Yadava leaders with the clear-cut agenda of electing a crown prince. But do not reveal to anyone that we have decided in favour of Brihaddal. Then, leave the rest to me; I will handle things from there." Now, what does a drowning man want but a hand to pull him out of water?! Besides, grandfather usually agreed with everything I said, and since he trusted me completely, he was bound to side with me. All the pieces had fallen into place. I had even made the first move and was pleased with it. With a single masterstroke, my consciousness had opened several doors to countless possibilities. This is why I say, how can anyone defeat Krishna as long as his consciousness and intelligence support him?

Well, there were scores of things to be taken care of and very little time to put them into action. For now, I had only devised the plan; success had not yet knocked on my door. So, I reined in my soaring ego and took leave of grandfather. But yes, before leaving, I did not forget to play my next move, thinking of the solution to the second part of the problem, which was Rukmini's *swayamvar*. While taking my leave, I said to grandfather, "Do not tell anyone about Rukmini's *swayamvar* and the fact that Mathura has not been invited. It will give us a bad reputation unnecessarily. If Jarasandha and Rukmi want to forcefully marry her off to Shishupala, then so be it...why should it concern us? Our pride and honour lies in not letting this news spread across Mathura."

Truly, at this moment, I walked with a spring in my step, and my intellect too was functioning at its peak. This was no doubt incredible, but I was even more incredible, for, as soon as I left the palace, my thoughts turned to Rukmini. Sigh...my Rukmini! The queen of my dreams! How could she be married to someone else? Even if she wasn't married to me, she certainly should not be married off to the evil Shishupala, and that too, coercively, as part of a plan. No! This must not be allowed to happen! The fiend, Jarasandha, was already the enemy of my life, but now, he had, wittingly or unwittingly, become the enemy of my beloved's life too. Nah, I would foil his plans, come what may. Argh! I felt like piling a thousand curses upon Jarasandha's head, but that alone wouldn't save my dear Rukmini from this grave injustice. Oh well! I had the rest of my life to vent my anger and hurl as many curses at him as I desired. But for now, it was better to focus on the tasks at hand. With only a month left before the *swayamvar*, there were many things to take care of. Foremost was the problem created by Satrajit, which hung like a sword over my head. Hence, my first priority was to deal with Satrajit and the rogue, Brihaddal. Only after tackling them could I save Rukmini.

With this thought lodged firmly in my mind, I once again focused on *karma* (action). And presently, my only task was to ensure that the meeting of the Yadavas took place in accordance with the plan I had chalked out. With that goal in mind, I asked grandfather to hold the meeting in the most spacious ground of Mathura. To grandfather's credit, despite his grim mood and the despair he was caught in, he had arranged the meeting in just a week's time. For me, these seven days passed by in a whirl, and the day of the meeting finally arrived. Wasting not a moment, I set off for the venue well in time with grandfather and bhaiya in tow. Most of the Yadava leaders invited to the meeting had already reached the venue. Indeed, everyone was visibly excited about the pronouncement of Mathura's crown prince. The entire council of ministers could also be seen in attendance. Well, their enthusiasm was understandable. But now, let me tell you a secret. My decision to accompany grandfather to this meeting was also an integral part of my strategy. My intention was clear: I wanted to give the impression to everyone that grandfather was going to announce my name as the crown prince so that when Brihaddal was nominated and appointed to the post, Satrajit and the others would consider it their victory and not an outcome of my strategy. As soon as we reached the venue, a commotion greeted us from all around. As I had mentioned earlier, all the Yadava leaders including Satrajit were already seated on the podium and they squirmed in their seats on seeing me arrive with grandfather. I, of course, ignored their uneasiness, for, it hardly mattered to me; in fact, I even climbed up the stage with grandfather. As for the common people of the Yadava clan, I could clearly see about a thousand youths seated in this assembly. Most of them seemed to have been brainwashed, and this was perhaps another reason behind the ruckus prevailing on the ground. Regardless of the situation, grandfather and I took our seats. Naturally, I sat in the front row with grandfather, and as soon as we were seated, shouts supporting Brihaddal erupted from all corners of the ground. The mood, especially in Satrajit's camp, was explosive. And as for me, I was forced to witness my pitiable position in Mathura in the eyes of the people. Actually, all of this was the result of my own strategy. This entire fracas was proof of the illusion I had created by arriving with grandfather. Everyone was under the impression that grandfather had called this meeting to elect me the crown prince. However, occasionally, a few voices could be heard shouting in my support as well. And I was content with that alone; otherwise, the mood of the assembly was ample proof of Satrajit's hold over Mathura and my own pathetic position.

Needless to say, this public display of the dismal stature I held in Mathura continued for a while, with voices raised disparagingly against me. Finally, as per plan, grandfather invited me to speak and I rose from my seat. But just as I had expected, as soon as my name was announced, the chaos swelled and the moment I tried to put in a word, a still louder ruckus rose from the crowd, effectively stopping me from saying anything. It was with great difficulty that grandfather succeeded in pacifying the crowd with the assurance that the candidate would be chosen by popular opinion, but everyone should first lend an ear to what Kanhaiya had to say. Did you see the position I was in? Only after grandfather gave such a strong assurance did everyone agree to hear me out. So, before another disruption could arise, I hastened to speak, "Greetings, my friends! First and foremost, I would like to clarify that I have no desire whatsoever to become the crown prince of Mathura."

Hearing this, a wave of delight coursed through Satrajit's camp. This was natural, but what happened next completely exposed the impression my personality had created on the collective mindset of Mathura. Someone in the crowd shouted sarcastically, "O *Rannchhod Rai*![53] What makes you think we will even consider making you the crown prince?"

Hearing this, the entire ground rang aloud with peals of laughter. Standing on the podium, my face turned red with embarrassment, while I could clearly see rage emitting from bhaiya's countenance. The taunt was sharp indeed. Well, before I could compose myself or pacify bhaiya, another heckler shouted, "If we make Krishna the crown prince, he will once again run away as soon as he hears the news of Jarasandha's attack. We will then have to search for our prince everywhere, over hills and dales, mountains and forests!"

In fact, many such jokes were made at my expense as I stood before everyone, a thousand emotions flitting through my mind in the span of a moment. Perhaps, the situation might have turned out differently had the circumstances been different, but since the present issue concerned Rukmini, I ignored everyone; and before I was ridiculed further, I once again made an attempt to steer the meeting in the right direction. Addressing them yet again, I spoke in a serious tone, "As you all know, King Ugrasena has called this meeting to elect the crown prince of Mathura. Thus, I request all of you to collectively propose the name of the potential crown prince. The palace's wish would be the same as everyone's choice." And as I had expected, only one name echoed throughout the ground, "Brihaddal, Brihaddal!" In the end,

53. *Rannchhod Rai* - The one who deserts the battlefield.

respecting everyone's wishes, Brihaddal was declared the crown prince by collective choice. My strategy had been successful; Satrajit believed this to be a victory of his charismatic influence over the Yadava leaders, and I too wanted him to nurse this delusion. Encouraged by the success of the first step of my strategy, I enthusiastically invited Brihaddal onstage, embraced him and congratulated him. Seeing this, cheerful cries of "Long live Brihaddal!" began to ring out with increased fervour. A few slogans were shouted in my praise as well. The excitement was such that even the people who had been sitting all along had stood up, while some had even begun to sing and dance. The ground resonated with joyous cries, and soon, a celebratory atmosphere took over the ground. A queue of people had formed to personally congratulate Brihaddal and Satrajit. I, on the other hand, was blatantly ignored. In fact, I stood silently, watching this drama of victory unfold. There was a reason behind this as well. So far, only the first phase of my carefully laid out plan had been executed. I still hadn't played my trump card. I was now patiently waiting for the commotion to subside. So, as soon as everyone's enthusiasm whittled down a little, I addressed the gathering once again, "On everyone's behalf, I congratulate Brihaddal on becoming the crown prince of Mathura. As you all know, Prince Brihaddal is a very brave man. I am convinced that if Mathura ever finds itself facing a threat, he will not baulk at the danger—instead, he will leave no stone unturned in his role as the crown prince of Mathura to protect its honour." Then, looking pointedly at him, I asked, "Am I right, Brihaddal?"

Now, has there ever been a prey that failed to walk into a trap laid by me? The foolish, unsuspecting Brihaddal fell for it, hook, line and sinker. Indeed, my innocent query filled him with such enthusiasm that he stood tall and declared with great fervour, "I affirm that if anyone even looks at Mathura with an evil eye, I will chop off his head!"

After this short but impressive speech by Brihaddal, the meeting came to a close. I was chuffed, for, everything had gone according to my plan. For that matter, you know very well that in my presence, everything plays out the way I want it to. Still, one can only be sure once the task is actually accomplished. And now that things had transpired as per my plan, naturally, my ego had begun to rear its head. But I controlled it, for, a few more phases of my plan still awaited implementation. I'm sure you must be wondering whether this was a single plan or a series of plans! Well, you'll find out soon enough. But first, I had to rein in my ego. Obviously, there was no question of gratifying it before the entire plan was implemented successfully. So, I controlled myself and, focusing my entire attention on Rukmini's impending *swayamvar*, set off for home. How could I tolerate the queen of my dreams being forcefully married off to a scoundrel like Shishupala? Incidentally, Shishupala was my maternal cousin. But so what? Brihaddal was my cousin too! He was my maternal aunt's son. I am not sure why but for some reason it seemed as if I had entered an era of waging strategic wars with cousins! Oh well, now that the war was upon me, I was not one to back down.

I somehow whiled away the next couple of days, but the time had now come to execute the next phase of my plan. For this, I needed Brihaddal's help. Fortunately, this did not pose a difficulty, for, unaware of my political skills, the poor, innocent man was actually quite pleased with me at present. Thus, after a quick discussion with him, I arranged for a grand chariot race to be held in Mathura after ten days. I could easily convince him that this festival would not only entertain the people, but also increase his popularity among the masses. And the poor fellow readily agreed, believing this to be my brotherly affection for him. The matter was thus settled effortlessly. Now, for the next phase of my formidable plan, I wanted as many people as possible to participate in this race. To ensure this, I had myself enlisted ten of my chariots, and going a step further, I even decided to personally participate as a charioteer in the race. For, the next set of events depended entirely on the success of this very race. No one knew of the hidden political agenda behind arranging this race; in fact, I had kept even bhaiya in the dark. Everyone was under the impression that this festival was being organised by Krishna to celebrate Brihaddal's appointment as crown prince. An air of festivity had taken over Mathura, with enthusiasm and fervour reigning supreme. Every *Mathurawasi* was elated, for, this was perhaps the first time in the kingdom's history that a chariot race was being held. Well, this wasn't new to me; after all, in Krishna's presence, unprecedented events were bound to happen.

It was heartening to see the joy and enthusiasm of all the participants, and the chariot race was the only topic of conversation in Mathura. I had asked Brihaddal to specially invite all the Yadava leaders including Satrajit to watch this race. Funnily, everyone was under the impression that it was just a chariot race; not a single person had any inkling of the real reason why I had organised this event. Thinking about the fervour with which everyone was preparing for the race, I would chuckle to myself in the solitude of my chamber at night. What intricate, far-reaching and cunning plans I had begun to devise! Truly, with the passage of time, I was turning more and more dangerous! Just look at the many convoluted schemes my devious mind was able to concoct! Perhaps, this was the reason why the *chakra*[54] with its convoluted design was my favourite weapon. Oftentimes, I would wonder, 'What if all this convoluted scheming causes me to forget to do things in a simple and straightforward manner?'

---

54. *Chakra* - Discus.

Well, the day of the competition was drawing close. My preparations were already in full swing, and so far, everything was proceeding as per plan. On one hand, I had instructed scores of my own soldiers to be armed and present at the chariot race, and on the other, I had also ordered a hundred of the best soldiers from the palace to be stationed at the event. Concurrently, another development had transpired, which was not a part of my plan. These days, I was compelled to put even my charming smile to full use; indeed, it had proven to be an incredible weapon in my arsenal. Whenever someone enquired the purpose of the chariot race, I would flash a mysterious smile, effectively silencing them. It is quite simple really…when one does not want to give a straightforward answer to a question, all one has to do is evade the question with a smile. Incidentally, just like me, my smile was also multi-faceted. It would help me immensely by extricating me from many tricky situations. Whenever I wanted to hide some information or tell a lie, my enchanting smile would come to my rescue. If I wanted to confuse someone, there was no better weapon at my disposal than my smile. In fact, if I wanted to plant a doubt in someone's mind or instigate them, my smile would accomplish it with astonishing ease. Amazingly, neither could anyone fathom its mystery, nor could anyone shield themselves from its spell.

Well, spreading the charm of my smile ever so often, I patiently waited for the day of the chariot race to arrive. And finally, it did! I had reached the contest venue quite early. Naturally, the contest had been arranged far from the city, in a huge ground, close to the main highway. As expected, the whole of Mathura had thronged to see the race. The air pulsated with excitement, and everywhere my gaze fell, people were engaged in animated chatter. Indeed, the entire kingdom wore a festive look. The ground was already at full capacity, yet thousands more were thronging and jostling on both sides of the racing track. Close to a hundred chariots were participating in the competition. Brihaddal had marched into the ground, accompanied by his mentor, Satrajit, while all the prominent Yadava leaders had also reached well in time. Even grandfather had reached the ground with bhaiya in tow. All in all, everyone's enthusiasm was at its peak. And why would it not be? This was, after all, the first time that Mathura was hosting such a grand event to celebrate the coronation of their beloved prince, Brihaddal.

Once the mood was set and I saw nearly two thousand spectators eagerly awaiting the contest, I became fully alert. At this moment, I was seated along with grandfather, bhaiya, Brihaddal, Satrajit and the other Yadava leaders on a stage constructed adjacent to the racing track. In front of us, a hundred chariots stood lined up and ready, surrounded by a huge crowd. Meaning, the mood had been set and the time was ripe to start the proceedings.

Since the arrangements for this chariot race were in my hands, I inaugurated the competition with a formal speech—which was nothing but the final phase of my plan. Thus, standing up from my seat on the podium, I began, "I am pleased that such a grand chariot race is being organised under the leadership of our beloved Prince Brihaddal. For this, I first want to congratulate our prince. I proudly recall the moment when, at the time of his coronation, Prince Brihaddal had shown us a glimpse of the determination and courage hidden within him. I am sure, all of you clearly remember how, on the day he was crowned, the prince had promised to protect the pride and glory of Mathura under all circumstances. That's not all, he had even sworn to sever the head of anyone who dared to question Mathura's dignity. And just see the ways of Nature! Today, our beloved prince has got an opportunity to demonstrate his valour and make good on his promise to Mathura!"

Hearing my words, the audience erupted in surprised chatter. Everyone began wondering what this new threat to Mathura's glory could be, one that was compelling their prince to prove his mettle. Naturally, Satrajit and Brihaddal's camp was alarmed. They too wondered what possible threat required the prince to demonstrate his bravery, a threat that they knew nothing of but Krishna was well aware of! Even grandfather looked at me in astonishment. No one could fathom the great mystery! Now, how could anyone understand the import of Krishna's words, unless he himself explained it? In any case, this was the final move of my elaborate plan, which I had made with the very purpose of knocking everyone out. Of course, I thought it best to reveal the mystery right away rather than keep everyone in the dark. So, I continued dramatically, "This morning, I received news from grandfather that a *swayamvar* for Rukmini, the princess of Kundinpur, has been scheduled... but alas, Mathura has not been invited! This is an affront to Mathura and especially to Prince Brihaddal." Then, raising my voice, I spoke even more dramatically, "Prince Brihaddal will not tolerate this humiliation at any cost!"

Saying this, I incited the crowd to shout slogans like "Glory to Brihaddal! Glory to Mathura and its crown prince who will ride on the fastest chariot and avenge Mathura's honour and pride!" The crowd, as I had orchestrated, was instantly roused by the commotion I had created. Slogans in favour of the prince and Mathura resonated from every corner of the ground, while Brihaddal, Satrajit and the other Yadava leaders wore a dazed look, unable to fathom what exactly had hit them. Indeed, their demeanour reflected the thoughts racing through their minds. In fact, they were scratching their heads wondering, 'Where did this news of Rukmini's *swayamvar* come from…and what was the connection between the *swayamvar* and Brihaddal's vow to safeguard Mathura's glory?' The situation had turned comical indeed.

The members of Satrajit's camp were cowering in fear, while the inhabitants of Mathura were in raptures. Amusingly, with every surge in the enthusiasm of the crowd, the nervousness and fear in Satrajit's camp shot skywards. As for me, I just stood in my place enjoying this spectacle thoroughly. Honestly, I wanted to laugh out loud on seeing Brihaddal and Satrajit reeling in a state of confusion. Deep within, I was elated, even gloating with pride that so far, everything was going according to plan. But there were still many layers yet to be revealed. This was certainly not the time to watch the drama as a spectator or get carried away by emotions. I still had to pull my enemies out of uncertainty and push them into an abyss of fear.

Thus, making my final move, I asked Brihaddal, who was sitting close by, to stand up. Then, raising his hand, I announced, "Everyone, please be quiet. Prince Brihaddal can empathise with your feelings. He is committed to do anything it takes to safeguard the glory of Mathura. Having said that, this *swayamvar* is being conducted under the supervision of King Jarasandha. But so what? Our prince cares little about who the organiser of the *swayamvar* is. In fact, if you ask me, our prince is incredibly lucky to have quickly secured the opportunity to fulfil his pledge of upholding Mathura's pride. We want our brave crown prince to leave for Kundinpur right away, taking all the chariots and soldiers with him, to protect the glory of Mathura, either by thwarting the *swayamvar* or by abducting Rukmini and bringing her to Mathura. We all know that for centuries, it has been a long-standing practice to protect the glory of a kingdom not invited to a *swayamvar*. I am fully confident that our crown prince will not back down either."

Hearing my impassioned speech, the naïve crowd was roused to such an extent that it once again began to shout slogans glorifying Brihaddal, but this time, with double the fervour. Satrajit, in the meantime, threw a spiteful look in my direction. Clearly, it was he alone who understood my strategy better than anyone else. So be it! I was now ready for my final strike. Very calmly, I continued my speech, "Of course, since the *swayamvar* is being conducted under Jarasandha's supervision, it is quite likely that our crown prince might have to face his ire. But even so, I am convinced that to protect the honour of Mathura, our brave Prince Brihaddal will not hesitate to behead even the great Jarasandha!"

With this, I once again shouted, "Glory to Brihaddal!" This served to stoke the fire of patriotism even more and the crowd zealously began to chant slogans glorifying their Prince Brihaddal. After all, it was a question of Mathura's honour. Within no time, the entire ground resonated with slogans and chants glorifying my dear cousin as well as Mathura. To be honest, tears welled up in my eyes at the respect being shown to this brother of mine. It was only natural to become misty-eyed on hearing everyone cheer for him so heartily. I even threw a benevolent glance at him, but what was this? Brihaddal was quivering like a leaf tossed in a storm, trembling with fear. And what do I say about his mentor, Satrajit, who sat unmoving in his seat. Caught in this vexing situation, none of the Yadava leaders could fathom what course of action they should take next.

The situation had turned awkward. All across the ground, the crowd was roaring, demanding that the prince save Mathura's honour. And on the dais, sat that very prince, frozen with fright. A single move by Krishna had forced Jarasandha's minions to clash with him directly; the poor men were truly trapped. If they withdrew now, they would lose face in Mathura. If they accepted the challenge and raced off to display their bravery, their death at Jarasandha's hands was certain. Caught between the devil and the deep, blue sea is exactly where Krishna's deviousness had landed these poor men! The bone was stuck in their throats in such a manner that neither could they swallow it, nor spit it out. Seeing how brilliantly my devious plot had unfolded, my theatrical abilities came rushing to the fore. I thus walked towards Brihaddal, dramatically threw an arm around his shoulder and said, "Come, my brave prince. It is time to crush Jarasandha's pride to smithereens. The whole of Mathura stands in solidarity with you. In fact, it is eager to see you off."

Hearing this, Brihaddal quaked with fright and broke down completely. Body racking with sobs, he pleaded, "I do not want to be the crown prince of Mathura! Let me go!"

Well, couldn't he have understood all this earlier, when it was being explained to him so clearly? And now, he had understood it so well that right after uttering these words, he broke into a sprint and fled from the ground. Seeing him run away, the crowd began to jeer at him. As for Satrajit and the other Yadava leaders, they sank further into their seats, holding their heads in their hands. Their plan and their pawn, both had been beaten and battered. And with this, all their ambitious ideas of taking over the kingdom of Mathura were ground to dust. As for the masses, they were plunged into gloom with Brihaddal's disappearance. Despair was etched on every single face with the realisation that their prince had turned out to be a coward. Satrajit's prestige had been blown to bits and he could not dare to raise his head and look anyone in the eye. Now, I may have succeeded in ruining his plans, but this in no way was going to solve the problem related to Rukmini. But do not worry, because I had an ace up my sleeve to tackle that problem too. Indeed, I may notch up victory after victory, but if I was still unable to save the light of my life, then what was the use of all my efforts? And since this final move concerned me and my 'life', I played it with utmost caution, treading very carefully.

Raising both hands to calm the uproar, I began addressing the crowd. Adopting my most melodramatic tone, I said, "Please do not feel so dejected. If Brihaddal cannot safeguard Mathura's honour, I will shoulder this responsibility myself. Anyone who dares to threaten Mathura's honour—especially someone like Jarasandha—will find that I will not tolerate it. No! Never! Besides, as you all know, I have already fought and defeated this very Jarasandha not once, but twice. So, rest assured I will do so again!"

Hearing my powerful speech, the gloom that had descended on the ground lifted. Enthusiasm found its way back to everyone's hearts, as chants glorifying me began to resound all around. A litany of voices rose in unison, "Mathura's true hero was, is and always will be Krishna…and only Krishna!" Well, there's no denying the truth in these statements. However, right now, I did not care about the slogans glorifying me or the jeers aimed at Brihaddal. I was more interested in rescuing my beloved. So, I immediately set off for Kundinpur with an army of hundred chariots and a posse of soldiers and servants to rescue Rukmini, the queen of my dreams.

Needless to say, the enthused inhabitants of Mathura gave me a hero's send-off. Of course, these innocent people had no idea that there was absolutely no chance that I—who had never fought for my own honour—would rush off to defend Mathura's honour! The poor simpletons had no inkling that Krishna had fooled them and was rushing off to Kundinpur only to save the queen of his dreams. Oh, what a fabulous plan I had hatched! I had not used a single weapon, yet all my enemies had fallen like ninepins. Hats off to you, Krishna, for devising devious plans that would flummox even the sharpest of minds! To be honest, I was feeling quite proud of myself today.

Our chariots thus raced off to Kundinpur, with all the soldiers and charioteers bursting with enthusiasm. And why would they not? After all, they were getting a splendid opportunity to save the honour of Mathura! However, these naïve and innocent men were unaware that I was using them to save the woman of my dreams—Rukmini. Did you see the trick I had played? In the name of upholding Mathura's honour, it was a game played by and for Krishna! And now that I have revealed my game plan, let me also tell you a secret. I had hoodwinked not just Satrajit, the Yadava leaders and the inhabitants of Mathura, but I had duped bhaiya as well.[55] Actually, I had no intention of taking bhaiya along on this adventure. For, taking him with me on such a sensitive mission was like tying a millstone around my neck. Thus, it had become necessary to trick him too. Poor bhaiya, I had told him that in the current circumstances, it was not advisable for both of us to leave Mathura together. What could I do, pulling the wool over his eyes was the very demand of time! For, had I let him accompany me, and in the event that the situation

55. Harivansh Puran, Vishnu Parva, Chapter – 47, Verse – 15-18.

compelled me to abduct Rukmini, I knew for certain that his presence would have put a spoke in the wheel, hindering my plans. And I did not want to take any chances in matters concerning Rukmini. At present, she was not only my dream, but also the very breath I took, my very life. And there was simply no question of Krishna taking chances with his life. For that matter, there was another aspect to this issue as well. My poor brother could have proved helpful if he was aware of the secret I held in my heart. But both bhaiya and Uddhava were unaware of this particular storm of love raging in my heart. For that matter, even Rukmini was not aware of it herself. In short, your dear Kanhaiya was badly caught in a one-sided love affair!

However, I was assured of one thing—due to the clever trap I had laid for Satrajit and his puppet, Prince Brihaddal, and the ignominy that had fallen to their lot, the problem of the Yadava leaders had been dealt with, at least for the time being. In fact, I had left them in no position to raise their heads anytime soon! All in all, I was quite pleased with the respite I had found in Mathura. I also felt extremely proud of myself. But this was all about Mathura; speaking of Kundinpur, my mind was still caught up in a thousand misgivings about the situation there. For, the success of this elaborate plan of mine hinged on being able to rescue Rukmini. After all, the primary objective of this entire ploy was to save the life of the 'light of my life'. But this was not easy by any means. Oh, what do I tell you? Although I had set off on this journey by putting my life at stake, entering Jarasandha's stronghold with these hundred-odd soldiers and rescuing Rukmini from his clutches was nothing less than sheer audacity. I wondered, what if I was voluntarily handing Jarasandha the opportunity to finish me off, a chance he had been waiting for most ardently, just because I had lost my mind due to my love for Rukmini? What if I failed to save the light of my life and, in the process, ended up losing my own life too?

'Krishna, stop it! You are falling prey to despondency,' the inner voice chided. Well, the voice wasn't wrong. When negative thoughts begin to overwhelm the mind, one is bound to be engulfed in despair. Hence, shrugging off the despondency threatening to swallow me, I reassured myself saying, 'O brave warrior, when you have killed despots such as Panchajanya and Shringlava in their own stronghold, when all odds were against you, of what consequence is this fiend, Jarasandha? Trust me, for a master strategist like you, it is not a difficult task to be able to save the light of your life while also saving your own skin.' No sooner had these thoughts filled my mind than my entire being was suffused with positivity and I could feel a gradual surge in my confidence. At the same time, I vowed to myself that I would not let Rukmini be forcefully married to Shishupala under any circumstances.

I loved her more than life itself, and now, I was willing to risk my own life to save her! Oh, just see, I was back to where I had started. Killing was one thing, but where did all these morbid thoughts of death come from? It was one thing to die for Rukmini, but that did not mean I would offer my head on a platter to my arch enemy, Jarasandha. Indeed, I had gone off track in my thinking, for, there was no question of killing or being killed. The handful of soldiers at my disposal were far too few to engage in a battle with the mighty Jarasandha. At the most, I could create an obstacle to effectively put a stop to the *swayamvar*. At the same time, abducting Rukmini was out of the question, for, given my current situation, neither did I consider myself worthy of her, nor did I have a palace or kingdom of my own to welcome her as a princess! Thus, in the present situation, my biggest achievement would be to stop the *swayamvar* somehow. If I could stop Rukmini from being married off and return to Mathura safe and sound, I would consider my mission successful. Ah, this was a great development indeed! My plan had become crystal clear while revisiting the strategy I had devised.

It was on the evening of the fifth day that our small army reached the outskirts of Kundinpur. So engrossed was I in my thoughts that I had completely lost track of time! Well, after reaching the outskirts of the kingdom, we took a halt at an *ashram*. We were already exhausted from the continuous journey; besides, from a security standpoint, it was unwise to enter an unfamiliar city at night. But there was nothing to be gained by waiting unnecessarily either. So, the next day, we rode into Kundinpur at the break of dawn. Our grand procession of hundred chariots caught everyone by surprise, and consequently, the news of my arrival spread like wildfire throughout Kundinpur. Well, this was exactly what I had wanted, and this was why I had entered the city early in the morning, flanked by a royal caravan. Thereafter, I kept this stately procession moving up and down the streets of Kundinpur for hours together. Wherever our caravan turned, an inquisitive crowd would gather to see us pass by. My objective was clear: I wanted the news of my arrival to reach not just Jarasandha and Rukmini, but also the inhabitants of Kundinpur as quickly as possible. And by afternoon, I had successfully achieved this objective, as the news reached every nook and corner of the kingdom. By evening, we retired to a splendid guest house situated in the heart of the city.

Rukmini's *swayamvar* was eight days away, but my problem was that I could not seek an audience with King Bhishmak by striding straight into his court. It was not as if I had been invited to the *swayamvar* that I could simply march into the palace. What I mean to say is, I was totally deprived of the king's hospitality. In fact, I was enacting all this drama only to intimate him of my arrival and secure an invitation for myself. Of course, I was well aware that Jarasandha was at the helm of the *swayamvar,* hence it would be well-nigh impossible to wrangle an invitation. But I felt assured by the fact that although the reins of the *swayamvar* were in Jarasandha's hands, it was King Bhishmak who had to observe royal protocol. And as the *swayamvar* was of his own daughter, it was his prestige which was at stake. Now, Bhishmak was no ordinary king who could be pushed around and compelled to obey Jarasandha's decree. And, frankly speaking, it was only because of this conviction that I had made the audacious decision to come here. Well, whether Bhishmak was able to invite me or not, it was certain that he would not give Jarasandha the opportunity to make any rash move against me. Meaning, Bhishmak would bind Jarasandha by royal protocol and prevent him from seeking revenge. In other words, despite entering the lion's den, I was perfectly safe. Indeed, I was no fool to have come this far just to be slaughtered at the hands of Jarasandha!

Well, I heaved a sigh of relief, happy in the knowledge that no harm would come to me. But all said and done, I was still anxious about Rukmini—not just anxious, but deeply worried. And from that perspective, the good news was that my move had proved successful. My arrival, with a splendid caravan in tow, had compelled the royal palace to extend an invitation to me. After all, it was impossible to continue ignoring the hero who had twice defeated Jarasandha and killed the likes of Panchajanya and Shringlava. The very next day, the Deputy Commander of the Kundinpur army came to see me, bearing gifts from King Bhishmak. Well, it was reassuring to know I was being accorded at least this much respect.

But wait a minute! This man, the Deputy Commander, looked very familiar. Then it dawned upon me that he was my dear friend, Shwetketu, a classmate from *Acharya* Sandipani's *ashram.* My heart leapt with joy on seeing him. This was the first time since my birth that Nature had cast her benevolence on me and favoured me with kindness. Indeed, this was an unexpected blessing. Also, the arrival of gifts from King Bhishmak, despite the *swayamvar* being in charge of Jarasandha, was in itself a big breakthrough. Indeed, on just the second day of my arrival, I had received two pieces of great news from the kingdom of my beloved. First, the king's adherence to royal protocol was proof of my safety. Second, the Deputy Commander of the enemy turning out to be my friend boded well for my future.

But time was short and there was a lot that needed to be done. So, after spending a few moments catching up, I came straight to the point. Upon enquiring, I learnt that Shwetketu had been appointed as the Deputy Commander in King Bhishmak's service for the past year and a half. Ah!

There could not have been any happier news for me than this. His appointment to such an important position was tantamount to gaining a secret entry into the royal palace. Now, it was mere child's play for me to know what exactly the palace was thinking, and more importantly, the arrangements that were underway for the *swayamvar*. Indeed, it is said that if you know beforehand what the enemy is thinking and planning, it is as good as winning half the battle. And presently, this seemed to be the case with me. As proof of this, I had very diplomatically wormed out a number of secrets of the royal palace from Shwetketu. In a way, it could be said that he had opened the doors of victory for me. Shwetketu revealed that the *swayamvar* was planned upon the insistence of Jarasandha and Rukmi, while King Bhishmak was not in favour of it at all. But the poor king was helpless before Rukmi's insistence. This being the situation, the only person who could help Rukmini at present was Grandfather Kaishik. He was so vehemently opposed to Jarasandha and Rukmi using force that he had walked out of the palace in protest and was now living at a nearby *ashram*. That's not all! At present, the person Rukmini shares the closest bond with is him; in fact, she even confides all her sorrows to Grandfather Kaishik.

Hearing the entire narrative, I was caught in a vortex of emotions, while several thoughts raced through my mind. But all said and done, the news was definitely encouraging. Firstly, Rukmini was not happy with the *swayamvar,* and secondly, from a political standpoint, it was heartening to know that her grandfather was also against this alliance. However, seeing the bigger picture, the increasing clout of unruly sons in Aryavarta was truly a cause for concern. In Hastinapur, King Dhritarashtra was being browbeaten by his uncontrollable son, Duryodhana, while here, King Bhishmak was helpless in front of his son, Rukmi. King Damghosh also had to bow down to the wishes of his son, Shishupala; and in Mathura, Kansa had usurped the throne after having his father, King Ugrasena, thrown into prison! The worrisome aspect was this: would the ongoing struggle for the throne and dominance between fathers and sons eventually lead to the downfall of all of Aryavarta?

Oh, just see! Overcome with worry for Rukmini, I had wandered far, my mind now consumed with thoughts of the greater good. However, I reined in my thoughts, for, this was not the time to worry about the greater good. The inner voice mused, 'My dear Kanhaiya, first think about yourself and the light of your life. What is the use of worrying about the future at this moment?' Thinking thus, I immediately returned to the topic of Rukmini. Actually, Shwetketu had not revealed much about her, and unable to curb my curiosity, I straightaway asked about her. Alas, what he revealed upset me even more! Distressed by the forced *swayamvar,* Rukmini had expressed her anger and opposition to it a thousand times over—however, her pleas have fallen on deaf ears. As a result, she has been crying incessantly, day and night! Overcome with exhaustion from the constant weeping, her tears have now run dry. But even this sorrowful condition of his sister hasn't melted the heart of Rukmi, who has chosen to turn a blind eye. And on the off chance that he feels pity for her, he finds himself helpless before Jarasandha and Shishupala, who are manipulating him like a puppet. And now, as a final attempt to pressure them, the poor Rukmini has refused to eat or drink, hoping that this form of protest will soften their hearts. Oh! I was deeply distressed upon hearing this. How could a lover not be engulfed in misery when the life of his beloved was at stake?

Well, this was the end of our informal conversation. And it was only now that Shwetketu remembered that he had been assigned the task of enquiring the purpose of my visit to Kundinpur. After all, the king had sent him here with that very purpose. Great! I had asked everything I wanted to and gathered all the information from him, but he was still clueless about why I was asking all these questions. Well, he would know only if I told him, right? However, I was faced with a dilemma, for, what should I tell him? He was no doubt a good friend, someone I could confide in. In fact, at that moment, he felt like a saviour, and it didn't seem right to keep secrets from him. But then, I reckoned, there would be ample time later to reveal my true intentions. For now, it was crucial to send a strong, politically appropriate message to the king. So, I said, "Actually, Mathura did not receive an invitation for the *swayamvar*. Perhaps, we were excluded on Jarasandha's orders. Either way, Mathura sees it as a grave insult. That's why I've come here with a posse of soldiers to express our indignation over this humiliation, and of course, to get the ceremony cancelled."

Shwetketu was dumbfounded. He realised that his friend, Krishna, had come with a very dangerous intention. Well, regardless of my motives, he had come to understand the purpose of my visit—and he had succeeded in his task. However, as he was leaving, he gave me a peculiar smile and shared the good tidings that he had recently tied the knot. That was wonderful news! I was thrilled for him, so enveloping him in a warm embrace, I congratulated him wholeheartedly. Well, he left soon after, but not before offering me a sense of reassurance. Indeed, one does feel reassured on finding a friendly face in enemy territory.

Our meeting had been fruitful in more ways than one. First, feeling reassured, the restlessness I had been experiencing since the past several days had gone. Indeed, I slept soundly after many nights of sleeplessness. And after enjoying a good night's sleep, I was brimming with energy the next day. As soon as the sun rose, I stepped out to explore the kingdom of Kundinpur. I reckoned, the king's reaction to my message would come in due course, but until then, why not find out what the inhabitants of Kundinpur thought of the *swayamvar*? In just one day of roaming around the city, I learnt that the people were not particularly pleased with the *swayamvar*. On the contrary, the majority were upset with Prince Rukmi. They were unhappy with the idea that their darling princess was being forced to marry against her wishes. Actually, this did clear up the air to some extent, for, I too was wondering, with the *swayamvar* just around the corner, how was it possible that no one in the city was in a celebratory mood? Well, the unhappiness of the people was actually good news for me. My enthusiasm soared upon realising that not just the king and the grandfather, but even the masses were completely against the *swayamvar*. Indeed, when I had left Mathura, I had been clueless, riding into pitch-black darkness with not a glimmer of hope in sight. But now, after just two days in Kundinpur, things were beginning to look up—bright and clear. Naturally, my happiness knew no bounds. Now, I was only waiting for Shwetketu to return with the king's response, as my next move hinged on the king's reaction to my message.

I, however, did not have to wait long, as Shwetketu arrived on time. But the moment I opened the door to welcome him, I stood stunned. He had brought his wife along, who was none other than Shaivya, whom I had adopted as my sister not too long ago. I was astonished to see her, and she too was dumbfounded on seeing me. Instantly, the atmosphere turned joyous with the reunion of a brother and his sister. Along with this came the conviction that I had the full support of Nature—this was precisely why I was running into my friends, one after another, in this unfamiliar city. Recovering from this pleasant surprise, Shaivya was the first to speak. In an incredulous tone, she said, "Brother Krishna, is it really you?"

Hearing her voice, I was jolted back to my senses; otherwise, I would have remained lost in thought, caught up in the beauty of the moment. I promptly ushered them inside, and as they entered, I replied in my characteristic style, "Yes sister, it is really me, Krishna!"

Seeing us talk with such ease and familiarity, Shwetketu was surprised. Naturally, the fact that Shaivya shared a close bond with me was nothing less than a surprise for him. So be it! Interestingly, even though we had met for political reasons, a warm and familial atmosphere took over this small gathering. The three of us sat down on the bed itself and made ourselves comfortable. In the course of our conversation, Shaivya revealed that it was she who had gotten Shwetketu appointed as the Deputy Commander of the armed forces in Karvirpur. Eventually, they had fallen in love and later tied the knot. But after marriage, Shwetketu did not want to stay in Karvirpur as the Deputy Commander; his self-respect would not allow him to do so. Hence, they had both come to Kundinpur. However, the best news Shaivya gave me was that she had become a close friend of Rukmini ever since. Now, this was news that truly interested me! In fact, I couldn't have imagined better tidings than this! Really, everything falls seamlessly into place when Nature's wish synchronises with yours. That is why it is said that Nature has a thousand hands!

Well, what more could I have asked for? Taking cue from this, I revealed to them what was in my heart. As a matter of fact, this was the first time I had revealed the love I harboured in my heart for Rukmini to anyone. Hearing that I, her brother, was in love with Rukmini, Shaivya jumped for joy, but the very next moment, her shoulders slouched, her happiness turning into anxiety. For, Rukmini was about to get married, and the most distressing aspect of this *swayamvar* was that it was being held against her wishes. Moreover, the stress that Rukmini was undergoing was gradually deteriorating her health, leaving her extremely weak. Unburdening all her worries, Shaivya looked at me helplessly. The very manner in which she looked at me pushed me into the depths of despair. I failed to comprehend how any father or brother—and that too, not an ordinary person, but a king—could come under pressure and meekly watch his darling daughter be married off to an evil man like Shishupala. Honestly, hearing Shaivya's account of Rukmini's suffering caused me immense pain, making each breath I took unbearable. I wanted to run to her and console her, but unfortunately, the present circumstances made that impossible. Oh, I had never felt so helpless before! Moreover, Shwetketu had not been able to gauge the king's reaction to my message. For that matter, the king's opinion did not hold much weight either, as he more or less depended on Jarasandha. And Jarasandha's intentions towards me were crystal clear.

In essence, Shwetketu did not have any news for me at present; his visit today was prompted purely by personal reasons. Besides, with only six days left until the *swayamvar,* there was a mountain of tasks to be completed. Hence, they departed after promising to return the next day with fresh information. As for me, I was left alone, curious about the road ahead. Most importantly, I could not plan my next step until I had some idea about the royal palace's reaction to my arrival. Meaning, despite a thousand complications, I still had to wait for fresh information from Shwetketu. On the other hand, I was certain that after hearing the news of my arrival, my three sworn enemies, Jarasandha, Shishupala and Rukmi, must have surely considered hatching a

plot to eliminate me! Although I was prepared for any unexpected attack on my life, the possibility of my being attacked in Kundinpur was close to nil. I could say this with conviction because I had come here simply to register Mathura's protest—not to start a war. And Mathura was entitled to do this from a political standpoint. Seen from this perspective, I was King Bhishmak's royal guest, albeit an uninvited one. Therefore, if anything untoward happened to me here, King Bhishmak would be disgraced in all of Aryavarta. It would also create a big wave of opposition against Jarasandha, and that in turn would surely ruin his plans to become the emperor of Aryavarta.

In short, I was confident that Bhishmak, who was a politically astute king, would not entertain any childish suggestion put forth by Shishupala or Rukmi. This was the only reason why I felt reassured. In fact, let me admit that it was based on this assessment alone that I had entered the jaws of death in the first place. Circumstances had connived in such a manner that neither could they attack me, nor object to my being present here; in fact, they could not even order me out of the kingdom. On the other hand, I must say, my very presence in Kundinpur must be pricking them like a thorn. Meaning, I had proved to be a bone stuck in their throat, which they could neither swallow nor spit out. However, all these considerations, though amusing, were of little consequence at present. The paramount task before me was to stop Rukmini's *swayamvar,* and this problem remained unresolved, fraught with complexities. Despite the many positive developments that had occurred recently, I had not been able to come up with a foolproof solution to tackle this problem. Meanwhile, it was also certain that after learning the purpose of my arrival, the security at the *swayamvar* venue would be reinforced to such an extent that even considering abducting Rukmini would be insane. In short, all the good news and promising signs I had received since my arrival had turned out to be nothing more than fleeting bubbles, vanishing into thin air! They held no practical significance, as none of them pointed to a viable way to save Rukmini.

Oh, what do I tell you about my condition? I spent the entire day pacing up and down in my chamber, lost in these thoughts. The only hope flickering in my heart was that Shwetketu would bring some positive news about the king's reaction to my arrival. However, there was still no sign of him, and I wasted the entire day waiting for him. And as night came trundling in, I spent it tossing and turning in bed. With my patience wearing thin, I decided, enough was enough; I could not waste these crucial days twiddling my thumbs in anticipation of the king's reaction. Come what may, I had to stop the *swayamvar* under all circumstances. I reckoned that even though I may not be able to change the royal palace's intention, I could very well stoke public sentiment against it and mount pressure indirectly. At any rate, with nothing else to do, this was the least I could do. Thinking thus, the following day, I set my plan into motion and spent the next two days instigating the people against the *swayamvar*. All I had to do was provoke those who were already disgruntled with the *swayamvar,* by reminding them that the princess of any kingdom is the pride and honour of not just the king but the entire kingdom too. Playing the emotional card, I told them that Princess Rukmini should not just be seen as their own daughter, but that there must be strong opposition to her being forced to marry a rogue against her will. Finally, my efforts paid off and voices denouncing the *swayamvar* erupted from various pockets of Kundinpur. Gradually, the protests gained so much traction that the very walls of the royal palace rattled under their onslaught. As for the people, when they could be so easily instigated even for a wrong cause, how difficult was it to provoke them over something that was right? All it needed was a few emotionally charged words, accompanied by a suitably sad face, and the masses were fired up. Moreover, I had painted a painfully poignant picture of Rukmini's condition, so how could their sentiments not be stirred? Indeed, unable to bear the sight of their darling princess in such a plight, they were bound to be enraged.

Suffice to say that this move of mine turned out to be a success. The same royal palace, which had been studiously ignoring me so far, had now sent me a formal invitation. Shwetketu himself came bearing an invitation from King Bhishmak. Naturally, the vociferous protests all around had put pressure on an already weakened Bhishmak. At any rate, he was not in favour of the *swayamvar,* so this had perhaps given him the chance to hear what he wanted to. Otherwise, it is usually very easy for the palace to dismiss trivial protests from the people. Whatever the case may be, my work was done and I was elated. Wild with happiness, I embraced Shwetketu and even kissed his cheeks a few times. Indeed, my plan to put pressure on the royal palace had produced the desired effect. And now that the door to dialogue and discussion was open, I was confident that many others would open on their own. This was certainly a big victory for me, and I felt justifiably proud of it. Truly, my plans never failed! Perhaps, my determination was so strong that circumstances simply had to bend to my will.

Actually, another key reason for my string of successes was that even in the most difficult situations, I never accepted defeat as long as there was some option available. Despondency could never tie me down. I made it a point to completely understand the situation at hand, analyse it thoroughly, and then try to do everything to tackle it, and that too, without any self-interest… such being the case, why would I not be able to achieve the desired outcome?

I knew that Rukmi and Jarasandha would never get pressured by the public. But King Bhishmak carried on his shoulders the responsibility of running his kingdom, hence he could not ignore public opinion beyond a point. He had to respect their wishes under any circumstances. Indeed, the people's revolt had accomplished what I had been aiming for since the time I had arrived. King Bhishmak's formal invitation had laid the groundwork for my victory in the battle for my love. After all, since the time I had set foot in Kundinpur, my only motive was to be invited to the palace to engage in a dialogue. For, I knew that in the course of a discussion with me, I could turn the very tide in my favour. That was precisely why I had been anxiously waiting to visit the palace ever since my arrival in Kundinpur. And now that the moment I had been waiting for had arrived, why delay it? So, I quickly got ready and left with Shwetketu, brimming with confidence and attitude. Shwetketu had come with four chariots to escort me to the palace, but I was not one to be left behind; to make a grand impression, I accompanied him with scores of my own chariots. After all, I was heading to my in-laws' house, so I had to travel in style. On a serious note, today was the day of judgement—the real test of my eloquence—and needless to say, I was more than ready for it.

Contrary to my expectations, the court was filled with kings and princes. I had thought that I would be taken straightaway to meet King Bhishmak, but no, an entire royal assembly was in attendance. Perhaps, Bhishmak wanted to take all the decisions in everyone's presence so that no one could point a finger at him later. Regardless of the reason, his attempt had ensured that my eloquence would be put to the ultimate test. It was easy to prevail upon Bhishmak alone, but to persuade all the kings and princes…well, never mind! To fire up my enthusiasm, my most beloved friend, Jarasandha, was also present in the assembly. Not only was he present, but he was also seated with an air of pride. The elevation of his throne itself indicated his special status. His acolytes, Shishupala and Rukmi, were seated on either side of him. As for me, seeing my foes seated so proudly with their wicked intentions writ large on their faces, my enthusiasm was bound to soar. Indeed, I followed a simple principle—the higher the waves rolled, the more expertly I swam. Meaning, the grimmer the situation, the more astute and agile I became. And this was proven by the fact that I had not forsaken my humorous nature even in such a formidable situation. I glanced at Jarasandha and gave him my most supercilious half-smile, as if he was just a lowly minion. For that matter, even Jarasandha had not discarded his usual demeanour. He stared at me fiercely, as if he would swallow me whole. But what difference did it make to me? Irrespective of Jarasandha's status in Aryavarta or his position in Bhishmak's court, as far as I was concerned, he was just an ordinary king, who while fighting against me, had fled from the battle on two occasions. Now, tell me, would I perceive Jarasandha through my own lens or would I see him through the eyes of what the world thought of him?

Standing at the entrance of the courtroom, I was quietly watching this entire scene, a little smile playing at the corner of my lips. The entire court had its eyes riveted on me, watching me keenly, especially the kings and princes of other kingdoms who were taking a special interest in sizing me up. And why would they not? For, an ordinary cowherd, barely twenty-four years old, stood boldly as a distinguished personality in front of such reputed kings. Honestly, my ego soared skywards at the very thought of this. On the other hand, the condition of the kings and princes was no less strange. They kept darting glances between Jarasandha and me, as if trying to make a mental comparison of our respective strengths. Looking at me, they found it hard to believe that this young lad had defeated Jarasandha twice! And interestingly, even Jarasandha was not oblivious to these glances of comparison that were being levelled at us. In his heart of hearts, he was agitated, but he was a seasoned king after all, so he controlled himself and adopted a stoic demeanour, maintaining a marked silence.

Well, let us forget about him for now and talk about King Bhishmak, in whose royal court I now found myself. The king left no stone unturned in following protocol and offered me a seat as soon as I arrived. This was the first time I had the opportunity to sit among so many kings, and naturally, I could not contain my elation at receiving such an honour. Indeed, this was a matter of great pride for an ordinary cowherd like me. And I saw it as an opportunity, for, if I managed to make an impact in this court, it would be certain that this cowherd would be recognised and accepted as a king across all of Aryavarta. Sensing this, I too observed protocol, just like a seasoned king. To begin with, I paid my respects to King Bhishmak and then turned my gaze towards Jarasandha and offered respects to him and the other kings. It was only then that this cowherd took his seat in style, on par with the other kings. Honestly, this single gesture made me feel worthy of Rukmini. If nothing else, this delusion at least emboldened me, making my enthusiasm soar to the skies! After all, my enthusiasm was all I could bank on in this difficult situation.

Well, only time would tell how the situation would unfold from here on. As soon as I sat down, a palpable silence descended over the court, making it evident that everything had been discussed at length long before my arrival. Besides, everyone's presence had also proven this beyond a doubt. Obviously, the matter could not be resolved by either Bhishmak or Jarasandha, which is why I had been summoned before an entire assembly of kings. Needless to say, Jarasandha, Rukmi and Shishupala were not thrilled to see me being invited here. But why should that matter to me? Well, as was my wont, I tried to lock Jarasandha's gaze with mine, but he pointedly refused to look at me. However, I could see the effort it took him to control the rage simmering just below the calm countenance he was displaying. Meanwhile, silence continued to prevail in the court. Since it was King Bhishmak's court, it was his prerogative to begin the proceedings, but the poor king seemed utterly at a loss for words. This made me wonder: what if this silence continued indefinitely, until it was time for the *swayamvar* itself?! No, this certainly would not do. Hence, losing my patience, I decided it was better to present my case in my own way, before Bhishmak parroted the words put into his mouth by Jarasandha. With this thought, I rose from my seat and addressed King Bhishmak confidently, "O King, I express my gratitude to you for the invitation. However, I believe this invitation should have been given to me the very day I had set foot in Kundinpur."

My opening statement was so incisive that it left not just Bhishmak but everyone else speechless too. It also managed to create a great first impression on this imposing assembly of kings. To my amusement, King Bhishmak completely lost his equilibrium with my first strike; still fumbling, he managed to say, "Well...actually, I was about to send you an invitation but then…"

I refused to let him complete his statement. Indeed, when his tongue had slipped, why would I not take advantage of it? Thus, cutting him short with a laugh, I said, "But Jarasandha must have not approved of it. Well, so what? I am sure you are well aware that he and I go back a long way. And if I'm not mistaken, Kundinpur is still under your rule!"

Although provoked, Jarasandha displayed maturity by managing to remain silent even after being subjected to my sarcasm, but Rukmi was riled up. Well, it hardly mattered. Who cared about him anyway? Besides, now that I was regarded as an equal, I had acquired the right to speak as an equal too. Indeed, only if I spoke as an equal would I truly be convinced that I was on par with all these kings. However, by now, King Bhishmak had completely regained his composure. This time, showing maturity, he did not respond to my sarcastic remark at all. On the contrary, he took over the reins of the conversation and started afresh. Ignoring my sharp sarcasm, he spoke very calmly, "Kundinpur is as much your kingdom as it is mine. You may come and go whenever you please. But I fail to understand the purpose of your arrival on the occasion of Rukmini's *swayamvar*."

I laughed and retorted, "O King, you are playing a fine game of pretence. Everyone is aware that you have not invited Mathura for this *swayamvar*. So, what choice did you leave me with other than to come here

as an uninvited guest?" Did you notice; now that I had the opportunity to sit among kings, I was completely in my element. Inspired by this great mood and seeing Jarasandha seated in front of me, it was only natural that I felt the urge to needle him. To be honest, I wanted to annoy him and make him lose his composure. So, with this objective in mind, I pretended to sympathise with King Bhishmak and spoke dramatically, "It appears that you have committed the audacious act of not inviting Mathura under the influence of some foolish people whom Mathura has cut down to size on a number of occasions!"

Well, I said what I had to, but the very next moment, I realised I might have said a bit too much. But so what? It brought about the effect I had hoped for. Hearing my sarcastic jibe, Jarasandha went wild with rage; in fact, he shot up from his seat and even unsheathed his sword. Watching this act of his, the entire court froze. Perfect! This was exactly the reaction I wanted. Indeed, until an opponent is roused to anger, he does not commit a mistake. Well, this was as far as the interaction between Jarasandha and me was concerned, but seeing the atmosphere become tense, King Bhishmak grew worried. He somehow managed to calm Jarasandha down by repeatedly entreating him with folded hands. However, seeing Jarasandha's condition, I could barely hide my amusement. The one who held unquestionable sway over entire Aryavarta had been humiliated by an ordinary cowherd, but all he could do was swallow the insult and bear it quietly. Tell me, how could I not feel like laughing? Having pacified Jarasandha, King Bhishmak now spoke to me in an irritable tone, "I would appreciate it if you could simply state what you mean, instead of making sarcastic remarks."

I thought, 'Alright then, I will present my case. The king's wish is my command.' This time around, I spoke gravely, "You are all well aware that I have come here merely to register my protest. If an invitation had been extended to Mathura, there would have been no need for me to come here at all. For, neither Mathura nor I have any interest in Rukmini. Therefore, my visit should be viewed as one undertaken purely for political reasons, and most importantly, one driven by compulsion."

King Bhishmak replied immediately, "We have understood the purpose of your visit, but we fail to understand why you have been instigating the people against us."

Ah! Finally, he laid his thoughts bare. But I was not one to be outsmarted. Putting on an innocent expression, I declared guilelessly, "Actually, when I came here, the common people began requesting me to put a stop to this *swayamvar*. Your own subjects think that this *swayamvar* is just a farce and that Rukmini is being forced to marry Shishupala. But contrary to what you have accused me of, I tried to defuse the situation, explaining to the people that this couldn't possibly be the case. I pointed out to them that several brave and promising princes from across Aryavarta have been invited to this *swayamvar*. In the event that such a vile attempt was made, would they not draw out their swords and put an end to the ceremony?" I had been asked for an explanation, and just see, I had cleverly used the opportunity to shoot another arrow from my quiver, successfully hitting the mark. Hearing me speak in an inciting manner, Jarasandha and Bhishmak's faces fell, taking on a sick hue. But how could I be satisfied with this alone? I couldn't let them off the hook so easily. So, looking around at all the assembled princes and addressing them directly, I said, "My brave brothers, did I say something wrong?"

No sooner had I finished speaking than many of the princes, nodding vehemently in agreement, rose to their feet and drew their swords. One of them even shouted, "If such an attempt has really been made, then mark my words, there will be bloodshed in this court!" Aha! My work here was done. The court had more or less turned into a fighting arena. Seeing the tumultuous turn of events, King Bhishmak began to quiver like a leaf, for, he could see the situation spiral out of control. He was so frightened that he couldn't even muster the words to salvage the rapidly deteriorating situation. With Bhishmak losing control, Jarasandha swung into action. He tried to handle the situation in a different way. Addressing me directly, he said, "Clearly, you were not invited, but despite that, I wonder why you have come all the way from Mathura to disrupt the *swayamvar*! Moreover, you have incited the masses and are now pretending to be innocent, trying to deceive everyone. And if that wasn't enough, you are now provoking these princes too, right before our eyes!"

His words and stance clearly revealed his helplessness. Casting a pitying glance at him, I spoke in my head, 'O Jarasandha! Whether it is the battlefield or the political arena, you will always find yourself helpless before Krishna. And just look at the extent of your helplessness! I will continue to embarrass you, and you will be forced to watch the drama as a mute spectator!' But Jarasandha was seasoned and intelligent enough to gauge the situation. He had understood that I was embarrassing him repeatedly so that he would get incensed and the situation would spiral out of control. His dilemma was that while he could endure the pangs of humiliation, he could not allow the situation to escalate any further. For, the disruption of the *swayamvar* would irrevocably weaken his grip over Aryavarta. Everyone would mock him, questioning why they should fear a man who couldn't even manage a *swayamvar* properly. Ultimately, seeing no way out, the great Jarasandha almost pleaded with me saying, "What is it that you want? Why are you determined to disrupt this auspicious event?"

Aha, it was only now that I had him exactly where I needed him! Actually, I could very well understand his helplessness, and if truth be told, it was precisely this helplessness that I was using to my advantage. To become the emperor of Aryavarta was his heart's earnest desire, and this being the case, it was imperative for him to conduct this *swayamvar* without any disruptions. Having said that, I too was well aware of my own limits and current position. Jarasandha was, after all, the uncrowned emperor of Aryavarta, and to cross my limits and instigate him beyond a point was extremely risky. Thus, I instantly changed my stance, and although I still wanted to make inflammatory statements, I had to veil them under the garb of humility. So, adopting a calm tone this time, I said to Jarasandha, "Actually, I want to save King Bhishmak's reputation from being tarnished. As you can see, Grandfather Kaishik has already left the royal palace in protest of this *swayamvar*. Just think, if even the subjects, the very people of Kundinpur, as well as these princes turn against the king, what will be left of his reputation? Wouldn't it be smashed to smithereens? And God forbid, if his daughter's wedding is stained by bloodshed, it will affect not just her future, but that of the entire kingdom too. Now, of course, the king can do as he pleases, but in my opinion, I would strongly insist that King Bhishmak cancels this *swayamvar*."

Hearing me, the entire court fell silent. Only Shishupala and Rukmi continued to glare at me with angry, embittered eyes, and the look they shot me was proof enough of the malicious thoughts raging through their minds. Indeed, if they had the opportunity, they would not think twice before pouncing on me and tearing me apart right this moment. As for poor Jarasandha, he could not wrap his head around what he had just heard. The very court was now pulsating with an undercurrent of tension. While Jarasandha was baffled, his acolytes were seething with rage. And if this wasn't enough, the princes I had instigated were standing by, swords drawn, ready to kill or be killed. Some kings were trying to help Jarasandha save face, while others were engaged in discussing the future of King Bhishmak and Rukmini. And the best part was that I, who had created this entire ruckus, stood calm in my place watching the drama unfold. Oh, I cannot tell you how much I was enjoying myself! Meanwhile, King Bhishmak had broken down completely on seeing chaos and disruption take over his court. The court too was trapped in the complex web of my arguments. Jarasandha was tongue-tied, as if he had taken a vow of silence for the rest of his life! Did I not say from the very beginning that, if given the chance to speak, I would turn everything on its head before anyone even realised what had come to pass?! Ultimately, what I desired did materialise. Helpless as he was, King Bhishmak spoke in an almost whining tone, "My daughter Rukmini has been unconscious since yesterday. The royal physicians are not happy with her condition. I too am not feeling well. I request all of you to maintain peace and calm."

Out of pity for him, everyone did calm down, but Shishupala couldn't keep his cool any longer. Well, his anger was justified; after all, with the *swayamvar* now in jeopardy, it was the potential 'bridegroom' who was bound to be upset the most. However, there is a limit to that as well, but this fool had completely lost his composure. Boiling with fury, he launched a personal attack on me bellowing, "So what if we did not invite Mathura? It's our wish! Why have you shamelessly come here to create hurdles in the *swayamvar*? Besides, only kings and princes are invited to a royal *swayamvar*, not cowherds!"

There! He had put his foot in his mouth. The poor fool had vented all his anger in one go. But displaying maturity, I maintained a dignified silence, and in spite of being called a cowherd in a packed courtroom, I did not lose my temper. I had to tread the same path as Jarasandha and Bhishmak by not behaving childishly. So, I merely turned to Shishupala and spoke calmly, "Whether I am a cowherd or a prince is not for you to decide. That decision lies with King Bhishmak and he has already made it by according respect to me. As for my coming here, let me make it clear that this court will definitely have to pay the price for humiliating Mathura."

Hearing this, it was Rukmi's turn to explode with anger. He stood up at once and shouted, "Do you mean to say you will abduct Rukmini?"

As soon as he said this, the atmosphere in the court became even more tense. This was exactly what I was aiming for. An increasing level of tension would mount pressure on King Bhishmak and this in turn would serve my purpose. In fact, I wanted the situation to deteriorate so much that the king would become a nervous wreck. And this was precisely what happened. When he saw the discussion veering towards his darling daughter's abduction, he was shattered. Indeed, which father would not feel devastated on hearing his daughter's abduction being discussed? But Bhishmak had become a little too distraught. He was so overwrought that he broke into tears right in front of everyone. Seeing the king sob in this manner, the entire court was stunned into silence. Honestly, I too did not enjoy seeing the king in such a pitiable condition. This was certainly the anguished cry of a loving father. Naturally, as a gesture of sympathy, silence reigned in the courtroom. No one could muster the courage to utter a single word. I too fell silent. What else could I do? After all, it was I who had masterminded the whole drama. Finally, King Bhishmak himself broke the silence. Addressing the assembly in a sad and broken voice, he said, "As mentioned earlier, my daughter Rukmini has been unconscious since yesterday. The royal physician has advised that it would be unwise to conduct her *swayamvar* in her present condition. Therefore, it is with deep regret that I declare the *swayamvar* cancelled. I also offer my sincere apologies to all the honoured kings and princes for this unexpected turn of events."

Then, turning to me, he said, "I apologise to you too for the grave mistake of not inviting Mathura to the *swayamvar*."

Hearing this, I was overjoyed. For, I had finally accomplished my goal. My love was safe! The danger looming over Rukmini had been averted at least for the time being. A wave of renewed enthusiasm surged through my entire being, and in its wake, I even imparted a piece of advice to the king, "It is my humble request to you that when you hold the *swayamvar* next time, kindly do not forget to invite Mathura."

I reckoned, this would at least ensure my candidature for the next time. Meanwhile, a dark, brooding silence descended over the royal court after the king announced his decision. Jarasandha, Shishupala and Rukmi looked miserable, as if they had just lost an epic battle. Of course, the worst hit was Shishupala, the honourable 'bridegroom', whose most cherished dreams were shattered. And as for poor Jarasandha, with the cancellation of the *swayamvar,* he had to taste defeat at the hands of a cowherd yet again. Well, did he not know, this was bound to happen if one tried to match wits with Krishna!

Well, I would pamper my ego later. Coming back to King Bhishmak, he had regained his composure soon after announcing the cancellation of the *swayamvar*. It was evident from the look of relief on his face that this announcement had fulfilled his heartfelt desire too. Perhaps, that was why he graciously invited everyone to the feast arranged for the *swayamvar*, signalling that he had normalised enough to fulfil his obligations. Most importantly, he remembered to invite me this time. Needless to say, I was pleased by this rare honour. First, I had been given the opportunity to sit among the renowned kings of Aryavarta, and now, I was invited to dine with them. This cowherd was really going places, but his childishness refused to let go of him. Everything had worked out the way I wanted it to, but I still could not hold myself back, and while leaving, I made another sarcastic remark. I said to the king, "It is good to know that although you may not have authority over the *swayamvar,* you at least have the right to decide whom to invite for the feast."

My taunt was so acerbic that it left the trio of Jarasandha, Shishupala and Rukmi fuming under their breath. Meanwhile, Bhishmak, who had lowered his eyes in shame, refused to look up. Soon after the announcement, everyone returned to their royal quarters in a dejected state of mind. I too wore an unhappy look on my face; however, inwardly, my heart was performing somersaults, dancing with joy. Oh, what do I say? My head was floating in the clouds, gloating over the cancellation of the *swayamvar*. Indeed, I was thrilled to the core for having succeeded in saving my world of dreams from being devastated. Moreover, I was likely to catch a glimpse of my beloved Rukmini at the feast too. Additionally, I was mighty chuffed about the fact that I had walked right into Jarasandha's lair and checkmated him yet again. In short, Kanha's heart was soaring to the skies! But I was such a fine actor that while stepping outside the royal palace, I maintained a solemn expression on my face.

Of course, once I reached my chamber, I could no longer hold back the feeling of euphoria. I jumped for joy, and even tried to embrace myself repeatedly. And the devil that I was, Jarasandha's downcast face kept looming in front of my eyes, which only served to boost my mood. Indeed, there was a strange kind of enmity between Jarasandha and me. He was after my life and I, after his prestige. He would pull out all stops in his attempts to kill me, while I would repeatedly blow his reputation to smithereens. However, I could not compare myself to him by any measure! Jarasandha had some of the most reputed kings of Aryavarta paying obeisance to him...and what did I have? Nothing! I had neither a kingdom nor an army. It was also worth noting that despite his obvious advantages, it was he who had to concede defeat every single time. As for me, although I did not have an army, power or influence, I was brimming with self-confidence; moreover, I had a firm resolve and the ability for deep contemplation too. And, of course, I also possessed an exceedingly sharp brain. But most importantly, I possessed the quality of selflessness and a strong desire to act for the greater good, because of which even the most challenging tasks would become easy to perform. And this is not a baseless brag, for, I had once again proven my capability by getting the *swayamvar* cancelled in the court of a king like Bhishmak, despite the presence of a 'guardian angel' in the form of Jarasandha! Really, I must say, I was more than a match for all the royals in Aryavarta, solely because of my unique qualities and skills.

Well, having scored a stupendous victory, there was no question of my falling asleep tonight. On one hand, I was lost in dreams of Rukmini, and on the other, I was puffed up with pride. Besides, my ego also kept rearing its head every now and then. Ah, what do I say about my ego—it was manifesting itself in a variety of forms. On one hand, there was the smugness for having devised an ingenious plan, and on the other, there was the pride arising out of the joy I felt on being able to save Rukmini from a potential disaster. On one hand, while I was bursting with delight on being seated among kings, on the other, I was dancing with joy on being invited to the royal feast. And just when I managed to gain control over all these emotions, sweet dreams of Rukmini and her enchanting face would dance before my eyes, playing havoc with my senses. Oh, what can I say! I spent the entire night tossing and turning in bed.

Well, the night passed somehow, but a fantastic idea struck me in the morning. I wanted to meet Grandfather Kaishik before departing for Mathura. After all, he was the only one who had opposed the *swayamvar* from the very outset. So, I thought, let me be the bearer of good news and boost his morale as well. However, I also had other compelling reasons to meet him. For instance, he held great sway over Rukmini while he despised her brother Rukmi. Considering all these aspects, he could prove to be an extremely useful ally in my quest to attain Rukmini. With so many good reasons supporting my intention, there was no question of postponing this visit. Thus, I lost no time and went to meet him early in the morning at the *ashram* he was living in, on the outskirts of the city. As I entered the vast, sprawling *ashram*, I could see that in terms of comfort, convenience and security, it was no less than a palace. Well, no sooner did Grandfather Kaishik receive the news of my arrival than he invited me to his chamber. Perhaps, he had already received the news that I had succeeded in thwarting the *swayamvar*. Be that as it may! On meeting him, I was pleasantly surprised. His personality was quite impressive, and age seemed to have only enhanced his appeal. Speaking of his reaction, he appeared far more pleased to see me than I was to meet him. This meant that my guess was correct; he had already heard about my role in getting the *swayamvar* cancelled. This was excellent news, as it meant that he was aware of my capabilities. Now, let me share a little secret with you: on the face of it, this meeting appeared to be just a courtesy call, but on a deeper level, I wanted him to meet his future grandson-in-law! So, in truth, I hadn't come to meet him, but to give him the chance to meet me. And judging by his reaction, this meeting was a resounding success, even from that perspective.

After spending considerable time with Grandfather Kaishik, I returned to my quarters by noon, enveloped in the warmth of his blessings. And the good news was, just like him, the people of Kundinpur were also extremely pleased with me. Praises in my honour could be heard all around, with everyone giving me full credit for saving their beloved princess. In stark contrast to them, the trio of Jarasandha, Rukmi and Shishupala was on the verge of exploding with fury. So, in a way, they too were giving me full credit for foiling their plans. And verily, they should! For, I invariably take charge of the proceedings wherever I am present. In short, the moment I returned to my chamber, I was gripped by ego yet again. Oh, but let us leave that aside; why become so smug or mar such a beautiful moment by talking about Jarasandha and his coterie of foolish men? Instead, let me talk about Rukmini. In other words, let me talk about my poor heart and the woman who ruled it. Honestly, after this victory, I was yearning to make Rukmini mine. That's not all! I was also becoming more and more determined towards that goal. For that matter, I could no longer see any obstacles in my path to make her mine, for, I had clearly proven that I was worthy of her. Moreover, having saved her from Shishupala's clutches, I had become her saviour as well. Viewed from this perspective too, I felt I did have some right over her. All in all, I was so intoxicated by my success that I kept pacing up and down my chamber, lost in my daydreams.

Well, I had my whole life ahead of me to weave beautiful dreams about Rukmini. So, as soon as the headiness wore down a little, my mind shifted to positive thoughts. It soon turned to Shaivya and Shwetketu's unflagging contribution to my success, leaving me filled with gratitude towards them. But my mind changed track once again, losing itself in thoughts of Rukmini. It seemed as if I had lost my senses due to the sudden and stupendous victory I had scored! Indeed, my mind was hopping and jumping from one line of thought to another. Suddenly, I began to view even Shaivya and Shwetketu in the context of Rukmini, which was quite understandable too. Because, as things stood at present, they were the only ones who could act as a bridge between Rukmini and me. If I wanted to win her hand in marriage, I would have to use this bridge wisely. Thus, my attention latched onto these two while thinking about Rukmini, and my mind became engrossed in making plans for the future wherein these two could play a pivotal part. And what were these plans? Of course, they revolved around just one thought—to attain Rukmini, to open up the paths that led towards this objective. Immersed in these thoughts, little did I realise that it was evening already. A while later, Shaivya and Shwetketu arrived to congratulate me, their faces wreathed in joyous smiles. In fact, Shaivya appeared even more delighted, for, she was happy not just for me but for her friend too, who had been saved from a fiend like Shishupala. For a while, all we did was congratulate each other over this victory, exchanging warm hugs and pecks on the cheek, but soon, I returned to serious discussions. I first requested them to promptly bring me any information concerning Rukmini, especially that which was related to her marriage or the *swayamvar*. I also asked them not to apprise Rukmini of the love I nestled in my heart for her. For, I feared, what if all my lovely dreams were crushed in a single stroke? Nah, I could not let that happen! It was far better for this cowherd to allow this dream to blossom than watch it end abruptly! This was all fine, but I ended up putting forth a very strange request to Shaivya. I asked her to keep singing praises of my plan and bravery in Rukmini's presence whenever she got the opportunity. I told Shaivya to repeatedly tell her how I had heroically saved her from Shishupala and the *swayamvar,* which would have otherwise turned into a hell for her! Of course, there was no ill intention behind asking Shaivya to do this. I simply wanted to create a good impression on Rukmini and hopefully spark some attraction in her heart by having Shaivya sing praises about my bravery and clever planning ever so often. I wanted to kindle the fire of love on both sides, instead of having it burn on this end only. Now, this crazed lover was entitled to at least try tugging at the heartstrings of his beloved. Needless to say, both Shaivya and Shwetketu were more than willing to help me in every way they could, and with the firm promise of setting my love story into motion, they took their leave. Actually, I was likely to meet them again on the day of the feast, but it certainly wouldn't have been possible to speak to Shaivya about these matters.

With their departure, my thoughts veered towards the upcoming feast, and with that, I had once again made arrangements for staying up all night! Soon, I was lost in dreams of the feast, of standing before my darling, Rukmini, and gazing deep into her eyes! I even dreamt that she would serve me food with her own hands. Oh, how happy she would be to see me seated among all the kings and princes. Then, suddenly, the voice within warned me, 'That is all well, Kanhaiya, but please do not faint…and do keep your wits about you!' The feast was just a few hours away, scheduled for the next day, but my condition could best be described by someone who, sitting on the bare ground, had dreamt of touching the stars and had suddenly found an opportunity to soar straight to the skies!

Well, the night came to an end, heralding a day that would yet again be a decisive one. Undoubtedly, I had to take full advantage of the opportunity I had received to sit among kings—I had to leave a lasting impression on Rukmini! Thus, the grand ritual of getting dressed, which I had started in the morning, stretched on almost until it was time for the feast. Choosing the garment I would wear at the feast with great care, I really lost count of the number of *pitambars* I must have worn and discarded. Meticulously choosing the jewellery to be worn, I just could not make up my mind on what to wear, but finally, I was ready in time for the feast. Dressed in finery, I set off for the palace with great pomp and splendour. And though it was unnecessary, I had still departed with a caravan of ten chariots. I was dressed so immaculately that even Yashoda and Radha together couldn't have adorned me better than this! After all, this was the day I was going to meet Rukmini; besides, I had

to overshadow all my rivals—the kings and princes. I'm sure it's not difficult to imagine how much care I must have taken over my attire. And when one dresses up magnificently, it also affects one's overall personality. So, it goes without saying that I made a grand entry into the palace. Everyone was being welcomed with *ittar*[56] applied to them, and I was welcomed in the same manner. This signified that I was considered one of them. My chest puffed up even more as I strutted into the dining area. The feast had been organised in the vast, sprawling garden in the rear portion of the palace. This area was adorned with stunning, brightly coloured fabrics on three sides, fluttering merrily in the breeze. Arrangements were made to seat nearly a hundred princes and kings. And no, I wasn't the first to arrive. Obviously, I hadn't lost my senses—I did care about my image and reputation. Several princes had arrived before me. As for the food arrangements, the seating was set up in three rows, and I had been placed in the last one. In addition to these three rows, arrangements were made for six more individuals to be seated very close to the palace. Perhaps, King Bhishmak, Jarasandha, the Chief Minister and a few others were to be seated there. Meanwhile, kings and princes continued to pour in. However, despite all this, the overall mood refused to lift. The dejection everyone felt over the *swayamvar* being cancelled hung heavily in the air. Nonetheless, the dining area was now filled to capacity. Moreover, nobody had to wait for too long, as King Bhishmak soon arrived, accompanied by Jarasandha, Shishupala and Rukmi. In a show of respect, everyone rose to greet them, and after acknowledging the greetings, they too took their seats.

As soon as everyone was seated, the serving began. The platters, bowls and cutlery were already set out in front of us; and on receiving the signal, scores of servants began to serve an assortment of delicacies. The mood was set now, and as you know, good food was one of my major weaknesses. But on this day, my mind was not focused on food. I was anxiously waiting for someone who was a far greater weakness of mine. Indeed, like a true love-struck person, I sat nibbling at my food, my eyes never losing sight of the entrance. Rukmini would enter the dining area through that very doorway at any moment. I yearned for a glimpse of her, longing to gaze into her eyes to my heart's content, as I was not sure when I would see her again...or if I would ever see her at all! Finally, after what seemed like an eternity, the wait came to an end. It was about time too, else this lover would have died with his eyes fixed on that cursed doorway! Oh well, let's not talk about something that never happened! The door opened, and there she stood, like a resplendent moon descended straight from heaven. It seemed as if the full moon, in all its radiant glory, had stepped down daintily on earth! Dressed in shimmering silk in various hues of gold, Rukmini was a sight to behold. Her sparkling radiance

56. *Ittar* - A type of traditional perfume or fragrance made from natural plant oils, flowers or herbs.

almost blinded me even from this distance. I was too mesmerised to take my eyes off her. Indeed, this lover was about to faint when, with a herculean effort, he immediately composed himself. For, if Shishupala or Rukmi got so much as a hint of my love for Rukmini, all my future plans could be jeopardised. This fear alone helped me regain my composure. Indeed, I did not want my eyes to betray me and let loose the avalanche of love that was waiting to burst forth from my wildly racing heart! So, rather than lose Rukmini forever, it was better to presently sacrifice the pleasure of gazing at her. And Kanhaiya was quick to grasp matters of self-interest. Thus, I sat quietly, assuming a calm and composed demeanour. Of course, this 'normalcy' was just a pretence; within me, a storm of feelings brewed, raging uncontrollably. On one hand, while I was overjoyed that I had been able to save the princess of my dreams from an undesirable fate, on the other, I was thrilled by the fact that I was seated in her palace as an honoured guest, and that too, alongside kings and princes, as their equal. Besides, the wave of ecstasy I felt wash over me on seeing Rukmini was simply indescribable. But that's not all! My changed circumstances were not allowing me to calm down either. As you may remember, when I had first felt the stirrings of attraction towards Rukmini, a huge chasm of the difference in our status had stood between us. She was the princess of Kundinpur and I, a poor, illiterate cowherd. However, now, I was not only educated but affluent too. And on this day, the power of my personality was no less than that of a king either. Indeed, seated among other kings and princes, I was invited to a grand feast by her very own father! What better proof could one want of my rise in status than this?

Nevertheless, I was in a strange state of mind. The person who could make my heart race just by crossing my mind had come to serve me food today. Naturally, I was thrilled to the core of my being, but I had to bear the torture of sitting quietly without expressing any of my feelings. All that my heart desired stood right in front of me, yet I sat in silence, as if my eyes were shut tight and my lips sealed. Oh, I alone knew the state I was in! Coming back to the feast, four servants followed Rukmini, carrying platters of delicacies to be served. I could also see Shaivya accompanying Rukmini, arm in arm. My sweet princess appeared somewhat weak because of the trauma she had undergone, but that had not affected her beauty in the least. With downcast eyes, she kept serving food to the kings and princes. Shishupala, however, was so enraged that when Rukmini served him, he angrily pushed away the food. The wounded lover that he was, he was certainly venting his anger in the wrong place and at the wrong time. However, unmindful of this, Rukmini went about fulfilling her duty, unaware of what she was serving—or even whom she was serving. Considering the condition she was in, it was commendable that she was at least able to do this. Watching her closely, with Shaivya standing next to her, I felt quite relieved on seeing the close bond they shared. Truly, the rapport they shared had turned out to be a boon for me, opening the biggest door towards attaining Rukmini. Incidentally, though I did not look at her directly, I continued to cast furtive glances at her. Suddenly, while serving in the row in front of me, her eyes fell on me. Seeing me, a great many emotions flitted across her visage. Certainly, she must not have expected me to be present at the feast; and my being seated on par with the kings must have left her completely nonplussed. And as for me, what do I say? The moment her gaze locked with mine, I could feel myself melting like wax! Finally, it was my turn; she reached my seat and began serving me. However, it didn't appear that she paid me any special attention. Well, I did not take offence to this either. It was fine that she did not treat me with any extra regard; she had at least served me with her own hands, and that was enough to make this lover lose his senses. Forgetting royal etiquette, I devoured every morsel, licking my fingers like a true cowherd. Truly, I had never tasted such sweetness in delicacies before!

Well, the feast was over and so were Bhishmak's worries. My task had also been accomplished, and I was eager to return to Mathura quickly. Waiting unnecessarily after completing a task often brings trouble in its wake. And here, it was even more crucial for me to remain vigilant. For, Jarasandha and his cronies would just be waiting for an opportunity to strike, and they were quite capable of creating trouble at any moment. So, as soon as this thought flashed through my mind, I left for the rest house and commenced preparations for my departure. As for preparations, all I had to do was change my clothes. That done, I instructed the caravan to be ready to leave for Mathura, while I set off for the royal palace once again. Yes, after two days of mixing and mingling with kings, I too had become adept at observing royal protocol. So, before departing, I did not forget to meet King Bhishmak and take his leave. However, I was one of a kind! Compelled by habit, I thought, why not meet Jarasandha too before leaving, and more importantly, gauge his mood? He was anyway housed in the chamber right next to the king's. Besides, for the sake of the future and also as a precautionary measure, it was imperative for me to gauge his mood. This was like shooting two birds with one stone! I would accomplish an important task while also fulfilling my desire to indulge in some mischief. So, ignoring all rules and formalities, I went straight to his chamber. Seeing me at his door, Jarasandha was momentarily stunned. Actually, I enjoyed shocking people, and this was Jarasandha, after all! He had the exclusive right to witness all my antics first-hand. But yes, on entering his chamber, I observed all formalities and greeted him respectfully. Of course, there was no question of him acknowledging my greeting. He was seated on the bed, a look of pure hatred emanating from his countenance. He did not even ask me to take a seat. Incredibly, the moment he saw me, he too forgot his royal etiquette! But I hardly needed an invitation. Brazenly, I took a seat opposite him and watched him struggle to control the emotions raging within.

Naturally, it was I who had to take the initiative to begin the conversation; he was obviously not going to speak to me. So, losing no time, I spoke with great humility, "Having spent the last few days under your aegis, I plan to set out for Mathura tomorrow early morning. So, before leaving, I reckoned, I should come see you and hopefully take your blessings."

It was strange! I was respectfully asking for his blessings and permission to leave, but he still did not deem it fit to answer or acknowledge me. Well, what difference would it have made to a shameless person like me? I brazenly continued, "For that matter, I have enjoyed your benevolence for many years, and I must admit, you are the only true guiding force in my life." Saying this, I took a pause once again. Although Jarasandha was listening to every word I spoke, he still refused to give a reaction. But yes, I could feel the heat of the rage simmering within him. After all, my actions were not aimed at calming him down! But contrary to my nature, so far, I had neither said anything to provoke him nor made any sarcastic comments. But truth be told, since I was meeting my 'guide' alone for the first time, it did not seem appropriate for this meeting to end on such a sour note. Yes, you got it right! I felt like mocking him a little. At present, he was nothing more than a tiger locked in a cage. He was bound by royal etiquette, and even though he would have loved to, he could not harm me in any way. So, when there was no real danger to me, I thought, why not take the opportunity to mock him? In an open battlefield, I lacked the courage to face him; in fact, in the open ground, he had made me run for my life. Given that, why would I pass up this golden opportunity to needle him? So, just as I stood up to leave, I aimed a sharp barb at him saying, "I sincerely hope we meet again in Mathura. But this time, please come prepared, or you may end up biting the dust..." Then, after the briefest pause, I added, "...yet again!"

Hearing this, Jarasandha bristled with rage, his hands itching to strangle my neck and squeeze the life out of me. Yet, despite all this, he did not utter a single word. This was enough to satisfy the notorious imp in me. I had managed to mock him and had also gleaned what I wanted to. Moreover, I had conveyed to him all that I wished to. And my inference was clear—Jarasandha did not have any plans to attack me on my journey back home, so I could travel safely with a mind free of worry. I thus took my leave, with no response from him. Still, as you all know, it was in my nature to remain vigilant at all times. Even though it did not seem that Jarasandha intended to attack me, I could not rest assured. Oh, what do I say to you? I had told him that I had planned to leave the next morning only to mislead him. The fact was, I intended to leave Kundinpur that afternoon itself. If Jarasandha had any nefarious plans in store for me, I wanted to keep him waiting till the next morning while I escaped immediately. Agreed, he could not attack me in Kundinpur, but he could always pounce on me once I crossed the border of this kingdom. My life was really strange—I had to constantly plan and plot just to stay alive. I sometimes wondered whether Jarasandha's plan was to kill me simply by draining the life out of me, forcing me to run for my life all the time! Well, now that we are on the subject, let me tell you a little more about my hidden motives. There was a bigger, more significant reason behind my meeting Jarasandha, keeping the long-term future in mind. By provoking him, I actually wanted to gauge the intensity of his hatred for me. It was pretty evident that the failures he had suffered, one after the other, had wounded his ego. It was also certain that sooner or later, he would launch a final, deadly attack on Mathura. And I was also sure that the attack would be so lethal that it would wipe out not just me but the whole of Mathura as well. Now, these were eventualities that were bound to happen; in other words, these puzzles had already been solved. But when would Jarasandha make that final strike? That was the mystery I wanted to solve and I had finally managed to do so. After meeting him, I had ascertained that he did not have any such plans at least in the near future. You could very well say that having gained this information, I had secured yet another victory in this trip. My life was safe, even if it was just for the time being, and this pleased me immensely. Coming back to my astuteness, you may not have noticed, but the final statement I had made to Jarasandha before departing was quite effective. While getting up to leave, I had said to him, "This time, please come prepared, or you may end up biting the dust…yet again." Did you not get it? I had said those words so that he would refrain from attacking in haste. I wanted him to take his time to prepare well so that I could buy more time. After all, what did we have in Mathura to counter him? Even a small regiment of Jarasandha's army was enough to wipe us out. Well, so be it! For now, having notched up yet another victory, I rode off towards Mathura with my splendid caravan, a lilting symphony playing in my heart. The only difference was that this was my personal victory. Purely personal!

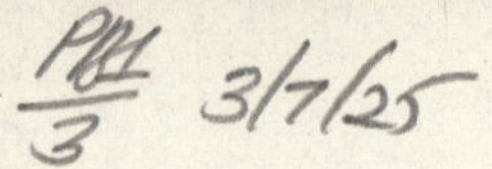